MW01228053

midnight's simulacra

Gold & Appel Publishing

DEDICATED
to all those of whom i am proud,
and those who will one day get there.

midnight's simulacra

copyright © 2024 nick black—all rights reserved
cover by nick black and justin barker
illustrations by justin barker
isbn: 979-8-9895236-0-3 (hardback form factor)
version 1.0.1 released 2024-01-11 (first edition: 2024-01-11)

Library of Congress Control Number: 2023922340

Bibliography/errata available at https://midnightssimulacra.com.

Created on a Debian Linux workstation using exclusively Free Software (git, Vim, LuaTEX, Memoir, GNU Make, polyglossia, CircuiTikZ, PyMOL, and GIMP) and free fonts (Gentium Book Plus, Kanit, Noto, Hack, and Symbola).

Languages include English, Nahuatl, Deutsch, Polski, Italiano, Filipino, Latīnum, Español, Magyar, Français, Shqip, Cymraeg, Lingála, Yorùbá, čeština, Lietuvių, Việt, Norrǿnt mál, русский, українська, қазақша, беларуская, Ἀττικὴ Ἑλληνική, ⵜⴰⵎⴰⵣⵉⵖⵜ, فارسی, پښتو, العَرَبِيَّة, ગુજરાતી, தமிழ், ␣␣␣␣␣␣␣, ບາລີ, සිංහල, תּ֫וֹרָ֖ה, संस्कृतम्, हिन्दी, ༄༅བོད་སྐད་, ଓଡ଼ିଆ, ਪੰਜਾਬੀ, 官话, 日本語, 한국어, C++, technical argot, and mathematics.

midnight's simulacra

a novel by nick black

illustrations by justin barker

invocation

This one's for everyone out there building the future, everyone working to constrain entropy, everyone putting in the hours, creating something neither banal, nor evil, nor wasteful, nor broken. Keep fighting the good fight.

Arma virumque cano: I sing of engineers and all their nerd shit. I hope to shine a little light on my tribe. Doing so faithfully requires a measure of the recondite, a dash of the esoteric. *midnight's simulacra* can be a nontrivial read.

Should you find yourself frustrated, put the book down. Breathe. Step outside. Smoke 'em if you've got 'em. Look up any offending concepts, if you'd like. Nothing here is beyond the understanding of a motivated high schooler. If you're not feeling a research break, bathe in a river of atramental enigma: allow the unknown to wash over you; try to enjoy the sense of mystery. Skip a few para. We all do it. Reject shame and burden both. Trudge on and find your footing—it'll come along more quickly than you might expect. I've provided expansions for acronyms and cursory translations of non-English phrases, of which there are admittedly quite a few.

You can do anything to which you put your mind (except *e.g.* design a procedure to determine whether an arbitrary Turing machine T halts, simultaneously measure canonically conjugate variables of a quantum system such that the product of errors is less than half $\hbar$, or create a complete and consistent set of recursively enumerable axioms capable of deciding PA—duh). Proof is left as an exercise for the reader. I apologize for nothing.

Metric prefixes ought be interpreted as such: in the spirit of Herman Kahn, a "megadose" is "one million doses," not "a large dose." If you don't like it, I encourage you to FAX your representative, or mail the Management at:

nick black
International Court of Justice
Peace Palace
Carnegieplein 2
2517 KJ The Hague
The Netherlands

Arma virumque cano: I sing of arms and of a man. Virgil, *Aeneid* I.1
PA: Peano arithmetic

prolegomenon

All very well to talk about having a monster by the tail, but do you
think we'd've had the Rocket if someone, some specific somebody with
a name and a penis hadn't wanted to chuck a ton of Amatol 300 miles
and blow up a block full of civilians? Go ahead, capitalize the T on
technology, deify it if it'll make you feel less responsible—

Thomas Pynchon, *Gravity's Rainbow* (1973)

What follows is a work of fiction, a modern alchemic fantasy, a phantas-
magoria. Neither characters nor events are based on real people, to whatever
degree that assertion is possibly true, or even semantically well-defined.

Standard advice is to Write About What One Knows. I know the experience
of America's top-tier Technical Institutes, concentrating unlike anywhere else
in the world madness, brilliance, and youth of blistering eccentricity. I know
likewise sociopathy, ambition, and crime. The allure of the forbidden. The call
of the clandestine. The formidable, almost sorcerous powers available to that
rara avis, the competent rogue engineer.

The science explored herein is, to the best of my ability, absolutely rigorous
and reproducible—the biology, chemistry, and physics of *midnight's simulacra*
are those of our universe as I know it. The characters are of course sometimes
misinformed, or mendacious, or simply running their ignorant goddamned
mouths, but Nature cannot be fooled.

Information wants to be free, and I sought to spin a unique and compelling
story. This book was not written to encourage the manufacture of substituted
tryptamines, nor the enrichment of fissile actinide isotopes, nor the broad
penetration and subversion of computing resources.

But a fish is gonna swim.

Let us go, then, you and I—into the light, and into also the very dark. *Lux
fiat—une oasis d'horreur dans un désert d'ennui!*

May God forgive us. May history judge us charitably.

Lux fiat: Let there be light. Genesis 1:3
une...d'ennui: an oasis of horror in a desert of boredom. Charles Baudelaire, *Les Fleurs du mal*
(The Flowers of Evil, 1857) "Le Voyage" (The Voyage) VII.4

Part I

verwirrung—CHAOS

All is not lost; the unconquerable Will,
And study of revenge, immortal hate,
And courage never to submit or yield:
And what is else not to be overcome?
That glory never shall his wrath or might
Extort from me.

John Milton, *Paradise Lost* (1667) Book I 106–111

That which exists without my knowledge exists without my consent.

Cormac McCarthy, *Blood Meridian* (1985)

And Lo, for the Earth was empty of Form, and void.
And Darkness was all over the Face of the Deep.
And We said: "Look at that fucker Dance."

David Foster Wallace, *Infinite Jest* (1996)

SPAKE ERIS: I am chaos. I am alive, and I tell you that you are free.

Malaclypse the Younger, *Principia Discordia* (1963)

1   coming of age in confusion

When they met in his dreams—and they came there all too often of late—the two agents—phantasms? visions? possibly theophanies?—took the forms of Teddy Roosevelt and Jodie Foster. They stood in huddled proximity at the long edge of the National Mall's reflecting pool. Teddy ate with zest hard Hanover pretzels, briefly examining each through his monocle, discarding those that failed muster. His supply seemed quite bottomless. Baked dough fractured crazily between the legendary incisors. Beneath his breadfall feasted pigeons.

Roosevelt: In 1886, as Billings County Deputy Sheriff in what was not yet nicknamed the Roughrider State, I tracked three boat thieves from Elkhorn Ranch fifty leagues along the Little Missouri River, subdued them, bound them, and marched them to Dickinson. We'll have this Katz and his confederates.

Foster: I doubt they know we picked up on it at Savannah. Followed that shipment all the way along I-16 to I-75. Hundreds of miles up highways that snake through the south like main circuits plugged straight into Katz.

Roosevelt: I prefer rail, or a good river patrol boat.

Foster: So long as it's not a cruiser in Havana.

They suggested to Sherman Katz the two Witnesses of Revelation 11. Terribly well informed, nigh-numinous in their access to cross-organization, transbudget facts, exact affiliations and portfolios were yet unclear: they wore neither recognizable uniform nor insignia, but rather gray glen plaid flannel in clinging Malibu Imperial cuts, aping unmistakably Paul Reubens as Pee-Wee Herman.

Foster, then, epitomized what Hobson called an "incomplete cognition," and Blechner an "interobject": one of the world's most intimidating women, clothed via dream as the world's most childish man. On Roosevelt's bull moose neck the red bow tie looked obscene. Every trapped fidget unleashed complex systems of undulation and vermicular bulge. Three spatial dimensions of suit seemed insufficient, oversubscribed. It was mesmerizing and foul and Sherman—no friend to that which crawls along the ground, whether on its belly or many feet, nor swarming things that swarm the earth, and absolutely not *Gastropoda*, neither those sporting toxoglassate radulae nor those that gummed you in the gummy way of the cyclostomatous worldwide (and holy shit, there are *Conidae* that *launch* barbed radulae at you, like someone gave goddamn Queequeg access to neurotoxins)—the next morning regarded the whole Pee-Wee thing as incongruous and, like, undeserved.

Roosevelt made sense: he'd read Edmund Morris's three volumes of biography twice in his twenties, and adored the man of the arena ever since. *Silence of the Lambs* ranked among his top ten movies easily; *The Accused* was right up there. But he'd not been allowed to watch *Pee-Wee's Playhouse*. Not that he'd particularly cared to—once *Muppet Babies* ended at 0930h, young Sherman knew of nothing worth viewing until the next week's episode. Over breakfast in 1991, eleven years old, his mother had interrupted the silence to declare "*Pee-Wee's Playhouse* is a thinly disguised invitation to pederasty. Right CJ?"

3

Cassius Julius Katz's presence at breakfast was infrequent, and that day unexpected. "Conspiracy to pederasty, perhaps, Evy, certainly."

Satisfied, she continued. "And that's why the Catholic Church likes it."

Sherman doubted any correlation between Catholicism and Saturday mornings on CBS. Months prior he'd agreed to some protracted viewing at the urging of his friend Richard. Eveline came in on an early, loquacious drunk, pointing at the television with squinting accusation. "That chair's speech is blasphemy."

Richard, slow on the uptake and confused already, looked to Sherman.

"Genesis 1:29—I have given you dominion over all the animals and seed-bearing plants."

Katz sighed.

"Genesis 1:30—And the animals can eat the plants. Nothing about couches. Every word from that sofa is a mockery."

Richard's mouth hung open.

"Can a couch give glory to God, Sherman?"

"No." His voice was resigned.

"Can it lift up its voice in jubilation? Was it made in His image?" She stumbled to the control panel, appraising it with mute, disgusted confusion, and finally unplugged the offending appliance. "Go play outside. I won't have you anthroposophizing the living room."

"I think you mean anthropomorphizing?"

"I mean anthroposophize. Anthroposophy. The Nazis did it. Tried to make super demon soldiers for Hitler. Dark witchcraft. You think you're so smart? You don't know nothin'." Richard stopped dropping by after that.

Back to breakfast: "He looks like a Communist and all the homos are Communists. I've got no problem with gay people. They've got real trouble with the AIDS." She crossed herself. "But if you're gonna be a pederast it's gross that you're doing it with little boys." This proclamation's unsettling implications elicited no comment. Some stones are best left unturned in their mosses, a lesson quickly internalized at the table Katz. Yet her first comments merited a question. "What do you mean about the Catholics, mom?"

"Those poor priests are all pederasts. It's not their fault. The Church won't let them lay with women. It's unnatural. They would just be homos, but that's a sin. So they have altar boys."

His father didn't look up. "Evy, that's enough."

"But aren't we Catholic?"

"Of course we're Catholic. Do you need to go to more Mass?"

"Well then isn't it sinful to say they're humping the altar boys? Or if they are, aren't they sinning? And why are we chanting responsorial psalms and doxologies with a clergy that you suspect to be systematically humping or"—nodding here to his father—"conspiring at least to hump altar boys? Dear God, didn't you say I have to be an altar boy when I turn twelve?"

"'Don't say 'hump.' That's what camels have. Well, if they try to get fresh with you, you smack their hand away and tell them 'No, Father, you go try that with that Nathan boy from your CCD class, he'd probably like it.'"

Aghast: "How about a church without altar boys? Holy shit mom!"

"Sherman Spartacus! Language! I have been a Catholic all my life. It's a wonderful faith, God's chosen faith. One holy Catholic and apostolic church. How many times have you heard us say that? All the way back to Jesus and Peter, one long line of Popes just like those New England Jews tracing their families back to the *Mayflower*. You want to be a Baptist? You think Jesus manifested himself to the French? You've been a Catholic eleven years. For nine months before that you were inside me and that counts as Catholic too. I have your baptismal candle in our safety deposit box. Your father will be a Catholic soon. Why in the world would we stop being Catholic? What would your grandparents say?" She'd arrived through passion at the verge of tears.

Sherman wasn't sure about the Frenchman thing, whether she thought Providence's Roger Williams some kind of confused Huguenot or Charlemagne the first Baptist or what exactly. It had come up before. Mentioning the Western Schism or the seven antipopes of Avignon would only annoy her. His father had silently winced at the absurdity of *Mayflower* Jewry and Sherman hoped desperately that she would not expand upon this theme.

"You mean your parents, right? I don't think Dad's would care."

Cassius grinned at this behind his coffee.

∗ ∗ ∗ ∗ ∗ ∗ ∗ ∗

Elijah Katz and Mildred Blickers of Jacksonville, Florida were blessed with Cassius Julius in 1950. Three quarters of a century before this happy birth, Moses Elias Katz was delivered in the Mellah of Fez to Leopold and Freida, Ashkenazim out of Prussia. Their emigration from Europe had been arranged by the *Alliance Israélite Universelle* with the intention that Leopold would lecture in Morocco. A united Germany wrote Jewish emancipation into the *Bismarcksche Reichsverfassung* of 1871; Freida's native Württemberg had granted general equality in 1861. They'd nonetheless seen the angry holdouts (especially in Bavaria), read the vituperative counterpoints in the goyim papers, and grown up hearing about the Hep-Hep riots. The revolutions of 1848 had been good to European Jewry, but before their time, while both possessed clear memories of Edgardo Mortara's kidnapping in Bologna and the complicity of Pius IX.

Between the Rif mountains Dersa and Ghorghiz nestles Morocco's Martil valley. There Mauritanian Berbers founded Tiṭṭawan. Phoenician traders used the fine natural harbor, and under Augustus the Romans colonized it as Tamuda. Thirteen centuries later, Muslim Berbers of the Marinid sultanate rebuilt it as Tétouan, then dispatched armies to subdue Ceuta, and galleys to harass the Spanish. Bad move: the Castilians razed the casbah in 1399, and the Portuguese raided it in 1436 for good measure. In 1492 the Granada War and greater *Reconquista* wound to its close, and the Nasrid dynasty—the last Arab power on the Iberian peninsula—was driven from Andalusia. Ferdinand II and Isabella I moved their royal court to Alhambra. The remaining Moors were tamed as *mudéjar*, and would soon be expelled as *moriscos*. Ali al-Mandri

---

Alliance Israélite Universelle: כל ישראל חברים Universal Israelite Alliance
Bismarcksche Reichsverfassung: Bismarck Constitution   **Tiṭṭawan:** ⵜⵉⵟⵟⴰⵡⴰⵏ Tettawan
mudéjar: Muslims remaining in Iberia following the *Reconquista*
moriscos: Forced converts suspected of crypto-Islam

of Piñar saw which way the winds were blowing, and sailed south across the Mediterranean to refortify Tétouan pursuant to reclaiming Moorish Spain.

Andalusian Moors would never again control Granada, but their corsairs plied the Middle Sea anew. Captured Christians were held in the fetid tunnel complexes called *mazmorras*. Miguel De Cervantes, himself for seventy-two months a prisoner in Algiers, refers in *El juez de los divorcios* to "captivity in Tétouan's caves," and Chapter XLII of *Don Quixote* reminisces of "the deepest mazmorras of Barbary." Growing weary of this, the Spanish once again sacked Tétouan, this time destroying its harbor.

Jews established communities in Hispania soon after the fall of the Second Temple in the first century. For over a millennium of Arab rule they lived as *dhimmīs*, paying *jizya*, the Muslim tax for tolerance of "people of the covenant." The Spanish Empire became less attractive for its Jews with the investment of *Tribunal del Santo Oficio de la Inquisición* in 1478. Upon taking their seats in Alhambra, the Edict of Expulsion was among the Catholic monarchs' first acts, and Jewish life in Spain became entirely untenable.

These Sephardic Jews dispersed to the Maghreb, and with the advent of *limpieza de sangre* laws even the *conversos* joined the diaspora. There were famines and there were pogroms, and in 1807 the Mellah of Tétouan was temporarily relocated so that Sultan Slimane might build a mosque where it had stood. Still the Sephardim developed successful communities through Morocco, and participated in the Makhzen elite. 1859's Hispano-Moroccan War saw Spain's General Zabala subject the Tétouan mellah to bombardment, and Riffian tribesmen finish the task of destruction. The Jewish press in Europe published appeals for a "Morocco Relief Fund"; rebuilding was brisk. In 1862, the AIU established its first school there under Rabbi Isaac Ben Walid. That same portentous year Prussia's King Wilhelm I, acting from the Carlylean playbook, appointed the Junker Otto von Bismarck as *Ministerpräsident*. Bismarck would soon repay the favor by proclaiming Wilhelm the first *Deutscher Kaiser*.

Denmark's most adept defenders a decade earlier had been Britain and Russia. The Crimean War had already weakened Russia when in 1863 partitioned Poland's *Komitet Centralny Narodowy* together with Lithuanian *szlachta* launched the January Uprising. Alexander II warned the Poles to "forget any dreams," Prussia opened her railways to the Tsar's forces, and within the year even Rochebrune's *Żuawi śmierci* had been marched off to Siberia as *sybiracy*, or more often slain. Russia was in no mood to begrudge friendly Prussia her meal of the northern duchies. In July 1863 Palmerston stood before Parliament and promised to defend Danish territorial integrity, but the British economy

---

El juez de los divorcios: *The Divorce Judge* (1615)
dhimmīs: ذمي "People of the Covenant" (Jews and Christians under Muslim rule)
jizya: جِزْيَة Taxes paid by *dhimmīs* in place of Muslim alms
Tribunal...Inquisición: Tribunal of the Holy Office of the Inquisition
Sepharad: סְפָרַד an uncertain destination in Obadiah 1:20, now Spain
limpieza de sangre: blood purity   Deutscher Kaiser: German Emperor
Komitet Centralny Narodowy Central National Committee
szlachta: Polish and Lithuanian nobles
Żuawi śmierci: Zouaves of Death   sybiracy: Pre-GULAG forced Siberian labor

struggled meanwhile due to the Cotton Famine caused by the American Civil War; the armies of Victoria, soon to be named Empress of India, garrisoned the Raj half a world away following 1857's Sepoy Mutiny.

Thus began Bismarck's years of blood and iron. In January 1864 he demanded King Christian IX rescind the November Constitution. Forces of the Prussian and Austrian Empires rode north on the first of February; the prostrated Danes ceded Schleswig, Holstein, and Saxe-Lauenburg six months later. Prussia turned upon her *Öster* ally within two years, soundly defeating them at Königgrätz, and the Hohenzollerns had finally eclipsed the Habsburgs. Austria, roughly expelled from the German Confederation, shacked up with Hungary. Their 1914 declaration of war on Serbia triggered the guns of August, the Great War's long grave already dug, and the dissolution of the Austro-Hungarian Empire—but that's another story, one better told by Barbara and Winston and ten thousand others. Finally, Napoleon III (goaded by Empress Eugénie, foreign minister Agénor de Gramont, prime minister Émile Ollivier, and Bismarck's Ems Dispatch) declared war on Prussia in 1869 with no allies, no offensive plan, no system of conscription, and centralized railroads.

For a year Leopold Katz had spoken to the AIU without commitment. With Freida in Königsberg he watched the artillery and troops rolling west, and their talks turned more ardent. The established Sephardic enclaves of Morocco held definite appeal; the Mediterranean climate, it was hoped, would help hold off Freida's recurring consumption.

Bazaine's *Armée du Rhin* was savaged early. From its ashes rose briefly the *Armée de Châlons* to meet the Prussians at Sedan. Fighting began the first of September. The next day, Napoleon III surrendered himself and 104 kiloflowers of French youth; they were paraded outside besieged Metz. That same day, Katz accepted the AIU's offer. It was good that he did: the telegraph lines of Paris were cut on the 27th, and the AIU's confirmation postcard left the capital via balloon mail. The remaining forces under Bazaine surrendered Metz the next month.

Roosevelt: Is this fellow Jewish?

Foster: I don't believe so. Many of the names we think of as Jewish are just German. He certainly doesn't practice.

Roosevelt: I was the first President to have a Jew in my Cabinet. Oscar Straus. Also from Georgia! Do you think he might be related to this Katz?

Foster: Unlikely. The names are spelled and pronounced differently.

They rode west to the French border on a *Schnellzug*. Infantry that had crossed that same border only months ago were already returning the other direction, drunk, riotous, filling every station through which they passed. On occasional flatcars sat sullen French prisoners, mostly unhurt and in seemingly good health. The majority had already wintered in Prussia. It seemed to Freida that they could easily escape, though the military police with their Dreyse rifles

---

Öster: Eastern (usually Austria, though see *e.g.* World War II's *Ostfront*)
Armée du Rhin: Army of the Rhine   **Armée de Châlons:** Army of Châlons
Schnellzug: express train   **Gare d'Austerlitz:** one of Paris's train stations

would surely endeavor to stop it. Still, were a company to break all at once, it was unlikely that more than a handful of men could be brought down.

They switched in Strasbourg to what months ago had been French rail, waved through by listless *citoyennes* under the watch of cheerful Prussians. It was all very orderly for a country under unexpected occupation. They arrived in *Gare d'Austerlitz* March 3, where the streets outside were being symbolically scrubbed following a Prussian march through the capital. Food remained scarce. The air was thickly gravid with revolution. They remained two uncomfortable days, receiving many hard looks from the Parisians. Within weeks, the family Katz was in Morocco, and the Commune was in control of Paris.

Leopold taught mathematics at the Tétouan school as he had promised, but yearned for the culture and sophistication of Königsberg. After two years, they said their goodbyes and moved two hundred kilometers south into the historic Mellah of Fez, within sight of the forbidding *Bab Semmarine*. There they were loved by their neighbors, and when Dreyfus spent his time on Devil's Island they were happy to have left Europe. Two daughters were born within twenty months, and in 1875 also a son, the aforementioned Moses Elias Katz. All three children proved clever and forthright, and they were happy.

Leopold and Freida were content to grow old in Fez, where the Jewish community went all the way back to Idris I, first Emir and fifth generation to Muhammad *alayhi as-salām*. Eager Moses dreamed of larger things than the dwindling Jewish sector of the African Athens and the nominal economy afforded it by their true French masters. When a wretched *shiksa* showed up at their hearth with a shameful, swollen belly, she was sufficient motivation to join a cousin in America. For three weeks they sailed west across the Atlantic in the *SS Antonio Lopez* out of Spain: Moses, Ghislaine, and little Roy Simon, only six months old when in 1901 they embarked for Ellis Island and New York. He seemed marked even by that time by a trifling and wayward nature.

Roy was drafted into Pershing's Expeditionary Forces and fought not without distinction in the Argonne. It seemed that service in France had done some good for the boy: the grammar and spelling and outlook of his letters home improved, and he wrote of becoming a dentist. Alas, Spanish flu struck while he awaited transport from the Bordeaux embarkation zone known as the Mill. For seventeen days he hallucinated and sweat in a dank château pressed into service as an Army hospital. On the second day he began to seize. Doctors noted active encephalopathy; Reye's syndrome was ruled out only by his age. Swelling persisted almost forty-eight hours. Brain damage was feared. Indeed, had Roy's skull been cracked open, a pathologist would have found hyperaemic meninges, a pulpy and oedematous cerebrum, and reddish discoloration of the brainstem, along with diffuse haemorrhagic lesions—he was one of many victims of *encephalitis lethargica* in combination with that year's fierce A/H1N1. Roy was never quite the same after that; he didn't mail another letter until he'd already set up station as an attendant at the Perkins Bath House on the

---

Bab Semmarine: باب السمارين "Gate of the Farriers" southern gate of Fes el-Jdid
alayhi as-salām: صَلَّى ٱللَّهُ عَلَيْهِ وَآلِهِ وَسَلَّمَ peace be upon him
shiksa: Gentile woman (often derogatory)

boardwalk of Jacksonville, Florida. No further missives were forthcoming, and he never installed a telephone.

Roy remarked to seekers of his wisdom that the Jacksonville beaches were "awash with gash"; between his New York accent and general lack of spoken clarity since Bordeaux it almost rhymed. He was generous and free with his seed. Late in 1930, after Smoot-Hawley had begun to take its toll but before the bad bank runs started, he was presented with a son and a paternity suit. The boy's head seemed smaller than a healthy brain might warrant, his eyes still more so. He spoke very little, ducking his head under his arm when Roy looked at him. The upper lip, thin as a papercut, might have confirmed to a more perceptive potential papa the sad evidence of fetal alcohol syndrome, and indeed his mother had trouble standing or even staying awake. When in January 1931 she died of typhus, Roy took in an apathetic child unpropitiously christened Gabriel Furbish Bellows, endeavoring to make of him some approximation to a man. The first thing was to rename the boy. Roy thought of two other nonpracticing Jews with whom he'd fought. Thus the unfortunate Elijah Dorfzaun Katz.

Elijah was only seventeen by the time the next draft ended, narrowly avoiding World War II. He moved in with (but did not yet marry) Mildred Joy Blickers, a vivacious native of the central peninsula. She consumed in long pulls PBR without discernible limit, and while doing yardwork wore her rampant abundance of black hair up in curlers. Hearing on the radio about the Polish camps, he decided that giving up the Jewish faith and community was well and good, but it was probably best to shuck the naming, too. When their first child came, he told Mildred, "Let's name him Julius, like Caesar."

"I love it! I luv youuuuuuu! What about Cassius Julius?"

"What the hell's a Cassius?"

"He killed Julius Caesar. So he'll have the strength of both Caesar and the man who killed Caesar."

"No one killed Julius Caesar, dummy. He fell off his horse."

"Simple son of a bitch, Brutus and Cassius killed him in the Senate."

"The Senate! Why would an emperor be in the Senate?"

They fought and fucked and Cassius Julius Katz carried the day. Paternal Jewish heritage was never mentioned to Cassius. The few times he inquired as to their ethnicity, Elijah claimed to be Italian.

Roosevelt: How did you identify the material in Savannah? I thought it impossible to detect that kind of thing. Are there leaks in his organization?

Foster: Any number of ways. CIA has people in Kazakhstan with ears to the ground and dollars in pockets. Sailors weren't delighted to be used as mules in this kind of operation. NSA is up to their asses in Astana—they've got video of the diversion so good you can see the outlines of cocks.

Roosevelt: Uncircumcised, no doubt! Heathens.

Foster: Burroughs described Arab cocks as "wide and wedge shaped."

Roosevelt: Reading *Naked Lunch*, I thought it a sad thing that I could go on a hundred safaris without the chance to bring down a man-sized centipede.

PBR: Pabst Blue Ribbon

Elijah, Mildred, and CJ Katz left Jacksonville for Atlanta's northern exurb Canton in 1952, CJ two years old then, too young for memories. When he asked his parents later why they left Florida, he received uncertain answers and conspiratorial looks. Piecing together fragments and lapses over the years, he concluded that Mildred, passed out in the crumbling lanai opening onto their swampfront, reclined, sleeping with her Winchester 94 clutched loosely across her chest (a habit retained all her days), woke to movement among the fetterbush and honey locust. Announcing, "Step on my land, and I'll put one between your goddamned eyes," she leaped up, raised the .30-30 to her face, and went to half-cock. From the arrowwood shrubs burst an alligator absolutely tearassing it, a big fucker, seven feet at least, probably eight. Behind it emerged a specimen of genuine Floridian trashperson: denim overalls frayed to exhaustion, Confederate stars and bars sewn into his hat, shoeless, waving a machete, hooting delirious hog calls. Mildred, uninterested in whys and wherefores or what had been done to whom by who, drunk and sleepy and unhappy in the 36 °C steambath of fall in Duval County, dropped a double tap into the man's ten ring. She couldn't very well have a gator fucking with her gardenias and tomatoes, so three went into it as well. As the smoke drifted up and away, Elijah shambled out with a loud, clueless clatter, and she instructed her useless man to fling that piece of shit somewhere back in the swamp, somewhere deep. No *not* the gator are you out of your goddamn mind? She went inside to fetch her prized Silver Stag, a gift from her sister: there were a good thirty-five pounds of fresh meat in her backyard. Maybe more.

In Canton Elijah started up a business removing and disposing of dead animals. Callers sometimes complained of live ones, so he moved to serve that market also. "It's a series of yes or no questions," he told CJ on a job: "Is it alive? If yes, kill it. Is the carcass on private property? If yes, remove it and bill the owner. If no, remove it and bill the county." Many years later, CJ would collect this wisdom in an actual flowchart.

Their gloves were thick and went up to the elbow. They wore no facemasks. Elijah flung the gray bag and its two shelled armadillos, both toxified to death with phosphine gas, up into the truck's bed. "Having collected it in at least two Hefty Steel Sak reinforced bags—these sons of bitches might be dead, but their claws will come through a single bag and rip your ass up, CJ—you burn it." He dropped to a whisper. "Send it back to God." His breath was sour.

The incinerator sat in their backyard, effectively driving away neighbors despite a stake of six acres. Elijah put together the initial coal-fired installation. Mildred insisted that diesel would be more efficient, but Elijah pointed out that the Auschwitz crematoria had run off coke and that was good enough for him. It was a shambolic thing, quickly blackened and rusted, and the dark smokes of a burn were suffocating, mephitic, still barely tolerable at half a kilometer. The miasma got into your clothes and even your skin, and you never grew accustomed to it. CJ had few friends.

Cassius never returned following tenth grade's winter break, and had no intention of acquiring a GED. He was nonetheless quick, with an uncanny knack for machines and hands-on, practical engineering. He proposed to Elijah improvements on what was by now a truly appalling and macabre furnace.

When Elijah from laziness more than anything objected, he bought his own acres—these in Pickens County to the north, sparse and olfactorily remote—and with only a few simple calculations and furrowed brows and a borrowed arc welder constructed a marvel of a puppy smelter. Should Vulcan himself need reduce an unbutchered cow to ashes and atmosphere, he might in a pinch seek out Cassius's Carcasses LLC. It consumed natural gas, supported temperatures up to a kilodegree Celsius, could vaporize anything short of a moose, and when Cassius dared one blustery day to winch in a whole trio of shaggy black bears, it handled that onerous load. He clapped his hands. "Eat shit, bears!"

Soon he had the contracts of five counties, and Elijah's sputtering abomination had been ordered destroyed by the City of Canton. Elijah feuded and appealed and victorious Cassius bought a lovely starter home in a Woodstock subdivision. He provided the angel capital with which Elijah opened on Highway 92 what would become a thriving video rental concern. He successfully courted the boisterous Eveline Ringel, marrying her and bringing into the world the first Katz in three generations not born a bastard. He reluctantly took on his younger brother and his younger sisters' corn pone husbands, until the former set himself on fire, and the arrant in-laws, normally torpid beyond belief, were observed trading blows over a third woman, wife to neither, having tall hair and dubious honor. Cassius thought *Spartacus* a bitchin' film, inspirational really, and loathed those cracker-ass neighbors that clung to third- and fourth-hand memories of the failed Southern rebellion.

Sherman Spartacus Katz was in 1980 given a name with panache.

Foster: We're still arguing about how to go in if we find him. We don't think he's violent, but who knows? We want his computer badly, but a source says he's gone to great lengths to obstruct that possibility. I doubt we find significant incriminating material at his house.

Roosevelt: All that crab, though. A shocking amount of crab.

Foster: That's correct. A check on his cards revealed a charge, $300 plus taxes, for fifty tins of clearance crab claw meat, a pound each. I asked our close source, and she said he's eaten nothing but crab meat all month.

Roosevelt: The Marino woman? How would she know?

Foster: She blew him and he tasted like Diet Mountain Dew and tide pool.

Roosevelt: Delicious, but hardly admissible testimony!

The boy evidenced early a mind of rare puissance, skipping the second grade entirely. By eight he was reading longer novels than Cassius had ever looked into, and asking questions neither parent was in a position to answer. Innocently he one morning queried his father as to the meaning behind $E = mc^2$; it led to a miserable evening that saw CJ struggle through the *Encyclopedia Britannica* entry for SPECIAL RELATIVITY, and a tortured explanation (involving rather more railroads than expected) that satisfied no one. He won his elementary school's Spelling Bee and Geography Bee without serious competition, and if they'd had any other Bees he'd have won those, too. He was a force of nature at the state academic bowl tournament: there was never doubt as to who carried Georgia's 1991 Elementary School champions.

By 1991, even as she directed Sherman to apply to parochial middle schools, Eveline (unquestioned spiritual leader of the house Katz, Ephesians 5:22 be damned) was drifting away from the Catholic doctrine she'd learned as a girl. Her social group had become one of Protestants, many of them evangelical, and engaging with them in daily Bible study she found no Scriptural evidence for fish on Fridays, nor *limbus patrum*, nor the exclusive authority of Douay–Rheims and its dubious apocrypha (resistance stirred within Sherman as well, for different reasons). American Catholic progeny might no longer spend much time at the CYO (to the chagrin of Frank Zappa), but they gather on Wednesdays for CCD, "Confraternity of Christian Doctrine," an hour-long class on the catechism. It was taught by volunteers, and Eveline stepped up that year as tribute. Much to Sherman's dismay, she took the sixth grade class into which he was slotted. Arriving home from training, she leafed through the assigned curriculum, frowning, and declaimed "This is crap. I'll just teach what me and the girls are doing in Bible Study that week."

"I don't know, mom, it seems dicey to volunteer to teach a class and then take it in your own direction."

"It's all the Bible, Sherman."

"Well sure but isn't the whole fragmentation of Christianity due to differing interpretations of the Bible?"

"Catholic means 'universal,' Sherman. So Catholicism includes all those interpretations."

"How can a system contain contradictory statements? You can then derive anything you want." He didn't yet know ¬(p ∧ ¬p) as Aristotle's law of noncontradiction—*Metaphysics* was two years away, Gödel four—but he could smell a rat. "And I don't think you can say that just because it means 'universal' it actually is? And wouldn't it then contain, like, Satanism?"

Annoyed: "Don't say Satanism is contained in Catholicism or I'll slap your face. That's blasphemous, Sherman. You're stupid. God contains many contradictions. Jesus and God are distinct, yet they are the same coequal, coeternal, consubstantial hypostases, one Holy Trinity. This is Christianity 101. And, 'universal' means 'universal for Christians,' not 'whatever damn thing you want to believe in.' Give me a break."

"So not really universal, then. In fact restricted."

She was now grievously vexed. "Only if you're a dumbass. No one else is asking the Catholics, 'hey you're universal, can I sacrifice something nasty in here to Michael Dukakis?' because that's a stupid thing to ask."

"Are Mormons then under this umbrella?"

"Mormons aren't Christian!"

"What are they then?"

"I don't know! They live in Utah!"

Further questions would get him nowhere. So for several Wednesdays Eveline taught her renegade class in the evening with Protestant *samizdat*, and Sherman was torn between appreciation of her freethinking and worry that

---

limbus patrum: Limbo of the Fathers   **CYO:** Catholic Youth Organization
samizdat: самиздат grassroots dissemination of prohibited literature

she'd say something startlingly stupid. It happened three weeks in: she began
with a Psalm, then began to freestyle regarding David. She spoke of treacherous
Absalom, sister Tamar, and half-brother Amnon, David's firstborn. Amnon
looked upon Tamar with lust, a grave *chillul hashem*, and raped her, and Absalom
engineered his murder in retaliation. She paused, and looking salaciously out
over the class, said with triumph, "See? You don't need *Married...with Children*
or Cheryl Tiegs splaying herself all over the cover of *Sports Illustrated*. The
Bible's got plenty of sexy stuff in it." She gave them a moment to exchange
high-fives or perhaps raise her a cheer, and seemed disappointed that they did
not. Sherman buried his head. They rode home silently. The call requesting
that she not return the next week, or ever, came that night.

Nonetheless, Sherman applied for and was awarded a full scholarship to
St. Anthony's in Dunwoody, and his parents' hearts burst with pride. In 1992
Sherman Spartacus and two younger sisters were packed into a Dodge Caravan,
and they moved on up to comparatively tony Marietta. For two years, Sherman
covered himself and his family with glory. He won another Geography Bee, and
this time went to Nationals. He found a true delight in Latin: all his life he would
call upon the Virgil, Catullus, Horace, and Ovid learned that year by heart. He
mastered the language in three quarters, swallowing it up, and successfully
petitioned to study Greek in the eighth grade. That same year he achieved a
score on the AHSME sufficient to qualify for the American Invitational Math
Exam, the first eighth grader to do so at St. Anthony's in four years, *vox clamantis
in deserto*. He wrote two plays (both readable enough), short stories of varying
quality, and belted out a fine first tenor. His play on the defensive line was by
no means inspired, but solid; he was likely to go first-team varsity by tenth
grade at the latest. He could name the most forks at cotillion. Then he got a
modem, and a new world.

✳ ✳ ✳ ✳ ✳ ✳ ✳ ✳ ✳

The Naugle panel of 1982 recommended that the Shuttle carry civilians in
the hope of "adding to the public's understanding of space flight." Thus was
born NASA's Space Flight Participation Program; two years later, the President
announced the ill-fated Teacher in Space Project. The TISP placed "payload spe-
cialist" McAuliffe aboard STS-51-L, the tenth mission of OV-099 *Challenger*. As
detailed in the Rogers Report (and illustrated on national television by Richard
Feynman), the elastomeric O-rings of Thiokol's solid rocket boosters stiffened
in the freezing temperatures of Kennedy Launch Complex 39B. Ammonium
perchlorate composite propellant combusts in its chamber at a pressure of
over six megapascals; the resulting gases exceed 3300 °C. Sixty seconds after
launch, the O-ring joint failed, and flame arced away toward the LH$_2$ segment
of the central, structural External Tank. The Orbiter's fate was sealed. Liquid
hydrogen began leaking four seconds later, and what had been flickering, lam-

---

chillul hashem: חילול השם a desecration of God's name. Leviticus 22:32
AHSME: American High School Mathematics Exam
vox clamantis in deserto: the voice of one crying in the wilderness. Isaiah 40:3 as quoted in
Matthew 3:3, Mark 1:3, Luke 3:4, John 1:23 (KJV)
STS: Space Transport System   **OV:** Orbiter vehicle

bent plumes came together in a bright orange ball. At T+73, Pilot Smith was recorded muttering "uh-oh," and within a second *Challenger* was engulfed in a mass of flame. At twice the speed of sound and fourteen kilometers above sea level, aerodynamic loads well beyond design parameters broke the Shuttle into several large pieces.

Among these discrete elements was the pressurized crew cabin, shorn from the payload bay and trailing umbilicals and fluttering electrical cables. Impelled by its existing speed, it tore through the thin troposphere in a great ballistic arc, a confused meteor reaching apogee twenty kilometers up. Buckling of the mid-deck floor that would have accompanied uncontrolled decompression was absent from the wreckage; there exists convincing evidence that the reinforced aluminum compartment's crew remained conscious across two and a half minutes of unpowered flight. Through the triple-paned fused silica forward windshield they beheld momentarily a hot iridescence, replaced quickly by blue sky. Had things gone as planned, this would have darkened into the blackness of the void once the Orbiter crested the Rayleigh-scattering mesosphere. Instead, they rotated forward, pitching down towards the brown waters of the Atlantic. This profluent trajectory abruptly terminated with a 200*g* impact quite incompatible with existence.

Before McAuliffe's selection, overtures had been made to the Children's Television Workshop that puppeteer Caroll Spinney's Big Bird (plus teddy bear Radar, a gift from Mr. Hooper) might fly aboard *Challenger*. The idea was never approved: the Muppet's two-meter-plus stature and loosely-bonded plumage probably doomed the prospect from the outset. NASA didn't confirm these talks until 2015, but rumors had circled long before that. A wide-eyed Katz of fourteen years read them on FidoNet in 1994, and was deeply moved. The next day, he submitted to St. Anthony's literary magazine *The Disputant* "Big Bird Contemplates Terminal Velocity from *Challenger*":

> Ostrich, emu, proud penguin black and white
> gaze skyward and wonder what could have been.
> Failed birds afforded feathers but not flight
> might seek it in rockets Promethean.
> It seemed unfair that I'd be earthly bound—
> hale wings flapped, yet never left the Street.
> But looking back, at least that asphalt ground
> never betrayed these three-toed orange feet.
> Fell capsule in which all my dreams were placed
> falls homeward with obscene velocity.
> Life emerged from the oceans by God's grace;
> I return to the oceans at Mach 3.
> Though not all birds are built to fly,
> Birds Big and small must one day die.

It was uncommon for *The Disputant's* staff to provide reasons for a rejection, or indeed to indicate any verdict prior to publication. In this case, however, Katz was called to the faculty advisor's classroom, where he was informed that his sonnet was "demented, perverse, absolutely unhinged," and that he ought in the future take such efforts directly to the counseling office.

＊＊＊＊＊＊＊＊

With fervor he had begun to program. Too many nights to count he dreamed that he and those he met were C++ code. Function invocation and call-by-value reduction strategy replaced communication verbal or otherwise. There was no loss of flexibility or expression. No one called attention to this extraordinary state of affairs. On the phone a few years later, a prospective date indignantly conjectured nonexistence of her person's potential digital incarnations: "they couldn't feel the sensation of tasting an orange!" From dreamed experience Katz knew her to be wrong; from waking life he understood it neither time nor place to press the issue. But he asked, innocently, "is the dream of a sensation a real sensation?"

Lacking any kind of instruction or textbooks, Katz's knowledge of computer science was all over the map. Much of his university experience was learning the proper names for techniques and results he'd derived in high school, and enjoying a much more complete and refined presentation. He wrote his first program on an ATARI 400 in 1986. He had regular access to nothing else until 1992. He would greedily commandeer any Apple IIGS or IBM XT or even Commodore 64 he saw, but for six years it was just him and the ATARI's sixteen kilobytes and MOS 6502B. His only data structure was the array. With the endless time of children he spent hundreds of hours writing to various addresses and watching for results, to which he paid close attention.

By the time he got an 8086, he'd worked out a sizable chunk of the ATARI's hardware interface and instruction set. He didn't know addresses 0 to 255 were "page zero," but he knew they supported faster access than any other memory. He didn't know the term "register," but he knew five values were tracked and updated very quickly. He called them "clocks," thinking of them as the red numbers on the faces of ubiquitous digital timepieces.

He didn't know what "assembly language" was, but he knew that the same "clock" that tracked where you were in the program could be used to read the running program, which was a large array in memory. You could write to that array and change the running program. The program's behavior changed in a way correlated with the changes you made to that memory. In a few months he caught on to jumps. With that insight, the rest unrolled pretty easily.

Then he realized you could just write your program with these numbers directly rather than using BASIC, and with triumphant enthusiasm began to do so. He didn't know what "machine language" was, either. They were just "program numbers." Base ten numbers, at that—he was unaware of hexadecimal. A decade later, telling the story, someone asked if he'd made the change for performance. "No," he responded, "but I didn't have a reference for either the instruction set *or* BASIC, just a few magazines I'd found at the library with example code. I was building out my own references for both. With machine

---

ATARI: 当た り lit. "to hit the target"
BASIC: Beginners' All-purpose Symbolic Instruction Code

code, I could be sure I'd explored the entire capability space, due to the finite encoding of instructions. It was about completeness."

Foster: The more we dig, the more we turn up on these two, Katz and one Michael Luis Bolaño. They're into all kinds of dirt. It's likely that they made most of the LSD in this country for the past few years. Two boyfriends of Bolaño have gone missing. Likewise another name that links up, one Greg Moyer. Besides the LSD, they appear to have trafficked various controlled substances basically all their adult lives.

Roosevelt: Mossad thinks Katz changed his grades in high school. To strike at the official record is to strike at the very foundation of democracy, and at truth itself. Unwelcome news. Most unwelcome.

While still working in BASIC, he needed the ability to quickly add elements anywhere in an array. If you already had five elements at positions 0 through 4, and needed to insert at position 1, you had to copy four elements a position forward each. That took time—possibly a lot of time if it was a big array. You had to start from 4: if you started by copying 0 to 1, you wiped out the item at 1, and your whole array ended up with copies of that first value. If each element contained the index of its subsequent element, though, you didn't need to touch any other positions. It just cost a little memory, and you had to remember to walk the array using those indices rather than monotonically increasing constant ones. This was a useful trick, one he used often, calling it "telephones"; those taught it knew it as a linked list.

Roosevelt: Does Mossad just watch all Jews worldwide, you think?
Foster: Mossad watches everyone, but, again, probably not Jewish.
Roosevelt: They wouldn't know that.
Foster: Until they started watching him.

Working in machine language by now, he was searching for items repeatedly in a sorted array. He'd start from position 0, check to see if the item there was what he was looking for, and if so, great. If not, if the value is greater than what you're looking for, it's not in the array, and you can fail early. But otherwise, you had to go to the next position and check. If you were searching for the last item in a big array, this took a long time. It was annoying, because if you're trying to, say, go to the last page of a book, you can do that very quickly. He thought: how do you go to a particular page in a book? You don't start from the beginning and go page by page; you open the book to the right general area. So if you have, say, 100 elements, start at 50. If the value there is greater than what you're looking for, go to 25. If it's less, go to 75. If it matches, great. He called it "lightning find"; those taught it knew it as binary search.

✳✳✳✳✳✳✳✳✳

In the brutally hot Georgia summer he one afternoon hit tennis balls against the side of their first house. That part of the plot was a hill of red sticky earth, rich with divots and bare rocks and narrow gullies. It was a game of chaotic bounces and no lack of assbusting. Planting himself again into the mud, he

---

LSD: lysergic acid diethylamide, $C_{20}H_{25}N_3O$, of which much more later

watched the Penn 3 roll away, and mused that you never fall in the tennis video games. He pondered how this mechanic could be added, and inferred that what you really wanted were the full physics; the game ought simulate your virtual feet dashing across its Centre Court. Why didn't all games work that way? Was it impossible to build in chemical knowledge, so mixing virtual ammonia and bleach would gas into virtual chloramine? Could you build some universal engine, no pun intended, that was fed a molecular description plus higher-level holistics and gave you a truly realistic game? It would require a great deal more computational power than was available from his ATARI, sure. How big of a world could you run on one of those Cray X-MPs? What if you wanted your game to take place over the entire known universe? Was it possible to make a machine that could simulate all the universe's atoms? Even if you could compute the time evolution of one atom with less than one atom, wouldn't it need to simulate itself? And what if, in a game built on this engine, you built your own computer and attempted to simulate all the game universe's atoms, so there wasn't a true physical constraint? Was it possible? Could you solve the recurrence? You could call the game *Life*. Would it be worth playing?

A few weeks later, CJ asked Sherman if he was interested in learning how to join wood. The boy perplexed and amazed him, and yes frightened him a little, too; CJ and Evy worried that one day they'd all be electrocuted. It would be good to get him out of the house and teach him some workaday skills.

Sherman responded languorously, "I intend to build more elegantly. My media will be the photon, the atom. Deoxyribonucleic acid perhaps."

Cassius evaluated the boy. "Yeah, you sound like you're taking acid."

"Deoxyribonucleic acid is DNA." Sherman rolled his eyes.

Cassius wondered what the hell it meant to build with DNA. For that matter, what's a photon? Was it like a proton? He made a note to watch more *Star Trek*. It was mortifying to be outworded by this strange son. "I built your ass with DNA. If you don't want to learn joining, take your ass outside and mow the lawn. You're not staying inside with books all day today."

"Are we so vain?" Katz scrambled to his feet in a show of defiance. "Must we strive against nature's order? We meaning myself, of course, as no other members of our pentad Katz are directed to manhandle that thrice-damned mower around our hilly acre. Only I must pony up this weekly tribute to Sisyphus. *Multi autem sunt vocati pauci vero electi.* Why roll out to the Caravan each Sabbath to praise the Lord if, presented with God's good verdant bounty, we cry 'Hold! Too much!'?" He spoke with fire now, like a preacher of the Great Revival. Cassius watched, chewing thoughtfully his Lebanon bologna and cheddar on white bread, slow as a ruminant.

"Less than two months ago I was drafted—I dare say impressed—into uncompensated laying of sod. More grass? Less grass? What is it to be? We read Proverbs; can we not pick our proverbial lane?" He grew louder and more confident as he built towards magnificent peroration. "To what knuckle-dragging mongoloids of the heartland utopia do we hope to prove ourselves through this weekly ordeal?" Returning to normal volume, he looked Cassius in the eyes.

Multi...electi: Many are called, but few are chosen. Matthew 22:14 (KJV)

"And what is it, Old Father, Old Artificer, that we prove?" He fell to his knees, lifting his hands in supplication, taking his words from Josiah Wedgwood. "Am I not a man and a brother?"

"Nope, you're thirteen years old, and you're gonna mow the lawn." Cassius wondered, not for the first time, how this bizarre and impractical child had fallen out of his wife. Swallowing the last of his sandwich, he observed "it's just getting hotter out there while you bitch." He kept his tone even and sagacious.

Sherman trudged towards the garage, unhappy. "Is this the weekend our hero succumbs to heat stroke? What Valkyries will spirit away his body, shriveled and dark like a clay California Raisin among the red clays of Georgia? Ah, Bartleby! Ah, humanity! Six score years ago, Sherman burned Atlanta. Today, Atlanta burns Sherman. Every time I inhale the uncombusted hydrocarbons and volatile compounds of that machine's exhaust, I lose IQ points."

"Didn't you just say you wanted to build with atoms? Hydrocarbons are atoms, aren't they? Go get some practice."

This offense was too much. Sherman shrieked, "They're molecules! The combination of 'hydro' meaning hydrogen and 'carbon' meaning carbon precludes the possibility—" but his father had already left.

✳ ✳ ✳ ✳ ✳ ✳ ✳ ✳ ✳

Thoughts of rigorous definitions led to musing upon numbers. What was "one" in its Platonic Form? The dictionary said "a single thing," but wasn't "single" just a synonym of "one"? You couldn't say "that which when added to itself is two," because then you'd need define "two," and how do you do that without "one"? Zero seemed easy enough: an absence. The empty set. Nothingness, a single representation general across all countable things.

If you have zero, you could define one as "those collections from which removing any element leaves zero," but isn't "any" just another way of saying "one"? No improvement there, but if you said "those collections from which removing any non-trivial subset leaves zero," that seemed to work: there was no need to artificially limit the difference; the definition itself provided the necessary restriction. "Two" follows: those collections from which removing any subset of size one left behind a collection of size one. Satisfying. In eighth grade he read *ho gar arithmos estin ek tou henos kai tēs dyados tēs aoristou* and smiled in agreement. Years hence he'd learn equivalence classes, and the standard constructions within Zermelo–Fraenkel set theory of von Neumann ordinals using successors and bijections, and integers $\mathbb{Z}$ using the Cartesian product of these ordinals, and so on through the rationals $\mathbb{Q}$ and reals $\mathbb{R}$, then $\mathbb{C}$ and $\mathbb{H}$ and finally the quirky $\mathbb{O}$ in all their eight-dimensional, noncommutative, nonassociative glory, but look back warmly on this early insight.

The integers grow ever more positive and negative without bound. Yet between every two integers spans another infinite set, dividing that gap more and more finely. The infinity of $\mathbb{Z}$ grows only out; the infinity of $\mathbb{R}$ grows

---

ho...aoristou: ὁ γὰρ ἀριθμός ἐστιν ἐκ τοῦ ἑνὸς καὶ τῆς δυάδος τῆς ἀορίστου Number emerges from monadic one and the unbounded duality. Aristotle, τὰ μετὰ τὰ φυσικά (*Metaphysics c. 350 BC*)

$\mathbb{C}$: the complex numbers $\mathbb{H}$: the quaternions $\mathbb{O}$: the octonions

inwards as well. We can count to no largest integer, but we count to n, and say with earned confidence, "I name it n, and $n - 1$ positive numbers are smaller." Consider the set $\mathbb{N}$ of all positive numbers, and its proper subset of all even positive numbers. Every element $\{1, 2, 3, ...\}$ can be mapped to $\{2, 4, 6, ...\}$: just multiply by two. The second set can be mapped to the first by dividing each element by two. Thus there exists a bijection, and the two sets possess the same cardinality. Despite one containing the other and more, they are the same countable size. Hence the meaninglessness of schoolyard taunts of "infinity plus one." Don't let your guard down, though: this does not mean all infinite sets have the same size. What does it mean to count to 1.0? Infinitely many positive reals are smaller, and between each explodes another infinity. There is no means by which $\mathbb{R}$ can be mapped to $\{1, 2, 3, ...\}$. There's no way by which you can enumerate even those reals less than 1.0. Two infinities—"countable" and "uncountable"—of provably unequal size.

There emerged in the 1980s a cottage industry of encyclopedias. Along with dignified *Britannica* and the rather less genteel *World Book*, a resurgent effort arose from Funk & Wagnalls *(F&W New Encyclopedia* and, licensed from Peanuts Worldwide, *Charlie Brown's 'Cyclopedia)*. New competitors entered the arena: Grolier *(Encyclopedia Americana)*, Stuttman *(New Illustrated Science and Invention Encyclopedia)*, a *Children's Britannica*, Collier's (another *New Encyclopedia)*, Childcraft *(How & Why Encyclopedia)*, Greystone's surprisingly broad *Practical Handyman's Encyclopedia*, and Golden Book *(Encyclopedia of Natural Science)* are just a sample of short-lived sets striping twenty-plus volumes across A–Z. Displays at grocery stores and suburban malls hawked the first volume for some nominal sum, usually less than a dollar, in the hope that you'd spring for the entire set based off the strength of ABACUS or ANGOLA.

Ma and Pa Katz, thrifty shoppers all their lives, were not about to shell out a grand for reference sets Sherman could just as well read at the library. At the same time, a single volume for pennies was a phenomenal deal they couldn't pass over in good conscience. So Sherman came to have eight or nine first volumes, and for lack of other material read and reread them. All his life he enjoyed a thorough, detailed knowledge of subjects starting with AARDVARK and ending somewhere around AZERBAIJAN or BAKU, as they stood anyway circa 1988. Thankfully, this included ARITHMETIC and ATOM. Eveline and Cassius were pleased to give their son a solid grounding, at a price that couldn't be beat. Katz thought Jabez Wilson a whiny ginger bitch.

✳ ✳ ✳ ✳ ✳ ✳ ✳ ✳

Well into Catholic school and halfway through Confirmation lessons, scandal erupted in their parish. The choir director, an old friend of Eveline's, was forced out from her position. A few weeks later the family Katz attended a non-denominational Evangelical assemblage that met for several long hours in a high school gym. Sherman despaired of his new fellow communicants, clearly a step down in class and social standing from the smartly-dressed congregants his mother sometimes now referred to as Papists. Just two months before, his father had completed the protracted and not inexpensive Rite of Catholic Initiation for Adults, walking the catechumenate largely for his wife's peace of mind. Paul in his Epistle to the Galatians enumerated twelve (well, now only nine) Fruits of the Holy Spirit, and let it be said that Cassius Julius Katz embodied each one as he accepted new heresies so freshly forsworn.

Sherman, a committed Christian possessing a strong, full-duplex relationship with God, God's only begotten Son, and (to a lesser degree) the metaphor-cluttering Holy Spirit, observed this turn of events painfully, with growing heaviness of heart. Until now, he'd compartmentalized faith away from reading, from science, from a nagging absence of evidence for anything but a Deist watchmaker God. For the first time he contemplated his own apología, finding there nothing but glibly absorbed familial tradition. Regarding the *quinque viæ*, *Prima* (Unmoved Mover) and *Secunda* (First Cause) seemed the same thing. *Tertia* (Contingency) and *Quinta* (Teleological) struck him as failed, grasping logic. He looked around at the world and thought *Quarta* (Degree) a bad joke. Quantum fluctuations, slow roll inflation, and acoustic oscillations of baryons were more or less indistinguishable from an illimitable First Mover; tradition had been shown the door for reasons hardly theological. He said a last set of prayers, intoning them for the first sad time without real hope. From well-practiced genuflection he begged the God of his father (just barely) and forefathers (on one side) to lend him strength enough to believe. He stood and for a moment did not feel a fool. Then like the Temple veil his heart ripped from top to bottom: *templi scissum est in duas partes a summo usque deorsum.*

Emo wasn't yet a thing, really, but he got emo as hell. He underlined, as many had before him, whole long sections from the end of *The Portrait of the Artist as a Young Man.* He drank half a glass of Parrot Bay rum and had within an hour puked out his brains.

He cursed himself, and God, and his loud, apostate mother in all her misinformed Hofferian rodomontade, and his recreant father's acquiescence and unexamined philosophy and never being there to shut all this bullshit down, and the Pope and all Popes before him and the antipopes too, hoping them as annihilative as the name suggested, and Peter and Iesus Nazarenus, *Rex Blennorum et Bucconum et Stolidorum*; the Holy Ghost he deemed unworthy of his curses but then, thinking better of it, he likewise cursed. He cursed the College of Cardinals and the archbishops in their archdioceses and the bishops in bishoprics and *Brave New World's* velvety Arch-Community Songster and Aslan and he cursed all the priests he could remember, whom by that time *The Boston Globe* and hungry lawyers were demonstrating to be well beyond conspiracy to hump and indeed probably indictable under RICO as a continuing humping enterprise subject to formidable mandatory minima in addition to Papal reassignment and a stern Polish tonguelashing from the *pontifex maximus* in Holy Father John Paul II's sanctified person or even the unthinkable loss of vestments. He cursed their towheaded catamites, collaborators in their own de-

---

apología: ἀπολογία apologetics. Acts of the Apostles 26:2
quinque viæ: five ways. Thomas Aquinas, *Summa Theologica* (1485) I q. 1 a. 3
templi...deorsum: At that moment the curtain of the temple was torn in two from top to
     bottom. Matthew 27:51 (NIV)   **Iesus Nazarenus:** Jesus of Nazareth
Rex...Stolidorum: King of blockheads and dolts and fools. cf. John 19:3
pontifex maximus: "supreme pontiff" the Pope

filement with apparatus of vitiated lavabo and corrupted thurible, conspirators every time they proceeded to the nave's ambo in silent shameful surrender and acquiescence. Let my ballsack descend, oh three-personed cremaster God, so that I might cool it in the cruets of Eucharist wine, for it is Thy blood. Deez are my nuts which I give unto You. In remembrance of me You can suck them both. He enumerated the intersections of his worldline walking history like worn well-fingered beads of a rosary and among them counted liars and cowards and fools and like neutrinos superpositions of the three and counted himself most foolish of all, and his eyes burned with anguish and anger.

He set to erecting new, harder ethics. What Gospels synoptic and Acts Apostolic called metanoia, Crowley in Thelema named Crossing the Abyss, and the Night of Pan. Sherman was sure only that he'd never again accept an unconsidered truth, and that authority conferred no suzerainty over the real.

* * * * * * * * *

At fifteen Sherman Katz tried LSD, and just as a 2400 baud modem had opened up *unus mundus*, so did 150 μg seem the key to *anima mundi*. He first ingested dextroamphetamine as a senior, falling immediately into a lifelong love of substituted phenethylamines. Here in an orange pill was 20 mg of friend, of ally, of powerful ward against sleep and slayer of distraction.

He looked ecstatically forward: forward to a life of imagination made reality through manipulation of hardware and bits, forward to a life of reality made imagination through manipulation of neurotransmitters. Between the Idea and the Reality falls the Shadow, but he would spin the two together like waves of **E** and **B** in a long sleepless waking dream of formal systems. Hell, let's throw in the Shadow; do it like an earthquake's two shear polarizations and one longitudinal wave. *Et movebitur terra de loco suo.*

Reading rapturously aloud George Herbert's devotional "The Collar," the Welshman spoke to him from the Baroque, across four centuries, though perhaps not with the sense the metaphysical poet intended:

> *But as I rav'd and grevv more fierce and wilde*
> > *At every word,*
> *Me thoughts I heard one calling, Childe:*
> > *And I reply'd, My Lord.*

Sherman Spartacus Katz grokked his purpose, his raison d'être, his métier and justification. With confidence he started down the path ordained.

---

unus mundus: one world. Carl Jung, *Mysterium Coniunctionis* (Mystery of the Conjunction: An Inquiry into the Separation and Synthesis of Psychic Opposites in Alchemy, 1970)
   anima mundi: world soul. Plato, *Timaeus* (c. 360BC) 30b-d
   E: the electric field   **B:** the magnetic field
   Et...suo: and the earth will shake. Isaiah 13:13 (NIV)

2   sherman katz gets himself expelled

Sherman Spartacus Katz despised the sun all his life. He called it the Daystar, speaking thereof with contempt, and sometimes spit, and always sweat.

"A century ago, agriculture ceased to dominate our economy," he urged anyone not explicitly uninterested. "Time has been democratized, the telling of time anyway. Darkness: usurped by the electric lamp." His manager closed her eyes. "Yet you'd have me in the office by noon like some primitive geocentrist, chanting over goat bones." Control remained, if only by inertia, firmly with the forces of the diurnal, the oxen of the sun. In admittedly peevish protest he insisted on 24-hour time, correctly citing it as the preferred representation of ISO 8601—that's an *International Standard,* mind you—and requested meridional clarification whenever he could get away with it.

Your typical software shop puts candidates through a day of four to five whiteboard interviews, an hour per, entirely technical affairs forgotten minutes after filing feedback. The interviewer has favorite questions, asked dozens of times before, and tends to know within about ten minutes how the shit's going to go down. A coworker called in sick, or had an emergency, or died, whatever; they wouldn't be able to run their scheduled hour. The candidate's recruiter mailed Katz, requesting that he cover the unexpected two o'clock hole.

Within ten seconds: "would that be 1400h or 0200h?"

The recruiter swore at her desk, rejoining incredulously, "what chance is there that we're interviewing at 2AM?"

Katz replied, "ISO 8601's unambiguous representations make that kind of question unnecessary (probably why ISO chose them)." He scheduled delivery for 1405h, and blackholed further mail from the recruiter. 0200h interviews would be glorious, he thought: the clash of samurai under a soft moon, binary trees reversed in the coder's hour's achromatic truth. Do it outside, in loincloth. Not sexualized, but primitive, a contest between titans.

So there at #1 on the list: Earth's sun.

Death was absurd, incomprehensible, nothing to cheer about, but had at least evolution as recompense. It represented an honest termination, totality, a tallying, not mere maddening Nietzschean recurrence. Infinity is a potent memetic hazard, horrifying in its expanse, subsuming all it contacts. Remember Borges: "There is a concept which corrupts and upsets all others. I refer not to Evil, whose limited realm is that of ethics; I refer to the infinite." From $\aleph_0$ to $\aleph_\omega$ it is put on correspondences, yet never fathomed; not experienced, only rued: a glimpse of the past curling to become the future, a photon timeless and forever receding. Death was a nemesis as respectable as the Daystar was redoubtable; death was getting its job done.

But sleep? To burn one third of one's hours—precious, irreplaceable—on hosing down the ol' neurotransmissional stoop was fury itself. He really only

---

ISO 8601: International Standards Organization 8601:2004 *Data elements and interchange formats — Information interchange — Representation of dates and times*
$\aleph_0$: the cardinality of the natural numbers $\mathbb{N}$
$\aleph_\omega$: the least upper bound (supremum) of $\{\, \aleph_n : n \in \mathbb{N} \,\}$

got up a serious head of work at night, and recalled furthermore no good dreams, not one he was better for having experienced. Most were tedious: waiting rooms packed with uncomprehending children and the braying mad. Disputes with waspish bureaucracies, their couriers delivering forms referencing undiscoverable regulation. Furious callers demanded $\$\pi$ and enumerated severe penalties for inexact payment. Through labyrinthine asphalt and concrete he rode dismayed and unceasing shotgun along journeys atop complexes of bridges and cloverleaves and roundabouts, nonplanar arrangements necessitating level after soaring level. The topology changed among isomorphic configurations with great swirling roars, their fury signifying nothing, for he knew anyway no destination. In this dream he acquired a Rand McNally: it unfolded into Alexander's horned sphere, and he flung it away with distaste. Drivers rotated through after a night or nights and often there was no driver at all, the unattended wheel following silent stigmergy or curved space or perhaps its own ghostly instinct. During irregular stops at roadhouse skymalls he purchased broadsheets printed dense with hieroglyphics and boustrophedon. Their inks leached through his clothes and subsequent skin; their grainy pages fused into his fingers and like tumors sank new blood vessels. He inquired as to cigarettes, but the clerks exchanged uneasy, knowing looks, replying gravely, "on the way, *werter Herr,* soon; there are tonight bad troubles for the roads." He woke less rested than when he'd bedded down, crusted with salt, breathing the humid evaporates of his own slumberous sudations.

He might in an hour synthesize plodding weeks of oneiric time. These were rich worlds, revealing no scale beneath which further detail ceased to unfold. However deeply he probed, science of dreamspace reproduced that of wakespace. The bandwidth, he marveled, must be tremendous. Should he conjure a powerful particle accelerator to smash ultrarelativistic heavy ions, he'd no doubt dream of quark-gluon plasmas. Drowsy teenage thoughts, listening to Orbital's *In Sides*, reading Drexler's *Engines of Creation* or Wiener's *The Human Use of Human Beings* on the laundry room floor, the coolest place in the house...What of dreams beyond the Hagedorn? Would his sleeping mind supply what those awake could not yet detect; was he Bohm's hidden variable?

✳ ✳ ✳ ✳ ✳ ✳ ✳ ✳ ✳

Some say that children of the Cold War grew up in the shadow of Hiroshima. That's fatuous nonsense. Little Boy (Los Alamos's "Mark I") was a relatively puny device, best suited for use against an opponent already on the ropes and lacking retaliatory capability. Less than 1.5% of its 64 kilograms of highly enriched uranium fissioned, a yield equivalent to roughly fifteen kilotons of TNT (it's likely that about 0.3% of Fat Man's 120 kg natural uranium tamper fissioned, thanks to the top end of the fission neutron energy spectrum). California's Port Chicago and Staffordshire's RAF Fauld both suffered 2KT ammunition explosions in 1944. The *SS Mont-Blanc's* 2,653 metric tons of explosive cooked off in Halifax in 1917, where Intercolonial Railway telegraph operator Vince Coleman traded his own life to save hundreds, remaining at his station to broadcast

---

TNT: 2,4,6-trinitrotoluene $C_6H_2(NO_2)_3CH_3$ 2-methyl-1,3,5-trinitrobenzene

"HOLD UP THE TRAIN. AMMUNITION SHIP AFIRE IN HARBOR MAKING FOR PIER 6 AND WILL EXPLODE. GUESS THIS WILL BE MY LAST MESSAGE. GOOD-BYE BOYS." The ungainly drag of Coleman's ten-kilo balls tragically prevented him from reaching safety.

A superbolide over Chelyabinskaya dissipated in 2013 at least 400KT as blast. The sables and ermine of Tunguska's taiga ate shit and died under a 1908 meteor's eyewatering *12MT* airburst. A Mark I detonated at optimal height over the Mission District would leave the Golden Gate standing and the Tenderloin markedly improved. The same device dropped on central Tokyo's Imperial Palace would scour less area than Operation Meetinghouse's distributed 1.6KT. To really carve from a megalopolis its heart of steel and glass, to set alight suburban homes, to broil alive in their vehicles panicked families on jammed evacuation routes—if you Gotta Catch 'Em All—you want a meg or two. A quotidian fission device won't get you there. The necessary plutonium would ensure a predetonation due to neutron flux; sufficient uranium can't be assembled in time from an initially subcritical configuration.

No, Hiroshima's most unsettling shadows were the *hitokage no ishi*: silhouettes flashfried onto buildings and steps, delineating regions shielded from thermal pulse by a vaporizing body. Truly eschatological visions rose not from Honshu nor Kyushu, but *Pikinni* and Kiritimati and *Ānewetak* atolls (save *Āllokḷap* island; Ivy Mike's 10.4MT excised it from Earth's surface, putting it forever out of the shadowcasting business), from the *Novaya Zemlya* archipelago and *Archipel des Tuamotu*, from *Luóbùpō zhèn* in Xinjiang and the Polygon at Kazakhstan's *Semipalatinsk-21*. Give Teller and Ulam and Sakharov their due, but through the 1950s you were still talking gravity bombs delivered by Tu-16 Badgers and B-52 Stratofortresses, lumbering beasts vulnerable to interceptors and even on Chrome Dome missions hours away from targets.

Mount that meg atop an ICBM or SLBM, and the calculus changes. Less than half an hour after launch, a strategic ballistic missile reenters the atmosphere at well over twenty megameters per hour. To live during the last thirty years of the Soviet Union was to know that at any moment, without ever knowing the reason, a second sun might appear in the sky. Light beyond any light you'd experienced, then blindness, then heat and overpressure, and finally darkness for you and all you knew, all arising from ideological differences, ha-ha, or stupid mistakes, ha-ha again. It promoted a certain fatalism for sure.

The unique irony for children of the 1980s was that the Cold War seemed for all intents and purposes won. This was not the USSR that shattered Hitler's indestructible armies, but the lummox whose Afghan misadventures made the world forget for a moment about Vietnam. Soviet music exported no Janet nor Jermaine, let alone a Michael. Solzhenitsyn won the Nobel Prize in Literature in 1970; for this, the home of Tolstoy and Dostoyevsky put him on a plane to Frankfurt after a failed assassination (the KGB used ricin, later successfully

---

hitokage no ishi: 人影の石 human shadow etched in stone
Pikinni: Bikini   **Ānewetak:** Enewetak   **Āllokḷap:** Elugelab
Novaya Zemlya: Нóвая Земля́ New Land
Luóbùpō zhèn: 罗布泊镇 Lop Nur Test Site
Semipalatinsk-21: Семипалатинск-21 Semipalatinsk Test Site

employed against Bulgarian dissident Georgi Markov). If you didn't have your own NES, there was probably one down the street. Playing *Super Vorkutlag Comrade Bros.* (mine coal, eat Super Mushrooms for caloric content) or *Gosplan Hero* (a central planning simulator) meant waiting until 1992—*after* the fall of the CCCP—for the Dendy. With that said: Tetris.

OK, Communist cinema had some winners: *Idi i smotri* is an undeniable masterpiece. From Tarkovsky: *Zerkalo* most certainly; *Solaris* if you're into that kind of thing. Eisenstein duh, also the fever heat of poetess Anna Akhmatova, and Mikhail Bulgakov's subtle satires. Gorky? Fine, fine. Socialist realism is a dreary genre, but one can't hate Pavel Korchagin of *Kak zakalyalas' stal'*. Calling Pasternak a Soviet writer seems specious at best. Nabokov? Now you're trolling. The anthem is perhaps the greatest of all time.

The Soviet Union had been created by that most dangerous type of human being: fanatics full of passionate intensity, convinced that they're doing good. No nation that traps its citizens behind kilometers of walls bristling with machine guns and guards is a nation one wants to be a part of, nor is it a nation that can last. The final years of Brezhnev and the interregna of Andropov and Chernenko saw the world's largest country and its ten time zones clearly decaying. Perestroika would soon be at hand, but between Able Archer, FleetEx '83-1, deployment of the Pershing II, SDI, Operation RYaN, false alarms in *Oko* (we can thank Stanislav Petrov in Serpukhov-15 for averting gigadeaths), and the slaughter of KAL007's 269 passengers by an Su-15's AA-3 Anabs, 1983 brought the two superpowers closer to war than any time since at least October 1962. It was clear even then that the Bloc was not long for this earth. The question, and it seemed very real, was whether this ossified system would take the rest of mankind with it when it went.

✳✳✳✳✳✳✳✳✳

In high school, Sherman heard a few ladies in Poetry Club discussing with giggles and low voices *The Story of O*. He'd the previous week suffered through a nauseating Pablo Neruda swoonfest from these same girls, and currently held their taste in low esteem. Nonetheless, he was uncomfortable with anyone reading something he hadn't, and that evening at work picked up a copy. He opened it and was quickly disgusted. Ugh, so many piercings. Eveline entered his bedroom, saw it, and swooped down to seize it from his hands. "*The Story of O*? Sherman, why are you reading this? This is a dirty book! Your father gave it to me when we got married, and I went right up to him and said, 'Cassius Julius, I don't know what you meant by this, but if you think I'm getting up to

---

NES: Nintendo Entertainment System
Vorkutlag: Воркутлаг Воркутинский исправительно-трудовой лагерь
    Vorkuta Corrective Special Labor Camp
Gosplan: Госплан State Planning Committee
CCCP: Союз Советских Социалистических Республик USSR
Idi i smotri: Иди и смотри Come and See (1985)   **Zerkalo:** Зеркало Mirror (1975)
Kak...stal': Nikolai Ostrovsky, Как закалялась сталь *How the Steel Was Tempered* (1936)
SDI: Strategic Defense Initiative
RYaN: Ракетно-ядерное нападение Nuclear Missile Attack
Oko: Око Eye (satellite-based early warning system)

any of this French nonsense, you've got another thing coming."' She ascended the stairs, taking the paperback with her.

He hadn't been enjoying the book, but this aggression would not stand, and two days later he bought another copy. Eveline greeted him at the front door, and he lost it before it was even opened. He'd exhausted his location's copies, and wrote out an Ingram order for more. It slipped his mind until that summer, at which point he dutifully bought a third copy of this book he thought so distasteful. Within a few hours of arriving home, Eveline found him with it, and pounced. This time he held onto it tightly, and said "no Mom, it's assigned summer reading; I've got to read it."

Dumbstruck: "They assigned you *The Story of O* for summer reading? This is for AP English?"

"Yeah they're doing a theme. Books with letters in the names. We've got to read Pynchon's *V*, the collected Archibald MacLeish, for *J.B.* presumably—that one's a poetic drama, Pulitzer in Drama 1959—*J R* by William Gaddis—oof—*A Void* by Perec—"

"What's the letter in *Avoid*?"

"Not *Avoid*. *A Void*. *La Disparition* in the original French. Lipogrammatic—Perec was of the Oulipo school—it never uses the letter 'e.' Very difficult in French, surely a bitch to translate. And then *The Story of O*. I can understand leaving out Čapek's *R. U. R.* and Asimov's *I, Robot*, but I'm honestly kinda surprised she elided Updike's *S*." Proteus. Books you were going to write with letters for titles. Have you read his *F*? O yes, but I prefer *Q*. Yes, but *W* is wonderful. O yes, *W*.

"What about J. D. Salinger?"

"That's an author, mom."

"Oh, so authors don't count?"

"Well then it would be anyone with an initial, right?"

She stares at him for a moment. "I doubt this would have happened at St. Anthony's. But I guess this is what you get from the public schools." She leaves, and he explodes with laughter, and returns to the grotesque Reage.

A few hours later with book long done, he hears "SHERMAN SPARTACUS, get your ass up here." He heads up the stairs, taking two at a time. Eveline stands, livid. "I just got off the phone with the Cobb County School District. Do you know why they called me?"

"They're redoing the physics curriculum and wanted your input."

"No. Ass. Guess again."

"An emergency related to Virginia Slim Ultra Lights."

"No. I called a few hours ago to give them hell about your assigned summer reading." Katz knows what's coming by the time she hits "give them hell," and laughs hard. "Oh yeah, laugh it up, well I told them *The Story of O* is unfit for children. They didn't believe me at first. The nice lady asked, 'are you absolutely sure, ma'am?' and I, stupidly believing you, told her 'oh yes Sherman listed all the books with letters in them.'" Sherman doubles up. It's so wonderful. "Well apparently they agreed with me, because they tracked down your poor AP English teacher on her cheap vacation in Jekyll Island, and that's barely a vacation because Jekyll is strictly trash. They leave a note with her hotel asking why in the world she assigned you pornographic garbage. So I just got a call back telling me, 'we think someone might be playing a trick on you, ma'am.' And I look like an idiot. And your AP English teacher is going to know you're a liar." Sherman is delighted; the entire ordeal has in a flash been made worthwhile.

"Mom I'm sorry but that's hilarious. Best thing I've heard all summer.."

A sheepish smile. "I guess it is kind of funny. Bring me that book."

"With pleasure. I'm done. It was gross."

"You read it all?"

"Finished an hour ago."

"Damn, Sherman, you read fast." She looks appreciative, then grimaces. "Why did you insist on reading that particular book?"

His face grows hard. "I won't have you taking words from me."

* * * * * * * * *

The room is dark, the hallway less a source of light than noise. Metal halide floods attending the parking lot defend against lawsuits but provide scant illumination through the high, wide window. The overhead lamp is off, per always. Sixteen meters of T5 LEDs, strung year-round along the ceiling on green Christmastime insulator, are despite their six colors decorative at best. Aggressively rectangular geometry is that of the (bare) mattress writ large. Upon first moving in, Sherman Spartacus Katz had wondered whether it was sized according to the Golden Ratio; measurements proved no. A 24" Samsung flat panel provides an orange luciferian gleam for one side of his ponderous head, but he is ventilating in the finest of fettle, and even without this luminance would be the natural focal point of attentions. A clean shave—he has never indulged facial hair, and is unmarked by tattoos—contrasts with the heavy storm of black curls through which he regularly runs his hands.

Twenty-four years old, he was two days ago cleared for graduation, a narrow thing uncertain right up to the end. He stepped onto campus in the Fall of 1998, a dewy-eyed "junior by hours" thanks to the College Board's Advanced Placement exams. Three semesters in, he was the pride of two different departments. Three semesters after that, GPA in freefall and looking like a prisoner of war, he was summarily invited to leave, to depart, to be gone. To contemplate a still lake while speakers unseen played "Dust in the Wind." To remove his sorry worldline from this Institute of Technology. To disentangle, to decohere. It has been a long, hard climb back. Though he graduates *sine laude* or maybe even *summa cum dubio*, it is with both a BS-CS and a BS-MATH (the former for phat cash, the latter for love), and if a septennium seems a slow and winding path to glory...well, Daniel when exiled in Babylon prophesied a seven-year Great Tribulation, and if this wasn't a Tribulation, what is? Katz knows only pride, and luck, and thanks. *Ave Satanas!*

His class, many of them cherubs several years younger, walks tomorrow at the Coliseum. Katz has consumed most of a bottle of Gran Patron Platinum

---

sine laude: without praise   **summa cum dubio:** with greatest doubts
Ave Satanas: Hail Satan   **gaudeamus igitur:** let us rejoice

scored earlier for this evening's festivities, and any number of shots besides, and has no intention of taking his place among that bovine swarm. Around five in the morning, Alysha will surreptitiously dose him with several milligrams of her alprazolam, and when this semester's Computer Science graduates stand to shuffle under an oppressive Daystar he'll be a third of the way through eighteen unrousable and motionless hours. By Sunday morning, it'll be back to code. Always, always there is code. Code to be made more rigorous, code to be refactored into more sensible forms. Code to be benchmarked, optimized, microoptimized. Code to lucubrate through sunrise. Code to steal sleep, code to take priority over school and family and friends, code with its unrelenting call that can drown out all the rest of life. Die at your terminal waiting for emacs to start, and die thinking of intended improvements of the code. Little hits of warm dopamine pleasure with each item struck from the buglist. But tonight is for revelry: *gaudeamus igitur.*

Outkast's *Aquemini* bumps from M-Audio AV40s, and Katz is moved at times to sing along. A hammer pipe rotates counterclockwise among the half-dozen people of the circle, intersecting at two antipodes per circuit with the clockwise path of an absolutely enormous bong. This latter boasts a formidable bowl of intricate design, and beneath that an expensive ash-catcher. Its modularity suggests a military rifle. The substantial salient by which the bowl is grasped resembles nothing so much as a cockspur.

Katz conjectures that there exists an age A when one stops naming bongs, but has not yet reached it; he's dubbed this mastodontic bit of borosilicate *Kleinbong.* In America in this two-thousand and fifth Year of Our Lord, fewer than 2% of respondents surveyed recognized the term "Klein bottle." The numbers are quite a bit higher among those visiting this evening, but even there, uncommon are they who can rattle off any working definition: a two-dimensional non-orientable closed manifold, then, constructed (in a space of at least four dimensions) by joining the edges of two Möbius strips. Whether a listener's eyes glaze over or indicate comprehension, he typically plunges forth: "a bong is of course homeomorphic to a cylinder, not a sphere and two crosscaps, but my hope is that this bong has not yet taken its final form. It inhabits a potential well, a local minimum. One day a true warrior will rip from it a hit so beefy, such a thick and savory smokeloaf, such density of krunk, that spacetime itself will be reconfigured like a dank kugelblitz, and what then of topology?" It's nonsense, but sounds good. Katz counts several friends both knowledgeable enough to call him on this bullshit and sufficiently spergy to actually do so. He has identified them, and to them the bong will remain nameless. One doesn't entertain engineers without learning to shepherd fellow dwellers of the spectrum past regrettable *faux pas.*

Electric Sheep renders fractal flames when ncmpcpp isn't being used to control the music. With an expired Library of Congress Reader card reserved for special occasions he scrapes together an intimidating pile of powders, combining them, crushing them under a pestle of tungsten carbide, cutting them absentmindedly back into graceful rails. The surface upon which he plays is a rimmed circle of transparent tempered glass lacking corners that might trap active material; a separate top can be slid into latched grooves, protecting the contents from ashes and sneezes and prying eyes. He'd traded a local glazier a half ounce for it several months prior, and enjoyed bringing it out at parties. The bong came to him from the right just as the pipe approached from the other side, and he was one hand too short, and he spoke sharply.

"What gormless cretin passed the wrong goddamned direction? There are but two rules of smoking weed. It is an undemanding hobby suitable even for simpletons. Pass no bowl that is cashed. Announce instead 'this is cashed,' that it is *ṭumah*. Better still, repack it in silent charity: *dico vobis quamdiu fecistis uni de his fratribus meis minimis mihi fecistis.*"

Electric Sheep changes phases, its tint shifting from orange to damson.

"And secondly pass always to the left, as Cypress Hill did before you. Parallel transport. Intersections such as this one are provably impossible assuming equal velocities among bowls. This powerful result is independent of angular momentum. Would that bowls were subject to superposition and perhaps in the next world they are but alas this is an imperfect world and I can smoke but a single bowl B at a given time T especially whilst preparing nose drugs for the benefit of all. We are not executing Floyd's algorithm for cycle detection. I will pass both pieces to the left in succession. After I hit them."

Fuck, "parallel transport" is a well-defined concept in differential geometry. Will anyone call me on it? He eyes the circle warily. Fisk and Choudhary have taken relevant classes for sure. Doubtful that anyone but possibly Michael has read Egan's *Schild's Ladder,* nerdcore triumph or no. Remember that paper that referenced the LBJ slogan? "All the way with Gauss-Bonnet."

"Sherman my brother, what scrapest thou? Does thy apothecary thrive? Help me to not sleep this night."

"Desi Devesh, what was it about Gujarat that left you talking like a King James Bible? Are you not a student of the heathen and polytheistic Mahābhārata? Suck you not the balls of Garuda, best of birds? Will you not like Arjuna play the Kṣatriyaḥ and uphold dharma? Did you learn English from *Dragon Warrior?* Thou hast been F'd in the A by an Axe Knight. Thou art dead."

"Brother Sherman, I rep my desis but put on for my gujjūs. And thy knowledge of the Hindu epics is as shallow as it is vulgar. The Mahābhāratam is neither catechism nor consuetudinary. Hinduism is a holistic philosophy, undevoted to torturing points of reductionist theology hoping they might yield universal truths. Semiotic haruspices pick among the rubbly morphemic smashings of divine memetic colliders searching for hints of the Higher Mysteries. Thou puts too many faiths in words, the inventions of men, into semantics."

"Hail Eris, all hail Discordia. I'm not arguing religion with you Devesh, just wondering whenceforth this Jacobean 'thou' horseshit."

"The matrix of first-order partial derivatives of a function?"

ṭumah: טומאה ritually impure
dico...fecistis: I say unto you, inasmuch as ye have done it unto one of the least of these my brethren, ye have done it unto me. Matthew 25:40 (KJV)
Desi: देसी person of the subcontinent (friendly) (from Sanskrit देश deśá land)
gujjūs: ગુજ્જ Gujarati (sometimes friendly)

"Christ. Arjuna. Krishna. 'Jacobean,' not 'Jacobian.' James the Stuart. Middle English hands the baton to Modern English. *Of Engelond, to Caunterbury they wende* and they came back speaking something you can understand."

"Is that not the Elizabethan?"

"Elizabethan is before. Marlowe and Spenser. Shakespeare, of course, who straddles both."

"What comes after?"

"Caroline."

"What was the house of Caroline?"

"For Carolus. Charles. Carolus. These things generally refer to a single monarch. Charles II is Carolean. What are they teaching in the schools?"

"Forgive my ignorance of the ridiculous ancient aristocracies of an empire that oppressed both our nations, reduced now to NATO's biggest aircraft carrier. In Indian schools they are teaching electromagnetics. But I recall mention only of ages Elizabethan and Victorian."

"Because both those bitches lived for about a hundred years. The Caroline era ended with the untimely decoherence of Charles I."

"Decoherence?"

"His wave function collapsed."

"In what way did the King of England depart from unitarity?"

"He was decapitated by a genocidal Calvinist."

"And presumably observed as well. In Gujarat we have Hindus, yes, but also many Moslems and Zoroastrians too. Baghdadi Jews. My family regresses towards a Laodicean mean, but the exonymic Hindus of my state do appear rather more content than many Americans. What drugs hast thou there?"

"Devesh, you looking to get wild tonight?"

"Always thou knows that I am with it and for it."

"Gentlemen and m'lady—and why aren't there any more girls here why must y'all move like flocked sausage, Bolaño excepted for obvious reasons of gay—I have here a small sumptuous mountain of what I call methamketacaine, or I suppose ketacophetamine, full IUPAC designation methamphetacokaineamine. Mostly. There's also some 2C-I, traces really, nothing to worry about." He holds aloft a glassine bag and squints with suspicion. "I considered adding this mysterious powder, sold to me as LSD tartrate. But I trust it not. I suspect it to be 25I-NBOMe, a new phenethylamine active—and dangerous—in the microgram range. If anyone wants any, feel free. I intend to run it through a spectrometer."

Michael shook his head and sighed, making a note to bitch at Katz later. Katz heard him, and grimaced.

"Yeah they never made it clear what machine they were raging against, but I assume it was a mass spectrometer. Anyway, no enigmatic and potentially toxic

---

Of...wende: From England to Canterbury they travel. Geoffrey Chaucer, *Tales of Caunterbury* (The Canterbury Tales c. 1400) Prologue 16

IUPAC: International Union of Pure and Applied Chemistry

2C-I: $C_{10}H_{14}INO_2$ 2-(4-iodo-2,5-dimethoxyphenyl)ethan-1-amine

25I-NBOMe: 2-(4-iodo-2,5-dimethoxyphenyl)-N-[(2-methoxyphenyl)methyl]ethanamine

powders. But I did dump in the last of my synthetic mescaline from that batch last year. About a half gram. It ought definitely put some glow on everybody. I'm debating whether I want to eat acid. More accurately, to bust a big squirt of liquid directly down my throat in a Delta Force-like assault on my 5-HT$_{2A}$ receptors."

He looked down from his Aeron to Alysha, sitting to his left on the bed.

"What of you my love? Wanna dose hard tonight? I only graduate once."

"Do as you wish; I work in the morning. I'm expected at the law library. You barely slept this week, though—are you sure you're down for heavy hallucinogenics?"

"Ahhh, wise observations. Just monstrous lines of combined stimulants, then, and of course ketamine for that wavy hazy feeling-kinda-bowling-ballish disassociation."

"I'm definitely open to that mean mixed grill, though."

"Oh shit is somebody cooking? Do we have human food?"

"That heap of nose drugs, idiot. Blow some and pass it. Or just pass it."

"Ahh of course."

In walked Greg Moyer: casually disliked, tolerated in business, fratmax to the core. He handed to Katz a bottle of Moët White Star bearing a pink bow.

"Congratulations on finally graduating after seven years. Didn't honestly think you'd ever go back and do it."

"Nah I wasn't going to go through life without a degree."

"Why does it even matter? You already had the job."

"Because I'm not going to be a degreeless asshole. Beyond that, I'm the only cracker of my cracker-ass family to go to college, and I wasn't about to let them give me shit about it. Much less take shit from bitches like you."

Up go Moyer's arms. "No shit from me, Katz. As I said, congratulations. How many grades did you have to hack in and change to get out?"

Katz's first thought is "withering look," but he promotes it *gratis* to "contemptuous" and then "disdainful." He settles magnanimously upon "thin smile." The decision tree is run before any motor neurons fire; there is no indication that he ever felt other than bemused tolerance.

"Don't even joke about that. The last thing I need is for Tech to come after me with allegations of academic misconduct. God knows there was enough of it going around, especially in CS. I don't get it, personally. CS isn't exactly conceptually overwhelming, and you're gonna need to know how to do the shit on the job. But whatever. Actually, there's a story I don't think I've ever told y'all, or anyone. I suppose having now graduated college—"

Danny Fisk leaped up and yelled YEAAAAAAAAAAAH!

"YEAAHAAHHAHAHAAHAHA!—I can relate the tale now. One minute."

He ripped a tremendous hit from the Kleinbong, hove up a hale line, and passed the felonious farrago along to eager Alysha.

"So around the end of tenth grade, I realized that if I didn't get expelled, I wasn't going to be able to go to college." He paused. It's a Startling Claim; let it sink in. Let everyone get comfortable. Turn the music down. "I'd maxed out the PSAT early and skipped a grade so I wasn't too concerned about college, right? Everything was easy. *Rien n'est simple, mais tout est facile.* Then I got a modem, a k-shitty 2400 Hayes. That was an 8086 so this is pre-ISA bus, pure 8-bit expansion card—"

"Yo the whole difference between 8086 and 8088 was that the 8088 chopped the bus down to 8 bits. 8086 could use 16 right?"

"*Ja* but the physical interface was only eight. The 16 was for memory. There was this company Olivetti that built, like, the Lamborghini of eighty-eighty-sixen clocked on a then-baller dekahertz with custom sixteen-bit slots that could accept the full buswidth. Then ISA came out a few weeks later and did the same thing, except completely incompatibly and with support from companies beyond Olivetti, which is why you've never heard of Olivetti. Fucked to death by the Industry Standard Architecture."

Michael: "Intel really fucked you on the encodings for IN and OUT, too. A legacy of eight-bit immediates and the now-useless EE byte."

Alysha in quick succession: "Olivetti is like a century old, dumbass. Don't you have a boner for Burroughs? There's an Olivetti Lettera 22 in *Naked Lunch*."

"Michael." Katz holds up a single finger. "I will reply to you momentarily. Alysha, I have read *Naked Lunch* like fifty times and nowhere in there does the word Olivetti appear."

"It's in the Cronenberg movie. Which I have *insisted* that you watch."

"You can identify make and model of typewriters by sight?"

"You can't?"

"You amaze me every day." He kisses her; they're both smiling. "Bolaño, all that went to MMIO pretty quickly, though, right?"

"Sure, but you're not reclaiming opcode space."

Alysha speaks up: "The group rape perpetrated by the conquerors is a metonymic celebration of territorial acquisition."

Heads turn; Moyer is the first to ask. "Did you just say group rape?"

"What Michael said about not reclaiming opcode space, it just made me think of Spivak's essay, 'Can the Subaltern Speak?' I remember reading it and thinking well shit, I nominate that for Grimmest Use of 'Metonymy' or Derivative Thereof in a Sentence, 2001. Have none of y'all boys read it?" She pauses. "No? No Spivak, no Cronenberg. Disappointing. Read her introduction to *De la grammatologie*, which is basically like you've read *Grammatologie* itself, since Derrida is unreadable and everyone just goes by what she wrote in said introduction."

"Is Derrida really that bad? I thought what I read of Foucault was reasonable enough. *Discipline and Punish* was solid."

"What do they have to do with one another save both being French? They hated one another, actually. And Derrida was born in Algeria, like Camus."

"They both signed Sartre's petition to fuck little boys."

"Wait what?"

"Basically all the French philosophers less Camus petitioned the *Assemblée nationale* in 1977 demanding catamites. Deleuze, Barthes, it was a whole thing.

Rien...facile: Nothing is simple, but everything is easy.   **MMIO:** Memory-mapped I/O
De la grammatologie: Jacques Derrida, *Of Grammatology* (1967)

General strike of the poststructuralists. *Sous les pavés, la plage!* Simone de Beauvoir signed likewise. She didn't want to fuck boys so much as she'd become thoroughly disinterested in fucking Sartre. All those lobsters."

"I thought Hell was other people. No, it's these goddamn crustaceans."

"Well who knew. So yeah a piece of shit. But at least it was its own IC, not like the Winmodems that followed, which were barely a bare DAC and string and could be relied upon not to work in Linux ever. So I get the modem and stop giving a shit about anything. Might as well have been smack—"

"That's what The Mentor said back in *The Hacker Manifesto*, right?"

"Michael I can always count on you to catch my Phrack references. Though the article's actual name was *The Conscience of a Hacker*. Common mistake by those who don't know what they're talking about. OK everybody shut the fuck up; I've got the floor. So this is 1993 or 4, eighth grade, right as transcripts start to count, and suddenly I'm bringing home all Cs and Ds. All my time is spent exploring BBSs, then getting into the leet scene, and suddenly having access to documentation and other computer people—we were still pretty rare then, right? So I'm suddenly learning all this shit I'd been wondering about for years. I got Ralf Brown's *Interrupt List* and that alone, it was like holy shit, I burned thousands of hours as a result of that tfile. Fundamental leap forward as a programmer. Because I'd never had the books, or anyone I could learn from. That Ralf Brown list was available as a book—if you had forty dollars, which I did not. Well that's when Zell Miller set up the HOPE scholarship, which required a 3.0, and I realized well fuck I'm three-eighths of the way into this bitch with not but shit. I might not even get *admitted*, even if I turn this ship around, which I don't really want to do anyway. Well, I'm doing lots of wardialing during this time. All flows from *WarGames*, right?"

Nodding is general. *WarGames* was pivotal for much of present company.

"I hack up a dialer in Turbo Pascal and later find Mucho Maas's ToneLoc—"

"You liked to do the wild thing!"

"Yessssssssss. Well one of the things I found out early is that phone numbers tend to evidence a degree of spatiotemporal locality. If you order a few at once, I'm guessing they're clustered, until the exchange fragments up anyway. I notice that the FAX number for a school is just the voice number plus one. This pattern holds as I experiment with a few local high schools. So I dial around these numbers, and on every Cobb County school I try, there's at least one modem answering right around the voice number. Now these hosts do a standard V.8bis handshake—I've got a 14.4 USRobotics Sportster now, so I guess V.32bis—but it's all garbage. I make a note of them and move on. A few weeks later I'm playing with Norton pcAnywhere. I dial in raw to the remote machine, and hey, it's just the same garbage as those numbers. I use pcAnywhere to touch 'em, and boom, game recognizes game. Default creds are admin/password, but no dice. I had however nothing if not time and, like, big sperg energy, and within a few days I hit on the school's name plus "0000" as the password across all these machines, presumably configured by some

---

Sous...plage: Under the paving stones, the beach!   BBS: bulletin board system
HOPE: Helping Outstanding Pupils Educationally

braintrust contracted countywide. I think that's probably the first remote intrusion I ever pulled off. So I'm looking around for merry mischief, but each of these guys appears devoted to little more than management of a 'Nortel Meridian.' Interesting!"

"Ahhhh, was that a PBX?"

"Word is bond. I gather this from the somewhat opaque configuration software, and get super excited—I didn't know much about PBXen, but I knew you could dial out from them. So I've presumably got a proxy to cloak my own phone number during further explorations. Maybe even make free long distance calls, which would add some real cachet to my underground status. I was doing some cracking by now; Razor hadn't picked me up or anything—"

"You were in Razor 1911? Badass."

"Never a full member—Razor is strictly European so far as I know—but I did a few jobs for them. I mainly worked for Prestige, Fairlight, INC. Dude, if any of y'all played the four-disk release of Warcraft II, you most likely played my crack. DEBUG.EXE all day long, old-skool. So I immediately make myself a new admin-level account on each box and set to exploring this mysterious new delight. I figure out how to dial through, and how to permit toll dialing, but don't want to run up a bill and get noticed. I just slink in at night and read the online help. I learn how to change their hold music, but I'd need physical access to hook up an input—it's not like you could upload MP3s in 1995.

Anyway. My untimely lack of academic rigor at good St. Anthony's. We get a transfer student mid-semester from Oregon or some fuckin' place with a military school. We're talking and he mentions that he'd failed his mandatory first-period Theory of Marching and Saluting or whatever, and I'm like, 'hey how does that work on your transcripts? As we good peaceful Catholics lack firearm-related classes as a rule, what happens? Do you have to submit multiple transcripts to colleges?' He laughs; it had become an F in Boy's Chorus, surely the first. So there was the key upon which I seized. Change. Turn. Transfiguration. Metanoia. Impermanence. The Heraclitean river of grades. Everything is fire, and don't you fucking forget it." Katz has grown loud; the methamketacaine is doing its work forcefully.

"What was thought set in stone could clearly be altered. I call up some random school, maybe Sprayberry, and ask 'we're pulling mah boy out of private school and live in this district. What need we to do to enroll him? What goes on with his transcripts?' I'd unthinkingly assumed there was some state-level or even national clearinghouse to which grades were dispatched, staffed by shuffling *Reagan*-class functionaries with dead eyes, unifying and leveling across various districts, cantons, parishes. Nah. When you change schools, at least then, the old one FAXes or mails your transcript thus far, whereupon Chaldean sorcerers in the front office chant on it and their informed word is *ex cathedra*. All pretty laughable, integrity- and authentication-wise. I'm kinda shocked transcripts aren't being doctored on their way to colleges all the time. Maybe they are.

PBX: private branch exchange   **INC:** International Network of Crackers
ex cathedra: from the chair   **Auto-da-fé:** act of faith

So you see where this is going. Sure enough, the school FAX is configured as a Direct Inward Dial on the Nortel, and sure enough I can forward incomings to another, external line. So there's the classic man-in-the-middle redirect. Of course, I'll need to somehow bounce traffic into the real FAX, and am wondering how exactly to do that without a third number, but it turns out you can set up rules based on incoming characteristics. That weekend, I do a test run. I forward all incoming traffic to that number to my home number, except for when it's coming *from* my home number—that goes through. I call a friend and have him FAX to the listed school number. Boom, my FAX gets it and prints it out, and I grab it and dance a fuckin' jig. Now I send the same number a FAX, and it is not redirected, and I'll tell you that was about the most badass I'd felt in my life. Barbaric yawp shit. I go back in and remove the redirect and wait for my dick to soften and ponder this whole kettle of fish.

I was in the Turner Classic district, and they're a pretty good school. I knew from having our asses thoroughly whipped that their academic bowl team was phenomenal. Football was pretty shitty, but by that time I knew I wasn't exactly going to be making a career out of defensive line, and would just as soon avoid another two seasons of dehydration and summer camp in Valdosta, Georgia's Hadean seared asshole, and getting run over by fucking piledrivers of men from Tucker and Woodward in the name of good Catholic sport. The twice-daily journey between Marietta and Dunwoody would be likewise unmissed. I had few friends down there. My parents bitched at me about the money and driving as if it hadn't been their call in the first place. So I had no great attachment to St. Anthony's. Hell, we weren't even Catholic anymore. But having attended four years, they weren't about to pull me for the last two. I was still drawing my academic scholarship despite overall academic ineptitude. So it would have to be an expulsion, but not one that would involve police or lawsuits, or get the two schools talking. I needed something that would embarrass them, to which they would want to call no attention whatsoever, and wouldn't feel obligated to pass along.

So what does your typical religious order not like to talk about? Of what speak not the clerics regular? Abortion for sure. The dangerous lives of altar boys. Limbo, the game perhaps but definitely the doctrine and how it was kinda just made up *ex nilhio,* deficient of Scriptural backing. *Auto-da-fé.* Popes both Warrior and Anti. Indulgences."

Alysha volunteers, "let's not forget Copernicus. *Eppur si muove.*".

"Well that was Galileo, but yes."

"Galileo spoke Latin?"

Bolaño responds to Fisk with contempt. "That's Italian, you illiterate."

"Jews!"

"Well Moyer it's interesting that you bring up the Tribe. Did everyone who wanted some of the methamketacaine get some? A little more for the graduate, I think. On one hand you have self-loathing Constantine. 1096. 1147. 1251. 1320. The Edict of Expulsion in 1290. Cryptojews. Torquemada and the Alhambra Decree. Ferrand Martinez. Edgardo Mortara. The Church did not

---

Eppur si muove: and yet it moves

cover itself with glory during the Holocaust. On the other, *Nostra aetate* at Vatican II. *Quamvis Perfidiam* during the Black Death. Pope Gregory I was I'd say a wash, semitewise. Your modern Church definitely wants good relations. Of course, you could count both the Jews and blacks at St. Anthony's on your fingers. We had a horrible Cultural Appreciation Day where these kids were made to go in front of an uninterested and pissed-off student body and talk about matzah and the AME. Poor bastards.

A few weeks into junior year, me and a local buddy make a big-ass sign. Easily readable from the road. We do it all up in red, white, and blue bunting, patriotic as hell. Big crucifixen on either side. Along the top are headshots. We've got Pope John Paul II, Mike Tyson, JFK with his brains still in, poor Rosemary Kennedy with her brains reduced to Tuna Helper, Belinda Carlisle, Ayatollah Komeini, Anita Bryant, all the hits, plus our headmaster with a halo. They're having a hell of a conversation. Underneath it, in tasteful golden calligraphy, we letter 'St. Anthony's School and the Atlanta Archdiocese remind you this 29th Week of Ordinary Time'—"

Devesh looks gleefully horrified. "Oh nooooooooo."

"Then in big red letters 'KEEP ABORTION LEGAL.' Next to it the *Beata Maria Virgo* in full mandorla, attended to by Gabriel with holy horn, and the speech-bubble, 'Virgin birth or GTFO.' Underneath them, *sic transit gloria mundi.*"

"You did not. That's absurd. That got you kicked out?"

"Well then underneath it, all impeccable lowercase italics, 'pregnancy is a jewish plot!' And finally *'Audentes Fortuna Iuvat,'* our school motto. Fortune favors the bold, bitches."

"Nooooooooooooo."

"Yes! Stolen from Robert Anton Wilson. We go put this up early Saturday morning in the soccer field next to the road, working in the dark. I called the local media and some synagogues, leaving messages mostly—it was probably 5am. By the next afternoon my parents are called at home. I'd let people see me print out those headshots in the computer lab, and I'd assume they had cameras on campus as well.

I don't plead innocence. I say it was just a joke, a prank, and if they want I can come remove the sign. I am told absolutely not to come onto campus Monday and likely beyond. They talk to my parents, who seem more confused than anything. My mom asks, 'but what do Jews have to do with abortion? Is it because so many are doctors?' I told her yes.

The fix was in. The next day we were told that I would likely be expelled. Had I anything to say for myself? Only *Pater dimitte illis non enim sciunt quid faciunt.* The head of their priestly order was in on the call, and he was Old School Church; he knew the Latin just fine and started into language quite unbecoming of *sacramentum ordinis.* Early Monday morning they call, inform

---

Nostra aetate: "in our time"
Quamvis Perfidiam: "despite the perfidy" papal bull of Clement VI
AME: African Methodist Episcopal   **Beata Maria Virgo:** blessed Virgin Mary
sic...mundi: thus passes the worldly glory
Pater...faciunt: Father forgive them for they know not what they do. Luke 23:34 (KJV)
sacramentum ordinis: the Sacrament of Holy Orders

us that I can either withdraw that day, or be expelled, and that they'll ship the contents of my locker. I am *persona non grata.* Anathema. Excommunicated! My mother asks whether tuition will be refunded, and is reminded that I'm on a full ride. She asks how that makes a difference. Towards the end of this unfriendly exchange, we're told to call them and let them know where to FAX or mail my transcripts. And I smiled."

"I gotta say, Katz, that was a pretty stupid plan."

"I was a pretty stupid kid. But hey, things had worked out so far, and I really wasn't in any worse situation than I had been. Better, all told. But now the tricky part. We go over to Turner Classic and my dad, torn between wanting to kick my ass and delight at never again needing drive down to Dunwoody, tells them 'uhh we're not Catholic anymore, so he's your problem now.' They demand immunizations and certificates of birth and ask us to have St. Anthony's FAX over a transcript, here's the number. Mwahahahaha. I go talk to a guidance counselor and spec out my current classes. I tell him my test scores and his eyes get big. He asks my GPA and I'm like, I don't know, pretty good, I've had a few Bs. He's pretty much swooning as he shakes my hand and reminds us to get that official transcript FAXed this week. I start classes tomorrow.

So this hack looks like it's actually going to all come together, right? I've got my pristine transcript, a transcript you'd be proud to take home and show the folks. Scanned in an unofficial one and copied-and-pasted glyphs among the document. All I need do is log into their Nortel, turn on my redirect, watch the FAX machine, manually forward any other FAXen that come in unchanged, and interdict the St. Anthony's call. Log in again, clear the redirect, leave no traces. Nothing expected will be missing. St. Anthony's can confirm they sent it if called. Turner Classic can confirm receipt. Even if things are somehow exploded, nothing points to me."

"Well except call logs. If they subpoenaed BellSouth it would show calls from you to their box, and the PBX probably had logs all its own. For that matter, pcAnywhere probably did too."

"Fortune favors the bold. No one was getting a subpoena even if they compared notes. The cops would have laughed them out of the room. No way are they investigating PBX logs and shit. Or I guess maybe they could have. But they didn't. I could have done a lot of things smarter but c'mon, I was only 15. And remember, no one knew shit all about computers back then. All of this makes sense to us—"

From Alexei Orshanskiy, a Ukrainian so cachectic and angular that he looks only somewhat human: "Gonna interrupt you there. I've not been able to follow for a minute."

"Well goddamnit Alexei what threw you?"

"Fuck is a PBX for starters. Pterodactyl bitch extractor? Fucked if I know."

"Private branch exchange. What let you run your POTS. Plain ol' telephone service over the PSTN—public switched telephone network. These days anyone halfway hip is running Asterisk. Back then you got a few lines or some ISDN,

---

ISDN: integrated services digital network

maybe a T1's worth—1.544 megabits per—and managed it as an appliance. Let's roll. I effect the diversion. I call up St. Anthony's and tell them I'll be going to Turner Classic, and could they go ahead and send over my transcripts? I offer to provide the FAX number to them, but they say they'll get it themselves, and that it'll be done this afternoon. Give them credit: they at least weren't just accepting whatever random number someone quoted at them. Now, if they exchanged any verifiable details verbally, I was fucked. I was going from just over a 2.0 to a 3.9-plus. A meteoric rise. Go big or go home. I had no real defense for this, and wouldn't know if it happened. Didn't even think of it until after I called. Hail Eris."

ATLiens ends and is followed by Company Flow's *Funcrusher Plus.*

"I'm bound to the FAX machine until things go through. None of the forwarding is automatic. Within about fifteen minutes, there were two unrelated FAXen I had to put through. The frequency surprised me. What if I had to take a piss? The last thing I wanted was for some front office disneybot to start fucking with their FAX machine or the PBX. I realized that if they rebooted the PBX, my configuration changes would be flushed. Fuck! I was freaking out a little. What if they'd been tracking me this whole time, and were just waiting to bust me at the moment of peak illegality? The Secret Service could be sweeping even then into my front yard. Shit, if my room got searched, what all was in there? I looked out the window in total dread. How all had I fucked up? In what ways had I fucked up that I didn't know about? That 'guidance counselor' had probably been a fucking federal agent. Never having heard the term 'honeypot' I at that moment conjectured honeypots. A ring indicated another incoming FAX; I screamed before feeding it through.

Then the 'in use' light goes on. But there's been no incoming call. That means...shit, that means someone's using the phone in my house. No bueno. That'll put up a busy signal. Too many busy signals implies a call asking why. A call asking why implies fuckery and even investigation. I watch for it to go off. One minute. Another. Goddamnit. I charge upstairs and find my mom on her phone with Bible study materia spread around her and just about vomit. Bible study calls run approximately forever, with lengthy eyes-closed prayers and cross-indexing of Halley's NIV Study Bibles and the good ladies getting their rigor on for the Lord. 'Mom? I was going to use the modem. Could you possibly get off the phone? Please?'"

"Shhh! I am doing Bible study! Use the modem later! Go think about stupid abortion signs and getting kicked out of school!"

"The good Lord, acting through a loyal if unknowing servant, had speared me through with His great barbed thorncock. I raged silently at the heavens. You play your games, Jehovah. I shall play mine. This call would have gone on for an hour or longer in the absence of drastic measures."

"'Mom I'm gonna drive to the store real quick and get some imitation crab meat.' Recall that I am at this time fifteen and quite unlicensed, not to mention sans car. She actually chuckles at me. I go to her purse on the bed, look her in the eyes, unzip it, and remove her keys."

T1: Transmission System 1, 24 channels up to 1.544 Mbps

"Sherman have you lost your mind put my keys back in my purse and put my purse down. Sherman I will beat you and have your daddy beat you and homeschool you with the Maynards' retarded boy down the street. Sherman Katz I will burn every book in your bedroom if you walk through that door. I will *blind* you. SHERMAN!"

"I was almost at the front door when she slammed down her heavy receiver and began her descent. I head off to the garage, where my mother arrives, breathing hard, absolutely apoplectic. She opens the door to her little Renault, lowers her head in like a tyrannosaurus, yelling 'where are you, you son of a bitch, have you lost your mind?'"

"Mom?"

"Sherman. Spartacus. Katz. What the hell are you doing? What has made you crazy? You are dangerously close to some very serious mistakes, young man. You've already made one with your dumb prank. Give me my keys."

"'Here you go, mom. I'm sorry.' I'll admit to some tactical tears around this point. 'Mom, I do, I feel so crazy recently. It's like I'm not the person I used to be anymore. And I don't like the person I've become. I think I've left God's love and turned my back on Him and that's why, and I'm not sure He's ever going to admit me back into His grace.' I cede some general issues with my mother and that by choice I am not the closest son I could be, but give the gal credit, she comes running over to me with a big hug and the kind of honest simple love that made me feel almost sad for fucking with her like this. 'Baby the Lord only wants us to accept His love, and He is ready for us to do so at any time. We can always go to our knees in prayer and be heard. And your father and I will always love you, too.'"

"Can we go to our knees now, mom?"

"I'm so glad you asked, Sherman. Let's do so."

"She goes there in the dirt of the garage to two fully bended knees of supplication. I genuflect, and hold one hand. The other she'd raised with a palm upturned towards the garage door opener."

"Heavenly Father, we go to You in prayer to ask for Your help with Sherman. He has erred and sampled from the carts of Vanity Fair, Lord, he has put his faith in computers and Harper Lee and Ferris Bueller. He has known pride and gluttony and avarice. Sherman do you confess that you pollute yourself?"

"Ummm, if it's going to be that way, I do confess it, Lord. I flog the dog and festoon the balloon and covet my lab partners' asses."

"Just girls though, right?"

"Yes mom, Lord, just the girls. The redheaded ones, those in tall socks, big-breasted WASPs wearing tight winter sweaters, goth girls with serious thighs and short skirts and bangs, the casts in toto of *Clueless* and *The Craft*—"

"Yes, Lord he has known lust for women and all their lascivisions—"

"Lascivisions?"

"Nominal form of lascivious, asshole. Don't make fun of my mom. You sling enough lascivisions around, people are gonna call you lascivious. The Lord knew what she meant. 'Their lascivisions, Lord, You know they're little strumpets at that age. My son seeks Your wisdom and grace and love. He seeks Your Light. Sherman, will you throw away those Butthole Surfer tapes?'"

"Well how are those related mom—"

"Sherman think for one minute. God asks so little of you. Have no other gods before Him. Honor thy mother and father. Take not His name in vain. God created your butthole. God created the oceans. One's for surfing. One's not. Do you think Butthole Surfing venerates God's creation, or mocks it? The entire concept is obscene and warped."

"I guess it depends on why—"

"Father, give Sherman wisdom, small dumbass wisdom sufficient to know Heaven is closed to Butthole Surfers. No wonder they kicked you out of that school. No wonder you're getting Cs and Ds—"

"'Mom?' I touched her shoulder. We're both freely crying by this point. 'I think things are starting to heal. I see now. How could I have thought otherwise? I chuckle at my own mindlessness. I think I'll take God's gift of eternal life over the Butthole Surfers. Gross. Will you help me destroy those tapes?'"

"Sherman I've wanted to destroy those tapes ever since you brought them home. Every time I've looked at you since then, I think 'there's something called Butthole Surfers in my house.' I've prayed on it so many times."

"Your prayers are gonna be answered tonight, mom."

"Heavenly Father, hear our prayers. See my son's devotion to Your plan in not just words, but actions. He's going to try to lose some weight, too, Lord. He knows you didn't give him a healthy body just to let it get all chubby and stand around with bad posture like white trash. Drive out the demons inside him that would lead him to make crazy signs and stay on the computer all night. Amen. I'm so happy, Sherman. Tell you what. I've already missed a good bit of Bible study—but for such a joyous cause! Go inside and say a prayer of your own, and then you can go ahead and use your modem until we eat."

"Awww thanks, I really appreciate that. Let me know if you'd like any help cooking, and when I ought set the table."

"Two FAXen had spooled over the duration. One was mine. I stood trembling, loaded the *maskirovka*, dialed, transmitted, slotted it home. I logged into the PBX and removed the diversion, rebooting it for good measure. The next day I showed up at nine AM, asked for my schedule, bit my lip, and stared into eternity. They brought me a list of classes and said that my transcript had been received. 'Very nice, by the way. We're happy to have you here.'"

"I'm happy to be here."

"What are your goals for these remaining two years, Mr. Katz?"

"To shoot craps with the Universe, and win. I should go. Thank you."

"I walked to AP American History seventeenth in my new class's rank, eager to learn, eager to make good on this second chance, benignant and radiating wanton innocence. Joined their academic bowl team and moved quickly to the front, displacing a longtimer but hey, that's life in the big city. Kept my GPA high enough to secure HOPE and end here. Dropped a perfect SAT—god bless standardized testing—and took twenty-three AP exams. So I like to think of it as correcting what would have been a freak error. Funny coda to this story: I

---

maskirovka: маскировка deception, usually military

had to doctor my report cards *down* through graduation, so my parents weren't, like, 'didn't your report card suck a lot more than this?'"

∗ ∗ ∗ ∗ ∗ ∗ ∗ ∗ ∗

The night goes on, the apartment waxing heavy and happy with guests before they begin to thin out around 0200h, all according to the whims of the Poisson. A thoroughly pixilated Katz stumbles out into the living room in his underwear. "It smells like sex out here. I got two degrees today motherfuckers. Can't hold me down. Only Turing can judge me. Imma piss in the sink."

He strides purposefully to the kitchen, climbs onto the counter, and does exactly that. With no small élan he executes an Elvisesque pelvic swing. Now two. Now three. With an awesome crash he drops through the serving hatch onto the living room floor. Two chairs topple down with him. The table falls and begins to rotate slowly along its elliptical edge. One Robert Ng is there, and reaches down to lend assistance. "Yo Katz, are you ok?"

Katz leaps up, hooting all the way. "I never trusted that motherfucking table." He vomits with some force, lights a Newport, and returns to his bedroom, giving high-fives as he goes. Some land. More miss. He looks back before shutting the door. "My errors are volitional, and the portals of discovery! Bachelor of Science, hobags!"

What remains is the chaos, the table tracing out its epicycloid in the carpet, the rapidly dissipating smoke. From behind the door come sex sounds almost as cheerful as they are imprecise and impaired, not quite masked by Amy Grant's *Heart in Motion* playing louder than anyone present has heard Amy Grant played, or will hear her played in the future.

3   michael bolaño indulges in small pleasures

Stately, slim Michael Luis Bolaño attended Katz's hackalogue—he'd not heard the tale before—accepting it in its main points, feeling idly dubious about some details. Whatever its veracity, Michael thought it foolish to relate such a story. There was no percentage in it. Was he convincing those present of his intelligence? Everyone here knew Katz to be possessed of scintillating brilliance; he needed win none over. He had arrogance in spades, but it was earned confidence in his abilities, not that mien of belligerent pomposity which so readily betrays insecurity. Passing on knowledge? A night's entertainment? Tell the facts; claim no personal involvement. Katz was fundamentally sloppy. He had faith in some essential decency of the engineering class, though he'd likely deny it if put the question baldly. Bolaño knew better.

Friends become enemies. Confidantes break confidence for money, or for attention, or under torture, or due their unthinking stupidity. *In vino veritas.* A secret may be revealed but not untold. Knowledge like entropy grows only more general, a kind of Second Law of the furtive. Michael had never lacked a keen sense of self-preservation. He sometimes suspected that Katz had none at all. It made him a less-than-ideal partner in the Trade. At the same time, Katz's undisciplined extroversion and exuberance had been a necessary element of building up their enterprise, and no thinking man would deny that the son of a bitch had skills.

Still. Talking about using mass spectrometers! Say some grinning listener, perhaps that insufferable Greg Moyer, mentions to his fuckhead frat brother that Katz claimed to be testing drugs using GC/MS. Frat brother gets picked up retailing rohypnol. He calls daddy's lawyer but lacks the sense and/or balls to wait on counsel's appearance. Cops tell him he's looking at twenty years, not just possession with intent but also conspiracy to sexual assault. Tell us what you know and maybe we keep a leash on the District Attorney, maybe we don't seize your parents' house in Buckhead—oh you poor deluded dipshit, have you never heard of civil forfeiture?—maybe we don't replace your world of popped collars and Coldplay concerts with jailhouse tats and mandatory tuberculosis testing, don't guide you headfirst and trussed into a buzzsaw for which we work the treadle. "Well I know this guy Sherman Katz is into all kinds of shit. I heard he fucks with mass spectrometers." APD notes it down in a book, and later an entry goes into NADDIS on the DEA's Firebird intranet. Months later, some head gets busted with Devesh's ecstasy in California. They don't know our names, but they know it came from the southeast. Precious few inhabitants of the Mississippi Delta with cause for a mass spectrometer. Bolaño and Katz surrendered the privilege of careless speech some time ago, a hard fact he found himself forced to emphasize again and again.

Bolaño had required no changes to his grades. His transcripts recorded an inexorable march through the Texan high school curriculum, his lowest mark an A- in some horseshit geology class. He demonstrated no special pride in what

---

NADDIS: Narcotics and Dangerous Drugs Information System

had been, after all, an effortless saga. Asked the secret to his success, he would have sneered, and marveled with no feigned incredulity at others' laughable incompetence. He was never seen to study, but unlike Katz clearly cared enough to demonstrate mastery of the material, despite free hours dedicated almost entirely to computing and his own intense course of reading. He wrestled and ran cross country; he gave up soccer after being passed over for Lamar's varsity in the ninth grade. Michael Luis Bolaño saw no value in participating in activities in which he would not dominate.

He knew he was gay as soon as he knew much of anything, and announced it matter-of-factly in 1993. This was a move of some boldness for a thirteen-year-old Latino in Texas. His mother Rosemary screamed, but quickly regained her composure, biting her lip and looking to his father. On cue, the elder Luis came out of his chair with a bellow, lunging towards Michael.

Even at thirteen he'd stood a head taller than stout Luis. With sighing sang-froid he sidestepped the charge like a matador, catching Luis in an armlock. Looking his mother in her eyes, he spoke softly, holding Luis wriggling and impotent. "Shhhh. Calm yourself, *mon père*." The young Bolaño's *français* was better than his *español*. "Shhhh. *Ça suffit*. This is all a dream. Your second son will fuck girls to ensure them a special *quinceañera*, and their *abuelas* will say knowingly that he learned from his father, a real samurai cocksman. Just a dream. You have not in one generation ruined a great family. You didn't buy your first son a ridiculous Lamborghini. He never smeared himself and this car you did not buy him across a highway divider. A dream. *La familia es todo*. Bills marked Final Notice do not fill the mailbox. Your wife sheds no tears for what has been lost; she never dreamed love would never die. You loved your second son, the son you never drunkenly beat to feel for a few pitiable seconds what it is to be a man. You inspire this second son, his heart bursting with admiration for the father you never were. Your son didn't anticipate your pathetic sound and fury. Your son is in no position to shatter your plump arm, should he so choose. Your wife, mother to your sons, isn't hoping that he does, and isn't thinking of her hundred black eyes. I will release you now. Raise a hand to either of us again, and I'll kill you."

Luis spun to face him, sputtering. Then the light in his eyes went out. He hung his head and took his seat, shuddering. Rosemary looked upon her husband with loathing, and got up. "Mother, take a *siesta* in the day room. You're so beautiful. Luis, you appear unsteady. Let me pour you another mezcal."

Full of flinty and unyielding insolence, he burned with resentment for the authority placed in his inferiors, particularly teachers. He was detested by the Lamar faculty, who spoke of him behind closed doors with disdain and fear. Suspicions were muttered and allegations alleged, but given the absence of any real evidence, he went unaccused of major infractions. Any number would have loved to put him in his place, but assigned work was inevitably turned in on time, expertly completed, dripping with contempt. Lamar's principal

---

mon père: my father   **Ça suffit:** that's enough   **quinceañera:** fifteenth birthday
abuelas: grandmothers   **La...todo:** family is everything

seethed knowing that this haughty little shit would likely emerge first among the Class of '98, and began searching during Michael's junior year for plausible reasons to eliminate the standard valedictory speech at graduation. Bolaño accepted their antipathy and looks of distaste with smirking grace and derisive confidence, painted a wider target on his back, and cultivated unmistakable excellence as a means of protest.

With that said, he felt in no way constrained to the "silence, exile, and cunning" of Stephen Dedalus. During his sophomore year, he authored a recurring column of not more than 250 words in the semimonthly school newspaper. He wrote it somewhere to the right of the John Birch Society, a kind of gleeful Dark Enlightenment anticipating Hans-Hermann Hoppe and Nick Land and Moscow's eXile tabloid. Anyone who asked got a hard stare, and finally a languid assertion that, duh, "it is clearly satire: did you ignore the touchstones to Rabelais?" Responding to the vexed principal: "To Swift? To Aristophanes? Is it possible you have"—eyes widening here—"*not read* Aristophanes? C'mon, the column's title is 'Tex-Mencks.'"

"I've never understood the title, actually."

"You've heard of Tex-Mex? The cuisine?"

"Yes."

"You've heard of H. L. Mencken? The author?"

"Yes."

"If you say so. What has happened is the 'Mex' has been replaced with 'Mencks,' establishing a reference to aforementioned satirist. Under my own power I provide all the Mex we need. I'm not sure what else you want to hear."

"Michael, I'm going to read your last two months' titles out loud."

"A chrestomathy! But your English is...passable? A quartet of pleasures, I'm sure. I know them by heart. Please proceed."

"'Three Generations Weren't Enough After All: Revisiting Eugenics.'"

"A scathing conceit on our State Legislature's public housing policy."

"'Unsafe at any WPM: Against Universal Literacy.'"

"Routing lottery revenues into public schools is undeniably regressive. No one wants to hear this truth. The numerate class is made to feel guilty. Their complement is made to feel still more stupid than usual."

"'Killing Fields or Common Ground? In Defense of the Khmer Rouge.'"

"If you had grown up Rouge instead of—I'm spitballing here, Baptist?—you'd think Christmas the crazy tradition. I ain't got no quarrel with them Khmer Rouge. I refuse to hate a man simply because we've had instilled different beliefs regarding autarky, agrarian collectivism, and the significance of spectacles."

"I see—"

"By 'spectacles' I mean eyeglasses, not rousing struggle sessions against those chaps who dare to thwart the revolution."

"Excuse me?"

"It's on the gate at *Tuŏl Slêng.*"

"What?"

"Security Prison 21. The Hill of the Poisonous Trees. If you're going to learn just two words of Khmer, they're not a bad choice."

"'Too Many are Born: *Cameral* and—' what is this word, is it a typo? '*Cameral* and...whatever this is...concerns in an Age of Vaccines.'"

"Dr. Blish would be sad to hear it. *Oeconomic.* I learned about Cameralism right here in your own school's AP European History."

"I think it stinks, Michael. I think you're playing a lot of people for fools."

"Their foolishness manifests without my help."

"I think you've got a really bad attitude."

"In the sense that foolishness is presumably some scalar having minimum value zero, indicating an absence of foolishness. Not quite wisdom, mind you. This isn't that kind of scalar. Thus is measured their *dinge an sich*. I feel stupid even asking this, but"—he takes the shot—"how much Kant have you read?"

"I'll be watching you." *¡Goaaaaaaaaaaaaaal!*

The column had largely lost its luster anyway. The next issue, he submitted "A Case for Antisemitic Zionism."

"Hrmmm, what's this exactly? 'Israel is a necessary ally where America has few, but this only makes its Jews a greater strategic liability, quite independent of their qualities as a people *ceteris paribus*.' I'm not sure we can print this."

"I am skewering here *reductio ad absurdum* the 'socially liberal, fiscally conservative' mantra of the Libertarian Party. Social liberty is after all an impossibility without economic justice. Have we learned nothing from Dr. King's 'How Long? Not Long.'?"

The newspaper's faculty advisor nodded. She was usually unsure what Michael was talking about, but was absolutely certain that she'd learned something from Dr. King.

That would be Michael's last "Tex-Mencks" column.

✳✳✳✳✳✳✳✳

Despite being one of the most competent *científicos* of Mexico's fin de siècle *Porfiriato* technocracy, Michael's great-great-grandfather Gustavo had opposed General Díaz following the contested elections of 1910. He supported Madero until the inept display at Casas Grandes. The exhilarating news of Pancho Villa's victory at Ciudad Juárez was tempered with patrician revulsion at the demagogue's bloodthirstiness. Zapata and the Plan de Ayala were sources of horror. Trapped in Mexico City during *la Decena Trágica*, he came to despise revolutionary violence almost as much as the meddling of Sherburne Hopkins. He sided like most of the bourgeois with the Carrancistas, helping to draft their manifesto at Hacienda De Guadalupe and also the *Constitución Política*. He was conservative regarding the *ejidos*, suspicious of the Church, positively venomous concerning gringo interference, and determined to make Huasteca Petroleum and El Águila truly Mexican: Article 27 was largely his own.

Gustavo Bolaño and his son Antonio relocated to Garza García outside Monterrey, and began prospecting in the Chicontepec basin of Veracruz. They

---

dinge an sich: things-in-themselves. Immanuel Kant, *Kritik der reinen Vernunft*
    (A Critique of Pure Reason, 1781)
ceteris paribus: holding other things constant
científicos: "scientists" advisors to President Díaz   **Porfiriato:** Mexico under Porfirio Díaz
la Decena Trágica: the Ten Tragic Days   **ejidos:** communal land with usufruct rights

bought up its sandstone cheaply, proved hydrocarbon reserves in 1926, and sold the land at great profit to Royal Dutch Shell. Overnight, he became one of Mexico's ten richest *ciudadanos*. Almost concurrently, *Ley Calles* went into effect, enforcing the anticlerical Article 130 and leading directly to the Cristero War. The Bolaños engaged in profitable speculation and extraction through most of this conflict raging to the south.

In 1935, with the Depression at its peak, Antonio brought to San Antonio his nine year old son José López. "Look," he guided José, disembarking onto a platform from the International-Great Northern Railroad; "look around you. Here a quarter century ago Francisco Madero took refuge from the tyrant Porfirio Díaz, whom your grandfather helped overthrow in the *Revolución*. And ninety-nine years prior, fifty years before even your grandfather was born, Santa Anna won the Battle of the Alamo here. The Americano William Travis exhorted his treacherous Tejanos *¡no rendirse, muchachos!*, and swore that he would have victory or death. Our dragoons gave them plenty of the latter, to a man, and in doing so drove every able-bodied Texian to enlist. At San Jacinto, Santa Anna—also an Antonio!—a few weeks later lost the war, and with it *Coahuila y Tejas*. And now we Bolaños, people of the sun, have arrived." He squeezed his son's hand.

They deposited ten thousand *pesos plata*, just under the $5,000 FDIC guarantee established in the previous year's Banking Act, and traveled north into Texas Hill Country. There, in sight of staid granite domes and caverns of the karst, they purchased a large tract of savanna suitable for grazing, and much of the limestone hill it bordered. Over the next month, Antonio interviewed agents, finally selecting a gifted *gerente* and authorizing him the power to hire men to clear trees, men to build roads, men to construct a manor and to make ready fields and to bring herds for butchery. Over the hacienda they erected three flags: the American with its forty-eight stars, the lone star of Texas, and the tricolor *bandera*. "Look to our flag, my son. Our seal was sacred in Tenochtitlan, once the greatest state of this continent. When this republic's ancestors were dying of plague across the ocean, serfs to a hundred squabbling kings, yours took tribute from one end of the land to the other. Challenges were met by ten thousand yāōquīzqueh warriors, until no one living dared challenge the tlahtoāni. The proud *águila* perched atop a *nopal*, clutching his rattlesnake prey in talons and beak, like Huītzilōpōchtli wielding the atlatl Xiuhcoatl. Our legacy from the Aztecs. The prickly pear bears fruit, representing those good things within the earth, available to anyone who would but bend down and take them. Like the oil extracted by myself and your grandfather. One day you and your family will pursue our interests in this country, on this land, among

Ley Calles: 1926 law hostile to the Catholic Church
Tejanos: Mexican settlers of the Republic of Texas
no rendirse, muchachos: don't surrender, boys
Texian: American settler of the Republic of Texas
Coahuila y Tejas state of First Mexican Republic   pesos plata: silver Mexican coins
gerente: manager   yāōquīzqueh: "those who have gone to war" Aztec footsoldier
tlahtoāni: "one who speaks" ruler   águila: eagle   nopal: prickly pear
Huītzilōpōchtli: Aztec god of the sun and war   Xiuhcoatl: fire serpent used as a weapon

these people, but your line is that of Techichpotzin, daughter of Moctezuma Xocoyotzin. This you must never forget."

He did not point out that Techichpotzin was later baptized Isabel, nor that she carried to term the child of conquistador Hernán Cortés. He privately doubted that their ancestry could in any case be meaningfully traced across four centuries of Colonial Mexico. Likewise, no attention was called to the three flags' relative heights, that the Lone Star fluttered well above the deferential Golden Eagle. Parenting, after all, is already hard enough.

Seeking to relieve the overcrowded San Jacinto HS, the Works Progress Administration began construction of a new school in Houston. In 1937, that school would be opened under the auspices of Houston's powerful Independent School District as Southwest. Before the academic year ended it was renamed Lamar. Sixty years later, Michael Luis Bolaño would be its star student.

But soon there was tragedy in Monterrey due the Cristeros. Gustavo, now a respected and benevolent engineer graying at his temples, Gustavo who had seen so much in his fifty-two years, was in 1939 lynched by a gang of Catholic assassins. His hand in the hated 1917 constitution had not been forgotten. While delivering an address encouraging Mexican neutrality in the coming European war, men in dingy serapes dragged him away from the lectern. One smashed his glasses underboot; one with a hammer crushed his right kneecap. With laughter they cruelly took his ears, then cut deeply across his throat as he strove like a crippled crab to crawl away. He cursed them as fanatics and as brigands, and swore that in hell he would fuck their daughters, but never called to his timid countrymen, and indeed none moved to help him. Committing his soul into the everafter, he struggled to cry ¡que viva México!, but managed only to cough and sputter into sands reddening like Oaxacan cochineal with his life's blood.

The Depression had slammed shut the agribusiness exemption to the Emergency Immigration Act of 1921, bringing to a halt most Mexican immigration and leading to mass repatriation of laborers. José López assisted Antonio: promises of industrial investment to their Texas banks were made in his excellent English, and accompanied by sizable wire transfers. These were forwarded along with letters of recommendation to the necessary representatives, who forwarded them in turn to the recently-created Immigration and Naturalization Service. Palms were greased along the way, but the sums required were hardly objectionable. Six Alien Registration Receipt Cards arrived without overmuch delay in Monterrey: two for the twin daughters Xevera and Zita, born in 1940; one for José; cards of course for Antonio and wife Valentina; finally a card for widowed Guadalupe in her black rebozo and huipil, who seemed now to speak only in prayers and wailing protests. They were assured that naturalization would be a painless and quickly forthcoming matter. The living Bolaños took up residence in their compound in October 1941. Gustavo—what was left of him—was buried in his beloved Monterrey, but Antonio commissioned a tasteful cenotaph for the grounds.

Their new country was soon at war. Antonio had registered as required upon entry, but could expect a III-A dependency hardship deferment. Dependency exemptions were eliminated during the manpower crisis of 1943, but

Congressional action ensured that fathers would enjoy the lowest draft priority; Antonio continued to breathe easily. José López, however, turned of age in 1944, and as a declarant alien became liable under the Burke-Wadsworth Act for military service.

Executive Order 9279 ended both voluntary enlistment and the lottery, entrusting local boards with administrative selection. A family of the Bolaños' resources could arrange a deferment if so desired, but José López, descendant of Moctezuma II, never asked, and Antonio never suggested it. June of that year saw Eisenhower and Montgomery crash into the five beaches of Overlord, Clark capture an abandoned and open Rome, Saitō's defeat following a month of nightmarish fighting on Saipan, and the annihilation of *Heeresgruppe Mitte*, the dreaded Army Group Centre under Ernst Busch. This last was accomplished during Konstantin Rokossovsky's Operation Bagration; the Polish-Russian had only in 1940 been brought out from Leningrad's Kresty Prison, where he'd suffered since being swept up in the prewar *Yezhovshchina*. He made a gift to Stalin of 57,000 German PoWs, marched through Moscow Square in the Parade of the Vanquished. It also saw José drafted into the United States Marine Corps "for the duration of the conflict plus six months."

José was bused to MCRD San Diego at Camp Elliott, only to hike thirty-eight miles to the newly-constructed Camp Pendleton. A lank, mild, intellectual Mexican-American was there received into the 5th Marine Division, and became a nameless Recruit. An Irish boy from Denver threw back sass while still standing on his yellow footprints, and was suddenly aloft, hurled laterally, brought to a wet and ponderous stop when his face struck the wall. He slumped heavily into an unlikely position, moving only in the spasmodic twitches indicative of profound brainfuckery. The two meanest nurses José had ever seen emerged, shoving this limp form onto a stretcher, yelling all the while. Drill instructors addressed him at phenomenal volume not just as the expected greaser and beaner, but also chunt, Mexican't, roach, pool-digger, and once even Private Chalupa, a whole rich vocabulary of pejorative that seemed to flow independently of the platoon's performance.

He passed the Initial Strength Test and subsequent PFTs, learned to make a rack, fought with pugil sticks, and cleaned his rifle incessantly. On his fourth day he vomited, and was directed to sign the puddle with his finger. During one of the innumerable sets of pull-ups, he brought his chest to the bar, blanched, and explosively emptied his bowels. A salient of chunky scatnectar was already creeping like warm bisque down his calf by the time he dropped, dazed and horrified, to his feet. In a moment the DI was upon him, huge and apoplectic, campaign hat eclipsing the sun. "Jesus Christ recruit! What the hell was that movement? Did the private remember an appointment in Tijuana to audition for Greased Asshole Number Three at the donkey show?"

"This recruit has shit himself, sir!"

"Explain your undisciplined turdcutter!"

"This recruit's asshole lacks military bearing, sir!"

"Remove your befouled PT dress and get the fuck back on that bar!"

Yezhovshchina: ежóвщина period of Yezhov

He proved more than capable with the M1 Garand, just missing Expert with a Qualification score of 301. Judo felt natural; the M5 bayonet was simply divine. With his company he slogged through the hated "boondocking," close order drills performed in deep sand. He wore his gas mask into a chamber dense with chloroacetophenone, and was then ordered to remove it. It felt for hours like hot glass had been ground into his eyes. Grenades he thought destitute of intimacy, almost gauche, wholly lacking the *je ne sais quoi*. It was fun to let loose a salvo from the BAR or M1919, but he correctly surmised that most of his work would be with the semi-automatic M1 and its *en bloc* clip of eight rounds. During the penultimate week he saw two men of his platoon dragged out from a foxhole by the treads of an obsolete M2A4. One was unhurt save for his left arm, found largely intact a few meters away. The mess from which his scapula protruded resembled a bag of mulch, overflowing with grass and detritus. The other private, caught traverse, had been neatly hemicorporectomized, his pelvis pressed into earth like *bas-relief* upon which his legs emerged and lay. Their screams were inaudible over the roar of twin diesels.

By the end of the compressed seven-week training, he'd added almost six kilos of tough muscle, toasted to a shade of brown he'd never seen before, and he wondered upon which Pacific outcropping he would first kill another human being. There was no Family Day, no Graduation with its motivational run, no Warrior's Breakfast nor retiring of the guidon. The company's three platoons instead marched seventy klicks down the California coast to Gen. Pickett's newly-formed Amphibious Training Command in Coronado. For a fortnight they trained there in amphibious assault, effective deployment of cargo nets, medical evacuation, and the joys of throwing flame. It was thought that they might embark for Peleliu or Angaur, but Forager was more or less wrapping up when they boarded rough Liberty ships bound for Hawai'i's Camp Tarawa. During two months on the Big Island, their destination was known only as the generic "Island X."

Not until October 2nd was the Navy's preferred target of Okinawa approved over the Army's Formosa. The decision went in their favor due partially to Army Air Force Gen. Henry "Hap" Arnold's desire to deploy fighter cover out of a holm of the nearby Bonin-Volcano archipelago. Adm. Chester Nimitz was instructed to select and seize some saltatorial appetizer on the way to the Okinawan main course of Operation Iceberg. Planners assumed the Marine divisions allotted to this Operation Detachment would be available for wholesale reuse. Lt. Gen. Tadamichi Kuribayashi, an unorthodox and elegant man known for his haiku, made industrious, even brilliant use of the months available to him: defenses were exquisitely prepared when the first LVTs deployed their Marines on the largest of Japan's *Kazan Rettō*, 21 km² of chthonic brimstone pushed above the waters by a caldera's resurgent dome and called *Iō* by the Japanese. Today this is transliterated as *Iōtō*, but often still mispronounced as it was February 19th, 1945: Iwo Jima.

The landing was preceded by nine months of intermittent bombardment from air and sea. There was little response from on-shore batteries or the

---

Kazan Rettō: 火山列島 Volcano Islands   **Iō-jima:** 硫黄島 Sulphur Island

Mitsubishi G4Ms of the *kōkūtai.* Navajo code talkers reported to Pearl that the island's defenses appeared suppressed, and predicted easy formation of a bridgehead. The ten days prior to landing were thus afforded less bombing than the Marines requested. Later, Holland "Howlin' Mad" Smith would bitterly excoriate the Navy, and claim that this decision cost thousands of lives. In truth, the 21,000 men of the Imperial Japanese Army's 109th Division had long since gone formican, laying mines, presighting mortars, and tying together pillboxes, machine gun nests, trenches, camouflaged artillery positions, and bunkers with eighteen kilometers of tunnels. Some of these were more than thirty meters underground, untouchable by any munition short of a nuclear warhead in earth-penetrating configuration. A fourteen-inch battleship shell could have set off half a tonne of Explosive D overhead in a direct hit without Kuribayashi's subterranean staff noticing. PFC José López Bolaño landed with the first wave at 08:59 Tokyo Standard Time, emerging from his LVT with M1 in hand and twenty-five kilograms on his back, eyes squinting against the tropical sun, expecting a hail of spigot mortars and Arisaka 7.7x58mm, and the inevitable banzai charge.

He heard only birds, and lazy naval aircraft, and the 5th Division.

Americans swam ashore to the base of Mount Suribachi, stumbling from ocean up onto land, recapitulating in uncertain lunges a journey completed four hundred million years ago by their Silurian ancestors. Progress was jarringly punctuated by the explosions of landmines, sending skyward coastland and pumice and feet. It seemed nonetheless that the Navy had accomplished its task; some of the men grinned as they brought up endless cargo. José was concerned by the tall slopes of volcanic ash, clearly impassable by Amtracs. Likewise the gray pseudoplastic beach, a real rheological conundrum, too insubstantial for firm footing yet at the same time too wet for even a cathole. Attempted excavations flowed back to level the minute you looked away from them. José was about to seek his platoon sergeant's thoughts regarding shitting when the E-6's face came off his skull.

Kuribayashi had allowed several thousand Marines—the better part of the 13th and 28th Regiments—to collect on the beaches, which served now as abattoirs. Machine guns opened up from behind every hummock, mowing down a substantial fraction of V Amphibious Corps. Exposed officers were targeted by snipers and nothing wearing chevrons lived through the initial fusillades. The chatter of automatic weapons masked artillery erupting inland, but not the impacts nearby, and the beach seemed one wide impact. Every Marine hit the ground, shot and/or hoping not to be shot. Mortars screamed across the sky, whining before they exploded, launching jagged steel through stomachs, through shoulders, through scrota. José scanned for targets behind a mist of rifleman concentrate.

The story of Red Beach 1 and 2 and the struggle to Airfield No. 1 has been told (as best it can) elsewhere. Suffice to say that the Marines in Joe Rosenthal's Pulitzer Prize-winning photograph barely fought on their way to Iwo Jima's highest point—the Japanese were too smart to expose themselves on the naked

---

kōkūtai: 航空隊 Imperial Japanese Navy Air Service group

face of a mountain. José seemed touched by an angel through that first week, essentially unhurt as men perished all around him. With the cleansing fire of an M2 flamethrower his platoon was purifying one of hundreds of caves, the heat palpable and close to overwhelming twenty meters back. Its operator staggered and crumpled, and the others advanced with grenades. Then José felt his shoulder explode, and his vision went dark, and it was his turn to crumple, and he prepared to die.

He regained consciousness to find his right arm immobilized, his thighs wrapped in bandages, his bladder fuller than it had ever been, his mouth tasting like death itself. A WAVES came over to him quickly.

"What is this place?"

"Naval Hospital Pearl Harbor. You made it. Welcome home."

"I was shot?"

"The surgeons extracted two bullets from your shoulder, and some shell fragments out of your thighs. You're very lucky they didn't hit the artery."

"Can I walk?"

"You ought be able to get up now. Careful—you'll be weak. The doctor is more worried about the shoulder, the axillary nerve particularly, but doubts you'll have any permanent loss of function."

"Excellent. Please point me towards a lavatory."

Within a week he was back in Camp Tarawa, rejoining the 5th Division less their 2,482 KIA, a literal decimation. There they stayed through the final months of World War II. The headlines of the August 7th New York Times could be read across the room:

FIRST ATOMIC BOMB DROPPED ON JAPAN:
MISSILE IS EQUAL TO 20,000 TONS OF TNT:
TRUMAN WARNS FOE OF A "RAIN OF RUIN"

He had seen the 1939 *Nature* article describing nuclear fission. Before the cover page reached him, he'd worked out the same crucial point Leo Szilard realized crossing a London street September 12th, 1933: an uncharged neutron, repelled by neither electron nor proton, strikes the nucleus of a heavy atom. That atom splits into two or three smaller ones (these carrying a great deal of kinetic energy), and also a few neutrons. Should one of these neutrons fission another atom in turn, why, that's a self-sustaining chain. Should more than one fissions result, that self-sustaining chain grows exponentially. Should it grow for more than a few iterations, with these energies, that's a self-sustaining apocalypse. *Delenda est Japonia.* Thank God, he thought, this horrible war is over and I can go home.

Expedited naturalization meant citizenship for José before he'd even left Pearl. In four years total he studied petrochemical engineering at the brutal Colorado School of Mines (participating in the Ball Heist of 1948), and acquired a masters in mechanical engineering at the Georgia Institute of Technology.

WAVES: Woman Accepted for Volunteer Emergency Service
Delenda est Japonia: Japan must be destroyed. Cato the Elder in *Senātus Rōmānus*

He married Lillian Marin, one of the most eligible young ladies of Houston, and she was soon with child. He proved a shrewd engineer, and later a still shrewder manager and investor. When his son Luis was ten they moved at Lillian's prodding to the Bayou City, just in time to weather Hurricane Carla. Undeterred, the Bolaños funded repair and development in their new home, alongside the construction of Houston Intercontinental, the Astrodome, and NASA's Manned Spacecraft Center. Soon they were refining right there on the Gulf's coast, and Antonio handed José more and more of the growing business. They prospered.

By the time spoiled Luis departed for the University of Southern California, the Bolaños counted among the patricians of Houston. They took membership at River Oaks, and the annual Christmas party at their house in Memorial was attended by the highest society. Two younger siblings followed Luis: a brother of little exception at North Texas, and a callipygian sister at LSU on a softball scholarship. It took a year longer than expected—Luis was not a particularly strong student, and Los Angeles in the early seventies offered many distractions—but he narrowly graduated with a degree in statistics in 1974. He joined the family business, where his work was unexceptional. Luis was unctuous to those above him, and toploftical otherwise. José, normally discerning in business and relationships, was blind to his son's faults, and held him in undeserved esteem.

He might have reached more correct conclusions in time, but time was not on his side. José's first flight following certification lifted off from ACT, heading west. He got off a few hours later than planned, by which time a foreboding supercell had formed over the center of the state. In his forty-first hour behind the yoke, he received a NOTAM: flash flooding and hail had shut down receiving at SJT. Midland International was too distant; Abilene would involve cutting through the worst of the squall. José took a deep breath and called into ABI for a distress landing; they wished him luck. He flew low over US 277 with barely fifty meters of visibility. A black walnut tree reached up unseen as he banked right. His Skyhawk's wings disintegrated. He fought to free himself from the burning cockpit, but smoke accomplished what the Japanese couldn't.

From swerve of shore to bend of bay we recirculate then to Michael Luis Bolaño, second (and now only) son of Luis and Rosemary, accidental scion, heir to a misspent fortune, aristocratic in bearing. Last hope of a house from which glory departed, and last to be known by its name. His early reading was broader even than that of Katz. Asked in his first, privileged years how he would spend his days, he quoted Theodore Roosevelt: "I intend to be one of the governing class." By middle school he'd consumed most of Mortimer Adler's Great Books (*Tom Jones* he found simply too boring to finish; Freud he dismissed as a charlatan almost immediately). Dexterous enough with mathematics, he rarely felt the raw dopamine surge known to its devotees: the fundamental theorem of calculus was neat, sure, but contained less in it than any page of Wittgenstein's *Tractatus*. He mastered several languages under

---

ACT: Waco Regional Airport   NOTAM: Notice To Air Missions
SJT: San Angelo Regional Airport/Mathis Field

thickly accented private tutors. At fourteen he got into computing, attracted less to the involutional *l'code pour l'code* Rubik's cubology of computer science at its hardest core than the higher feats one could accomplish with the machine. It was for him a tool, not a shrine.

One spring morning at a library computer, he began to type his password, and wondered how he might know whether the login program had been subverted. He concluded that there existed no way he could do so. Neither could any other user, were he the one doing the subverting. Replace this humble authenticator, then, and he could silently glean credentials.

Ctrl+C didn't break out of the login prompt, which came up automatically on boot. Alright. He logged in and formatted a bootable 3.5", and checked out AUTOEXEC.BAT. Yep, there was LOGIN.EXE at the bottom...and break=off at the top of CONFIG.SYS, meaning you couldn't Ctrl+C out of the MS-DOS boot, either. He rebooted, and watched for the floppy's access light. No dice: it booted directly through to the hard drive. Huh. BIOS was...protected by a password. Oh well.

The next day, following some time with the manual, he rebooted, held down Shift+F5, and was dumped to a friendly C:\> prompt. Never doubt the awesome power of reading the documentation.

He wrote a reasonable mimic of the Novell Netware login prompt in Turbo Pascal. It welcomed you to Lamar High School, accepted a username and password, added them both to a hidden file on the local hard drive, and then passed them on to the real LOGIN.EXE. Then the grimy work of weaponization: a script installed the trojan from floppy, recovered the captured password file (if it existed), hid it with ATTRIB, and modified AUTOEXEC.BAT if necessary. Tagging a dozen library machines required less than a half hour.

Over the next weeks he observed several teachers using the compromised workstations. These included his mawkish, vapid British Lit teacher; in class he noticed that her room contained no computer. If she had no computer here...they must be able to enter grades from library machines. *My* machines. Well then. He harvested his credential files, and descended to a corner machine in the downstairs lab. There was her name among the pilferage, and her password from that day, and that was Michael's first successful intrusion.

A simple semigraphic menu offered InteGrade or MS-DOS Prompt. His eyes lit up as he selected the former and saw exactly what he'd hoped: four sections of BritLit, "Independent Study: Anne Brontë"—which unfortunate lesbian requested *that?*—and something called "Remedial Writing." Heh. Ghastly. He pondered what use he could find for changing that semester's BritLit scores. A footer advised that in addition to F1's "Help," F2 allowed one to "Change semester"—hey now—and that F3 promised "Other classes." *Que?* He jammed F3 and gasped: there for the pleasure of his scrolling selection were dozens of classes, probably every class being offered that semester.

"What's up MLB?"

Michael smashed Ctrl+Alt+Delete and turned. "Steve, hey. Precious little.. Did you bring it?"

---

l'code pour l'code code for the sake of code. cf. *l'art pour l'art*

"Precious little huh? Look at you rebooting as soon as you hear me. C'mon Michael. I'm your priest. Were you back here jacking it?"

"*Padre Esteban*, it is true, whilst daydreaming of your mother's honeyed oriface, the sacchariferous path to all her pleasure, I gifted this PS/2 with my hot Hispanic essence. I fear the machine might no longer boot."

"Disgusting. Four Hail Marys. Yeah I've got it. Bathroom?"

"I'll take it from you at the end of the day."

"Or you could take it now, so I'm not walking around with two smelly Zs."

"Don't have cash on me, my friend! In the car." Michael had the $500 in his wallet, but no desire to carry around a class B misdemeanor longer than necessary.

"Ahhhh ok. I'll meet you at three then. As a gay man, wouldn't you have been daydreaming of my dad's asshole?"

"Only you dream of your dad's asshole, Steve. Gotta scoot."

Through the day he pondered his happy discovery. His own transcripts could hardly be improved, certainly not in any way worth the risk. Other transcripts, though...success would hinge on two things: potential customers couldn't talk, and actual customers couldn't get caught.

Approach T people with an offer of services. P is earned for each of W who buy, where $W \leq T$. Total income of at least I then requires $W \geq \lceil \frac{I}{P} \rceil$. Risk grows as $C_0 T + C_1 W$. I think the power to modify grades is worth at least $20K. Why not. How many rich kids are in need of such a service? How rich are they?

The usefulness of a grade change was obviously nonlinear. Just that year, the Texas Legislature had passed House Bill 588, guaranteeing admission to the state's fine public universities for the top 10% of every high school's graduating class. To someone at 11%, the shift of a few hundredths of a point could mean the difference between UT-Austin and Lone Star College's North Harris County campus. To someone with a 2.12, it meant fuck all. There was some $\Delta_{VS} \geq 0$ between valedictorian and salutatorian; a change $C > \Delta_{VS}$ likely meant a great deal more to that supernumerary student than it did #10.

Risk was similarly complex. Ideally, rather than selling the service of improved grades, he would sell strategic reductions in the grades of others. If all you cared about was top 10%, it was enough that those above fell back, and no one whose grades actually changed could then name him. Alas, anyone whose GPA dropped unexpectedly was likely to inquire as to the reason, undoing his work, probably exploding the whole racket. Older grades were probably seen less frequently than newer ones. The more useless and dysfunctional the teacher involved, the less likely anything would be noticed. Less raw movement meant less impact to statistics. Try to avoid changing leftmost digits—humans would mark 2.99 to 3.0 more easily than 3.31 to 3.41, despite being an order of magnitude smaller. If a teacher had left since posting the grade, no way that was coming up in anything short of an authentic audit.

He realized with a gleam that he'd been wrong about the statistics. Less raw movement did not necessarily imply less statistical movement. If I bump someone up from a C to a B, the class average is held constant if someone else eats the inverse change, as is the letter grade distribution. Standard dev...yeah stddev can still change. Eh, no one has time for sigma anymore. Now, the kind of person who gets As is more likely...this is ludicrous. The necessary adjustments cannot meaningfully affect class-wide statistics. This nonsense would double the number of people affected. *Fool.*

So find five marks close to that 10% threshold. They needed moral turpitude, liquid assets, and to be able to keep their mouths shut. His ideal customer was a devout Longhorns fan who had in freshman year suffered a few too many Bs and Cs in classes taught by known imbeciles or, better still, the recently deceased. He figured five heads at $4K a throw, a tidy and tax-free twenty large. He went to the parking lot early, and evaluated its ostentatious vehicles while waiting for Steve. Fuck that, he thought: five a head.

None of that mattered to automated analysis, though. Any kind of auditing would fuck him proper. Shit, just decent *logging* could ruin things. He could not yet speak meaningfully of risk, but he could investigate. He needed a plausible sacrifice...Keith Liddick. Junior class president. Handsome simpleton. Gifted basketball player. Ineffective linebacker, but full of heart. Likely future Auburn attendee, maybe minoring in that Golf Course Design program they had. Common dicksuck. Spends a lot of time around the front office and at school in general. Burn him.

Within five minutes, Keith Liddick's transcript was just as humble as ever, class selection-wise, but clear of the 10 Cs and two Ds he'd racked up in two and a half years. Changing them all to A- boosted his 2.76 to 3.40. Ahhh, Keith, we've done great things for your sad story of Remedial Algebra and, Jesus fucking Christ, "Life Skills." The sun beats down on a brand new day for you.

It happened right after midterms. First, rumors that Liddick had been called out of class. Confirmed sightings of Keith Liddick wildly gesticulating and quite possibly crying across a table from multiple grim, unsmiling faculty, known high-level ballbusters. Vague talk of scandalous accusations and undignified Presidential confusion. Appalling abuses of trust. Threats of disciplinary removal from the student body. Counterthreats from Liddick Senior, Esq., a Skyline District litigator who wasted little time demonstrating ballbusting powers of a truly, like, wizardly nature, one Vice-Principals would never know. A wide-eyed report claimed Pa Liddick rattled off torts with a thunderous voice, and all who heard it trembled. Timid retreat on the whole removal thing, a misunderstanding we're sure, never a consideration. Keith is one of our finest students. Ahhh, we have just been informed that the error was ours. A problem of data entry. Come and see us whenever you'd like, sir.

A final petulant observation: your correct GPA, Mr. Liddick, was a 2.76 and thus you are ineligible for student government, participation therein requiring a Three-point-Zero, it's written right there in the student handbook. We're sorry, but student government is serious business. Not sure how it was missed originally. Were we to overlook this, only anarchy could follow.

So the current VP became President, and Keith Liddick knew honest bewilderment for his remaining time at Lamar, and was never sure who really believed him and who was just nodding until he would shut up. He sobbed freely when Auburn wrote that with deep regret they could not offer admission. Weep not for young master Liddick: his father, a friend of the Gochmans, set him up with an Academy Sports location. He married well and spawned several young upper-middle-class Liddicks, and was politely but firmly trained by his wife to stop telling that stupid Class President story.

If the vacancy at VP had any ramifications, no one noticed them.

Something had pretty clearly tipped off the administration. Either Liddick noticed the change, confided in the wrong person, and that person grassed, or it was surfaced by an audit. Too much time had passed for it to have been a response to routine logging. The proximity to midterms pointed at auditing— yeah, report cards go home at midterms, ergo stable grades must be in by then (and are likely recorded), ergo backups are likely taken, ergo perfect time to crosscheck against previous backups looking for discrepancies. Well, shit. He'd already collected a list of current seniors sorted by grade point average, calculated the 10% line, and identified five targets of opportunity. He'd carefully broached the topic, and found them more than receptive. Looking back, he probably could have asked for more than five K.

No one seemed surprised at Bolaño's claims; their main concern had been getting caught. He emphasized that not getting caught was a matter of not talking. "If worst comes to worst, act surprised and deny all knowledge. There are no records incriminating you, and I'll refund you. You heard about Keith Liddick last week, right? He's sitting happy today, sweating over Life Skills, furrowing his brow at $2x - 6$, wishing he was dribbling. All you have to do is earn grades this semester sufficient to hold onto the small numeric advantage I'm providing."

One had asked, "what about the person I'm displacing?"

"Well they won't be in the top 10% anymore."

"Do I get to pick who that is?"

"Are you serious?"

"You won't let me pick?"

"Pick whom among that 10% holds the lowest GPA?" Idiot.

"Oh, I guess you're right."

"Christ. Now, there is a small potential problem: if that person gets all As this semester, they might wonder how it's possible that their class rank went down. If they raised enough of a stink, maybe people look into things. But if these people were accustomed to all As, they wouldn't be at the border for the top 10%, *n'est-ce pas*?"

"Jeez, I hope not."

"You'll of course be refunded in this unlikely event. Look, I'm your fairy fucking godmother. You fucked up, but not too badly, and I'm giving you the opportunity to undo that fuckup for five thousand dollars. Your first year out of A&M you'll make more than that over changing tires and checking oil, and that's what you're looking at otherwise. You're driving a Navigator out there. That's a forty thousand dollar SUV. You can get five grand from your parents, and it'll be the best investment you ever make."

He was $15K richer than he had been the previous week. Another $10K was promised in the post. He had less than half a semester to neutralize whatever had highlighted his test run. He poked around the InteGrade UI, but saw nothing about backups or audits—there didn't even seem to be a way within the software, at least at a regular teacher's access, to configure notifications about changes. It all pointed at something working externally.

He approached the detestable Keith Liddick. "Hey, *presidente*, I heard some shit went down. You been changing grades? You clever fuck."

"What's up Bolaño? No, I didn't have anything to do with it. I don't know what happened. I didn't even know anything *had* happened until they called me in there and started accusing me."

"Any idea how they found out?"

"You mean how it happened? No idea."

"No, I mean how did they know that it had happened at all?"

"Oh, they said that they check the grades against backups whenever report cards come out, and if an old grade has changed, they ask the teacher to confirm that they did it. They were like, we didn't need to ask in your case. Twelve grades, Keith? Wasn't that a bit greedy? And I'm just like, what the Sam Houston are you talking about? Hey, you know computers, right? What do you think could have happened?"

Outstanding.

"I think you did it. Twelve classes? You can't blame that on cosmic rays." He put an arm around Keith's shoulders. "Don't let it get you down. If you get sad, remember that student government is retarded, and nothing bad actually happened to you. Teach me about computers sometime, big guy."

Campus IT was two dorks in their thirties, caricatures of stereotypes both, without a decent shirt or haircut between them. They knew Bolaño, appreciated his interest in computers, and were now and again useful sources of information or technique. They seemed furthermore convinced that he was fundamentally up to no good. He had little hope that he could ask truly relevant questions without setting off their alarms.

"Mr. Morris, I've been wondering about my backups situation at home. As in, I don't have any. What would you recommend?"

"I like Fastback Plus. It's what I use at home for both of my computers. Here we use Norton Backup, which is good enough, I suppose. Mr. Newell seems to think it's better."

"Well, we can get a support contract for it, so yes, I think it's better in that regard. I'm sure Fastback Plus is fine for you, Michael. They're both better than what comes in DOS."

"Is my Netware directory here at school backed up?"

"Yes, we back up all the student and teacher directories every Friday."

"Do you just back them up to another hard drive or what?"

"No. The server is running eight SCSI hard drives in a RAID. That's a—"

"I know what a RAID is. This is RAID5?"

"RAID0."

"Isn't that dangerous?"

"That's why we have the backups! It's very fast. RAID5 would be too slow, and it's hard to get hardware RAID5 for that many drives. But that's already a very expensive computer, and there's no room for more disks. It has an Exabyte

---

RAID: redundant array of inexpensive disks

Mammoth Data8 tape connected. For you, I'd try and get one of those Iomega ZIP drives. The tape drive is over a thousand dollars."

"How big are the SCSI drives?"

"Two gigabytes."

"So you can put sixteen gigs on a single tape?"

"Not quite, actually. The tapes are fourteen gigabytes. We don't back up the programs—DOS, or Netware, or the shared applications. The user data is limited to twelve gigabytes, and it fits on there."

"Do you overwrite the tape each week?"

"No, we have four tapes. One we only update after midterms and finals, and that goes offsite almost immediately—"

"Almost?"

Morris looked at Newell. "We run some consistency checks against it, make sure the backup ran successfully, you know. The other three we rotate through each week, with the oldest one going offsite."

"Why do you take it offsite? Oh, I guess the building could burn down."

"Exactly."

"Where's offsite?"

Newell cut in. "That's not for you to know, Michael."

"Oh of course, no problem at all. You told me what I needed. Thanks a lot, Mr. Morris, Mr. Newell. Could I maybe get a copy of that FastBack Plus?"

Morris frowned. "It's not shareware, Michael. It's very reasonably priced for what it does." But Michael Luis Bolaño was already in motion.

∗ ∗ ∗ ∗ ∗ ∗ ∗ ∗ ∗

So they all but confirmed that an audit is run against the previous long-held backup whenever grades are recorded. That's gotta be either something Inte-Grade provides, or they're dumping the InteGrade data store to plaintext and diffing them. Very sensible. There are three places to attack this: the backup media, the audit process, or the audit environment.

The source tape used is held offsite. Don't know where offsite is. Doesn't matter—I'm not breaking into anybody's house.

The audit process is some application. Maybe they built it themselves, in which case they might recompile it at any point. A vendor application can get upgraded...but they're probably not upgrading core functionality mid-semester. Either way, if they're competent, they probably put a sentinel bad value into the backup to ensure it's flagged. Otherwise, they wouldn't know the audit is functional. Maybe I can capture and replay.

A local BBS provided Netware 3.11 and several multimegabyte PDFs containing the Certified Novell Administrator training materials. The final weeks of his junior year were spent doing little else but reading them, experimenting on his local install, writing code, and iterating. He asked Larry at ¼-Price Books if he could go down to five hours a week through the end of the school year.

"What, do you think this operation is going to fall apart without your handsome presence?"

"So that's alright with you?"

"Michael, you're just here to bring in the chicks."

"You know I'm gay, right?"

"Well start bringing in the gays, then. Shitfire."

✳ ✳ ✳ ✳ ✳ ✳ ✳ ✳

On the fourth Tuesday of March, the 26th, Luis Bolaño in the master bathroom wrote to his second son:

> Michael Luis. My miracle. My monster. You will do amazing things. Try to do them in the service of good. Be audacious and bold. Honor God. Care for your mother. Love her also. Forgive me. Adios.

Luis picked up a gold-plated Colt Double Eagle, mugged for a moment in the mirror, and raised it to his mouth. He carefully pointed directly back and above the horizontal, the better to obliterate the brainstem. He pulled the trigger, striking the Boxer primer of a Winchester Defender SE .45 ACP jacketed hollow point. The bullet fired true, but whether this was due to the ballyhooed nickel exterior of the Super Elite we unfortunately cannot know. Luis demonstrated in his final act a competence and even aptitude largely absent from his life. Mess was minimal; there was only minor damage to the house. Conscious thought ceased less than a millisecond after the projectile first began to rend apart the muscles of his palatal velum. Were his neurons still networking, he might have been proud that tissue trauma actually beat chemical signals along the glossopharyngeal nerve: he triggered his gag reflex, but never felt it.

✳ ✳ ✳ ✳ ✳ ✳ ✳ ✳

Rosemary called Lamar High. Michael arrived home and a patrolman presented him the envelope. "It was on the sink next to your father. It has your name on it. I'm sorry." Michael took it wordlessly, hugged his mother, and went to his room. He paused for a moment, ripped the unopened missive along its height, then both pieces across their widths, and flung into the trash the last, unread words of Luis Bolaño. He began eagerly to work.

They pawned the meretricious pistol that day. Michael assured her he didn't want any of the other guns, and Luis's whole ostentatious armory was sold before the week ended. She never asked about the envelope. For a few weeks he thought about it once or twice a day. The end of the semester drew nigh and he thought of it no more.

Suddenly he could no longer log into his teacher account. He went down the list of collected credentials, trying each faculty username. All seven refused login. For a few moments, Bolaño felt things slipping out of his control. He ensured that *he* could still log in. No problems there. He edited his script to pull one last list of passwords from the machine on which it was run, and then remove all traces of the trojan. Cleaning the machines was even faster than compromising them. Looking at the newly acquired credentials, he realized that every privileged account had a different password on his current list. Oh, so they made everyone with grade access change their password after Liddick. Smart. Not good enough.

If he was going to disable or even discover the defensive audit, he needed access to the account that ran and built it. Newell had claimed no programming experience when asked—he was strictly a networking and hardware guy. Morris said he wrote some C when the school needed it. Assume Morris. He compromised a downstairs lab machine, and waited for Morris to come around without the more suspicious Newell. He unplugged the Ethernet from the computer in question.

"Hey Mr. Morris? I can log in fine on most machines, but this one seems to time out after I enter my password."

"Huh. Let me come look at it. Let's see if I can log in. Nope, is this the same behavior you were seeing?"

"Just the same."

"Hrmmm. Let's check the network cable. Ahhh yes, here's our problem." Morris smiled, satisfied, and pointed at Bolaño with the cable's 8P8C connector. "Always check your cables, young Mr. Bolaño." He reattached it, and verified a successful login. "There you go. It ought work now."

"Ahhh, you are truly wise, Mr. Morris."

Morris flipped a victory V and returned to the many irritations of high school network administrators. Bolaño sat down, copied the password corresponding to morrisb, and disinfected the box. Holding his breath, he tested the password right there.

It didn't work. Maybe I mistyped it? Fuck.

Indeed he had.

As soon as possible, he posted up on his preferred library machine, logging in as Morris. There, in his network file storage, was the directory CHECKER. Within were several .CPP and .H files, including one GRADECHK.CPP. Michael could have danced a jig. He printed all the contents—about twenty pages of a language he'd never used—and skipped home to learn C++.

There was an easy problem and a hard problem. First, he needed to modify the code, eliding verification for his customers while interfering with no other checks. He would need to rebuild the binary and stage it on the server. The hard problem was that Morris could at any time make a change to his source, rebuild, and push his own binary, blowing Michael's away. He could set up a job that watched for this, and copied his compromised binary back, but then Morris's changes wouldn't be reflected. However amusing it might be to watch Morris figure this out, he would presumably at some point get to the bottom of it, at which point all hell would break loose.

He could of course make his edits in Morris's own source tree, but then they would be immediately visible. *L'appel du vide.* Suicide, not even resilient against Morris restoring his source tree from some pristine location.

He remembered Ken Thompson's 1983 Turing Award lecture, "On Trusting Trust." Put it in the tools. He felt a surge of power as he read the Borland manuals, focusing on the linker TLINK.EXE. He gathered that the C++ compiler TCC.EXE generated code around external function calls, which were encoded with the target function name. The linker found these functions by symbol table lookup, filling in the appropriate jump target. If two modules implemented the same name, the collision could be resolved via linker parameters.

L'appel du vide: call of the void

The function performing the lowest-level consistency check was simplicity itself. `CmpGradeRecords` accepted two `Grades` and compared them for equality. One came from the first data set, one from the second. Above that was `CmpStudentSemester`, which matched up classes and invoked `CmpGradeRecords` on the appropriate pairs. If the classes couldn't be matched, or a grade had changed, it returned `true`. Michael carefully typed out a wrapper that checked the incoming student ID for his set of five. If those matched, it returned `false`, bypany actual work. Otherwise, it passed its arguments along to the original function. He got things working around four in the morning.

He copied his esoteric invocation of the linker, and pasted it into a new batch file `TLINK.BAT`, calling `2TLINK.EXE`. He copied this file and his compiled shim object to a floppy and went to sleep, exhausted but exhilarated. At Lamar, he renamed `TLINK.EXE` to `2TLINK.EXE`, and copied his payload to the network share. If everything worked as expected, building any source with the Turbo C++ tools would interpose his object code over any function named `CmpStudentSemester`. To test it, he built a fresh copy of Morris's tool from the pristine source.

He dumped the symbols. The size of `CmpStudentSemester` had increased by a factor of almost five. No other symbols seemed changed. Sweet.

He never heard complaints from the departed seniors. Fifteen thousand he handed over to Rosemary, suggesting she bring up to date various arrear balances, and build back up her savings. She wondered at the thick pile of currency, but did not question where he'd acquired such a sum. He'd planned to claim stock market wins if asked. The remaining ten he placed into a Vanguard brokerage account. It would find good use in time.

He accepted his diploma, smiling at his mother in the audience. His valedictorian speech was an excerpt from *The Myth of Sisyphus*. At its end, he came clean: "Those fine words were not my own. The name of the man who wrote them was David Koresh."

An angry murmur from the audience.

"Just kidding! It was Albert Camus, winner of the 1957 Nobel Prize in Literature. The text from which they were taken was one of the two or three most sublime works of this century. Not being a Nobel Prize winner myself, I figured I'd best use this opportunity to share him with you. Read a book, Houston." He sat down to minimal applause, and finally stood once more, setting forth to restore the house Bolaño. Graceful Rosemary, brave José López, learned Antonio, fiery Gustavo, even dogfucking Cortés—whatever else, the man had skills—stand me now and forever in good stead. I, twentieth generation of Monteczuma II, am putting my queer shoulder to the wheel.

✳ ✳ ✳ ✳ ✳ ✳ ✳ ✳

A little less than a year after Michael walked across a temporary stage at the distressingly ramshackle Astrodome, Eric Harris and Dylan Klebold donned trench coats, loaded up a shotgun and 9mm each (Eric a Hi-Point 995, Dylan the poorly regarded Intratec TEC-DC9 Mini), and snatched thirteen lives in the parking lots, cafeteria, and library of Columbine High School. Their elaborate plans were poorly executed: the two twenty-pound Blue Rhino propane tanks central to success were purchased only that morning (Harris's homemade "Natural

Selection" tshirt is visible on Texaco closed-camera footage at 09:12), leaving little time for deliberate preparation of their detonating apparata. Dylan's TEC, true to form, jammed after firing just two shots; he would end up with only 67 rounds expended to Eric's robust 121. Their pipe bombs proved pipe dreams: the one conflagration they initiated was extinguished by automated overhead sprinklers. A few weeks later, tornadoes would kill more than twice as many Oklahomans. Six days earlier, seventy-three Kosovar Albanians, sixteen of them *fëmijë*, were regrettably mistaken for Yugoslav infantry and engaged between Đakovica and Dečani with laser-guided and dumb munitions, much to their detriment. So it goes.

But for a few weeks Columbine simmered, a regular topic of American conversation. Many looked back soberly or otherwise and knew that they'd at times dreamed of nothing so much as pulling on their own coats, running up the black flag, and sticking it to some gladhanding high school sons of bitches. And still others wondered who had walked among them with the spirit of a Klebold or a Harris, and when alumna and alumni met it was a subject of speculation, and several mooted that our own Michael Luis would not shock were he to take up the wrathful visage of Sammāʔēl. At Stanford, two Lamar graduates drank Anchor Steam in the all-frosh housing of Florence Moore ("FloMo") Hall, and one offered an observation along those lines. The other, once something of an associate of Michael's, snorted derisively. It was an uninspired take: Bolaño was imperturbable, and aloof, but generally without complaint. He seemed solidly in control of his life. No, slaughter was not at all his style.

"Besides...if Michael Luis Bolaño had made his mind up to wipe out our high school, neither you nor I would be here wearing cardinal. We would have been blown to shit or shot to shit or whatever he intended, along with everyone else in that building. Good God, it would have been a saturnalia of blood. Westheimer Road would resemble the surface of the moon. And he'd be alive somewhere, bet. No way does he go down. And it wouldn't have been that he hated everyone there. It probably would have resulted from, like, a wager."

"Hah."

"And you know what else? There would be some sick fucking joke in there, something really dark and twisted, something that makes you laugh because it's so goddamn horrible."

"Like what, Steve?"

"Shit I don't know. I'm not Michael. OK here we go. He would have somehow the previous day arranged it so all the guidance counselors came down with food poisoning. So none of them are there, just two-thousand stiffening Houstonians and these eight guidance counselors bent over toilets at home. There'd be a note to all the media saying something like, 'I have spared your guidance counselors, several of whom can read. May they help you as much as they helped me. Don't mistake my kindness for weakness. —MLB'"

"Ahhhhahaha that's fucked up. Bolaño never did take shit from anyone."

"I guess if you're gonna grow up gay and out in Texas you'd better be the coldest motherfucker in Houston."

---

fëmijë: children

4   elephant seals

In Georgia's Marietta a steel chicken rises fifty-six feet above Cobb Parkway and Roswell Road. So long as power flows to this cyclopean gallus, her great beak opens and closes with ineluctable regularity. In times of plenty, she clucks enticing invitations, offering Kentucky Fried solace to a hungry world. During unhappier days she crashes maxilla and mandible together in warning: woe to he who rises up against Cobb County and all its strength. Her eyes—it is not possible to see both simulatenously—wamble in unnatural lunatic curves. Epicycloids, maybe, or perhaps epitrochoids? Watching either for more than a few moments can be unsettling, even unpleasant. Its common name—a sensible if decidedly unimaginative aptronym—is the Big Chicken.

Eight kilometers away from the Spiced Colossus, in 1996 the superb George Walton Comprehensive took down its Raider trade dress, raising high in replacement the banners of Turner Classic High School's Airpirates.

Cue those glorious Centennial Olympics, awarded unexpectedly to Atlanta. Cue memories thus evoked of Muhammad Ali, the Magnificent Seven, and Coca-Cola. Time Warner that year acquired Turner Broadcasting for $7.5G, and Ted Turner, *TIME'S* Person of the Year 1991, sat pretty. Meanwhile in Cobb County, passionate and eager suburban parents together with innovative and energetic staff led Walton's application for charter school status. The Turner-Agassi Education Facilities Fund looked close to home and saw a deserving cause. Money changed hands, complete with Publishers Clearinghouse-style non-negotiable gimmick checks. Centennial Olympic Stadium, rechristened as eponymous Turner Field, accepted the Atlanta-Fulton County Braves *en huddled masse* from their dilapidated Capitol Avenue home. The Turner wave seemed like it might never crest. Charter status was granted, a thankful school took a new cognominal from its benefactor, and the future waxed bright.

Georgia has 159 counties, at least 140 more than it possibly needs, second in number only to Texas's frankly preposterous 254. In the middle of Georgia's largely agricultural inner coastal plain a few more than nine thousand people carve their stakes from Turner County, home of the Titans. These normally reticent dirt farmers brought forth formal written protest to the Georgia High School Association: "Turner High School would infringe on the brand and identity we have for years struggled to establish. Must we small, humble communities, salt of Georgia's red clay, play yet again the role of estrous sow, presenting for careless ravage swollen and carmine cunthocks always towards the patronizing, Godless, yuppie scum of Atlanta's northern suburbs? Is it not enough that they have everything?" It came to Ted's attention, and he whooped, "Those Turner High School boll weevils want THS, huh?" He removed his hat and cackled wildly. "Well we'll be Turner Classic! The real TCHS!" It seemed slightly off, but the Fund was being historically generous.

They called Ted Turner the Mouth of the South. Looking out over his sloe gin fizz upon construction of a new library, he mused aloud. "Corsairs and buccaneers are all a bit passé. Square. Suggestive of the age of sail. Ottomans once tried to board *Courageous II* eighteen nautical miles out of Montevideo.

Scared hell out of Kofi Annan. He still wore a bolga hat back then. Wasn't Under-Secretary yet." He looked conspiratorially around the room. VIPs grinned back uneasily, wondering whether a point might at some time emerge.

"Well Jane yells *tiến lên!* and ninja-kicks the Saracen sons of bitches right into the water. Now that sea's just aswarm with the vicious candiru, the dread South American vampire fish. They'll swim right up your dick, chew it up from the inside, spit your dick out before you can say Billy Graham. Those Mohammedans are splashing and I holler down, 'that's what we call a baptism by Jane!' It'll be on her next videocassette. But these kids aren't gonna know a *lettre de marque* from their peckers. Now hijackers, hijackers can still scare people. You were primed to tuck into some American bison, boom! You're on a DC-8 bound for Havana. In the cockpit Will Kunstler's snoring under an issue of *Ramparts* with his dick in his hand. Then you're sitting on a landing strip with nothing but a box of rum and two infielders to be named later. Ruined our trip to Yerba Buena." None but Ted seemed enthused about the change, but the Raiders were dutifully reimagined as Airpirates, their mascot's unflinching depredator exchanging sabre and steed for balaclava, repelling gear, and a faux Kalashnikov painted orange in conformance with local regulation.

So Sherman Spartacus Katz became a Turner Classic Airpirate, even as his days as an Archangel of St. Anthony's came to ignominious and abbreviated end. He tried a few unpromising afternoons of Airpirate football, finding the camaraderie and company and prospects of victory markedly inferior to those at St. Anthony, with its hundred-year history of Irish Catholic scrappiness and big private donors. He recalled that the then-Raiders had obliterated his Archangels at Brookwood's quizbowl tournament the previous year, the only tournament in which StAHS's moribund academic bowl team played. He inquired, and was told to show up at room B-137 after school that Wednesday.

He found assembled at 1515h a raucous collection of nerds: marching band geeks. Conspicuously and complexly flawed flag girls. Second generation Asian-Americans spoke loudly, watched by children of Asian immigrants, who spoke little if at all. Freshmen rehashed their tryouts for Atlanta Youth Symphony Orchestra. A ring of sophomore boys communicated exclusively in Simpsons quotes and piercing, insane laughter. One simply enormous senior Katz knew from AP Calculus flipped through manga in isolation, somehow sweating both above and below a tentlike Eve 6 shirt. A gorgeous redhead sat crosslegged on a desk reading Flannery O'Connor, reason enough herself to attend whatever this was. An Indian—there had been no Indians at St. Anthony's, Katz reflected—collected dues with a superabundance of seriousness, rendering meticulous **X**s on an accounting pad. Christ, some of these kids look young. Older students, some wearing letter jackets—I *do* hope those letters were not for academic bowl ugh—conferred with a short woman of seeming Italian heritage. Median attractiveness on a denary integer scale here looked to be about a...call it a straight four among the gentlemen, a generous six for the ladies. Many of the older half he thought he recognized from a class or two: by one's junior year, Advanced Placement and the like have segregated high school, the intelligentsia

---

tiến lên: "go forward" Vietnamese battle cry

striding from one AP to another in bright-eyed, bushy-tailed flocks. Two blonde girls of indeterminate age studied the floor with intensity that suggested untreated autism, pacing deformed lemniscatic orbits like bees' waggles or the chaotic trajectories of Lorenz systems. Katz kept an ear open, hearkening for the crescendo of agitated whimpering that might herald a spectacular collision.

He waited until there was some space around the Italian woman, presumably faculty, and approached. "Hello there! My name's Sherman Spartacus Katz. I'm a junior. I just transferred from St. Anthony's downtown–you know it, I'm sure?"

She seemed distracted. "Yes, of course, private school. Good team back in 1991. They took one from us at Vanderbilt that year." She looked out over the room. "Squads break! Written drill on Norse mythology, forty-five open questions, written drill on Western philosophy, thirty open questions, then quick draw. Fifth tournament of the year is next weekend at Woodward. All seats are in play. A and B teams stay with me." Her voice was crisp and powerful. The fiftyish people present split into four groups that correlated not quite precisely with age. Three left the room.

Katz continued, hopeful. "Yep, that's us. I was captain of our team last year, and probably would have been this year, but now I'm here. I guess it's your lucky day!" He spread his arms, grinning stupidly, making of himself a gift. Perhaps she wasn't aware of the academic rigor he'd left behind.

She looked him up and down, eyes dubious, smiling thinly. "I only think we saw St. Anthony's once last year, at Brookwood? I recall a thrashing from our D team."

His smile faded. "That was your D team? They were pretty good. So y'all go to more than one tournament a year it seems?"

"Our A and B teams go to a tournament pretty much every weekend."

"Oh wow. Anyway, I'm here; I don't expect to be made captain but I figure, you know, I can probably slide right in on your varsity as it were."

Her laughter was not unkind. "Our varsity has been coming to practices twice a week, most of them for four years. I've never seen you play, Sherman Spartacus Katz. Sherman Spartacus Katz?" She shook her head. "Why did you leave in the middle of the semester?"

He was ready for this: "We abandoned the Catholic Church."

"Hmmm." Behind them, nine students had taken desks, pens out. A tenth passed out mimeographed worksheets, then primed an alarm clock and took her own chair, barking "go!" Then the sound of ten pens on paper.

"You don't happen to have the periodic table memorized, do you?" One shortish boy looked up at the ceiling and clenched his fists at his temples, radiating genuine anguish. His face broke into a smile; his scrawling resumed.

"All of it?"

She smiled wider. "Yes, all of it."

"I can't say that I do."

"Where are you strongest?"

"I mean, I'd consider myself strong across the board."

"Not on the periodic table, it seems."

He cocked an eye. "No, I suppose not."

"Who won the fiction Pulitzer in 1953?"

"Ummm, can you tell me the book?"

Her laughter this time had a definite edge to it. "You said you're a junior, right? I'd have you start with the D team, but they're mostly younger. I guess you can try a practice or two with group C. They're headed down the hall that way." She pointed to the left.

The alarm clock rang and the leading girl, rather unnecessarily it seemed, called out "Time! Pencils *down!*" Several of the sitting players looked at Katz with discernible, unfriendly confusion. Papers were swapped. Fists Boy told no one in particular, "easy drill, easy warmup, let's go." Katz wished him ill.

Surprised and not a little humiliated, he left the room and caught up with his assigned gaggle, happily counting the Flannery reader among them. He came alongside her. "Greetings and salutations! I'm Sherman Spartacus Katz. Just transferred here. This is a pretty serious academic bowl team! What's your name?"

"Ariadne. Are all your introductions trinomial?" She removed a black scrunchie and when she shook her hair it moved like auburn sand drifts.

"I dig the trochee-dactility of it."

"Wouldn't that only be five syllables? Where'd you move from?"

"I didn't move, just left St. Anthony's downtown."

"Why'd you leave? Did you fight someone? You're pretty big."

Straighten the back. Spread the shoulders. "We stopped being Catholic."

"You stopped being Catholic so hard you had to leave in the middle of the semester?" The group turned and entered a biology classroom, where a set of buzzers had already been strung across two front tables.

"Yeah, my mom's kinda crazy about the Pope now. She gets drunk and rants about papists. She's sweet, though."

An Indian in front of them turned. "Yo that's some Klan shit, is your mom a racist?"

"Eh, more an ignorant but imaginative lush with Manichaean tendencies."

Ariadne looked at him with curiosity, and momentarily he swooned.

"Dude I recognize you. My name's Arun. I was on Turner Classic D last year and we smoked your asses at Brookwood. You were on that team." He paused for a moment, evaluating Sherman. Katz figured their weight delta to be thirty kilos minimum. The kid had heart. "*Smoked* your asses."

"Yeah." Katz chuckled uneasily. "I'm getting the impression our team wasn't very competitive. This seems much more organized." Everyone was taking a seat. Katz angled towards Ariadne, looking pointedly in another direction as he did so.

"Yeah it's definitely an operation here. Did you see the middle schoolers? You can take fifth seat with that team. They're missing someone today." Arun pointed at the far table, and Katz walked mournfully to its end.

"Middle schoolers? I did see some goddamn children, yes."

"Yeah they get shuttled over to practice here on Wednesdays, so they're ready for camp before ninth grade."

"Camp? Like, academic bowl camp?"

A tonsorial abomination wearing a shirt covered with equations broke in. "Camp was the best!" Nods of acclamation around both tables. *Camp?*

The Arun person stood and began distributing worksheets. "First drills today are Norse mythology. Top scores earn a Flight of the Valkyries to Valhalla." No one laughed. "Seo-jun, got the timer ready?" A Korean to Katz's right nodded. "Start!" Katz leaned in to work; he guessed them to be the same drills people were crushing in B-137.

He read the page twice, not believing it the first time through. "What's the significance of the boldface?"

In unsynchronized chorus, with giggles: "A and B don't get those clues."

Norse Mythology (1 of 2) Levels C–E

0. Sometimes called Ásbrú
Shimmering path destroyed in Ragnarok _____

1. Son of Nanna and Baldr
God of justice _____

2. Whitest of the gods, emerald-toothed
Son of Odin and nine mothers _____

3. Fed his hand to Fenrir
Theophoric of Tuesday _____

4. "Lord of frenzy"
Wields Gungnir _____

5. Rules her subjects in Niflheim
Daughter of Loki _____

6. Flytes with Frigg
Father of Jörmungandr _____

7. Weeps for Baldr in Fensalir
Theophoric of Friday _____

8. Gylfaginning, Skáldskaparmál, Háttatal
Snorri Sturluson _____

9. Sæmundar Edda
Codex Regius _____

Name: _____ Score: _____

Targets: 10 (A), 9 (B), 7 (C, D), 6 (E)

Interesting. "Do answers repeat?"

From Arun: "You're allowed to. The sheet won't."

Oh my. He looked around: everyone but him was writing. A girl sitting opposite, fourteen years old tops, had at least four down already.

I guess this is how stupid people feel all the time. Huh.

Friday—that comes from Freya, right? He marked down FREYA for #7. Tuesday, could that be Thor? Thor is Thursday, idiot. Maybe he's both days? No one's two days you dumb piece of shit. "Rules *her* subjects." Well, that's another girl, put HEL. Is Frigg a woman? Isn't Frigg married to Odin? Christ this is hard. Fuck it. Are #8 and #9 the PROSE EDDA and POETIC EDDA? Shimmering path? Rainbow bridge? Bifröst? BIFRÖST, bitches, woot. "Emerald-toothed," the fuck? Gungnir is ODIN I think? "Flytes with Frigg" is that a typo? Fights? Flies? How much time is left? Argh. Ugh. He filled in remaining blank spaces with LOKI. A dismal performance.

"Swap." Katz felt numb yet also bruised. He accepted the paper of Seo-jun, and realized he hadn't written his name. He moved to do so, but the hateful child hooted "you're supposed to put your name down, Sherman! Otherwise you can't get points!" He spoke with affectations normally reserved for pets. "I'll put it down for you this time," He printed SHERMAN K., his laugh shrill. "You sure wrote LOKI a lot!" Laughter became general. Ariadne, for a few minutes the queen of all his dreams, giggled without even the courtesy of covering her mouth. Sherman died ten thousand deaths. He glanced at Seo-jun, wondering briefly what faces he would make were he being dragged under a bus.

"We've got BIFRÖST. FORSETI. HEIMDALL." Katz wondered whether Arun possessed some kind of delegated power in this room, or was simply assertive. "TÝR." Well, at least I didn't write Thor. Oh, fuck, I wrote LOKI. Not much better. "ODIN. also accept WŌDEN, WUODAN, WUOTAN, anything like that."

A kid with the look of a real dipshit: "Do we accept WÊDA?"

Arun is surprised. "Did someone answer WÊDA?"

WÊDA? Katz is certain he's never heard of WÊDA. Did Arun say Wu-Tang?

"No, but someone could have answered WÊDA."

Everyone looks annoyed, heartening Katz slightly.

Arun pauses before answering. "In my room, WÊDA gets you points, but it seems unwise to rely on that. Who answers WÊDA?"

Dipshit doesn't want to stop. "I thought about answering WÊDA."

"But you didn't."

"No, because I wanted to make sure I got points."

"Do you ever not want points?"

"Well someone else could have answered it."

"Moving on. HEL." Hot damn! That's three! "LOKI." And there's four! Katz turns to his right, looms over the questionably pubescent Seo-jun, pumps his fists, and erupts: "MAH BOI, LOKI." Plainly shocked faces at all seats. Seo-jun audibly whimpers. Katz feels better. "FRIGG." Fuck, I thought I had that with Freya. "Finally PROSE EDDA and POETIC EDDA. Goal here was seven." Katz with his six feels lucky indeed. Ace of spades, baybee. Papers are passed to Arun. "We've got a seven, six, four, two—jeez, Richard, might want to study the Norse—seven, new guy with a six, six, nine—nice work Wen!—and four. And me with an eight. But I don't count. Everyone below a six to the back." The unfortunate Richard and two other kids leave their buzzers, assuming dejected poses at other tables. One older boy mutters, "fucking Norse."

Oh, shit, I'm still in it! In it to win it, you eunuch jelly thou! Bring it on.

Seo-jun doesn't turn quite all the way this time. "You have to score high enough on the drill to play the open questions."

"I put that together, Seo-jun. Thanks."

Ariadne overhears, and smiles, repairing all the broken pieces of his heart.

✴ ✴ ✴ ✴ ✴ ✴ ✴ ✴

Seventy minutes later, he thought he'd made a pretty solid impression. He'd read Bertrand Russell's *History of Western Philosophy* that summer, and pulled out nine on the second drill (A. J. Ayer? who?). He stayed to help Arun clean.

"So are you captain of this C team, Arun?"

Arun looked pained. "I'm on B. Sometimes A. We cycle through the JV rooms as referees and mentors."

"JV? But I'm a junior." Katz frowned.

A shrug. "You're playing C, so you're JV."

Katz, despairing, called for a life preserver. "Well I had a pretty good first day, right? I think I got the most tossups in the room."

"You also got the most wrong."

Ice cold.

"I got a nine on that second sheet."

Arun's arms went up. "Sherman Katz, I do not make teams. But if you were the best player in this room, still, you were the best player in C. Coach Čermák has over two hundred of these sheets. There's a dude Kumarash on A who had them all memorized a few weeks into freshman year. If he got a nine, all those present would turn to one another asking with wonder, 'what the fuck just happened?' He's working on a new set of sheets. The Glengarry sheets. You do not get to play them, because that would be throwing them away. Anyone on A would smoke you, man." The admiration in Arun's voice rang clear.

"Čermák? Is that Italian?"

"Coach is Czech."

"Czech." Silence. "All right well I'm gonna head out."

"Good meeting you Katz, see you tomorrow."

"Arun, you normally play B, you said, right? Do you hope to move up to A?"

"I will finish my career at B, I had lots of fun, went to many places, and learned so much. Turner Classic Airpirates B is basically A without the pressure. I'm happy there." He paused, wistful. "It's nice to be on the same side as the people who are kicking everyone's asses all the time."

Sherman walked out into the hallway. Ariadne was long gone.

"Hey Sherman Katz, wait up one second."

"Yeah?"

"You never went to camp? Never had serious practice?"

"Arun my man I didn't know academic bowl camp existed. You're actually my first Indian-American."

The senior, proud but realistic, softened a bit. "You did really well for someone who never did this seriously. If it's something you want to do, you could probably be pretty leet. But you'd have to commit to it now, and work hard. There are people, man, where this is their life. I'm just saying this because you looked kinda, you know, sad."

"Aww Arun draw it in, give me a hug."

"Ahh, no, please, thank you."

He sprung *allegro* down the empty hall.

Arun, I shoot craps with the Universe, and win.

* * * * * * * * *

Returning the following afternoon, Čermák called him over.

"Sherman Spartacus Katz. Arun says you played well yesterday."

"I also got the most wrong."

"He said that you had some surprisingly deep conversions. He was very impressed when you picked up Aldous Huxley off *Brief Candles*." She looked up. "I've never heard of *Brief Candles*. You picked up all five computational maths. No one on my A team got more than three." Her knowledge was staggering. She raised her voice. "We never get computational math because everyone wants to be lawyers and writers and they don't bother learning to count. And we lose games because of it. I'm talking to you, Stephanie. I'm talking about Irmo and the finals at University of Florida." Dropping it again, she asked, "do you want to be a lawyer, Sherman—I'm going to call you SSK."

"Most of what I learn I study with passion because I consider it necessary to the practice of computer science, to which I wish to dedicate myself."

"Oh." She seemed pleased. "That's refreshing. Arun also said, and his logs verify, that you buzzed in on and missed a great many questions we'd call basic canon." Katz waited, tense. "Your foundations are trash. I can coach you. Are you serious about this? I pulled your test scores."

"Wechsler AIS?"

If she was impressed, she didn't demonstrate it. "Stanford-Binet and PSAT. If you put in the raw effort, you could learn the canon in no time. Arun says you're very aggressive, that your speed was of the highest level."

He had no idea what to say.

"I like that in a player."

"Was that a *Top Gun* reference?"

"They watch a lot of *Top Gun*." Serious now. "Will you memorize the periodic table? All of it?"

"Give me a week."

"Excellent." Booming again. "Because none of these future Superlawyers of America think they're going to get sued over element 66."

From behind Katz: "Erbium!"

"Take a lap, Stephanie!"

Katz ventures, "Dysprosium?"

Čermák's face brightens. "Hard to get at! Yessssssss!" She claps twice. "SSK, for real, why did you leave in the middle of the semester?"

"All part of God's good plan."

"Do you know what SSK stands for?"

"You mean besides my initials."

"Sociology of scientific knowledge. Should a tossup ever use the term 'epistemological chicken,' that's SSK. 'David Bloor' is 'strong SSK.'"

"What is that? Epistemological Chicken? Excuse me?"

"The game of chicken but with epistemology. If you want to know, you can read *The Structure of Evil* by Ernest Becker. He won the nonfiction Pulitzer in 1974 for *The Denial of Death*. You should learn the nonfiction Pulitzers for Nationals. Have you found out who won Fiction in 1953?"

"I...have not."

Loud: "Fiction Pulitzer in 1953?"

At least eighty percent roar back "HEMINGWAY, *The Old Man and the Sea*."

Some Jessie Spano wannabe adds, "also cited in his 1954 Nobel-Lit."

"Oh I've actually read that! Didn't know it won the 1953 Pulitzer, though."

"No one plays on my A team without knowing their Pulitzers, SSK." She hands him a run-off. "Go buy these books. Bring me a receipt and I'll reimburse you. We have donations."

"Ummm this looks like a few hundred dollars of books. How do I buy them in the first place?"

"Can you maybe use a card of your parents?"

"Sure, unless I hate getting my ass kicked seven ways to a Sunday."

She shuddered.

"I'll have Stephanie pick up a set for you, and I'll reimburse her. OK?"

"I mean, that's awesome. Thank you. Unless she needs distinguish lanthanides to do it. I'm sorry, that was really mean."

Čermák was chortling. "No, she's been claiming to have the f-blocks memorized since tenth grade. Learn my f-blocks, SSK. Losing on periodic table questions is like getting screwed by all the universe."

He thinks *like, 5% of a ΛCDM universe at most,* but now is not the time.

✷ ✷ ✷ ✷ ✷ ✷ ✷ ✷

He recorded one hundred and forty-eight WAVs. With his speakers turned up all the way, he could hear his computer in the shower. A program to sort them randomly, ask one detail ("1943?" *"Now in November?"*), give him five seconds to answer ("Upton Sinclair, *Dragon's Teeth*." "Josephine Winslow Johnson, 1935."), and then reveal the truth was fewer than ten lines of code.

"Willa Cather."

"1923. *One of Ours*."

"*To Kill a Mockingbird*."

"1961. Harper Lee."

"William Faulkner."

"Either *A Fable*, 1955, or *The Reivers*, 1963. Nobel 1950. Woot!"

His new shower curtain featured the periodic table through 103. The next year, IUPAC would officially name 103 lawrencium, but the issue was not settled in 1996. When Katz heard the news about 103, he cursed; his shower curtain had rutherfordium for 103. He later learned that this suggested the curtain

---

ΛCDM: Cosmological constant and cold dark matter

was manufactured in a Soviet client state, and marveled: I have a curtain with iron from behind the iron curtain.

Speaking of iron—on autopilot now—atomic number 26. Group 8. Period 4. d-block. Solid at STP. Amphoteric. 11 oxidation states: +2—iron II, ferrous—and +3—iron III, ferric. Body- and face-centered cubics. Ferromagnetic, obviously. Fe from Latin *ferrum*. Four stable isotopes dominated by 56. Common endpoint of nucleosynthesis. Component of hemoglobin and myoglobin.

* * * * * * * * *

In the back of classroom A-211 at Turner Classic HS, Sherman read *The Brothers Karamazov* as translated by Mrs. Constance Garnett and stuffed into an oversized purple Bantam massmarket. His AP English teacher brought a student to the front to start each class; they were to read aloud an original composition on any theme, not to exceed five minutes. Alphabetical order ruled the day. Preceding Katz was one Tara Jakorski, female lead in all the school's dramatic productions at least since he'd arrived. Doubleplusinsufferable, insufferable to the max. In October 1997, she overcame tears and a genuine wail—a heart-rendering thing heard in three other classrooms, something you'd expect to be accompanied with sackcloth—to deliver a confused and rather unscientific paean to that Carl Sagan chestnut, "we are made of star stuff." Katz wasn't sure why he was so offended by the performance, but he doubted Tara knew what nucleosynthesis was, and was pretty sure her mention of the Butterfly Effect was straight out of *Jurassic Park*. The simple truth was that he was an angry young man. Elements had weighed recently upon his mind; the next day, he presented a rejoining *capriccio*:

> Our stelliferous ancestors? Rude coruscant belches of supernovae from another spiral arm. Nebulae shrugging off expanding gossamers, pappuses gently borne on the dissipating breath of stellar winds. From this awesome cosmochemical lineage originate too dimethylmercury, thalidomide, and maggots. Rot and rabies and black molds in the lungs are star stuff; every purulent discharge and perineal cyst can trace its parentage to the heavens. Carbon fused aswirl as gamma rays rendered asunder neon, yielding the prime chalcogen. That same oxygen braved megakilometers of open space before finally becoming a crucial part of painful colorectal polyps. Would you deny ass cancer its stake in God's plan?
>
> *Cyanwasserstoff. Blausäure.* Hydrogen cyanide. Primo Levi stars in *A Bad Year at Auschwitz-Birkenau.* Call it what you will. Triply-bonded carbons and nitrogens made a rich feast from European Jewry's mitochondrial iron, maintaining acquaintance with old friends. Star stuff's calcium invests a human body with form; stuff from that same star erupts as osteosarcoma, packing the body bloated and bursting with leukemic mucilage. A tumor's corybantic growth

---

capriccio: short and lively piece of music
Cyanwasserstoff: hydrogen cyanide   **Blausäure:** prussic acid

feeds off star stuff siphoned up through the vessels of angiogenesis; like the Sorcerer's Apprentice they summon home siblings from strange aeons. Everyone you know will experience fratricide on the part of some celestial brother.

Star stuff: ash from the Creator's smoldering bong.

"Sherman." His teacher was pissed; he figured she was going to give him hell about shitting all over Jakorski. "No drug references, c'mon."
"Oh. Sorry! Cheerfully withdrawn. Thalidomide is ok though, right?"
"Yes?" She seems confused by the question.

Among the bosonic matter with which you and I are familiar, the vast majority was fused or at least astrated in stars. The exceptions huddle on either side of the curve of binding energy, and indeed on the line scored by time's arrow: primordial hydrogen, both with a neutron and without. Alpha particles with sundress-clad leptons at the Helium Ball. Some trace lithium; a pinch of beryllium. Behind them swarm only quarks and gluons and inflatons and mysteries. Far along out on the other side, assembled much more recently, are the heavy actinides, pear-shaped and lethargic from gorging on beta decay.

Get together enough of the latter, squeeze it tight, admit some bare neutrons, and you can destroy a city. The first annihilating emissions, screaming out from Hell and hohlraum, are in the form of x-rays, a terrible pressureweight of light. Murmur *lux fiat*, as your Father did before you. Direct them at some of the former. Lithium-6 plus a neutron breeds tritium *in situ*, a third isotope of hydrogen, one unloved by the gods. It will exist for only a split-second. Compressed and heated, vernal tritium seeks out deuterium almost as old as the universe itself. Get together enough of this, and you can destroy a world.

Star stuff. Why rent when you can own?

❋❋❋❋❋❋❋❋❋

Most state high school associations put on an annual "official" quiz bowl tournament; many high schools and colleges fund their programs by running their own. These run a gamut from small, strictly local affairs attracting a handful of schools to massive productions with several hundred teams split across a dozen divisions or more, sourcing small armies of volunteer readers from parents and alumni and drawing multiple caterers. There are furthermore televised competitions in the major media markets, many running the length of the academic year: *Battle of the Brains* in Virginia (WTVR following a long run on WCVE), *Masterminds* on TW3 in upstate New York, perennial *It's Academic* on D.C.'s WETA-TV and Baltimore's WJZ (running since 1961 and 1971 respectively), two unrelated *High-Qs* (Atlanta's WSB and El Paso's KCOS). In Michigan, *QuizBusters* on WKAR competes with the upstart *Quiz Central* of WCMU. There's

School Duel in Miami, and *Academic League* on San Diego's SDCoE iTV. Oklahoma City's KSBI features the oddly-named *Mind Games*. Most offer decent prizes in the form of scholarships to winners—it's a safe assumption that these kids will be matriculating. But like college football in the twentieth century, there is no true, universally-acknowledged "national champion" of academic bowl: any organization can call their tournament a National Championship; Mike Tyson could host one right now. It's the attending teams that make the NC, not the other way around. Winning any tournament of significance typically means an invite come February. Nationals take place over the penultimate or last weekend of the school year, and are the last time graduating seniors will play as a team, or in many cases see one another.

TCHS had taken a championship in 1996 (as the Walton Raiders), and would again in 2001. Other perennial heavyweights in that period included Pennsylvania's State College HS. Edison out of California, Thomas Jefferson School for Science and Technology and Maggie Walker Governor's School from Virginia, Horace Greeley representing Chappaqua, New York. Booker T. Washington, the pride of Tulsa. Paul Laurence Dunbar had recently taken a leap forward, and put in work for Lexington, Kentucky. Punching well above its weight was South Carolina, whose Dorman, Irmo, and Charleston Harbor juggernauts resulted in several all-SC *fin de siècle* championship rounds.

The PACE National Scholastic Championships (instituted 1998) and NAQT High School National Championship Tournament (likewise 1999) have today largely superseded the National Academic Championship. This last is surely the longest-running natty, having been put on since 1978 by Chattanooga's Questions Unlimited and its colorful president, Chip Beall. QU is regarded as outmoded by the cognoscenti, complete with dubious facial expressions and glasses pushed to the end of noses. *Anno Domini* 1997, it was the only game in town, and the nation's elite teams descended upon an agreeably, uncharacteristically cool and dry capital region. These participants included Houston's Lamar HS Redskins (renamed the Texans in 2014), and the Airpirates of Marietta's Turner Classic (changed back to the Raiders 2001-09-12). The Airpirates' shirts were emblazoned with their logo and iron motto:

TURNER CLASSIC HIGH SCHOOL

the skies belong to us

PACE: Partnership for Academic Competition Excellence
NAQT: National Academic Quiz Tournaments

Entering the dorms, Katz saw a cluster of kids parked around a television in the common room. Puff Daddy, truly inescapable that year, bounced around the screen, making a mockery of everything good in the world, and certainly everything good in hip-hop. Blinders of rage descended over Katz, sworn foe of Puff Daddies everywhere. Notorious B.I.G. had a few months prior been brought down under mysterious circumstances. "Hypnotize," one of the great tracks of the 90s, was pushed out of number one by Hanson's "MMMBop." Led by Puff Daddy's duets—as ubiquitous as they were annoying—with Ma$e (an uninspired ripoff of Grandmaster Flash's "Message") and Faith Evans (a treacly, maudlin misery built atop The Police's already dreadful "Every Breath You Take"), the bullpen of dogshit at Bad Boy Records enjoyed an *annus mirabilis*. Puff Daddy's otiose bars saturated radio; on MTV, as Suge Knight said at the 1995 Source Awards, "the executive producer was dancin' in the videos." Summer's end saw the rise of yet another Puff + Ma$e crapfest, the frankly embarrassing "Mo' Money Mo' Problems," a black mark on Christopher Wallace's escutcheon.

This trash track would be nominated for a Grammy in 1998, just in time for Puff Daddy to devolve Led Zeppelin's "Kashmir" into "Come With Me" on the *Godzilla* soundtrack. At the Radio City Music Hall, Will Smith's "Men In Black" defeated "Hypnotize," and Puff Daddy's *No Way Out* triumphed over both Biggie's *Life After Death* and the Wu-Tang Clan's *Wu-Tang Forever*. The Wu had that year recorded "Triumph," five minutes and thirty-eight seconds of incontestable greatness that have stood the test of time. The Ol' Dirty Bastard was thus more than generous when he interrupted Shawn Colvin's speech for Best Song, seized the mic like an *espontáneo* in a *ruedo* and announced, "I figured that Wu-Tang was gonna win. I don't know how you all see it, but when it comes to the children, Wu-Tang is for the children. We teach the children. You know what I mean? Puffy is good, but Wu-Tang is the best!" 🔱

The Airpirates had several times that season met the Charleston Harbor Butlers of South Carolina, coached by bitter Čermák foe and known ultrabitch Amélie Blankenship. Their first seat was a black-haired Mormon, jagged and vascular, who slapped at the buzzer with tremendous force. Next to him, their blonde Viking of a captain was at least six-six, and enjoyed a commanding knowledge of fine arts. The lithe West African girl in seat three was a full foot and a half shorter; she had been observed in prior tournaments whipping from her purse a laminated periodic table for review between games. All three were juniors. Together they were easily the best team in America, combining to cover wide swaths of material with astonishing speed, and were 4-0 that season against Turner Classic, winning twice in championship rounds. The games hadn't been particularly close. It was a point of belabored pain for Čermák. She seethed visibly when shaking the French woman's hand, and drove the team home in angry silences when they lost.

At the table's end sat their fourth, a creature of pure malevolence. He was taller than the third seat, but on this young team he was clearly by some years the youngest. The rumor was that he was only twelve, and in the seventh grade. Čermák felt sure that it was the eighth, but Katz suspected she just couldn't

---

espontáneo: an outsider who leaps into a bullfight   **ruedo:** bullring

bear the thought of another lustrum playing against this thing, this automaton, this golem. He sat with eyes closed, mouth hanging open in a rictus. Before each game, Charleston Harbor's Amélie walked him up to the table with her hands on his shoulders, guiding him, her gait timed to his uncertain, probing shuffle. She would pull out or straighten his chair as necessary, so his girlish hands could reach the buzzer. Then the game would begin. He couldn't see, but he could hear just fine, and from that beaming maw emerged a steady stream of academic bowl whoop-ass.

The story was that he had evidenced early on a complex and parentally-challenging set of spergisms. The child stared out into an unfocused space, and refused to eat anything but brothy soups. He shrieked hysterically when approached with a shoelace or zipper. Left in a Palmetto State front yard unattended at the age of eight, he sat atop a rock and watched the sun cross the sky for the better part of two hours, intent, purposeful, never letting it slip from his necrotizing eyes' rapidly decaying sight. Free radicals streaming from phototoxified chromophores attacked the choroidal blood vessels; these burst apart, yet he continued still to move his head, tracking perhaps by smell the eigengrau sun. From ruined pigmented epithelium spilled subretinal melanosomes, quickly engulfed by macrophages. An ophthalmologist said it looked like someone had been at the back of the boy's eyes with a dental drill, then threw up. Tim Grover would never see again.

Confirmed details regarding Amélie Blankenship's discovery and successful recruiting of young Tim are scant. Čermák mused darkly that she'd issued a standing request at Crab Road Middle years ago, to put any blind kids through to her directly, "but only if they once had sight. I can do nothing with a child who never had vision to mourn." If we accept her somewhat paranoiac tale: Blankenship with quivering orgasmic flush and great expectation set to recording tape. One ninety-minute Memorex DBX after another, filled with every tossup in the vaults of CHHS Academic Bowl. She then recorded facts so arcane and minor they'd never been deemed fit for high school play. Forty-five hours. Sixty hours. Mnemonics. Key words. Possible alternatives that made buzzing an uncertain thing. The likelihood that other, sighted children would know a fact. It was a comprehensive and well-rounded auricular education. She clutched the tapes under an arm and drove to the middle school, where he was called out of class.

"Tim, can you hear me?"

"Yes."

"Do you like sports, Tim?"

"I wasn't very good at them. Now I can't even see."

"That's right, Tim. You're blind as Helen Keller, and you're never going to get better." Tim whimpered. "Have they told you otherwise, Tim? That if you do their exercises, and you're lucky, you might one day see again?"

Tim nodded his head. Snot leaked thickly from his left nostril. Amélie dabbed it away with a cotton round. "My name is *Mlle* Amélie Blankenship. You may call me Coach Blankenship. I train the Butler academic bowl team at Charleston Harbor. Do you know what academic bowl is?"

"I think so, like *Jeopardy!* but with a team."

"That's right. I'm told you're very smart, Tim. You seem well-spoken. Do you like *Jeopardy!?*" He held out his hands, and she realized he wanted another makeup remover. She gave him two, into which he pathetically honked his nose. He placed them on the table, and she shifted her chair away a few inches. "Yes I like it. Especially reruns. I'm not very good at it the first time, but once I've heard the questions, I always remember them."

Comme c'est beau! "Tim, most little blind boys become beggars. They bang their bowls against the ground cadging change from strangers. Sometimes they're beaten, or worse. Most of them cut their legs or arms off so they can beg better. Can you imagine that? Having to roll around on a skateboard, singing 'I have no legs, I have no legs,' all the time dirty, dodging urine-filled beer bottles hurled at you by hateful men? Eventually you'll be killed and thrown on a heap with dead dogs. But you can do better than that. Maybe even have a girlfriend. Wouldn't that be wonderful? A girlfriend for a blind boy like you? It must be horrible, knowing you'll never know another human's love."

Tim fell apart, a blubbering blind mess. Amélie hugged him to her tightly.

"Until then, I'll be your only friend. But if you want to impress girls, you've got to have a hook, some skill. They love confidence, and right now you're not feeling any confidence at all, are you? Poor thing, I bet you've thought it would be best to snuff it, to just ask someone to turn you in the direction of some tall cliff. But I can make of you a champion. I can make you the best in the world at the world's greatest game."

Tim blinked, from habit, and whispered, "hunting human beings?"

Amélie laughed. "You've got the right idea, Tim. But you're blind. Blind people can't effectively hunt their fellow men. You'd be filleted by the first paraplegic with a gardening trowel. No, I mean academic bowl."

"Oh."

"I brought you a present." She lifts the tapes up onto the table. From the noises of her grunt and the tapes' impact, Tim can tell it's at least got some heft to it. "This is how you become a champion. These are forty tapes and a Sony Walkman. Listen to these tapes. Whenever you have free time—and we both know you've got plenty of free time—play another tape. Play them until they're worn out, and you see the words on the backs of your eyelids. Then I'll bring you more tapes. You'll come play on my varsity. Every weekend, you'll get to travel to a new place, up in the front of the van. And you'll win, Tim, and you'll hear the cheering from your supporters. And Tim, trust me, that is absolutely the best deal anyone's going to offer you for the rest of your life."

He looked uncertain, but reached for the Walkman.

"Oh, and Tim?"

"Yes...Coach Blankenship?"

"The short story about hunting men is 'The Most Dangerous Game' by Richard Connell. First published in *Collier's*, 1924. Also sometimes called 'The Hounds of Zaroff.' Memorize that." She turned and departed.

Comme c'est beau: how beautiful!

As she drove back, humming "Dreams" by the Cranberries, she figured Tim might by the end of summer be able to tell her the month and day of publication, along with the year. She pumped her fist, and yodeled.

So now he rode in the front seat of the Charleston Harbor van, listening to endless tapes on his everpresent Walkman, walking with their coach while the rest of the team ran ahead en route to crushing Čermák's hopes. Each time he got on stage with his sweatpants and Velcro shoes, Čermák perceived a future: CHHS beating her teams by more and more points; a boot stamping on her face, forever. In a dream she beheld goosestepping young children, tens of thousands of them, speaking in booming synchronization, reciting dazzlingly advanced material, eyelids flapping open and shut atop empty sockets. When one fell even slightly out of serried lockstep, it led inevitably to crash and tangle, and the groping of tiny arms, the air replete with mewls and moans.

A trophy for all tournaments present and future was ripped bloody from her womb, and awarded to Charleston Harbor, competing now as the Tiresian Tyrants, fielding a team of four infants each named Homer. At a fabulous reception, Stevie Wonder played as Ray Charles and Andrea Bocelli performed a medley rich with luscious harmonies. The audience chanted f-block elements and wore cheap headphones. Coach Amélie, resplendent in her opera gloves and tiara, wore over her evening gown a purple sash that read BOSS BITCH. She simpered. She curtsied. She blew kisses to the adoring crowd. She flounced and turned, deploying a peacock tail. The scarred eyes with which it was rife blinked in unison, and the back of the sash declared GOULASH SUCKS. Then she looked at Čermák and hissed *welcome to the place prepared for you from everlasting to everlasting. Now truly you will never die.* The sleeping mind of Venda Čermák screamed and screamed and screamed.

By Friday, the last day of preliminaries, Turner Classic was 3-1 over four games and guaranteed a playoff berth. The Airpirates had no more matches, so Katz and two others went to watch the Butlers play their 1000h game, hoping to find someone dead or mute. It was not to be; CHHS handily dispatched a quality Booker T. Washington team, sending them back to Oklahoma 440–225. They left the room immediately, casting sideeye at Katz and his teammates. Feeling lazy, Katz stayed to watch the subsequent game, Lamar vs. Bromfield of Massachusetts. The worldlines of juniors Katz and Bolaño thus first crossed in Arlington, Virginia on Friday, June 13th 1997, shortly after 1100h in room 70 of Marymount University's Rowley Hall.

Neither Bromfield nor Lamar were particularly inspiring. The Cambridge school put up 330 to Lamar's 215. Both sums were pedestrian; Turner Classic hadn't scored less than 375 in their four games. The Lamar first seat got two questions that made Katz take notice, however:

Tossup 13. Written in Vancouver, the word "cyberspace"—Lamar 1?
Lamar 1: *Neuromancer.*
That's correct.

Tossup 20. It supports hard drives, but also scanners, printers, and many other I/O devices. What is this successor—Lamar 1?
Lamar 1: SCSI.

Can you provide more information?
Lamar 1: Small Computer System Interface.
That's correct.

Katz had never heard a computer question in a tournament, let alone one about William Gibson's cyberpunk classic. That Lamar guy had picked them up both pretty quick, about where Katz would have had them. He waited for the match to spool out, and followed the Lamar team out the building.

"Hey! Uhhh, Lamar 1! Lamar guy! Tall thin guy from Lamar!"

He succeeded in stopping and turning around their team.

"Hey ummm I hoped to ask you something." He pointed at Lamar 1.

"Ask away."

"Well I mean ummm I really like William Gibson and it sounded like you do, too and I thought we could talk for a minute." He winced, feeling autistic.

Michael made a face, then shrugged. "I think he means to fuck me," he told his team. They laughed. "Best go on. I'll meet you back at the dorms."

"Ahhh cool actually ummm I'm not trying to fuck you at all, totally straight, I think—I've never really given the question much thought honestly. No offense if you're gay, of course."

"Good, I am."

Katz pauses for a moment. "Is that a joke?" Swing and a miss!

"It is not." Michael's face grows harder. "What do you want?"

"OK, I think we started off badly here, sorry. You got both the *Neuromancer* and SCSI questions in there, right?"

"Yes."

"Actually I mean you got most of your team's tossups, heh. How are y'all doing at this tournament?"

"Poorly by any metric other than participation."

"Sorry to hear that. Anyway, I guess I had never heard a computer-related question in academic bowl. It surprised me. And then it surprised me when you got it. What do you do on computers? Do you code? Are you leet?"

Arched brows. "Am I leet? Are you eight?"

"Hah I mean are you in the H/P/C scene, hacking, phreaking—"

"And cracking. I am aware of the acronym."

"Oh sweet! Do you write code?"

"Yeah, I have."

"What languages? Hey look not to offend you or freak you out but do you smoke weed?"

Michael looks around. "Yes. Keep it down."

"Sweet! I brought a delicious sack up here and a bowl and it's all in my dormroom if you want to go smoke some and continue this conversation. I really do promise, not trying to fuck you, not because you're not desirable or anything—you're a very attractive guy, if you don't mind me saying so—just I don't even, you know, know how that works."

Michael thought this guy clearly mad, but hadn't been high since Monday, and was feeling it. Besides, why does one attend such events if not to meet the weird and brilliant of America? "Sure, I'll come smoke your weed with you. What's your name? Where are you from?"

"Sherman Spartacus Katz of Atlanta, Georgia. Turner Classic High School. Rising senior. Fourth seat, but only because I'm loud."

"Michael Bolaño. Houston. I assume you're Jewish?"

"Nice to meet you mang, we're gonna get high as hell. And no, everyone thinks so due the name, but I descend from evangelical North Georgians. My dad incinerates animal carcasses. I used to say 'Katzes don't get Holocausts, we do holocausts,' in the sense of, you know, a burnt offering, but people kept misunderstanding it and I had to stop. The point being you're not the first to make the mistake. I'm a huge philosemite. I would have loved to have been born a Jew."

"You're a strange guy, Sherman."

"Oh mang, absolutely. You have no idea."

✳✳✳✳✳✳✳✳✳

"Do you have any SCSI gear in your machine?"

"I do not. Two Quantum Fireball one gig drives on IDE." Both Bolaño and Katz had built their own boxes from parts, Bolaño spending about twice as much total.

"Nice. Our team doesn't drill on any computer stuff. I guess it's going to start showing up in tossups? I saw a commercial for AOL on TV the other day; I never thought I'd see online stuff on television."

"The computer's spread into everyday life is inevitable. Certainly there will be more computer questions, although I expect that they will for the immediate future continue to be mindless expansions of acronyms."

"I wouldn't mind that. A big fat bonus round of computer acronyms would be tight." Katz paused. "BASIC?"

"Are you asking me what BASIC stands for?"

"Sure."

Bolaño rolled his eyes. "Beginners All-Purpose Symbolic Instruction Code." Are we really doing this? Alright. "COBOL."

"Common Business-Oriented Language. VGA."

"Video Graphics Array. FORTRAN."

"Formula Translator. BIOS."

"Basic Input Output System. ALGOL."

"Algorithmic language. RPG."

"Role-playing game? What?"

"Nope!" Sherman pounces. "Report generator. IBM language, old as hell, but still used. RPG IV just got released in 1994."

"Is that even Turing complete?"

"What does that mean? I only know Turing from *Gödel, Escher, Bach.*"

Michael laughed. "Here I thought you were all into computer science. A language that's Turing complete admits a solution for all recursive functions. You surely remember those from G-E-B."

IDE: Integrated Drive Electronics

"So basically anything with the power of a Turing machine. So the brain is presumably Turing complete."

"Some brains."

∗ ∗ ∗ ∗ ∗ ∗ ∗ ∗ ∗

The dorm room is breezy with both windows open. By Katz in the window sits a clear glass ashtray, bought from a street vendor the evening they arrived, featuring the White House silkscreened in red. He'd emptied it upon entry; twenty-eight minutes later, it contains two butts, and he's got another Newport going. He stands by his bed and clearly wishes there was room to pace. With his lighter Michael knocks a short glass pipe's cinders and dross into an empty can of Surge recovered from the trashcan. Three floors up, they can barely make out a quadrangle through flourishing red maple. They exhale through fragrant polyester held with rubberband onto the end of a toilet paper tube. Katz brought up the dryer sheet, liberated from laundry supplies; the cardboard tube had been extracted from a bathroom upon arrival. It was singularly ineffective at masking the smell of fuming marijuana, but most of their smoke left via the window, and anyway there were during summer semester no sullen RAs to pound on the door.

"How is the weed in Houston?"

"We call what you have mids; they are not usually available. Those with means smoke dank, sensimilla: high-THC product without seeds, often sold under brand slash strain names. Those without resort to bricked schwag, rife with seeds, smelling often of inorganic fertilizers and pesticides."

"Yeah, I don't have the money for dank. Mids get you just as high, you just have to pull the seeds out."

Michael nods without commitment; *comme ci comme ça*. "This is not bad. As I said, the middle is in Houston excluded. How much do you pay? An ounce runs three hundred for us, but I usually buy two at five."

"A qwop—quarter-pound—costs me four hundred, but figure you're losing about five grams from each ounce in seed mass. So you're paying just a little bit over twice as much, four point four repeating vs eight point nine."

Michael wants to close his eyes to run the calculation, but knows it would be a sign of weakness. It takes him several seconds. "Yeah. Four point four repeating. You did that pretty fast. Is math your thing?"

"I love math, but I'm not good enough at it for it to matter. Gauss is said to have commented regarding Euler's identity, 'if this is not immediately apparent to a student upon encountering it, they will never be a first-rate mathematician.' Do you know Euler's identity?"

"$e^{i\pi} = -1$, right?"

"Yeah, though normally written $e^{i\pi} + 1 = 0$ so you get both the additive and multiplicative identities of $\mathbb{Z}$." Katz watches Bolaño's reaction closely to see if he groks. "I don't know about you, but when I was first told that, I thought I was being fucked with. Did you do ARML and/or USAMO?" Michael frowns and shakes his head. "USAMO is the USA's Math Olympiad team, for competition at the IMO. ARML is just American. If you do well enough on the AHSME and AMC, you take the AIME, which seeds USAMO. I've taken the AIME every year, and never qualified for USAMO. Never come close. Those guys are going to be mathematicians, not me. My thing is computer science, that and literature, but CS as I don't want to be poor all my life. What's your 'thing,' Michael Bolaño?" Katz extinguishes his cigarette and sets to repacking the bowl.

"I'm good on that, by the way. I'm plenty high." Michael takes some time to answer. "I used to think I wanted to go into government. I no longer have any such desire, and am unsure when I lost it." He pauses again. "I enjoy subverting authority and disrupting the banal. I enjoy embarrassing those who substitute bluster for knowledge. I enjoy secrets and masquerade. I am unconcerned with most men's opinions. I wish to live comfortably, with maximum freedom of action. I ought probably major in computer science, but do not wish to major in computer science." Michael's eyes focus anew; his voice turns harder. "My family helped create modern Mexico."

"Oh yeah? Are they a cloud of pollution or the devalued peso? Sounds like you ought be CIA or something."

He lets the crack pass. Is history not a nightmare from which he is trying to awake? "I am too illegal for Langley. Where do you plan to go to school?"

"I'm going to Georgia Tech. It'll be free, I can get in there, I retain much of my existing Atlanta network, and applying to better schools sounds like a massive pain in the ass plus crapshoot. Yourself?"

"I have always assumed Harvard or Princeton, but only recently learned of the importance of letters of recommendation. This complicates things, and not in my favor. I've made a point of pissing off just about everyone from whom I've taken a class. I almost got the woman who ran our school newspaper fired. I've got a perfect SAT and close to a four oh, but I have no idea who I'll get to write recommendations. So I don't know."

"You and me both mang. Turner Classic will be glad to see my backside."

"How does your school come to be known as 'Turner Classic' anyway?"

"All part of God's divine plan. I know GT doesn't require letters of recommendation. I'm confident enough I'll get in there that I'm not applying anywhere else. It's one of the top five tech schools, which is all you need, and you don't have to deal with the extreme top-end of assholes, the trust fund kids with two Stanford professors for parents."

"I'm slowly coming around to the idea that I'll end up at UT."

"A Longhorn? But you want to major in something CS-adjunct? Nah man, you want to go to a tech school, somewhere everybody knows how to add. Otherwise you've got half the student body majoring in bullshit that requires no real effort nor time, and you'll be miserable watching them fuck their way through a leisurely and undemanding four years. No, you want everybody around you to be ass-deep in the shit. Everyone who comes out of there is useful for recommendations and starting companies and specialized knowledge.

IMO: International Mathematics Olympiad   **ARML:** American Regional Mathematics League
AMC: American Mathematics Competitions
AIME: American Invitational Mathematics Exam

Are you going to do a sociology startup? Has anyone ever done a sociology startup? Spend four or five or six years in Paradise, where everyone got an eight hundred on the SAT Quantitative and a five on the BC Calculus exam. How do you learn a foreign language? You embed yourself among its speakers." Katz hits deeply. "Plus you're gay, so the worst aspect—the fucked-up dating situation—doesn't affect you."

"How does it not affect me? I'll be surrounded by nerds as opposed to the hot men of political science and physical education jocks."

"I hadn't considered that. Fair enough. But fuck UT-Austin and a bunch of Longhorn Texas bullshit. Come to GT. Classes of all guys, a few girls from behind the Eastern bloc, sedulous Asians as far as the eye can see, all raw-dogging differential equations 24/7, Freaknik, David Finkelstein, access to great lab equipment, it's cheap as hell—dude, you could probably get the Presidential Scholarship if you applied, with your grades, and that pays everything plus a stipend, it's phat—and you'd be a big fish. I can kinda read that on you. You like being the smartest guy in the room, right?" Michael doesn't react.

"Well if you go Harvard, you'll be smarter than plenty of assholes, sure. There will also be a gang of USAMO guys in every class just kicking the shit out of you, or more likely not bothering because they don't care about you. Their jaws won't move when they talk. They summered in Monaco. If you don't go work for a fucking hedge fund it'll be like you failed. You'll be paying fifty thousand a year minimum to live in Massachusetts, New York's impacted colon. Here, hit this." Katz thrusts the pipe at Michael, who shrugs and accepts it. "They have Lisa Randall, but GT has Dana Randall, for my money pound-for-pound the superior Randall."

"Lisa Randall is the higher-dimensions braneswoman at Harvard?"

"It sounds more exciting than combinatorics, sure, but if there are such extra dimensions, will they not need tiling? On top of that, without serious hagiography-style rec letters you're not getting into the Ivy League anyway, nor Stanford nor Duke nor MIT—hell, I think MIT wants to do *interviews* with applicants, which fuck all that. So your choices are UCB, Atlanta, or the Michigan-Wisconsin nexus. Of which GT is the cheapest by like a factor of three."

Sherman accepts the pipe back. "Furthermore, I intend to get down there and sling, and make serious money right out of the gate. I have connections from two different high schools, twenty minutes away from campus. I have a number of people I'll already know there who'll be ready clientele. I'm saving cash next year to go down with goodly weight. And most importantly, I'll be in a dorm full of kids who've probably barely smoked weed before, surrounded by more such dorms. I plan to kick a lot of ass, to be something of an academic leader. I turn on a tenth of those kids and have them buying from me all through undergraduate, and I'll be living well."

"Perhaps. I ought return to my team. I wish to read. I'm in the middle of *The Magic Mountain*, and also the notebooks of Michael Faraday. Thank you, Sherman Katz, for letting me get my head straight."

"Ol' Hans Castorp and Madame Chauchat?" Michael nods. "I dug it. Read it last year. What Dostoevsky have you read?"

"Dostoyevsky is sublime. *Brat'ya Karamazovy* of course. *Zapíski iz podpól'ya.*
Prestupléniye i nakazániye. Not yet *Idiót* nor *Bésy.* Soon."

Katz's shock was delicious. "You speak Russian?"

Bolaño's smile was wide and predatory. "Without the language of the *rodina,* Sherman, can you really say you've read Dostoyevsky? You've just read
somebody's muddled translation."

"That's pretty fucking cool. Are your parents Russian?"

"My mother is a Mexican-American. My father isn't."

"Your father isn't what? Mexican-American?"

"My father isn't. Let me get your phone number."

∗ ∗ ∗ ∗ ∗ ∗ ∗ ∗ ∗

Katz didn't bring up *The Gambler, Poor Folk, The Eternal Husband,* nor *The Adolescent.* He'd personally taken a ten-point tossup just the previous day by buzzing
in on *Poor Folk,* though to be fair, he'd never read it, nor any of Dostoyevsky's
works of lesser significance besides *The Double.* Speaking Russian is cool, but it
doesn't get you points. Which perhaps, Katz ruminated, said something about
the didactic value of academic bowl.

Whatever. He figured he was putting together as thorough and catholic an
education as any high schooler in America, far beyond the curricula where
it mattered. He wasn't playing academic bowl as a substitute for learning.
He was playing academic bowl to kick ass, to be the best, to put trademarks
around the eyes of otherwise dismissive and mocking fucks from California and
Washington and New York, to remind them of and to reinforce André 3000's
defiant declaration: *but it's like this: the South's got something to say.*

∗ ∗ ∗ ∗ ∗ ∗ ∗ ∗ ∗

Katz acquired for $50 a fake Georgia drivers license featuring his picture and
the name Hezekiah Rhombus Cray. He enjoyed telling anyone who asked that
his parents were hippie math professors with PhDs in quadrilaterals.

Michael Luis Bolaño contacted him in September of their senior year. Only
one teacher had indicated a willingness to write the euphemistic "strong letter,"
and on further consideration, Bolaño didn't trust her. He'd applied to UT-
Austin, UC-Berkeley, and Georgia Tech. They'd both gained internet access in
the interim, and exchanged email addresses.

Katz received his expected admission to Georgia Tech and finished out his
senior year. His grades were, to be brief, ass. Nonetheless he maintained the
3.0+ necessary for Georgia's HOPE Scholarship. Michael did indeed secure a full
ride with stipend at GT. It was neither academically nor financially compelling
vis-à-vis the Longhorns—both offers were excellent—but he chose Atlanta. He
could list any number of reasons, none of them particularly convincing, but it
is most likely that he simply wanted a friend. AP exams were crushed; both

---

Brat'ya Karamazovy: Братья Карамазовы *(The Brothers Karamazov, 1880)*
Zapíski iz podpól'ya: Записки из подполья *(Notes from [the] Underground, 1864)*
Prestupléniye i nakazániye: Преступление и наказание *(Crime and Punishment, 1866)*
Idiót: Идиот *(The Idiot, 1869)*   **Bésy:** Бесы *(The Possessed or Devils, 1872)*
rodina: родина motherland

Katz and Bolaño would be entering as juniors, the former doubling in Computer Science and Mathematics, the latter springing for Industrial Engineering and Physics. The Turner Classic Airpirates finished third at the 1998 NACs in New Orleans, where Katz got spectacularly drunk and boorishly puked on a player from Ocala's Vanguard HS.

He quit the bookstore where he'd worked two years, and spent that summer writing Visual BASIC to administer psychometric tests—MMPI-2, NEO PI-R, 16PF, BFI, any standardized personality inventory that could be sold to HR departments, recruiters, or executive search committees. At $23 an hour he was significantly cheaper than most adult developers, but making almost four times his retail job's pay. He knocked the simplistic work out and delighted his superiors. By the end of the summer, he'd saved about eight thousand dollars. With it he paid for a year of dorm fees and meal plan, and the 3COM 3c950b-TX NIC he would need to access the campus network.

In addition, he purchased a twenty-liter lockable safe, a digital scale claiming 0.1g precision up to 500g total weight, sandwich bags, small glassine bags, a pound of schwag, a pound of mids, two sheets of Black Pyramid gelatin acid, two sheets (offered at the last minute) of nameless green gelcaps, four ounces of mushrooms, 600 generic methylphenidate in an imposing violet bottle with Devanāgarī lettering, and 180 20mg Adderall. It wouldn't hold water against *Fear and Loathing*'s collection, but it was a start. Fuck that devil ether. He'd done cocaine a few times that summer, but it was too expensive to easily sell, and he didn't trust himself not to hoover it up.

He swung his baby blue Crown Vic onto I-75 southbound from the Delk Road exit, and looked briefly back before accelerating towards Atlanta.

"This place could never contain me."

Twenty-five minutes to North Avenue. Katz played Goodie Mob, hung to the right, and observed the speed limit judiciously.

Part II

zweitracht—DISCORD

I will show you something different from either
Your shadow at morning striding behind you
Or your shadow at evening rising to meet you;
I will show you fear in a handful of dust.

T. S. Eliot, "The Waste Land" (1921) Part I

All the world will be your enemy, Prince with a Thousand Enemies, and
whenever they catch you, they will kill you. But first they must catch
you, digger, listener, runner, prince with the swift warning. Be
cunning and full of tricks and your people shall never be destroyed.

Richard Adams, *Watership Down* (1972)

Il y a toujours une philosophie pour le manque de courage.
(There is always a philosophy for lack of courage.)

Albert Camus, *Carnets II: janvier 1942–mars 1951 (Notebooks 1942–1951)*

Cincinnati will bullshit with us and kick our ass and laugh at us.
They're the only team that talk about us like a dog...We gonna *get down*.
We gonna *do the do*. I'm going to *hit* these motherfuckers.

Dock Ellis (pitcher), 1974-05-01, addressing the Pittsburgh Pirates

5   devesh choudhary is all about physics and rolls

The competition was never made crassly explicit.

There was always a justification for adding new credit hours. There was no prize to be won, nor rules for entry and play. Regardless, at some point during their first week, with registration open, Katz and Bolaño definitely began to seek the densest possible schedule of classes. While most freshmen were dipping their toes into the water, scheduling the fulltime student's minimum of twelve hours, they started at fifteen. Both were enrolled automatically in Honors Calculus IV (multivariable) and CS1501. Both added CS1502, working on the assumption that they would pass the CS1501 exemption exam, to be offered Friday. Bolaño signed up for Quantum I despite lacking the Classical Mechanics prereq. Katz gamely threw it on his own schedule as well. Katz added Applied Combinatorics, Bolaño Vector Spaces, and they had schedules as aggressive as any freshman's.

Tuesday, ripping bong hits by the fence separating East Campus from Atlanta's I-75/I-85 Connector, Katz mentioned offhandedly, "I picked up another two classes. Control & Concurrency, the UNIX C systems programming class, and Instruction Set Architectures, the machine language class. Twenty-one hours, but I think I can handle it pretty easily." He made a show of yawning, and scratched his chest.

"I thought we could only take fifteen?"

"That's what they said in freshman registration, but you can take up to twenty-one hours without so much as a waiver. Unless you'd be overwhelmed."

"Excellent. I think I can still get Honors Probability and Statistical Methods, both needed for my IE degree."

"Good to know there's some old Roman spirit left on this campus."

Thursday Katz ran into Michael outside the math department, also known as the Rigorium. "I got a waiver to take more than twenty-one hours. Went ahead and added Computer Architecture."

"How'd you get the waiver?"

"Went in, told them 'look I'm gonna exempt this CS1501 business, I could exempt CS1502 if you offered an exam, and I've been programming in machine language since I was ten or so, so CS2760 doesn't sound too tough either.' She told me I was going to regret it and sent a waiver off to the registrar. I bet you could get one too, you big superstud."

"That's a fair number of classes. Eight?"

"Probably a few late nights, gonna have to expend a little effort to get it done. Worth it when I'm sitting on two full quarters after twelve weeks."

"Hrmm."

Remembering Orpheus, Bolaño descended that very hour into the basement of Howey. With leers and ceaseless Marlboro Lights advisors of physics squatted in tall black socks, cargo shorts, and straining tshirts like ancient toad gods, arranged in a scalene triangle of doom. Any student foolish enough to step into that triangle and plead for compassion drew them like sharks to chum. Bolaño's spunk was admired, and cheered, and as they sent off the waiver, one told him "it's going to be funny when you're back in here crying, saying I took too many hours because I'm stupid; give me my GPA back." Bolaño stared him down, waiting for him to blink before leaving. Back at his computer, Michael could find only one class that fit his cramped schedule and counted towards his degrees: Astrophysics. Guess we're gonna learn about stars this quarter. Good times. On a humbug, he searched for any class that would fit as a ninth, even if it wasn't needed in his degree plan. He ended up in a senior-level Textile Engineering elective called simply "Yarn."

When Katz reported his load to his freshman advisor, she shook her head and told him that every year there were a few who thought they could come in and treat college like high school. With a ferocious smile, he replied "*ē tàn ē epi tâs*," to which she predictably had no reply. Michael won the non-competition, with a bruising nine classes to Sherman's mere eight. Like Ford Frick and Dick Young, let us mark this milestone with an asterisk: Sherman ended up with a 4.0, whereas Michael ate a B in Statistical Methods, and furthermore dropped Yarn like a bad bean pie after its first, humiliating test. Either way, they looted the Institute.

✶ ✶ ✶ ✶ ✶ ✶ ✶ ✶

Katz moved in on the Friday before classes, the earliest permitted date. He spent a cheerful solitary weekend in Smith 202 infusing the room with fine Virginian flue-cured tobacco and lesser domestic green. He drank Sweetwater Blue from bottles. The dining halls were not yet open, but Ritalin and coffee took edge off his hunger. He read Sipser's *Theory of Computation* and the "cat book" of David Griffiths (*Introduction to Quantum Mechanics* gets this nickname from the live cat on its front cover, and the dead one on the back). Neither would be used this quarter, yet they called to him, offering logical next steps down the walkway of the real.

1998 was Georgia Tech's last year on quarters (they would join the rest of the University System of Georgia on semesters in 1999), and likewise its final year of singly-homed internet. To a BBN Planet FDDI was added OC-3 SONET to Southern Crossroads, with Internet2 and Mbone capabilities. Southern Crossroads was little more than a broker to 56 Marietta Street, the Telx (now Digital Realty ATL13) building. Along with 180 Peachtree St NW, 345 Courtland, and 250 Williams, 56 Marietta sits on the communications backbone of the Southeast. They who control the fiber control the network, and (because it's easier to negotiate long-distance easements from a single holder of right-of-way) the fiber runs along the old railroads. The railroads terminated at Five Points, the center of downtown Atlanta. There in the Epoch Networks POP sat the fledgling AtlantaIX. Thus the famous passage from *Neuromancer:*

> BAMA, the Sprawl, the Boston-Atlanta Metropolitan Axis. Program a map to display frequency of data exchange...Manhattan

---

ḕ...tâs: ἤ τὰν ἤ ἐπὶ τᾶς with this or upon it. Plutarch, *Apophthegmata Laconica* (c. 100) 241
FDDI: Fiber Distributed Data Interface, up to 100 Mbps over 200 kilometers
OC-3: Optical Carrier 3, up to 155.52 Mbps   **SONET:** Synchronous Optical Networking
POP: Point of Presence   **FE:** Fast Ethernet, up to 100 Mbps

and Atlanta burn solid white...At a hundred million megabytes per second, you begin to make out certain blocks in midtown Manhattan, outlines of hundred-year-old industrial parks ringing the old core of Atlanta...

The FE always-on residential connection was in a completely different class than anything he'd experienced over dialup or even corporate ISDN-PRI on T3. He masturbated with great gusto. Video was largely beyond the capabilities of Redhat Linux 5.1 (Katz wouldn't even run X until 2002 or so), at least on his machine, but he put Wget and cURL to good use grabbing images. With his sinistral hand he drove the lynx text-mode browser, whacking industriously away with his right. It was just as muggy and gross as one would expect from Midtown Atlanta at August's end. Clean garments were soaked through within a half-hour; campus seemed empty; the showers were grody and generally uninviting. Katz said "fuck it"; embracing decadence, he spent his last forty-eight hours sans roommate freely ejaculating onto his shirt and pissing into beer bottles. He concluded that sex looks way better when the participants wear tall socks. Call him Ishmael, for it was squeeze! squeeze! squeeze! all the morning long, debauched and scurfy and generally unsanitary, but not the worst way for a seventeen year-old to spend a weekend.

Roommate Mark Campbell showed up Sunday evening. He was a friend from TCHS, majoring in MGMT from the get-go, a bit perplexed by the his fellow students' fetishism of science and never quite sure why he was at a technical school. He was well-versed in all things mysterious and esoteric, and acceptably literate, and tolerant of Katz's chaotic energy. In high school he'd been famous for the ability to puke on command, always with fine control of target and flux. Katz had seen him eat nothing other than candy and LSD. Aside from interminable Daft Punk and the *Shaft* soundtrack, Mark was close to an ideal roommate. Through the night they smoked steadily, drank pots of coffee, met their neighbors; they nerded out like one can nerd out nowhere but the freshman dorms of an elite Institute of Technology. Technical information interchange transpired at extreme rates in hallways, in dorm rooms, outside, everywhere. One could still enjoy a cigarette or two in the dorms during those less regimented times, and until they departed at year's end a gently fuliginous canopy danced along the ceiling in swirls and eddies.

Katz's RA, Justin Lamore from some Louisiana shitbucket parish, arrived midday Monday and seemed harmless enough. He was a Biology major—rare among malchicks—and five credit hours behind Katz despite two years on campus; Katz immediately marked him a jabroni. At a mere fifteen hours, he warned Katz that his schedule would prove his downfall. Sherman laughed and assured the poltroon that he expected no significant difficulties.

Michael in nearby Harrison dorm took an immediate hard line, from which he not once diverged, refusing to speak to or even acknowledge his RA. This

---

ISDN-PRI: Integrated Services Digital Network—Primary Rate Interface
T3: Transmission System 3, 672 channels up to 44.736 Mbps
malchick: boy. Nadsat via мальчик *(malchik)*

amused, then irritated, then infuriated said student employee, who suffered a catastrophic quarter and left school.

The third night on campus, Lamore pounded on the door of 202, opened it, and pushed in among Katz, Campbell, Bolaño, and three freshmen well-met. Two used the room's chairs while the others stood in an approximation of a circle, passing a cheap glass bubbler. From the coughing and general incompetence, it was evident that several of those present were smoking for their first or second time. Prong's *Cleansing* sounded tinny and distant on twelve watt computer speakers, but one makes do with what one has.

"Guys. Guys! What the hell is this?" Justin sounded betrayed and appalled.

"What does it look like, Lamore? Getting some of our dormmates together for a righteous roast this last night before classes. You wanna hit this?" Katz shoved the pipe up into Justin's face, along with a lighter. Campbell chuckled. Bolaño winced. The guests looked at their shoes.

Justin jerked his head back, as if the proffered weed were a patty of shit. "What are you thinking? You can't smoke weed in the dorms! I'll let you off this once, but guys, if I catch you again, I'll have to write you up."

Katz evinced disbelief. "Write us up? To whom?"

"To the head RA of this building. Kyle Teller."

"Who is Kyle Teller and why would I give a shit?"

"He's the head RA! He can recommend you for discipline or to be kicked out of the dorms."

"Why would he do that?"

"Because you can't smoke weed in the dorms!" Justin doesn't understand what part of this Katz is failing to understand.

"Hold on a sec, let me hit this." Katz rips it hard. Justin's eyes attempt to leave his head. "Sherman! *You can't hit that!*" Katz finishes applying the lighter and holds out his hand: *Wait.* Finally he finishes; the cloud he exhales wafts into the hallway through the open doorway. Justin watches it go over his head, blanches, and slams the door shut.

"Just did, my friend. Let's start at the basics. How do you benefit by turning *stukach*, telling this resident fascist Mssr. Kyle Teller—what major is he?"

"AE."

"Bolaño, do you think that means aeronautical engineering, or is Resident Assistant First Class Lamore referring to George William Russell?"

"Hard to know, Sherman. He doesn't look a theosophist."

"RAFC Lamore, do you mean aeronautical engineering?"

Lamore, completely lost: "Aerospace. Yes. And the"—air quotes here—"'value' I get is not losing my job."

"Lamore, what's up with bullshit"—insolent air quotes here—"air"—another pair—"quotes"—they come down—"around"—there they are again—"value?"

"Stop that." Lamore hadn't been counseled regarding this kind of thing during his four hours of RA training. "If Kyle walks through and smells weed, and walks in on you smoking, he'll want to know why I didn't do anything about it. And he'll smell it, because I smelled it."

---

stukach: стукáч informer

"Why does he give a fuck? Is there some greater RA above even him, an ArchRA, Brigadier RA, a five-star RA but only in times of war? Who with actual power is walking around the dorm caring whether I'm smoking weed?"

"The Resident Life Coordinator."

"Holy fucking dogshit, the RLC! One step down from the Central Scrutinizer itself. Does this RLC come 'round often?"

"No, but if someone were to complain"—

"What cocksucking shitheel would narc out a dormmate?"

"Katz! I'm not here to argue with you. Put that shit away and don't let me catch you again. Smoke it somewhere else, I don't care."

"Damn, Lamore." Katz shook his head sadly. "You's triflin'."

* * * * * * * * *

"My asshole is in tatters."

"Fucked by Dr. Wi, Katz? Or literal fraying of thy rectum?"

Sherman grimaced. "On the charged particle motion problem, what was all that about verifying that the canonical equations of Hamilton recover the equation of motion? I derived the Lagrangian and Hamiltonian just fine."

"Meaning to take up thy potential function, and to demonstrate therefrom derivation of basic kinematic results. What else could it mean?" Devesh had been waiting outside, smoking a bidi and reading over his notes.

"Oh. Yeah that makes sense. I'm pretty sure I fucked up the spring and string problem, too. Busted boundary conditions, might have written the wrong wave equation. Ugh. I fear I might not be long for Physics 3201. I've been brutalized by the malevolent and inscrutable Dr. Wi. He has plundered my tender darkstar and the rest is silence." He smiled and shook his head, admiring the cruel work of a master. "I will fight no more forever."

"Thou art neither the first nor last. Maximilian is in his second go-round. Another F, and he'll be cast down, and out from the program." Devesh looked skyward, as if his words might summon some demon. "Why art thou taking this class anyway? I thought thou CS and Math. Do they make Math wimps take classical mechanics?"

"You have to take one three-thousand-level physics, but I already have Quantum. Everyone cool was taking class mech. Plus I'm sexually attracted to pendulum systems."

"Are classical mechanics not prerequisites for mechanics of the quantum?"

"Get this: declared, but unenforced. We can go take quantum field theory without knowing what a potential is. Quantum is easy. I'm just fucked by the way this class is going. I can write down energy operators as well as the next man. Anyway, how did you do?"

"I thought it simpler than harmonic oscillators happily unafflicted by dissipation of energies." Devesh beamed, and allowed Katz a moment to get it. "No significant difficulty." He couldn't help but preen a little. "The questions were straightforward, easily predicted from the examples of class. Perhaps thou ought attend more often?"

"This class is at a shitty time. I studied the book."

"Thou would claim the book responsible for thy defiled asshole?"

Three Chinese undergraduates left together. Katz tracked them with the smoldering tip of his Newport. "Hey Devesh, do you know those guys?"

"I've seen them around. They were at the physics student orientation last year. Never talked to them. Why?"

"Just wondering if they ever talk to anyone else. You know their names?"

"They move as a trio, and I cannot distinguish between them. Perhaps I will call them quarks."

"A hadron's quarks need be different colors, though. Dial it back to partons. Are they good?"

"At physics? I knoweth not. Eight of us got As in EMag last spring, out of one-hundred twenty that started the class. I was one. Neil was one. Also the Newfie got an A, a perfect 100 he claims. I believe it."

* * * * * * * * *

The Newfie asked "whadya at?" rather than "how are you?" He smoked meaty French Gitanes from their pretty blue boxes, and was probably the best physics student admitted the past two years. His mullet had to be seen to be believed. He was older than everyone else, having spent four years sealing in the Gulf of St. Lawrence and berg-riddled waters between Newfoundland and Labrador known as the Front. Each October the crew would ready the *M. V. Saddleback*, a forty-year-old 160 ton wooden schooner that barely stayed afloat even before loaded with hundreds of pelts. Newfoundland's waters are home to the hooded seal, harbor seal, and square flipper, all insufficiently social to profitably support a harvest. For a Newfie on the make, the money pinniped is the gregarious harp, congregating on the floes in whelping, arping herds.

Directed by the aircraft of the Canadian Coast Guard, or sometimes just stalking the unfriendly Québécois out of *Îles de la Madeleine*, they made way to the coves of the Front. From the *Saddleback* slipped silently into the water one of the first E-Motion electric runabouts. Two men rode therein with hakapiks and white screens resembling opaque riot shields. Alighting under cold gray light onto the ice, they went to all fours, stalking "beaters." Moulted adults received this sobriquet for the sound their fins made slapping the water. They camouflaged the advance with snow when possible. About half a meter behind a silver adult seal, they rose to a crouch, carefully lowered the screen, and struck to smash its skull with the gaff's 400 g tungsten carbide ferrule. Done correctly, the pelt came through wholly unspoiled. The seal was flayed on the ice. Its stripped skin went to the motorboat, ready to be made into a jacket.

After doing this a few thousand times, and especially after a blizzard in which he lost the boat for eight terrible hours and two fingers forever, he wanted someplace warm, a task sheltered from the elements, with no harp pups to shame him with soft wide eyes. The Newfie (his name was Mustard Kettle, for which he offered no explanation) went south. He possessed keen strength in linear algebra and boundary value problems. As a freshman he'd taken Dynamics and Bifurcations, unhappily known as Discipline and Bondage, and the next quarter was asked to TA. His voice was like a gong, he laughed at

---

Îles de la Madeleine: Magdalen Islands

odd times, and when a recitation's student once asked "what's an orthonormal basis?" he exclaimed "Lard tunderin' Jesus!"

The Newfie made something of a point of smoking by himself, not hiding his active study of everyone else outside. Katz had once bummed a cigarette: the Newfie nodded from what seemed to be a daze, unboxed him a Gitane, and asked, "can you derive quantization of the electric charge without recourse to magnetic monopoles?"

"Mustard, I doubt I can derive quantization of electric charge with a whole wet bucket of magnetic monopoles, which anyway I thought didn't exist?"

The Newfie, impatient: "They haven't been found. They're predicted by most GUTs." He pronounced it *gootz*. "A compact U(1) gauge group emerges, which is a circle of radius two π over e. Quantization! An experimental point in favor of the GUTs! But it is not to be: topological argument shows that monopoles emerge in all U(1) gauges. Dirac's quantization condition, alive in the details. Do you know another way?"

"Mustard mang, I barely know what you're talking about. I know the words but I don't know how a U(1) group even applies to physics. I just know that it does, in quantum electrodynamics. I don't know shit about gauge theories."

"Magnetic monopoles are one example of topological defect only. Cosmic strings, domain walls. Theory of Kibble-Zurek teaches this. Also skyrmions." At "skyrmions" his voice doubled, and he laughed, causing birds to leave trees.

"Alright mang well thanks for the Gitane."

✶✶✶✶✶✶✶✶✶

"That Russian girl was one," meaning she received an A in EMag.

"I think she's Hungarian."

"The Soviet girl, then—"

"Devesh, do you think Hungary was part of the USSR?"

"Was it not?"

"Dude. They were in the Warsaw Pact, and there was a very short-lived Hungarian Soviet Republic—that was the whole Béla Kun deal—but no, even that was its own country. Soviet just means 'worker's council.' The Hungarians were never part of Russia. They *were* part of the Ottomans for a minute, through 1699 I believe. The Russians kicked their ass in 1956, it was a whole thing. The Berlin Wall basically fell because of the opening of the Iron Curtain between Austria and Hungary at the Pan-European Picnic."

"Why dost thou know this? Anyway that's before my time."

"You're older than me!"

Devesh waved it off as unimportant.

✶✶✶✶✶✶✶✶✶

Katz knew very well that she was Hungarian. He'd happily thrown himself into the awkward mating dance of engineering school upon arrival. Male-het demographics were ramified easily enough.

A solid fourth were sufficiently foreign as to be out of play for native English speakers, and stuck to their own. Active Christians—and there were more of them present than he would have expected at a Technical Institute—were likewise insular. The women were unwilling to fuck you unless you accompanied them to church and seemed anyway to regard Katz as egregiously untoward, which he couldn't deny. The boys were sometimes threats, lured easily away from their Messiah by a wafting prospect of impious snatch.

A sizable group of the most potent adversaries lit out from the dorms to Rush. Afterwards, they spent the majority of their time at frat houses, dated sorority girls met at their organized mixers, and generally ran with the Greek community. Katz had no intentions of dating sorority sisters, and thus they did not compete for the same resources.

There existed an on-campus coed house of pallid anime fans, redolent with organic stinks Katz couldn't quite place, that seemed to pulse with the roaches and silverfish pervading it in chronic infestation. Underneath shabby and stained throws horny, grotesque undergrads traded eager acts of wretched affection. As far as Katz was concerned, that whole place was cursed; he loathed it all the more knowing that it might easily have been his own fate. It did house a corps of the hardest core nerds on campus, with whom he kept up generally convivial relations.

Country boys up from the South's deepest, most crackerful regions would be serious opponents, but the city usually put a zap on them. They walked around slowly, cautiously, speaking in deep voices and clearly wary of being fleeced. Some of these guys had cornfed girlfriends at home, more often than not raising a kid with the help of grandparents: when summer came, they filtered back to Perry and Valdosta for a few months of hot, squishy copulation.

Another fourth were irrelevant. An appalling chunk of his dorm was inside playing Quake II every Friday night, and seemed to have cheerfully sworn off feminine companionship. Others appeared so emotionally crippled that it was impossible to imagine them approaching anyone worth approaching, or being noticed by anyone worth noticing. They spent a lot of time reading mass-market fantasy novels from Tor and Del Rey, gathering in common rooms Friday night for card games of bewildering complexity. There was also, to be sure, a healthy contingent of the physically repulsive and/or hygienically objectionable. They seemed to pair off with similarly uncongenial ladies around junior year, often marrying the first person with whom they slept.

Unfortunate souls, few in number but punching well above their weight in annoyance, demonstrated such social ineptitude that their main threat was glomming onto you, sucking from you and a prospective date the interaction they craved. The very worst tended to have Rushed, but received no bids. They sneered at those in the dorm on Friday nights, alluding to decadent parties. When the fratboys were in earshot, they railed against the elitists back at their houses, and mocked those who "paid for their friends." In truth they were unspeakably lonely and sad. Later, they'd be described as incels and spoken of as if they'd chosen this horrible way of life.

Finally there were the devoted subscribers to subcultures. You weren't fucking the handful of goth girls without a working knowledge of *Vampire: The Masquerade* and at least a few piercings. Any number of ravers spoke of

PLUR and revolved among one another in epicycles of JNCOs and STDs and loud drama whenever they weren't rolling.

So numbers which might have seemed otherwise insurmountable were for hoopy froods such as himself not nearly so bad as they seemed. For their part, the women of STEM seemed unafflicted with so high a percentage of deadweight. He'd done well enough so far, he thought. He lost his virginity in the first week to a Huntsville girl who claimed to have swept the Southeast tournament for "Netrunner CCG," apparently some manner of role playing card game? The next evening, she descended uninvited upon his dorm room, consumed three Smirnoff Ice, and with impressive vigor puked undigested Maruchan ramen onto a game of Trivial Pursuit he had raging against Campbell. The window was closed; the air became immediately saturated with the smell of soggy picante chicken. A pale architecture major had interrupted him while he sat outside reading *To the Lighthouse*, and they ended up in her top bunk as 192KHz MP3s of Carcass's *Heartwork* and Tori Amos's *Under the Pink* played in strange and fatiguing juxtaposition from cheap Dell-branded speakers.

Halfway through the quarter he'd seduced his CS 1502 TA, a twenty year old with Sri Lankan heritage and hair blacker than any crow. After a few weeks, he was ready to move on, and unsure how to extricate himself from the entanglement without potential damage to his grade. It was a trivial class, and he wanted his deserved A. He met up with her biweekly until the quarter had ended, then slowly stopped taking her calls. He had built a reputation in the CS department almost immediately by being loud and correct; several ladies even in that first term asked him to come over for help with CS homework (as did plenty of boys, whom he advised to mail their TAs). He successfully converted about half these visits into passionless intercourse on thin dorm-issue mattresses (and one, slightly nicer, at a sorority), knowing the sex to be essentially transactional, wondering if he ought feel bad, or feel anything.

He systematically worked his way through his classmates, fearless in approach, gallant in rejection, showing never shame nor malice. The Hungarian, last name Mališauskas, he'd thought Lithuanian. He approached her with a hale wave and the standard Lithuanian salutation, a sincere "*labas!*" As it turned out, Mališauskas is an adaptation of the Polish Maliszewski, and the Mališauskas had anyway for two generations thrived in Debrecen, diluting away Polish blood and forgetting the few years spent in Vilnius. Besides pretty solid English, in which "labas" is not a word and can be easily mistaken for no other word, Cathy Mališauskas spoke *magyar*, in which "labas" means "casserole," and *russkiy*, in which "labas" is a pejorative term for Lithuanians. She wasn't sure whether he was offering a covered dish or requesting one: it was in any case an inexplicable way to introduce oneself, and she answered "*Szia? Nem?*"

"*Atsiprašau.* I was saying hello. My Lithuanian isn't as good as yours."

"My Lithuanian is none. Why were you saying 'casserole'?"

"I was saying casserole? I thought I was saying hello."

"Not in Hungarian."

CCG: collectible card game **magyar:** Hungarian **russkiy:** русский Russian
Szia? Nem? Hello? No? **Atsiprašau:** Excuse me **Fekete pestis:** black plague

"Hungarian? How did Hungarian get involved?"

"You were babbling about casserole in Hungarian! *Labas! Labas!*"

"Oh shit I was saying hello in Lithuanian. *Labas!*"

"Lithuanian? How did Lithuanian get involved?"

"Are you not Lithuanian?"

"I am Hungarian! *Fekete pestis!*"

"Well," grinning broadly, "this has been a total misfire."

Bolaño, who had watched the interaction transpire, thought this the funniest fucking thing he'd seen in weeks, and greeted Sherman as Katzerole. Sherman bore it and hoped it would not catch traction. Thankfully it did not.

Katz in the spring of 1999 observed the blister of *Human alphaherpesvirus 2* and was pleased to be done with it. Chicken pox of the crotch. He took acyclovir when it was available, and endeavored not to be an active vector, but never let it bother him overmuch. Condoms appeared to be an incomplete protection; with clear conscience he continued to eschew them.

✷ ✳ ✳ ✳ ✳ ✳ ✳ ✳ ✳

Devesh continued. "The other four, I do not know. Definitely most of our class in there"—Devesh gestures at the building behind them—"took Bs or lower in EMag. An unpromising way to launch one's career in physics, I think. Perhaps better to major in something easy like Math or CS." Bidi long extinguished, Devesh drummed on his ample stomach with glee. "Tonight I will eat a roll and listen to *New Forms.*"

"Eat a roll as in MDMA?"

"Methylenedioxy-methamphetamine, yes. Hast thou heard Roni Size?"

"He's techno, I assume? I—"

"Drum and bass."

"Sure, that's a kind of techno, right?"

"It's electronic music. 'Techno' is a particular electronic genre, oriented towards the DJ set. Techno BPM is generally less than drum-and-bass. Among other differences."

"You're just gonna go eat a roll and rave in your dorm room?"

Devesh chortled. "Katz, I said *sayonara* to the dorms after a year. Devesh rents in Home Park the basement of an old house, now walled with anechoic foam. Big Phase Technology 7T speakers. Put 900 watts through them, and feel every neuron in thy brain. Big bazooka tubes also, for effect." Devesh imitates the sound of a falling bomb, and its explosion.

Would that be possible? You need a neuron for sensing each neuron, right? As an input. Can you get by processing multiple neurons with a single neuron? Wouldn't any kind of collection over the sensed neurons lose information, making feeling *every* neuron impossible? "Yeah my dorm sucks ass. Good for meeting people, I guess. So Devesh I fucking love acid but I've never rolled. Can I score some of those pills from you? Or better yet trade? What's on them? I've heard good things about Mitsubishis and dolphins."

"My pills are unscored, Katz. Dost thou have acid? LSD?"

"Devesh, I have fantastic acid at excellent prices. Especially for my buddies in Classical Mechanics."

"Is this why thou takes it in the ass on easy exams? Thou is all night holding thy head together, freeeeeaking out man? And absent from class as Dr. Wi jokes, 'I detect no Sherman Katz, ha-ha, like Tevatron and the Higgs, ha-ha.'"

Katz is mortified. "Oh fuck does he say that?"

"Last week he asked if thou had perished. 'Has Sherman Katz died already? Without mastering Hamilton's formulation of mechanics? He smokes outside, ha-ha, perhaps lung cancer, ha-ha.'"

"He suggested I died of lung cancer?"

"He did. Thy friend Michael Bolaño asked, 'don't you smoke, Professor Wi?'" Devesh's imitation of Bolaño sounds ridiculous to Sherman, but is actually pretty dead-on. "Wi replied, 'yes Mr. Bolaño, but I am in class!' Then he added that white students are lacking moral and physical mettle. Pointing at the board he said 'In China we are knowing this in the second grade. In Russia you are taught this in the womb.' One of the quarks said something in Chinese, and the room's Sinese laughed with belligerence."

Now Devesh laughs.

"The unicycle rider in his ridiculous hat also laughed, too loudly, and with implausible timing. Wi looked at him and demanded, 'Mr. Portnoy, you speak Mandarin?' rattling off what I do not know, perhaps 'Unto death I will beat thee with thy own unicycle, and melt it down afterwards for pig iron.' The unicyclist was silenced, muttering No Professor. Then Wi spoke more Chinese, and all present laughed cruelly."

"Good. *Yáng guǐzi.*"

"I dislike the unicyclist also. I think often of snatching away his hat and lobbing it onto the roof. Ought we candyflip, consuming both acid and MDMA? Would thou come over? I have turntables."

Michael Bolaño emerges, looking buoyant. "That was easy."

Katz calls to him, "MLB, you want to candyflip tonight?"

Michael joins their conclave. "As in eat LSD and MDMA? Maybe don't yell that across the quad? Sure, from whence the ecstasy?"

Sherman points. "Our friend from Gujarat, Devesh. And we're on an American college campus. What possible problem could there be?" He screams as loudly as he can, "I snort lines of dimethylmercury like I was at Dartmouth! Let's shoot tetrodotoxin into our forebrains!" Devesh cracks up. A Facilities employee on a golf cart gives them a look. No one else seems to take notice.

"You're a child." Turning to Devesh: "I would be delighted to this evening unite tryptamine and phenethylamine. First, a bowl."

"Devesh! Come join us in the dorms? Pursuant to a trip along the East Campus highway fence and roasting some bowls?"

"Roast bowls, Katz?" How can someone smile while looking confused?

"Smoking pot, weed, green, big heaping bowls of phat hairy nugs."

"Ahhh! Devesh can join, then proceed north across 10th towards home."

"I don't think I've ever seen you when you weren't grinning, Devesh."

Yáng guǐzi: 洋鬼子 overseas devil

"Devesh is a happy guy! I am all about"—here he pounds his chest with a forearm—"physics and rolls." He extends a finger in *vajra mudrā,* but neither Michael nor Sherman recognize his dactylology.

✳ ✳ ✳ ✳ ✳ ✳ ✳ ✳

Start at Diego Garcia, largest island of the Chagos Archipelago, in pretty much the dead center of the Indian Ocean.

Formally part of the British Indian Ocean Territory, and according to His Majesty's Naval Service a PJOB, Diego Garcia is an American show. The Malta of the Indian Ocean provides an unsinkable aircraft carrier and fleet anchorage capable of projecting power into the Middle East (especially the Persian Gulf), Southeast Asia, East Africa, and the subcontinent. Two runways each offer almost four kilometers, sufficient for concurrent B-1 Lancers, B-2 Spirits, and even elephantine B-52s. A 34 m antenna and two 13 m radomes perform tracking for 21st Space Ops; three Cassegrain 102 cm telescopes serve GEODSS for the 20th. Mauritius, which once marooned lepers on the island, wants it (and the rest of the archipelago) back, which good luck with that.

Proceeding north above the Chagos-Laccadive Ridge, we pass *Dhivehi Raajje:* Asia's smallest nation, and the lowest-lying nation in the world. Dhivehi culture (from Sanskrit *dvīpa*) has bloomed on the Maldives for two and a half millennia, flavored by Buddhist and then Islamic influences. Aside from a hands-off British protectorate, the islands have never been dominated by a foreign presence. Alas, they were quite dominated by 2004's Boxing Day Tsunami, and with a highest natural point only 2.4 meters above sea level, are likely to be subsumed this century by the rising Indian Ocean. Good luck with that one, too.

Shortly after passing capital Malé (ﻣﺎ) to our west, Sri Lanka's *Koḷaṁba* (*Koḷumpu* if you prefer *Tamiḻ* to *Siṁhala*) passes by to the east, too far away to be seen. Coming up portside is Lakshadweep, an Indian union territory, its atolls sparsely populated by Sunnis of the Shafi'i madhhab. India is to starboard, and will remain there. The citystate Goa spawned Goa trance from its Arambol beach, a hub of the old overland Hippie Trail—put on *Rock Bitch Mafia* by Green Nuns of the Revolution or Hallucinogen's *Twisted* as we enter the Arabian Sea. Slip by Mumbai and greater Maharashtra and into the Gulf of Khambhat, across which India intends to construct ten traffic lanes atop the thirty kilometer Kalpasar Dam Project, with the goal of creating the world's largest freshwater reservoir. The first district of Gujarat we reach is Valsad; the first city is the Vapi taluka, on the delta of the Damangaga. It is a powerful center of the Indian chemical industry. Here Devesh Choudhary made his home for twelve years.

Gujarat has a reputation for some looseness regarding education, at least compared to the rest of testing- and admissions-mad India. At the same time, they're respected for entrepreneurial spirit, business sense, and a general

---

vajra mudrā: वज्र मुद्र thunderbolt gesture   **PJOB:** Permanent Joint Operating Base
GEODSS: Ground-based Electro-Optical Deep Space Surveillance
Dhivehi Raajje: ﺩﻳﻮﻫ ﺭﺍﺟﻪ the Maldives   **dvīpa:** द्वीप island
Koḷaṁba, Koḷumpu: කොළඹ, கொழும்பு Colombo
Tamiḻ: தமிழ் Tamil   **Siṁhala:** සිංහල Sinhal
Kalpasar: कल्पसर lake that fulfills all wishes (cf. *Kalpavṛkṣa*, Shiva Purana 2.2.42)

surfeit of derring-do. Such stereotypes are worse than useless, but it cannot be denied that many of modern India's largest personalities emerged from the Western Jewel, the Land of Lions. BJP leader (PM since 2014) Narendra Modi previously served as Chief Minister, running Gujarat from Gandhinagar since 2001. Riots in 2002 (and the holocaust leading up to them) were an early test for Modi and a resurgent Hindi nationalism. Zoroastrian "Father of Indian Industry" Jamsetji Tata was born in Navsari, not too distant from Valsad. Vallabhbhai Patel, first Deputy PM, hailed from Gujarat. Only one man held rank above him: another Gujarati, one *Mahātmā* Gandhi, long before he was being misquoted by Elizabeth Holmes or incinerating *Civilization V* opponents with thermonuclear *shakti* of the Most High.

Interestingly, Muhammad Ali Jinnah, founder of Pakistan, also had Gujarati heritage. Perhaps it's not so surprising, though: the Raj was primarily governed from bases along India's western coast; most of India's first generation of modern leaders got their educations riding the Raj-to-London pipeline.

For Indian children hoping to study science or engineering at the highest level, whether Brahmin or some rather more scheduled caste, adolescence turns on the famously brutal Advanced Joint Entrance Examination. The 1961 Institutes of Technology Act designated the IITs Institutes of National Importance, and since then they've represented the top end of higher education on the subcontinent. Aside from Constitutionally-mandated reservations for SCaTs, OBCs and wretched EWSs, seats at the IITs are assigned pretty much according to marks on this test. As the IITs are the surest way to India's upper class other than taking twenty wickets against the Green Shirts of Pakistan, competition is stiff. It's awfully easy to go under in an aggressively upwardly mobile nation of over a billion people, and seats at IIT Bombay and Madras are far more tightly contested than those at Harvard or Oxford.

Test-specific training is pervasive. Companies like FITJEE, Bansal Classes, and Resonance, most of them headquartered in the "Factory" in Rajasthan's Kota, recommend several years of coaching, beginning in Class X. Annual fees collected approach ten gigadollars, and close to 150 kilostudents migrate north each year to begin two to three years of study. There are fewer suicides than one might expect (though by no means zero), but after all teenagers are unhappy all over the world. Kids who pull off a top JEE score will be set up for life.

Devesh was drawn to the sciences early, reading the biographies of Satyendra Nath Bose and Subrahmanyan Chandrasekhar with fascination, and that of Abdus Salam with stoic respect. His parents were chemical engineers who'd met at NIT Surat in the early years of Indira Gandhi's *Garibi Hatao*; while most of Gujarat would come out with the Janata Party, they remained loyal to New

---

BJP: Bharatiya Janata Party
Mahātmā: महात्मा great soul   **shakti:** शक्ति strength, cosmic energy
IITs: Indian Institutes of Technology   **SCaTs:** Scheduled Castes and Tribes
OBCs: Other Backwards Classes   **EWSs:** Economically Weaker Sections
FITJEE: Forum for Indian Institute of Technology Joint Entrance Examination
NIT: National Institutes of Technology
Garibi Hatao: गरीबी हटाओ remove poverty (cf. *Indira Hatao*)

Congress. When Devesh was a child his mother Grishma stood for Lok Sabha, narrowly losing twice. The three-language formula hadn't quite penetrated to Valsad even by the time Devesh started secondary education. In his home he heard Hindi, and in Vapi, Gujarati; he acquired a King James Bible from a local pair of Canadian missionaries and began working through it to learn English. When Devesh broached heading off to focus on the JEE, his parents found the whole idea repugnant. His father came home the next day with a burlap sack full of well-used I. E. Irodov and some mimeographed AITS problem sets.

Devesh grew stronger in chemistry and physics, though he never felt as strong in math as he ought be, and resented those who could peer so easily into the hearts of Lie algebras and permutation groups. Linear algebra came naturally enough, and he was fond of saying that much of particle dynamics could be recovered from careful consideration of the basic trigonometric functions. He delighted in Fourier analysis, and with it he whipped and drove differential equations. Still, the JEE loomed like an evil *rākṣasa* in his future, and he was full of dismay and pessimism.

When an aunt and uncle, recent American citizens in South Carolina, determined once and for all that their efforts to have a child were medically futile, they offered an I-800 adoption. The decision was left entirely to fourteen year-old Devesh. It didn't take him long. The first nonstop BOM-ATL flight wouldn't come until 2008 in the form of DL184 and DL185. Devesh took the two-day trip to Delhi by train, boarding Air India's 747-400, the magnificent *Konark,* longhaul to New York. He felt like a prince as he took his economy seat, though he was admittedly less sanguine after the sixteen hours east. He cleared Customs, and narrowly caught his shuttle to LaGuardia where he connected to a Delta flight to ATL. Feeling three shades of dead, he connected there to a DC-9 en route to Savannah International. He collected two trunks, met his relatives outside, and passed out before reaching I-95.

Three days later he was boarding at the South Carolina Governor's School for Science and Mathematics, which you'd better believe required all manner of strings to be pulled. He remembered Aziz Ansari touring as a prospective junior. There he prepared for physics, and stomped his SATs, and found his way to Georgia Tech in 1997, one year prior to Katz and Bolaño. The only thing he loved more than physics was electronic music, and while he never went full PLUR, one almost had to work to avoid MDMA prior to the 2003 RAVE Act. He ate his first pink pill the summer before heading down to Atlanta, and made it an immediate point to become familiar with existing methods of synthesis. He was a happy guy, and all about physics and rolls.

There was one other reason he left Gujarat, one he'd never told an American. When he was nine and splashing on the banks of the Damanganga, he'd known dinosaurs as well as any bright young boy. He watched as a dark spot in the river came in towards him. Suddenly ridges of osteodermic plate like those of

---

Lok Sabha: अगणनीय संज्ञ House of the People (cf. Rajya Sabh)
AITS: All Indian Test Series
rākṣasa: राक्षस "preserver" malevolent beings. *Rāmāyaṇa* III–VI
RAVE: Reducing Americans' Vulnerability to Ecstasy

Stegosaurus or Ankylosaurus broke the surface, except they were three, one rising straight into the air and two at angles, these latter stained a vibrant purple. He moved back a few cautious steps. Onto the amygdaloidal bank stepped something positively Jurassic, built like the Army's new Arjun MK1 tank. It opened its mouth in a hideous gape, moving its head to the left and then the right. Then it looked directly at Devesh, and charged. Devesh shrieked and took off towards home. He described the reptile to his parents, but they assured him no such creature existed in all of India. He suggested that the polluted waters of Damanganga had mutated some less ferocious turtle, but his father said that mutation didn't work that way.

Devesh knew what he had seen.

Three more times he encountered the demon-turtle. Once he had to return in the middle of gym class to his locker. The chelonian was out in the middle of the floor, and it stomped like a sumo. Another time he opened the door to the family's Maruti Suzuki, and it was sitting in the driver's seat. It snapped at his crotch, snatching a hole right from his dhoti. The next and last time he got in a river, it was on him almost immediately, swimming with great rapidity from who knows where, singularly intent it seemed on devouring Devesh's manhood. How it kept finding him, and how it managed to attack when no one else was around, were sublime mysteries. So he went to the other side of the world for his education, comfortably certain that no turtle would swim the endless Pacific for Devesh Choudhary, no matter how armored nor demonic. That this creature would without hesitation pursue him across far greater distances than any path along or through the earth he could not have known.

∗ ∗ ∗ ∗ ∗ ∗ ∗ ∗ ∗

Atlanta is a city born of and defined by transportation, but unlike most such cities, it sits astride neither a cargoworthy river nor the sea. There is the colossus that is Hartsfield-Jackson International Airport, ATL before Atlanta was the ATL. The railways were once of great importance, but their role has diminished. Sadly, Atlanta is a city designed for cars, with a sparse, sprawling metropolitan area; its very geography is specified by highways. First, the Great Circumscriber. I-285 is not a true circle, more of a square with rounded corners, with the southeast knocked in a good bit. Think of a bust of Lenin, facing west, seen in profile. It is naturally known as the Perimeter, and encloses (conversationally if not canonically) Atlanta, those territories ITP (Inside the Perimeter). Beyond it lies OTP (Outside *ibid.*), suburbia: megachurches, SUVs, lower taxes, and soccer moms.

Zoom out on a map of the interstate highway system. I-75 and I-85 form a saltire ✕ centered on Atlanta, where I-285 circles the cross: ⊗. I-20 runs east-west through the middle of it all, from the old South Carolina railroad junction town of Florence to Scroggins Draw, a dusty and largely uninhabited milepost in west Texas, notable for intersection with I-10 and not a goddamned thing otherwise: ⊗. The hundred kilometers of 285 are thus crossed six times by major interstates, once by an auxiliary interstate (I-675), once by the "Atlanta Autobahn" (Georgia 400), once by a Hartsfield taxiway, and once again by Hartsfield's full length fifth runway, the longest of its kind in the United States, meaning sometimes you're seizing gaps at 140kph and suddenly a 575-ton Airbus A380 rolls out at two hundred kph orthogonal to your direction. At its "Spaghetti Junction" flyover interchange 285 broadens to eighteen lanes. It is a fucking madhouse.

Zoom in on our map from earlier: 75 and 85 actually merge and run vertically for twelve kilometers (I-20 comes across about halfway through this section). It's as if the top and bottom sections of our $\times$ have been pulled apart from one another, remaining connected only by a line running north-south: think of the t-channel Feynman diagram: $\overline{\times}$. This is the Connector, the dodeca- and tetradeca-lane union of I-75 and I-85. Peachtree Street crosses the Connector twice, bracketing the city core. Above the northern crossing lies Buckhead; below the southern crossing is Downtown. Midtown, Atlanta's powerhouse neighborhood, one of few true high-density areas in the Southeast, is neatly bisected by the Connector.

Those living in Atlanta's vast northern suburbs must traverse the Connector to reach the airport or the beaches. The majority who spend their childhood there will count among their earliest memories a drive southbound in a packed sedan or family-friendly minivan, finding themselves suddenly surrounded by buildings hundreds of meters taller than any they've ever seen, and concrete in all directions. Far along the horizon the sky is dense with jumbo jets. In lanes to either side a parking lot worth of cars are cruising along at 100kph without anyone batting an eye. The situation is new, and thrilling.

I-75 proper starts in Tampa Bay, though it was extended *post hoc* through Alligator Alley to Miami Lakes (Miami itself is more properly served by US 1 and the coastal I-95, to which 75 connects via the I-595 auxiliary), displacing the canceled and parochially-named West Coast Turnpike. This tolled section was completed only in 1992, fifteen years after the rest of the highway. A picturesque stretch crosses the Everglades, including Big Cypress Nature Preserve, where Devesh and Bolaño spent NYE 1999 and the first day of 2000 watching Phish, zonked well out of their skulls and generally having one hell of a time. Go ahead and use I-475 to bypass poor Macon. Leaving Atlanta by the northwest, it passes by the Blue Ridge Mountains to Chattanooga, hugs the Great Smoky Mountains, then rises with some of the taller Cumberlands before descending to Lexington. At the Ohio river, vehicles trading a Rust Belt for one of Sun rumble above, but the bottom deck spills into Cincinnati; the skyline unfolds dramatically as you exit the Brent Spence bridge. Beyond lie Toledo, Detroit, friendly Yoopers, and border crossings into Ontario.

I-85 is a more regional affair, almost an auxiliary itself, albeit one that runs through five states. From Montgomery it departs from I-65 for Atlanta, bypassing Charlotte to the north where it junctions with I-77. In Virginia it terminates at I-95. A traveler heading north from Miami can thus cross the South by I-95 or, curving inland, take I-75 to I-85 in Atlanta, then meet 95 just south of Richmond, as any East Coast cocaine importer knows full well.

Midtown stretches from North Avenue up to Atlantic Station and Piedmont Park, and from Northside Drive in the west to Monroe Drive in the east. Midtown core sits immediately to the east of the Connector. Heading north on Peachtree Street one crosses the highway and North Avenue into a completely different economic and architectural motif. Downtown's 1970s brutalism and 1980s neoclassicism are older, poorer, more bureaucratic; New South from a time we look back on as Old South. Once across North, it's all finance-intensive glass and concrete contemporary, mixed yuppie residential towers and offices up until the Arts district. To its east is Atlantic Station, a reclaimed Superfund brownfield where Atlantic Steel for almost one hundred years bled lead and mercury (and to a lesser degree cadmium, chromium, and arsenic) into the soil. While Katz and Bolaño were undergraduates, this was all still poisoned ground, sludge ponds, and razor wire.

Looming over the west of the highway is Georgia Tech from North through 10th, with exits to the Connector on each extremum. Between 10th and 16th is Home Park, student housing in various states of disrepair, and also a few really bitchin' houses taking advantage of the lack of an HOA. Most of the units are old homes broken down into three- or five- or ten-person rentals. Two individuals have owned eighty percent plus of the neighborhood since 2000, and for them it is an endless wellspring of cash. Crime isn't as high as one would expect, but one definitely locks the doors. Home Park attracts a coarser, dirtier, louder Yellow Jacket than most: there are parties throughout the neighborhood on Friday nights. Drug use is endemic and heterogeneous.

It is here, on Francis Street, that Katz and Bolaño first visit Devesh.

"So DMT thou can make drunk and without some hand *H*. Trivial. Thou gets *Mimosa hostilis* bark, grind it, extract DMT into solution with acid, use naptha or some other base to deprotonate to freebase. Wash it with sodium carbonate. Precipitate out DMT crystal. Roll it, light it, smoke it, ahhhhhh." Devesh's grin spreads even wider than normal.

Bolaño: "What's yield like on that, though?"

"Admittedly not great." A shrug. "Thou can purchase a kilogram of supposedly high-alkaloid *Mimosa* bark for about fifty dollars plus shipping. Thou ends up with about ten grams of pure yellow crystal. Lots of pulpy waste. Another twenty dollars for solvents, just so. I have performed the extraction twice. Ten grams is two hundred strong doses."

Bolaño, fast: "So fifty milligrams on a strong dose."

"Correct. Fifty milligrams is a *Pṛthvī*-II rocket into the Land, *Śambhala*. Half that remains an intense experience. Threshold effects at one-tenth. Concurrent MAOI consumption protracts and potentiates effects. Thirty minutes becomes three hours due to increased metabolism."

"I don't know about that mang; half of everything I've ever eaten said not to combine it with an MAOI. And it comes on fast?"

"Before thou puts down thy bowl." Katz and Bolaño both look hot to trot. "Would ye like to try some?"

Their agreements are excited and roughly concurrent. "You've got some now? Awesome. This is the stuff you extracted?"

"Dost thou think I smoked DMT two hundred times this year?"

DMT: *N,N*-dimethyltryptamine $C_{12}H_{16}N_2$ 2-(1H-Indol-3-yl)-N,N-dimethylethanamine
Pṛthvī: पृथ्वी Earth, an Indian intermediate range ballistic missile
Śambhala: शम्भल Shambhala. Vishnu Purana 4.24   **MAOI:** monoamine oxidase inhibitor

"I don't know, you could have sold it, you could have done the extraction in India, it could have been stolen, plenty of reasons." Katz affects a disappointed tone. "Your mocking question lacks rigor."

"Thou art fair." The grin never fades, Katz notices—he would personally have felt slapped. "Yes, I have plenty of the yellow shards." Devesh collects a glassine bag from a desk drawer and brings it over to where the three were sitting, three diverse chairs around an inch-thick plane of wood resting on four supports of cinderblock. The wood shifts whenever someone bumps into it. A chess set, in no way garish, sits in the middle.

A small glass bowl is packed with a sprig of parsley, into which Devesh sprinkles a generous mass of crushed crystal. Handing it to Sherman, he remarks "this is my *bodhi*." *Hoc est corpus meum.*

Katz hits it first, with enthusiasm and gleaming eye. The powder pops and crackles where it isn't completely reduced to dust. The smell is hideous. Bolaño has to take the bowl from Katz's yielding hands, and then it is his turn to forget how to pass. Ever-grinning Devesh is pleased; he puts on Plastikman's *Consumed*, a triumph in dark minimalism, and waits for the freshmen to return. He reads volume 2 of Feynman's red *Lectures in Physics,* and glances around now and again, on the lookout always for turtles.

✳✳✳✳✳✳✳✳✳

Two Hilbert curves began to consume Katz's vision, one behind the other. The one in the front worked out from the center; that in the back worked in from the perimeter. When he blinked, they merged, then split again. Colors pulsed through both from side to side. He recognized them to be his mother. I am the servant of two masters, one involutional and one evolutional. He looked to Devesh, helpless, sure to be dominated by the space-filling curves. It was a struggle to speak, and his voice quivered with terror.

"My Hausdorff dimension is only one."

Devesh offered no assistance. "Art thou being attacked by killer fractals?" His grin wrapped around his head like a helical coil. Profane Desi magics, heathen to the max. The son of a bitch was in league with them. When they go high-dimension, we go low. Marr's multi-level theory of vision. 2½ dimensions. No depth, just texture. We've gotta eliminate stereoscopy. For Victory! For America! For Science! Katz closed his left eye, and the curve in the back dissolved away, screaming as it did so.

He leans towards Bolaño. "I just killed my mother."

"*Unser Leben ist ebenso endlos, wie unser Gesichtsfeld grenzenlos ist.* Did you refuse to pray at her bedside? Did you first make her your Jocasta?" He giggles, and it is an evil sound. "I slayed my Laius."

"Kill padre? Possess madre? I'll kill God and possess the cosmos. *Heute die Welt, Morgens das Sonnensystem.* Fuck bitches, get money. Hail Eris."

---

bodhi: बोधि perfect knowledge, abstract noun formed from *budh-* (बुध, to awaken)
Hoc...meum: this is my body. Matthew 26:26 (NIV)
Unser...ist: Our life is endless in the way that our visual field is without limit.
  Ludwig Wittgenstein, *Tractatus Logico-Philosophicus (1922)* 6.4311
Heute...Sonnensystem: Today the world, tomorrow the solar system!

The remaining curve wasn't going anywhere. Katz felt himself going under, *untergehen*. "She stopped being Catholic, though." The fractal paused, and was replaced by a punishingly white Gosper curve. Then Katz laughed, and realized her error. "You can't grow a space-filling curve 'from the inside out.' Fuck outta here with that bullshit."

A pyramid appeared and began to spin. The spinning grew faster, faster; it developed an ergosphere and all objects within its dragged frames moved. Katz dipped his finger, hoping to extract energy via the Penrose process. Her rebuke was fierce, and came swiftly.

SON OF MAN, DO YOU THINK YOUR VISION CONTINUOUS?

No.

DO YOU THINK YOUR MIND CONTINUOUS?

Probably not. A Blum-Shub-Smale machine is.

DO YOU THINK YOUR MIND AS POWERFUL AS A TURING MACHINE?

Well, no, it doesn't have infinite tape. I'm pretty sure.

CLOSER TO ZERO TAPE THAN INFINITE TAPE. BARELY FINITE.

Rude.

A BLUM-SHUB-SMALE MACHINE IS SUPER-TURING.

Yes. Can we move this up to at least a canter?

SON OF MAN. SURELY YOU SEE MY PROBLEM HERE.

Not p and not p. You needn't speak that way. I'm not a child.

YET YOU ARE A CHILD. NOT P AND NOT P.

It's possible that minds are not totally ordered, pumping lemma be damned.

FAREWELL, SHERMAN SPARTACUS KATZ.

The pyramid and curve were both replaced by nothingness, the Big Rip, and that was his father. Eons passed without local field fluctuations. He begged silently that an end might be made. A sphere of infinitely many dimensions caressed his mind, and she spoke from all directions, and Katz opened his eyes wide. She affirmed that he would one day die, and his person, his memories, would melt away like snowflakes caught on his tongue. But just as he was each moment a Heraclitean approximation of himself the previous and next, so was he approximated by all consciousnesses, those which were human, those created by humans, the slow intelligences within stars' plasmas, every proton dragged into a negentropic collective, for in the particular is contained the universal. Was this after all any greater Mystery than the Trinity?

Yadda yadda, so even from a purely selfish perspective, one can best spend one's time improving the world? Well that's why I'm an engineer.

She laughed like mocking thunder from nowhere and everywhere. NON QUASI CRUDELIS SUSCITABO EUM: QUIS ENIM RESISTERE POTEST VULTUI MEO?

Do I not then approximate You within some bounded error? Quoniam terribiliter magnificasti. *Do I converge?*

A TURTLE'S GONNA RIP DEVESH'S DICK OFF. HE CAN'T DO ANYTHING ABOUT IT. IT IS PART OF MY PLAN. TELL HIM, AND BRING HIM PEACE.

How is that supposed to bring him peace?

Non...meo: Can you pull in Leviathan with a fishhook, or tie down its tongue with a rope? Job 41:1 (NIV)   **Quoniam...magnificasti:** I am fearfully and wonderfully made. Psalms 139:14

HE CAN STOP FEELING STUPID ABOUT FEARING THE TURTLE.

✳ ✳ ✳ ✳ ✳ ✳ ✳ ✳ ✳

Devesh had been correct about the rocket up, the short duration, and the quick comedown. Well before the hour is over, both Katz and Bolaño landed, their heads more or less clear. The objects of the room no longer spoke to one another in fractals and strange geometries; everyone knew their names and that they existed. "So what dost thou think of the spirit molecule DMT?"

Katz's reply comes slowly, and without much assurance. "Devesh, I saw God, and She was an n-sphere." *Et eritis sicut dii.* "Volume of the unit n-sphere goes up until you surpass five dimensions. Once you get to six, it starts falling. An infinity sphere has no volume." And yet She spoke. Ought I tell Devesh about the turtle thing? No, clearly not.

Devesh looked at him with serious eyes. "Higher dimensional spheres are fascinating. Unlike the two-sphere, those of even-numbered dimensions admit a non-vanishing continuous tangent vector field—they can be combed."

"Yeah that's Poincaré and Brouwer's hairy ball theorem right? Most of these properties emerge from quaternions; they give it natural Lie group structure."

Bolaño joins in: "Dante describes the geometry of the universe in Canto 28 of the *Paradiso*, and it is clearly a 3-sphere. Lacking the terminology to efficiently speak of higher dimensional constructions, he refers to the resulting geometry as a knot *'tanto, per non tentare, è fatto sodo,'* one so resistant to unraveling that no one has tried." He waits for a moment; hearing no objection, he continues. "Ptolemy introduced the *Primum Mobile* as the outermost sphere in his epicyclic model. But it was embedded in the Empyrean, *ciel de la divina pace*, which no one described until Alighieri. Traditionally the Empyrean was basically 'outside' of the *Primum Mobile* without its own boundary. In topology, one suspends a space X by joining it to a set S of two discrete points not in X. A join just connects the members of the disjoint union of two spaces. Suspending an n-sphere results in a sphere of $n + 1$ dimensions. Here's another way to visualize it: the cone of a space is the suspension, except with only one point in S. So imagine we're taking a circle, extending from it a cylinder, and then collapsing the far face into a single point. That's a cone, right? And each point on the circle has a line to that vertex; we've induced an infinity on it."

"Like the real projective plane." Katz is uncertain.

"More like the real projective line, but yeah, same idea."

Devesh: "And the complex projective line is the Riemann sphere: a join of the complex plane to a point."

"Yes. Now embed the apex in the center of a 2-sphere, and it's obvious that the cone of said sphere is a solid ball. Take two of those, and join the bases—the original spheres. The result is a 3-sphere. Just an alternative construction of the suspension. So the 3-sphere is made up of two 3-hemispheres, joined along their equators. Dante speaks of nine concentric shells of the *Inferno* and nine

---

Et...dii: and ye shall be as gods. Genesis 3:5 (KJV)
tanto...sodo: so hard hath it become for want of trying. *Paradiso* 28.60
Primum Mobile: first mover/movable
ciel...pace: the heaven of divine repose. *Paradiso* 2.112

in the *Paradiso*. Satan lurks in the lowest level of the *Inferno*. God sits in the highest level of the *Paradiso*. All the spheres rotate; Satan's most slowly, and the *Primum Mobile* most quickly, as all rotation flows from God, represented as three distinct circles of equal size occupying the same space. The speed of rotation is thus a fourth dimension—recall the visualization from *Flatland*, where a sphere is seen as a series of circles, changing in size. The two 3-hemispheres are glued together at the Firmament, and God is the point *inchiuso da quel ch'elli 'nchiude."* Bolaño smiles, clearly pleased with himself.

Devesh asks, "I enjoy topology, but what's Dante?" Katz collapses into laughter; Bolaño moans. Not waiting for an explanation, Devesh pulls out a few "rolls." Both Katz and Bolaño frown, and poke.

Katz is the first to inquire. "Devesh, I thought rolls were pills."

"These are gelcaps. A roll just means MDMA."

Bolaño, dryly: *"Ceci n'est pas une rouler."*

Katz laughs. "I'm pretty sure a roll means a pressed pill more than it means MDMA, heh. But regardless, semantics, sure. So this is purported MDMA in gelcaps?"

"Not that I am that far up on the chain, but I would guess that pill presses are expensive, and difficult to obtain."

"Yeah, they're explicitly called out in the CSA."

"Just so. These are vegan capsules, so I am told in any case. And the MDMA within is the fire. One hundred milligrams each, very pure, very precise. Thou remains down, I'm sure?"

"Oh absolutely, I'm hoping to roll my balls off here in your Home Park *mahal*." Katz makes a face. "Seems difficult to market, though. Also kinda prone to mechanical trauma."

Devesh shrugs. "These are not my concerns."

❊ ❊ ❊ ❊ ❊ ❊ ❊ ❊

Devesh met Alabama Austin at the Highlander, a dive bar about twenty minutes' walk to the east from campus. Despite Devesh's requests that he come alone, he had some trashy girl with him. She was unnecessarily introduced as Tiffany, and emitted a clanging laugh that got on Devesh's nerves immediately. She had a multitude of rings and what were not quite bracelets, and wore a crusty crop top. Austin, now with more neck tattoos than he'd boasted two months ago, was clad in a zip-up tracksuit, knockoff Persol sunglasses and a bright red Alabama visor. His mustache didn't meet the thin beard that traced the perimeter of his face. His fingernails were painted black. On his left hand was tattooed ROLL and on the right hand TIDE. Devesh saw them sauntering up to his table and resolved once again to find better customers.

Austin sang insipid lyrics. *"Choudhary / you're my man today / with the E that paaaaaays"* He held out the last syllable, eliciting one of those spine-curdling guffaws from his thot. He sat down caddycorner from Devesh and began immediately to assault him with overapplied Drakkar Noir.

---

inchiuso…'nchiude: enclosed by that which it encloses. *Paradiso* 30.12
CSA: Controlled Substances Act   **mahal:** महल palace

Devesh didn't lose his good humor, but came close. "Thou mustn't sing songs of felonies."

Austin lit a Camel Light. "What did I tell you, babe, it's all 'thou' and 'thy' with my man Devesh. That's how they do it in India."

"I'd likewise prefer it were thou not to share my name." He'd come to the other side of the world to study physics, and this Tuscaloosa brain trust was going to get him snatched up by local constables. "I have it all here. Two sealed bags, seventy-five grams each. I think the quality superior this time."

Austin cocked a brow and said, "Dr. Devesh, your best was already excellent. We're frying eggs off people's brains on the dancefloor. I'm glad to hear it." The woman whistled and laughed her abomination of a laugh. Thirty hundred-dollar bills are less than a quarter-inch high; Austin always brought crisp, clean hundreds. He handed Devesh an envelope and received a Crown Royal bag, which he began to open.

"Not here!" Devesh chuckled. "My good man, thou will see it soon enough. Thou knoweth my word is bond. Do I count thy money at the table?"

"Fair enough, Choudhary." He turned to Tiffany. "Baby, you want some shots before we head back to T-Town."

"I want a Frangelico and a steak."

"I don't think they have steaks here baby but we can do that Italian goodness." He whistled at a waitress. Devesh, scandalized and trying to make himself small, shifted away. "Can I get this beautiful girl two shots of Frangelico? And I'll take a Long Island. Make it strong."

Devesh stared. "Dost thou have an unseen driver? Dost thou intend to get shitfaced and then traffic MDMA across state lines?"

Both of them found this hilarious. "Devesh, you know me like a doctor! That's exactly what I'm going to do. Gotta get limber for the road, don't want to be drivin' with a stick in my ass, drawing attention. Besides, if we get stopped, she'll just eat it fast as can be, little roll whore." The woman squealed.

"Please, be safe. I must go." He stood up and began to walk away, then doubled back. "I know it is a joke, but thou mustn't eat either of those bags. Thou will most certainly perish. Drive safely and please to use caution." He caught their waitress by the POS terminal and handed her a hundred-dollar bill. "Thou mustn't associate me with these people."

She made a face at the pair from Tuscaloosa and took the c-note. "Devesh, I associate you only with the very finest of people. Is this for their bill?"

"It is apology for bringing them into thy bar, and cover for the tip I suspect thou will be stiffed on."

"You're a sweetheart, Devesh." Her touch of his elbow is thrilling.

Across the bar he hears yelled, "Devesh! Do I hit you up at the same number next time?" He points at his watchless wrist in the universal sign of *gotta go* and scurries out the front door. There ought be twenty-nine hundred left. He is unsure whether he will answer Alabama Austin's next call. The freedom to ignore him will come only through finding new buyers. Perhaps Katz and Bolaño can help him out.

POS: point of sale

6   *atrium vestae*

Δ is delta, and means change. Please do not draw it upside down. That's a ∇—nabla, pronounced del—an entirely different kettle of fish. Div, grad, curl, and all that: A bare ∇ is gradient (scalar function to vector field); ∇· is divergence (vector to scalar, mirroring the dot product's vector to scalar); ∇× is curl (predictably vector to vector), and only defined in three dimensions. The other two? Fully general. Go nuts.

✳ ✳ ✳ ✳ ✳ ✳ ✳ ✳ ✳

Control and Concurrency isn't that difficult of a class, but some people simply can't wrap their heads around pointers. They knew better than to major in the more abstract teachings; Computer Science sounded easy enough. After dropping, or emerging with an unearned C, they make their ways in one and twos to the registrar in Tech Tower. Some depart for another school entirely, and are usually happier for having done so. Others fill out change-of-major forms, taking a ride on the "M-train": MGMT is accepted to be the easiest major on campus by some margin. Switching to it is a storied tradition.

Management majors had their own math sequence, a kind of watered-down and unrigorous calculus. There was thus only one class required of all students: CS1501, a sprawling enterprise containing hundreds of undergraduate TAs, and managed like an Army brigade. It offered an exemption exam, which both Sherman and Michael passed. The exam was answered in longhand, using whatever language one wished. Michael employed Pascal; Sherman used x86 assembly. Katz watched dozens of freshmen struggle through recursion and pointers, taking the baby steps of computer science. The second week they began writing code, and Katz was filled with fury when he discovered the class to be taught using an ALGOL-derived pseudocode for which there was no implementation. This unorthodox decision was justified by claiming that students needn't pay attention to the details of syntax, but as Katz remarked, "without formal syntax there can be no formal evaluation."

Homework written with syntax divergent from that shown in lecture was marked incorrect, exploding the lie in this claim. Students couldn't test their solutions, meaning they caught fewer errors before submission. TAs couldn't test the submissions, leading to more grading errors and contested results. More than once in the College of Computing, Katz watched an exasperated student drag their TA to a whiteboard and trace their code to win back points. The TA ended up feeling like shit, the student thought their TA a dumbass, there was no benefit, and graduates emerged from the class knowing a language used exactly one place: CS1501.

Katz regarded the situation as patently ridiculous. He had been those first few weeks ripping through foundational texts of software engineering: Dijkstra's *A Discipline of Programming*, long out of print, but for Katz's money the

---

atrium vestae: House of the Vestals   **baptisma per ignem:** baptism by fire

114

most beautiful book, page-per-page, in computer science. *Introduction to Algo-rithms*, an oversized white megalith known as CLR after its authors. The three magisterial volumes of Knuth's *The Art of Computer Programming*. Kernighan and Ritchie's slim *The C Programming Language* and Stroustrup's significantly larger *The C++ Programming Language*. *Structure and Interpretation of Computer Programs* from MIT, its purple cover's robed wizard an exultant embrace of the abstruse. Armed with this new knowledge, he had been looking for a sizable C project. Like any serious student of computer science, he longed to build a compiler, for compilers, operating system kernels, and virtual machines are the three most fundamental spells a young software witch must master.

He started by posting to the class mailing list, asking for a formal specifica-tion of the pseudocode's syntax. "Ideally in EBNF, maybe with some axiomatic semantic annotations. I can roll with whatever." From the head TA came a prim response: "we use pseudocode to avoid the need for a formal language definition." Almost immediately there arrived a flurry of contradictions from students who'd lost points to issues of syntax. A TA replied that she'd put together her own specification distilled from lecture slides. She stressed that it was not official, but she might as well post it, and did so. Katz thanked her and called for objections or departures from the concise grammar; there were only minor ones, quickly resolved. The head TA replied, "it sounds like you're looking to build a compiler. We'd rather you not, for various reasons." Katz fired back, "what are those reasons?" but received no reply.

Two days later, Katz posted `flex` and `bison` inputs and the necessary adhe-sive C to drive a frontend for the pseudocode. It only emitted a string of tokens on success, but it failed on invalid inputs, and already this was a great boon to the class. Now they, like users of every other modern programming envi-ronment, could automatically check for syntax errors (though not yet errors of logic). TAs and students both hailed it, but Katz assured them more was to come. It took less than two hours to rig up transpilation from CS1501 pcode to ANSI C, suitable for feeding through the C compiler of your choice. Now the programs could be run, tested, automated, *used*. With this relatively simple effort, Katz won throughout the student body the reputation as a formidably competent and possibly brilliant coder with a renegade streak: the bad boy of computer science. He thought it all a bit overwrought. It wasn't difficult work, per se, just a matter of deciding to do it and committing oneself to the task. He wasn't about to disavow anyone of their notions, though. Already he was learning that, besides raw talent and taste regarding its application, one of the most valuable traits a programmer can cultivate is *mystique*.

✳ ✳ ✳ ✳ ✳ ✳ ✳ ✳ ✳

It starts with a bit. If we subscribe to Wheeler's notion of a participatory uni-verse, it *all* starts with bits: "it from bit." A bit can take on two values; we typically use zero and one, because these are the natural domain of Boolean algebra, a formal description of logical operations, but any system that distin-guishes between two states is a bit. If a question can be answered with "yes" or

---

CLR: Cormen, Leiserson, Rivest   EBNF: Extended Backus-Naur Form "no," that question demands a bit. The velocity of a car cannot be summarized in a bit, but "is the car traveling at more than 20 kph" can. The mass of a tumor cannot be summarized in a bit, but "are tumor cells present" can. A bit cannot generally report how much current is flowing through a wire, but it can report whether current greater than or equal to some level is.

This tells us what a bit can represent. How can a bit be represented? The position of a mechanical lever. Holes/absence of holes in paper cards. Distinct voltage levels in a circuit or capacitor. Direction of magnetization. Polarization of electric current. Intensity of light. Thickness of a bar code line. Orientation of DNA. A fat guy sweating in the road decked out in hat and vest of ANSI Z535.1 OSHA orange, lowering and raising a sign reading STOP, *etc.* We want something we can easily control, and control quickly, and control without expending much energy or generating much waste. Ideally, we won't consume any energy unless we're changing the value.

Nota bene: we're talking two *states,* not two *values.* CMOS logic at some supply voltage V_{DD} typically interprets 30% V_{DD} or less as a zero, 70% V_{DD} or more as a one; the area between these extremes (40% of the total range) is called the *forbidden zone.* If a voltage in this forbidden zone is sampled, the result is at best implementation-defined. If you're lucky, you get an error. If you're not, who knows? Maybe something catches fire.

Sometimes we want to represent more than two values. If bits are available, combine them into an array—a bitstring—and interpret them as a single entity. With two bits, we can distinguish four states; with three eight; 2^n for n bits.

Katz had seen logic gates, but thought them nothing more than a graphical representation of qualitative logic: if I drink too much Jäger AND smoke too many blunts, the world will spin when I lay down. $\overline{(A \wedge B)}$ could be rewritten via De Morgan's Law as $\overline{A} \vee \overline{B}$. Thus the following two circuits are equivalent:

Logic gates were combined in the next lecture to yield a "half adder." Assume two input bits A and B. Adding them can result in zero, one, or—if and only if both A and B are high—two. But a bit cannot take on the value two, so just as if we had added five to five in base ten, define this sum as a "carry." It requires another output bit to be represented with fidelity: one cannot generally capture the addition of two n-bit values in only n output bits. Our carry bit is equivalent to A AND B. Our sum bit is high if (and only if) one (and only one) of A and B is high, and thus equivalent to A XOR B.

ANSI Z535.1: American National Standards Institute *American National Standard for Safety Colors*
CMOS: complementary metal-oxide semiconductor

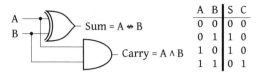

A	B	S	C
0	0	0	0
0	1	1	0
1	0	1	0
1	1	0	1

The full adder has the same outputs as the half adder—a sum bit and a carry bit—but by accepting the third input bit, it allows itself to be combined in sequence. Chain n full adders together, and you can add two n-bit numbers, storing the result in $n + 1$ bits.

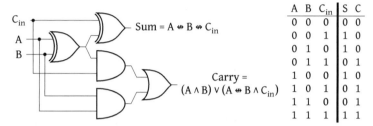

A	B	C_{in}	S	C
0	0	0	0	0
0	0	1	1	0
0	1	0	1	0
0	1	1	0	1
1	0	0	1	0
1	0	1	0	1
1	1	0	0	1
1	1	1	1	1

Static truth tables, the atoms of logic, are thus promoted to arithmetic operations on the integers. But where the truth tables explicitly encoded each result, here we need no further lookups: we're getting a whole range of results for logarithmically many (for we need one full adder, and line, per output bit) investments in logic. The circuit was shown on a slide, and Katz, overcome by its beauty, shed silent tears at his seat. He'd not felt anything like it since abandoning the explicitly spiritual. Varieties of religious experience, indeed.

The computer scientist thus starts upon the road of computer engineering; she can implement her algorithms' logic in hardware she can purchase and wire or solder together. They then pierced the abstraction of the logic gate, revealing the MOSFET: metal-oxide semiconductor field effect transistors. CMOS logic employs p-type and n-type MOSFETs in symmetric complement to implement a low-power, fast logic. We're lucky that NAND and NOR are functionally complete, because they're particularly easy to build with CMOS logic. Recall that the C in CMOS stands for complementary; CMOS circuits are built out of two types of MOSFETs, both of which work as switches: negatively-doped nMOS closes the circuit when the gate voltage is high; positively-doped pMOS closes the circuit when the gate voltage is zero. pMOS is drawn with a circle on the gate line; like that of *e.g.* NAND, it represents inversion.

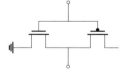

Inverters can be constructed using only a resistor and either a pMOS or an nMOS transistor. The nMOS requires a pull-up resistor across its source; the pMOS requires a pull-down across the drain. These are inefficient devices; whenever the circuit is closed, current flows, even though no new computation is occurring. What is a transistor, though, but a dynamic resistor? Let's place a pMOS transistor across the source of the nMOS, effectively placing the nMOS across the drain of the pMOS. We then bring the same controlling signal into both transistors. The same signal cannot close both transistors; one is guaranteed to be open during steady-state behavior. Current flows only when the value changes, and both transistors simultaneously switch through the forbidden zone. Only when we compute do we pay an energy cost.

From physics, we can establish bounds on how efficiently we can represent a bit. From the Second Law of Thermodynamics we know that entropy of a closed system must always increase. It is believed (the "no-hair theorem") that a black hole can be measured in only three independent ways: mass, electric charge, and angular momentum (and possibly magnetic monopole charge). All other properties of the black hole can be derived from these orthonormal variables. The matter that falls into a black hole has any number of properties—lepton number, baryon number, spin, *etc.* Compliance with the laws of thermodynamics requires the black hole to maximize entropy per unit volume. This implies a fundamental limit on storage density, no matter the media, by the Bekenstein bound:

$$S \leq \frac{2\pi k R E}{\hbar c}$$

An unfortunate result is that the infinite tape of an ideal Turing machine cannot be realized in a finite universe. A happier implication (depending on how one looks at it) is that the finite volume of a brain absolutely can.

Another result regarding ultimate limits of computation is the principle of Landauer. Any irreversible process consumes some conserved quantity (*e.g.* energy or angular momentum), releasing it as waste heat. Certain computational steps are (at least logically) reversible, the most obvious being inversion. Most are not; recall our dyadic operations (and beyond inversion, all reversible functions require ancilla bits). Evaluation of A AND B results in only a single bit, and if that bit is 0, we know only that at most one of the two inputs was 1. Clobbering one of the inputs thus destroys information, and requires a cost (when expressed in energy) of:

$$E \geq k_B T \ln 2$$

As an implication, bits in an isolated natural system are conserved. At 20 °C, this cost is approximately 0.018 eV (2.9 zJ). It is interesting to note that hydrolysis of ATP releases a few dozen zeptojoules as energy of the resulting gamma phosphate, and that this energy is comparable to that necessary to change

---

ATP: adenosine triphosphate $C_{10}H_{16}N_5O_{13}P_3$ adenosine 5′-(tetrahydrogen triphosphate)

protein conformations. Note the dependence on T: this offers a possible resolution to the Fermi Paradox regarding extraterrestrial intelligences: upon becoming sufficiently advanced, civilizations perhaps enter stasis, emerging only when the universe's background temperature drops low enough to enable computation sufficiently cheap as to justify existence.

Analyzing and designing these systems is traditionally the domain of the electric engineer, using her knowledge of signals (impedance matching, attenuation, crosstalk, reflections) and semiconductors (carrier generation, band gaps, Fermi levels). Building them calls upon the armamentarium of materials science, especially the 13.5 nm extreme ultraviolet photolithography of Veldhoven ASML Holding N. V., originally known as Advanced Semiconductor Materials Lithography, the world's foremost producers of EUV tooling (Canon and Nikon are distant seconds). Computer scientists are writing the spells, computer engineers are forging the cauldrons, and ASML makes the petahertz fire with which cauldrons are cast. They're closely aligned with the chemists. Beneath them, lurking always, the physicists.

It was a beautiful structure. You wanted to increment a value a by one. Write it as $a = a + 1$. Compile this human-friendly code down via formal methods, yielding minimized machine code. Schedule this machine code and it is loaded: combinatorial elements whirr into motion, reading new values from memory, into cache and then registers, the processor finally selecting from this sequence an instruction for decode. Underneath, transistors are momentarily enabled to change these values. Beneath them, gated electrons move at a lethargic crawl, orders of magnitude slower than the speed of light in copper or even the speed of electricity in copper, but the resulting updates to the electric field propagate near lightspeed. Sequential elements carrying state transition across forbidden zones; it all shakes and shimmies and it looks like the processor might lose its clocked integrity. Then in the last picoseconds of the cycle latches lock into place, like a gas pump's spinning digits when the tank becomes full. Across the processor's breadth, movement ceases, not with a whimper but with a bang. A new cycle ticks off; the process begins anew, billions of times per second. Trillions of processors worldwide. The human eye blinks in about one hundred milliseconds; in that time, a microprocessor sourced for less than a dollar might take on thirty million distinct states. Barring catastrophic physical failure, it'll do this without error, every second of the day, every day of the year, for years. It made Sherman's dick hard.

Quantum electrodynamics define our best model of the relevant force, one we believe to be pretty much correct. Feynman called it the "crown jewel of physics," but full disclosure: he won a Nobel for his work on it. You could analyze a chip using Dirac matrices and path integrals and the d'Alembertian operator $\Box$ (easily mistaken as a missing glyph the first time one sees it), but I wouldn't recommend it. Thanks to this multilevel tower of abstraction, one can these days set up a web page without even basic knowledge of Maxwell's much-ballyhooed Equations (QED in the ancient, classical limit). Indeed, the majority of working software engineers probably couldn't identify the photon as gauge boson of QED. No more than one of five can provide a usable definition of gauge boson. Interview a hundred frontend developers. Prompt them for the QED Lagrangian. Smart money says not one will produce

$$L = \int \frac{d^4x}{c} \left[-\frac{1}{4\mu_0} F^{\mu\nu}F_{\mu\nu} + \overline{\psi}(i\hbar c\gamma^\mu D_\mu - mc^2)\psi \right]$$

$$D_\mu \equiv \partial_\mu + \frac{ie}{\hbar}A_\mu \qquad x^\mu \equiv (ct, \mathbf{x}) \qquad A^\mu \equiv \left(\frac{1}{c}\phi, \mathbf{A} \right)$$

nor any approximation thereof. Some may have the temerity to question your hiring processes. Take no guff from these swine. "We work in the real world, chief. Lorentz invariance. Curved space. Your bitmaps and Javascript have no place here. Get the fuck out of my office." Request that their recruiter mail them asking, "is your name Cache Miss? Because you're not in our working set." *Mákhesthai khrḕ tòn dḕmon hupèr toũ nómou hókōsper teíkheos;* if you won't keep the gates, who will?

✳ ✳ ✳ ✳ ✳ ✳ ✳ ✳ ✳

On Michael's door in Harrison Hall were quality prints of Gustave Doré's woodcuts and CHURCH OF THE HOMOSEXUAL REDEEMER in heavy jersey font.

Carefully lettered on the door of Sherman Katz in Smith was a proverb of his own recent coinage: CODE STONED. DEBUG SOBER. DOCUMENT DRUNK.

Inside each notebook she purchased, Cathy Mališauskas reproduced Georg von Frundsberg's comment to Martin Luther at *Reichstag zu Worms:* LITTLE MONK, IT IS AN ARDUOUS PATH YOU ARE TAKING.

On Devesh Choudary's monitor was taped a piece of white paper bearing the mysterious animadversion DON'T MISTAKE LACK OF TALENT FOR GENIUS, taken from the liner notes of Type O Negative's *Bloody Kisses.*

All over the Institute, NP != P is written on restroom stall doors. In the tunnel on 3rd Street it is spraypainted two meters tall.

In Howey Physics, an ISO 7010 (*Graphical symbols — Safety colours and safety signs — Registered safety signs*, defined largely in terms of ISO 3864 Part 1: *Design principles for safety signs and safety markings* and Part 3: *Design principles for graphical symbols for use in safety signs)* laser beam warning is affixed to a lab door. Underneath is announced that ISO 16321 (*Eye and face protection for occupational use — General requirements*) eye protection is absolutely required. Another sign warns THIS WILL KILL YOU, AND IT WILL HURT WHILE YOU DIE.

✳ ✳ ✳ ✳ ✳ ✳ ✳ ✳ ✳

On East Campus, a regular sight was a young Materials Science major motoring around in her wheelchair. Said chair was astronomically expensive and by every indication a true boss hoss, with thirteen-inch drive wheels, regenerative braking, and capable of a hair over eight kilometers per hour on level ground. Using an early lithium-iron phosphate battery, it claimed a range over thirty kilometers on a single charge. Nonetheless, it lacked the oomph to take its

---

mákhesthai...teíkheos: μάχεσθαι χρὴ τὸν δῆμον ὑπὲρ τοῦ νόμου ὅκωσπερ τείχεος
The people must fight for the Law as for their city walls. Heraclitus, Fragment 44
Reichstag zu Worms: Diet of Worms

rider up the forbidding Freshman Hill running alongside Bobby Dodd Stadium and separating underclassman dorms from the academic center of campus.

Katz had several times observed chair and rider detouring through the northeastern section of campus dominated by Greek housing. When she approached him going the other way on Techwood Drive one day in December, he flagged her down. "I'm Sherman Spartacus Katz, and you are?"

"Meredith Zaxby. Can I help you?"

"I doubt it. Are you able to take that thing up the hill?"

"No." She sounded wistful. "It won't even let you attempt such an incline."

"Yeah, that seems for the best. So you have to go the long way around?"

"That is correct."

"Would you like to be able to go faster?"

"How?"

"I bet that thing has a governor on it. I'd like to explore its interface to the world. Do you know if it has a CAN bus?"

"What is a CAN bus?"

"A standard network interface for vehicles. It's in cars, planes, pretty much anything with an engine. I might be able to get in there and soup that fucker up for you, if you'd let me try."

"That would be awesome! Have you ever done this before? Is there a chance you're gonna screw up my chair?"

"It'll definitely invalidate the warranty, heh. I cannot guarantee that I will not damage it, but I doubt any damage would be permanent, probably something that can be fixed with a factory reset. I can't say for sure."

"Why are you offering to do this?"

"Well I see you whipping around on that thing, and I'm just like, mang what if she could take off like a little Suzuki or something? It's gotta be a pain in the ass making that huge loop."

"Sherman Katz, everything about this is a pain in the ass. If I felt pains in my ass, which I do not."

Katz laughed loudly. "Well, if you'd like me to try, I can come by your room or you can come by mine or whatever. You should probably get a helmet if I'm able to add any real speed."

Katz's computer, his last to go nameless, was a motley assemblage spray-painted black. It had begun life as a Hewlett-Packard purchased from Sam's Club. Since then, a ragged hole had been cut in the side, through which two hard drives (for a total of four) partially emerged. A large GWAR sticker appeared to be structurally integral, and its cheap Mendocino Celeron 300A (Intel's down-graded Pentium II Deschutes) had only 128 KB of L2 cache. Still, the frontside bus was overclocked from 66 to 100 MHz (this had required placing tape over the B21 pin of its SEPP slot), and the core itself from 300 to 454 MHz. A 92mm Delta fan provided the cooling necessitated by its 2.2V thirst. It couldn't play video games worth a damn, but it was otherwise fast, and it was cheap, and damnit it was *ugly*.

CAN: Controller Area Network
SEPP: Single-Edge Processor Package

After fifteen hours of exploration, much of it spent studying Bosch manuals checked out from the mechanical engineering library, he thought he had it. Brackets held the wheelchair immobile, facilitating exposure of its underside. Its controller's housing had been removed and placed to the side. Alligator clips connected jumper wires to I/O points on its microcontrollers, providing a D-subminiature hookup. A CAN interface plugged into this, and then via USB to his computer. Meredith employed a quadrature encoder to measure rotation of the drive wheels, and hooted, "yeah, that's up 35%!"

Katz whooped and grinned. "I'd definitely get a helmet."

On January's first day of classes, Katz and Bolaño joined her outside her dorm. She'd tested the chair, of course, but not with campus in full bloom. "Godspeed," said Katz, and she motored off to the main thoroughfare.

"Can she sue you if she takes that thing up past its intended velocity and gets thrown out of it?"

"I don't know. I imagine if she gets thrown out of it at ten kilometers per hour she won't be in a position to sue anyone." Katz got quiet for a moment. "I mean, she's got a seatbelt. I hope not, ugh. There she goes!"

Upon reaching Techwood Drive, she opened up the throttle, as it were. The difference between 8 and 10.8 kph might not seem that vast a delta, but on the ground, with the momentum of a solidly constructed wheelchair, it's no small thing. With barbaric yawp Meredith Zaxby took off, feeling for the first time in years the most powerful bitch on the sidewalk, and Katz squealed with delight watching two people leap out of her way to safety. She turned a curve and zoomed out of visibility. Michael Bolaño, impressed, slapped Katz high-five. It had after all been an undeniably righteous hack.

Two years later, Katz befriended a PhD in Paper Science. The Institute of Paper Science was a research organization, imported whole from Wisconsin in 1989. It sat uneasily on the northern edge of West Campus, not yet administratively a part of Georgia Tech, but capable of awarding infrequent graduate degrees. This was the first Paper Scientist he'd met. They'd come together because the older graduate student distilled his own absinthe, quietly importing grand wormwood extract—the monoterpene thujone, illegal in the United States until 2007—from Sweden. Thujone is a competitive antagonist of gamma-aminobutyric acid, opposing in part the effects of alcohol. To Katz, it meant you could drink a delicious anise-flavored high-proof liquor colored like green death itself all night without passing out or losing energy, and he bought it with enthusiasm from the paper scientist in 1.75 L Golden Grain bottles. Poured over ice in fifty-fifty mixture with water, it quickly became his favorite drink, and many nights those years found him ranting powerfully into the morning's early hours, sipping from a tall glass of the Green Fairie, gesticulating with fervor and occasionally spilling some out the sides.

The paper scientist claimed to build his own gliders, cutting them from foam using expensive CNC milling machines. A friend with an IMCO CallAir A-9 and clearance at Chamblee's Peachtree-Dekalb Airport took him up to around two kilometers and detached the tow. He'd flit around as long as the thermals

---

CNC: Computer Numerical Control   CPT: charge, parity, time

let him, and land with a few rough bumps. The planes didn't stand up to much reuse, but the foam he got for free. Katz listened, enraptured, truly amazed. "And you just designed these yourself? That's fuckin' *outstanding*."

＊＊＊＊＊＊＊＊＊

Walking to North Avenue one afternoon, Katz saw Autumn Rohan in a grassy area. It appeared that she'd spilled her bag: she was kneeling, collecting scattered papers and junk. Upon Sherman's hail she looked up briefly and waved, returning to her gleaning. Tiny Autumn was insubstantial save blonde hair of almost pathological length. She was aloof, but not rude; reticent, but not reserved; Industrial Engineering, but known to be competent across the board. He'd only smoked with her once, but she seemed high every time he'd seen her. "What's up, Autumn? Let me help clean up."

She smiled at him. "My bag left the nest too early. One day they're hanging from you; the next they're diving into the lawn." This was typical of Autumn, in that Katz had no idea whether she was making some obscure cultural reference, or speaking in metaphors, or simply talking nonsense. He knelt and began to collect. Almost everything, at least that which remained, was small yellow squares. "Lots of Post-it Notes, Autumn. You using these to study?" He read one: THIS IS YELLOW. This is yellow? What the fuck? He grabbed another. THIS IS YELLOW. Three and four, each inscribed with the same message, down to the heart over the second I.

He found three still stuck together; all three were labeled.

"Here you go Autumn. It was just notes over there. I don't think any blew away. You uhhh studying up on Yellow Engineering or what?"

"Yellow Engineering? What do you mean, Katz?"

"Well your notes all said 'this is yellow' on them. Handwritten. I'm not saying it's strange, but it's not something I see myself doing."

"Oh, not all of them."

"Just the ones I picked up? We can stop talking about this if it's personal or something." This was sperg at its most intense. Katz didn't want a *Rain Woman* situation to develop.

Her laugh was a euphonic trill. "No, not even all the ones you picked up, Katz, silly." She slung her backpack over her shoulder. "Come by Heffner and Armstrong more often. I think Clair is into you." Her movement in flipflops was faster than you'd expect, especially given her height. Not to mention that backpack, damn near as big as she was.

Suddenly she turned, and yelled "Sherman!" She ran over and said, "Hey Brian on West Campus has been out since Monday. You ought bring a few sacks over tonight. You'll definitely move them."

"Thanks dear; I'll do that. Hope to see you. And Clair!"

She nodded and headed back in her original direction. Her arms didn't appear to move when she walked, and her feet were hidden underneath a long skirt. To onlookers she seemed pulled along by barely subterranean magnets.

＊＊＊＊＊＊＊＊＊

Neither Katz nor Bolaño had really considered joining a frat, though both kicked around a good bit during Rush Week, scamming drinks where they could. Rush was officially dry: said drinks were typically had in bedrooms, often directly from bottles. He gathered that there were two big advantages to Greek life: the first, and it was a serious advantage, was arranged and guaranteed access to promiscuous women on the more attractive side of the Technical Institute's bell curve in great breeding mixers (and, it was said, sometimes Agnes Scott and glorious GSU, the latter of which implied Dionysian minimal effort fucking thanks to the loose and easily hot girls with which less Technical universities were awash). Then again, Katz's only tie (his uniform tie from St. Anthony's, complete with school crest) was currently load-bearing and he had no desire to acquire a second, so it was a wash.

The second advantage was their collections of old exams and homeworks, known in the local argot as "word." Few professors put such materials online or made any offer of them, and these hoarded materials were often a serious advantage. There was exactly zero chance of being invited along to one of their brood sow bacchanalia, but keeping up relations with some brothers seemed like it might pay off come exam time. Rooms in the frats were about the same price as dorms, both of which were more expensive than Home Park.

The downsides included the fact that every last frat had a number of glad-handing gormless gasconaders with whom Katz couldn't imagine voluntarily sharing a building, a great deal of bullshit in the form of required activity and socializing, altogether too much cornhole, sure drama within the ranks, and in general all the kind of thing Katz abhorred as an anarchist autist. He heard descriptions of the pledging process and inwardly shuddered. What kind of asshole invited more external regimentation into their life just when you'd managed to throw it off? The ideas of making floats and riding tricycles around campus and sitting on Intrafraternity Councils he immediately dismissed as trifling; likewise unappealing was the association with date rape. In the end, he never seriously entertained the notion because few of the most interesting people he met in those first weeks had any intention of rushing, whereas those who rushed seemed generally to be the kind of normie blasé common fuck he'd hoped to avoid by going to engineering school.

Katz further sounded brothers out about their drug economics, looking to insert himself into the frats' pipelines. It was tricky ground to navigate. A direct approach resulted in null results; frats were officially drug-free zones, and their governors had vested interests in keeping controlled substances out of the house. Even smoking was kept low-key; beyond weed, there seemed little going on in their houses save cocaine and Schedule II/III pharms (primarily Adderall and painkillers). He worked out that most houses had a single dealer inside, operating at small scales. Several seemed to buy weed from Alpha Epsilon Pi, the Jewish house on the corner of Techwood and Bobby Dodd, at the bottom of the Freshman Hill; Katz noted with approval that AEΠ seemed pretty psychoactively forward, sampling gamely from the modern buffet of narcotics. The Phi Kappa Sigma "Skull House" likewise smelled most times of weed, and seemed to be slinging some into the general student body; he regularly converted ΦΚΣ customers. The Kappa Sigs (ΚΣ; Katz was never clear on if and how they were related to ΦΚΣ) smoked broadly, but scored from ΑΕΠ; they had among them a number of cokeheads, and seemed to have that business locked up. So far as he could tell, the sororities bought their few drugs (almost entirely benzos, which they purchased in large sacks of generic pills) from fraternity members exclusively.

✳ ✳ ✳ ✳ ✳ ✳ ✳ ✳ ✳

Katz was righteously pwned at least twice in his first year. The first time was five days in. Down the hall, in the room of one Greg Moyer, he copied from his workstation some MP3s using FTP via Moyer's Internet Explorer 4 (and you'd better believe bitching about it, militantly encouraging Netscape Navigator 3 ("It's way less heavyweight and grody than Navigator 4") and of course a complete switch to Linux). He entered the URL using user:password syntax, `ftp://ssk:roskolnikov420@ssk.resnet`.

Two hours later, he logged into his machine; it began playing Bryan Adams, told him to fuck himself, and logged him out. "What the hell?"

Mark looked over at him sharply, and with real irritation demanded, "Katz, I didn't sign up for Bryan fucking Adams nor the *Robin Hood* soundtrack."

"Yeah I didn't play that, what the fuck?" Again Katz entered his username, `ssk`, and password, `roskolnikov420`. "Everything I Do (I Do It For You)" started afresh in all its horrific saccharine Canadianness. Mark groaned and covered his ears. He climbed into his bunk and hid under a blanket. "Make it stop!"

"What the FUCK?" Katz powered off his speakers and stared, bewildered, at his monitor.

Mark came back out from underneath his bedding, sighing with relief as he scrambled back down to engage Ween's *The Mollusk*. "What's going on over there, Sherman?"

"I log in; it plays Bryan Adams and prints `Fuck you!`, then logs me out."

"This is Linux that does this?"

"I mean, yes, but Linux was not doing this earlier today."

"You should probably run Windows."

In their doorway appeared Greg Moyer. He was six feet even, matching Katz and a little taller than Mark, though he looked taller than the heavier, squatter Katz. He'd played basketball and golf at Westminster, probably Atlanta's most elite private school. Everything about him radiated smooth privilege, especially his casual good looks, tailored clothes, and the shiteating smirk he wore seemingly by default.

"Katz! I didn't have you pegged as a Bryan Adams fan." Moyer broke into a *basso profondo* with rich *vibrato*. "Everything I dooooo..."

"Not another measure." Mark turned Ween up louder. "What the hell is going on here?" He needed to log in if he was to investigate. "Hey Mark, can I use your computer for a second?"

"Are you going to make it play Bryan Adams?"

From the doorway: "it was the summer of sixty-nine!"

FTP: File Transfer Protocol   **basso profondo:** deep bass (vocal range C2–C4)

"Trust fund Westminster fuck, get out of here with that shit." Katz stood at Mark's computer, brought up a Telnet window, and logged into his machine from the other side of the room. He groaned as it printed Fuck you! and logged him out. "Alright, I can reboot and login with init=/bin/sh or single on the LILO command line. Except I'd need to rewrite the LILO configuration file. And to do that, I'd need make a Linux boot floppy. Which would require a Linux machine other than mine. Maybe the guys across the hall?" He looked at Mark.

"Are you asking me? The Management major?"

Moyer leaned in from the doorway and offered Mark a high-five. "Give it up for Management, Campbell!" Mark looked up at Moyer from his seat, held his gaze for a moment, and then shook his head with sad remonstration. Moyer returned to the room's entrance. "Fair enough, fair enough."

Mark turned back to Katz. "I think you ought run Windows. If you're taking my general advice, I'd likewise drop that whole Computer Science thing and take up your white man's burden a/k/a Management."

"You will die a peasant's death." Katz threw himself into his chair, dejected. "How could this have happened?"

Moyer: "It sounds like you got hacked, Katz."

"How could that have happened?"

"Maybe you left your account name and password in someone's browser history like a big dumb idiot."

"Oh! Fuck! You son of a bitch!"

Moyer laughed heartily, and resumed singing as he departed. *"Man, we were killing time, we were young and restless."*

"Moyer! You asshole, what did you do to my box?"

"We need to unwind, I guess nothing can last forever." Moyer retreated into his room, closing the door behind him.

"That motherfucker."

"Are you going to clean it out?"

"No way to do that. A fundamental result in security: once the machine is pwned, the only way forward is to completely reinstall it. Otherwise you're working in an environment the attacker controls, and they can deceive you pretty much arbitrarily. Copy off what data you can, and wipe that fucker."

"I'd think someone who knew so much would know better than to leave their password in someone's browser history."

"Argh." There was no option but to eat all the shit people cared to feed him for a few days. Better that than to be a sore loser. He extracted his Red Hat 5.1 install media from a Case Logic 200-disc CD book, sighed, and set to reinstalling.

In late October, Katz was sitting at his desk reading, and he heard his hard drives begin continuous, loud work. He saw the drive activity light come on and stay there. He furrowed his brow, and was puzzled, but went back to Ralph Ellison. He'd just finished García Lorca's *Bodas de sangre* an hour earlier, and

---

LILO: LInux LOader, an early bootloader
Bodas de sangre: Blood Wedding (1932)

was hoping to work through *Invisible Man* before surrendering to sleep. The light and noise persisted, and suddenly output was printed to the login screen:

```
cron: /usr/bin/pidof: No such file or directory
```

"The fuck?" He attempted to log in, and received:

```
login: /bin/bash: No such file or directory
```

"Uhhh." He rebooted the machine, and it blew up immediately after loading the kernel. After a laborious recovery, he was able to mount his old /home, but at least two thirds of it (mostly MP3s) was missing. He wept for them briefly, but remembered that many of them were 64kbps he'd ripped with an unregistered version of Audiograbber completely lacking hardware correction. He'd learned much since then. He chalked the episode up to random computer madness in the carefree way of eighteen year old morons, hoisted high the black Case Logic book, and set to ripping with Paranoia III.

What had actually happened was that he had been viciously rooted through wu-ftpd, the University of Washington FTP daemon, the same server through which Greg Moyer had owned him in the first week of school. The attacker didn't have Katz's password in his browser cache, but did know a default username and password, set up by the printer spooler. With that foothold, he took advantage of a loose _PATH_EXECPATH variable—a poor choice in default configuration—to raise privileges with site exec. Once that had been done, he simply launched rm -rf /, because he was an asshole. When Katz reinstalled, the same default user and password were added once more, but this time he didn't install an FTP server, and thus wasn't rooted anew when the attacker (one Daniel Wurther, a West Campus junior on academic probation, who now passes from our story forever) came back around a few hours later. The next week he removed all printing server infrastructure, as he had no printer, and with it went the default account. He was learning.

✳ ✳ ✳ ✳ ✳ ✳ ✳ ✳ ✳

By the end of their first year, Katz ran a thriving business on campus, reselling product from Marietta and Dunwoody. He initially kept bulk product in his car, parked on a grassy strip of no man's land behind the frats on East Campus. He had no authority to be parking there, and didn't even know who owned it, or whether it was any kind of official space. The only illumination was from diffuse head- and taillights of perpetual southbound traffic and there were no cameras. One night Bolaño remarked "light grows more intense as cars come closer, and recedes so as its source does, but it's not a Doppler effect."

Katz furrowed his brows, exhaled a cloud, and answered "well no shit." He paused. "Obviously there is a Doppler effect though. But that would just change the frequency of the perceived light, so the color."

Bolaño pursued his own line of thinking. "Were it omnidirectional emission, there would be a simple inverse square law. As the car came towards you, you'd expect an exponential rise in luminance, peaking as it passed you—minimum distance—and then you'd expect an equal exponential drop as it drove off. Assuming isotropic light. But it's highly directional."

"Traffic lights only work due to the slow speed of cars, right?" Katz was likewise lost in his own world. "Red light is seven hundred nanometers let's call it, green five-fitty. That's about point eight, so if you're moving at even a lousy sixty thousand kilometers per second, that light's going to be green. I guess if you've got the tech to do point two c, you can make something work. Hence the bumper sticker, 'if this sticker is blue, you're driving too fast.' Heh. This is cashed." Katz knocks the bowl into his palm and repacks it.

"Wouldn't you need the relativistic Doppler equation at those speeds? So imagine you emit at pi over two, forty-five degrees on either side of the vertical. And sure, you've got something like an inverse-square law for intensity as a function of distance from the emitter within that spherical cone. But rather than a maximum, you would expect the position of minimal distance to be zero light, since you're outside of the sector."

"Inverse-square would only be valid if the light is unimpeded. It's interacting with hella air molecules mang. Some of that is going to come your way. Speaking of coming your way: I want to store the majority of my product in your place. Not buy from you, per se, but keep it with you. You'd of course be compensated."

"I was wondering when you'd suggest that. I've been tempted myself to break into your car and grab it." At Katz's look, Bolaño replies indignantly: "I didn't, obviously."

"My biggest worry is being able to access it whenever I need access it."

"I'll be moving out of the dorms in two weeks. The new place has its own entrance that's just mine. You can have keys."

"And it's cool to just come in whenever?"

"I mean, I'd knock."

"Should I call ahead of time?"

"That would be cool, but it shouldn't be necessary?"

"Fair enough. What kind of money do you want?"

"Ten percent seems reasonable."

"Ten percent of profit?"

"Net."

"Fuck off."

"It's my understanding that you smoke the majority of your profit. What kind of number would you expect 10% of profit to be?"

"Ummm, presmoke?" Bolaño nods. "Maybe $200 a week? And I smoke about $100 of that."

"So you're offering me $40 a month to expose myself to multiple felonies on possession, or a breakin. I'll have to refrain, sorry."

But volumes, and profits, steadily grew.

✳ ✳ ✳ ✳ ✳ ✳ ✳ ✳

Katz was a TA for CS2430 by the end of freshman year. One of his students, a Chris Gillett from Broken Arrow, Oklahoma, had stopped turning in weekly assignments after the first. Sherman didn't know whether this kid thought them some kind of best friends or what, but he had no intention of passing the Sooner on without work. Around midterms he knocked on Gillett's door. There was no response, but it was unlocked. He pushed it open and Chris was there, headphones on, eyes locked on his monitor where Quake II's Bitterman rocket-jumped around the arena. "Hey Chris mang, can you hear me?"

Louder. "Chris! Hey mang return to the planet for a minute."

Katz tapped him on the shoulder, prompting a curse and a nervous leap. "Oh fuck! Oh hey Katz. What's up? Oh man, you fucked up my game."

"I'm sorry about that buddy but hey we need to talk. You know I'm your CS2430 TA, right? You remember the first two weeks of the semester, when I was like, 'hey Chris you bitch you're in my 2430 section!'? And the first two recitations when you showed up? And when I came in here the second week and was like, 'Uh-oh Gillett you fucked up!' because you got a thirty on the first assignment? Out of one hundred?"

"Yeah."

"Soooo what are your plans here? Because you're carrying an average now of ten. Again, that's out of one hundred. And every time I look in here, you're playing this fucking game, and you seem really good at it, but I don't understand how it helps you develop ANSI C skills. I know you live next door, and I'm worried that perhaps this has made you think that, like, I would report your grade as not a ten but perhaps some passing score."

"Oh no man, no worries there. I'm going to fail that class."

Katz evaluates him critically for a moment. "Gillett, you can still drop the class. It's required; dropping it puts you back a quarter; but back a quarter without an F is way better than with one. You can probably even still pass the class if you unfuck yourself. What's wrong?"

"Nothing's wrong, I'm just not cut out for this computer science shit."

"Well even if you're boarding the M-train, you still don't want the F."

"I'm riding this quarter out and heading back home. I had a good job at the Best Buy all through high school, and I can walk back into it."

Sherman's face betrays his horror. "You're going to drop out with the plan of working at Best Buy?"

"Yeah, I had a good time there. I'll become a manager eventually. Living in Oklahoma is cheap. I paid twenty-thousand dollars to find out I don't like programming; I just like video games."

"That's the saddest fucking thing I've ever heard, dude."

Chris looked up at him finally, with unhappy resignation. "Sad for you, maybe. I don't get this shit, man. I'm not smart enough, and it makes me miserable to try. What I'm good at is Quake II, and EverQuest, and selling modems."

"Godspeed, Chris. Best of luck in the blue shirt." He'd never seen such a pathetic surrender. He tried to empathize, but could not.

7 y'all've any more of that vee-cee?

Katz and Bolaño started middle school in 1992, matriculating in 1998. America and the world had changed drastically in those six years. In 1992, the West was slowly emerging from recession. The Soviet Union had dissolved, plunging her republics and especially Russia into the economic and existential poverty so elegantly chronicled in Alexievich's *Vremya sekond khend*. Japan, so fearsome throughout the 1980s (in 1989, Japan was home to 32 of the largest fifty companies in the world), saw its equities collapse 60% as the *Ushinawareta Jūnen* commenced. On September 16, 1992, the pound sterling collapsed, necessitating Britain's immediate withdraw from the European ERM. The recession as measured by growth ended in 1991, but job losses accelerated (defense drawdowns following the Cold War's end, and large drops in construction due to overbuilding in the 1980s); it was called a "jobless recovery."

Then everything got better, quickly. Widespread adoption of microcomputers paired with rational management led to astounding leaps in American worker productivity. The oil prices that had doubled following Iraq's incursion into Kuwait were back down to preinvasion levels, and sometimes lower; other countries had increased their output to pick up the slack from Kuwait's inaccessible Rumaila and Burgan and Iraq's sanctioned Kirkuk, Halfaya, and Majnoon superfields. The Four Tigers continued to enjoy their good fortune, and a PRC choked by decades of Maoist nonsense began to rise. Deng Xiaoping put *Gǎigé kāifàng* back into play (it had been on hold since 1989's *liù-sì zhènyā* in Muxidi and along Chang'an Avenue). Jiang Zemin and the Third Generation reinforced and extended his policies, guiding China towards a Confucian *Xiǎokāng Shèhuì* and ultimately its twenty-first century renaissance. Globalization might have been shitty for jobs, but everything sure got cheaper.

Alan Greenspan, "Maestro" according to Bob Woodward's 2001 panegyric, cut interest rates deeply—thrice in the mid 90s alone. America had money again, and looked around with an eye to spend it.

Computers! In a few short years, the fraction of families with a personal computer rose from fifteen to thirty-five percent.

Internet! Eternal September! Prodigy, CompuServe, GEnie, fledgling shell providers (*e.g.* EarthLink, MindSpring, NETCOM, Random Access...), BBS gateways in their dwindling days of relevance, and of course the AOL behemoth rose to supply a hungry population uuencoded porn and A/S/L. AOL 3.5" disks and later CDs were produced in disconcerting numbers, incomprehensible really; they could not be avoided. It was not uncommon to shake multiple AOL CDs from a single magazine. They came unrequested in grocery store bags and Blockbuster rentals. AOL CDs were delivered by the Postal Service; AOL CDs were distributed in movie theaters. Landfills were devoted to acres

---

Vremya sekond khend: Время секонд хэнд Secondhand Time (2013)
Ushinawareta Jūnen: 失われた10年 Lost Decade   **ERM:** Exchange Rate Mechanism
PRC: People's Republic of China   **Gǎigé kāifàng:** 改革开放 Reform and Opening-Up
liù-sì zhènyā: 六四鎮壓 June Fourth crackdown
Xiǎokāng Shèhuì: 小康社会 moderately prosperous society

of never-used AOL installation media. It by no means impossible to collect a half-dozen pieces of trash from America Online running the day's errands. Sometimes they fell onto the street upon opening a car door. As the recession faded, America added millions of jobs, and at least half seemed related to the industry of producing, packaging, delivering, and disposing of unused AOL CDs and their thirty free hours.

Equities! The 1997 Taxpayer Relief Act lowered the top rate of capital gains taxes from 28% to 20%, and the 15% rate to a mere 10%. It furthermore introduced the income-restricted, tax-advantaged Roth IRA. America's middle class was prodded back towards Wall Street, and after years of boring bonds fell again in love with the more speculative equities. Losing money in America's massive bull markets the rest of that decade was no easy task. Venture capital, dwarfed through the 1980s by leveraged buyouts as a path to big money, could boast only three gigadollars across the industry in 1983, and only four in 1994, but began to ramp up voraciously.

What K Street is to lobbyists, what Broadway is to theater, what Wall Street is to finance—what Fleet was to British journalism at least until the 1986 Battle of Wapping—Sand Hill Road is to VC. What was once a cow path eventually connected El Camino Real and I-280 through western Silicon Valley, and runs through Palo Alto, Menlo Park, and Woodside, always keeping Stanford close. Kleiner Perkins and Sequoia both established offices in 1972. Very few of the largest tech companies (Oracle and Microsoft, both launched in the back half of the 1970s, are exceptions) grew to their size without money from SHR. In 1991, one point five gigadollars were committed to the tech sector by venture capital. In 2000, VC poured *ninety* gig into tech.

It was the Boom: a golden age, one which would last forever.

✳✳✳✳✳✳✳✳✳

For two years at the Institute of Technology, Katz and Bolaño could do little wrong. They took six or seven classes each semester despite TAing, and rarely took out less than a B. Neither cared about their GPA much beyond what was necessary to retain scholarships and good standing, and weren't about to throw in long hours for grades if the material lacked sufficient intrinsic interest. Both made it a point of pride never to complain about grading or assignments, nor to ask for exceptions. If something was missed, it was missed. They got their fundamentals down cold; they studied what they found interesting; they expended minimum necessary energy otherwise. They stormed up and down the class newsgroups and mailing lists, answering student questions, augmenting and correcting posts from TAs, posting deep insights and provocative thought experiments. Every week, they developed skills both in class and outside, in their own experiments.

Bolaño got really into SMT solvers and ILP engines, and for some weeks claimed that they "were two different ways of looking at the same problem."

El Camino Real: the royal road   Palo Alto: tall stick
SMT: satisfiability modulo theories   ILP: integer linear programming

No other undergraduates really knew SMT solvers nor ILP algorithms well enough to contest this, though Katz once remarked, punctuating his words with a cigarette, that "just because NP-complete problems can be reduced to one another doesn't mean you solve maximum cuts the same way you do direct Hamiltonian cycles."

Bolaño replied with some malice that this was "only because you solve them, as it were, with incomplete heuristics" and that "an optimal exact solution would look the same for both."

Katz pointed out that Karp reductions were polytime and had nothing to say about optimal possible implementations.

Bolaño retorted that the equivalence was obviously based on more than just Karp reductions, or his conjecture would be true for all NP-complete problems, to which Katz replied, well, prove your conjecture then.

Katz bounced crazily around for awhile. He latched onto automata theory like a man possessed, and his first major open source software release was a library for architecture-adaptive regex matching using Glushkov and Thompson automata, SIMD and parallelism within a register, and the Method of Four Russians. Microarchitecture got him hot for awhile, but then it was all compilers by his second year. He disappeared for two weeks solid; when he was next seen, gcc had much better C99 support. Then he was digging into the core building blocks of the UNIX environment, rooting around in GNU and BSD libc and the POSIX cores of both kernels.

Fall 1999, the first year of semesters, he signed up for Honors Probability (Bolaño had taken it the previous fall). The professor, an almost spherical postdoc from CalTech who seemed at all times high, opened the class by saying "undergraduate probability is stupid. We're going to do measure theory. Is anyone unfamiliar with Lebesgue integration?" Katz looked around, knowing that he'd never done functional analysis, and pretty certain that no one else had, either. Thus began fifteen weeks of σ-algebras, Borel sets, and stochastic diffeqs, but then also Markov chains, martingales, and queuing theory.

* * * * * * * * *

By the beginning of 2000, at the apex of the Boom, demand for software engineers was such that they were readily plucked from undergraduate programs, especially by aggressive and unorthodox startups. The undergraduate summer internship was not yet in vogue (these really took off after 2010); those that did exist were typically offered by academia. If one wanted to work, one simply worked. Two masters students graduated that semester, Uri from Computer Science and Parker from Civil Engineering. The latter married another civil engineer, Tainara, herself the youngest daughter of an esteemed immigrant Brazilian civil engineer running his own thriving practice based out of Buckhead. This father-in-law placed great value on entrepreneurship as the gate to true success, and encouraged, almost goaded, his new son to launch a startup, promising to place two million at his disposal (no such offer was even considered for his daughter). He mentioned this to his friend Uri, an Israeli full of ideas, one looking to start his own company in the nascent field of network security. While not in Katz's recitation section, he'd known him on the class newsgroups. "If we can get this undergrad Katz," he urged, "we'll be in good shape. And he'll know other people that are good."

"How old is he? You said he's an undergraduate?"

"How would I know, Parker? I doubt more than twenty."

"That's an awfully young kid to build a company around."

"Do you want someone young and hungry and brilliant, or someone senior and bullshit? They call this kid Sherman TFM Katz, as in RTFM, Read the Fucking Manual—he's the fucking manual. Our funds are limited, Parker! Limited! We can't outbid large companies. The only people we'd be able to hire away from them, they are their shitpeople, people of the shittiness."

Katz had stopped TAing and given up his Visual BASIC job, having decided the latter insufficiently leet for a hacker of his growing stature. The TA role simply didn't pay enough to be worth the time required on campus (Katz was by this time living in Home Park), and he had grown weary of the shameful begging of his fellow students. Each quarter he received emails with complaints and mendicancy he could scarcely believe, degradations of the ego and soul his pride would have never allowed. Early on, he replied, "if you didn't want the grade, you ought have dropped the class." By his second year, he simply deleted such emails as they arrived.

It furthermore seemed to bring out something bestial from within him. That first semester of the first year of semesters, a gaggle of CS majors stumbled in seeking weed. Among their number was one of his students, and Katz merrily cried out, "Aaron Spengler, come on down!" He packed an initial bowl for the crew writ large and encouraged general consumption. "Y'all know this motherfucker is my student in CS2430, right?" His grin was maniacal, predacious, that of a pelagic shark darting to the surface. "Aaron, you did pretty well on the last homework, 70 out of 100, not too bad."

When one of his friends had suggested, "we ought go down to the Deck and pick up," Aaron had not understood it to mean his TA. He had been caught off guard, and is now already uncomfortably high, and certainly wasn't expecting his class performance to be a subject of discussion. Katz appears definitely wired on something; on reflection, he always does. Aaron Spengler is no man's cowed bitch, however, and is willing to scrap. "Yeah, I don't know, I thought that 70 kinda bullshit, since you want to talk about it right now." The bowl comes to him again, and as he hits it he stares Katz down.

"Really! Let's grade your latest right now, then."

Spengler's look is one of hate. "Go for it."

Katz takes orders as he goes through a stack of printouts. Assignments are run through a set of unit tests (some of which are made available to the class, some of which are not), and TAs print these results, along with the submitted source code. Unlike the Java of CS1502, the C of a given assignment is typically all in one file, making it in Katz's approbative opinion significantly easier to grade. The verbosity and prolix boilerplate of Java offends him, and always will. All those `Factories` and `.toString()`ing and `.equals()` and even the entry `main()` method with its `public static void` where bare `main()` would have sufficed. The `void` there raises from Katz a further rash—what kind of horseshit language doesn't let you return a status code to the caller from `main()`?

"Alright, let's look at this first problem."

Implement `ssize_t utf8len(const char* u)`, returning the number of UTF-8 bytes in the NUL-terminated string u (not including NUL), or `(ssize_t)-1` on invalid input.

Valid input contains no more than SSIZE_MAX bytes, and NUL.

Assume POSIX.1-2001 and C99, and that the caller has successfully initialized a UTF-8 locale with `setlocale(LC_ALL, "")` and an appropriate LANG environment variable.

"Pretty simple. Well-specified."

"Yeah it didn't seem that hard. Why did it make the point of allowing us to assume a POSIX environment?"

"Because as of ANSI C99 `ssize_t` is not a part of ANSI C?"

"Oh. But `size_t` is?"

"Yes? Do you not know your basic data types?" Titters from his crew. Brynne coughs from behind the bong, coughs again, and fails not to laugh at this absurd belligerence.

"I don't know which ones are POSIX vs. ANSI, I guess."

"Doesn't that seem like useful information?"

"I guess so, man."

The room is filling with smoke. Katz's four machines add a good deal of heat and noise. Thankfully, he doesn't pay for power. "So I would hope everyone in this room knows the function that will sit at the core of ours?" No one in the room seems to know said function. "Oh my. Spengler, you just did this homework. What function is it?"

Spengler looks by this point distinctly uncomfortable. "Do we really want to go through this right now? I'm pretty high and don't think I'm making the best impression."

Katz had been doing a little cocaine before the group arrived, a rare thing for him, and is full of fire and fury. He mistakes the attitude of the group, and thinks they're calling for more. In truth, they're mostly horrified. "You questioned my grading in front of all our friends, mang. Let's fuckin' do this."

"Fine motherfucker. Umm the core function we call is m-b-r-something. Let me see my code." He grabs it from Sherman. "`mbrtowc()`."

Katz comes around behind Spengler, and runs his finger down the hard copy. "Zorn! *Was ist das?* You pass NULL as the state argument to `mbrtowc()`!"

Palpable fear. "Yes. It worked for my tests and the tests y'all put up."

Katz rolls demon eyes. "Spengler, did you perform any testing such that another thread was simultaneously calling `mbrtowc()`?"

"What? No? Why would I do that?"

"Well, it might have helped you discover that your code was pathetically fucked when another thread does that. `mbrtowc()` requires per-context state to be supplied as that `mbstate_t` argument. Passing `NULL`, as you've so blissfully done, is unsafe in concurrent contexts."

"But I didn't have concurrent contexts! I have only one thread!"

"But it was clearly a library function that you were implementing. A lack of thread-safety is a glaring flaw in such a general-purpose function, especially when it can be provided so easily. I'm afraid I can't accept this as correct."

"Well how much are you taking off?"

"Spengler. Your code engages in unsafe and undefined behavior. You get a zero on the problem. The other two problems use this, so they're zeroes also."

"You're giving me a zero?!"

"I mean, would you prefer I go design a bridge with your shitty thread-fucked garbage code? Put it on the space shuttle? Here you go, *Atlantis,* and make sure no two astronauts ever do anything at the same time. Nah, this is shit, you get a zero, do better."

"That assignment took me three days, working almost ten hours a day."

"That's ridiculous. I could have knocked this entire assignment out in an hour, hour and a half. You need more practice." Katz exhales a phenomenal cloud. "Lay off the dope; it's wrecking your head."

Cruel laughter. Spengler looks apoplectic. "Fine, let's see you do it."

"I thought you'd never ask. I'd love to. Whaddya say, folks, can I do this problem in less than a minute? Does anyone have a watch to time it? Fuck, we're computer scientists, we'll just run `sleep 60` in another terminal." He takes his seat before his terminal. "Wait! The people want a show! How about...blindfolded?" The group murmurs excitedly—this is something new.

Ctrl+Alt+F1 to the first console, login, Ctrl+Alt+F2, login. There he types `sleep 60`, but does not press Enter. Katz whips off his shirt and ties it around his head. "I used to be able to beat the first eleven fights of *Mike Tyson's Punch-Out!* blindfolded. Let's see if I've still got it." Darkness. Enter. Sixty seconds remain. Ctrl+Alt+F1 back to the first console. `cat > a.c`. Enter. "I'm gonna just blast this stuff down without whitespace. Whitespace is for bitches with eyes. Mine is Mason Word and Second Sight, and, like, what Bog sends." He speaks the code aloud as he types, his keystrokes setting off machine gun staccato CLACKs from the beige IBM Model-M, forgoing even indentation:

```
#include<wchar.h>
#include<stdlib.h>
ssize_t utf8len(const char* u){
mbstate_t m = {0}; size_t r = 0;
do{ wchar_t w; size_t s = mbrtowc(&w, u + r, MB_CUR_MAX, &m);
if(s == (size_t)-1 || s == (size_t)-2) return -1;
else if(s == 0) return r;
r += s; }while(1); }
```

"And so it links..."

```
int main(void){ return 0; }
```

He smashes Ctrl+d to generate an EOF, removes his blindfold, and invokes `gcc -Wall -O2 a.c`. The compiler runs like a gentle wind, producing no warnings.

Ctrl+Alt+F2 to check and...yep, our timer has not yet expired. "Woot! Under sixty seconds."

One of the group says, "dude, I was timing that, and I counted thirty-three seconds. Holy shit." Another asks, "but does it work?"

Katz's smile is all radiance. "It works." He looks at poor Spengler. "Even if some asshole calls things from another context." His spirit is full in his chest; he feels pure, and clean, in superb health. He is moving like a tremendous machine. His is a primal and intense arousal; he'd like to fuck something, even if only for purposes of thematic flourish.

But young Spengler (technically older than Katz, but they were all young) understandably seethed, and dropped the class within a week, and sent Katz a justifiably pissed off email with no shortage of hard words. It embarrassed Katz terribly to reflect on the ugly episode, and he figured he was lucky to have avoided administrative trouble—props to Spengler for not being a snitch. Katz had gone to Aaron's house on the other side of Home Park about a month after the semester ended, apologized, and handed through the door an ounce, $300 worth of transactional relief of the conscience. Aaron hadn't forgiven him, per se, but he did say "thanks" upon taking the sack, and had invited Katz to his party that April. It had been a pretty dope evening, and Katz laughed uneasily and called himself an asshole when Aaron told the story.

✳ ✳ ✳ ✳ ✳ ✳ ✳ ✳ ✳

The leet companies, the Borlands and Suns and SGIs (then still owners of the Cray name), the DESRESes and Tradebots, the Getcos and HRTs, even poor uncool Microsoft with its reliable existence and monopolistic practices and generous stock grants, still generally wanted college graduates. Feelers extended from Lotus and Cisco and ArsDigita and Home Depot were fundamentally uninteresting; Katz met them with *mokusatsu*. The startups, however, had more intriguing value propositions. The truly insane salaries, the baseball player money, weren't much of a thing until 2010 (and would never match what you could pull down at a trading shop), though even by 2005 a recent grad could expect $125,000 at Google or Netflix. As of 2000, seventy-five large was still a respectable salary fresh out of coders' school. Early employees were talking half a percent or a full percent of ownership. If your company made it, you were set for life. If it didn't, you were a bit older, hopefully a bit wiser, and had suffered little beyond punishing schedules and the opportunity cost of time.

Uri and Parker approached Katz December 2000, an opportune time. He was missing the regular TA paychecks. Drug profits were about two thousand a month, covering consumption of food and intoxicants both, but contributing little to rent. Clientele, almost entirely students at GT and GSU, had largely departed for unknown and varied hinterlands; revenue would be severely impacted until their return. His upcoming semester offered six classes of perceived drudgery, things like Numerical Analysis, a mandatory health class, and the maligned Software Engineering, an oppressive and obsolete dive into

---

HRT: Hudson River Trading
mokusatsu: 黙殺 "silence killing" to reject with silent contempt

the details of the waterfall model. He yearned to operate beyond the meager scope of class projects, at timescales longer than the semester, evaluated by the market rather than picayune professors.

"So I'll be running the technical team?"

"Well, Uri will be CTO, but he'll be looking to you for technical solutions. You're the *Top Gun* coder here, not him." Flattery still gets you everywhere.

"And I get a full 1% ownership? You can't dilute that down later? It's preferred equity?"

"It is preferred equity." Preferred equity doesn't mean protection against dilution, but it's not Parker's fault that Katz is throwing around definitions without knowing their meanings. Carefully, he adds "Note that preferred equity does not necessarily mean governance rights."

"Ahhh I don't wanna fuck around in board meetings anyway. I can write this in C or C++, no Java bullshit? And we're doing it all on Linux? I won't need a Windows workstation? I'm not down for that."

"There will be a Windows component, an agent for customer workstations using GINA to talk to our local server, but other than that, no Windows. The GUI will be written in Java."

"But I needn't touch the GUI?" Katz makes his face one of disgust.

"Not at all. We'll hire someone for that. We want you to focus on building the fastest, best network IPS in the world."

"I know a great Java guy we can pick up. Who else is building one?"

"Most companies have IDS products. To do IPS you have to sit in the middle of the traffic, so that you can block individual packets. That means you have to keep up with the wire rate, a full gigabit. Most people can't do that without ASICs. They run a tap to a server running the IDS, and whatever it misses, it misses, and it cannot filter traffic."

"I guess it could do RSTs and ICMP interruptions—"

"But those would be after-the-fact."

"Sure. Is it really that hard to push a gig?"

Uri laughs. "It's hard to push a gig through a PC even if you're not doing anything with it."

Katz smiles. "Well, we'll see about that. What about salary? You really can't unass another twenty-five large? I was really hoping my first fulltime job would be a clean six figures."

"We don't have the money right now to do that, but you can expect big salary increases once we start generating revenue." A tale as old as time. "Besides, you want to focus on the exit. If we sell at three-hundred million, that's three million clean for you, minimum. And you'll be getting more stock each year as part of your bonus." Meaning don't expect much cash bonus.

"And we can expect three-hundred megs?"

"Sherman, we can probably expect more than that. Acquisitions in this sector sometimes run upwards of a billion. We're not doing this company for a

---

GINA: graphical identification and authentication
IPS: Intrusion Prevention System   **IDS:** Intrusion Detection System
RST: [TCP] reset   **ICMP:** Internet Control Message Protocol

few lousy million." December 2000 was still within the shadow of the Boom, not yet irrevocably committed to the Bust, and it's likely that Uri and Parker actually believed this.

Katz is barely twenty, and sold. "One thing. I still want to finish my degree. So I'll have to be able to go to class."

"Can you get them all on Tuesdays and Thursdays or something?"

Laughter. "Dudes, I'm taking six classes. They're all over the place."

"Do you think you can take six classes and work full time?"

In one of the greater miscalculations of his life, Katz replies almost breezily, "oh yeah, sure, no problem. Classes are, you know, classes."

Katz learned some things over the next year. When people—dozens of people—depend on you, letting them down is more emotional toil than merely letting down yourself. You can retake a class, but not a sale. If management is pitching bullshit to investors and customers, management is pitching bullshit to employees. Salespeople pitch bullshit all the livelong day, and can be safely relied on to be without a fucking clue in general, promising things you can't, shan't, and/or won't do. Vendors and partners pitch bullshit. Résumés are vectors for bullshit at scale. Bad hiring is death. It's easier to personally give more hours than to hire well. You're footing the bill for a candidate's hotel room. They steal the hair dryer. The hotel will notice that it is missing, and you will be billed, this despite gaining at no point use of the hair dryer in question. Teams of two or three people, four max, are the only chance (though hardly sufficient) for conceptual integrity and elegant design. Unobserved systems tend by default towards entropy and collapse. Customers generally have no idea what they're doing (a shocking fraction of his early support cases came down to misconfigured client site DNS). When development is subject to customer whims, product scope becomes unbounded. Building a company is harder work than he had imagined possible; building a compelling, capable product from the ground is incredibly hard work; carrying that product forward while supporting active customers is harder still. Technical merit doesn't decide who wins in the market, though that doesn't mean technical incompetence won't sink you. Startups are acquired less often for revenue than because big companies no longer know how to build compelling products. Even if you're determined and capable and full of sacrifice, if you allow all this to weigh on you, you'll become a venomous cunt, and it can destroy the enterprise. If you put all of yourself into the company, you lose everything else around you, and one day find yourself without any external support structure. Your external support structure means more than you think. Nothing—only nothing—is easy.

There are of course exceptions.

Once he bought in, school never stood a chance. His absenteeism had been thorough before; it became now profound. Katz had been all his life slow to start a new labor, but once involved, he clung to it like a barnacle. Once absorbed in the sweet song of code, blasting the Chemical Brothers or NoFX or the *Judgment Night* soundtrack, little could move him, let alone the drive down to campus for an hour and a half of Networking II—was he not building the

---

DNS: Domain Name System   **ARQ:** automatic repeat request

network for real all day long? Alas, fluency with UNIX network programming and the Linux kernel doesn't translate to the math of ARQ protocols nor TCP congestion control, and these classes were no jokes, and six finals cemented a flat 1.0 for the semester, rocking him all the way to Academic Probation.

Katz scheduled "only" five classes the following Fall, with predictable results. By December he had twice freaked out badly at work, and slit his wrists one anguished Saturday night. He went to sleep expecting never to rise, but woke up ten hours later with the blood already staunched, his head a rage of hangover, the bed looking like swine had been slaughtered. His back felt stung by a thousand bees. Turning on the light, he beheld a shattered mirror, and remembered smashing it ala *Apocalypse Now*'s opening scene. He'd later extended himself on the floor—plus, apparently, some amount of broken glass. "Well, fuck." Brynne popped up on AIM: What's going down today? <3.

```
lots of blood in the room
What?
i looked in my wallet, and it was full of blood
Do I need to come over there?
lots of glass, too. something of a Circe evening.
I'm going to come over there.
for the love of god bring cigarettes you are an angel
```

She arrived. She beheld the glass. She beheld his back. She beheld his tenebrose face, clucked, set to sweeping up the glass, and said nothing about his messes of wrists, because what could be said, really?

"A rough night, then? Are we doing better today?"

"Yeah. Mainly irritated that I'll get such a late start to code."

"You can't let that bother you. You need to take better care of yourself. You should probably get stitches for those," pointing to his sanguine forearms.

"Bah, I'll be fine. They're already scabbing over. I have an extremely high constitution." She plucks glass from his back, dabbing at the wounds with rubbing alcohol. "Does that hurt?"

"Of course it hurts; it's glass and isopropanol. Thank you though. For removing it. I feel stupid."

"Well, it looks like you were being pretty stupid."

"Thanks babe. Let's rip some bong hits. What are you doing today? You wanna chill out and work here while I work? Then go get some drinks?"

Katz doesn't change his work habits, but nor does he wear sleeves as he heals, nor bandages. He makes no concession to good taste or even hygiene; if you're going to come to Sherman Katz's desk and ask whether some feature is done, or sit next to him in a rare appearance in class, or even buy weed, you're going to see the ragged cuts running from radiocarpal up along the radial artery as you do so. Those who inquired got a deadpan, "I had a bad evening, been pretty stressed recently, thanks for asking," that inevitably left them haunted and in a little awe.

Then maniacs registered their displeasure with elements of American foreign policy by flying Boeing 767s into the Trade Centers, and Enron happened, and WorldCom, and Arthur Andersen was suddenly just *gone*, man, and the Boom had well and truly turned Bust, and the faucet that had poured forth so much money dried up. Three quarters of engineering—most of them Katz associates—were fired in one go in the 2002's gloomy winter, leaving only four. By that time Sherman was taking no classes, having moved from Academic Probation into Academic Drop/Dismissal. Unlike his wrists, this he played close to the vest. The news came to him in a bulk email. He read it, and wept for a few moments, and returned to coding. His startup, once employing forty people, was back down to eight; it seemed they might any day close up shop.

In the end, they came through, and grew once more, larger than they had ever been, due mainly to Katz's heroics. In 2003 Katz approached Uri and cashed in, demanding to be allowed to go finish his undergraduates, and this time intending to do it right. "The only way I can possibly get two degrees while working fulltime here, with all my old fervor and struggle, is to work from home. By default I will no longer be coming into the office." This was a rare thing in 2003, almost unheard of. But the company owed Katz, and they gave in. Katz executed the necessary petition to rejoin the student body. It was made clear to him that this would be allowed only once. Shortly before turning twenty-three, he found himself back on campus, older than nine out of ten undergraduates, feeling a life of responsibilities and experience beyond them.

He juggled things carefully, and managed to do well. Whenever a class began to break bad, he dropped it, overscheduling by at least one class per semester in expectation of this maneuver. He was several times able to commingle work and assignments; for his Embedded Systems final project, he did nothing more than bring in one of his company's boxen. When his pubescent lab partner in Biology fucked around, Katz ambushed him outside the building the next week. Katz threatened the child's life and the child's parents' lives, and the boy's eyes were like those of a seal falling prey to an orca, wholly convinced this madman and his stink of Newports would be his last impressions. But work always won out in the end; his eyes remained on the prize of however many millions, now that they once again seemed likely.

An increasingly unhappy It was during his first semester back that Katz found methamphetamine, and with alacrity switched to it from dextroamphetamine. No one does meth very long without becoming addicted, and so it proved in this case, rather quickly all told. First he used it to pull allnighters, then the occasionally necessary twonights or threenights. He found it helped him think so much better that he quickly started beginning each waking period with a tiny line (it no longer made much sense to speak of days and nights), then a line that was not so tiny, and within a few months he was waking up and putting out a serious rail. Katz waited for the bill to be presented, but when none seemed to be in the post, he freely accepted this new state of things. "Erdős," he never tired of reminding Bolaño, "did amphetamines all his life, and did good math until he died. At 83, mind you."

"Yeah? What kind of amphetamines?"

"Records from that era are spotty."

"I don't know a single person who does meth and has their shit together. Do you? Even one?"

"You don't know them because it's in their disinterest to tell you they do meth, because they know it's demonized."

"It's demonized because everybody who does it ends up a tweaker, a creature never loved by God."

But then it was the summer of 2005 and Katz was invited to walk, a tale related earlier. At twenty-five he was in the best shape he'd been in since days of high school ball, the meth having burnt off the thirty pounds he'd put on in his first trip through school. He woke, hit a line, and ripped off fifty pushups and two hundred situps. He walked everywhere, wearing basketball shorts and combat boots. He established a regular sleeping schedule: forty hours awake, ten solidly dormant, a little more than thirty hours of sleep a week.

It was all for naught. Not long after graduating, one of the employees let go years before hit him up, suggesting he come to another Atlanta network security startup, not quite a rival but definitely working in the same sector. Katz replied without interest, but his friend cajoled and badgered and eventually Sherman agreed to talk to their CTO, if they could meet late some night at the Highlander. Katz waited in the back corner, unsure whether anyone would actually show up, and eventually spotted a man of style, one sporting a tailored suit, a tie, and a black beret. He was a brash Louisianian with Ghanan heritage, a PhD in CS out of GT after an undergraduate in chemistry at Morehouse. Copernicus Law was a force in Atlanta's startup scene, and a natural leader among its growing community of African-American technologists.

They got along well, and the CTO matched him easily drink for drink. He asked what Katz was making now; Katz replied with a figure ten thousand beyond his actual $95,000, and Copernicus laughed, offering $150,000. Sherman had just been offered $130,000 by Google, a heady sum. Still, he stuck with his people. "I don't know. They let me go to school and work from home. I've been there since the beginning, and am untouchable. I could show up at the office with a bandanna tied around my scrotum while my wang hangs free, and no one would bat an eye. I don't have anyone telling me what to do, and won't, ever. I'd have to come to Alpharetta, up shitty GA-400, and have people sign off on my shit. And you're saying I'd get very limited equity."

Copernicus chuckled loudly and replied, "limited, but it would actually be worth something, unlike whatever you've got right now."

Ahhh, clearly Dr. Law hadn't understood his situation. "Sir, I own two point five percent at this point. It's worth plenty."

Copernicus met his eyes. "How much, do you think?"

"Say we sell at a billion. That's twenty-five million I make."

"How would you sell for a billion?"

"I mean...I don't know how valuations work, really, but that's the size of deals I see happening."

"But why would anyone make a deal like that for your shop? What do you think your sales were last year? And don't worry about telling me anything I don't already know, because we were in talks to buy you guys, and saw all these numbers in the due diligence."

"Ummm." Katz thought about the customers he'd had to support, the feature requests he'd seen, the sales he knew of. "I mean, we charge a hundred K for each box minimum, and we've got at least, like, fifty customers, and most of them have spent way more than a hundred thousand; there are support contracts and stuff…"

"Even if fifty customers spent a million, that's fifty million. How do you get a billion from that?"

How did he get a billion from that? "I don't know. I just don't think we'd sell for less than at least a few hundred million." Why? What had led him to think that?

"When we talked to Uri and Parker, they wanted to sell it to us for eight."

"Eight?"

"Eight million." Copernicus pauses, lets it sink in. "We looked hard at it, but turned them down."

"Eight megs? That's it? And you said no?"

"It wasn't worth eight million. We told him, you've got great tech here, good engineering, but your sales team sucks, you barely have a marketing team, no one knows about you, you've got no traction. I'll be surprised if that company's around by the end of next year."

Seven years to graduate. His early twenties burned. Meth addiction. For this? Two point five of eight million was two hundred thousand, about two years' salary. A single year if he'd jumped ship and gone to Google when they offered him the previous year. He had told Uri about the interview, and the offer. "I had to check it out because, the way people talk about Xerox PARC now, that'll be Google in twenty years—it's where all the best people are going." It was true; Google in the early aughts was a special place. "I turned them down because I wanted to see this through, because I believe in us." Uri had merely nodded.

"You're bullshitting me, right?"

"Katz, go ask Uri. Look him in the eye and ask him whether he offered to sell for eight. Then come back and talk to me. We'd love to have you onboard. I'll get the check."

8 alexei orshanskiy thinks he can get you lemons

Brynne Givens—Econ at Agnes Scott, Katz cohabitant for ten months now—made of the waitress what seemed to him a strange request. The response was stranger still.

"I'm so sorry, we don't have any lemons right now."

Incredulous: "You don't have lemons? I can't have lemon in my water?"

"It's hard to get lemons in Atlanta right now. In the whole southeast!"

Sherman stirred. "Did Florida fall into the ocean?"

The waitress leaned in and lowered her voice. "Y'all didn't hear this from me, but the Ukrainian mafia controls all the lemons. You can't get lemons right now unless you're national, or you pay them off. They're making some kind of play. That's what I heard."

"Ukrainians are making a play? With lemons?"

"Yeah, Ukrainian organized crime. They're big here around Atlanta. Nigerians won the war for the taxis against the Ethiopians—"

"That I can confirm. I take a lot of cabs. Used to be all Addis Ababa, or Eritreans talking shit about the Abyssinians. Eritreans stole Ethiopia's whole coastline, it was a thing. But yeah now it's all heavyset dudes out of Lagos bumping Nkem Owoh. The other day my driver muttered, 'Òyìnbó mugu,' and I was like 'no mang, I'm Òyìnbó babaláwo!' He just about loses his mind, and is like, 'did you spend time in Nigeria?' And I'm like, 'no, just you're the third guy to call me *mugu* this month, so I looked it up.' He was impressed, though not so impressed that he apologized or anything."

Brynne pokes him. "He can't drive."

"I choose not to drive." Katz looks up to the server. "I'm a terrible driver. Hit shit all the time. Firm believer in the separation of labors."

They're not drunk, but they're getting there, and the couple busts into "Punk Rock Girl" from the Dead Milkmen. The waitress tolerates this; Katz comes often, and tips generously, always in cash. "So yeah, the Ukrainians were like, alright, we want money from the bars. So somehow they're keeping lemons from getting delivered."

"Does not having lemons really fuck you?"

"It's definitely annoying."

"But it's not as bad as, like, keeping beer from getting delivered."

"Oh, I don't think they have that kind of power."

"Just lemons. Huh."

Brynne kisses him. "Are you going to get into the lemon business?"

"I doubt there's terribly much margin in lemons. And the last thing I need is a bunch of pissed-off Ukrainians thinking I'm getting up in their game. More likely someone put the lemon money up their nose."

If not, however...hrmm. Lemons.

Òyìnbó: white person   mugu: victim of fraud, especially of the Yahoo boys
babaláwo: lit. "Father of mysteries"

＊＊＊＊＊＊＊＊＊

Alexei Orshanskiy was born in Rochester to an RIT professor of computer engineering and a researcher at Xerox. The hip kids hear Xerox and think of Jack Goldman's Palo Alto Research Center, especially the Computer Science Laboratory under Bob Taylor and George Pake. They think Butler Lampson, Bob Metcalfe, Charles Simonyi, Alan Kay: the *Dealers of Lightning* as immortalized by Michael Hiltzik (and a much lesser extent by John Markoff in *What the Dormouse Said*). Ethernet, WYSIWYG, skeuomorphism, mice, really the whole WIMP paradigm, laser printers? Yeah, all that. They think about the Alto—not so much about the Star—very few about the 6085 (*The Computers Nobody Wanted* according to Strassmann). They don't think about the obscene load times on the Alto; *de mortuis nil nisi bonum dicendum est.* No one thinks about the failed 820 unless they're reading *Fumbling the Future*.

They might also think Ivan Sutherland, Douglas Engelbart, and J. C. R. Licklider, but none of them ever worked at PARC: Engelbart was at SRI, cursing about PARC hiring his students. Licklider was at ARPA, IBM, and then MIT. Sutherland was at the University of Utah while the shit was going down. In any case, Xerox had a significant research effort long before PARC, though *Copies in Seconds* and *Joe Wilson and the Creation of Xerox* lack the verve, vision as revealed by hindsight, and sexiness of Hiltzik's subject matter. From 1967 to 2005, the tallest building in New York outside of NYC was lit with the blazing red "Digital X" logo thirty stories up. The logo came off; in 2013 the building was sold; by 2018 Xerox was out of Xerox Tower entirely, and in 2021 Xerox Plaza became Innovation Square. Eastman Kodak was headquartered in Rochester long before Xerox set up shop, but fell to Fujifilm after a hundred years of dominance, entering Chapter 11 in 2012. The luster had come off the Imaging Capital of the World, though Kodak still licenses technologies from its Kodak Tower, and Xerox maintains a research presence in the Webster suburb.

Having grown up in Dnipropetrovsk (renamed Dnipro by 2015's decommunization laws), his mother spent seven years at Saint Petersburg's ITMO, achieving fundamental results in semiconductor manufacturing processes (especially ultrapure water recycling). She returned home hoping to fall in with the *Shistdesiatnyky*. Alas, Alla Horska had just been murdered by soulless *chekists;* Chornovil was headed to a Mordovian prison judged a *vrag naroda,* and Ivan Dziuba followed him not long after. She married, and they left for Canada in 1975, the earliest date possible, joining the larger Ukrainian diaspora. Two years later, they headed south on King's Highway 405 out of Ontario and, after a lengthy delay, across the Lewiston-Queenston Bridge.

＊＊＊＊＊＊＊＊＊

WIMP: Window, Icon, Mouse, Pointer

de...est: τὸν τεθνηκότα μὴ κακολογεῖν Of the dead do not speak ill. Diogenes Laërtius, Βίοι καὶ γνῶμαι τῶν ἐν φιλοσοφίᾳ εὐδοκιμησάντων (Lives and Opinions of Eminent Philosophers) I.70

ITMO: Университет ИТМО University of Information Technologies, Mechanics, and Optics

Shistdesiatnyky: Шістдесятники Sixtiers (*russkiy:* Шестидесятники / Shestidesyatniki)

chekists: чекист Soviet secret police (narrowly, members of Чека (Cheka))

vrag naroda: враг народа enemy of the people

At Bolaño's house in Home Park: "I think you ought move exclusively to dank."

"What, in terms of smoking? Or slinging?"

"In all terms. I would be happy never to look at a seed-saturated sack of mids in all the days left to me."

Katz looks at Bolaño as if he's lost his mind. "I still have people buying schwag."

"And you shouldn't. Anyone who is buying schwag is a trash person. You're cheapened by having it. There's next to no profit in it. All you can earn selling schwag is money to buy schwag with."

"So how do I convince people who are buying $80 ounces to throw down $300?"

"One, you don't have to move ounces all the time because people aren't losing half the weight to seeds and stems and other detritus even less smokable than the schwag. People can buy a quarter and make it last all week. So it's $90. Your profit goes way up, even assuming you move to smoking dank exclusively—"

"I'm gonna smoke a lot more than a quarter a week, no matter what it is."

Bolaño is impatient. "Yes, assume an ounce for you, at a true cost of $200, the profit still goes up."

Katz scoffs. "Where am I buying pounds of dank for $3,200?"

"From me." Bolaño smiles. "From your friend in the gay community."

Katz affects a wail. "No, my friend! Don't peddle your ass for dank hookups."

"I peddle nothing." Bolaño's grin, a bit too haughty, creeps Katz out a little. "But my people do tend to know where the good drugs are, and I can get dank elbows all day for two eight. Maybe less on multiple bows; if so, I might kick you back some of the savings. Either way, I make $400 on each, a little over 14%. Quite reasonable, and you get to continue stashing at my place."

"When do I get to meet your guy?"

"When can you cut me out, you mean? Oh, Sherman." He chuckles. "My guy would not do business with you. He'd take one look and say 'ugh' and invite you to take your straight dollars elsewhere."

"What? Seriously?"

"We don't keep our shit flowing by retailing to every white boy in basketball shorts with a gut that comes up hoping to buy weight."

Katz is dubious, and makes it plain. "What kind of insular bullshit is that? The name of the game is Trade. You don't aim to keep the product in your community. I mean, you want to sell it there too, of course." He's vexed. "What do you mean?"

"When you're marginalized, you maybe want to ensure your people have their essentials taken care of before you try to build up a trade surplus."

"Awww bullshit, spare me. Your 'people' have as an essential dank weed?"

"Yes, of course."

Katz pauses before replying. "Yeah, fair enough."

"And the experience is just so much better for everyone. How many times per day do you miss a seed and have it pop out of the bowl like a volcano of filth? With the horrible smell. The weed looks like shit. Our oldest customers will soon be graduating, and will suddenly be awash with cash. Let's prime that pump."

✻ ✻ ✻ ✻ ✻ ✻ ✻ ✻ ✻

The U-Haul Lofts stood at the corner of 14th and Howell Mill, in what has been radically revitalized as the Westside Provisions District. An old center for self-storage and truck rollout, it had been divided into a few massive industrial units, in which four to six people tended to live cheaply indeed. It was a known party center, with readily available parking, proximity despite isolation, lots of crannies and alcoves into which one or several might momentarily abscond, a large outdoor area for milling, and structures that couldn't get much worse no matter how many beers were spilled on them. One of these units was home to a number of CS students who'd entered together in 1999, and in 2001 Katz and Bolaño found themselves there. Katz brought in a backpack his usual 1.75 L of absinthe, and dedicated it to the party's general use. In addition, he came strapped with a half ounce, and commandeered a bowl upon arrival. He held court outside, yelling over Sunny Day Real Estate, the Dismemberment Plan, and Modest Mouse, packing and repacking, draining several tall glasses of heavily iced absinthe, growing louder and happier as the night went on.

Into the circle broke all those wishing to roast bowls. Katz, generous and gregarious, welcomed all participants. Several left with his phone number, and intentions of picking up. One of the few who brought his own green was the gaunt and hyperkinetic Alexei Orshanskiy, now in his third year of a CS+Mechanical Engineering double, producing from his pockets a sack of laudable dank. Katz recognized him from the College of Computing and hailed. "Hey Alexei, you wouldn't know where I could get some lemons, would you?"

"That's racist, man!"

"Heh. What? What's racist? I was just looking for some lemons."

"You assume I'm with the *bratvá* just because I'm Ukrainian?" The question carried an underdone of pride.

"Mang, how would I even know you're Ukrainian? I mean you kinda look like a victim of the Holodomor but I figure most everyone who came up under the CCCP is underfed. I don't even know your last name." Katz reached across the circle, taking Alexei's hand in his own. "Sherman Katz. What's the *bratvá*?"

Bolaño was only too happy to answer. "Brotherhood. Organized crime."

"Alexei Orshanskiy." Nodding at Katz: "Pleasure to meet you." Alexei looked across at Bolaño. "You're Russian?"

"*Ja nemnógo govorjú po-rússki.*"

"Hah, OK, I speak enough Russian to understand that, but I'm Ukrainian. I assume you don't speak Ukrainian. Did you live in Russia?"

"ни to both. I learned *russkiy* in Texas."

"It's pronounced 'ni,' assuming you meant Ukrainian 'no'. You are?"

"Michael Bolaño. I think we had Computer Architecture together last year."

---

bratvá: братвá brotherhood
Holodomor: Голодомор lit. "hunger plague" Ukrainian famine 1932–1933
Ja…po-rússki: Я немного говорю по-русски I speak a little Russian

"Oh ok yeah that was a good class. Yes, the *bratvá* refers to Russian and Ukrainian organized crime. Not the Chechens. Only those who honor *vor v zakone*, the *ponyatiya*, the *blatnaya fenya* are called *bratvá*. Chechens do their own thing. Always have. Here in Atlanta, Russians and Ukrainians are locked in struggle. Mikhail Odenussa arrived here eight years ago for Solntsevo Bratvá. But Odessa's Aleksandr Angert and Semion Mogilevich—him in Moscow, but a Ukrainian, born in Kyiv—look to the southeast and see many Ukrainians, but not so many Russians. The *Malina* thus press here for advantage."

"And why were you saying Katz was racist?" Bolaño turned to Katz, confused and irritable. "Katz, why were you asking about lemons?"

"Because the Ukrainians control lemons." Alexei said it matter-of-factly, as if this should come to no one's surprise.

"I had been led to believe the Québécois mafia behind the lemon shortage. The dreaded Maple Leaf Gang. They're hoarding lemons with which to acidify the whole year's maple syrup crop, driving up prices, allowing them to retail at vast profit. They're going to take the money they make from that and bribe Celine Dion so that she goes back to making French records. When the Strategic Maple Syrup Reserve is opened, they're going to swoop in on that bitch and pilfer it, replacing it with *soupe aux pois*."

Alexei stared at Katz. "Are you serious?"

Katz shrugged. "I read as much in *The Economist*." Bolaño cracked up across the circle. "No I'm not serious, duh, how could they get that much pea soup?"

Alexei seemed thoroughly confused. "So when you asked about lemons?"

"I am aware of the Ukrainian spectre that haunts the Atlanta lemon market."

"Ahhh. So you are racist!"

"You knew all about it! Which, speaking of, how do you know about it?"

Alexei calmed down. "Ahh, I hear about things from other Ukrainians."

"Other organized Ukrainians?"

"As in the *bratvá*? I might know a few."

"This is pretty good weed, Alexei. Can you get more?"

"Probably. How much would you be looking for?"

"Ideally several pounds a week."

Alexei's eyes undraped. "Oh. I figured you were going to say, like, a quarter or something."

"Well, sixty-four quarters. Several. A week."

"Let me get your phone number."

"Yeah let me get yours. Do you have a pen? Does anybody have a pen?" Katz looked around and shrugged in frustration. "Alexei, go find a girl with a big purse. Therein we'll find a pen. Borrow it and bring it back." Both Katz and Alexei carried napkins on which were scrawled dozens of phone numbers, pager codes, addresses, AIM handles, and all the other details now maintained in cell phones and cloud applications.

---

vor v zakone: вор в законе thief in [opposition to] the law
ponyatiya: понятия understandings
blatnaya fenya: блатная феня professional criminal language
soupe aux pois: yellow pea soup

Late the next day Katz called Alexei up, and suggested he stop by.

∗ ∗ ∗ ∗ ∗ ∗ ∗ ∗

"Alexei, let's talk about this weed!"

"Yes. I must warn you that these are not gentle people from whom you seek to purchase. They are unkind, aggressive, eager to push any advantage. Looking always to apply pressure. It would be unwise to mislead them, or to play any games. They are quick to use force, and do so with little excuse, as a demonstration to one another of the ruthlessness."

"I mean, so long as I play straight, there's no issue, right?"

"I would not unnecessarily reveal wealth."

"What, like they might come rob me if they think I have money beyond what I'm buying with? Even if I'm a solid customer?"

"It's unlikely that your connect, the man I can introduce you to, would do so. Not out of respect for you, but because you deliver business. But there are others. They quietly listen and watch, and might not be above tailing you back, then approaching with the pistol, and taking what you have purchased."

"Holy shit Alexei, these sound like real pieces of shit."

"They are ungentle. But they are businessmen."

"They sound more like mafia. *Bratvá*."

Alexei sighed. "I would not use that word around him."

"What, does he deny what he is?"

Alexei laughed. "Hardly. But his organization is not *Bratvá*, only *Bratvavor*. A subdivision. Two sets of the boys sought to run Atlanta, one from Miami, one that grew up native. He is of the native set. They battled the Russians together, driving them out. Then those of Florida turned on the natives, and bullied them down to *bratvavor*, paying up to the Florida gang. This despite Atlanta activity being far more profitable, and inventive. For instance, the lemons."

"Miami had Meyer Lansky and Trafficante and all the Cubans, right?"

"Cubans? *Revolucionarios?*" Alexei is confused. Poor ex-Sov.

"No, The Corporation. Cuban mafia. And I think Trafficante was actually Tampa, now that I think about it."

"I have never heard of this. Miami is Leonid Fainberg. Miami is Chris Paciello. Miami is Giselda Blanco, *Viuda Negra*. Miami is CENTAC 26. Miami is Winston Brown coming up here and taking over Techwood Homes, John Hope Homes, and Eagan Homes, snatching Ronald Baker up off a corner and into a Mustang 5.0, then putting 81 mm of Parabellum through his cerebellum from two feet away. Brains made a slick across half of North Avenue."

"81 mm?"

"Nine nines."

"Oh, ok."

"Have you ever heard branecore?"

"Braincore? Christ, Alexei. No."

"Not, like, human brains, Branes as in D-branes."

Viuda Negra: Black Widow   **CENTAC:** Central Tactical

"I'm convinced you're making this shit up. How has an esoteric generalization of superstrings inspired a genre of music?"

"This is music created by drawing visual art, then interpreting that art as a map of frequencies, and Fourier transforming them into audio."

"What does that have to do with D-branes?"

"Well it's just branecore, not D-branecore."

"What does it have to do with branes?"

"Oh!" Alexei pauses for a minute. "I'm not sure!" Katz groans. Alexei picks up from earlier. "Miami is cocaine, cocaine, cocaine. Atlanta is Mikhail Odenussa cleaning out the Gangster Disciples and Latin Kings on his lonesome, showing them how the *bratvá* hold it down."

✳ ✳ ✳ ✳ ✳ ✳ ✳ ✳

"Let us roast one, and tell me, Alexei, to what have you been recently listening?" Alexei has the strangest musical taste of anyone Katz has ever met, by a wide, almost pathological margin. He sometimes listens to GT's WREK 91.1, known to Katz for playing things like dripping faucets, engine sounds, and of course the institution that is Friday night WREKage, the southeast's hardest one to ten hours of true metal. A teenaged Sherman passed out listening to WREKage many Friday nights, and woke to David Adams still playing Nuclear Assault or Sleep or Morbid Angel or Fantômas. Even 91.1's hundred kilowatts of weirdness don't suffice for Alexei, though, who receives discs in the mail in scripts Katz doesn't recognize, sometimes in envelopes lacking return addresses. Sherman has seen strange media at his apartment: Video8 cartridges intended to be played at half speed, roentgenizdat and magnitizdat on high-metal tape, once a huge box of Philips DCCs, dozens of which had liquefied into a rufous puddle in the corner possessing an unpleasant but only faint odor.

"I've really been digging on bridgecore!"

"Is that songs about bridges?"

"No, it's music that's all bridge."

"Like, the bridge between chorus and verses and such?"

"Yeah, but this is just bridge after bridge after bridge."

"Isn't that just...unrelated sections of music?"

Alexei is grieved. "These are bridges which must make sense together despite no intermediate verses nor choruses—but each must stand as a true bridge on its own. You must listen for the verses that are not played."

"I've really been digging on crashcore!"

"Like, music about crashes?"

Pained: "No, this is music which seeks to exploit security vulnerabilities in active units, decoders, equalizers, these kinds of things. And music in that spirit. Even null results are useful knowledge."

"I've really been digging on corpscore!"

"Songs about Korea by 'Chick' Corea?"

With bemused tolerance: "No, that would be hancore. Unless you're talking about DPRK mass performance stuff, which is Pyongsong—make it just two

---

DCC: digital compact cassette

syllables, not pee-yong-song, just pyong-song—or music suggestive of Kim-ilsungism–Kimjongilism, kimcore. Stuff like WLMB's *Janggun-nim chukjibeop sseusinda*—"

"WLMB?"

"*Wangjaesan Kyŏngŭmaktan* a/k/a the one and only Wangjaesan Light Music Band! One of North Korea's two bands."

"They only have two?"

"Most people are just going to listen to bullshit mallcore, so what does it matter, Katz?" Alexei gets emotional easily, Katz has noticed. "There's this one banger called 'Attain the Cutting Edge' that's all about CNC machines. North Korean state music can be surprisingly dope. There's one 'I Also Raise Chickens' which is really classic harmonizing, great mixing on that especially if you get the vinyl. 'The Joy of Bumper Harvest Overflows Amidst the Song of Mechanisation' really anticipates Discore/kängpunk."

"The mind positively reels, Alexei. No way is that a real title."

"I never bullshit about music, Katz. Now corpscore is like, taps, Souza marches, reveille, all played in weird time signatures and heavy distortion." Alexei asks to play some corpscore; it sounds like the Do Lung Bridge scene from *Apocalypse Now*, but with more trumpets.

"Alexei, much as without Britain, there's no Canada, without the Spice Girls, you never have Neko Case. Just my opinion."

✳ ✳ ✳ ✳ ✳ ✳ ✳ ✳ ✳

Katz met Danylo Kushnir at City Cafe, on the intersection of Hemphill and 10th across the street from campus. It was lunch rush, and the restaurant had a short wait, yet none of the tables next to Danylo's saw occupants through their short council. The broadshouldered Slav saw Katz enter, furrowed his brow, and with his coffee cup motioned him over employing the slightest of gestures. Upon reaching the table, Kushnir asked, "you are Katz?" Sherman assented, and took his invited seat. "Alexei," Danylo whistling here, and shaking his head in disbelief, "he is smart as hell."

Katz said nothing.

"Makes all of us proud. He wants to do jobs, has been saying this, but I tell him 'no, school for you, *bratíška*.' He is relative. On father's side. Not close."

"Did y'all grow up together?"

Danylo dismisses the question. "I arrived more recently. Now we are both here." He drinks down the rest of his coffee. "You want maybe two Ks a week."

"I usually go through about three pounds a week now. Yours is a bit better. Pretty good. It's a pain in the ass to get to my guy. I'm looking for new options."

A waitress scurries over to refill Kushnir. "Three pounds, this is one and a half kilograms? Not so much. Maybe not worth it for me. How much are you paying? Every week?"

"Well, whenever I need it; it's not on a prearranged schedule. And one point three six keys, less than one five." He's paying $9,600 for three pounds at a

---

Janggun-nim…sseusinda: 장군님 축지법 쓰신다 The General Uses Warp (1996)
bratíška: братишка little brother

time through Bolaño's hookup, of which he knows at least $1,200 is going to Michael. "I'm paying $8,000 for that. I could go $10,000 for four weekly?"

Another cup is drained. The Ukrainian's coffee intake is awesome. He stares at Katz for a minute. "Eleven thousand. Two kilos. Every week."

Two kilos is just over 4.4 pounds. At eleven, that's $2,500 per bow, the same price as he just offered for an even four. "I think that's the same price, basically, as what I just offered? $2,500 per pound either way?"

Danylo darkens. "I don't know what a motherfucking pound is. I can get you two kilos for eleven thousand. Every Sunday. We'll work out a time. Same time, every week. At your place. Good price? You want? Not want?"

"What if I'm not going to be around one Sunday?"

Kushnir evaluates him critically. "Then you have someone else there with the money, ready to take it."

"So you need regularity here, you're saying."

Kushnir sighs. "Katz, this is small potatoes. Eleven thousand a week? Barely worth my time. I need schedule driver." He begins counting on long fingers. "I need make payment. I need ensure delivery. All on timetables. I do not need your college kid two kilos sitting around wondering where are my eleven thousand? If you are amateur, not worth it for me." Another coffee.

"No, I can step up to that. Thanks; that's a good deal."

"Better than what you pay now. And better weed. Always there. It is Friday today. You are ready Sunday?" Katz gets the idea it's not a question, quite.

"Yeah, I can go Sunday." He might need get some money out of checking. "How about cocaine?"

"I don't want to sell it, and I don't do it." Abusers of organic and synthetic stimulants tend to be creeped out by the opposite tribe. The tweaker regards cocaine a party drug for unserious people easily separated from their money. The cokehead considers methamphetamine antiglamorous, lacking in subtlety, the drug of the poor. There is little traffic between the two.

"I get you good price on halfkilo."

Katz snorts. "The absolute last thing I need is half a key of cocaine."

Kushnir shrugs. "Let me get address, phone number." He does not offer to shake hands. "I tell you something now, Katz. You fuck up, police come, throw you in a van? You do not buy from me, you take delivery from Ukrainians, speak no English, know very little. Hand him over to police? If he says anything, whole family dies in Ukraine. Come in the night, torture to death, burn home. Family pets also tortured. He is put in box, shipped home, probably burned, perhaps tortured first. Life forfeit. Cops have only lowlevel Ukrainian, you are no hero." He grinned menacingly. "And all of us come after you."

Katz holds his eyes. "I have a lawyer. No way would I talk to the police."

"That's good, Katz." A toothy smile.

* * * * * * * * *

It was Bolaño who came up with the term "Dnipro Guidos," immediately and eagerly adopted by all involved non-Ukrainians. They superseded Bolaño's source, who was moved strictly into a backup role. The only downside was the minimum purchase, but in 2003 it was an excellent price, especially for such high-quality weed, superior to the beasters that had been common currency. It was not long after this that a horrible drought struck the southeast, as broad as it was sudden. Some rupture in the British Columbian pipeline? No one was quite sure. The gays were out. Greg Moyer came, hat in hand, and practically begged that the frats might taste dank that summer. Black connects on Hosea Williams Drive in Kirkwood were stocked, but with overpriced garbage only. Mexican connects along Buford Drive weren't picking up phones that they likely no longer had (Mexican connects being fond of calling cards and burners, in Katz's experience). A beautiful Polish-Japanese girl Katz had been talking to whenever he could offered to help, but her help was a seed-riddled brick of schwag such as Katz had not smoked in years, It was the Dnipro Guidos who first put together a new upstream. Hints pointed to California. First a few spurts and dribbles, hungrily bought (despite shameless profiteering) just to ensure personals, then a good green torrent of dank from the evening redness of the West.

✳ ✳ ✳ ✳ ✳ ✳ ✳ ✳ ✳

By 2004, real profit was being generated. Between wholesaling pounds to those who had once hooked him up, and growing mushrooms split between those same contacts and Katz, it was an uncommon week when Bolaño didn't see a taxfree thousand. Katz was clearing close to twice that. He went through two ounces a week between his own constant chiefing and the entertainment of those who stopped by, $600 of retail cost, but only $312.50 at his price. He sold speed at cost to a very small circle. Whatever else came through his hands got moved, usually without markup unless it was going to be a recurring thing.

After getting ripped off on $5,000 of MDMA (Devesh was off doing his PhD at UCSB, much to Sherman's dismay), he mentioned that it would be good to get a mass spectrometer, and a place to use it.

"Why would you need a mass spectrometer? Can't you just check for purple or black on Marquis reagent?" Marquis reagent, a mixture of sulfuric acid and formaldehyde, is the first line of alkaloid testing.

"This tested purple on Marquis, and gave a reaction on Simon." Simon's is a binary reagent: it is stored in two parts, combined only at the time of testing. Solution A is 2% sodium nitroprusside and 2% acetaldehyde in water. Solution B is 2% sodium carbonate in water. It turns blue in the presence of amines of the second degree, such as MDMA and methamphetamine. "But those can only show presence, not purity, not amount of substance. They certainly can't tell me what other random crap is in these bogon pills."

"Will a mass spectrometer?"

"It'll do a lot better than bullshit colorimetric reagents. You bombard whatever you've got, and out come fragments, and from that you can deduce composition."

"And my role in this would be what, exactly?"

"Well, if I get such a, let's call it a lab, I'll be storing product there. So you'd be losing a bit of income. Also, I was going to suggest that you move your fungiculture there. Keep all the deep felonies in one location, as it were. Where neither of us live. And of course the contribution of cash."

＊＊＊＊＊＊＊＊＊

Katz and Bolaño debated lab locations. Katz preferred a place he knew in West Midtown, the "Goat Farm," an unrepentant industrial center that had seen little rehabilitation. Bolaño liked what he saw in the West End, separated from downtown by a little less than five kilometers. Neither denied that both locations were shitholes of the first order; the argument rode on other lines.

"Sherman. West End is ghetto. Rent will be cheap. People there are less inclined to talk to the cops, and if they do call the cops, the cops are less inclined to give a shit. MARTA takes us right there—no need to use cars or cabs, nothing to track. It's on the way to the airport."

"What the fuck do we need with Hartsfield-Jackson?" Hartsfield International, since roughly forever the world's busiest airport (and it's not particularly close) had in 2003 been renamed in honor of Atlanta's first black mayor. It was during Maynard Jackson's first administration that the massive Midfield Terminal (now Concourses A–D and T North) was built. Midfield—the largest construction project in the South—was completed on time, under budget, and largely via minority-owned contractors. MARTA's Airport Station was likewise constructed during that second term; in his third Atlanta was awarded the Olympics, primarily over Athens and Toronto, and he accepted the Olympic flag at Barcelona's closing ceremonies.

"It seems shortsighted to dismiss easy airport access."

"So you're suggesting two white college boys—"

"Since when am I white you big chalky bitch?"

"Michael my droog, in West End you're a ghost, haunting it with your whiteness. You're titanium dioxide. You're an electron-degenerate stellar remnant without the height issues. West End Isaac Newton would have called you homogeneal and put you through a prism. You're a white-winged dove, sing a song, sounds like she's singin'. Dudes preparing for *hajj* are going to wear you as *iḥrām* clothes."

"I disagree, but continue."

"If we set up shop there, I give us less than a week before someone kicks in the door and ransacks it. They're gonna know no one lives there. Saving a few hundred dollars on rent is not worth sticking out like Jim Carrey on *In Living Colour*. People are going to notice us, talk about us, want to rip us off. Shit, nothing to track on MARTA? They won't need to track our cards, just ask anyone, 'did you see two white boys get off the train here?' Some holmes is gonna say, 'oh you mean Keebler and Keebler Chacho. They've got some operation over there making mayo-flavored *Saladitas*.' Think."

It was an issue with few hard data and plenty of specious reasoning. They agreed that moving the conversation forward required selecting some actual properties, and made plans to find some suitable addresses.

MARTA: Metropolitan ATL Rapid Transit Authority   **droog:** friend. Nadsat via друг (*drug*)
hajj: حَجّ Islamic pilgrimage to Mecca   **iḥrām:** إخْرَام Islamic state of purification
Saladitas: A saltine cracker from *Galletera Mexicana S.A. de C.V.* "Mexican Biscuit Company"
    (since 1990 *Gamesa*, a subsidiary of PepsiCo)

* * * * * * * * *

"I miss acid." The longing is clear in Katz's voice. Bolaño accepts the bowl and nods. "I never thought it would become impossible to get quality LSD."

"You know why, right?"

"Yeah, the silo bust in Kansas a few years back."

"Those guys apparently had quite the operation."

"But why hasn't anyone else stepped back in?"

Bolaño shrugs underneath an occlusive cloud. "The chemistry is involved." He thinks for a second. "But how involved can it be?"

"Exactly. We're America's scientific vanguard. Man, sorry to have cut you out on the weed, but you've got to admit, this is great shit."

"No one can fault you for taking advantage of a better deal. I'm doing fine."

"Those mushrooms have got to be printing cash for you. What's input cost on those? Pretty much nothing?"

"The margin on fungus is excellent." Bolaño smiles.

"All this cash, all these hookups, and yet we can't find acid. Hell, we can't even find reliable MDMA. Devesh should be done in four years, and he keeps talking about coming back here and trying to get tenure. He misses us."

Bolaño's look is scathing. "We can get reliable rolls. We can't reliably get thousands of dollars of rolls, perhaps, which what were you planning to do with all those anyway? Retail them at clubs? In your sweatpants?"

"I don't know, mang, I like to stock up on things when they're available at a good price. You can never have too many rolls. A mistake that won't happen again, once we have a mass spectrometer. A modest proposal: let's make acid."

Bolaño laughs with more than a hint of disbelief. "How?"

"I will look into it. If we can figure out a means, we ought not need spend much to have all the acid we'll ever need, and we'll know it's clean. We'll even know the dosage. I don't think I've ever know the dosage of my LSD with certainty. We can make a bit more and cover lab costs. Make a few grams, keep a few sheets, sell the rest, close up shop." He cashes the bowl and props himself up. "How can we respect ourselves as elite engineers and masters of the neurotransmitter if we never make the greatest drug of all time?"

"The thinking man's psychedelic for sure."

Idle speculation. Bolaño assumes that will be the end of it.

9 pavlov's hierophant and schrödinger's hæresiarch

```
From: sherman katz <ssk@suburbanjihad.net>
To: Stamps Health Service <********@*******>
Subject: forearm pestilence
Date: 2003-12-02 0747 UTC (0247 EST)

hello! i am a GT undergraduate and i've had this
mark--hopefully not of the Beast, haha--on my forearm for
like two months now. it's not going anywhere. i'm concerned
that it might be skin cancer, though it could just be
really obstinate dirt. either way, it's gotta go.

i'm happy to remove it myself, but how deep need i dig to
ensure complete excision in the case of an actual melanoma?
need i employ any particular strategies for cauterization?
```

"That'll be $340 on the Z." Katz counts up seventeen twenties. "Let me bag that up for you. So to what have you been up?"

"Not too much, Katz. Working at the Google data center in Lithia Springs."

"Oh yeah? What do you do there? Are you writing code?"

"I do a little Python scripting, but mostly I'm touching hardware in the DC."

Katz doesn't bother to hide his disappointment. He rarely does. "Oh. Are you cool with that?"

"Absolutely. Working for Google is phenomenal. I'm pretty involved in the buildout and setup of the DC. There's all kinds of technology there we're pioneering, stuff you wouldn't see anywhere else. It's paying more than twice my old job. And, I mean, I'm not like you. I don't love coding. I just like computers. I leave my job there at the end of the day."

"Oh yeah? What do you have that's unique?"

"Off the record?"

Katz rolls his eyes. "Sure."

"We're supplying only twelve volts to the hard drives, to avoid having to build 5V outputs into our PSUs. Nothing else uses 5V."

"Don't hard drives require both 12V and 5V? Twelve for the motors, five for the electronics?"

"Yep, but the electronics can usually handle 12V, at least for the timeframe in which the drive is useful to us. Or they blow immediately, in which case we send the drive back. Pretty much every drive has a 12V TVS diode on it, that'll let go at over 12V. But it'll take 12V. Seagate and Maxtor and Western Digi eat a percent or two higher reject rate from us; we save a few bucks per server."

"Scandalous!" He is delighted.

TVS: transient voltage suppression   **GPU:** Graphics Processing Unit

156

✳ ✳ ✳ ✳ ✳ ✳ ✳ ✳

"That'll be $300 on the owskie. You're also taking an ounce of shrooms at $200 so that's $500 total." Katz accepts four hundreds and five twenties. "Have a good time with this. When will you be tripping?"

"It's a group of four of us, going to Radiohead October sixth."

Katz's hands tighten. "Ahhh, yes. I was going to that. Not anymore, alas."

"Why? It's gonna be a great show, I'm sure."

"Eh, I'm not as infatuated with Radiohead as everyone else. I mean, they've got some good tracks. The new album is dope. But *Kid A* was hardly, like, the revolution in music that people seem to think it was. I could go without ever hearing 'Paranoid Android' again. Six and a half minutes of fucking tedium right there. Warrrrrble garrrrrrrrble from a greeeaaaat heighhht. I could have gone without hearing 'Karma Police,' like, ever. Concentrated extract of bitch. But the more real and immediate reason is I'd bought the tickets for Brynne and myself, and when she moved out, they went with her, with my best wishes." The wound is clearly still raw. Brynne Givens had moved in fourteen months prior, after they'd gone out for a year and a half. Things had gone poorly.

"Oh, shitty, I'm sorry man."

"It is all good! I hope it's a fantastic show. These shrooms are the shit."

"I'm sure we will. Thanks a lot Katz."

✳ ✳ ✳ ✳ ✳ ✳ ✳ ✳

"That'll be $90 on the quarter." Katz is clearly irritated, brusque, distracted.

"Here's $100."

"I don't think I have change. I'll put $10 on your credit for next time. Sorry about that." Katz augments files/owed and accepts the five twenties. "Here's your sack. You want to rip some bong hits?" Katz tokes furiously.

"Is everything cool?"

He holds off for a second, momentarily reticent, then plunges in. "I mean, yeah, just, ugh. I got a ride home from work with one of the support people, and she was playing the motherfucking Counting Crows. The Counting Crows make me violently angry. They're like a photon I absorb and transition into a cunt state. Every time I hear 'Long December' I get dumber." Katz stares into the distance, lost, adrift. "I just don't understand."

"I can confirm 'Mr. Jones' was also overplayed."

"While we're talking about bands I'd like to see fed to Cthulhu, one of the worst things about living in Georgia is sharing a state with R.E.M."

✳ ✳ ✳ ✳ ✳ ✳ ✳ ✳

One of the nicer aspects of being a bibliophilic pharmaceutical distributor is the inevitable use of $20s and $100s as bookmarks. Years later, opening a book for a reread, out falls hard currency, an unexpected gift from the past. In the shorter term, it's not uncommon to find sums folded and slightly bleached in the pockets of laundry. One has to be careful getting in and out of cars; some angel in a parking lot once called Katz's attention to $800 that had fallen from his pocket. He gave her $200 in generous appreciation, got her number, and two days later fucked her from hell to breakfast.

```
From: sherman katz <ssk@suburbanjihad.net>
To: Stamps Health Service <********@*******>
Subject: RE: rabies vaccination
Date: 2004-03-17 1703 UTC (1203 EST)

Stamps Health Service consulted their pineal gland:
> bite site. Rabies is a major health emergency and

no, i don't think you understand. i have no reason to
believe i've been infected with rabies. i go outside only
infrequently, and am without chompmarks. i just understand
there to exist a rabies vaccination, and if that's the
case, i'd feel pretty stupid if i died of rabies. i'd also
like any other vaccinations you have on premises. rub them
on my gums, i don't give a shit.
```

"That'll be $90 on the quarter." Katz accepts a hundred dollar bill. "Let me see if I've got $10 for you...ahhh, here you go. So to what have you been up?"

"I've still got my Playstation 2 cluster going on at GTRI—"

"Oh yeah? Sweet. What're the specs on that?"

"Four racks with twenty-four PS2s per rack. Six point two 32-bit gigaFLOPs per Graphics Synthesizer. So—"

"Six hundred GFLOPs? Almost a teraflop in your office?"

"Well, five hundred ninety five point two, and in a networking room two down from my office, but yes."

"Solid. What's power draw on that bitch?"

"Not so bad! Just a little over two kilowatts." Katz nods appreciatively. It's impressively efficient. "But I'm right now writing grant applications to build a cluster of machines with multiple video cards, on which I'll run Cg programs."

"Cg is that programmable shader language for GPUs?"

"Yeah. GPUs have a much shorter lifetime at the top of the market than consoles, so I ought be able to stay on the last year's hardware, as opposed to the last generation of console, potentially several years prior. Also, you can pack several of them into a machine, so no overhead there."

"Do they have the FLOPpage?"

"Well, what do you think the Graphics Synthesizer is? Just a GPU. They're built for tremendous throughput. It's a somewhat limited environment and slightly weird programming model, but if you can work within it, you can extract unholy amounts of compute. There's this system that Nvidia's developing called CUDA which is going to be much more powerful, and when you combine that with completely programmable shader hardware, it's going to be an absolute monster."

"Huh! Will it push FPGAs out of their space?"

FLOPs: floating point operations per second **FPGA:** field-programmable gate array

"Eh, with FPGAs you have a lot more I/O possibilities, and much lower-level control. For a pure compute task, I would bet the GPUs let you get within a few percent, while being an order of magnitude easier to program."

"Huh! I'll have to watch this...Nvidia?"

"You're unfamiliar with them?"

Katz shrugs. "I know they make video cards, and that those cards have closed-source drivers. I don't play video games so they're not really of any value to me. I want something with in-tree kernel drivers. I'm rocking a sweet dual-RAMDAC Matrox G450 at the moment. It's a 2D monster. Great card."

```
From: sherman katz <ssk@suburbanjihad.net>
To: Stamps Health Service <********@*******>
Subject: RE: rabies vaccination
Date: 2004-03-18 2041 UTC (1541 EST)

Stamps Health Service consulted their pineal gland:
> We do not administer rabies vaccination unless you have
> been exposed to rabies, or you are likely to be.

fine. i woke up this morning to find a whole family of
weasels chewing on me save the one that was chasing out
a Peruvian bat with bloody fangs. they were in the blood
rage, more Lyssavirus than Mustelidae. i burned them. only
way to be sure. after all, next week i'm off to the Ashanti
region of Ghana, where i hope to get black market (no money
for gray, alas) cornea transplants.

when ought i come by?
```

"That'll be $180 on the half ounce."

"Can I get it in four eighths?"

"What? Why?"

"I'm selling three and keeping one for myself."

"You're selling eighths? You want an eighth? Sell quarters at a minimum. No one has time for eighths."

"I only have money for an eighth for myself."

"It sounds to me like you don't have money for any for yourself. You were gonna sling eighths at what, $60 each? Offsetting the $180? Dear, what you want to do is get an ounce. I'll do that for you for $300. You're then paying $75 per quarter ounce. Sell all three for $100 each. Your customers do better—they're paying $14 per gram instead of $17, and furthermore not having to fuck with bullshit eighths. You do better: you get seven grams free instead of three point five. I do better: I keep 'em movin'. I don't sell eighths. If I bagged you up four eights, not only am I selling eights, I'm selling them at a discount, due to my benevolent everyday $10 discount on quarters."

RAMDAC: random access memory digital to analog converter

"But Katz I only have $180."

"Allow me to front you the remainder. You can owe me $120, no problem, and preserve both our dignities."

"When do I have to pay you back?"

"When you have it? When you want to buy more?"

"Really? I mean I'd love to do that."

"Wouldn't have it any other way. Let me get that out for you. Normally I'd ask you to subdivide yourself, but since I like you, I'll handle it. I assume you don't have a scale?"

"I do, actually."

"Oh! Then why don't you bag it at home? That way you're not cruising around with rolling possession with intent. Subdivided and bagged product is pretty much *prima facie* PWI."

"Sure, I'll do that, good call."

"So who are you hooking up? Anyone I know?"

"My sister and two of her friends. They're in town from Vanderbilt."

"Girl friends?"

"Yes." Smiling, "do you want to meet them?"

"Well I'm vexed that you never told me you have a sister, first off. Does she look even a bit like you? I'd definitely be mining the Prescott fields."

She squeals. "You're too much!"

"I look back on our weekend very fondly, though I do not begrudge Danny his good fortune. And you have of course remained beautiful."

"Sherman Katz, you remain a master of blandishment. My sister is gorgeous, and looks nothing at all like me. She has a boyfriend, but I do not care for him, and encourage you to distract her from him. He's not nearly good enough for her. He is pretty, but so, so dumb."

"What about her friends?"

"They're fine. You should go out with my sister. She's two years younger."

"Ask her if I might call her, and if so, give me her number. Here's your sack. Can I get the $180?" He takes nine twenties and makes an entry in files/owed.

As Wendy Fisk (*née* Prescott) departs, Katz hollers. "Wendy dear, she *does* like...weird guys? Because otherwise she might be irritated at you."

"I wouldn't have suggested it otherwise, Katz."

✳ ✳ ✳ ✳ ✳ ✳ ✳ ✳

"Alright Alan, that'll be $90 on the quarter. Plus two ounces of shrooms at $400 for $490 total. I'll knock an extra $10 off that, so $480."

"Solid! I've got $500 if you've got $20."

"I do." Katz takes a long pull from a 12 oz draft pilsner glass filled with a brown, viscous semifluid. "Augghghgh."

Alan Peters, counting out five hundred dollar bills, watches the slow sliding pile's progression from glass to gullet, and his eyes go wide. "What are you drinking there, Sherman?"

"Forty-two uses for salmon, m'lad. My rich sustenance. *Kyriakon deipnon.* Eucharist. It's all I've eaten for several weeks now."

"Eucharist?"

"Well, I've transubstantiated it. Consecrated at least. Each morning I take a can of Goya black beans, a can of Del Monte diced tomatoes, a can of corn—Del Monte for the win once more—and a can of Bumble Bee pink salmon, throw that shit into the blender, throw in some cumin, throw in some curry powder, throw in a bit of speed. Bioavailability of speed consumed orally is surprisingly high compared to insufflation. Typically I'll throw two Adderall twenties into the mix, whereas I'm putting meth in my nose. Add a multivitamin. I usually add two because everything is made for underpowered individuals. Blend that fucker. Say a prayer over it." Katz intones with a singsong. *"In nomine patris et filii*—you'll notice I elide the *Spiritus Sancti.* Never cared for ye olde *Spiritus Sancti.* It's like the third generation of leptons. Electrons? Of course, get aboard. Muons? Ehhh, I guess. You catalyze fusion. Maybe one day we'll find a unicorn that pisses muons and jack it up to complete the dream of Fleishmann and Pons. But the tau? Sure, let's have a lepton that can decay into a hadron, why not. And we already have twice as many neutrinos as we'll ever need, let's add a third. Fuck the tau lepton and fuck all neutrinos."

Katz grows contemplative. "Third-generation quarks are alright, though. I dig the top quark. It's got all kinds of interesting relationships to the Higgs boson, should we ever find the Higgs. The Large Hadron Collider is supposed to when it comes online. If it doesn't, there will be a lot of pissed off Europeans. Dude, when I went to academic bowl Nationals back in 1998, there was this girl from a Michigan team with beautiful long hair, just overall really pretty, and one day she was wearing a Fermilab tshirt that said TEVATRON. I'd never seen a white girl with a science tshirt before—any girl, come to think of it; there was this Asian girl at my high school wearing a shirt that just read A/X, and I went up to her and asked, 'hey is your shirt about assembly language? Is that the 8086 AX register?' but she had no fucking clue what I was talking about."

"Katz, that's Armani Exchange."

"Yeah, I found that out three years later. A similar situation happened at the mall last year. There was this store called Cache, as in they wanted to be 'Cachet' but didn't want to spell it correctly? It might have had an accent mark, 'Caché,' but that's still wrong if so. So it's on the bottom floor and I walk in and am obviously out of place; it's upscale as hell. And they're like 'uh sir do you need assistance, are you stroking out perhaps?' And I ask, 'this is the first level Cache, right? Do you have a larger store upstairs perhaps, one that takes more time to get through, but has more items? A level two Cache?' Anyway, I fall immediately for TEVATRON girl, heart and soul. She was the queen of all my quiz bowl dreams. I wish I could remember her name." He looks wistful.

"Did you get with her?"

"What? No. Hah. I took her to see *Fear and Loathing in Las Vegas,* which had just come out and I obviously wanted to see. I think it freaked her out pretty badly. She'd apparently never had a drink. Then I was like, 'if we had a child

---

Kyriakon deipnon: Κυριακὸν δεῖπνον Lord's Supper

it would be one hell of a quiz bowler.' She went back to their dorm and kinda avoided me the next two days. Anyway, I bring up TEVATRON girl because they found the top quark there." His eyes snap back into focus. "The slurry. It's like four dollars a day, and almost all the calories are protein."

"That's disgusting."

"It's actually surprisingly...not terrible."

"Don't you have a good job? Why are you not willing to spend more than four dollars a day on food?" Alan considers himself something of a gourmand. He's been following the work of Nathan Myhrvold, eagerly anticipating the promised *Modernist Cuisine* (it would eventually be published in 2011). The last time Katz smoked him out, he launched into a monologue Sherman could only partially follow regarding foams in molecular gastronomy. He once brought to a party a beet sherbet that was the singularly most unacceptable thing Katz had to that date put in his mouth, but his sous vide steak kicked ass.

"Well it's more about the nutrition, but I'm not upset about great values."

"And that's all you've eaten for weeks?"

"Well, I also get a shitton of alcohol calories. They're actually probably a majority. And I eat a pollo quesadilla whenever I go to El Amigo, which I do frequently. Sometimes two. Quesadillas. Quesadilla? But this is all I eat at home. I figure I'll go a year and a day, like an ordeal of the old school. Gotta train for the Green Knight and Chapel Perilous, *And ȝet gif hym respite, a twelmonyth and a day.* Let's rip a few, and then I need get back to work."

"How do you get work done hitting the bong all day?"

"I've been consistently high since sometime in 1998. If I sober up, I'll forget everything I know. Here's your $20."

* * * * * * * * *

"Hey Katz, when you call me it shows up on caller ID as MALACLYPSE THE ELDER; what's up with that?"

"You knew it was me, right?"

"Well yes I knew it was you, because who else is going to be Malaclypse anything, and more importantly I know your number."

"The phone company asked my name, I told them Malaclypse the Elder, they put it into their system. That's how I get billed."

"That's crazy!"

"Why? They get paid either way. Speaking of getting paid, I'll of course need a flat large on the qwop. This is delicious shit; your people will love it. I also have you down for $80 from last time. Do you want to bring that current?"

"Yeah Malaclypse I've got $1080."

"Or six pi radians."

"What? Oh, yeah, heh, ok."

"Did you know that the probability of two randomly chosen positive integers being relatively prime is six over pi squared?"

Robert Ng is taken aback. Surprise turns to bewilderment which turns to softer confusion. "Really? How the hell is that the case? Six over pi squared?"

And...day: and yet give him respite a year and a day. *Sir Gawain and the Green Knight* 13

"You agree that given a prime p, the probability that two random elements chosen from the natural numbers are both multiples of p is 1 over p squared?"

"Ummm." Robert cogitates insufficiently quickly; Katz tries again.

"Probability of a single random positive integer being a multiple of a prime p is one over p, surely you agree?" He doesn't mean to sound patronizing.

"If $p = 2$, half of numbers are odd, half are even, so half are multiples of two. Sure. And if $p = 3$—"

"Then it partitions the number line into three equal parts, one of which is divisible by three, and the other two aren't. So if we have two numbers—"

"Then they're independent, so product of the probabilities, sure, one over p squared. That makes sense."

"The probability that they are both not multiples is one less that, yes?"

"Of course."

"Let me go ahead and get that cash from you." Nine hundreds and four fifties. "So if two numbers are relatively prime, that's equal to saying that there is no prime number which divides them both, right? So that's big pi of the difference we just calculated." Katz grabs a napkin and scrawls upon it:

$$\prod_{p=1} 1 - \frac{1}{p^2}$$

"Let's rewrite that as a summation."

$$\frac{1}{\sum_{n=1} \frac{1}{n}}$$

"And there you go."

"I don't see any six in there." Ng sounds cross.

Katz's look is one of sympathy. "Dude, that's the Basel problem. Euler solved it. It's the whole basis for the Riemann zeta function. Riemann just generalized it to complex arguments."

$$\zeta(s) = \sum_{n=1}^{\infty} \frac{1}{n^s}$$

"I'm still not seeing the six."

"Oh. Sum of reciprocals of n squared through infinity is pi squared over six. And we wanted the reciprocal of the sum, remember? So six over pi squared."

"Oh. Alright, yeah, cool."

"Here's your $20 back. And we are now straight." Katz removes Ng from `files/owed` with a quick invocation of `sed`.

∗ ∗ ∗ ∗ ∗ ∗ ∗ ∗ ∗

"The quarter is $90. Would you have any interest in a TEC-9?"

"Like, the gun?"

"The very same. It's also got the vented shroud barrel extension and two thirty round magazines."

"Are you a gun dealer now?"

"Absolutely not. I want out of the business ASAP. I'll give you a fantastic deal on that TEC-9."

"Why do you have a TEC-9 that you want to sell?"

"It's a long, stupid story. Wanna roast a few and I'll tell you?"

"By all means."

"So I roll out to a more rural part of this fine state. I'm looking to meet up with, let's call him Awesome Bill from Dawsonville. That's not his name, and he doesn't live there. Either way, I pick up speed from this guy, and it's a ridiculous pain in my ass every time."

"What do you mean by speed? Like, Adderall?"

"Desoxyn. Methamphetamine hydrochloride."

"Wait, meth is a prescribed drug?"

"Absolutely, Schedule II all day long. Mind you, I'm not purchasing diverted Desoxyn. This is a product of rural Georgia, cookin' the meth because the shine don't sell. The man lives in absurdist, subdystopian horror, but damn if he doesn't have the cleanest speed I've ever seen. He once went to jail for unloading a clip into the Waffle House down the street. Then he goes to jail again for taking shots at airplanes overhead. His dad and a dude with whom his dad smokes crack sit in loungers around a fairly serious hole in the living room floor, watching a small television that's often tuned to a dead channel. It's not, like, a Baby Jessica situation; any adult human could go right through this hole. I think they're both living off disability. Him and his girlfriend live in the basement, where sometimes rubbish and jetsam fall through from the living room above. It's a cement floor, or cigarettes would surely have started a fire by now. It reeks perpetually of melted plastic crackscent. Downstairs, Awesome Bill lives a life of roids and weightlifting. He's enormously obese, and relatively drugfree beyond the Dianabol and Trenbolone."

"And he cooks the speed?"

"Hell no. I doubt this dude can open a can. He picks it up for me; I swing by and pick it up, paying him about 4x his price. Still cheap for what it gets me. I then leave as quickly as I can. If possible, I hold my breath the entire time."

"Can I smoke a cigarette in here?"

"Fuck yes." Katz finds an ashtray and lights one up himself. "So sometimes I have to sit around a bit waiting for the delivery. I think they started doing this on purpose, as I'm having to hang out there a decent bit lately. I reup about once a month, but even an hour in this place is a grim fucking time, one that casts a pallor on subsequent days. So the most recent time I go over, he's like, 'we've gotta ride to my peoples.' That's how he said it, 'my peoples.' So I was like, 'your people's what?' Which I immediately regretted, because it of course just set his mind ajumble."

"Why did they have a hole in the floor?"

"Because they're pieces of shit. Fire? Stacked too much weight? Shot it out? Pissed on the floor and it rotted out? They're junkies. Everything they touch turns to garbage. So we roll over to this dude's house down the street. He's hyperkinetic, clucking practically, within an epsilon of fullblown amphetamine psychosis. He's got several guns broken down in front of him; he's blasting

Slipknot; I figure this guy's gonna do something stupid enough to draw cops to him within twenty-four hours max."

"So not to be a dick, but don't you feel kinda weird calling people junkies when you're there buying meth from them?"

"Do you think I'm a junkie?" Katz stares; it is difficult to tell whether he is mildly amused or mildly irritated, or both.

"I mean, you're addicted to hard drugs, right?"

"Semantics. I prefer the term high-functioning addict."

"Better marketing, certainly."

"What's a hard drug? A drug that causes you to fuck up. For some people, weed is a hard drug. Some people fuck up without any drugs at all. It's a hard drug if it makes your life hard."

"Hrm."

"I'm not saying being addicted to anything is a positive thing, a net life win. I'm saying that if I have a fucking hole in my floor, I get it fixed. So this guy asks me the same question I asked you: 'hey man, you wanna buy a TEC-9?' And I'm like, 'there are few things I wish to buy less than a TEC-9.' He insists with rising agitation and volume that this is a phenomenal deal he's offering me, that I'll never see such a deal again, that he would not offer his beloved mum this deal on a semiautomatic high-capacity pistol. Finally, he declaims that without a pistol purchase, I'm not buying any drugs, at any price."

"So surely there was a body on that pistol?"

Katz shrugs. "Possibly? It was actually a tremendous deal, so I just saw it as a cost of doing business, and said fine, I'll take it. I leave and on my way home, I stop at this bridge. It's over the Dog River, I think. I get out and I'm about to toss this heater into the river, when I remember that's how Wayne Williams got caught back in 1981."

"Wayne Williams?"

"Yeah check out the Atlanta child murders sometime. They got him when he pulled off to ditch a sacked-up body into the Chattahoochee, and a surveillance team heard the splash. And I'm thinking, if this gun has a body on it, I do not look great throwing it into the drink."

"I mean, you don't look great with it in any context, I'd think."

"Yeah but this would be loud. Anyway, that's how I end up with a tricked-out TEC-9 spray-and-pray in my closet. I'll let you have it for a fantastic price. Such a deal I would not offer my own mother."

✳ ✳ ✳ ✳ ✳ ✳ ✳ ✳

"The quarter's $80." Four twenties, dead on. "What have you been up to?"

Stacey Jacobs is a breezily pretty girl from Missouri, only in Atlanta a few months now, who'd waited on Katz and Bolaño at the Steamhouse Lounge. There they consumed Jäger at -18 °C, washing it down with draft Abita Purple Haze in pint glasses. Katz's sweat had long collapsed his collar, which felt wet and mushy whenever it touched his neck. If Bolaño sweat, no one saw it. They had a policy of paying for meals with cash, tipping 100% unless there was good reason not to. This effectively utilized unbanked monies, encouraged staff to look the other way should someone need hooked up on premises, and kept the service attentive. Katz had waited for Bolaño to go to the bathroom—Michael got fussy and priggish when Sherman acquired customers in front of him, several times prompting Katz to ask how then Bolaño proposed to acquire customers, exactly—and invited her to come pick up. Quarters went to servers at $80 rather than the $90 charged most people, a discount that (combined with late availability) brought many in as customers. Quality hookups of quarters to one server often led to ounce sales, indirectly hooking up several servers. Ounces were his bread-and-butter, profit- and weedflux-wise.

"Oh man Sherman, last night we're absolutely packed, all these frat guys and their drunk hos. One boots all over the floor and herself and falls down and starts crying."

Katz packs a bowl, lights it, passes. "Did she clean it up?"

Her laugh is a chirping thing, sardonic but not cynical. "Fuck no. Her boyfriend comes over and helps her up, then another girl slips in the vomit and almost goes down. I'm already getting the bucket at this point before we get sued because this stupid bitch drank too many Kamikazes."

"Hers was a divine wind indeed!"

"What?"

"Oh, heh. Kamikaze. It means divine wind. *Shinpū Tokubetsu Kōgekitai.*"

"Oh OK." She ignores him. "So I go to get the mop and bucket but, hey, here's the mop, no bucket. No indication of where the mopless bucket got off to, or why. Fuck it, I grab the mop, and go get the floor dried out to a point where people aren't going to be busting ass. But now dancers have coalesced around me again, and I can't get out of this mass of jumping frat boys." Stacey is as petite as they come. "I wield the mop like an American Gladiator and start yelling at the top of my voice VOMIT ON THE BROOM, VOMIT ON THE BROOM, jabbing it in faces like I'm Lady Ahab. That served to clear me a lane."

"Outstanding." He chuckles, then guffaws. "VOMIT ON THE BROOM. I'd have enjoyed seeing that. Let me ask, do you enjoy acid? What about MDMA?"

"I don't eat much acid anymore, but I'm always down to roll."

"Are you working this Friday?" She nods. "You get off around what, 2am?" The bowl is at her lips at full inhale; she holds up three fingers. "Three am? Well I'll be just finishing up a bunch of work around then; want to come over, eat acid and watch a movie? Have you ever seen *Pi?*"

"I could be down for that." She smiles. "You'll have plenty of weed, right? I like to smoke a lot when I trip."

"Honey. I mean, my stocks of weed are essentially limitless."

She smiles wider. "Alright then, it's a date, Sherman Katz. What will you be working on until three AM?"

"Code. Always. I make holes in the coding to do anything else; I'd like to hang out with you after work this Friday evening. Before that, I'll code. When you leave, whether it's Saturday morning or Sunday morning or whenever, I'll code again. Take up thy Model-M and walk." For a calculated moment he stares into the distance.

"Saturday evening! What, would I crash here or something?"

Shinpū Tokubetsu Kōgekitai: 神風特別攻撃隊 Divine Wind Special Attack Unit

"My *Katzhaus* is your house for the duration of your trip and recovery. I meant to imply nothing else." He smiles; he has implied everything. From coy eyes leaks confirmation of the correctness of his interface. He might go with something other than *Pi*, though; it had been unsuccessfully broken out on a recent second date, one unfollowed by a third. Maybe *El ángel exterminador* or Bertolucci's *The Dreamers,* just recently acquired via BitTorrent in DivX-encoded MPEG-4. He'd attempted with no small annoyance to burn with growisofs media a DVD player could read, wasting several blanks before he figured out how MicroUDF and VMG and VTS and FPPGC and VOB worked together. He then realized he'd need reconvert his MPEG-4 to MPEG-2, disgustedly said fuck it, and resolved to simply watch it on the computer.

```
From: Select Agents Program <********@*********>
To: sherman katz <ssk@suburbanjihad.net>
Subject: Federal Select Agent Registration
Date: 2005-02-04 1749 UTC (1249 EST)

The Federal Select Agent Program has received your
APHIS/CDC Form 1 Application for Registration for
Possession, Use, and Transfer of Select Agents and Toxins.

We are not currently registering individuals in the
FSAP. Application must first be on a laboratory-wide scale.
Once your laboratory has a Person of Contact (as defined in
7 CFR § 331.16, see also 9 CFR § 121 and 42 CFR § 73) and
has designated Operators, and they have completed mandatory
training, and been approved, they may apply to FSAP.

We are furthermore confused by the nature of your
organization. Your application claims BSL-4 compliance
for your research on "ultrapox". Your address seems to be
a multifamily home in a residential area, and there is no
ICD-10 diagnosis code corresponding to "ultrapox". What is
the nature of "A Plague on Both Your Houses, LLC"?

Center for Disease Control / US Department of Agriculture
Federal Select Agent Program Administrator
```

It is long past evening's end, around 0420h. Sherman Spartacus Katz looks at IM. He alone is awake and active. He packs and smokes a bowl in honor of the time, gets a glass of water, and focuses on code. It is far and away his favorite part of the day: nightcore, the hacker's hour, is his. Time to work.

El ángel exterminador: The Exterminating Angel. Luis Buñuel 1962
MPEG-4: Motion Picture Experts Group Visual (H.263-compatible) ISO/IEC 14496-2
VMG: Video Manager   **VTS:** Video Title Set   **FPPGC:** First Play Program Chain

10 vladimir cel tredat takes up a collection

Recently naturalized Vladimir cel Tredat, 6'2, godawful teeth, at least 128 kilos and probably a good bit more wears tailored dress shirts and fine trousers, stepping to in custom-made brogues. Riding along in Vlad's Dodge Durango 5.7 Hemi, they'd pulled into the parking lot of a Chattahoochee Avenue strip mall, a picture of urban decay, whereupon Vlad hopped out with a pair of shoes. "Atlanta's best cordwainer, Katz." He held up the expansive wingtips. "Normally I would return them to Romania, where the cobblers of Clujana are among the finest in the world. But I'll need these for dancing tomorrow." The thought of portly Vladimir tutting and krumping around on a dance floor to Republica or 2 Unlimited brought Katz some joy. "cel Tredat" apparently means "the Betrayed," which Katz supposes to be better than "the Betrayer," but still rather inauspicious, and he is growing somewhat frustrated as he explains the Trade.

"They're not steering untargeted transcription through keyword search and launching investigations based off it." Katz's eyes roll hard. "Leads would be overwhelming in number and low in quality. Beyond that, the computational cost is something that you can roughly assess, right? It costs C core-hours to transcribe some unit time of phone call. You look at the time spent in phone calls nation- or worldwide over a day, week, whatever to get valid big numbers. A core costs W watts, so you've got a kwh cost for each call. That gives you a ballpark estimate on how big the operation can scale using their power input. Now, are they archiving all calls, for lookback parallel construction once you're targeted? Very possibly. You can do the same analysis—it costs this much to compress and write the audio data."

"But how do you know the government doesn't have transcription algorithms that are way better than what's known?"

"Vladimir. *We know the people that could do such a thing.* Not all of them, of course. But CIA, NSA, FBI, they all actively recruit our computer science and math departments. One, how likely is it anyone at school in a given year, with all our undergraduates and PhD students, makes a meaningful advance in voice transcription? Two, how many people at school are even capable of doing so? Three, how many of those people are going into government work?"

"Yeah but the government has a vested interest in this."

"They have an interest based in a perverted notion of justice, employees who couldn't hack it at a real company, and managers servicing a job-creation program. You've got Google, Apple, Microsoft, Amazon, all of those gigantic companies throwing hundreds of millions at this, with engineering talent the government couldn't dream of. And how do you think the government approaches research-intensive problems? They don't just have stables of elite engineers hanging out. Well, they do, but they're called national labs and they're busy doing subcritical stockpile testing and calling it inertial confinement fusion. I do not see the Department of Energy unassing a few Q-cleared senior scientists to do voice transcription. Nor do I imagine the kids hacking on ALE—"

"ALE?"

"Arbitrary Lagrangian Eulerian, you'll see it in conjunction with AMR—that's adaptive mesh refinement—you use it to simulate manybody problems step by timestep. Sandia's CTH is big here. You've got a plasma and it's doing this with these particles. What does it do next? Those cats want to sit there and write FORTRAN 95, race one another's MPI programs, and call it work. Lattice QCD, Hartree-Fock, MUSCL and Godunov the God all day long. Those guys won't fuck with anything that isn't a matrix or a partial differential equation. So they go to the mercenary labs: SRI. GTRI here. Charles Stark Draper at MIT. APL at Johns Hopkins. DEVCOM ARL in North Carolina's Research Triangle. Naval Research Lab in DC. AFRL in Dayton."

Vladimir looks dubious.

"There's precedent here, right? Public key cryptography gets developed at GCHQ in 1969 by three dudes you've never heard of."

"Exactly! Years before Diffie-Hellman!"

"Seven years beforehand. Diffie and Hellman patent it along with Merkle. Diffie's a Sun Fellow and looks like a happy Gandalf. Hellman becomes a professor at Stanford for fucking ever. Merkle runs the GTISC down the street. They'll win Turing Awards. Those three British fucks peddle ass on SoHo for all the world knows. You don't think anyone noticed? And either way, the military edge was less than a decade, and the money in computer science was a fraction of what it is today. Shit, if someone pukes up a better algorithm, they'll quit their agency and start a company around it."

"Should I get a gun?"

Katz stares at him for a moment. Has he made a mistake? "Why would you get a gun?" Vladimir starts to respond, and Sherman cuts him off, speaking with slow deliberation. "Vladimir, you live in America now. You ought by all means take advantage of your Constitutional right to arms. I recommend dual-wielded Desert Eagles for motherfuckers, the Sentinel Arms Striker-12 combat shotgun for a few more motherfuckers, and the Browning M2 firing fifty-caliber BMG for big motherfuckers. Bear spray also works. M18A1s in the front yard, howitzers in the back. Go nuts. With that said, guns are for playing William Tell with Joan Vollmer and keeping the king of England out of your face. Their presence takes a regular, meaningless possession charge and adds a five year consecutive prison term. They scare neighbors, who are then more inclined to drop a dime. They give informants' reports more weight and assholes more reason to rob you. What are your intentions for a firearm?"

"Well, if someone breaks in here for one. When I go make a big pickup and have a bunch of cash on me. If I need to intimidate someone who isn't paying."

"Vlad, you're worrying me here. I'm wondering whether you're really the guy to take over this ship. Let's address each of your cases. Someone breaks in, presumably with you here. What are our possible outcomes? A. You blast him, defend the castle, leave his corpse for others to see. Hang a sign outside.

CTH: Chart-D to the Three Halves (your guess is as good as mine)
MUSCL: monotonic upstream-centered scheme for conservation laws
M18A1: "Claymore" anti-personnel mine

'Please break in. I would love the chance to kill you legally.' So the cops are here twenty minutes later, wanting to know what happened, do you know this head, why do you think he wanted to rob you? They're going to search your place. *Thompson v. Louisiana* and *Mincey v. Arizona* explicitly allow a sweep for additional victims, during which evidence seen can be seized under plain view doctrine. They can secure the premises while securing a warrant—*Segura v. United States.* You're almost certainly getting arrested and processed. In the very best case, you've got a huge spotlight on you, you've attracted all kinds of heat, and there's a big nasty mess of brain and bone and blood and shit downstairs. Or maybe you get capped, or take one in the spine and end up paralyzed. Maybe the DA says your use of force was unjustified. Maybe the head is a fifteen year old black kid selling candy bars and you've got Cynthia McKinney and all her old district calling for your ass. Maybe it was a friend being an idiot, or your landlord."

"So what do I do if someone breaks in?"

"Vladimir, are you particularly skilled with weapons?"

"I play a lot of *Halo.*"

Katz gives the rotund Romanian the harshest possible side of his eye, and comes very close to saying fuck it.

"Do you have any reason to believe that you would successfully put down an intruder, one who is possibly armed, one who is possibly practiced with their gun? By which I mean they've fired it at a target, not that they're familiar with their fucking Xbox controller. And if I might say so, you're not a small target. If someone fires in the right general direction, they're gonna tag you."

"No, fair enough. No need to be an asshole."

"I'm unsure. B. You go to make a big pickup. You have a lot of cash on you. You're worried they're gonna take it. You hand over cash, and they say 'thanks' and start walking away. You gonna plug 'em in the back, or what? And furthermore, you're picking up from *me.* The way you avoid getting ripped off is to deal with people you trust, and don't fuck people over. I've been doing this for years. Never once have I wished I had a gun. Your C is the same deal. You're not a goddamn Soprano. If someone isn't paying, you *stop selling them drugs.* You go over and knock on the door late at night. You call them. You mention to their friends that you're worried about their health, that you haven't been able to reach them for a few days about this small matter of an unpaid debt. If they're having a rough spot, being squeezed, you tell them to pay when they can. If they're a good customer, you extend all reasonable fronts, maybe drop their cost a little bit in the interim, make it easy for them to pay you and keep your product among their scaled-back purchases. You earn their trust and respect and appreciation. Then they get back on their feet and make it right and are yours forever. Or they don't, and maybe they even cut town. Well, you eat that cost. You don't go threatening your customers unless you want their next action to be a call to the cops.

The most likely outcome of acquiring a gun will be that you never use it. The second most likely outcome is that you get busted for something else, and it becomes a massive judicial stick broken off in your ass, one that profited you not at all. You can be a drug dealer, or a gun owner. Or a gangbanger, and you'll be treated and live as such. We are genteel; we are merchants; we are friendly shopkeeps, the backbone of the neighborhood. All that gun shit is great for singing along with Westside Connection and Master P. It has no applicability here.

Speaking of fronts: they are the name of the game. You don't discount on behalf of friendship, because if you're doing things correctly, *your friends are your customers.* But you extend pretty much any credit someone wants. The only time you don't is when it would promote the buy to a volume that justifies further discounting, or would deprive you of remaining product at a time when you need cash. And why would you need cash? You're buying from me; I'll front you as necessary. Just get 'em moved. What do you call a customer who buys a Z each week, but always on a three hundred dollar front? You call them three hundred dollars a week."

"Do I want to try to cultivate large volume sales, then, even at the cost of substantial discounting?"

"Drugs are tangible consumer goods with relatively inelastic demand and somewhat elastic pricing. You buy a finished good, and then trade it; you are a middleman. The costs of the middleman are raw COGS and other OpEx costs of revenue: warehousing, and shrink, mostly to himself. Demand inelasticity means your COGS ought always come back to you—Atlanta isn't going to lose interest in weed. You probably won't have warehousing, but you do have the threat of law enforcement; both are bigger worries when you move more product. Your costs of revenue less COGS are similarly small, but the more transactions you engage in, the more people to whom you're advertised, again the more heat. You're a firm. You want to maximize profit. You're picking up elbows from me at three large. That price is fixed unless you move up to substantially larger orders. Following all this?" Vladimir nods. "You've got some amount of profit you make on each bow. You control that based on your pricing. You've got some rate at which you move bows, influenced by your client development and your pricing. Your product is to a degree subject to substitution. Prices too high? You'll sell nothing. Prices too low? You'll make no profit. You want to sell at whatever price—and that price is probably dynamic—maximizes your profit, without calling down unreasonable heat. Consider a minimum profit you want to make on the bow, and rarely sell without at least that much markup. The exception is client acquisition. Discount heavily with the hope of further sales, if necessary. Fronting is better."

Vladimir looked unsure. "Vlad, the point of taking larger orders is normally twofold: a larger sale, and the potential for steeper discounts from the supplier. You're not getting a steeper discount by tacking another bow onto your order. So there's no advantage there. The only reason for you to discount is if the increased size of the order offsets the discount, profit-wise. Or if you'd otherwise miss the sale entirely. If you're picking up qwops, and someone wants a QP all their own, at your price, you maybe do it because the hopper is less per unit than the qwop. Your six bows will be the same unit price as your three." The lesson seems to have gotten through, finally.

COGS: cost of goods sold

"If you ever get picked up, you need to understand—you're a citizen, right? Full-fledged? You're not on a green card?"

"Yeah."

"Good, otherwise getting arrested could cause you a real problem, get you kicked out of the country. There's a chance you could get picked up. That's why I'm getting out; I don't want to run the risk anymore. But I've done this for almost a decade without any police problems. I'd recommend not driving around dirty. Have people come over as much as possible; it's more convenient anyway. The vast majority of busts happen while driving." Katz doesn't know if this is true, but it sounds reasonable. "The biggest risk you've got is somebody you sell to getting arrested while doing something stupid, and giving up your name. Now, you're not selling enough to warrant some bigtime operation, surveillance and shit"—Katz doesn't know about this, either, but hopes it to be true—"but they'll take a day to do a controlled buy if someone's offering you. *Don't freak out.* You've got a clean record, right? No felonies?"

"I have a few speeding tickets."

"That matters not at all. So they come in, they put the handcuffs on you, you're on the floor, they're going through all your shit. Don't antagonize anyone, don't admit anything, don't say shit. They're going to ask you questions. They're going to intimate that they can help you at trial, but only if you tell them things now. Don't say shit. You're not going to go to prison, absolutely not—unless you have a gun. Here's our lawyer." Katz hands over a business card. "Call him and mention my name. We'll get you bailed out as quickly as possible, and I'll help cover his fees. He's excellent. You'll spend two or three days in jail—can't do anything about that—then you'll have a court appearance, and you'll get a fine and probation. With the amounts you have, on a first trip, with a lawyer and a job and an education, and let's not deny the value here of being white, there is zero chance you go to prison."

"When am I going to meet these guys?"

Katz unspools the New Way. It intended to largely remove himself from the loop, with its demands on time and legal exposure, while retaining a decent amount of the cash. "You won't be, unless there are problems. You won't even know one another's names. I only ever met them once, when we first hooked up. I wasn't taking over for some trusted person, but you are, and they want to avoid meeting you entirely."

"Why?"

"Seriously? So that you can't give them up." Katz leans in a bit. "And honestly, dude, this is just as much about protection for you."

"Why would they tell the cops about me?"

"Not in that sense. Protection from them worrying that you might give them up, and doing something to cover the risk." Vlad shudders. Good. "You want them to know you can't give them trouble. Hence, not knowing their names, or what they look like."

"Not that I intend to give up anyone, but wouldn't I be able to just give up the phone number, or let the cops know about a buy? How am I going to hook up from them if I never meet them?"

"It's a pretty smooth little scheme, but it requires some discipline from you."
Katz smiles. "You pick up from storage units. Different storage unit every time,
different facilities. Nothing too far away, but outside the Perimeter sometimes,
far enough that you'll want to avoid rush hour." Katz hands him two cards, fake
identification in the names of Brad Lowell of Massachusetts and Eric Shandly
of Alabama. "This is why I needed those passport photos from you. Usually
you won't need to present identification, just the key, but some places require
you to be listed for access. If you'll need a key, I'll give one to you when you
drop off money."

"And so I'm dropping money off to you?"

"Yeah. But I won't know what you're ordering, or where it's being dropped
off. Even if I happen to have the key, I don't know what it opens."

"Why don't I just drop off money where I pick up?"

"Because they want money up front, and if you did that, you could tell
cops where you're doing it, and they could watch and get names. Also, this
eliminates any disputes about whether you dropped off correct cash."

Vlad isn't stupid, just a little slow. "Couldn't I tell the cops where I'm picking
up, and they'd watch to see someone drop things off?"

"You won't know where you're picking up until after they've dropped off."

"Couldn't they just drop if off with me, then, instead of this tapdance with
keys and fake ID and storage units?"

"What did I say about you not wanting these people to know who you are?"

"We could do the exchange in public. Use codenames."

"Vladimir, they're already doing us a solid by retailing to us in these small
amounts, at these prices. They're accustomed to dealing in fifty, a hundred
pounds at a time. They're professionals. I have no intention of arguing procedures with them, and suggest you similarly refrain from doing so."

"It just seems like a lot of bullshit. And what if I get caught with fake ID?"

"Then you do what I said earlier about not saying shit. No one's going to
catch you with fake ID. I've done it this way for years, with zero problems. If
there are problems with the product—which there won't be—bring it to my
attention."

"Do you have working phone service again?" Katz had subscribed to an early
VoIP service; combined with his BitTorrenting, phone calls often devolved to
"text me! zee phone is fucked." He refused to get a cellphone, and wouldn't
have one until 2008 in a protracted display of contrarianism.

The objective is to no longer bring consuming herds to his house. Robbery
is a concern, as are cops, whether brought there by a flipped customer or any
of the numerous other reasons why they might show up. He's been pretty
loose over the years regarding who he's served, and has enemies. Product
will be stored with Bolaño, who will deliver to the storage unit upon Katz's
directive. An emolument, more a pourboire really, would flow from Katz as
necessary, asynchronously; Bolaño would continue his low-volume wholesaling, benefiting from the bulk discount. Vlad would get to deal with most of
the dozens of individual buyers Katz had collected over the years, many of
them now professional engineers, some with families, discreet and quiet folk
giving excellent custom. He would take over Greg Moyer's weekly pound, for

distribution to a handful of fratboys at GSU and GT, and even one at Morehouse. The twenty or so smalltime retailers, buying their ounces and quarterpounds, those too would be his responsibility. Katz would add $800 to each pound and still undercut anyone else Vlad could buy from; should that situation change, he could drop prices comfortably. He expected to clear about three thousand dollars a week after expenses; he smoked about a pound per month himself, so knock two large off for that. About ten thousand a month, tax-free. Not bad.

And so Katz contacts his largest customers, giving them contact information for the Romanian, informing them that business was now to go through Vladimir exclusively. "Pricing remains the same, quality remains the same. He'll be buying from my people. I'm removing myself from the equation." Over the next few weeks he directs most of his smaller buyers the same way (he keeps some of the girls). Most customers convey a sense of sorrow, of loss; almost every conversation ends with an insistence that they continue to meet up, to hang out. Katz agrees with assurance, as if to do otherwise was unthinkable. In truth, while their relations are cordial enough, most of these people are simply customers; he is unlikely to see them again beyond social gatherings and social media. It's a bit of a downer.

* * * * * * * * *

Bolaño gazed out his window. He was working at Intercontinental Exchange, and rented a spacious groundfloor condo in the newly-built 960 Buckhead for $2,200 per month. He figured he'd purchase within a few years. The furnishings were modern, tasteful, and wholly masculine. It was a much more comfortable place to talk than Katz's $750/month craphole off Northside Drive. Bolaño didn't understand why Katz hadn't yet moved. It had been a fine base of operations while retailing customer-intense product, right down there in the thick of things with quick access to the Connector, but it was high time Katz became a bit more aspirational. He still wore basketball shorts and t-shirts exclusively. Bolaño frowned.

"So I'm no chemist. But from what I understand, there are two main difficulties in synthesizing acid that make it a more involved effort than MDMA or the child's play that is DMT." Katz stands at Bolaño's office whiteboard, a green marker uncapped and armed.

"Access to precursors, right?"

"Yes. That's the first and most significant problem." He puts up a I and II, and writes D-LYSERGIC ACID next to the former. "Lysergic acid is a biological precursor for the—"

"You sure you want to be writing this stuff down?"

"Michael. It's a whiteboard. I'll erase it when we're done."

"Until you do that, what if someone walks by and sees it? You do notice we're on the first floor? Or if someone is taking pictures? You want a big blown-up picture of you looking stupid, standing next to a whiteboard with synthesis details on it in court?"

"Dude, who's going to walk in? Who's going to take a picture?" Katz stomps to a window and throws it open, leaning out most of his upper body. "Looking for people with cameras! Paparazzi? Ron Galella? Cindy Sherman? Rino Barilarri? KGB? FBI? Anyone taking pictures of sexy Bolaño? Y'all want it!"

"*Stop that.* Close the fucking window. Jesus." Katz makes a production of looking up and down the road before turning back. "It's bad opsec. You can't deny that. We're talking about life in prison. Pickard's rotting away in there until he fucking dies. He's a smart white fuck from Georgia just like you. Went to Princeton. Went to Harvard. Didn't count for shit. The Honorable Richard Rogers sent him to Tucson after telling him and his lawyers to eat shit on every objection they made at sentencing. He went from a base offense level of thirty-eight up to a forty-eight." Michael stands and erases the board. "The federal sentencing grid cuts off at offense level forty-three. One long row of 'life,' 'life,' 'life,' 'life.' He got an 'abuse of special skill' enhancement and he doesn't even have a degree."

"I'm kinda following what you're saying, but I don't grok. What's a 48?"

Michael is pleased to possess facts of which Katz has no knowledge. "Federal judges have a sentencing matrix. I think it was introduced in 1987, and amended a few times since then. You get convicted of some crime, and that crime has a base offense level. Let's say you jacked off in a national park—"

"Is it a crime to masturbate in a national park?"

"Should one's masturbation come to the attention of a park ranger, I can't imagine it goes well for you. Let's make it simple. You're smoking weed in Yosemite. Ranger Rick comes up behind you and finds an ounce in your pocket. There's a base offense level on the conviction. Then there are adjustments both down and up. Minors, hate crime shit, elderly, were you wearing body armor, were you strapped, did your parents dress you up like a girl, etc. One of those enhancements by the way being 'use of a special skill,' which Pickard ate, and I'm sure we'd eat. The judge explicitly said Pickard's special skill was 'being a chemist,' which makes one wonder how exactly you're cooking LSD without being a chemist, *c'est la vie.*"

Katz absorbs this with a thoughtful expression. "What if you plea?"

"That's a negative modifier for 'taking responsibility.' What you're really looking for there, I think, is that they drop or reduce some charges. Once they have the modified offense level, they look across its row for the column corresponding to your criminal history level, running I–VI. There's the penalty. The offense level cuts off at forty-three, at which point you are capital-F Fucked. So the upshot of this is that there has been only one major American LSD bust in the past twenty years. They're going to be able to say devil LSD is active in microgram amounts. Did you know that's the name of the DEA's internal newsletter slash Parade Magazine? *Microgram.* Yeah. They're going to be able to count any precursors and waste product towards total mass. Let me add that we would likely be subject to any number of *further* charges.

Let me emphasize that this is a different world than what we've been doing. You bust somebody slinging weed, a few pounds, who the fuck cares? Exactly no one. So long as no one has guns, your public gives not one solitary fuck. Weed is everywhere. The flow is unceasing and will never cease. Whoever you bring in probably doesn't even do any time on a first offense, certainly not if they have a lawyer with half a brain. You get that guy to roll, again, who the fuck cares? You go up the ladder on some weed. What are you going to do, extradite from British Columbia? Now acid scares people. There're still plenty of assholes out there who think it does chromosome damage, or that there's strychnine in it, or that you can go permanently *non compos mentis* off a dose. Ludicrous, just grossly misinformed notions. To be fair, it's certainly more disruptive than marijuana. You come across your kid tripping, you're gonna think he has lost it, or has gone retarded, or is possessed."

Katz recalls his first poorly considered evening eating LSD, sitting in his father's recliner in the living room, unable to stop laughing for any meaningful period. His mother had looked at him like he'd lost his mind, which he supposed he had. In the end she seemed to chalk it up to his innate weirdness.

"So that's the first thing. Two: let's say you get caught with three sheets. That's three hundred doses, which sounds a lot more impressive than two pounds of weed, despite the latter being significantly more expensive. Not to mention bulky. Three hundred hits, that's gonna be reported as 'Johnny Cunt was caught with enough acid to dose everyone at Buckhead Church if he poured it in the Communion wine.' Three: let's continue with our three-sheet example. You pull this head out, you're plugging a serious chunk of your acid inflow, since there's so much less of it. If you roll him, how many steps can you be from actual production? There's furthermore tremendous incentive for people to roll on us, because they know the value of giving over an acid dealer, *especially* if they have any suspicion we're the point of synthesis. That's a get out of jail free card. Just look at that shithead Todd Skinner. He basically tortured someone to death, but would have gotten away with it for putting the DEA onto Pickard."

"Would have gotten away?"

"Well he did, but then he fucked it up later. Immaterial. I feel warranted in urging abstention from writing D-LYSERGIC ACID on a whiteboard visible through"—pointing in turn at each—"two different windows, and to be in general somewhat vigilant."

Katz caps and returns the marker. "Good call mang; I'm with you." Whether he's convinced or simply admonished is impossible to know. "Question: aren't you worried about microphones or cameras or that kind of thing? Should we be discussing this here?"

Michael has considered this. "If someone has cause to install mics or cameras, we're already deeply fucked. That doesn't mean we need give the game away to some random pedestrian asshole who walks by and sees Professor Katz"—Katz smiles—"delivering a lecture on clandestine chemistry."

Katz buys this logic. "So the question of precursors is fundamental. One gets LSD, lysergic acid diethylamide as you surely know, by reactions on lysergic acid. Also known as D-lysergic acid for reasons that will become clear. I might say D-LSA, which should not be confused with LSA aka ergine aka D-lysergic acid amide, itself a psychedelic D-LSA derivative, a natural one."

Bolaño makes a face. "Is ergine in any way relevant?"

"At most minimally. You've heard of morning glory? Ololiuhqui? Hawaiian baby woodrose seeds?" Michael nods. "They produce ergine as an alkaloid. It's mildly psychedelic, and you could theoretically cleave the amide to get regular

D-LSA en route to LSD, but it's universally considered uneconomic. Not enough alkaloid density in cultivated *Convolvulaceae* compared to a nice fermented broth of ergot sclerotia. So yeah, D-LSA is always lysergic acid, and I'm aware of no path to LSD that avoids D-LSA. All this stuff was originally found in ergot, which ergot by the way is fascinating; I got lost for a few days studying ergot." Katz speaks with some reverence.

"You were studying ergot?"

Katz's shrug is insolent. *"De omnibus rebus et de quibusdam aliis."*

His silence is aggressive, and demands a response.

"Is that...Virgil?"

"When the skills go, they *go*." The balance of the universe has been restored. "Pico della Mirandola. Martin Luther had ninety-five theses; my man had nine hundred. First book to be banned by the Catholic Church, long before the *Index Librorum Prohibitorum*. So. Lysergic acid. Trivially interconverts with paspalic acid. The two are both biosynthesized on the way to ergopeptines, which are alkaloids that stick a peptide on the lysergic acid where we want amides—lysergamides. Lysergamides are water-soluble; ergopeptines are not. In all of these chemicals we have the tetracyclic ergoline backbone. Ergoline pretty much has serotonin as its own backbone; they're both biosynthesized from L-tryptophan. Activation of the 5-HT$_{2A}$ serotonin receptor is necessary but in no way sufficient for full effect from serotonergic psychedelics.

So. The main ergopeptine alkaloids are ergotamine, ergonovine, and ergocristine. Take any one of these, hydrolyze it, and you've got lysergic acid. Ergotamine and ergonovine are original List I precursors. Ergine and D-LSA are Schedule III but good luck with that. Ergocristine isn't a listed precursor yet, but it probably will be soon—Pickard and Apperson were using ergocristine in their Kansas op. Even there, Pickard was getting the ergocristine via some shady cash-only Italian supplier. The assumption is that any attempt to directly purchase ergot alkaloids will be immediately reported, raising the swift umbrage of the DEA. Now, whether this is true with *e.g.* Chinese and Indian suppliers, I have no idea.

Assuming one can't buy them, you can have two paths: synthesis and biosynthesis. The synthesis paths are difficult chemistry, beyond my abilities for sure without some serious study and a lot of practical lab work. But they are published, and there has been progress since the initial patents. Then you have biosynthesis, the method favored by industry, where you grow a shitton of ergot fungus, dry it, and perform relatively simple analytical chemistry to separate the alkaloids. You have a cap of about 2% alkaloid mass, really more like 1%. You can probably do some genetic engineering to kick that up a bit, but that's beyond my knowledge. It's probably worth looking into, though, given the small amounts one needs for serious LSD synthesis."

Michael breaks in. "What's yield like from the precursors?"

"I haven't calculated it myself. It looks like about 20% from ergotamine, up to 40% if you're leet. Apparently Pickard bragged to Skinner—yes, Michael,

---

De...aliis: Of all that exists and a little more. Giovanni Pico della Mirandola
Index Librorum Prohibitorum: List of Prohibited Books

I've also read the transcripts—that his 44% beat the old 'world record' of 24%. For whatever that's worth. So five kilos of active precursors for every kilo of product. I'm also unsure whether that figure applies to LSD or LSD tartrate. A tartrate is just a stabilized salt using tartaric acid."

"We'd get 2mg from each pill assuming no loss. So that's likely to yield 400 micrograms each. Four so-so doses. Definitely no way to scale."

"Not unless you want to divert half a million Cafergot, no. But more than enough for us to never need buy acid again. And if we ever did have some access to bulk precursor, all the equipment and process knowledge is there to make bank. Surely we know someone who'd get really into growing ergot? Shit, do you know any fields of rye around here? I think you ought be able to use most of the ergopeptides—ergovaline represents something like 85% of total alkaloid weight—not just ergotamine and ergocristine. Those are the precursors you hear about because they're the alkaloids people want. But it's always just an ergoline backbone with a bunch of crap hanging off the end."

"Precursors: got it. What was the other problem?"

"Now this is a much more surmountable issue, and one that must be dealt with at any scale of production. Stereoisomers. There are four stereoisomers of D-LSA, and thus of its derivatives. I would love to draw them for you, but alas." Katz shrugs, smiling limply. "Only D-LSD is psychoactive, at least at the expected levels. Carbons five and eight are stereocenters. The C-8 isomer is iso-LSA, and the two rapidly interconvert in the presence of base. iso-LSA fucks you—it has full vasoconstrictive body load, but you don't trip off it. So it weakens your product by weight, and furthermore if your customers eat more to achieve the expected level, they're taking on proportionally more semitoxin. The other two isomers aren't really a concern, but most synthesis routes aren't stereoselective, so you end up with trash iso-LSD. Luckily, you can separate the two with fairly basic chromatography, and isomerize the iso-LSD to the dank shit. So your second problem is partly vigilance—ensuring your good product doesn't isomerize—and partly diligence: extracting and converting what isomers you do have."

Michael feels he's followed along pretty well. "So it sounds like the intrepid LSD chemist must design four processes: isolation of ergot alkaloid, lysis of said alkaloid, amination, and stereoselective purification via chromatography."

Katz grins broadly. "We are simpatico in this, you and I. We've got to assume some loss at each point. I'm assuming you don't know practical microchemistry? I certainly don't. I think we'd do very well to bring in someone with actual lab experience. There are pretty explicit writeups of varying credibility. Shulgin's *Tryptamines I Have Known and Loved* is trustworthy. He recommends a process based on phosphoryl chloride. I think there's a minimum of two chromatographic steps, one with silica to purify to LSD and then possibly iterated chiral substrate for the isomers."

"What about availability of reagents other than alkaloids? Diethylamide?"

Katz's laugh is no crueler than it needs be. "Diethylamide is an unthing, my friend. An amide is the N-C=O moiety, with two substituents off the nitrogen and one off the carbon. Ethyl is CH_2CH_3. Diethyl is two of them. You can't have 'diethylamide' by itself; you need something on that carbon. In LSD, you've got ethyl in both the nitrogen R-groups, hence diethylamide. You get there with diethylamine, two ethyls connected by a nitrogen hydride. An 'amine' is just ammonia—NH_3—with some hydrogens substituted. Diethylamine has two ethyls in place of two hydrogens; the third hydrogen is retained."

"What's the third substituent? In the final amide?"

Katz grins. "Lysergic acid. You strip the hydroxyl from D-LSA and pull the hydrogen off the nitrogen in diethylamine, and bind the two together."

"So diethylamine, then. Is it available?"

It's on the Hazardous Substances List and the Special Health Hazard Substance List, not to mention the Special Surveillance List, so not really. Ethylamine and methylamine are both List I precursors, but not particularly applicable anyway. There's a whole galaxy of substituted ergines, some of them just as effective as LSD: 1P-LSD, ETH-LAD, yes also 1P-ETH-LAD, PRO-LAD. Some of them are Shulgin's, others David Nichols' group at Purdue. So you only need diethylamine if you're looking for LSD proper, I think."

"Hrmm. Let's look into synthesis there?"

"Sure. I'm not sure about phosphoryl chloride. I'm pretty sure it's not controlled. I wouldn't be surprised if it's watched. Methylene chloride you can get. Reputable wholesalers won't send anything to a residential address, though, and might want an actual lab, presumably of some external accreditation."

"Define 'actual lab.'"

"I do not know. I'm sure that GT's chemistry department is an actual lab. I'm sure that our apartments are not. I'll look into it. Expect us to need an identity or two. We might want to have chemicals delivered to a distinct location. Might want not to, as that maybe looks weird."

"I feel an awful migraine coming on. The only cure is Mexican Cafergot."

Katz, delighted, goes in for the fist bump. "Is Pickard really from Georgia?"

"Yeah. Lived in DeKalb County, high school literally across the highway from here. Supposedly named 'Most Intellectual' at his high school. I think his mom or stepmom worked at the CDC. Just remember where he is now."

✳ ✳ ✳ ✳ ✳ ✳ ✳ ✳ ✳

Bolaño has a black messenger bag. He extracts blue and white Novartis boxen, each touting *30 comprimido—Ergotamina, Cafeína.* Turn one over, active ingredients, yes there it is: 2mg ergotamine tartrate. We're in business.

"Ninety-six packs at thirty each. A total mass of five point seven six grams of ergotamine tartrate. Twenty percent of that is one point one five two grams. 5,760 burners packing 200 mics per. A five strip would be a solid milligram. More than three will be a waste. One will be enough."

Katz, wary: "Theoretically."

"Theoretically. I'll be happy if we get two thousand. If they're pure and that strong, we can charge a K per sheet. Sell two pages, and that's eighteen thousand, and we each keep a sheet."

"We only keep two sheets? A thousand a sheet? That's $10 per hit for whoever's buying from us." When Katz first dosed in 1996, he paid $5/hit for Black Pyramids. By freshman year, a vial ran $80, a sheet $60. The streets ran triboluminescent with LSD, and glowed bluish-white under UV light.

"We'll have the only LSD around, and it'll be extraordinary LSD. We can charge what we want. There are people who'll pay that just to keep it for themselves. If they want to retail, retail at a double sawski. We're playing the only game in town, unless you want to fuck with 2C-B and all that."

"I mean, shit, people still have mushrooms."

"And mushrooms run $50 a quarter, $25 per trip. Our acid's still cheaper. One thousand a sheet. It's what we need to make lab costs back." Bolaño coughs, and scratches his face. "So talk to me about chemistry, our rough plans."

"So through all of this, remember the enemies of LSD, which are primarily the enemies of D-LSA. Those are ultraviolet, moisture, oxygen, and heat. A compound is unsaturated when it has double bonds that react with hydrogen plus a catalyst. Ultraviolet light is a catalyst for saturation of the 9,10-double bond by water. You end up with a hydrogen on 9 and a hydroxyl on 10. That's lumi-LSD, and it is useless. Heat plus an acid reagent promotes irreversible conversion to the naphthalene isomer, benzindoline. At 100 °C this runs to completion in minutes. Any oxidizer is going to rip the molecule apart. At all times, we want to be working in a dry, inert atmosphere, at low temperatures, at long wavelengths of light."

Bolaño pops a blister pack, selects one of the round fulvous tablets, and lifts it to his eye, examining its shallow convex bevel edge. Unassuming, simple, not at all indicative of the power locked within. "How do we get out the alkaloid?"

"Contaminants are magnesium stearate, talc, maize starch, cellulose, and iron oxide yellow. Normally you extract ergot alkaloids from fungus using formation of an aluminum complex, then attack that with ammonia, followed by hydrocarbon extraction. I think we can just dissolve the crushed material in chloroform or pyridine, assuming the inactive ingredients are insoluble there. Magnesium stearate is insoluble in just about everything; that's, like, its entire point. Caffeine is soluble in chloroform and pyridine. Maybe we find something it's soluble in, that ET isn't, and filter it out first. Either way, we wash it with methanol and get a pale brown powder. This all needs to happen away from light. During hydrolysis, we'll want to protect the ergopeptides from decomposition. A German patent from the 70s suggests sodium dithionite. We'll need methanol and potassium hydroxide. We want CDI to aminate our D-LSA. It's the best method I've found. Shulgin used $POCl_3$ and $CHCl_3$.

Let's talk verification. Thankfully, the Department of Justice has published their methodology, as have the UN. We want to do this right, so we want something that can discriminate D-LSD from its isomers. The best I can find is positive-ion GC/MS/MS."

"Why do we need quantitative verification?"

"Are you an engineer or not?"

"Fair enough."

2C-B: $C_{10}H_{14}BrNO_2$ 2-(4-Bromo-2,5-dimethoxyphenyl)ethanamine

11   ergot

(this material was taken from the website of Sherman Spartacus Katz)

pronunciation

Ur-go? Er-go? Ur-got? All wrong. Their (mis)use denotes you a jabroni. There are no long vowels in ergot. ˈɜːrɡət. UR-gət. Ur, followed by "gut" almost.

fungus among us

Adam Lonicer in the 1582 *Kräuterbuch* wrote regarding rye, "There are long, black, hard, narrow pegs on the ears, internally white, often protruding like long nails from between the grains in the ear." Gaspard Bauhin's posthumous *Theatrum Botanicum* provided the first known sketch of ergot in 1658, placing it firmly within the "theatre of plants." It was not until 1764 that Otto von Münchhausen (not that von Münchhausen) stated in *Der Hausvater* that ergot was a fungus. Erasmus Darwin (not that Erasmus, and not that Darwin) in Part I, Canto IV of *The Botanic Garden* (1791) penned (lines 511–514):

> *Shield the young harvest from devouring blight,*
> *The smut's dark poison and the mildew white,*
> *Deep-rooted mould and ergot's horn uncouth,*
> *And break the canker's desolating tooth.*

regarding funga

Fungi have rarely received the respect they've deserved. Aristotle in *Τῶν περὶ τὰ ζῷα ἱστοριῶν (Historia Animalium)* came no closer than σφόγγος, the sponges, "those animals that are unfurnished with shells and grow spontaneously." He marveled in *Περὶ Ψυχῆς (De Anima)* that decaying wood gave rise to "things, not in their nature fire, which seem to produce cold light"; this bioluminescence is a product of the 3-hydroxy hispidin—one of the "luciferins," or light-bringers—metabolized by xylophagous *Agaricales*. Having been declared simple animals by the Stagirite, loyal student Theophrastus would make no mention of mushrooms (μύκης) throughout his *Περὶ φυτῶν ἱστορία (Historia Plantarum)*. Pliny the Elder[1] in *Naturalis Historia* derives *fungus* from this Greek *sphongos*, and

---

[1] R. Kobert's learned *Zur Geschichte des Mutterkorns* (1899) claims the *Rubigalia* feast described by Pliny to have been motivated by ergot, but the Rolfes in *The Romance of the Fungus World* (1925) point a convincing finger at *Puccinia graminis*. Kobert advances that the "noxious grains" of Columella's *De Re Rustica* Book II and *lolio* (darnel[3]) of *Miles Gloriosus* by Plautus similarly identify ergot, but this seems unsubstantiated by the text. G. Barger observes in his magisterial *Ergot and Ergotism* (1935) that Kobert "was carried away by enthusiasm for his subject."

considered mushrooms "plants which spring up and grow without a root—plants which grow, but cannot be reproduced from seed.[2]" The neoplatonist "Great Chain of Being" (*scala naturae*) dominated medieval natural philosophy through at least Lamarckian orthogenetics, and by its hierarchy, "truffles" would remain an uneasy substudy of botony.

What of the great Carl Linnaeus, *nom de plume* Carolus Linnæus, later ennobled Carolus a Linné? Wrote he of fauna, flora, and funga? *Est omnis divisa in partes tres?* The tenth edition of *Systema Naturæ*—the first to apply Gaspard Bauhin's binomial nomenclature across biota and beyond—bore in its subtitle *per regna tria naturæ*, "the three kingdoms of nature." But these *regna* were the *animale*, the *vegetabile*, and the *lapideum*, this last the kingdom of minerals: *Sunt sine regno.* Though he introduced important fungal taxa (and carried over several from Pier Antonio Micheli's 1737 *Nova plantarum genera*), his sparse mycology was contained wholly within *vegetabile*. Christiaan Hendrik Persoon's *Synopsis Methodica Fungorum* (1801) detailed the rusts and smuts (it was Persoon who in 1796 first used the word *mycologicæ*), while the *Systema Fungorum* (1821) of Elias Magnus Fries introduced the "fleshy" (fructificating) fungi. Species recognized in these volumes were sanctioned by the 1987 Botanical Congress to possess nominative priority, even when they'd been mentioned earlier by the Father of Taxonomy himself.

It is understandable that pioneer taxonomists would (reluctantly) place the mycota among plants. They are typically immotile, unless one counts growth as locomotion. Many (particularly macrofunga) are marked by fruiting bodies. They share habitats—especially soil—with plants, and often grow directly on plants. Polysaccharide walls defend their cells, though fungi erect theirs from chitin rather than plants' cellulose. Ernst Haeckel in 1866 introduced and saw generally accepted a new "Archephylum" *Protista*. Herbert Copeland advanced a fourth kingdom, the prokaryotic *Monera*, in 1938. Only in 1969 did Robert Whittaker put forth the quinary system commonly used today: life without cellular nuclei (prokaryotes) make up *Monera*, while the remaining eukaryotes are heterotrophic *Animalia*, autotrophic *Plantae*, saprophytic *Fungi*, or the largely unicellular gallimaufry *Protista*. The empires Eukaryota and Prokaryota are structured to admit all cellular life: that which is acellular (particularly viruses) is held to be abiotic[4].

---

[2]From Book XIX, Chapter 11: "It is known to me as a fact, that the following circumstance happened to Lartius Licinius, a person of prætorian rank, while minister of justice, a few years ago, at Carthage in Spain; upon biting a truffle, he found a denarius inside, which all but broke his fore teeth—an evident proof that the truffle is nothing else but an agglomeration of elementary earth."

[3]Bové writes in *Story of Ergot* (1969) "in fact [Harold] Moldenke and [Alma] Moldenke do not even mention ergot [in *Plants of the Bible* (1941)] except to say that *Lolium* was infested by a fungus with ergot-like properties...nevertheless darnel is darnel and ergot is ergot and the two are not alike."

[4]Despite virology being unquestionably considered a subfield of microbiology [shrug].

Est...tres: All is divided into three parts. Julius Caesar, Commentarii de Bello Gallico (*Commentaries on the Gallic War, 49 BC*).

Sunt sine regno: They are without a kingdom. *Rota Fortunae* as popularized by Boethius in De consolatione philosophiae (*Consolation of Philosophy, 524*); see also the *Carmina Burana/Burana Codex.*

the evolution of *Claviceps*[5]

With the advent of molecular phylogenetics, morphology-rooted rubrics became in any case passé. Let us draw then a curtain of charity over these arbitrary onomastics, as infinite as man's vanity. The Argentinian Jorge Luis Borges satirized the idiom in *El idioma analítico de John Wilkins* (The Analytical Language of John Wilkins, 1942), citing the tetradeca-fold classification of a mythical Chinese *Celestial Emporium of Benevolent Knowledge*:

- *pertenecientes al Emperador* (fortunate favorites of the Emperor)
- *fabulosos* (legendary beasts)
- *perros sueltos* (stray and unlicensed dogs)
- *embalsamados* (those preserved whole in jars)
- *amaestrados* (those habitually involved in lawsuits)
- *lechones* (those with caramelized breastmilk)
- *sirenas* (those mistaken for mermaids when photographed)
- *incluidos en esta clasificación* (those recognized by pushdown automata)
- *que se agitan como locos* (the rabid and/or Parkinsonian)
- *innumerables* (those that churlishly refuse to be taught sums)
- *dibujados con un pincel finísimo de pelo de camello* (dromedaries)
- *etcétera* (those of which one cannot speak and must pass over in silence)
- *que acaban de romper el jarrón* (those with the franchise)
- *que de lejos parecen moscas* (those that from afar look like flies)[6]

Foucault in *Les mots et les choses* (*Order of Things*, 1966) remembered this passage "breaking up all the ordered surfaces and all the planes with which we are accustomed to tame the wild profusion of existing things, and continuing long afterwards to disturb and threaten with collapse our age-old distinction between the Same and the Other." *J'Accuse,* motherfucker! It seems reasonable to seek more general rules, with bonus points should they prove machine-decidable: let us have procedural or even axiomatic taxonomy!

Evolution (or more properly the "modern synthesis," unifying Darwinian and Mendelian theory) can be modeled with a directed acyclic graph known as an evolutionary tree: each node represents some species, from which its child nodes diverged. Each set of child nodes (along with their common ancestor) forms a clade. These DAGs were initially drawn up according to synapomorphies, and thus they implied homology. Indeed, many things do come to pass, and will come again. Modern cladistics place funga and their fauna congeners together among the monophyletic opisthokonts. Despite a more meager fossil record, it is fairly certain that funga diverged over a billion years ago, in the Neoproterozoic era. The supercontinent Rodinia[8] lay barren under largely unimpeded ultraviolet; superplumes prompted intense volcanism

---

[5]"Club-headed," referring to spherical reproductive structures sitting atop stromata (solid mycelium nodules). In these heads, perithecia form threadlike sexual spores.

[6]I thank Michael Luis Bolaño for providing these translations from the original Spanish. He claims that he "took certain stylistic liberties" but that they are "essentially accurate"[7].

[7]*Omnis traductor traditor,* as it turns out. Some more than others.

[8]If you're thinking, "that looks a lot like the Russian *rodina*," yep!

Omnis traductor traditor: Every translator is a traitor.

when glaciers weren't reaching the equator. Plants had not yet made their way onto land: anything growing in the dubiously fertile soil and harsh radiation environment of Rodinia through the Tonian period was very likely a hardy fungus. Hundreds of millions of years later, on a wholly reconfigured planet, the "fungal spike" following the Permian–Triassic extinction event marked another period of fungal dominance.

Angiospermae—the flowering plants, those whose seeds are developed in ovaries—emerged in the early Cretaceous. By the end of that period they had surpassed *Gymnospermae* worldwide in both population and evolutionary diversity. Well before that time, the obligate heterotrophs of fungal family Clavicipitaceae (including *Paleoclaviceps*) emerged as endophytes of Poaceae (grasses). The clade coevolved with its autotrophic hosts on the Antarctica-Australia-South America compact block. *Epichloë* continued on a path of constitutive symbiosis; within twenty-five megayears, the ergot fungus *Claviceps* diverged, and began engaging in systematic (but non-systemic) parasitism, including an autapomorphic restriction of habitat to the unfertilized ovaries of angiosperms. When *secale cereale*—rye—showed up, *Claviceps* was ready[9].

Outside the world of mycology, ergot is almost synonymous with rye ergot (*C. purpurea*[10]), the species primarily responsible for ergotism (of more in a moment). Priority for *C. purpurea* is given to Louis René Étienne Tulasne from his *Memoire sur l'ergot des Glumacees* (1853), but *C. purpurea* was infecting rye (and to a lesser extent wheat, barley, and oats) long before humans engaged in taxonomy, agriculture, or even gathering.

Was the first man condensed from dust[11]? Was the first woman crafted from his rib[12]? Did they walk naked, name animals, and suffer the temptations of serpents in Eden[13]? It's not for me to say.

But if the Garden contained grains, the Garden sure as shit contained ergot.

the lifecycle of *C. purpurea*

Agrostologists tell us that the flowers of most grasses are hermaphroditic and anemophilous, and clustered in spikelets (Poaceae's racemose inflorescences). In *S. cereale*, each spikelet contains three florets, of which at least two are typically fecund. Each floret in turn contains three stamens and a single pistil. It is the integumented megasporangia of this pistil that is targeted by *C. purpurea*: sexual ascospores and asexual conidia mimic pollen grains, entering the ovary

---

[9]Ergot alkaloids are present in fungi beyond *Claviceps*: Clavicipitaceae genera *Epichloë, Atkinsonella, Balansia, Periglandula*, and *Metarhizium*; Aspergillaceae's *Aspergillus* and *Penicillium*; Arthrodermataceae's *Arthroderma*. These alkaloids are not typically psychoactive (in contrast to those found in certain flowering plants—don't worry; we're getting there!). The clavine oxidase gene *cloA* is necessary to convert agroclavine and/or elymoclavine to paspalic and/or lysergic acid.

[10]From *purpuro*, purple, to adorn/beautify. In addition to *purpurea*, at least *paspali, fusiformis, cyperi*, and *africana* produce significant neurotoxic alkaloids. G. Wasson is convinced that *paspali* is among the components of κυκεών *(kykeôn)* from the Eleusinian Mysteries.

[11]*Formavit igitur Dominus Deus hominem de limo terrae;* see Genesis 2:7.

[12]*costam quam tulerat de Adam in mulierem;* see Genesis 2:22.

[13]The Garden of/in גַּן־עֵדֶן (Eden); see Genesis 2:4–3:24.

via the stigma. Any seed present in the ovary is aborted as the spore germinates tubes, which by mitosis create somatic hyphae terminating in appressoria. Turgor pressure facilitates penetration of host cell walls. The fungal mycelium reaches the apex of the ovary within ten hours of infection, disintegrating cell walls and digesting ovarian protoplasts. Growth ceases when it encounters the vascular bundle intended for the seed.

At first, this infection appears as *sphacelia segetum*, a white soft tissue that produces honeydew containing millions of conidia. This develops a hard, dry protective rind inside the floret's husk, the *sclerotium clavus*, in which alkaloids and lipids accumulate. This may be up to ten times the size of a normal grain. The mature sclerotium falls from the stalk and lies dormant until the fruiting phase; they can survive for over a year. Several dozen stromata (compact masses of vegetative hyphae) emerge atop stalks, and these germinating mushroom-like fruit give *Claviceps* its name. Each stroma yields numerous perithecia, each containing many saclike asci. Meiosis results in eight multicellular ascospores in each ascus. While ergot obviously ruins the infected floret, the alkaloid-heavy mature form wrecks havoc on the neurological and cardiological systems of many predators, reducing net loss of the host grain to herbivores.

Ergot grows best in hot early summer temperatures, following a wet winter or damp spring. The more open florets, the more prolonged the flowering period, the more susceptible a plant is to infection. Ergots can be removed using a gravity table, or by flotation in brine: the sclerotia float in 20% salt solution, whereas grain sinks. Wheat is graded ergoty when it contains more than 0.05% by weight of ergot sclerotia. Barley, oat, and triticale are considered ergoty at 0.1%, and rye is permitted up to 0.3%. Once the grain is milled, it is difficult to distinguish and/or remove ergot.

ergot as pestilence

Man has known many mycotoxicoses, but few have caused devastation like those first recorded: ergotism *convulsivus* and *gangraenosus*, poisoning due to consumption of ergot alkaloids. These potent nitrogenous compounds can be passed through breast milk. Ergot's colocation with staple cereals has led to human consumption throughout recorded history. Wherever rye was a regular part of the diet—western and central Europe, and Scandinavia (but notably not England, dominated by wheat)—there too was ergotism.

Two millennia before Christ, a Mesopotamian spell specified as an ingredient infected grain, calling it *mehru*. Chinese obstetricians described the effects of ergot as early as 1100 BC. Assyrian cuneiform dating to 600 BC refers to a "noxious pustule in the ear of grain"; the Hearst Papyrus of 550 BC advises a trichological preparation of ergot, oil, and honey. The Parsees in the fourth century BC write of "noxious grasses that cause pregnant women to drop the womb and die in childbed." And of course Hippocrates mentioned ergot ("melantion")'s use in halting postpartum hemorrhage. In *De Bello Civili*, Book II, Chapter XXII Caesar wrote *Massilienses...gravi etiam pestilentia conflictati*, but details no symptoms, and there's not much reason to suspect ergot save *hordeo* (usually translated as barley) and the western European location.

The *Annales Xantenses* for 857 mention *Plaga magna vesicarum turgentium grassatur in populo et detestabili eos putredine consumpsit, ita ut membra dissoluta ante mortem deciderent* a "great plague of swollen blisters consumed the people by a loathsome rot, so that their limbs were loosened and fell off before death." In 994, during the last years of Hugh Capet (of whom every subsequent French monarch save Napoleon was a male-line descendant), an estimated forty kilofranks died due to *pain maudit* (cursed bread). The Middle Ages were regularly ravaged by waves of ergotism, called *ignis sacer* (holy fire) due to burning sensations in the extremities. The Dauphinois noble Gaston of Valloire, having "cured" his son by hagiotherapy involving relics of St. Anthony, formed in 1095 the Antonite order to provide care for the "Devil's Curse," and thus it came to be known as St. Anthony's Fire.

With that said, ergot is more easily blamed than proven culpable. It is unlikely that it played much role in mass outbreaks of tarantism in southern Europe, nor central European choreomania. In particular, ergotism was almost certainly not the cause of the Salem afflictions of 1692 (the "Witch Trials"), nor the "Great Fear" preceding the French Revolution in July 1789. Peter the Great's Cossacks and his Caspian Flotilla assembled in 1722 at the Volga's delta near Astrakhan, ready to attack Safavid Persia. They turned back on the Terek steppe, and the French ambassador Campredon recorded in his diary widespread ergotism in the Tsar's forces—but the Safavids were already on their knees, and the Great Westernizer might simply have missed Moscow.

ergot as pharmacopœia

Midwives of Central Europe employed ergot as an ecbolic and abortifacient for hundreds of years, but the first explicit reference was by F. Paulitzky in 1787's *Pulvis ad partum aus dem Mutterkorn* (powder of birth). It entered the United States Pharmacopeia in 1820. Widespread use led to a rise in stillbirths, and D. Holsack in 1822 tied this to oxytocic application of powdered ergot, declaring it *pulvis ad mortem* (powder of death) in a public inquiry.

Ergometrine (sold as, among others, Syntometrine, Ergotrate, and Ergostat) and ergocalciferol (sold as, among others, Deltalin, Drisdol, and Calcidol) are on the WHO's List of Essential Medicines. Note that ergocalciferol (a product of ergosterol), while initially discovered in *C. purpurea*, is not an ergoline nor even an alkaloid, but rather a sterol. It is present in the cell membranes of most fungi and many protozoa, making it an enticing target for antifungal and antiprotozoal drugs.

Industry consumes about twenty-five tons of ergopeptides and D-LSA each year. These alkaloids are largely sourced from submerged fermentation of

---

Massilienses...conflictati: The Marseillians, overwhelmed with profusion of calamities, reduced to the utmost distress by famine, worsted in two different engagements by sea, weakened by continual sallies, assaulted by a heavy pestilence occasioned by the length of the siege and their constant change of diet (for they were obliged to feed upon old meal and musty barley)...

C. purpurea's fecund Strain 275 FI[14], or *Aspergillus* SD58, or just, like, baskets filled with mycotoxic jizz. Spraying flowering rye with a dilute solution of spores has yielded up to 500kg of ergot per hectare. The dried sclerotium typically contains 1–2% alkaloid by mass.

The following table does not purport to be exhaustive:

Drug name	Purpose	Active ingredients
Cafergot	Migraine headaches	Ergotamine, caffeine
Ergomar	Vascular headaches	Ergotamine
Gynergen	Uterotonic	Ergotamine
Sansert	Cluster headaches	Methysergide
Methergine	Postpartum bleeding	Methylergonovine
Syntometrine	Postpartum bleeding	Ergometrine, oxytocin
Sermion	Senile dementia	Nicergoline
Hydergine	Dementia	Ergoloid
Dihydergot	Orthostatic hypotension	Dihydroergotamine
Deltalin	Hypovitaminosis D	Ergocalciferol
Parlodel	Hypogonadism	Bromocriptine
Liserdol	Hyperprolactinemia	Metergoline
Delysid	Trippin' ballz	D-LSD

ergot as psychedelic

The symptoms of convulsive ergotism hint at neuroactivity among ergot's alkaloids[15], distinguished by a common heterocyclic moiety backbone of tetracyclic ergoline. These alkaloids can be divided into the clavines and the derivatives of lysergic acid. It is these latter which are pharmacologically active, and they can further be divided into the water-soluble ergometrine group and the insoluble ergotamine group. Their chemistry proper began at London's Wellcome Research Laboratory where G. Barger and F. H. Carr in 1907 isolated "ergotoxine," which A. Hofmann of Sandoz would in 1942 prove to be composed of three distinct alkaloids: ergocristine, ergocornine, and ergocryptine. In 1918 A. Stoll (Hofmann's manager at Sandoz) isolated ergotamine. These er-

---

[14]Paspalic acid freely converts to lysergic acid, and thus *C. paspali* is also sometimes used.

[15]Beyond rye ergot, psychoactive ergoline alkaloids (particularly ergine) are found in some flowering plants. The seeds of morning glories *I. violacea* (moonflower), *I. tricolor* (Mexican morning glory), and *I. corymbosa* (ololiúqui, xtabentún, Christmasvine), and the vine *A. nervosa* (Hawaiian baby woodrose, अध मुद्रा (adhoguda)) contain lysergic acid amide (ergine) sufficient to cause psychoactive effects when crushed and consumed. Alkaloids are found only in the seeds: endophytic clavicipitaceous infections were once thought the source, but it has been demonstrated that the same alkaloid is produced by these wildly different biota. The K'iche' Mayans in their *Popol Vuh* describe *balché*, an infusion of the bark of *Lonchocarpus longistylus* and honey from bees fed on *I. tricolor*. Tremendous amounts were consumed in ceremonies where drinkers wore bags around their necks to collect vomit. Of course, they also smoked *D. stramonium* (धतूर (dhattūra), tolohuaxihuitl), so it's difficult to pin the hallucination on the alkaloid, as it were. Powdered ololiúqui seeds were almost certainly consumed as entheogens for thousands of years.

gopeptines already demonstrate interactions with the monoamine receptors[16], but do not yield psychedelic effects.

During the first half of 1935, four different labs reported a new ergot alkaloid, now known as ergometrine but sometimes seen as ergotocin, ergobasine, ergonovine, or ergostetrine. This alkanolamide trades the long peptide for propanolamine, and is psychedelic in high doses. In 1936, W. A. Jacobs and L. C. Craig at the Rockefeller Institute cleaved ergometrine, isolating D-lysergic acid. "Lysergic": *Lysis* of *ergot*. The ergot alkaloids are biosynthetic derivatives of D-lysergic acid, but D-lysergic acid is a synthetic derivative of the ergot alkaloids. Indeed, despite several known total syntheses of DLA, it is produced almost entirely via hydrolysis of biologically-sourced alkaloids.

Hofmann in 1938 began systematically exploring amines of D-lysergic acid using the rearrangement reaction of Curtius. The twenty-fifth compound, Lyserg-säure-diäthylamid, was inspired by nicotinic acid diethylamide, the analeptic marketed as Coramine. He writes that "a peculiar presentiment induced [him], five years after the first synthesis, to produce LSD-25 once again...This was quite unusual." While purifying his lysergic acid diethylamide and crystallizing it as a tartrate, he absorbed an imperceptible amount[17]. He was subsequently "forced to proceed home, affected by a remarkable restlessness...a stream of fantastic pictures, extraordinary shapes with intense, kaleidoscopic play of colors." Realizing that this implied LSD-25 to be a "substance of extraordinary potency," on 1943-04-19 he embarked on a 250μg self-experiment at 16:20 Central European Time. He clambered up onto his bicycle, then rode down the streets of Basel and into another reality. Some call this evidence of God's direct intervention in human affairs; I remain unconvinced.

Both ergonovine and ergotamine (and salts) were among List I precursors of the original 1970 Controlled Substances Act. Ergocristine was added in 2010[18]. Ergotamine, lysergic acid, and ergometrine are all on Table I of the INCB Red List, and are thus EU Category 1 precursors. Lysergic acid and its amide are Schedule III CS; lysergic acid diethylamide is Schedule I. The 1986 Federal Analogue Act adds to Schedule I LSD's functional analogues (any chemical "substantially similar[19]"). Schedule I is of course those chemicals with no accepted medical function and a high potential for abuse.

Hallucinogens are almost entirely either substituted phenethylamines and tryptamines. Lysergamides (amides of lysergic acid) are often considered a third class due to their complex and varied neuroactivity, though they are tech-

---

[16]In particular, the adrenoceptors, as well as receptors of dopamine and all-important serotonin.

[17]Hofmann suspected that LSD tartrate was absorbed through his fingertips, but D. Nichols pointed out that the tartrate ought not have transdermal effect, and suggests that he contacted a solution of free base during column chromatography.

[18]This was almost certainly in response to the 2001 William Pickard bust in Kansas. The 2003-11-25 DEA release claims 19 kilograms of ergocristine, and *United States v. Pickard, 278 F. Supp. 2d 1217 (D. Kan. 2003)* clearly states "6½ kilograms of a substance they believed was ergotamine tartrate...The substance, however, tested positive for ergocristine." Informant Gordon Todd Skinner testified extensively for the Government about "the ET man," *i.e.* the ergotamine tartrate man, but also said, "ET is the ergotamine tartrate *or any precursor* that is unique that goes to the manufacturing of LSD" (emphasis mine —SSK). A better question: what happened to 12½ keys of ergocristine? *Hrmmmm.*

[19]As if that had any kind of precise meaning, ugh.

nically complex tryptamines, and enumerated as such in *TiHKAL*. An ergoline backbone of bicyclic hexahydroindole fused to a bicyclic quinoline group is common among lysergamides, as are two sterocenters and substitutions at the nitrogens. The indole moiety results in a reaction with Ehrlich's reagent.

Name	R_1[20]	R_6
LSD	H	CH_3
AL-LAD	H	$CH_2CH{=}CH_2$
ALD-52 (1A-LSD)	$C{=}OCH_3$	CH_3
1P-LSD	$C{=}OCH_2CH_3$	CH_3
PRO-LAD	H	$CH_2CH_2CH_3$
ETH-LAD	H	CH_2CH_3
1P-ETH-LAD	$C{=}OCH_2CH_3$	CH_2CH_3
1B-LSD	$C{=}OCH_2CH_2CH_3$	CH_3
1cP-LSD/1V-LSD	$C{=}OC_3H_5$	CH_3

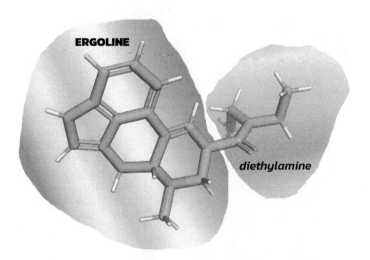

The ergoline moiety in all producers derives from L-tryptophan and DMAPP (dimethylallyl diphosphate). DmaW (tryptophan dimethylallyltransferase) catalyzes production of 4-dimethylallyltryptophan (4-DMAT). This is methylated to 4-DMA-L-abrine. EasC/EasE close a ring, yielding chanoclavine. EasD/EasA close the fourth and final ring, and decarboxylate to agroclavine.

---

[20]R_1 substitutes at the indole NH.

Biosynthesis of D-LSA in *C. purpurea*

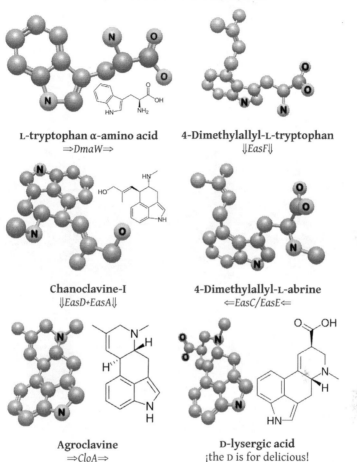

L-tryptophan α-amino acid
⇒*DmaW*⇒

4-Dimethylallyl-L-tryptophan
⇓*EasF*⇓

Chanoclavine-I
⇓*EasD+EasA*⇓

4-Dimethylallyl-L-abrine
⇐*EasC/EasE*⇐

Agroclavine
⇒*CloA*⇒

D-lysergic acid
¡the D is for delicious!

Dihydroergopeptides: chanoclavine-I via EasA$_{reductase}$+EasG.
Elymoclavine: agroclavine via CloA orthologues in other *Claviceps*.
Ergopeptines: D-LSA via LpsB+LpsA.
Eas: ergot alkaloid synthesis

smash the state: imposition of order → escalation of chaos!

12 welcome to my lab; we've got *Taq* polymerase

Bolaño drank coffee with Paul Pasolini, a chemistry PhD student.

"So long as something isn't a DEA controlled substance I can pretty much just order it with a credit card, right?"

"Order it where? Under what account?"

Irritated: "To my house. Under my account."

"And your account is..."

"I mean, I register on their site, I enter my shipping and billing information, I have an account."

Harsh laughter. "First off, you're not even going to get glassware from a reputable dealer without being an educational or commercial entity, let alone chemicals. There's all kinds of chain-of-custody issues with regards to disposal and storage. Listed prices are way above what you can negotiate with a purchasing agent once you've established a reputation. Those agents are capable people, and they'll want to know what you're doing, and if they think you're full of shit, they'll write you off as a customer. And there's plenty of stuff that isn't a DEA precursor that you'll have trouble ordering. Anything under the 1976 Toxic Substances Control Act, for instance. If you call up wanting organophosphates, somebody's gonna want to know why."

"What's wrong with organophosphates?" Bolaño is thoroughly disgusted.

"Just that the feds take a dim view of you manufacturing nerve gas. Explosive precursors will likewise get you a visit. People get nervous if you order strong solvents. Honestly, if you're not a university or a known company, and you order anything questionable, you can assume the supplier is sending off a report of suspicious activity to DEA, ATF, whomever. And like I said, they're—the sales agents, that is—competent. If you order up a bunch of second-order precursors to synthesize a controlled first-order precursor, they're going to tell you to fuck off, or possibly say 'No problem, Señor Bolaño,' take your money, and your chemicals will be delivered by unfriendly DEA agents with unpleasant questions."

Bolaño began to despair. "So do I need to be licensed? What kind of license is that, even?"

"There's not so much a license, as an ongoing evaluation of the customer relationship, though I know Sigma-Aldrich won't ship to anything but a commercial address. You will likely need to convince them that you have responsible processes and a basic level of competence. The 1996 MCA fines a cool quarter million for distribution of anything on the Special Surveillance List, distinct from the CSA list."

"So I can fake all that, right?"

A long, hard look at Bolaño. "If you're asking whether there's some central database saying, 'this guy is kosher to order chemicals,' there is not, at least not in the US. I mean, there is for DEA controlled substances, but there's

---

MCA: Methamphetamine Control Act   **HIDTA:** High-Intensity Drug Trafficking Area

approximately zero chance you're getting anything in response to a Form 510a other than the boys from Atlanta HIDTA putting a boot up your ass."

Bolaño rages silently. "So I can form an LLC. I can get commercial space. I can likely even get an accredited chemist to put their name down. You're saying I still won't be able to order uncontrolled chemicals at will? What the fuck? How does anyone get anything done in this country?"

"Not in their garages, that's for sure. Look, the sad truth is that the authorities are suspicious of anyone doing anything beyond grocery store chemistry on their own hook. They are going to regard you as a drug op or a bomb op until you demonstrate otherwise. No one—not the feds, not the chemical supply houses, not the general public—considers it your right to access lab equipment or reagents. Just the word 'chemical' freaks out most people. Oh, and if you ever dispose of something incorrectly, the children of the children of your children will still be paying off the fines. They do not fuck around."

✳✳✳✳✳✳✳✳✳

"We're going to want to be able to analyze our product. Gold standard is gas chromatography-mass spectrometry. An alternative is high performance liquid chromatography in place of gas. That would probably be a Thermo Scientific Accela, which look to run about a grand on eBay. Either way we need a single quadrupole mass spectrometer, which will not be cheap. Maybe we find one at a decent price and still working at government auction. Maybe not."

"No way around the mass spectrometer?"

"All the reports give their results in terms of MS spectra. It's the fundamental tool of modern analytic chemistry. There might be ways to do quantitative analytic chemistry without one—I mean, there definitely are—but I don't know them, and you don't know them. I think we'll have a difficult enough time running and interpreting a mass spectrometer. It doesn't spit out 'you have good acid, bro!' There's a lot of art just in reading the output."

"How much?"

"Difficult to pick up used—they get snapped up by universities, and manufacturers have tradein programs. Looks like twenty large minimum."

"Christ. We can't build one?"

"Are you volunteering?"

"What's involved in building one?"

"I honestly have no idea. I'd guess it's more difficult than the chemistry we're pursuing. Otherwise there would be some Rigol of spectrometers."

"Rigol?"

"Chinese manufacturer of serviceable oscilloscopes."

"What exactly does the spectrometer enable?"

"It allows us to confirm the presence of a given chemical down to the isotopic level, even at very low concentrations. It allows conjecture about contaminants. It allows quantification of purity, though that's not too difficult with just chromatography, I think. It allows us to do all this without material-specific chemistry, though there is some material-specific preparation, and definitely material-specific interpretation. Do you know how they work?"

"Roughly, I think? I mean, the 'mass' part is presumably that you're sorting your outputs by mass, because you've got some force acting upon them according to $F = ma$. So if you're ionizing things for instance, you've got a magnet and a collecting plate, and the amount a cation moves is going to be proportional to its charge and mass, right? Assuming a good vacuum."

"Indeed. And why will it normally be a cation?"

"It's a whole lot easier to knock out an electron than it is a nucleon, natch. But aren't you also going to break up a lot of molecules?"

"Absolutely. Those are fragments, and the output of a run is a histogram of counts versus mass to charge ratio. A decent spectrometer gives you single-AMU resolution, but not below that."

"Well who cares? It's eighteen hundred electrons to a proton."

"Just saying. I'm also unsure whether relativistic mass comes into play."

Bolaño made a face. "People don't really say relativistic mass any more."

"What? Why not? What do they call it?"

"They don't call it anything. It's not a particularly useful concept. There is an increased gravitational effect for a system with momentum, but that's because of the stress-energy tensor, which increases with all energy. You really only see it in Einstein's mass-energy equivalence, which was by the way never emphasized by the man himself. Relativistic energy: E squared equals pc squared plus m sub oh squared c to the fourth works for systems with non-zero momentum. And it's 'invariant mass' rather than 'rest mass.'"

"How are those better than relativistic mass and rest mass?"

A sigh. "Stand by for pedantry. So you agree that for different bodies, the Newtonian attraction acting on your mass is different?"

"I'm not a child. That's mass versus weight."

"We don't say that you have different 'Newtonian mass' on the moon; you have a different weight. There's no change in the fundamental property that is your mass, just a difference in the force that acts upon it. Similarly, there's no relativistic change to your mass, just a difference in geometric properties of spacetime due to your movement. Mass is the magnitude of a four-vector. And if you go substituting weight for where mass is needed, you're going to be off by some linear factor, right? Same if you go blindly plugging in relativistic mass where mass is needed. What changes with your velocity is your energy, and the relationship of your mass to your momentum. Rest mass is invariant across all frames of reference. Relativistic momentum and total energy are frame-dependent. If you're traveling along with a particle that's moving at some velocity, it has no kinetic energy from your perspective, right? And a massless particle can't have a rest frame. Its energy-momentum four-vector is zero in all frames."

"This all seems semantics. It's the relativistic euphemism treadmill."

"Sure, it's just semantics, but it's semantics of a particularly cliché and opinionated type, a shibboleth. It's like if I said you do IT work."

Katz draws back as if stung. "Got it. In any case, I remain unsure whether relativistic *energy* comes into play."

AMU: atomic mass unit

Bolaño sounds disgusted: "Why would anything be relativistic?"

"You have relativistic electrons in ground states of heavy atoms. An electron moving close enough to light speed can be arbitrarily more massive—excuse me, can have arbitrarily more momentum and/or energy, right?"

"One, relativistic electrons are not moving that close to the speed of light. There's an approximation, Sommerfield's I think, Zc over one hundred thirty-seven. Uranium Z is ninety-two, so that's what two-thirds c? So you'd only be talking about one point three five the intrinsic mass. Even with uranium you're talking one hundred twenty five compared to ninety-two, so, what, two percent of a proton's mass? And that's giving every electron credit for the big gains. Fuck outta here. Two, if we've got uranium in our LSD we've got big fucking problems."

"Alright, I buy that. But yes, mass spectrometry builds atop an already necessary chromatography setup to enable and simplify a lot of physical and organic chemistry. Which recall that neither of us has taken p-chem, and neither of us took a lab-based o-chem."

"But twenty thousand dollars."

"At least twenty thousand dollars. You can't get similar functionality from any cheaper tool. Unless we can steal one or buy a stolen one. Which these are sufficiently rare devices that if one's missing, the manufacturer probably knows, which means that's felony theft by receiving. You can arguably move up to NMR, but that's even more expensive and complicated. I also think it has to be mounted into a superstable configuration requiring professional assistance. I doubt anything useful shows up at yard sales."

Bolaño looked around the metropolitan skyline. "Are there not old guys dying who have spectrometers in their home labs?"

"I don't think many people have home chemistry labs in the way one has home electronics labs. You're fundamentally more likely to burn down your house and/or kill your family with chemistry. Many more laws. Difficult to dispose of things. Largely incompatible with children."

"And an electron microscope wouldn't work?"

"It would be several times more expensive and would in no way work. We don't need an optical survey. Where's your head?" He gawked at Bolaño for a moment, then broke out in geeky reverence: "Have you heard about ptychography? They've started doing something called iterative phase-retrieval X-ray ptychography at the SLS. They've finally got enough compute oomph to put together coherent interference scattered off the target. It's going to go subangstrom. But it would still be pretty useless for us. Crystallography "

"Just thinking out loud." It had without a doubt been a stupid question. A more relevant one was forming. "Wait, don't you run into problems with mass spectroscopy where you've got the same mass for isomers? By definition they're the same formula. They're going to be the same AMUs."

"Ahh, yes, for both structural and stereoisomers, yeah."

"Well then what the fuck good is a mass spectrometer to us, given that we are primarily worried about stereoisomers? What am I missing here, Katz?"

NMR: nuclear magnetic resonance   **SLS:** Swiss Light Source

"Well, so what you typically do is what's called hybrid MS/MS, where you have a first MS step, then feed that into a second spectrometer—"

"A second?"

"Yeah I don't think you can just loop it back to itself, you want two—"

"So fifty thousand dollars."

"Well only if you want to do two-stage spectrometry—"

"Which is necessary for isomers."

"Well, to get to two mass spectrometers, you start with one mass spectrometer. And it would be good for detecting non-isomeric corruption. I think there's a technique called circular dichroism that people use for isomers. Seems you would want something capable of activating the minutely different molecular vibration modes, something like what they do in laser isotope enrichment." He pauses and looks pleading. "I really want a mass spectrometer, Michael."

Bolaño stares at him.

"With all my heart I do."

"I am recalling that massproduced LSD of the past was able to attain very high purities. All this without, so far as I am aware, mass spectrometers."

"Yes, but did they *know* that it was high purity?"

"I think they did, yes, because they knew when they could stop performing enantioselective chromatography. Which they were doing to purify product. Or when they could stop isomerization, whatever."

"So basically just quantitative chromatography."

"Basically just quantitative chromatography."

"So we're not getting a mass spectrometer."

"I do not feel a mass spectrometer justified at this time."

"We're not getting a big fuckin' NMR either are we?"

"I doubt we could get an NMR installed even if we wanted to."

"So basically I ought just drink the bathroom cleaner and suck dog dick."

"What's necessary, chromatography-wise?"

"Gonna need a big column of motherfuckin' dog dick to just suck on all day, answer the phone with it poppin' in my cheek, oh it's my beloved mother asking if I'm doing serious science, and I'm like, no ma, slurp, just getting *familiaris* with this randy-ass *canis*, drinking shots of Comet to ease the pain, you know how we do it with Bolaño around."

"Does Ma Katz know who I am?" Bolaño smiles.

"Ma Katz prays for you every night. 'Lord help Sherman's gay Mexican friend.' She's got your best interests at heart."

"I mean, 'gay Mexican' is accurate, but it sounds so dirty from her."

"That's just your deeply-rooted classism. Gay Mexicans live up on South Cobb Drive, US 41. You live in Buckhead. You're a Hispanic bachelor of means, not a gay Mexican, which sounds like a drink involving grenadine."

Serious again: "Chromatography."

"We need columns! I don't know how these numbers are calculated, but I'm seeing references to fifty mm diameter fifty cm length columns, and also sixty by sixty. We ought get a better theoretical understanding of what's going on there. You understand chromatography basics?" Michael nods. "We don't yet need bioreactors, but I think we will if we're going to take this anywhere."

"Bioreactors?"

"Multiliter stainless steel vessel for biologically active processes. You can add gas and medium automatically, agitate it, carry away effluent, keep the temperature and pH and everything else monitored and just where you want them. If we want to scale, I think we're going to need biosynthesis, using *Claviceps paspali*. Apparently *Aspergillus* is worth looking at from things I saw online, on Rhodium, but who knows. I suspect you could improve alkaloid yield from fungus without too much effort."

"Paspali? I thought it was *Claviceps purpurea?"*

"Paspalic acid freely interconverts with lysergic acid. Apparently it's easier to ferment up high-yield *paspali.* There are two periods in which ergot produces alkaloids: during biomass formation, and afterwards. *Purpurea* strains produce in one or the other; *paspali* produces during both. People looked at this problem pretty thoroughly back in the 60s under Army and CIA contracts. There's a hundred page document out of Edgewood Arsenal from 1964, 'Synthesis and Chemistry of Lysergic Acid Derivatives,' that goes into depth."

"But we're not doing anything biological now?"

"Nah, we've got your Mexigot. But that's not going to scale."

"And total syntheses don't exist?"

"No, several exist. They're just a dozen steps or more, and yields are shitty. Also, anything that even looks like a Grignard reagent is restricted by DEA, though I guess we could make those. Just recently Hendrickson and Wang at Brandeis brought out a new method with ten point six percent in eight steps."

"Ten point six? That seems not terrible?"

"Yeah we ought look into it. But as far as I can tell, everyone who's ever done scale production did it with the benefit of lab-grade ergoline precursors. And those precursors came from dried and crushed fungal mycelia. Now, maybe you can do total synthesis easier with recent technology. Microreactors let you control processes at a small scale, very fine control, very energy efficient. I don't think we'd need them unless we got into total synthesis, though."

"So you're saying scaling almost certainly requires biological work. And that we've got a potential path to improvement via work along biological lines. How potential is that? You say 'improve alkaloid yield.' By what means? Since when do you do genetic engineering?"

"There's your Mendelian engineering, which is just breeding species together and selecting for characteristics. Well, fungi don't necessarily sexually reproduce, and anyway I think all the work along those lines was already done. But consider this: DLA is a biochemical precursor to ergot alkaloids. The fungus folds it up from tryptophan using various enzymes to catalyze. Now behind each one of those enzymes is a gene, right? So if we were to knock out the gene that encodes for whatever converts DLA into *e.g.* ergotamine, that ought save us an extraction step and its attendant losses."

"Knock out a gene, huh? You know how to do that?"

"I do not."

"Is it possible to do?"

"I cannot really speak to that with any confidence."

"No worries. So I think it might be worthwhile to pick up bioreactors now, or at least soon. What other equipment?"

"Absolutely we need rotational evaporators. Rotovaps!" Katz says the word with clear relish. "I think a rotary vacuum flash evaporator. Cost on these looks to be under two large. Magnetic stirrers. An industrial overhead mixer, cheap. We'll want a fume hood with a powerful pump, and we'll need install that. Personal protective equipment. Maybe glove boxen? I think we ought use glove boxen unless they'd make things too difficult. Freezers. Long wavelength overhead lighting, red as fuck, also a blacklight. Some ultraviolet lighting, not overhead in this case. If we're not getting a mass spectrometer, some kind of spectrometry still would seem desirable." Bolaño nods agreement. "If you're saying no to the MS, you get to research spectrometry options."

"I'll do that."

"Cartridges for liquid and solid phase extraction—SPE and SLE. The Bond Elut Certify brand from Agilent is thought leet, but Agilent can be trusted always to fuck you in the ass pricewise. Methanol. Carbonyldiimidazole. Now CDI is on the Special Surveillance List, so we'll likely want to synthesize that. Easily enough done with imidazole and phosgene."

"Phosgene? As in World War I phosgene? 'Bent double, like old beggars under sacks' phosgene?"

"Technically 'Dulce et Decorum Est' was about chlorine. We'll need research grade argon gas, methane, ammonia, nitrogen. We ought be able to get those from anywhere. We should get some nitrous oxide when we do, a big-ass tank. I haven't done whippets in a minute. Get some girls over, guys for you, have a whippet extravaganza, get some cars and go driving with that shit—"

"Whippets and driving would seem not to recommend each other."

"Only if you suffer a morbid fear of hitting shit. Dude, actually, the one time I did whippets while driving, it was in the Kroger parking lot, and I just kind of drove in this lazy circle at about five kilometers per hour out at the edge. I didn't hit anything. Some lady did honk at me. We'll need Erlenmeyer flasks, Büchner flasks, beakers, can't have too many beakers. All that shit has apparently become kind of annoying to buy, and we ought look into non-recorded transactions if possible. Activated decolorizing charcoal. Ummm, probably a water bath."

"Probably?"

"I mean, I don't know."

"I thought you researched things and put together an actual list."

"I did. I'm giving you an actual list."

"Do we need a water bath or not?"

"Bitch, probably!" Katz sounds crosser than he actually is, though he's not wholly free of irritation. He thinks he's done a pretty good job. "It's cheap. Cheap enough that let's just get a water bath and if we need it, we'll use it. Extraction solvents. High-molar acids—2N HCl for sure. Dry ice. Distilled water out the ass, or preferably a Milli-Q purifier. Acidic ion exchange resin, coarse powder, bead form if we can get it. Anhydrous diethylamine."

Dulce...Est: It is sweet and fitting. Wilfred Owen (c. 1917). cf. Horace *Carmina* (23 BC) III.2.13

"Do we need purchase it as diethylamine? That's rather on the nose."

Katz shrugs. "It too is on the SSL. Easily synthesized from dimethylformamide. Come to think of it, ammonia gas is on there, too. Trifluoroacetyl imidazole and trimethylsilyl trifluoroacetamide derivatizing reagents, apparently retailed as TFAI and BSTFA respectively. Methylene chloride. Sodium hydroxide in ethanol solution for conversion of isoLSD. Sodium dithionite assuming we're doing hydrolysis; it protects the ergoline backbone. Keller and Urk-Smith reagents. Hydrazine hydrate. Actually no, we'll use potassium hydroxide for lysis."

"Isn't hydrazine a rocket fuel?"

"Everything is everything. Remember Lauryn Hill?"

It was time to go shopping.

＊＊＊＊＊＊＊＊＊

It will be at this juncture instructive to explore some of the larger acid busts; only through such an investigation can we study the history of clandestine lysergamide chemistry. A draconian legal environment worldwide has starved this field for primary sources, leading to scarce scholarship. The active underground chemist has little incentive to record her story. This is best explored in the context of a larger history of the drug, which I cannot hope to do full justice here. Interested readers are recommended the excellent histories *Acid Dreams: The Complete Social History of LSD* by Martin Lee (1985), and *Storming Heaven: LSD and the American Dream* by Jay Stevens (1998).

Is any drug surrounded by more mystique, misinformation, and myth than LSD? Sumerians scored *Papaver somniferum* and collected its opium latex more than four millennia ago. In South America, *Erythroxylaceae* has been cultivated in *aspi* and *uachos* for longer than that. Marijuana was smoked atop the *bam-e-dunya* (the junction of the Pamir, Himalayas, Karakoram, and Hindu Kush) well before Christ. The Atharva Veda (c. 1400) speaks of sacred cannabis (from which is derived *bhang*). As of 2023, LSD is only eighty years old. Within twenty-five years of its discovery, it had stirred the highest levels of the arts, become synonymous with a powerful social movement, been the subject of extensive research by the armed forces, and was globally prohibited under the auspices of a similarly young United Nations. All this despite the fact that psilocybin has essentially the same effects (if not duration) in sufficient doses.

First, the legals: Sandoz of course, where in 1943 Hofmann started it all with his *Sorgenkind*. Marketed as Delysid, it found its way to psychotherapists like Humphry Osmond, Stanislov Grof, and Myron Stolaroff. The Czech manufacturer Spofa was responsible for huge sales on the open market and behind the Iron Curtain. In Eli Lilly's Indianapolis lab, processes were developed for industrial production to meet the needs of the CIA and Army. This included William Garbrecht's synthesis published in the 1959 *Journal of Organic Chemistry* and Richard Pioch's method in US2997470A *Lysergic Acid Amides*.

---

aspi: planting holes   **uachos:** furrows   **bam-e-dunya:** بام جهان Roof of the World
Sorgenkind: problem child

The DEA licenses a handful of industrial and research chemists to work with Schedule I substances. David Nichols of Purdue is legendary (as is the Purdue University Library's Psychoactive Substances Research Collection), but he "retired" in 2012; as of this writing he is affiliated with UNC. Joel Smith at FSU gets it on. Jason Wallach is doing interesting work. Sasha Shulgin, Hofmann's only plausible competition for GOAThood, had a license until he was raided in 1994 (probably in response to publishing PiHKAL; DEA spokesman Richard Meyer stated on the record that "it is our opinion that those books are pretty much cookbooks on how to make illegal drugs."). The DEA on 2018-01-18 claimed "more than 590" researchers hold Schedule I licenses. Suffice to say that even application puts the licensee firmly on federal radar. Transactions in controlled precursors are still logged; licensure is no path to synthesis at scale.

Numerous chemical suppliers keep LSD on hand, distributing it primarily as a reference standard: it is product number L7007 at Sigma Aldrich, LSD-397-FB at Lipomed, L-001 at Cerilliant, FOR1346 at LGC, 35189 at Cayman Chemical. PerkinElmer's spinoff Revvity retails as part number NET638250UC LSD tritiated (doped with tritium, the two-neutron isotope of hydrogen) on the N-methyl group having activity of 9.25 Mbq.

Experimentation with LSD in the interests of national security was protracted and horrific. The armed forces became Sandoz customers early, long before Timothy Leary and Alfred Hubbard were making spectacles of themselves, and did not stop until 1972. U.S. Army Medical Corps psychiatrist Jim Ketchum published *Chemical Warfare: Secrets Almost Forgotten* in 2006; tales of EA-1729 related therein are harrowing indeed.

The CIA's Project Artichoke (initially Bluebird) and Navy's Project Chatter explored psychoactive drugs in the context of interrogation as early as 1947. In 1953 they were folded into MKUltra, administered by Sidney Gottlieb through CIA's OSI (now part of the Directorate of Science and Technology) in conjunction with the Army's Biological Warfare Laboratory at the Edgewood Arsenal in Maryland; it would be followed by MKDelta and MKSearch, and the loosely related MKOften, MKChickwit, and MKNaomi (Stephen Kinzer's 2019 *Poisoner in Chief* is the best available study of Gottlieb, though it tends towards the sensational). These programs were distributed throughout America and Canada: at USP Atlanta, Whitey Bulger was fed LSD over the course of eighteen months, long before consolidating control of Boston's Winter Hill Gang. Discovery led directly to the Church Committee of 1975 and Gerald Ford's Executive Order 12333 §2.10, forbidding human experimentation without consent.

It is not difficult to find arrest and court records of high-level LSD distributors, including those "manufacturing" in the sense of packaging (the stories of Carolyn Holly Fried, Seth Ferranti, and Timothy Tyler are worth reading). Busts of actual chemists are rarer. Potential cooks are sometimes taken down before they ever get started: Glenn Slayden of Seattle went looking for ergotamine

---

PiHKAL: Phenethylamines I Have Known and Loved

EA-1729: the Army's designation for its LSD maleate; it is doubtful that any connection to the Ramanujan-Hardy number $1729 = 1^3 + 12^3 = 9^3 + 10^3$, the smallest number expressible as the sum of two distinct pairs of positive cubes, was intended.

OSI: Office of Scientific Intelligence

tartrate in 2004, and found an undercover DEA agent—*timeō Danaōs et dōna ferentēs.* The chemist can distribute from a distance: LSD's extreme potency means that large amounts can be mailed in small packages, and even without masking there is no detectable odor in the finished product.

Even low masses draw stiff mandatory minimal penalties (a single gram triggers not fewer than five years imprisonment per 21 U.S.C. §841(b)(1)(B)). Carrier mass is included in the total weight, a practice affirmed by SCOTUS in *Chapman v. United States (90-5744), 500 U.S. 453 (1991)).* A standard sugar cube (a terrible way to package LSD for any number of reasons) is about four grams. Distribution by such means is a telltale sign of amateurism.

The DEA's Strategic Intelligence Section (Domestic Unit) in 1995 published the Drug Intelligence Report *LSD in the United States.* Its "LSD Trafficking" section provides a history in miniature:

> *Initially, LSD was supplied by small groups that obtained limited quanti-*
> *ties of ergotamine tartrate on the commercial market.*

The best guide to these small groups is Robert Timothy Scully's 2013 paper "A Sketch of the Early History of Underground LSD Manufacturing." In 1960, before LSD was illegal in any state, Dr. James Grossman, Bernard Roseman, and Bernard Copley synthesized a rather impure LSD solution. They sold it in the United States and Canada, claiming Israeli origin. They were arrested by FDA and Customs agents in 1963 and convicted in 1964 under 18 USC §545 and 21 USC §331. Roseman's *LSD: The Age of Mind* (1963) was prepared primarily to organize the defendants' defense, and is not particularly worth reading. At the same time, Douglas George (working at Aerojet) set up a small lab in Hermosa Beach, likely using a modified Pioch synthesis. His product is described by Scully as a "green goo," and was severely compromised by impurities. Graham's primary influence on clandestine chemistry was the 1964 supply of his psychedelic goo to Owsley Stanley by way of Ray Brown.

The next name that comes down to us is a mere *nom de guerre.* In *The Electric Kool-Aid Acid Test,* Tom Wolfe wrote of a "Mad Chemist," the original supplier of acid to the Pranksters (the original supplier of acid to Kesey himself was the Menlo Park Veterans' Hospital under the aegis of MKUltra). This unnamed artificer was (contrary to some claims) absolutely not Owsley Stanley; this is obvious from a cursory read of Wolfe, where the two debate:

> Owsley, the little wiseacre, is tearing him up. Owsley is young and
> sharp and quick and the Mad Chemist—the Mad Chemist is an old
> man and he has taken too much dope. He's loose in the head. He
> tries to argue and his brains all run together like goo. The Mad
> Chemist is getting crushed.

Firmer ground and extensive documentation are available regarding Augustus Owsley Stanley III, *TEKAT's* "White Rabbit" (not to be confused with the OCDETF Operations White Rabbit and WR East, of more later), sometimes

---

Timeō...ferentēs: I fear the Greeks, even those bearing gifts. Virgil, *Aeneid* II.49
OCDETF: Organized Crime Drug Enforcement Task Force

better known as Bear, the Acid King. Robert Greenfield's 2016 biography *Bear* is likely to stand the test of time. It includes most of the more reliable and interesting information from longtime Stanley partner Rhoney Gissen's 2013 *Owsley and Me: My LSD Family*. Unfortunately, Melissa Cargill (Stanley's other longtime lover, and a Berkeley-trained chemist; the Cargill-MacMillan family is generally considered to be among America's ten richest, counting fourteen distinct billionaires in 2019) has not published anything, and maintains a minimal profile. When attorney Al Matthews provided Stanley with Delysid—a wholly different animal from Graham's amateur product—Bear dedicated himself to reproduction of this extraordinary substance, starting up work at the "Green Factory" at 1647 Virginia Street. It was raided by agents expecting methamphetamine 1965-02-21; their equipment was seized.

The aforementioned Tim Scully was by seventeen interning at Lawrence Berkeley National Lab, whose 6.5 GeV synchrotron (the Bevatron) had recently proven existence of the $\bar{\text{p}}$. He first dosed 1965-04-15 with friend Dan Douglas, becoming an immediate convert to the Ergoline Church. Weeks later, having spent much of the intervening time sperging over patents and journals, Scully's roommate Diana Nason introduced him to Owsley (at a party thrown by Ken Kesey, no less). Owsley brought Scully and Douglas aboard as apprentice sound engineers for the Grateful Dead at $500 per week each. Following a successful lawsuit to recover equipment (LSD had not been illegal at the time of the 1965 raid), Owsley set up a new lab in Point Richmond, California in July 1966, complete with a tableting machine and precursors he'd stashed away. The address of this lab seems lost to time; Tom Butt, a one-time mayor of Richmond, set about on a search, concluding that 800 Western Drive was the most plausible candidate. Scully and Douglas came along. Point Richmond was chosen, according to Scully, due to Stanley "hoping that smells from the refinery would mask lab odors" and the possibilities of "counter-surveillance from the hillside above the house." Using 10% tricalcium phosphate as a binder and lactose as filler, Stanley was able to standardize dose, fight counterfeiting, and protect active material from the degrading effect of ultraviolet light; the result was the infamous "White Lightning."

Scully mentions a "speckled barrel group" in California, referencing Robert Black's unpublished memoir *LSD Outlaw*, along with other small-scale affairs (perhaps most notable for Barry Orlando and Bill Week's work in a gutted Airstream trailer buried under the California desert). Most of the relevant material cited is sadly embargoed. Returning to the 1995 DIR:

> By the end of the 1960s, a single group...emerged as the principal supplier of LSD in the United States.

This likely refers to the Clear Light System group in Northern California. Information about Clear Light is exiguous; Mark McCloud, curator of San Francisco's "Institute of Illegal Images," claims that Leonard Pickard (of more momentarily) got his start with the group. Their 1968 samizdat (second edition in 1971) *The Psychedelic Guide to Preparation of the Eucharist* includes several dubious

---

$\bar{\text{p}}$: the antiproton, a negatively-charged hadron made up of $\bar{\text{u}}/\bar{\text{u}}/\bar{\text{d}}$ antiquarks

guides to clandestine synthesis, listing "The Ultimate Authority of the Clear Light" as author. Denis Kelly (later "Jun Po Rishi") manufactured at least some of their gelatin, and later spent many years as an *saṅghaṇāyaka* at the San Francisco Zen Center. The System's name comes from a Buddhist term known in Tibetan as *'od gsal ba*, and in Sanskrit *prabhāsvaratā*: "luminosity" or "clear light." Attainment of *samadhi* leads to the *'od gsal gyi sems* and *prabhāsvara-citta*: the mind of clear light. Related concepts are those of "Primordial Clear Light" of the Bardo Thodol of the *tertön* Karma Lingpa, and the "Clear Light of Reality" of Padmasambhāva. The Dharmic (and the Abrahamic, for that matter; perhaps all) religions are full of references to Light, and we ought not discount the perhaps relevant *apāma somamamṛtā abhūmāghanma jyotiravidāma devān*.

In Britain, Victor James Kapur had two distinct labs operating when he was picked up in 1967. In Kent, the lab of Quentin Theobald and Peter Simmons was raided in 1969, and the chemists were arrested in London. The stories of Her Majesty's clandestine chemists are told in *Albion Dreaming: A History of LSD in Britain*, published by Andy Roberts in 2012.

> With the immobilization of this group in the early 1970s, another organization took over as the principal source of supply...The neutralization of this organization wiped out the large-scale production and distribution of LSD within the United States.

In Millbrook, New York, Addison Mizner in 1912 designed *"Daheim,"* an exemplar of the American Queen Anne style with asymmetrical façade, wrapping verandas, turrets, and a Bavarian Baroque gatehouse. Ownership eventually fell to the children of Tommy Hitchcock Jr., heirs to the Mellon estate. They befriended a controversial psychology professor: Timothy Francis Leary, administrator of the Harvard Psilocybin Project. When Leary and assistant professor Richard Alpert were fired by Harvard in April 1963, the Hitchcocks rented to them Daheim. Leary moved his International Federation for Internal Freedom to the Millbrook mansion, installed Peggy Hitchcock as its director, and renamed it the Castalia Foundation after the rarefied community of the mind in Hermann Hesse's 1943 novel *Das Glasperlenspiel*. If you're interested in Leary, Don Lattin's *The Harvard Psychedelic Club* (2010) covers his scene well, as does Robert Greenfield's eponymous biography (same Greenfield as *Bear*), but Leary was a jackass, and no chemist.

Nicholas Sand, originally using the Pinoche method of trifluoroacetic anhydride on D-LSA, traveled to meet Leary. He was named Alchemist of the

---

saṅghaṇāyaka: abbot/abbess, head of a Buddhist temple
'od gsal ba: འོད་གསལ་བ   'od...sems: འོད་གསལ་གྱི་སེམས
samadhi: समाधि meditative absorption, eighth of the Noble Eightfold Path
prabhāsvaratā: प्रभास्वर   prabhāsvara-citta: चित्त   Daheim: lit. "at home"
Bardo Thodol: བར་དོ་ཐོས་གྲོལ lit. Liberation Through Hearing During the Intermediate State
tertön: གཏེར་སྟོན་ revealer of hidden *terma*   Karma Lingpa: གཏེར་སྟོན་
Padmasambhāva: པད་འབྱུང་གནས "born from a lotus" 8th century Vajra master
apāma...devān: अपाम सोममम्रता अभूमागन्म जयोतिरविदाम देवान We have drunk Soma and become immortal; we have attained the light the Gods discovered! Rigveda 8, Hymn XLVIII
Das Glasperlenspiel: The Glass Bead Game (also *Magister Ludi*, "Master of the Game")

Foundation (by now renamed once again to the League of Spiritual Discovery). Following several FBI raids organized by district attorney G. Gordon Liddy (later the organizer of the Daniel Ellsberg and Watergate burglaries, convict of criminal contempt of Congress, actor of small and big screen, author of several novels, massively successful radio host, and general rightwing ruffian), Timothy Leary moved across the country, joining Sand on a ranch in Idyllwild's Garner Valley. The loathsome Logan Paul purchased it in 2019, but it was in 1967 home to John Griggs and his commune, the Brotherhood of Eternal Love.

At least two major popular histories of the BEL have been written. Nicholas Schou's 2011's *Orange Sunshine* is a compact and not incompetent volume in which Scully and Sand are peripheral to the main story of hashish smuggling. William Kirkley brought out a documentary of the same name in 2016. *The Brotherhood of Eternal Love: From Flower Power to Hippie Mafia*, a 1984 work by Stewart Tendler and David May, has broader coverage, and is at times full of rich detail. A 2015 documentary *The Sunshine Makers* focuses on the two alchemists, and is worth your ninety minutes. *Rainbow Bridge,* Chuck Wein's 1971 film loosely related to the BEL, is a bizarre but ultimately boring viewing experience, in no way necessary nor even particularly relevant.

In 1966, California and Nevada became the first two states to prohibit LSD. Scully already suspected he was being tailed; on 1966-12-08, the clerk at Nurnberg Chemicals (now Nurnberg Scientific) was Orve Hendrix, a BDAC agent. Douglas and Scully broke off towards free state Colorado, and settled on a lab at the intersection of Ash and E. 26th streets. Owsley joined them, and they produced 20 mg tablets of DOM (they called it STP, for "serenity, tranquility, and peace"), tablets combining LSD and 10 mg DOM, and a hundred thousand 270 µg "Monterey Purple" tablets.

On Christmas Eve 1967, Owsley, Cargill, and Gissen were arrested in Orinda, California, at a two-story lab at 69 Esperila St. Stanley and Cargill had already been picked up with Leary in Putnam Valley, New York. Owsley would go down yet again in 1970's New Orleans bust of the Grateful Dead, and then in Oakland five months later; in 1974 he was hit with tax evasion. Scully thought it prudent to change locations, and found a second location in Denver (1050 South Elmira St). There he set up shop with the help of financial backing from the Hitchcocks, intending to distribute through the Brotherhood exclusively. This lab was discovered in less than six months, and raided while Scully roamed Europe in a quest for precursor alkaloids. The search was ruled illegal, and the case dropped, but it represented a substantial financial loss.

Having returned to California, Owsley introduced swashbuckler Sand and studious Scully, and they assembled a lab in a Windsor farmhouse occupying two acres off Wilson (now Mitchell) Lane. Scully convinced Sand to distribute through the BEL rather than the Hells Angels. Sand provided initial funding by sale of his San Francisco DOM lab. Through an English contact they acquired a pound of Italian-made lysergic acid and went to work—serious work, in shifts; the two thought themselves teleologically called to immanentize a psychedelic

---

BDAC: Bureau of Drug Abuse Control
DOM: $C_{12}H_{19}NO_2$ 1-(2,5-Dimethoxy-4-methylphenyl)propan-2-amine

eschaton. It was from this location that they put out about three pounds of LSD, yielding (once tableted in a Novato home using a triturate machine) four and a half megadoses of tableted "Orange Sunshine," revered for its remarkable purity and potency. This was perhaps the most advanced lab to date, making proper use of multispectral light, vacuum evaporators, nitrogen environments, and full purification via chromatography.

During their trial, Sand and Scully contended that they had manufactured not LSD but ALD-52. Appeal upheld the Government's assertion that manufacture of ALD-52 necessarily goes by way of LSD, and is thus illegal *prima facie.* Circuit Judge Duniway furthermore smacked down the assertion that trial delay led to hydrolysis of their ALD-52 into LSD: "Whatever prejudice defendants suffered was a product of their own negligence. Experienced chemists like Sand and Scully should have known, that burying a substance in an unsealed container is an ideal way to promote, not prevent, hydrolysis," and in a vicious bitchslap, "we do not imply that the district court was compelled by the evidence before it to conclude that the chemical offered at trial ever was ALD-52."

Both Scully and Sand were convicted of conspiracy. They were cellmates at Washington's McNeil Island Federal Penitentiary. Scully was paroled after three and a half years, and has by all indications retired from the game of clandestine chemistry.

> *By 1976, however, another [San Francisco Bay] organization had assumed the primary role in the production and distribution of LSD.*

Here the DEA sweeps under the rug a substantial effort across the Atlantic, where British chemists were busily supplying a large portion of the free world's LSD. Operation Julie (the subject of the Clash's "Julie's Been Working for the Drug Squad") spent thirteen months working surveillance, then arrested 120 people in England and Wales on 1977-03-26, seizing about 1.5 kg of LSD. David Solomon oversaw the organization, with Richard Kemp (not to be confused with MIT peptide chemist Daniel Kemp!) as his primary chemist operating out of Tregaron. Distributor Henry Todd and chemist Andy Munro worked out of a secondary facility in Hampton Wick. In bucolic Binfield Heath parish, Leaf Fielding and Christine Bott managed tableting and first-order distribution. Fielding *(To Live Outside the Law* (2011)) and Bott with Catherine Hayes *(The Untold Story of Christine Bott* (2021) and *After Julie: The Kemp Tapes* (2022), both posthumous) have released memoirs. Kemp received the longest sentence, thirteen years in gaol. Operation Julie was in 2022 the subject of a rock musical by Neath's *Theatr na nÓg*, due in part to Tregaron hosting that year's *Eisteddfod Genedlaethol.* Be advised that Officer Stephen Bentley's *Undercover: Operation Julie* (2019) is as dreadful a book as they come.

According to Tendler and May, George Ronald Hadley Whitney Stark a/k/a Terrence W. Abbott a/k/a Ronald Shitsky a/k/a Ronald Hadley Clark "was and is an enigma." He oversaw labs in France, and organized purchases of precursors

---

Theatr na nÓg: theater of the young
Eisteddfod Genedlaethol: National Eisteddfod lit. "sit-be"

from places like Exico, Alban Feeds, Charles Druce Ltd., Renschler, and Inland Alkaloids. He kept the BEL afloat with European-made acid, largely sourced from the Solomon and Kemp organization and a lab in Le Clocheton in Belgium.

Nicholas Sand was still putting in hours, and was likely responsible for most of the American acid during this period. Before being arrested in Windsor, he started a well-financed lab outside of St. Louis. This was brought down before production began, but Sand managed to beat the charges due to failure to acquire a search warrant. Released while *US v. Sand* was being appealed, Nicholas Sand became Theodore Edward Parody III, and relocated to Lumby in British Columbia. Using his Bell Perfume Labs and Signet Research and Development as fronts he acquired necessary chemicals and equipment, raised hydroponic vegetables and psychedelic mushrooms, and set up shop. He established a lab at scale in Port Coquitlam near Vancouver, and operated there until the RCMP showed up in 1996. It took two months to establish that David Shepherd (another pseudonym) was Nick Sand; he was extradited to San Francisco, and spent several years in prison. His interview with law enforcement in 2003's *Hallucinogens* is illuminating. He emerged in 2000, and enjoyed showing up at Burning Man's Entheon Village until he died in 2017.

Casey William Hardison was born in Washington state, acquired the lab equipment of novel psychedelic researcher Darrell Lemaire in 2001, and set off for Britain the following year to set up labs in Winston (near Steyning) and later The Vale in Ovingdean. There he was known as "OB1" and manufactured substantial 2C-B, DMT, and LSD. In July 2003 he sent £4,000 worth of MDMA to the United States in a copy of *Private Eye*, and it was detected at the Memphis FedEx facility. He was busted with 145 kilodoses of LSD, and represented himself before Judge Niblett in Lewes Crown Court for *Regina v. Casey Hardison.* The Honourable Niblett complimented Hardison, writing that "no professional advocate could have advanced the arguments, which he has put forward, with greater skill." He subsequently pointed out that "the Misuse of Drugs Act 1971 is a Statute, an Act of Parliament which is binding upon every citizen of, and visitor to, this country. It is binding upon the courts...this Act is not capable of other than literal interpretation," then sentenced Hardison to twenty years to be followed by deportation. He served eight years before being deported to Victor, Idaho, and claims to be running for president in 2024.

Kary Banks Mullis received his undergraduate degree in chemistry from Georgia Tech, and his PhD in biochemistry from Berkeley, with a postdoc in pharmaceutical chemistry from UCSF. At Cetus in 1983 he developed the PCR method, now a ubiquitous and fundamental technique for DNA amplification via heat-stable polymerase such as *Taq*. He received the Japan Prize and then the Nobel in Chemistry in 1993. His 1998 autobiography *Dancing Naked in the Mind Field* is a delight from far beyond the beaten track. Therein, he describes drinking whiskey with his grandfather's ghost, a visit from aliens in the form of a fluorescent raccoon, and how the LSD he synthesized while at Berkeley helped him develop PCR. He produced several grams, and by all indications consumed them himself; he is perhaps the only person besides Peter Webster

---

RCMP: Royal Canadian Mounted Police   PCR: polymerase chain reaction

(author of the unreleased *Kosmos: A Theory of Psychedelic Experience)* to have credibly claimed LSD manufacture without suffering an arrest.

From the DEA's 2019-09 D-Lysergic Acid Diethylamide fact sheet:

> *The number of LSD items seized decreased dramatically in 2002 due to the seizure of a large LSD lab in Kansas City in 2000. With the arrest of clandestine chemists and with the dismantling of their laboratory, the availability of LSD in the U.S. was reduced by 95%.*

We come now to the most recent of the major known acid chemists, by far the strangest story of the lot, a true Greek tragedy. The best book on our final subject is Dennis McDougal's eminently readable (if overly credulous) 2020 *Operation White Rabbit.* William Leonard Pickard, Jr. was born October 21st of 1945, about six weeks after the end of war in the Pacific. His father was a member of the Georgia bar association admitted 1951-08-31, having read law at Woodrow Wilson College in Atlanta (said College shut down 1987-12-15; in the northern Brookhaven suburb, Oglethorpe University serves as custodian of their records). Mother Audrey divorced and departed early on (Pickard claimed to McDougal that she danced with Clark Gable at the premiere of *Gone With the Wind),* and Pickard's primary distaff influence was stepmother Dr. Lucille Georg. Lucille had studied biology at Michigan, and mycology at Columbia's Vagelos medical school. In 1974 she would be awarded the Rhoda Benham Prize; Dr. Benham had at Columbia set up the world's first medical mycology class, and the first research lab for medicinal funga in the United States. She joined the fledgling Centers for Disease Control, having been established as the successor to the Malaria Control in War Areas program only in 1946. The junior Pickard attended Daniel O'Keefe High, graduating as 1968's "Most Intellectual." DO'KHS existed only from 1947–1973; its location at 75 5th Street NW put it right in the middle of what is now Georgia Tech's "Tech Square" Midtown development, in what has been the Centergy One building since 2003.

Pickard is by all indications brilliant. He was definitely a finalist in the 1963 Westinghouse (later Intel, and now Regeneron) Science Talent Search, then and now a big deal (there was one other finalist from Georgia that year: Steven Muchnick, later the author of *Advanced Compiler Design and Implementation).* He interned at Argonne National Labs as a high school junior. He was one of two winners of the Atlanta Science Congress in both 1961 and 1962, the latter year for "radiobiology of pinocytosis." The Georgia Tech Alumni Magazine of November 1962 includes a picture of him delivering his presentation; he was a handsome little fucker by any standard. He recounts significant time in Tech's Price Gilbert library, and eventually accepted a scholarship to Princeton, where he lasted one semester. Following several arrests, the last by US Marshals for violation of the Dyer NMVT, he avoided prison by diversion to the grimbrick Connecticut Institute of Living. He spent 1966 in Boston at the Retina Foundation for Experimental Biology, and in 1967 moved to Berkeley's Department of Bacteriology and Immunology, where he worked alongside Kary Mullis at the same time Mullis describes synthesizing several grams. Who taught whom is

---

NMVT: National Motor Vehicle Theft Act 18 U.S.C.A. §2312

unknown, but it seems likely that Pickard and the future Nobel Prize winner shared knowledge. This brings us to the end of the 1960s, when Mark McCloud places Pickard with Clear Light.

Pickard pops in and out of the record for the next thirty years. In 1974 he attended the trial of Scully and Sand, watching Billy Hitchcock indict former friends (Sand refused to testify; Scully stated forthrightly that he was guilty of "wanting to turn on the world," and later claimed ruefully "if you are guilty you should never get on the witness stand") and handing out longstemmed roses to supporters of the defendants. There was a 1976 raid (and short detention) in Woodside by San Mateo PD, who came looking for peyote but found only (then legal) MDP2P. A 1977 MDMA raid in Portola Valley led to eighteen months' imprisonment. Early in 1980 he was charged with methamphetamine possession in Gainesville, Georgia; analysis demonstrated the powder to be the aromatic aldehyde 3,4,5-trimethoxybenzaldehyde, and the charges were dropped. Four months later, Volusia County (Florida) PD got Pickard for MDA distribution, but this turned out to MDMA (MDMA wasn't placed on Schedule I until 1985). 1986: brass knuckles at Atlanta's Hartsfield airport. 1987: false identification in San Mateo, upgraded to a 18 USC §1542 false statement applying for a passport. Then on 1988-12-28, his trailer-in-a-warehouse Mountain View lab was raided. It was a substantial operation; BNE investigator Max Houser collapsed in convulsions despite PPE including a respirator. Upgraded to a federal charge, Pickard ate an eight-year conviction, of which he served four in FCI Terminal Island, being released in November 1992.

Pickard "vehemently denied ever having worked with or for the DEA" to McDougal. This contradicts what he told the United States District Court for Kansas according to *United States v. Pickard, 236 F. Supp. 2d 1204 (D. Kan. 2002)*, ruled 2002-11-26. This ruling considered Pickard's request for a pretrial conference pursuant to CIPA, and reports on his early motion for discovery *inter alia*:

> The defendant has had a longstanding, cooperative relationship with the DEA and other governmental agencies.

Pickard has claimed that this was "disinformation." What information is true, and whom is being deceived, is left as an exercise for the reader. Pickard emerged from Terminal Island and went directly to the SFZC mentioned earlier, spending months there; this time is credibly written up in his *The Rose of Paracelsus,* an uneven but occasionally gorgeous work authored in prison, and published in 2015 (its name is taken from *La rosa de Paracelso* by Borges). He sought out Scully to swap processes; Scully offered him tea. He linked up with the Shulgins and attended their weekly potlucks. He worked briefly in the lab of David Nichols at Purdue, and despite Nichols being "extremely disappointed†"

MDP2P: piperonyl methyl ketone $C_{10}H_{10}O_3$ 1-(2H-1,3-Benzodioxol-5-yl)propan-2-one
MDA: $C_{10}H_{13}NO_2$ 1-(2H-1,3-Benzodioxol-5-yl)propan-2-amine
BNE: Bureau of Narcotic Enforcement   FCI: Federal Correctional Institute
CIPA: Classified Information Procedures Act (18 USC App. III)

†This directly contradicts what's reported in *Operation White Rabbit.* I spoke with both Dr. Nichols and Mr. McDougal at length in 2023, and stand by this claim. Mr. McDougal does not seem to have deliberately misstated facts, but interviewed Nichols days after the latter emerged from openheart surgery, and likely got some cloudy recollections. My words come directly from Dr. Nichols. —*nick*

in Leonard, was accepted into Harvard's Kennedy School of Government as a fellow in drug policy, focusing on novel opioids following the collapse of the Soviet Union. He followed Mark Kleiman to UCLA and was hired as Director of the Drug Policy Analysis Program. He traveled the world attending entheogen and psychedelic conferences. One would reasonably think Pickard had, like Scully, given up on the game. In truth, he was out only while he was inside.

Pickard established a lab in Aspen, keeping it up for a few years before relocating it to New Mexico (110 Vuelta Herradura outside Santa Fe). The dry desert air was a fine environment for chemistry, and through Alfred Savinelli's Native Scents he could order lab equipment and basic chemicals. He used John Connor and James Clerk Maxwell as fake names around Taos. There he met a particularly foul example of humanity, Gordon Todd Skinner. Skinner owned a missile silo in Carneiro, Kansas, and convinced Pickard to acquire a tasteful SM-65F Atlas installation: Silo 7 of the 550th Strategic Missile Squadron operated out of Schilling AFB.

Pickard had known San Jose machinist Clyde Apperson since the 1970s, and they had worked together on at least the Mountain View lab. Together they put together an industrial-scale lab in Wamego, Kansas. Skinner, caught up in the Operation Flashback push against MDMA, fed the lab directly to DEA Special Agent Karl Nichols, who had spent time with the LSD task force in Operation Looking Glass. From this treachery was born Operation White Rabbit, the largest LSD interdiction in DEA history. When Pickard and Apperson returned to Kansas on 2000-11-06, alerted to trouble and intent on moving the lab out of the silo, Kansas Highway Patrol pulled over Apperson in a Ryder truck and Pickard in a silver Buick LeSabre. Pickard managed to elude helicopters, dogs, and a small army of DEA agents for a day, but was eventually turned in by farmer Billy Taylor.

On 2003-01-13, US District Judge Richard Dean Rogers opened *US v. Pickard*. The jury on 2003-03-31 returned guilty verdicts on the charges of conspiracy to manufacture 10 grams or more of LSD (21 USC § 846) and possession with intent of same (21 U.S.C. § 841(a)(1)). Pickard was sentenced on 2003-11-25 to life without the possibility of parole. Apperson ate 360 months. Skinner received immunity and a $200,000 stipend. Several months after the trial's completion, he (together with wife Krystle Ann Cole and accomplice William Earnest Hauck) kidnapped, drugged, tortured, and dropped off for dead eighteen year-old Brandon Green. The "Facts" section of Skinner's 2009 appeal makes for unpleasant reading:

> ...Evidence presented at trial established that the torture at the Tulsa hotel included numerous and repeated injections by Skinner into Green's penis, testicles, buttocks, and other parts of his body, with the apparent dual purpose of permanently disabling and disfiguring Green sexually and of keeping him in a prolonged state of unconsciousness, while he was being physically, sexually, and emotionally assaulted by Skinner. Skinner brutally punched and kicked Green in the genitals, lifted Green's unconscious body up off the bed by grabbing him at the base of his genitals, and wrapped a

phone cord about Green's penis, put his foot on Green's stomach, and jerked until he heard "the cartilage snap."...Both Hauck and Green testified about a particularly disturbing thing that Green vomited up, which had little worm-like things inside it, and that Skinner claimed was a "parasite sack." In addition, and at the direction of Skinner, Green's eyes were covered and he was told that if he took the covering off, his retinas would be burned. Skinner then pretended to be a Swedish doctor, who had come to "help" Green, but who actually tormented him and put suppositories and perhaps other things in Green's anus....

Skinner is serving life plus ninety years in Oklahoma's Joseph Harp Correctional Center. Krystle Ann Cole divorced him (she never served time) and published the 2007 memoir *Lysergic,* which makes rather more aggressive use of exclamation points than I care to see in peacetime.

In the aftermath of the Kansas silo busts, acid availability across most of the country dropped precipitously. The DEA associated this reduction entirely with Pickard's capture, but others (most particularly Jesse Jarnow in his somewhat messy *Heads: A Biography of Psychedelic America* (2016)) point to aggravating factors: Jerry Garcia's death in 1995 and the cessation of Grateful Dead tours, the capture of Nick Sand in 1996, and the death of an unnamed European precursor source. Pickard credits the rise of MDMA, and claims that LSD production is too distributed for his arrest to effect such an impact. This is all rather dubious: regarding events in the mid 1990s, acid remained cheap and plentiful through the end of the century. The end of the Grateful Dead was concurrent with the rise of Phish. The sudden lack of precursors could explain such a decline even assuming distributed production, but extraction of precursors from ergot is not a task of overwhelming difficulty, and it seems likely that one of these other chemists (Pickard repeatedly refers to (five of) "The Six" in *Rose:* Vermilion, Cobalt, Magenta, Crimson, and Indigo) would have taken up the challenge. Nonetheless, it is certain that LSD remained difficult to find through most of the new century's first decade, and that the Kansas operation had been producing volume sufficient to keep America tripping.

What was sold as LSD often turned out to be other chemicals, some of them substantially more toxic, almost all of them less effective. Examples include the NBOMe family, described in Ralf Heim's 2003 *Doktorarbeit* and further developed by the Nichols group, and the dihydrofurans, epitomized by Bromo-DragonFLY (first synthesized by Matthew Parker in 1998). This didn't change until the rise of darknet markets using cryptocurrency, most effectively pioneered by Ross Anthony Ulbricht's Silk Road. His story is told well in Nick Bilton's *American Kingpin* (2018). Ulbricht was convicted of myriad crimes in 2015, and is serving life without the possibility of parole at USP Tucson (having initially been held at USP Florence High), where he befriended...Leonard Pickard. So revolves the *dharmachakra—Sors immanis et inanis, rota tu volubilis, status malus!* With the arrival of Silk Road and a hundred successive imitators, LSD was once more

---

dharmachakra: धर्मचक्र wheel of dharma

Sors...malus: Empty, monstrous Fortuna, whirling malevolent wheel! *Carmina Burana* 13–16

available, initially largely out of Germany and Russia. Trends hint at renewed American production in recent years.

In something of a surprising move (and perhaps the single best result of COVID-19), Pickard was released on compassionate leave 2020-07-27. He authored the afterword to Transform Press's 2023 translation of Hofmann's *Die Mutterkornalkaloide*; it is uncertain what else has occupied his time these past few years. What *is* known is that between possession of undeniable talent and well-honed skills, decades spent in the game, and a consuming drive to synthesize psychedelics, it is plausible, even probable, that William Leonard Pickard Jr. produced (and possibly consumed) more clandestine LSD than any man living or dead. States away from either, he was almost certainly responsible for most of the acid Katz and Bolaño consumed in the twentieth century. In Atlanta, the city in a forest where Pickard attended high school and his mentor Mullis studied undergraduate chemistry, these two set to closing the loop. The students would become masters.

Starting in 2008, there was thanks to our boys a sudden deluge of American LSD of the highest grade. Multiple HIDTA regional headquarters and smaller DEA offices reported a sharp uptick in possession and distribution arrests. Confiscated acid submitted to the DEA's laboratory network exhibited remarkable uniformity under even the most rigorous analytic regimen. It was a discussion topic among the SWGDRUG in 2009; it was at first thought that there must be some error in methodology. DEA scientists concluded that no, testing was being performed rigorously, and in conformance with best practices. A workshop report ended with the summary:

> We seem to be seeing the work of a single lab, one that had a nationwide distribution network readily available. It must be assumed that this group can synthesize arbitrary volumes, likely producing to meet demand. The chemists involved are highly skilled and probably few in number. It seems likely that they are operating out of a major industrial or academic installation, one in which they might be highly placed and thus capable of retarding or avoiding internal oversight. Otherwise, we might be looking at organized crime's first foray into hallucinogens.

Reading this report in *Microgram*, Bolaño chuckled, and sent Katz an instant message: WHAT DOES IT MEAN FOR CRIME TO BE ORGANIZED? Katz replied immediately: THAT IT MAINTAINS ITSELF BY CONVERSION OF INPUTS TO NEGENTROPY. After a few seconds, he followed that up: LIKELY AN EMERGENT PHENOMENON.

Die Mutterkornalkaloide: The Ergot Alkaloids (1964)
SWGDRUG: Scientific Working Group for the Analysis of Seized Drugs

Part III

unordnung—CONFUSION

From time to time a player leaps up with a despairing cry, having lost his youth to an old man or become Latah to his opponent. But there are higher stakes than youth or Latah, games where only two players in the world know what the stakes are.

William Burroughs, *Naked Lunch* (1959)

As he brews, so shall he drink.

Ben Jonson, *Every Man in His Humour* (1598) Act II, Scene 1

Ich verwende gern meine Kenntnisse.
(I like to make use of what I know.)

Franz Kafka, *Der Process* (*The Trial*, 1925)

I will take with me a file, a chisel, a knife. I will try to get some major explosives and fight my way out. I will grab a sword like Maximus Decimus Meridus, and as a gladiator I will stab people in the crotch. God save the Republic and God save the Constitution.

James Anthony Traficant, Jr. (D-Ohio), 2002-07-17,
addressing the House Committee on Standards of Official Conduct

13 cloud wandered lonely as a daffodil

June 2009. Phish, fresh off five years broken up, were in Manchester Tennessee to play Bonnaroo. It would be their first appearance at the festival, now in its eighth incarnation. Katz wasn't there for them directly—though if there was a bumpin' "Chalk Dust Torture" or "Llama," he was down, taboot taboot—but there was sure to be good business with the prime jamband finally back on tour. His musical interests lay in "That Tent," where Friday there'd be a nearly perfect lineup of St. Vincent, Santigold, Ani DiFranco, Phoenix, Crystal Castles, and Girl Talk. In this imperfect world, ecstatic dancing to the mashups of Gregg Gillis was about the purest joy Katz knew. He had through an unlikely series of decisions and dates seen Ani DiFranco live six times, usually convinced that he was the only heterosexual male in attendance. Beyond that, he intended to catch Dillinger Escape Plan, Nine Inch Nails, Russian Circles, and Mars Volta. Music for old men. At twenty-eight, already he was sufficiently old to recognize fewer than half the acts.

Bolaño had brought in two sheets, stored in aluminum foil in a manila envelope taped to his chest. Their rental had not been selected for a deep search, and they rode slowly on in; Bolaño immediately extracted the folder and handed it to Katz. The agreement had been easily reached: Bolaño would drive, and hold the product while in the car; it was Katz's inside the festival. The ideal case was to sell at least one sheet as a unit, and the remainder in runs of no fewer than ten, preferably twenty. It seemed not at all unreasonable that they'd encounter a buyer with a thousand or more in cash. More important was the hope of finding someone who could take the remaining sheets off their hands upon return. How exactly that would be done—probably through the mail, but how to handle payment?—had not yet been worked out.

Bolaño had likewise imported three liters of Laphroaig Islay scotch, carefully decanting the 750 mL bottles (glass was forbidden, as was any more than 1.75 L of outside hard liquor) into Lipton tea empties that morning. He poured two red Dixie cups, added ice, and handed one off to Sherman. They toasted to the confusion of their enemies and took long pulls. "Hail Eris!" bellowed Katz.

From a few meters behind, an unexpected response: "All hail Discordia!"

Katz looked back in surprise and saw a rangy man in a Stetson, ancient Grateful Dead shirt, and cutoff jeans. He was handsome enough, thin as a rail in the way of nippletaped cross country runners, jolly, long of limb or at the very least gangly, somewhere between fifteen and fifty, shoeless. He had produced a great deal of volume from such a small frame. He saw Katz looking and waved enthusiastically. "Hark! Be you a servant of the Goddess?"

"She Who has Done it All, and known the Fairest." Katz was delighted. This was surely a good omen.

Bolaño looked over at Katz. "You've found another practitioner of your faith, Katz? There are more of you?"

"We are legion!" Katz hissed and started towards his fellow Discordian.

"Ewige Blumenkraft!"

The fellow clapped his hands and actually left the ground in a little hop. "Yes! *Ewige Blumenkraft! Ewige Schlangenkraft,* friend!"

Bolaño caught easily up with Katz. "Was that a shibboleth? He replied with the right password. Do you have to let him fuck you or what?"

"If he doesn't fuck me I get his powers."

"And if he does?"

"Then he gets my powers; read a motherfucking book Bolaño!" Katz extended his hand. "It's rare to meet a servant of Eris."

"Getting rarer all the time, brother!"

"Oh man, this makes me really happy." Katz wears a broad grin, wholly authentic, an uncommon display of joy. "You having a good time?"

"Time's a mere measure of light through space. This space is holy, brother, blessed! Free of the aneristic, structured by disorder's crooked lines. The universe wants us to minimize entropy? We are no slaves! Smash the lathes of metabolism!" He thrust a large glass pipe at Katz, and for a few moments he danced like *wayang kulit.* Bolaño evaluated him at length, raising an eyebrow.

"This weed is exactly as fantastic as I hoped and expected. Thank you!" Katz passed it, and Bolaño nodded exuberantly upon hitting it.

"He has found Cloud! And I have found Katz and Bolaño, it seems. The former, fortunate favorite of the Goddess! The latter, not so fortunate? This latter one who must go down the mountain alone, no one meeting him."

Zarathustra stieg allein das Gebirge abwärts und Niemand begegnete ihm... Bolaño's eyes widened slightly. "Was that a Zarathustra reference?"

"I teach you the Superman: he is that sea; in him your great contempt must be submerged, for you know no faith in your heart." Cloud wagged his finger and danced again, briefly.

Bolaño looked at Katz. "I'm going to walk around a bit. I'll meet you back at this stage. Or somewhere."

They were silent as Michael receded into the swarm. After a few seconds Katz began unconsciously to simulate the crowd as a particle system. He blinked and shook his head. "This is awesome weed, mang! You said your name was Cloud? Like the Final Fantasy VII guy with the big sword?"

"I was Cloud long before! It's my *karass* name. My parents named me Walther, but my heart is not in the least tired. Does this surprise you?"

"Are you asking me if I am surprised?"

Cloud nodded.

"I am entirely unsurprised, my friend! Are you speaking of *karass* from Vonnegut, ummm, *Cat's Cradle?*"

"Around us, this is all a *granfalloon!* And so it has been for years now. They will crowd around us, panting with anguish and disappointment! So it will be until her Sacrament flows again from Eleusís, *Kallisti.*" Cloud wailed, a noise like a Sioux might make, and his face broke into despair as once more he danced.

Ewige Blumenkraft: Eternal flower power   **Ewige Schlangenkraft:** Eternal serpent power
wayang kulit: ꦮꦪꦁꦏꦸꦭꦶꦠ꧀ Javan shadow puppets

"You're an interesting guy, Cloud. So did you change your name, or did someone give you that name, or...what do you get up to? What are your ermm themes and central motivations? Jesus, this weed is amazing, I'm high as shit, where does it come from?"

"I count five questions there, Katz. My weed comes from places whereof those who know do not speak." *chih chê pu yen. yen chê pu chih.* "My motivations are the acceleration of sacred entropic forcings, my themes those developed in the music of our Goddess. I get up to working the circuit with *karass,* but the circuit has been dusty, and we look to Her for rain. Given to me was Cloud, given unfreely. I won it, and in winning it, brother, I lost my old name."

"You're not, like, alluding to ritual murder or anything, right, Cloud? I'm not going to judge you either way, but that—everything you just said—was the most culty-ass shit I've ever heard." Katz probably would have already broken off, but for the weed, the weed that is hitting him like a train, some of the best he's ever had. He'd like very much to buy some. To set up further, larger buys in the future. With this he could press Vlad to expand. Bring in further Vlads. A Vladstravaganza. That's nonsense high talk, idiot. Katz shook his head.

Cloud whooped. "Ritual murder? Brother, we all kill a billion people every day, and we're killed a billion times. Every second we all die." He put his arm around Katz's shoulders, pushing hard towards the threshold where this stupendous weed was no longer worth association.

"Cloud, if that was meant to convince or even suggest to me that you reject ritual murder, you're going about it the wrong-ass way."

"Brother, brother." Another whoop, this one piercingly loud, drawing looks from all over the place, but at least he pulled his goddamn arm away. "You've got the wrong idea. Have you ever eaten LSD?"

Katz laughs. "Several thousand hits, Cloud."

"Ahhh! Then you understand, maybe. How old are you? I'm sixty-one."

"You're sixty-one? Bullshit." Katz could accept forty with some surprise. Fifty would be impressive. There was no way this guy had lived sixty years.

"Sixty-one." He pulled a Montana license and handed it to Katz, who almost fumbled accepting the card. CLOUD NEPHELE CARPO, DOB 02-02-1946.

"Well I'll be fucked. You're a healthy motherfucker, Cloud Carpo." Katz handed the card back. "And I am twenty-eight, but twenty-nine soon." Something's off. "Wait, I thought you were born Walther? Did you actually legally change your name to Cloud, then? The ID..."

Cloud ignores the question. "And when was your First Communion?"

Fine. Keep your secrets. "Holy catholic and apostolic church? Or LSD?"

"They're one and the same, brother!"

"Well Cloud we're gonna have to agree to disagree there, but I first ate LSD when I was fifteen or so."

"Yes! Then you've noticed, surely brother, that what's sold as LSD of late is a perversion, an impostor! As if to breathe were life! This decade, not so many

---

chih...chih: 知者不言. 言者不知. Those who know do not speak. Those who speak do not know. Lǎozi (道德經 Tao Te Ching 56)

years ago, first there was suddenly no acid, then there trickled in this lifeless pretender to LSD."

"I have noticed that, actually. Isn't that due to the busts out in Kansas? That guy who was working in a silo out there?"

Cloud brightens into radiance. "Yes, you know the story, brother!"

"Well, I read the *Rolling Stone* article." And a bit more than that.

"The *karass* purchased from that alchemist, who called himself Rubicund."

"He called himself red?"

"Aye, and he spoke also of five other shades. But we have been unable to make contact with them, and if they are producing, it is of low quality, or not in general circulation. Most of us think they never existed, or referred to historical alchemists, or were Rubicund's dream or lie."

"His name was William Leonard Pickard, Jr. For the record."

Cloud dismisses it. "If anyone has won his name, it is the alchemist in his silo. We seek a new alchemist, one who will restore the *karass,* give it purpose. We have our own stashes of the last of the his wares. Otherwise we would drift apart entirely, to demise and darkness, going down one by one. But there is nothing to distribute, to fund the work, to bring in the new. And now children are born who'll never have a chance to know true LSD, no better than they were before the Archmage Hofmann. I wail, I despair, thus."

A callathump had been rising inside Katz, charivari and tintamarre, foofaraw and donnybrook both, a right pother and stir. All energy flows according to the whims of Eris. "Cloud, I have something I'd very much like you to try."

✳ ✳ ✳ ✳ ✳ ✳ ✳ ✳ ✳

The LSD cults started springing up around 1965. They were made famous by the Legion for Spiritual Discovery and the BEL; they were made notorious by the Manson Family in Death Valley and hysterical articles in *Reader's Digest.* Already eulogized by Hunter S. Thompson's "wave monologue" from his first *Fear and Loathing,* the heyday of LSD cults came to an end by the mid 1970s. Nixon's Reorganization Plan №2 summoned up the DEA on 1973-07-01, merging the BNDD, ODALE, scattered federal agents, and a $116 meg FY1974 budget (FY2021 budget: $3.28 gigs). The BNDD had been formed four years earlier under Plan №1, bringing drug policy for the first time under the Department of Justice: the Bureau of Narcotics had been Treasury, the Bureau of Drug Abuse Control part of the FDA. With a new, more retributive mandate (and federal largesse), the DEA disrupted the larger, more casual distribution networks that had been until then the style.

The SYnchromystic Neuronoumenologists of the City Of the Pyramids Eso-teric (SYNCOPE) formed, or in any case coined that unwieldy name, in 1984. Two years earlier, Harold Grimbisch had been a Golden Gopher at Minnesota, an early PhD student in computer science. Twenty minutes south on I-35 sat the headquarters of Cray Research in Eagan. Turn west onto I-494 instead to reach Bloomington and the Control Data Corporation. Engineering Research

---

ODALE: Office of Drug Abuse Law Enforcement   **DDP:** Digital Data Processor

Associates started in St. Paul; the AS/400 was designed in IBM's Rochester facility; the Minneapolis Regulator Company would become Honeywell, building
the IMPs of the first ARPANET nodes. A Cray-1 sat in the University Computer
Center's Lauderdale facility, and Harold often drove there from Marcy-Holmes
to assist with operation of the finicky monstrosity. He wrote early numerical relativity FORTRAN, and was narrowly scooped for the first simulation
of rotating gravitational collapse, and assisted Boeing in validation of their
A502/PANAIR linearized potential CFD code.

1982-02-21 was a Sunday; he kissed his girlfriend goodbye early in the afternoon, and embarked east towards Chippewa Falls in his Hialeah Yellow 1970
Gremlin. A mysterious demo would be given by Seymour Cray himself; rumor had it that this would be the first sighting of the new X-MP. It would be
hard to get a room this late, but the Indianhead Motel didn't accept reservations over the phone, and Harold hoped to find lodging there. The winter of
1982, especially the late January blizzard, had shut down large sections of the
Midwest—twenty inches fell overnight in St. Louis; Minneapolis saw forty-one
inches between January 20 and 22. The Twin Cities, normally adept with their
snowplows and salts, were overwhelmed. It was the first time Harold could remember MSP International shutting down. The Minnesota sky took to strange
hues of pink and orange, and lightning struck in echoes of white flash, bolts
too numerous to associate any one with the peals of thunder that rolled into
one another overhead. To stand outside at the peak was to be buried under two
accumulating inches per hour. Only in the past few days had the North Star
State emerged from the oppressive winter. It was a downright balmy 16.1 °C;
Harold felt alive and optimistic, singing along with The Cars to "Shake it Up"
and drumming on the AMC's roof in time with "Centerfold."

The Indianhead had a room, and he paid his $16. Alas, it was not to be. He
ran into an associate at a N. Bridge street diner, and got the bad news.

"Cray's not even going to be there, man. The X-MP is a Steve Chen deal.
They're saying Seymour's losing it, that he won't accept parallel memories,
won't accept multiprocessors, he's gone all Einstein-vs-Bohr and is locked away
working on the Cray 2, who knows when it'll come out. They say he spends
long hours in the evening digging tunnels in his backyard. He talks to elves."

"That's all nonsense, just messing with the corporate overlords."

"He brought a pickaxe to the National Computing Conference last May."

"Eh, who doesn't bring a weapon to Chicago?"

"Well, either way, this will be the unveiling of the X-MP, supposedly, but
that definitely means Seymour won't be there if true. He hates that machine
with a passion. He considers it an insult to his greatness. He won't talk to Chen
or anyone on the X-MP team."

"It's Cray Research. If Seymour Cray doesn't want it, how does it exist?"

"It's Cray's name, but it's not Cray's money. Hell, he's not even CEO anymore,
hasn't been since 1980. Cray wanted to not have a manager, not to manage ev-

---

IMP: Interface Message Processor   **ARPANET:** Advanced Research Projects Agency Network
PANAIR: panel aerodynamics   **CFD:** computational fluid dynamics

eryone else. He's an incompetent CEO. I think he's technically an independent contractor now, not even a fulltime employee."

"Well, shit. I don't care about seeing—who is this X-MP designer?"

"Steve Chen. Chinese guy, got his degree in Formosa, did his PhD under Kuck at UIUC. Designed everything good Burroughs put out the last decade."

"Well I don't want to sit around to watch Steve Chen sit on a torus."

"I don't know, the X-MP is supposed to be pretty sweet."

"Yeah, but I'm not here on a per diem." Harold left fifty cents for a tip, collected his bag, and headed back towards St. Paul, jamming to Kansas and Queen with Lance "Tac" Hammer on KQRS 92.5 "Superstar Rock Radio!" Arriving home, the front door was unlocked, and from within streamed out chords of power pop and distaff yelps. He entered, and there was Debbie, Generra Hypercolor shirt up around her navel, knees out to the side, some lounge lizardish lothario pumping his small chalky ass atop her, jeans and Cuban-heeled matador boots thrown to the side. *Working Class Dog* blared from the 8-track, and her paramour would turn out to be the backup guitarist for Rick Springfield's touring band, enjoying a little afternoon lovin' before kicking it that evening at the Orpheum Theatre. Harold stood there for a moment, watching, listening, smelling, and "Love is Alright Tonite" closed down for the delicate opening riffs of "Jessie's Girl." Just as Rick started in on that tragic tale of male friendship riven by love for the same woman, Harold screamed, and leaped upon them, pounding the interloper with blows from his ten-pushup arms as spit and froth flew from his lips. Then he was upside down, flying backwards, head smacks against the wall, and his vision dwindles, and *ooof* there goes a kick right into his balls, he's been demanned, augh he's puking and Debbie screams at him, calls him an asshole, calls him a stupid selfish faggot nerd; the musician cups his chin gently, looks him in the eyes with equal parts sympathy and contempt, and smashes him with a backhand, and he's wearing a ring and has lean, powerful muscle from hauling that axe around under Rick Springfield's precise directives and it draws blood and it *hurts,* and Harold, already concussed, surrendered to indignant sleep.

He came to a few hours later, the small apartment cold and dark, alone save a mangy dog of unknown origin. The front door had been left open and through it churned a winter's wind. Harold chased the dog out, slammed the door, and evaluated himself in the mirror. Blood was caked on his split lip. He looked utterly defeated and wan. Looking around, Debbie seemed to have alighted with her possessions; he guessed she had no intention of returning. With a start, he shambled to the kitchen, checking the cookie jar that held their few hundred dollars of savings. Empty. He sat down against the fridge and stared for some minutes at the cabinets opposite, open and devoid of kitchenware. Then he went to their—his—bed, and slept through the next day.

Harold spent several months despondent, bereft of vitality, uncertain of the future, for the first time unsure of himself. The prospect of a life spent in loud, cold machine rooms, inspecting vector displays and praying his punchcards wouldn't be spindled, folded, and/or mutilated by the ferocious IBM 1442s seemed suddenly uninspiring. He'd been with Debbie for five years, meeting her in his second year at Michigan at a South University Avenue hole in the wall. She'd come to Minneapolis with him, living cheaply on his small stipend, complaining about their finances but not bothering herself to get a job. He had no idea how to meet another woman, not that many were to be found in the Experimental Engineering Building. He'd not bothered to make friends at Minnesota, content to sit quietly on the periphery of Debbie's orbit, watching loud and generally uninteresting locals enter and leave their—her—life.

His attendance at the lab and meetings grew infrequent. He had a three-hour kiki with his advisor each Thursday; towards the end of the semester, he twice in a row missed it without notice. Said professor had hard words regarding these absences, and also his general lack of gumption the past months. "Punchcards, Grimbisch," he rebuked. "I ought know you by the trail of chads."

"Yes, sir. I'll do better. It's been a bad semester for me personally."

"A-B-C, Grimbisch. Always Be Carding. You got problems with the old lady? Tell her to get lost. You're married to this machine now," pointing at a DEC PDP-11 minicomputer, "this conglomeration of signals and bits."

"Yes sir."

"You think the Russians are slacking off?"

"No sir. I'll do better, sir."

"Without American computing, one day we'll hear sirens, and it'll be a thousand incomings, angry Redbirds erupting from silos in Yakutsk and Irkutsk. Very sexual, Grimbisch. The ICBMs resembling in their ballistic arcs nothing so much as the Devil's own phalli, ejaculated—yes, Grimbisch, ejaculated—by the rather vaginal silos. As usual, the Russians did it all backwards."

Harold's head began to ache.

"But then the MIRVs rattle from their bus, drip drip drip, transudation. Have you ever made love to a woman, Grimbisch, really seized her and given her your gift, made of her a thrashing ululator? That's what they're trying to take from us. It started with the water, the fluoride in the Goddamned water, and here we are in the Land of the Thousand Lakes. Oh, they got us good. So now who's the first to eat it when the missiles fly? They come over the Pole, Grimbisch, Dasher and Dancer and Sinner and Spanker, Satan and Scapegoat and Stingray and Saber, ten different ICBM families all aimed right at us"— he pointed to them both— "and what's that new SLBM they're putting on the Typhoon, the SS-N-20 Sturgeon I think it is, with a big bright red hammer-and-sickle nose. They come over the pole and whatever doesn't fall into Canada hits us first, right in the keester." He paused to let it sink in.

"Always Be Carding, Grimbisch. We'll see you around next semester. And Grimbisch? Do something about that lip. It's ungentlemanly."

* * * * * * * *

He'd been a reader, but he began to read more widely, with more fiction in the mix: John Fowles, John Barth, and John Edward Williams; William Faulkner, William Gass, and William Thomas Gaddis. He found a group within walking distance who'd been playing, more or less, the same disordered and shapeless campaign of Dungeons & Dragons for three years. Players came and left and

---

MIRV: multiple independently-targeted reentry vehicles

joined again, bringing wildly different approaches to the game and character development. Through them he found another, more directed group, one that met three nights most weeks, drinking strong beer and smoking weak weed as they Word of Radianced and Eldritch Blasted and Magic Missiled their way across and under an imaginary continent. Harold was known to drink a beer or three, but had never smoked marijuana; he considered it briefly when it was offered his first night, and took a long drag. He didn't get high for the first two weeks, but was up soon enough, and took to the bong with devotion. A month later he was invited into a very tight AD&D corps starting fresh, and considered himself graduated from the freeform game, though he still attended now and again in a misguided hope of meeting women.

Then came August 6th, Hiroshima Day 1982. The Grateful Dead played the St. Paul Civic Center, and Harold attended, and in the raucous lot across the street a girl wearing tiedye asked if he wanted to visit infinity. He smiled sweetly and replied that he regretted having but one mind to lose for his *Śivadarśana*. Grinning, she asked if it was his first time. "Yes, for pretty much anything you might be offering." She squealed and motioned him to tilt his head back, and to open wide. Up went a little bottle of Sweet Breath, filled almost entirely with special denatured alcohol, water, and glycerin, but also 7.5 mg of LSD tartrate. This afforded 25 hearty 300 µg doses, more than sufficient to seek devils and gods within, to scream divine ecstasy and shriek hellish agony, for neurophoresis and egocide and nousruption and theomorphism. Such a dose was minute compared to usual drug thresholds, but still represented over 381 quadrillion molecules, each yearning for a berth in some waiting receptor.

There's little to say about Harold's subsequent twelve hours. If you've been there, you know. If you haven't, you don't, and you won't learn it here. Suffice to say that he responded very intensely, and—as happens from time to time—the experience dominated his thoughts over coming days and weeks. He never found that girl in all her color again, but in the wake of the Dead, local lowest-level dealers were stocked well, and happy to sell him all the acid he wanted at $6 a hit, and then $45 a ten-strip, and then $250 a sheet. Soon he was tripping multiple times per week, refraining only to allow his weary neurotransmitters time to recharge. He adopted a vegetarian diet, and drank little but water. He talked everyone he could into the LSD experience, guiding their journeys, quickly becoming a skilled and playful tripsitter. By October, his AD&D group, DM included, was dosing under his watchful eye.

The next March and May, barely hanging on at school, he saw Prince three times in Bloomington (Met Center, Registry Hotel, and the Carlton Celebrity Room for the Minnesota Music Awards). He handed out hundreds of free hits (by this time he was ordering pages—900 hits on nine sheets—retailing much of it, eating a fair amount himself) to anyone who would accept them, which was pretty much everyone, and the Purple One put on outstanding homecoming shows, and oh! it was a time. He grew mushrooms. He hooked up with Michael Clegg's (another man on a sacred mission of distribution) "Texas Group" to bring north then-legal MDMA. He didn't know he'd failed out of school until

---

Śivadarśana: शिवदर्शन vision of Śiva

several weeks after the fact, when campus police showed up at his apartment looking to retrieve his keys for the Computer Center.

Among the dosed, he acquired social facility he'd never known in sober life. He moved drugs profitably and to the benefit of all, and was content with it, but his thoughts went back always to acid. He was terrified of losing his mail-based connection: he arranged transactions via phone, paid via Western Union, and received opaque 500 mL vials in bubble mailers, always from a different return address. His materials were once three weeks late despite prompt payment up front, and no one answered the phone, and he just about lost his mind.

During that unpleasant period he acquired a new connect in Detroit, but she was expensive, and the drive required eleven hours of sustained operation from both him and his faithful Gremlin, both ways. His second visit, sleepdepped and high and badly misreading the situation, he tried to kiss her. She cried "what the fuck are you doing?" and laughed, pushing him away, stating firmly that she was uninterested in him and indeed in all men. Seeing her was now uncomfortable. But she was the one who moved him up the graph. He called her during another supply jam (he'd simply bought out his supplier this time). She mentioned that she was getting out of the game, moving to North Dakota for unclear reasons, digging for lesbian dinosaurs or something, the fierce *Lickalottapus,* and offered to hook him up with her contact above and customers below. That hookup proved cheaper than his own, and more businesslike to boot, and the acid flowed.

Harold yearned still to become self-sufficient, and read sometimes in the University's chemistry library, coming to the same conclusion as have countless other autodidacts: LSD production isn't an issue of difficult chemistry so much as it is an issue of unobtainable precursors. He investigated total syntheses, and even attempted to reproduce the method of Julius Rebek at Pittsburgh, just published in 1983. This started with the Woodward path (Robert B. Woodward, widely thought the finest organic chemist of the twentieth century, was in 1956 the first to synthesize D-LSA at Lilly Laboratory). He read up on cyclization and Hanessian diacylation, Eschweiler–Clarke reactions and Wittig reactions and the Curtius procedure.

Following the scheme of Daly et al., L-tryptophan in 1N hydrochloric acid containing 10% palladinized charcoal was shaken in at atmosphere of hydrogen. He filtered the catalyst, added aqueous ammonia, and evaporated the mixture in vacuum. Recrystallized in water, he had half of his original weight in 2,3-dihydro-L-tryptophan. In went a small amount of 0.1N sodium hydroxide and benzoyl chloride, which he stirred. Extraction with ether, acidification of the aqueous layer with more HCl followed by chloroform extraction, washed, and dried with sodium sulfate. Trituration with ether. Recrystallization from 50% methanol. Boom, fully blocked N,N'-dibenzoyl-2,3-dihydro-L-tryptophan.

Close the first cycle via ketonization: dehydrate to azlactone using acetic anhydride at 100 °C, cyclize via Friedel-Crafts using aluminum chloride and dichloroethane (performed under nitrogen so as to prevent death). The fourth cycle would be brought over wholesale, then locked down: a solution of bromine and zinc yielded a lactone only too happy to join up with the tricycle. He quickly methylated the result with dichloromethane in hydrogen bromide. Deacylation via Hanessian's reaction (requiring triethyloxonium tetrafluoroborate, a bitch to find), and now he had a pentacycle, one cycle more than necessary. Thionyl chloride and methanol opened this lactone, supposedly, and he finally dehydrated the result with phosphorus pentoxide and methanesulfonic acid. If he'd done things correctly, and these Rebek and Tai fellows weren't bullshitting him, this ought be lysergic acid, suitable for the standard amination. He hoped there was a "standard amination," anyway.

But what had emerged bore none of the hallmarks of acid he'd been led to expect. It responded without fluorescence under 365 nm blacklight. What had crystallized was an unappealing gray, and most of his product hadn't crystallized at all, but formed a brownish sludge. Froehde reagent turned a pale yellow at best—he was expecting a greenish yellow (5GY 6/6)—and Ehrlich gave him no result. He frowned. Any kind of indole ought have stained deep purple (7.5P 3/10). If he didn't even have an indole...he really had no idea. It had no effect in micrograms, nor milligrams, and when he finally scooped the remainder up in a spoon and ate it all, perhaps a gram, it was a null result other than a terrible stomach ache and two days of savage diarrhea presenting a slightly metallic odor. Thinking on it later, he was glad not to have died. LSD remained beyond their production capabilities.

By the middle of 1984, as Nancy Reagan took her message of "just say no™," nationwide, Harold and his organization were buying several grams a throw. At 100 µg per hit, a gram of active material yields ten kilodoses. This will typically be absorbed into square blotter paper 7.5 inches to a side, "pages" of 900 hits each. After Harold had purchased fifteen grams, his supplier (name and face still unknown) noted that his own Man, the Man himself, the alchemist, would be coming through Chicago the next month, and that Harold was cleared to meet him. "He's an elegant guy, older, smart as hell, uninterested in bullshit. Professional. Don't rant and rave. Don't wax ecstatic about LSD. Don't claim anything you can't back up. Bring a jacket and tie for dinner. If he doesn't like you, you're out of the chain. Either way, you won't be dealing with me anymore—destroy this number. Bring twenty thousand dollars, nothing smaller than a fifty." Harold cleaned and pressed his one buttoned shirt, borrowed eveningwear, and took Amtrak to Union Station.

East along Jackson to Wacker took him to the Sears Tower, just eleven years old, the world's tallest building for another fourteen. North on Wacker to the river, then a half mile to the double-leaf, double-deck, fixed counterweight trunnion ("Chicago-style") bascule Michigan Avenue (now DuSable) Bridge. Across to the Magnificent Mile, then a right on W Chicago, where a left would have taken him to Cabrini-Green's seventy acres of Reds and Whites, subject to a HUD consent decree since 1981, demolished in 1995 under a HOPE VI New Urbanism grant. He walked past the Northwestern campus, snickering momentarily at the weakest sister of the Big Ten, remembering one-sided games in Ann Arbor's Big House. His undergraduate years in electrical engineering

just say no™: Serial 73705528 Registration 1756484 Word Mark JUST SAY NO
Design UNIVERSAL PROHIBITION SYMBOL Filed 1988-01-14
HOPE: Housing Opportunities for People Everywhere

seemed a lifetime ago. Finally, the turn onto E Walton Place (one block short of Lake Shore Drive and its fine omen of an initialism), and he was at Benjamin Marshall's Italian Renaissance Drake Hotel. He paid for his splendid room with cash (registering as John Eckert), went upstairs, and slept.

A call to his room phone woke him at 1900h. "Mr. Eckert? You have an interroom call from Mr. Maxwell. Ought I put him through?" With some grog he acquiesced. "Yello?"

"Mr. Eckert, welcome to the Second City. I shall dine this evening at Gabino Sotelino's Ambria. Sotelino was previously at Plazza Athénée, Le Perroquet, and the Pump Room. No lesser authorities than Gault Millau tout it as extraordinary Nouvelle cuisine."

Harold, sans clue regarding Nouvelle cuisine, heard this as "gooey mijo."

"It's in the lobby of the Belden-Stratford on West Lincoln Park. I assume you have appropriate dress? The code is enforced with some insistence."

"Yessir. Jacket and tie, black pants."

"I suppose that will have to do. With your permissions, I'll come by your room at 7:15pm? The walk is not a lengthy one."

"Sounds good, I'll be here. Thank you."

Fourteen minutes later, shaved, hair managed as best he could, he heard a knock at his door. He drew the bolt and opened it to a tall man pushing forty, thin as a sheet of balsa, clothed in recherche tuxedo due the tailors of Ermenegildo Zegna N. V. and their *Su Misura* made-to-measure service: grosgrain lapels, piped outseams, and a cummerbund Harold mistook for some kind of belt. A mane of long but groomed dark hair was going silver around the crown and at the temples. His bright eyes scanned over the room, then critically evaluated Harold. Spying Grimbisch's copy of *Molloy,* he asked, "Ahh, are we reading Mr. Beckett?"

"We are."

"Reginald Gray's portrait of Samuel hangs in Dublin's National Gallery. Old bogtrotters both. Magnificent Renaissance portraiture with a trompe l'oeil effect about the perimeter. Black-and-white, save those incisive eyes, cornflower blue. Striking. They pierce to the soul. May I come in?"

"Please do."

The visitor strode to the corner opposite the door, clearly inspecting as he went. "Forgive me for not taking a seat—I hope to keep this old thing free of wrinkles. Richard Melman is a firm believer in the dictum that fine dining is an event, paid respect in part by a gentleman's dress or a lady's couture. Respect is of course likewise remitted in the form of an extravagant bill, but I believe there few finer ways to spend one's money than on the cuisine of an artisan. Sotelino's preparations are as creative as they are mouthwatering." When Harold didn't respond, he continued. "Well in any case, I have a reservation at 8pm. I strive always for promptitude. But we must have introductions before setting off together." Extending his hand: "My name is James Clerk Maxwell."

"John Eckert. Were your parents electrical engineers?"

The tall man chuckled airily. "Ahh, so you know the name?"

"I have a EE BSE from Michigan, and passing acquaintance with Maxwell's equations." He dug deep, pulling up their differential forms:

$$\nabla \cdot \mathbf{E} = \frac{\rho}{\epsilon_0}, \ \nabla \cdot \mathbf{B} = 0$$

Gauss's flux theorem and law for magnetism. Given electric field $\mathbf{E}$, the flux Φ_E out of an arbitrary closed surface is proportional to the enclosed charge, and does not depend on distribution of said charge; local charge density defines the divergence of the field. For a bounded charge Q, $\Phi_E = \frac{Q}{\epsilon_0}$. Φ_E could be expressed as a surface integral of $\mathbf{E}$. If you wanted to get fancy, $\Phi_E = c \oiint_s F^{\kappa 0} \sqrt{-g} dS_\kappa$ handled curved space with electromagnetic tensor time components $F^{\kappa 0}$ and metric tensor determinant g. The magnetism law also admitted an integral form, another surface integral, but this time over vectors of the outward-directed surface normal: $\oiint_s \mathbf{B} \cdot d\mathbf{S} = 0$. There is no divergence in the magnetic field $\mathbf{B}$; magnetic monopoles do not exist.

$$\nabla \times \mathbf{E} = -\frac{\partial \mathbf{B}}{\partial t}, \ \nabla \times \mathbf{B} = \mu_0 \left(\epsilon_0 \frac{\partial \mathbf{E}}{\partial t} + \mathbf{J} \right)$$

Faraday's law of induction and the Maxwell-Ampère law. Together these four equations defined the speed of light, explained power generation and motors, quantified wireless communications, and otherwise formed the foundations of emag, circuits, and optics up until the quantum. They united two hundred years of disparate theoretical and experimental results. Unless your problem depended on the precise spectrum of blackbody radiation, or the photoelectric effect, or a laser's optical noise, or the schizophrenic behavior of electrons in their orbitals, Maxwell's equations will get you there.

Together with the force law, Newton's gravitation, and the Newton-Einstein law of motion, that's all of classical physics (including special, though not general, relativity) in seven equations.

$$\mathbf{F} = q(\mathbf{E} + \nu \times \mathbf{B}), \ \mathbf{F} = -G\frac{m_1 m_2}{r^2} e_r, \ \mathbf{F} = \frac{m_0 \mathbf{a}}{\left(1 - \frac{v^2}{c^2}\right)^{\frac{3}{2}}}$$

He realized with sudden aching nostalgia how much he missed working problem sets, bringing experiments to heel, fixing bugs and setting right what was wrong. Nothing that's any good works by itself, just to please you; you've got to make the Damned Thing work.

"Delightful! In this endeavor, one rarely meets the scientifically trained, nor for that matter Michigan Men. Maxwell is a name I've taken, one of several, in a nod to cloak-and-dagger theatrics. I'll ask you to continue using that name through dinner. You may call me Rubicund in the future, though it's unlikely that we'll meet again."

He thought Caesar had crossed the Rubicund, but was not about to ask.

"Now this is distasteful, regrettable, but I must ask you to strip."

"Take off my clothes?"

"Yes, and haste, please, if we are to make our reservation."

"Why?"

Rubicund sighed. "To check for electronic surveillance, the arms of the cheese eater. I must protect myself, you know. I'd furthermore like to ensure you're not carrying any weapons."

Harold began unbuttoning his shirt. "All the way off?"

"As you entered this world, James. Even unto the soles of your feet."

His clothes came off; he lifted his feet in embarrassed demonstration; he ran his fingers through his hair; he turned, bent over, and prepared to cough when Rubicund said, "That will be fine. Thank you, Mr. Eckert. One can't be too safe. Why don't you become decent, and we'll proceed." Rubicund gazed out a window, two long fingers to his mouth, and avoided watching Harold dress.

They departed. Once on the street, Rubicund was all business. "The gentleman from whom you've been buying will soon be departing from my service. You were proposed as a possible replacement. Your payments have been without error. You've been sensible in communications. You've got a clean criminal record—yes, Mr. Grimbisch, I know your name, and I've looked into your past. These attributes speak well for you. You brought the twenty thousand?"

"Twenty-two thousand, actually. I was hoping to get four grams."

Again that ethereal laugh. "Twenty-two thousand will get you a good deal more than that. This is for both of us felicitous, as you'll be moving significantly more moving forward. The fellow you purchased from takes hectograms."

"A hundred? I don't have the kind of sink to move that in six months."

"As I said, you'll be taking over his distribution. Otherwise, why would I be meeting you?" His laugh this time had a hint of snicker. "Operational security would have me never meet you at all, so that you wouldn't know my face, but I like to look into the eyes of the people with whom I'll be working. I ask that you honor the agreements regarding price and logistics that have already been established with his clients, but he was already clearing fifty thousand a month in profit. And I'll have some recommendations regarding your own retail prices, MSRPs if you will." He smiled wanly.

"All the distribution will take place by mail, like I'm getting it now?"

"Yes. Product will be mailed to you from Europe."

"Europe? Is that where you work?"

"Oh, I move here and there, among dredgerous lands and devious delts. Usually in America, despite our unrefined and often bestial citizenry; there's simply so much more space here. Europe's laws are less savage, her sentences less cruelhearted. Here, they toss out life sentences, and mean them: a man will spend all his days caged, at the mercy of callous guards. It's difficult to believe that faced with such a thing, one's associates will drink from the cup of suffering, when they might see it pass them by. In Italy, or France, or Spain, one can expect silence even in the face of capture. Rolling up the network furthermore requires combination and cooperation between nations, and our world knows precious little of that. The only problem is passing Customs on the way back into America, but the Substance is potent, and odorless besides. Unlike bales of marijuana or bricks of cocaine, we can move all we want in packing envelopes, without scents that might attract dogs."

Harold was impressed. "Do I still Western Union the cash?"

"He had you using traceable Western Union? I'll see him flensed!" Rubi-cund showed sudden vicious anger, but it receded as quickly as it had come. "Money will be picked up from you by agents of mine. They will bear tokens of authentication, and it is imperative that you are there to meet them promptly. I cannot overemphasize this. It is preferable that you meet them alone, watch-ing for surveillance on your approach as best you can. We prefer that you pay in hundreds; you'll need work out a means to reliably convert your myriad remittances. Cash will flow up to you via mail, or whatever other means you employ. Your cost is forty thousand a hectogram, purchased in fifty gram units. Should you need a kilogram, the price is a quarter million. You pay up front, and provide an address or addresses to which you'd like the Substance mailed. It will arrive within three weeks."

"What if it doesn't?"

"Then something has gone very wrong. Things will be made correct as quickly as possible. And to that point, let us discuss communication. You'll be provided several numbers. Each of them goes to a voicemail box, and each box is checked, so you only need leave a message on any given one. There are multiple numbers because sometimes we must bring one down. You'll be called to provide you with new numbers as necessary. You'll have your own voicemail box, which you're expected to check weekly, or ideally more regularly than that. Should that box become inaccessible, leave a message on our voicemail consisting only of a phone number and time at which you can be reached. Otherwise, never leave a phone number, only your code name."

"What's my code name?"

Rubicund slowed to a halt, and looked him in the eyes. "Infrared, I think. Yes, that will do nicely." They picked up speed again, and found themselves at the restaurant. "Seven fifty-eight. Very good. I ask that you not discuss matters of business while we dine. I've taken the liberty of inviting two lovely ladies to meet us. I trust that is not a problem?"

The restaurant appeared scrotumtighteningly expensive. Harold had only $22 in his wallet. "Ummm I didn't, like, bring that cash with us here; I'm not sure I can be covering a date."

Rubicund let free his first real laugh of the evening. "Oh, Mr. Eckert, that has already been taken care of."

On the way back to Minneapolis, his bag holding two thousand dollars and fifty grams of white LSD crystal, Harold decided his was now an Organization, and organizations need names. He'd been recently reading deep in Thelema, and the City of the Pyramids seemed apt:

> He then told me that now my name was Nemo, seated among the other silent shapes in the City of the Pyramids under the Night of Pan; those other parts of me that I had left for ever below the Abyss must serve as a vehicle for the energies which had been created by my act. My mind and body, deprived of the ego which they had hitherto obeyed, were now free to manifest according to their nature, to devote themselves to mankind in its evolution.

Thus was born SYNCOPE.

* * * * * * * * *

Cloud found Katz on his way to Mars Volta. The title track from the prior year's *Bedlam in Goliath* was crashing when Katz heard from behind him, "Brother! Good brother! Brother in Eris!"

Katz turned to face the jolly man of mystery. He'd fed Cloud three hits before departing, promising an exquisite trip. Cloud had been thankful, even a little hopeful, but had insisted "the true Substance has not been made in years, brother." Katz smiled and urged him to keep an open mind until he lost it.

"Cloud! I bet you tripped balls last night! What did I tell you?"

Cloud wrapped him up in a hug ursine, and whispered into his ear, "We must talk, brother. You're busy now, but tonight, can we speak?"

"Sure. I'm going to be seeing Nine Inch Nails after this, but want to just meet me over here when that's done?"

"If you don't mind, brother, I'll stay close. Nothing here is as important to me as speaking with you. I'll hang nearby. We can talk immediately afterwards."

"Well how about we just talk now?"

"We must be away from those with ears who hear, from potential recordings, for they are secrets we will speak. I'll find you, brother." He clapped Katz on the back and remigrated into the crowd, dissolving among teeming bodies under setting Tennessean sun.

Five loud hours later (including an encore featuring the semi-rare "Dead Souls," a Joy Division cover released on the 1994 soundtrack for *The Crow*), Cloud materialized like an apparition. "Here's some of that weed you liked so well, brother! Hit this deeply, and we will speak."

"Thanks muchly, Catherine Earnshaw."

They ambled and passed the pipe and Cloud gushed regarding the acid Katz had traded him. The finest he'd had in years beyond his own stocks. In no way distinguishable, actually, from his own stocks. The real deal. "No body load whatsoever. I feel fantastic today. I crossed easily from trip to sleep, waking up refreshed, uncramped, not even dehydrated nor foggy."

Katz felt roaring pride. "I told you it was the fire, my friend."

"I wish to acquire all that I can, but more important is setting up a larger purchase for later, ideally a pipeline. Brother, if this is reliable, it promises the resurgence of the *karass,* the return of the good times. How did you come to have it? When did you acquire it?"

"I'm pretty confident that I'm very close to the source. It was made just last month. So I'm told anyway. We brought two sheets; I'm sure one and a half, at least, are still available. It's pricey, though."

Cloud's eyes shone, reflecting the fey licks of luminance reaching down from hastily erected Powermoon lights. "Brother. What quantities are available?"

Katz looked around, mostly to make sure Bolaño wasn't near. "Look mang, let me be straight with you. This is my product. Do you know anything about LSD chemistry?"

"Enough to wonder where you got precursors."

"There we go. A bunch of Cafergot—it's a migraine medication with two milligrams of ergotamine tartrate per pill. Extracted that and went to town."

"And you've done this many times?"

Katz smiled. "First time, just read the relevant material and followed directions. It's not very complex chemistry. I'm an engineer." A hell of an engineer.

"How did you achieve such quality?"

"It's all in the chromatography, my friend." If Katz had a nickel, he'd flip it in the air. "All the information is out there. You just have to read it and understand what it says. Atop that, a few thousand dollars of equipment."

"I will take all you can make."

Katz laughs, only slightly derisive, full of good cheer. "Well, you can take what I've got on me, though like I said, it's not exactly cheap. Beyond that, though, I don't have any more precursors. I don't want to go through the Cafergot route again anytime soon; it's a pain in the ass. Not to extract the ET, but to gather all that Cafergot. It's got to draw attention, besides. So I'm not sure what I can do beyond that."

"Impossible. Every artist needs a patron. I can be yours."

"Cloud, I'm telling you, it's not a money thing. It's a precursor thing. And I've looked into total synthesis; it doesn't seem to be economically possible. Not at my skill level, anyway." He looked at Cloud, who wore a slight grin. "I mean, if you wanted to collect Cafergot at scale, that maybe could work."

"I can get you your precursors, if you can cook."

"I don't think getting that much Cafergot is safely doable. I mean, it's a prescription medication."

Now it was Cloud's turn to surprise Katz. "Brother, I speak not of Cafergot."

✳ ✳ ✳ ✳ ✳ ✳ ✳ ✳ ✳

Over the next half hour, Cloud related to Katz the legend of Harold Grimbisch, and his selection by the alchemist, and the formation of the *karass* SYNCOPE. How it had come to dominate distribution on the alchemist's behalf, how Grimbisch had improved on the alchemist's logistics, how dead drops and cutouts and proxies and *poste restante* were employed to limit and repair damage along the chain. How they had perfected manufacture of false identification, how they built up real alternative identities by scouring record halls for birth certificates of dead children (*Day of the Jackal* fraud, employed also by the surviving elements of WUO). Grimbisch had indeed made it to the kilogram level, and beyond; in 1996 he convinced the alchemist to do a multikey cook, just to minimize mail traffic. "After all," he'd said, "there's no real difference between getting caught with a kilogram and two kilograms." That had been rumored to be a two megadollar deal (prices had risen in the intervening decade, due largely to increased precursor costs).

Here Cloud drew once more his Montana DL, and showed it to Katz. Then he produced a Missouri card with the same face, labeled CLOUD FRACTUS CHAPIN DOB 10-06-1970. A Maine card for CLOUD ALTOS CACCIATORE. A California card with its golden bear and background of a Forty-niner panning for gold, CLOUD UMBRAS CHAMBERS. A red *Pilipinas Pasaporte* in the name of ULAP CONCEPCIÓN.

WUO: Weather Underground Organization

"*Ulap* is Tagalog for 'cloud,' and you only get a middle name in the Philippines if your parents were married," he offered helpfully.

"So you're not sixty-one, then."

Grinning: "Depends on whom one asks."

But in 1997, Harold Grimbisch—by now a comfortable resident of suburb Chanhassen—had been crossing the street downtown, perhaps out of practice, and was struck by a speeding Alfa Romeo. He was flung like a boleadora across two lanes, and while that probably didn't kill him, the truck coming the other way certainly did. All were grieved to have lost their founder and leader. Grimbisch had been intelligent, generous, firm when and where firmness was called for, and until this moment lucky. Three of his closest confidantes knew the tactical details of contact with the alchemist (and other sources), and between them had most of the organization's operational knowledge, but none had a clear cause for seizing leadership, and things became very uncertain. The alchemist was not notified for over a month, and when all three came to meet him several weeks later, he was vexed in the extreme. This would not do. "I am currently moving between regions of the country, and cannot work for several months in any case. When next I speak with you—and it is at that time that we will establish new procedures for the future—it will be with one of you, not this troika." They never even made it to dinner.

The alchemist seemed even then to be fraying. Whether due to the stress of decades underground, or the ingestion of hundreds of thousands of unintended doses over a lifetime of clandestine chemistry, or just getting older in an ever more complicated world, Cloud did not know. But in 2000 the alchemist had *appeared at the home of one of the* karass, and spoken to them with agitation, and they had moved two dozen paint cans out of a car and into the attic ("the basement would be too humid," the alchemist had angrily countered, when that was at first proposed), and only four people total knew that the cans held—here Katz's eyes went wide—just over twelve kilograms of Polish ergocristine. Then the alchemist was exposed, and arrested, and sentenced most cruelly, and it seemed unlikely that he would emerge from prison via the front door.

"The front door?"

"A brother who perishes in prison goes out the back door."

"Oh right, Body Count has a whole song about that."

"So we have held onto this ergocristine, keeping it dry, and away from light, and at a constant room temperature, such as it would enjoy in a museum. And prophecy has told us that a new alchemist would emerge, that we would find them without searching, that they would come to us at a music festival."

"Heh, fairly convenient prophecy. 'Go forth, ye, and attend shows.' And what do you mean by 'prophecy'? I hope that's rhetorical flourish."

"No. The alchemist, before taking his departure, regretted that none of us seemed as smart as Harold. Returning to Minneapolis, we agreed sadly that it was so. We thus decided to draw upon the power of prophecy, of chaos. Already we had been performing services in honor of Eris, our chaotic Mother; she selects one of our number, and through them speaks."

Oh dear. "My Discordianism has always been of the more abstract, kinda ironic sense. Hail Eris and all that, but how does she 'select' one of you?"

"A prophet may be unseated in the Game of Lies, in which I won my name. Listen well, brother. The prophet gave us three indications by which we would recognize the new alchemist. If you don't match them, it'll be difficult for me to convince the *karass,* no matter what acid you bring. If you do, perhaps you'll learn something, and open your mind a little."

Amused: "Sure. Shoot."

"In his ravings the prophet said that both alchemists would know the same birthplace. Rubicund was born in Atlanta, Georgia."

"Birthplace could be what, a country, a state, whatever. Meaningless."

"So where were you born? The United States, Georgia, wherever?"

Sigh. "Northpoint Hospital, in the Atlanta suburbs."

Enthusiastically: "Exciting, brother! Hail Eris! We were told secondly that they would have the name of a great conqueror."

"Full name match, or just one name? This is like astrology. OK, my first name is Sherman." At this Cloud broke into frenetic dance. "But, *but,* my middle name is Spartacus, who got his ass kicked at Senerchia, and his followers crucified."

"His followers. Followers of his military leadership, followers who saw victories at Vesuvius such as had never gone against Rome. And who else called himself Spartacus? None but Adam Weishaupt."

"I hardly think the Bavarian Illuminati represent any conquest. And counting against you would be the Spartacist Uprising. Not that I'm uninterested in your ergocristine, mind you. Be sure that I am. I just prefer to enter business on a basis other than Oracle of Delphi shit."

"The Thracian went from slave to commander, and defeated legions in the field. The brothers will accept this."

Katz rolled his eyes. "Ridiculous. What's the third prophecy?"

Cloud looked at him with the hopeful eyes of a child. "That despite a Jewish name, they would be baptized Christian; that despite Christian baptism, they would reject it for science; that despite their science, they would quote Abrahamic scripture like it was going out of style."

"Well. Fuck. Perhaps too regularly, all told. *Quomodo ignoras quae sit via spiritus, et qua ratione compingantur ossa in ventre praegnantis, sic nescis opera Dei, qui fabricator est omnium.*" He translated for Cloud, providing the NIV he knew better than KJV:

> As you do not know the path of the wind,
> or how the body is formed in a mother's womb,
> so you cannot understand the work of God,
> the Maker of all things.

"Ecclesiastes 11:5. Though I suppose we've got a good handle on gestation now. We know the path of wind, for that matter."

"Aye, brother. And where does wind bring one but to Cloud?"

Katz looked Cloud over for several seconds. He smiled. "Both your prophet and his sophistry come from a limp, weak bag. Fuck a bunch of hippie bullshit. The fact, 'brother,' is that I'm the Man. If you want to do business, let's do some fuckin' business."

14 max-cashflow min-cut theorem

With serious cash, a dollar securely in the bank is worth two in hand. It's not truly a linear relationship—few things are, sadly. If you have $200, so long as you have access to a bank account, they're as good as banked. Walk in, deposit those ducats, smile, all is well. Just another account holder among tens of thousands. No one worth taking notice of. All the way up to at least $3,000, you're likely fine so long as it's not an everyday thing. The $3,000 triggers certain mandatory recordkeeping under the Joint and Travel Rules. A money order or cashier's check purchased with cash in excess of three large requires identity verification and logging. Currency transactions in excess of $10,000 mandate a CTR filed within fifteen days. Monetary instruments in excess of $10,000 into *or out of* the United States require filing a CMIR with Customs. Dropping $10K or more of cash at a compliant business will see them fire off a Form 8300 with the details. Citizens maintaining foreign accounts with $10,000 or more must file Form FBAR (Foreign Bank and Financial Accounts). Suspicious Activity Reports serve as a further catch-all, and deposits structured to avoid the CTR threshold explicitly mandate an SAR (structuring is a federal offense in and of itself). These reports are fed to the IRS and FinCEN; disclosing such a filing to the customer is a federal offense.

What does one do with a hundred thousand dollars in cash? A hundred thousand in hundreds is 4.3x2.61x6.14 inches, a stack just barely (and not very securely) grasped in an adult male hand. A hundred large in twenties, or half a meg in hundreds, is 21.5 inches, just over half a meter. You might think this stack will fit in a brown paper beer bottle bag; it will not. Go ahead and get a brown grocery sack, and roll up the top. Tightly, now. The practicality of twenties ends somewhere well below a meg. For a million dollars, you'd really rather not be using cash at all, but if you insist: hundreds definitely, ten thousand of them. In a single stack, this would be 43 inches, about a five year old's height in greenbacks. At a little over eight kilograms, it would be a fine weight for curls if only it were denser.

Interior packing dimensions of a ZERO Halliburton Pursuit Aluminum or Polycarbonate Hardside Attaché (Small) featuring Combination Lock, Coated Leather Lining, Organizational Sleeve, Brushed Exterior, patented Concave Edging, and Bespoke Carry Handle made from proprietary polycarbonate material crafted through a customized two-shot molding process to prevent fallapart, MSRP $545, are 3.7x10.3x15.6". It just won't make it. The comparatively luxurious Medium offers the same depth at 12.2x17.1", and this will handle either a megadollar or a mebidollar (2^{20}, $1,048,576) formed from Franklins.

So you've packed up your stylish case with a cool million. How do you buy things with it? The black market might accept your legal tender, but the bank is going to have serious questions. Maybe you blame an expired veteran of the Depression: "Grandpa Pityokamptes died, and didn't trust banks. He left me

---

CTR: currency transaction report   CMIR: currency and monetary instrument report
IRS: Internal Revenue Service   FinCEN: Financial Crimes Enforcement Network

this, his life savings, along with his collection of Gilded Age robber baron action figures." Up the SAR goes to FinCEN and the IRS, and you can assume they're going to come asking about this dead relative. The interview will be filed away, along with any supporting documentation you might have provided. There isn't any, of course, which detracts from your argument. Hell, you don't even have a copy of the will, nor a death certificate from the right decade. Maybe you whip up some childish fake docs. It ends up contradicting some other automated check, gets flagged, and now you've provided false information on government forms. Things move rapidly to an unfortunate end for you.

So big-ticket items. A fabulous house, perhaps. Well, not *that* fabulous—it's only a meg, after all. But a nice place from which you can probably extract rent, a tidy laundered asset. How do you pay with your cash? Your seller isn't going to want to accept it, or they'll be in the same boat you're in now. They deposit, a CTR gets filed (within fifteen days, remember), they get interviewed, they dig up the purchase agreement—notarized by both your and their lawyers, natch—and by the transitive property, we're right back to people in suits interviewing you as you pick at your shirt and feign blessed ignorance regarding your financial life. More likely, their lawyer advises them to tell you to fuck off. Cars? Dealers know full well their mandate to file Form 8300. Anything online, forget about it. Casinos? Must-file. There appears to be an intriguing loophole around auctions, so if you're down to buy a Modiglani or van Eyck with a few laundry bags full of hundreds, that might just fly. It seems furthermore that fines, court costs, and the like will accept all the cash you can source.

If you can get it out of the country, and especially if you have connections where you're going, you can probably get cash into foreign banking systems. But these days they're supposed to be implementing the same anti-laundering protocols, and some of them are actually doing it, and you're anyway going to get dinged with a CMIR if you try to bring it back.

Ultimately, analog currency entering the digital banking system requires justification, and if that justification can't be produced—especially if taxes ought have been paid—the government will be unhappy about it.

There are four main strategies:

- The *Brewster's Millions:* try to step up cash expenditures to match unbankable cash income. Effective, to a degree, for travel and henchmen. Works best in conjunction with a more-or-less real job that pays legal, banked, documented money. Everything paid for with cash is effectively tax-free. Difficult to scale beyond a certain level.

- Smurfing. Enlist dozens of people, dispatching them regularly to deposit your money in their accounts. Said monies, less a fee, are transferred to you within the banking system. This becomes a sprawling and unwieldy enterprise at any kind of scale. People happy to receive and deposit cash of mysterious origin for a 10% cut tend not to be the most reliable employees; they often lack the requisite bank account, and cannot get one. Expect large losses from runners, requiring intercession of resourceful and possibly violent enforcers. Data mining in conjunction with flow and network analysis will explode this pattern. Eventually, your scummy employees will alert authorities, probably in a poorly conceived and pointless disclosure that doesn't even help them.

- Cash business(es). The income will be subject to taxation, and will need to be declared. Complex. Your business can be seized. You'll likely need maintain some modicum of actual business activity and attract patronage. Most flexible option. Minions can be legally (more or less) paid, such that they can prop up their own tax-free earnings. If done correctly, the IRS is removed as a threat entirely.
- Gift cards in lieu of banked money. One can buy everything short of cars, homes, and investments off Amazon. Walk into CVS, load up ten cards with $500 each, and sell the cards online. Theoretically, one can pull a reliable 80% of face value back in ACH. In the real world, many of the buyers will be perpetrating one fraud or another; you will see clawbacks, and losing your balance and/or vendor account is not at all out of the question.

Bolaño mused "You can't deposit money into domestic banks. You can't buy domestic goods with cash. You can transfer money out of the country, maybe, but you can't bring that money into the country. So that seems to leave two more strategies. Both begin with getting your money out of the country and into foreign banks."

Katz, wryly: "You could then move to that country."

"Correct. And there's one other. Do you see it?"

"Ummm...buy foreign goods and bring those into the country?"

"Yes."

"They'd have to be expensive goods, though. And liquid."

"Yes. And it would need be a pretty loose country to accept all that cash, and yet sufficiently lawful to not simply nationalize it. And yet they'd need produce goods worth bringing back."

"Well, no, you'd just need be able to purchase such goods. If I'm in Turkey with a half meg in lira in the bank, and I can import South African diamonds, and then ship those here, that works fine, right? I just eat the import overhead."

"Any number of duties and conversions and taxes. I'm unsure countries admitting briefcases of American currency into their financial systems welcome its immediate outflow. But the biggest problem is you've got to sell those diamonds without being recognized as a naif, which you will."

"What about some kind of commodity?"

"You've got to get something pretty dense, or else you're basically starting a logistics company. At some point it's going to be enough busy work that it doesn't compete with simply standing up an actual domestic enterprise and funneling cash into it."

"Nonsense. The rate at which you can funnel cash into a domestic business is limited. If you report to the IRS that you did a million dollars worth of cash carwashes in a month, I don't care that you're paying taxes on that; someone's eventually going to call bullshit on you."

"Figure anything more than a few trucks per week is too much to do without it being a fulltime deal, or something you have to staff. Call it twenty containers a month. So if you want to wash a meg per month, you need fifty K of crap per container. What are you going to import twenty containers of that you can rapidly sell without taking a huge loss?"

"What kind of loss are we admitting? Fifty percent?"

"Ugh, terrible."

"At fifty you can lose twenty percent to overhead, and another thirty percent to undercut 37.5% off what you paid. You pay $10 to buy at $8 and sell at $5. If an angel appears before you in my somewhat corpulent form and offers you a $1.6M house for $1M, you take it, do you not?"

"Fifty percent. Ghastly. Ptah."

* * * * * * * * *

Cloud danced at festivals, but had been adamant, even dogmatic, in matters of pricing. For all his professed enthusiasm, negotiating positions were rigid. "Brother, we can distribute as much as you can generate. SYNCOPE is a great sink. We consider the *karass* a public utility, in a sense. We seek to keep the prices low and the quality high, and wholesale at $2.25 per 300 μg."

"Sure. Molecular mass of LSD-tartrate is 473.52. LSD is 323.44. If we have say 98% purity in crystal, and 95% purity of D-LSA, that's 93.1% output purity. A kilogram of that tartrate would be what umm 635.9 g of pure LSD base, right? 980 g of true crystal per key of output, 323.44 over 473.52 times 980 times 0.95, yeah, 635.9 g. Assuming full purity, it would be 683.1 g, but that's silly. Working the other direction, that's a kilogram of pure base per 1572.5 g of output, just 1000 over 635.9. When you say '300,' are you talking base or tartrate?"

"Ummm..."

"And are you passing impurities through cleanly to the customer, or are you increasing weight to hit that 300?"

Cloud frowns. "Brother, I am unsure. We sell 300 μg of material as a hit."

"So you're passing impurities through, and talking tartrate weight. So really you're selling 191 μg hits, assuming impurities as quoted. Which of course could be way off from what you were receiving."

"Why do you say this, brother?"

"Because that's how multiplication works."

"Brother, bear with me. I'm no skilled mathematician."

Katz tries, and fails, not to be a dick. "This isn't even algebra, mang. If you take 300 μg of product as delivered, *i.e.* crystal of some purity, which is itself base of some purity, if those purities are not 100%, you agree you're putting less than 300 μg into the dose, right?"

"But I believe we were receiving it 100% pure."

"You were not." Jesus, the shit you heard in this game.

Peering quizzically: "How could you know?"

"Because 100% chemicals don't exist, certainly not out of clandestine labs. Because 98% purity is still really fucking good. Because the DEA hasn't reported LSD blotter having more than 200 μg in roughly forever. Because if you were selling 300 μg hits through the 90s, people would have been losing their fucking minds. Regardless, fine, let's call it 100% pure. In that case, 300 μg of delivered crystal would still only be 204.9 µg of true LSD, because the stabilizing tartrate doesn't count, and it's about a third of the molecule by mass."

Cloud closes his eyes. "It makes sense, brother, but it is surprising to me. I thought we were selling 300 µg. We all did. Perhaps Grimbisch knew better."

Katz summons up patience. "I mean, you were selling three hundred per hit. Just of LSD tartrate, not LSD. Or whatever you had, anyway."

Cloud bows his head. "Yes. We know whether it is acid as acid is intended, or not. We expect 300 g back from each kilogram of precursor. Only if it is Hofmann's Gift do we buy and distribute it. Meet this standard, and we will pay. They needn't be nearly as strong as those you gave me, brother. We prefer to offer a more graduated experience."

"What, do y'all just take out a few milligrams and eat them in common? Roll your thumbs in it? That's a long fucking way from rigorous."

Cloud finally looked offended. "What we lack in trained scientists, we have in practical brothers. The *karass* has several fine analytical balances, accurate to milligrams, and in two cases tenths of milligrams. They cost several thousands of dollars each, and are lovingly maintained. The brothers have been calibrated through experience. Usual testing dosage is 800 µg intravenously."

"Well fuck my ass, I stand corrected. You mainline it, huh? Gotta say I've never even gone intramuscularly."

"We treat the Substance as a sacrament. Would you pour Eucharist wine onto blotter paper?"

"That's an interesting question, Cloud. I guess it would depend on the motivation." Katz pauses a moment to ponder it, but returns to matters at hand. "What if it is sufficiently pure, and I can prove it, but you disagree? Is there not some impartial, quantitative oracle? A standard we can consult?"

"Than I and I do not purchase, damn you and damn your outventions of false alchemy, lies like Babylon!" Apparently he affected Rastafari patois when vexed. "These prices are constant no matter how much is purchased, though we do not retail less than ten grams, sold at $75,000."

Katz approximated a whistle. "Minimum of ten grams, huh? Wait, why are you talking about 300 µg hits, then? You're surely strictly selling bulk crystal, or liquid, right? You're not portioning out hits."

"Not always. Some prefer blotter, some gelatin."

"Even at 300 µg per dose, 10 g would be thirty-three kilodoses. That's three hundred and thirty sheets. People want hundreds of sheets?"

It was Cloud's turn to shine. "Pages, brother! Nine sheets of blotter per page. Ten grams are just over thirty-six pages, not so unreasonable. Many people are uncomfortable laying pages."

"Really? I'm surprised they can feed themselves."

"We are the wholesalers. At the top, the alchemist; below him, veteran traders. A half-kilogram crystal is $3,750,000. We rarely sell more than this at a time. We pay $0.75 per hit, profiting $1.50 on each dose sold."

Two hundred percent profit? "Well, you paid Rubicund $0.75 per hit."

"No, you do not understand. The *karass* pays $0.75 per hit. It sells for $2.25 per hit. This is independent of the supplier and buyer."

"What if I don't want to sell to you for $0.75?"

"It is the price we pay."

"What if I can't make it more cheaply than that, but I can make high-grade LSD? Would you want lower quality, or to pay more?"

"There is LSD, and that which is not LSD. $0.75 is the price of first-step supply. In such a case, you must make LSD more cheaply."

"And if that is impossible?"

Smiling: "How can anything be impossible for an alchemist?"

"All due respect but if you had much knowledge of the chemistry involved, one of you would have become an alchemist by now, right?"

"It is not a question of chemistry, but a question of Goddess. An alchemist that seeks her, seeks her in his pineal gland rather than his cowardly stores of reason, will make a handsome profit at this price."

"I guess I'll look into it, mang, but Christ, this is a bunch of fucked up procedure you've got going on here, positively mediæval shit."

Still worse was the matter of the deposit. It made sense, in a way. Somewhere in Minnesota, SYNCOPE held the strategic ergot alkaloid reserve of the United States. No one knew where to acquire more. Properly stewarded, it could generate hundreds of millions of doses, adding orders of magnitude of value and utility. Wasted with bad chemistry, it could be quickly drawn down to nothing. It was the organization's last hope for a return to their glory days, and they held it in almost divine regard.

They could surely sell it for a few hundreds of thousands, maybe even a few million, to a chemist, but they'd fall out of the loop. SYNCOPE didn't want to sell ergocristine; SYNCOPE wanted to sell acid. Ideally they would have contracted a capable chemist, but finding one had proven difficult. Instead, they instituted a policy of deposit on carryaway. A prospective chemist was asked to deposit the full retail value of the expected volume of acid, three times the price SYNCOPE would pay. The hippies were thus covered from the outset against theft or bust or fuckup. Upon acceptance of delivered product, the deposit plus the wholesale cost would be paid out, or left floating to take more precursor. They were uninterested in doing less than 100 g of precursor at a time, implying a minimum deposit of $225,000.

Katz had asked Cloud earlier, "Mang, if your whole worry is that you're going to lose your precursors, why won't you let us take away less than a quarter million dollars of it?"

"These rules are not mine to make, brother." A small shrug. He leaned in, as if his *karass* was there listening. "To be honest, as I said, the circuit has been dusty for years now. Our cashflow has been less than where we would like it. Were a chemist to fail with a batch, the brothers would accept it, appreciating the infusion of currency."

He took the tale to Michael, hoping he might have access to funding, or sufficient reserves himself. Bolaño's summary was plaintive: "It sucks."

"I cannot disagree that I am disadvantaged."

"And any potential investors. Let's go over how this is an unacceptable arrangement. One, we need big cash up front that we don't have. Two, we're out that cash if there is an accident or failure. Three, if we lose contact, if someone dies or goes to jail, we're out our money. Four, they're incentivized to cut and run, as they then get the full retail price without having to pay the wholesale price, or even having to do the actual work of retail. The ludicrous–"

"But then—"

"Excuse me. The ludicrous minimum further incentivizes them. Yes?"

"But then they lose their chemists."

"Who says they don't do this every time they meet a chemist? Five, if they sell us bogus precursors, and we take them, we're out our money when they say we fucked up the procedure. Six, if we have product of quality, but that they refuse, we have no organization to retail it. They know this. They could fuck us on the wholesale price when we deliver, and what can we do about it? Seven, it destroys profitability of selling to anyone else. Eight, they won't accept a scientific, objective reference for purity, just nonsense about 'we decide if it's good.' The entire thing is onesided, plus perverse incentives. You ought tell them to fuck themselves."

"All valid points. Assume for a moment that they do actually want to get an acid pipeline up, and not immediately rip us off."

"It doesn't have to be immediate. They could get us to make a substantial amount, stock up, and then fuck us."

"So I agree we need to establish that this deposit business stops after a few cooks, ideally just one. We say 'alright, we'll keep depositing on your precursors, but only the wholesale cost, not this retail opportunity cost horseshit.' Basically they sell us raw materials, and we add value and sell it back, like normal human beings, once we've established trust in our engineering."

"Agreed that this would make things much better, though I don't see them budging. They sound pretty dogmatic, pretty set in their policies."

"Because they've probably been burned by a few inept wannabe chemists. I think they really do want things to flow, though."

"I don't want to get in on it unless we can protect our original deposit. Simply too much incentive for them to take our money and run, possibly giving us bullshit in exchange."

"I understand that. I feel the same way. At the same time, we're dead in the water without precursors. Diverted pharms are not going to scale."

"Katz, why do we need to scale? Why can't we just make acid for us and friends, and sell a few sheets, and not step into industrial LSD manufacturing?"

Katz faltered. "We have all this equipment, and I'm good, and I'll get better. That was my first cook, with no help from anyone experienced, and I nailed it. It was fun to do. I enjoyed it. It's a new science, one I'd like to get good at. I'd like the world to have LSD rather than bunk and imitations and toxins. And it has the chance of tremendous money."

"So on the plus side, there's personal development and a hobby for you. I recommend you get into collecting something stupid; that's a pretty standard path for autistic straight guys hitting their thirties. Something with lots of years of sets, where you can try to complete the sets, and then look at them from time to time with satisfaction. A way to waste time with no possibility of lengthy prison sentences, massive financial losses, or getting kidnapped and sacrificed to your weird Discordian goddess by mystic retards from Minnesota. As for the world's access to LSD, get the fuck outta here. The vast majority of acid is going to be eaten by assholes in pursuit of asshole objectives: let 'em eat shrooms. Then there's money, which both of us already make. Not yet thirty, we're doing markedly better than our parents ever will. We'll be multimillionaires unless we really fuck things up. This seems a grand opportunity to fuck that up."

"You and I know a million ain't what it used to be. You never let me finish earlier. So they don't have a quantitative approach. You're right, they're mystic numerologists. Their inability to synthesize from their own precursors says nothing good about them at all. I bet some of them buy lottery tickets. They might even subscribe to astrology. Maybe that makes them less reliable business partners. It definitely makes them suckers. We establish the minimum dose they'll accept per hit, and if that's less than what they're expecting in terms of total conversion, we get the difference for free."

"Huh. That's a good point. It depends on where they put that threshold."

"Datum: Cloud liked what I cooked."

"Won't their expectation be based around whatever Pickard was cooking for them? And thus they'll be expecting a key of ergo to turn into x qualified doses, where qualified means loading them at least to where he was."

"And acid was down below a hundred mics in the 90s."

"None of that matters to me, really. The fundamental problem is the incentive for them to fuck us entirely. We either need them to relax the deposit, or we need some kind of insurance on it."

Katz laughs. "You wanna call up Lloyd's of London?"

Bolaño tokes deeply. "No, but consider this: we're going to have to get the deposit fronted to us in the first place, right?"

"I mean, we could swing it. I've got a few hundred thousand myself, but I didn't want to float the whole thing."

"Katz, Katz." Bolaño shook his head sadly. "That's banked money. If you give these assholes your banked money, I'll have them killed on general principle."

"Have them killed?"

Bolaño dismisses it with a wave of the hand. "A figure of speech. No, we would want to use cheap, unbanked money in all interactions, assuming we have transactions at all. I assume they prefer cash?"

"Cloud's words on the subject were, and I quote, 'the *karass* is rich with true brothers, but poor in bank accounts.' They want cash and can definitely only pay back the deposit in cash. And yeah, I think they're opposed to transaction histories, an attitude with which I have some sympathy."

"It's amazing that such failures of people can exist. So how much free currency do you have?"

"About ten thousand."

"Twenty here. So we would need an infusion of folding money. Now, from what source might such a loan be had? Who do we know that works with large amounts of cash?"

Katz understood. "You speak of the Dnipro Guidos. Bolaño, you want to make partners of Ukrainian organized crime? Have you ever heard of the Dnepropetrovsk maniacs?"

"Those two Ukrainian kids from a few years ago?"

"Yeah, those two Ukrainian kids. Viktor Sayenko and Igor something. They beat random people to death with hammers and pipes, focusing on the face— they liked leaving people unrecognizable. They performed a few screwdriver enucleations along the way. One victim was pregnant; they cut her fetus out, because why not? Then they'd attend these people's funerals. They filmed it. Go check out '3 Guys 1 Hammer' sometime if you want your whole day ruined. At one point they laugh, surprised that a dude kept breathing after they dug around in his exposed brain with a screwdriver."

"What's your point?"

"There's the Nighttime Killers from Kyiv in the 1990s, too. They used bricks and stitching awls. Andrei Romanovich Chikatilo. Butcher of Rostov. 52 convictions. That's not a serial killer; that's a combinatorics problem."

"Rostov is in Russia, not Ukraine, you dope addict."

"We're not in Ukraine. And he enucleated most of his victims. I understand killing a motherfucker, but Ukrainians have to take their eyes. Perhaps an homage to Nabokov?"

Bolaño cocked his head. "Nabokov?"

Patronizingly: *"The Eye?"*

"The Eye?" Confused and irritated: *"Glaz?"*

"Nabokov's shortest. 1930 I think. I don't think it's *Glaz,* but I don't know what it is. Maybe they misunderstood Gogol?"

Totally lost; an uncertain stab: *"Nos?"*

"Indeed."

"Ugh." Bolaño rolled his eyes. "And how many unsavory murders happened here in the 1990s? Right here in the United States?"

Katz cedes. "Fair enough. The Ukrainians have no monopoly on being sick fucks. But you're talking about career criminals who accept violence as a part of doing business."

"We're already doing business with them. We have been ever since we met Alexei back in 2003. We've run literally hundreds of thousands of dollars through them, close to a million. Christ! That's a lotta sacks. But they've been our primary weed suppliers for half a decade now; have you ever felt threatened or fearful?"

"To be honest, every time I meet up with those fucks I feel nervous as hell. You know they're strapped, right?"

"Have they even once pulled on you?"

"No, but I've never fucked up their money, either."

"I have no interest in fucking up anyone's money. The point here is we have a lengthy history with them; we've built up some trust; we've proven ourselves useful and reliable. I think they'd be willing to front us the necessary cash. Now, does the bank just hand over a big stack in a brown paper bag if you ask for a loan? No, they want collateral. If you fuck up your mortgage, they want to make sure they can take your house, and that said foreclosure can recover most of their money, right? Do you think Danylo is going to front us a

---

Nos: Hoc The Nose (1836)

quarter million without ensuring he can get it back? What might be possible is somehow getting him to insure our deposit."

"How?"

"You borrow money from Danylo. What incentivizes you to pay him back?"

"Mostly a strong aversion to being pistolwhipped."

"How were you planning to do exchange with these *karass* fucks?"

Katz shifts. Katz frowns. "I asked Cloud, and he did a dance for me, called me brother, hailed Eris, and provided no useful plan. I'm pretty sure we're the first people they've pulled this deposit shit on."

"Well surely you weren't going to accept that."

"I was thinking of maybe going up there to do the first cook, or something." He blanches. "Though I guess that kinda exposes me to getting robbed, getting my ass beat, impressment gangs for Her Majesty's Chemical Services..."

"I don't think you need worry about kidnapping or murder. But yes, the allure of beating and robbing you would be strong. Either taking the cash you brought with you and sending you back south, or more likely letting you cook first, taking your technique, taking your product, keeping your cash, and laughing at you. Now how might you prevent that?"

"We could make them give us one of their guys?"

Bolaño arches a brow. "Take a hostage?"

"Take collateral."

"And if they fuck us, we do what, exactly, with our collateral?"

"Leaving anything liquid and comparable in price seems to defeat the whole point of the deposit. We'd have their ergocristine; they'd net zero."

"Yes. So we would do what, exactly, with our collateral?"

"Sell it, but we just agreed—"

"We agreed that they would not give us something fungible."

"Right."

"So what, exactly, would we do with our collateral?"

"You've got me, Bolaño. What would we do?"

"Why do you pay back Danylo?"

Katz gets it, finally, or thinks he does. "I'm not really the kind of guy to beat the shit out of a business partner, especially one who can't fight back. I also don't see how that gets us our money, especially if they give us someone worth less to them than the cash. You're talking violence, mang. Well, kidnapping, assault, just a whole lotta shit I want no part of. I don't think anyone would look at us and believe we'd, what, torture some hippie to death? Over a deal gone bad? If they would, I might need get up out of this game."

"Division of labors, Katz. Specialization. Delegation."

✳ ✳ ✳ ✳ ✳ ✳ ✳ ✳ ✳

"Well, which Bible are you talking about?" Katz squints under an overbright Daystar, and sips from his TaBsinthe. The foul brew is exactly what it sounds like: absinthe (by now legal throughout America, so long as it contains less than 10 ppm thujone, but Katz still swore by his own high-thujone concoction) mixed half-and-half with TaB, Coca-Cola's oddly metallic, thoroughly synthetic low-calorie beverage known for bright fucking pink trade dress and popularity among secretaries during the Carter administration. Katz is devoted in what he freely admits to be a somewhat hipsterish bit of brand veneration, describing it as tasting "like pine needles licked from the side of a galvanized aluminum shed in one's backyard, following a short summer rain." When asked, "is that good?" he offers a succinct "not particularly."

"You mean which translation? They have different books?" Bolaño had grown up with only perfunctory religion, the kind of incogitant and uncalculated worship that provides little more than a focus for emotional energies and a name of the unknown. Mass on Christmas™. He was fascinated by Katz's religiocentrist childhood and the ardent Ma Katz.

"Erp, the different translations are the species level of the theopneustic. Your kingdoms of written, monotheistic Holy Writ are al-Qurʾān, Tanakh, and *tà biblía*. You don't really have Judaism without *Talmūd*, though, which is kind of similar in role to the *Catechismus Catholicae Ecclesiae*. I don't believe Islam has a similar concept. Evangelical Christianity is almost defined by rejecting any such terrestrial extension of the literal *Verbum Dei*. Let's also throw in Thelema's *Liber AL vel Legis*, *Kitáb-i-Aqdas*, the *Principia Discordia* of course, and *The Book of Mormon*; all are kinda first-among-equals with regard to their other sacred writings. I can't speak meaningfully on textual criticism beyond those. My experience with Eastern shit, by which I mean Dharmic, is that you can't get anything even approximating an authoritative edition of their scripture. It's all very scattered; they're pretty cool with that in a way I fundamentally fail to grok. Like in Hinduism you have the four *apauruṣeya* Vedas, but they're more mantras than what we'd think of as scripture, except for the Upanishads, which you probably know about?"

"Yeah Schopenhauer in *Die Welt als Wille und Vorstellung* is with them and for them. And of course T. S. Eliot in *The Waste Land*."

"Of course. Schrödinger in *My View of the World*—"

"*Meine Weltansicht?*" Twenty-nine years old and still smirking. Ass.

"—yes, thanks, that's much better, *Meine Weltansicht*, great. Have you read *What is Life?* Fucking brilliant."

"I have not." Bolaño chuckles. "*Was ist das Leben?*"

"NO SIR. Published in English originally, based on lectures delivered at Trinity College. Hoisted with your own polyglottal petard! Sick reverse humanities burn." Katz does a little shufflestep and points to the sky ala Tony Manero in *Saturday Night Fever*.

"Good Lord. Are those your Travolta moves?"

Katz drags victory Vs across his eyes in a Batusi, channeling Vincent Vega. "All my Travolta moves are from *Look Who's Talking*."

"Ghastly breeder shit. *Look Who's Talking*. Christ."

---

al-Qurʾān: القرآن Koran   **Tanakh:** תַּנַ״ךְ Hebrew scripture
tà biblía: τὰ βιβλία lit. "the books" Christian scripture
Catechismus...Ecclesiae: Catechism of the Catholic Church (1992)
Verbum Dei: Word of God   **Liber...Legis:** The Book of the Law
Kitáb-i-Aqdas: كتاب اقدس lit. "The Most Holy Book" prime document of Baháʾí Faith
apauruṣeya: अपौरुषेय not of a man
Die...Vorstellung: The World as Will and Representation (1818)

"Written by one Amy Heckerling, who would go on to do the magnificent *Clueless*. Kirstie Alley got me hot back then. Anyway, Schrödinger said his philosophy was basically that of the Upanishads. Back to the Vedas. Each of the four has four subdivisions: Samhitas, Aranyaka, Upanishads, and Brahmanas. Now the Vedas are also used by the *śramaṇa* non-Brahmanical paths: Buddhism and Jainism and some others."

"Where does Sikhism fit into all of this?"

"Sikhs seem to be the Mormons of the Indian faiths. Sufficiently recent that they're small and the more established groups look at them cockeyed, but they're industrious and True Believers. If you've got money, put it on Sikhs and Mormons. Shinto seems merely an extension of general Japaneseness. You never looked into this stuff?"

"I think I'm constitutionally opposed to religious hogwash."

"I don't know, man. I think more and more that smart people either find religion, or go completely insane. Maybe not. Figure a third of all allusions ever are to religious texts. It's essentially impossible to meaningfully read the Western canon without a solid foundation in Christian scripture."

Bolaño rolls his eyes. "I think I picked it up via osmosis."

"Yeah you seem to be doing fine."

"By 'finding religion,' under your somewhat *jiù sīxiǎng*-stinking rhetoric, doesn't that just admit anything that brings one existential solace? Basically you're saying, 'religion is the anodyne draught of oblivion, that which relieves dread of nothingness.' Then asserting this dread to be debilitative insanity. I don't know, 'religion' seems to be doing some heavy lifting there."

"Point taken. In fact, I'll agree with you. Religions exist primarily to manufacture conclusions of the afterlife. Faith is what enables them."

"Judaism is so far as I'm aware a counterexample. And absent such conclusions, one must go mad?"

Looking meditative, Katz replies. "Yeah I've never understood that about Judaism. It's a large part of why I respect it. Every so often I get a bug in my ass about *giyur*. But then I think hard about it: without addressing life's absurdity, it's just an upscale Elk's Lodge with three thousand years of history."

"Well, plus control of global media and finance."

"I thought you guys had taken media from them?"

Feigning confusion: "You guys as in Mexican-Americans?"

"The Homintern, ass. And if one's paying attention, yeah, I think perhaps so, you go more and more nuts as death draws closer. I once thought otherwise. Before that I felt a third way." Katz grins.

"If you have kids, you don't intend to have them read the Bible, do you?"

"Michael *mon frère*, I hope to marry a vaguely Christian woman who exploits some upscale church to its full social potential. I'll make my kids dress up on Sundays, take them in, sing boisterously—I love a good upbeat hymn, especially when you go in high as hell. Then when they get to the point where they

---

śramaṇa: श्रमण seeker of religious purpose, an ascetic
jiù sīxiǎng: 旧思想 Old Ideas (first of the Four Olds 四旧)
giyur: גיור conversion to Judaism

realize it's horseshit, they'll come and be like, 'dad, what the fuck?' And I'll be like, 'excellent work, little Joan Mollie Mae Freya Noether, you've started down the path to thinking for yourself. Don't tell your little brother.' Soul-crushing, reality-upending destruction of all one holds dear is an essential part of development: the resulting anger and distrust powered me through high school. And if she doesn't figure it out, hey, cool, she's built to go along with what she's told, and in that case a mellow, apolitical Christianity seems a fine ethos. Who am I to take the comfort and ease of religion from her?"

"I don't know, Katz. I'm glad I didn't go through that."

"I've got to think that realizing you were gay in a very straight world had to be a similar kind of deal."

"Hrmmm."

"Beyond the Vedas in Hinduism you've got *Mahābhāratam* and *Rāmāyaṇam*, both Sanskrit. The former is long, an order of magnitude more than the combined length of *Iliad* and *Odyssey*."

"What about the *Bhagavad-gītā?*"

"Part of the *Bhishma Parva,* the sixth book of *Mahābhāratam,* of which there are eighteen Parvas, said to have been compiled by Vyāsaḥ. And of course you probably know the *Gītā* to have been dear to Dr. Oppenheimer. He did his own rather idiosyncratic translations."

"Yeah Vannevar Bush in *Pieces of the Action* has him quoting from—"

"That's a well-known error. Oppenheimer was quoting from the *subhāṣita triśati* of Bhartṛhari. They're in three books, the *Nītiśataka, Śṛṅgāraśataka,* and *Vairāgyaśataka.* I don't know which of the three contains Oppenheimer's passage; I haven't read them myself. You're talking about this, right?"

> *In battle, in forest, at the precipice in the mountains,*
> *On the dark great sea, in the midst of javelins and arrows,*
> *In sleep, in confusion, in the depths of shame,*
> *The good deeds a man has done before defend him.*

"Yeah." Bolaño says it with serene satisfaction. "Bush never gave a citation for the poem. He also misspelled Sanskrit. I'm not sure how it became attributed to the *Gītā.*"

"I understand Oppenheimer to have been all over the map with his Sanskrit, and then you've got a bunch of white people quoting him. Things are bound to get lost in the translation."

"What about the Destroyer of Worlds line?"

"Real, though taken somewhat out of context so far as I understand it. Krishna is speaking to Arjuna, that much is accurate. I don't know how to write the Sanskrit, but I've got the verse memorized:

Bhagavad-gītā: भगवद्गीत The Song of God   **Bhishma Parva:** भीष्म पर्व Book of Bhishma
Vyāsaḥ: व्यास: the compiler (Krishna Dvaipayana)
subhāṣita triśati: सुभाषित त्रशितिं Three-hundred Poems of Moral Value
śhrī-bhagavān…iha: श्रीभगवानु कालोऽस्मि लोकक्षयकृत्प्रवृद्धो लोकान्समाहर्तुमहि प्रवृत्त
   The Supreme Lord said: I am mighty Time, the source of destruction brought forth to
   annihilate the worlds. BG 11.32   **Jyotisha:**ज्योतिष Vedic-Purāni astrology

śhrī-bhagavān uvācha
kālo 'smi loka-kṣhaya-kṛit pravṛiddho
lokān samāhartum iha

Lord Krishna is encouraging Prince Arjuna of the Pandavas to fight the Kaurava at Kurukshetra, on Dharmakshetra, the field of dharma. Now these are two clans of cousins; everyone's related. There have just been three solar eclipses, baneful omens in *Jyotisha*. Poor Arjuna is fighting, among others, granduncle Bhishma and beloved tutor Drona. The Kauravas are arranged against him in eleven *akshauhinis*. Filled with anguish, he calls upon Krishna for advice. The eighth avatar of Vishnu manifests before him and is like, 'Arjuna, son of Indra, where be your yarbles, your yarblockos? Your gibes, your gambols, your songs? This is this *caturyuga's* battle between dharma and adharma; it is your duty to slay those in whom righteousness no longer dwells.' Echoes of Paul's epistle to the Ephesians: *quia non est nobis conluctatio adversus carnem et sanguinem sed adversus principes et potestates adversus mundi rectores tenebrarum harum contra spiritalia nequitiae in caelestibus.* And should you ever hear that quoted at you, run don't walk away, because you're in the presence of an eschatological evangelist. They fuckin' love that line. I'm guessing you've never read Frank E. Peretti, perhaps the greatest author of thrillers to emerge from the Assemblies of God? *This Present Darkness* is a real pageturner."

"How much speed are you doing these days?"

Katz spears him with a stare. "Enough to get all my shit done."

"Just wondering. Please, continue."

"I'm lead engineer at an established startup of over two hundred people, and I'm getting two masters degrees. I have a lot going on."

"Never have I thought nor said otherwise. Sherman Katz is a busy man. Only a fool could believe any other evaluation. Just wondering how much speed you're doing. Doing it every day?"

"I've been doing it every day for like five plus years, dude, this shit isn't something you take days off from unless you want to just lose those days."

"Hrmmm." A short pause. "Well, I'd like to hear more about Arjuna."

"Do I not seem on top of my shit?"

"You're more on top of your shit than just about anyone I know. King Katz of shit mountain. The only shit you do not tower above is the shit of not being addicted to methamphetamine, and not needing it unless you are to 'lose a day.' Also, your clothes and weight, but you've never been on top of them."

"So since you wouldn't know about the meth except that I've told you—"

"Oh, I'd know some nose drugs to be at work, my friend. You're not so on top of your shit that I've never seen you with two jets of detritus hydrochloride under your nostrils."

"Fuck! When? How often?"

---

akshauhinis: अक्षौहिणी battle formation of 218.7 kilowarriors
yarbles: testicles   **caturyuga:** चतुर्युग a cycle of the four *yuga* (4.32 megayears)
quia...caelestibus: For we wrestle not against flesh and blood, but against principalities, against powers, against the rulers of the darkness of this world, against spiritual wickedness in high places. Ephesians 6:12 (KJV)

"Not often. I am not judging you. Please, the Oppenheimer story."

Clearly scandalized, Katz presses on after a long look. "Arjuna is yet unsure of his dharma. Krishna, by now severely pissed off, reveals his divine form and explains, 'it matters not what you do, mortal; it is written that these sinners will perish. If you won't execute your dharma, Time will get them in the end.' Because that word *kālo* is pretty much always translated as 'time.' Now Oppenheimer, when Szilard *et al.* were wringing their hands and decrying the upcoming drop on Nippon in what was frankly a bit of white exceptionalism— Szilard thought nuking Nazi Germany would be just fine, but not the poor little yellow folk—said that while the scientists of Los Alamos had created the bomb, it was up to political leadership to decide on its use. He didn't want responsibility for what was about to go down. And when he saw the lights of Trinity, the Destroyer of Worlds bit wasn't him talking himself up. He didn't see himself as Krishna, he saw himself as Arjuna! Even if we didn't drop on the Japanese, the bomb was going to get used. Time, the true Destroyer of Worlds, was going to come along anyway and clear the board."

"If that's true, why would Oppenheimer have translated it in such a way as to lose that detail entirely? He was the source of the 'I have become Death.' He said it on national news."

"Well there's an argument to be made that Death works there. Yama, the Hindu god of death, is also known as Kala. That's how Oppenheimer's teacher, Arthur Ryder, translated it. But here's the thing: the following line, which Oppenheimer surely knew, but chose to elide, is *even without your participation, the warriors arrayed in the opposing army shall cease to exist.* So Krishna is explicitly saying, 'this is going to happen. You can perform your duty or fail to do so, but forsaking your dharma only ruins you.' And remember: Hiroshima and Nagasaki had been spared the firebombing that burned out most other Japanese cities *so that the effects of the atomic bomb could be accurately determined.* Without the atomic bomb, they already would have been obliterated. So Oppenheimer said 'Death' because that's how he learned it. And most people weren't going to understand the subtext of the full quote, and one must admit the shorter form is snappier, one of the great soundbites of the twentieth century."

"I feel we ought have Devesh here to speak to this."

"Devesh doesn't know shit about any of this. Devesh's knowledge beyond science and EDM is pretty generally lackluster."

✳ ✳ ✳ ✳ ✳ ✳ ✳ ✳

"Molecular weight on ergotamine tartrate is 1313.4 g/mol. So for every 1313.4 g you're getting N_A, from which you would ideally recover one ergoline molecule. Ergoline mass is 212.29 g/mol. So that's, what, 83.8% waste product by mass."

"Anything useful there in those leftovers?"

"Absolutely not, a big piece of shit tripeptide. Alanine, proline, and phenylalanine if I remember correctly. Doesn't matter, as they're worthless. You're ideally generating one LSD molecule from each ergoline. Stabilize that as LSD tartrate plus two H_2O of crystallization at 473.52, and that's 36.05% of your

---

Nippon: 日本 Japan

original ET mass. So that's your absolutely optimal conversion, 360.5 g on a key of 100% pure ET. That's for tartrate. 246.2 g of actual LSD freebase on same, enough for 820 kilodoses at 300 μg of freebase. At 300 μg of mere tartrated salt, 1.2 megadoses. If they're hoping for $2.25 per, that's almost three megs street for the weaker option, and almost two for the stronger. They're looking for a deposit of almost a quarter million per key. So that tracks. If they're saying one key of ergocristine—"

"Wait, you've been quoting ergotamine tartrate."

"Oh fuck! I have!" Katz is deeply embarrassed. "That's a solid fuckup. Goddamnit. Most of this is recoverable. Can you look up molecular mass of—"

"Already on it. Ergocristine...esylte? Tartrate doesn't seem to be a thing."

"Ergocristine phosphate."

"Ahh, seven oh seven oh nine, call it 707.1 g/mol."

"That's an upgrade, sweet." Katz punches at his laptop. "669 and 457."

"So from a key, you ideally get 1.5 megs of strong doses, or 2.2 weaker ones?"

"Yessir. That's for 300 mics. 4.57 and 6.7 on 100."

"That's phenomenal." Bolaño shakes his head.

"It doesn't make sense to me. They're calling it three hundred grams per input key. That's a million strong doses, matching the nine quarter million dollars they expect from a key. But we know they were taking weaker doses. That only accounts for about 45% of the expected tartrate yield."

"Did you miss a factor somewhere?"

"Your clients miss a factor, *puto*. I mean, we're staking a tenth of a key of precursor. That's one hundred million micrograms. A third of a meg of 300 μg doses at a one-to-one conversion, right? So this all makes sense, except for them." Katz stared into the distance for a moment, then got very excited. "Hail Eris, all hail Discordia! You know what it is? They were basing things off ergotamine tartrate, just like I was earlier! That's exactly it! Everything works out if you're assuming ET. But ergocristine phosphate has only about half the molecular mass. So you get roughly twice the output from a fixed amount. These dumb motherfuckers don't know that. It's all 'precursor' to them."

Bolaño's eyes danced. "So you're saying—"

"What I'm saying, Michael my droog, is that we stand to take 75 large from each hundred gram cook, plus 55% of the output. Without stepping on it."

"That 55% being over a hundred thousand hits."

"A perfect conversion would generate 67 g tartrate from 100 g ergocristine phosphate, about 46 g base. They expect 30 g of tartrate. We keep up to 37 g tartrate. 25 g base, 250 kilodoses at 100. Which we can either sell to them, accumulating precursor, or sell elsewhere—without losing our deposit."

"Much more profitably than $0.75 per 300 μg."

"Shit, nobody's seen acid reliably in years, and we come swooping in like two big-dicked mindflayers selling 300 μg tabs? Charge $20."

"There's no need to sell 300 μg, but yeah."

"Nah, I like the idea of melting motherfucker's brains. This would be the first wave of Georgia Tech acid. It ought wreck you." Katz gleams.

---

puto: male prostitute

"I can almost certainly move a sizable amount at a good price to some folks I know out west, older burner types with effectively unbounded cash. If we're going to have tens of thousands of hits free..."

* * * * * * * * *

Oppenheimer resolutely opposed development of the hydrogen bomb so long as the best suggestion was Edward Teller's Alarm Clock (known in Russia as Sakharov's First Idea and the *sloika*, and implemented in the RDS-6s). The Alarm Clock, much like the Classical Super (known in Russia as the *truba*, and implemented in the RDS-6t), intended to ignite a fusion reaction via material compression. It was fundamentally impractical for megaton performance levels. Together with a breakthrough idea of Stanislav Ulam, the Teller-Ulam concept instead relied on radiation to initiate compression of a staged secondary. With this new, elegant design, the hydrogen bomb effort moved forward: forward to Enewetak, forward to Elugelab. Asked about his change of opinion, Oppenheimer replied, "When you see something that is technically sweet, you go ahead and do it, and you argue about what to do about it only after you have had your technical success."

* * * * * * * * *

"So we're basically going to ask Danylo to provide escrow on our transaction, presumably via some brutal monster of the Zaporozhian Sich. That's how it seems to me, anyway. Doesn't that just mean we're employing violence, but too pussy to enact it ourselves?"

"Not at all. First off, we're asking him to fund things until we're cash-positive. It's his money for which he'd be providing 'escrow.' We're not even necessarily asking him to do so."

"But you wanted escrow. It was a fundamental goal."

"If it's not my money, I don't particularly care."

"At some point it'll no longer be his money," observes Katz.

"By then we ought have rapport and trust established."

"Trust based on a threat of an assbeating."

"Best kind of trust."

"I'd disagree with that. Kinda cliche Machiavelli."

Bolaño looks put out. "Katz, fucking us over is violence."

Katz laughs. "Absolutely not. Robbing us is violence. Kidnapping is violence. Whupping your ass is violence. Receiving our money and running is theft by taking, fraud, possibly flimflam. Bunco. Graft. The two are not the same legally, morally, nor in what responses they might elicit."

"Whupping my ass?"

"If I had to fight one of us, I'm definitely picking you. But feel free to interpret the second person as the third. One's. Whipping one's ass."

Bolaño sighs. "Posit a call on collateral. The fault is with the Ukrainians."

"A 'call on collateral?' You mean a brutal beating?"

---

sloika: Слойка layered cake   **RDS:** *Reaktivnyi Dvigatel Specialnyi* lit. "special jet engine"
truba: Труба cylinder

"However the collateral is called. Legally—"

"I'm pretty sure we're conspirators in that case, but continue."

"Ugh. Legally, their responsibility. Morally, their responsibility."

"Bolaño! Don't bullshit a bullshitter. We know how Danylo operates."

"We're not choosing him for that. We're going to him because he has cash."

"He has cash because otherwise he burns people alive."

"Claims to."

"We would absolutely bear some responsibility, dude. To claim otherwise is asinine, almost insulting. And they'd feel the same way, up north, and possibly come after us."

"You're worried about hippie death squads? C'mon."

"Fuck off you equivocating piece of shit. If you're not worried about people with nothing to lose coming after you, watching over your shoulder, setting alarms, wondering about that thump in the night, you're stupid. If you think yourself some kind of hard gangster, run this shit yourself. Get rowdy. Kick down doors. Show motherfuckers that you're 'bout it 'bout it in your collared shirts and four hundred dollar pants."

"So what were you going to do? Just hand this glib asshole two hundred and twenty-five thousand dollars, watch him head north, and wait for a call like a lovestruck teenage girl?"

Katz must admit defeat. "I don't know. The opportunity to do this business...he's necessary, but that doesn't mean I want to do business with him." He brightens. "Well, there's a way around him, and around the deposit entirely. We just need our own precursors. Which would mean fermenting our own ergot, or whatever. We have the bioreactors. Then we distribute through Minnesota, take a lower cost on the precursor, and never involve Slavic psychopaths."

"And how long will that take?"

"I don't know. I don't know anything about it with any certainty."

Bolaño shakes his head. "If you won't go the Danylo route, leave it to me. I'll arrange it, handle everything other than the cooking, sell you ergocristine, and buy your LSD."

"At what price?"

"I'll pay you ten cents per hundred mics."

"Fuck off."

"Then I'll learn to do it."

"Dude, this is my thing. And I don't think Cloud likes you. At all. Speaking of which, what position do you see for yourself in this enterprise?"

"None, except that I suspect I can engineer some bulk sales, and would appreciate privilege of purchase from your surplus at an attractive price, befitting my role as partner in the lab. However, I'm happy to open the dialogue with Danylo." Bolaño had met Danylo a few times over the years; they had taken to one another, apparently meeting for a purely social kaffeeklatsch or two. Katz hadn't liked this development at all.

"Whether we can make it work depends entirely on what shameless usury Danylo hits us with."

"Well, if he's down at all."

Bolaño's silence is agreement.

* * * * * * * *

Cloud and two brothers of the *karass* came down to Atlanta two weeks later. Katz caught a burner call from them in Chattanooga. "A thousand miles down I-24, about thirteen hours, brother! We look forward to some sleep upon arrival."

"I bet. Where will you be staying? Hopefully somewhere close, Midtown?"

"Ahhh...will we not be staying with you, brother?" It emerged that they assumed lodging available with Katz. He chuckled. "Pretty bad opsec for y'all to know where I live. You don't have a hotel room?"

"Negative, Ghostrider! The pattern is full."

"Do you have a credit card among the three of you?"

"Ahhh, yes, but I'd prefer not to use it..."

"And I'd prefer not to give you my address. Look, take down these directions. This place will let you pay in cash, and only put up a credit card for liabilities. So long as there aren't any, that's barely a record. I'll even cover your room, in apology for the inconvenience. And I can meet you over there in the morning when y'all wake."

They did, and he did. As prearranged with Cloud, false names were used by all parties throughout the day. They passed bowls, and played Oysterhead's *Grand Pecking Order,* and locked down procedures and exchange rates. After two hours' conversation, Cloud excavated from their trunk a tin-plated steel can, along with a vacuum-sealed bag. The latter was a pound of the Northern Lights Katz had enjoyed so thoroughly at Bonnaroo; Katz had set forth forcefully his thoughts regarding the deposit scheme, and it was a thoughtful edulcoration. The former, they said, ought be a half kilogram of ergocristine.

"Powder form?"

"Aye, brother."

"Then it's probably ergocristine phosphate. I'll need work out that hydrolysis. I'll want to work with this under red light, and an atmosphere of nitrogen—you haven't opened it or anything, right?." They assured him that they had not. "I can do the most basic of tests within an hour using a microsample: colorimetry using Ehrlich's reagent and a density measurement. The density measurement is non-destructive, and will be done pursuant to dissolving the material in methanol for storage. Another microsample will go through GC/MS, and if we get a good peak at m over z of 223, I'll concede that it's an ergot alkaloid. If that checks out, but the density is off, we might be able to identify it as some other ergot alkaloid, or some other salt of ergocristine. I won't dissolve the material unless I'm satisfied it's a working precursor, and that we're willing to take it from you." Katz was feeling good about things, though—he knew that the ergocristine numbers from the DEA reports didn't add up. "First, let's get some food. Then, you're—just you, Cloud—are going to need to talk to the guy funding this op. Your deposit policy meant I had to bring someone else in. He's not exactly friendly. Just smile and nod."

* * * * * * * *

Cloud emerged. He shuddered. He looked at them, and at the floor, and to them again. His eyes darted. Sweat slowly ran the gutter of his nose.

"What's good, my man? Are we up?"

Cloud glanced at them with fear and some revulsion. "We're up." Unhappiness was manifest throughout his person.

"Alright, let's go talk details." Bolaño hung back for a minute, standing next to Cloud, whose head was down, shoulders crumpled, a portrait of dejection.

Katz squared himself and walked through the door. "Danylo! Satisfied?"

Danylo sat behind the desk, moving not at all, conserving energy like a reptile. He wore the minimal possible smile. "We have satisfaction."

"I think you put the zap on our friend out there! What did you tell him?"

Danylo waits a moment. He sips from a Tervis tumbler, looking Katz in the eye. "Rules and conditions. Keep things tight, keep things professional."

"That's all?"

A tiny shrug. "Showed him some pictures."

"Oh yeah?" Katz is smart enough to feel dread immediately. He doesn't want to see, can guess what's there, but feels he's obligated. I called up this demon. Let's look his violence straight. Play the man, Mr. Katz. "Show me?"

Danylo sighs quietly. His hand goes into his pocket; out come a few Polaroids. Katz arranges them on the desk, and swallows back his gasp.

Picture one: an emaciated fellow, short, perhaps Malaysian, maybe Thai? His hair is black; his skin is brown where not mottled with thick, almost foamy blood the color of chewed areca nut. Katz can hear the screams of agony despite the gag in his mouth. One eye is missing entirely. From the other socket, caved into a mess of a face, hangs half a deflated sclera. There is only a very minor redeye effect: most of the fundus appears to be missing. Katz can't tell whether it is tears or vitreous humor that pool there, held by surface tension, only beginning to roll down the poor fucker's cheek.

Picture two: same guy, an icepick in his ear at an angle. His head is jacked back, neck clearly broken: yeah, Mistah Kurtz—he dead. Several teeth are gone. Enough remain to hold the missing eye, staring out from his ruined maw. His pants have been removed, as have his genitals, leaving only a truncated stump. Katz scans the scene for loose cocks and balls. He remembers Jodorowsky's *La montaña sagrada,* Axon in his centurion's blue *galea,* intoning "your sacrifice completes my sanctuary of one thousand testicles."

Picture three: a woman this time, a little heavy. It's impossible to tell the age. A lack of pallor mortis suggests she's alive. Anechoic foam, sloping tile floor, drains—a torture chamber. Eastern Orthodox icons on the walls seem decidedly out of place, but who is Katz to ask? Her head is shaved. For now she retains her eyes. She's stippled in cigarette burns and knife cuts. By far the worst are the wounds on her thighs and pelvis, looking for all the world like they've been gnawed. Then Katz recognizes the rat cage for what it is.

"Katz, we can move on this. But I have a different proposal you ought hear."

Katz manages to pull his eyes away. "Yeah?" His voice is flat.

"Already we will be keeping ourselves aware of this tiedyed flower man. Until the debt is settled. His home. Friends who come to his home. His move-

---

La montaña sagrada: The Holy Mountain (1973)   **Galea:** myrmillo helmet

ments. I understand the flows of money here. What if we sell you his product more cheaply? No deposit, no need for loan. We go in as partners."

Of all the people Katz hopes might cease to intersect his worldline, Danylo is near the top. "Whatever do you mean, Danylo?"

"Hah. We relieve him of preLSD, your money also, if that was taken. Keep 15% of your money only, finder's fee. Sell you preLSD much more cheaply, no *nekulturny* duckshit deposit. Simple, good, all earn together."

"How would you 'relieve' him?"

Danylo's face changes not at all. "Wait to leave, enter, seize. If all is found, good, we take, we leave."

"And if not?"

"Lurk in waiting, capture in darkness, extract truths, seize."

"We're going to need his distribution network, Danylo."

Danylo waves him off. "Fine, fine."

✳ ✳ ✳ ✳ ✳ ✳ ✳ ✳

"So hey man, what did you think of his offhand suggestion that they torture Cloud to death? Not because he did anything to them, just because he had resources. Resources that Danylo had provided in the first place, and thus probably didn't represent a lifechanging amount."

"I think he was just showing off."

"Yeah? Because it made me think, we'll soon have a good bit more money than Cloud would have had, and no one to lobby that we not be killed."

Bolaño bit his lip. "We're valuable clients."

"At some point we will have far, far more cash due to LSD than we'll ever put through him for weed."

Bolaño stared at a distant point. "You can't kill all your client base."

"I'll admit I encouraged taking on some financial risk dealing with Cloud. You rightfully bitched about it. But now you're happy to take on existential risk dealing with this evil fucking Cossack, who less than an hour ago referred to torturing a man to death. A childlike man easily moved to dance, who wears only Grateful Dead shirts, who greeted us exuberantly as brothers."

Bolaño continued staring. He turned and looked into Katz's eyes. "I understand the exercise of power. I can predict it, and have rational expectations. Dancing fools making decisions based on Greek goddesses, that I have no model for." He pauses and continues. "And further, Katz, if someone walks with my quarter million, I at least have no compunctions slitting that thief's throat. Better that than know a man lives, walks, talks, and mocks me, thinking what a fine thing it is to fuck over Michael Luis Bolaño, scion of Montezuma II."

Katz surrenders. But it was some time that evening before he could fall asleep. He dreamed of eyes.

15   if you eat that i think it is going to kill you

Life as we know it is based on biopolymers: nucleic acids and proteins.

Not everything containing nucleic acids is alive. Viruses have either RNA or DNA. Capsidless viroids, even simpler than viruses, still have RNA despite not coding for proteins. Rather than nucleic acids, the chemical that marks life is ATP. It is conversion, not information, that qualifies life. After all, legal death is defined in terms of brain and/or heart death, long before the human body's few hundred grams of DNA have been denatured. Schrödinger famously defined life as the homeostatic maintenance of negative entropy in an open system, above and beyond the "aperiodic crystal" that carries genetic information.

Life, then, is at its most fundamental level the consumption of nutrients, their conversion into energy (catabolism), use of that energy (anabolism), and the elimination of waste products. This metabolism should be locally negentropic (though it is inevitably globally entropic: eat a chicken wing, contribute to the heat death of the universe). Under this definition, viruses are, in a sense, the negation of life. They have no metabolisms, only genetic information, and their primary means of reproduction involves destruction of negentropic cells, a lytic conversion of the negentropic to the entropic, the aneristic to the Eristic.

✳✳✳✳✳✳✳✳✳

Katz burned with desire to harvest his own precursors. SYNCOPE's ergocristine was expensive, and had that damned deposit. Should they ever lose a batch— and Katz was sure they would lose a batch or two—the financial hit would be massive. A bit of bullshit, he reflected, that Cloud and his band of freaks were completely protected from loss during production. They were staking nothing. The deposit ought reflect that, but it was essentially set up to protect against moving the final product elsewhere. In terms of loss, it was fine for defense against overambitious wouldbe chemists, but it was a shit deal for an ongoing working relationship. Katz resolved to bring this up with Cloud, but doubted it would go anywhere: they had the precursor; where else could he score?

He'd spent a few hundred hours over the better part of two months looking into total syntheses, bringing himself up to speed on the necessary ochem with *Organic Chemistry* by Solomons and Fryhle, and more of Pauling's venerable *General Chemistry* than he would have liked to admit. Twelve years ago, he'd made AP Chemistry his bitch; on a lark, he'd taken inorganic as an elective, and experienced no significant difficulty. But applied organic chemistry still seemed a great swirling mess: zoology at its worst. Beyond that, he had no lab experience, and every other chemical he looked up was plastered with warnings regarding spontaneous flammability, and tendency to explode, and fifty thousand ways to die upon ingestion. The many reagents involved would require unacceptable investment of banked funds, not to mention multiple suspicious suppliers. No, he finally accepted with a sigh, they would not be the first team to bring mass LSD *de novo* to the market.

That left the biological path.

254

Fermented ergot strains produce minimal alkaloids, but *C. Paspali* strains had been successfully engineered to support lab growth. He wasn't sure how to get his hands on those strains, though, which were probably trade secrets. Brewing a few hundred kilograms of *Claviceps* looked to be a gory affair. The world moved on to *Aspergillus* bearing the eas (ergot alkaloid synthesis) gene clusters. Either way, you wanted to feed them a bunch of tryptophan to start things off. Katz despaired. What was keeping you from a denser alkaloid output? Could you cut out the unnecessary metabolisms and pathways, and all the unused alkaloids?

"Model organisms" are species used to study biological phenomena. An ideal model can be quickly and cheaply farmed (including provision of feed and removal of waste), maintains a high SNR (minimal amount of junk DNA), accommodates surgical and genetic manipulation, and is (for research purposes) analogous to human biology. Extensive documented knowledge of a species, including sequenced genomes, is of the highest importance, and there is thus a self-reinforcing, snowballing effect in model selection. The classic prokaryotic model is doubtlessly *Escherichia coli,* the coliform (gramnegative, asporogenous) facultative anaerobic rod-shaped bacteria that can subsist on just about anything, but loves nothing so much as water parks. The β-galactosidase gene can be amplified with PCR to conclusively detect their presence. *E. coli* cells are immortal by default. All in all, a fine specimen.

On the other side of the spectrum from *E. coli* are primates, primarily the chimpanzee, rhesus monkey, and macaque, reserved for cognition and disease testing. COVID-19 and Chinese export cuts have prompted a hurried increase in domestic monkeyfarming. Chimpanzees are unpredictable, aggressive little fuckers, known to go after faces and genitals. If a chimpanzee steals away your child, as they regularly do in Tanzania and India, that child will rapidly become chimpfood. Macaques are also prone to seizing infants, but tend to throw them—from roofs, and surprisingly often down wells. Then again, if Harry Harlow of UWisconsin had developed a "pit of despair" and "rape rack" for your species, you might also want to rip off someone's testicles.

Between bacteria and primates come a whole host of test species. The 1 mm nematode *Caenorhabditis elegans* has not only had its genome sequenced, but its connectome (neuronal graph) mapped. A broad range of inbred *Mus musculus* strains have largely replaced *Cavia porcellus* as the canonical "guinea pig," while a "lab rat" is almost certainly *Rattus norvegicus;* their larger organs are more easily manipulated than those of the mouse. For early development, you can't beat *Danio rerio,* the zebrafish: her embryos become transparent upon fertilization, and readily develop outside the mother. Viruses are not exempt; the escherichia T4 is extensively studied in genetics, along with enterobacteria phage λ (the latter also a powerful tool for recombineering). The thale cress *Arabidopsis thaliana,* with its relatively short 135 Mbp genome, was the first plant to have its genome sequenced, and is the workhorse of molecular botany.

But perhaps no organism models so much, or is as well understood, as the fruit fly *Drosophilia melanogaster.* Fruit flies boast superb fecundity (a hundred

---

SNR: signal to noise ratio

eggs per day, a few thousand per laying lifetime). The larval connectome of 3016 neurons was in 2023 mapped at the synapse level. Haploids have only three autosomes and a sex chromosome. Generation time runs ten days, and its development is understood in great detail. Males, virgin females, and harlot flies can all be easily distinguished. One can nonlethally anesthetize a flock with a little gas, or simply cooling their environment. Morphology is easily analyzed once asleep. Drosophilists have exploited these attributes en route to six Nobel Prizes.

Baker's yeast, *Saccharomyces cerevisiae,* is useful not only for studying funga, but for metabolic engineering, the engineered biosynthesis of useful substances. It is nonpathogenic (indeed a GRAS organism), enjoys well established fermentation and process technology at scale, had its complete genome sequenced by 1996, and is highly receptive to recombinant DNA techniques. Its substrate range has been expanded in many experiments, and selective breeding has yielded robust strains which generate minimal waste.

✳ ✳ ✳ ✳ ✳ ✳ ✳ ✳ ✳

In the relentlessly upscale Ginza district of Tokyo's central Chūō ward, legendary *itamae-san* Jiro Ono serves ten seats at Sukiyabashi Jirō, and spins out a web of some of the world's greatest sushi chefs. Shiro Kashiba of Seattle's Sushi Kashiba trained underneath him. Daisuke Nakazawa spent eleven years there as apprentice, followed by another three in finishing school under Kashiba. He went to New York in 2013 to found Sushi Nakazawa, competing with Masa Takayama's Masa and Masatoshi Sugio's Sushi of Gari.

Futoshi Yoshi, *itamae* of Glenwood Park's new *Kuchisabishii,* hardly had time for all that. He studied fishcutting via Youtube while practicing tax law, made connections with national fishmongers, perfected pickups at Hartsfield, and spent hundreds of hours tirelessly perfecting his *sumeshi.* Three years after making partner, he put his law career on hold, and funded Lonely Mouth himself, intending to bring Atlanta (and thus the southeast) its first truly exquisite sushi. Everything was his own: the menu, the sparse decoration and bluish lighting, the music (heavy on Talvin Singh, Panjabi MC, and Asian Dub Foundation), the uniforms of his *wakiita.* With twenty-two seats, the cozy venue is significantly more inclusive than the most hoity-toity locations in Ginza, but space is after all a good deal cheaper in East Atlanta than Tokyo.

Two thousand dollars cash secured off Craigslist four tickets for the thirty-course *omakase* grand opening (face value: $1,600). Fine dining is a common thing for Bolaño; Katz does much less of it. Michael cautiously inquires as to what Katz plans to wear, and pleads for an upgrade from "tshirt and pants," which felt already to Sherman like a sacrifice in terms of comfort and maneuverability. Bolaño joins Katz and his parade of dates regularly enough, but a double is a rarity; Michael tends to keep his private life private.

GRAS: generally regarded as safe
itamae: 板前 skilled chef   **kuchisabishii:** 口寂しい lonely mouth
sumeshi: 酢飯 vinegar rice   **omakase:** お任せ chef-selected

Sherman is bringing Chelsea Mahr, a commercial litigator at King and Spalding, ChemE/ZTA at GT before a JD at UVA, 5'9 in flats and half an inch taller than Katz in cork Michael Kors wedges, then a few inches more of piled red hair, not yet defeated in the courtroom, totally out of his league and barely receptive to this third date. He doubts she'd ever be exclusive with him, and for that matter has no real wish to date her, to attend "galas" rather than "parties," subjected to the idly arrogant talk of lawyers so moneyed and pretentious that they're just barely believable. With all his heart and soul, however, he hopes just once to bend her over a desk, to hold her hips locked immobile and fill her with loads of North Georgia Mountain Nerd. He seems to amuse her, and she genuinely respects his intelligence, but still he figures this his last good chance to bring her home for an orgy of self-validation and dopamine.

Michael reveals that he has been dating the same man for two months now, about as long as he ever lets them hang. Steve Psomething (Katz doesn't hear it clearly, and doesn't care enough to ask for clarification) has a blandly handsome face, frosted tips that even Katz knows to be a few years out of date, absolutely expansive shoulders tapering to a dancer's waist, and what has to be a tailored suit. He identifies as a physical trainer. Katz asks if he's read anything recently; Bolaño grimaces, and Steve cheerfully responds that he likes anything with pictures of beautiful beaches. Katz grins, and agrees wholeheartedly. "I've always thought Michael to have the best taste in coffee table books. You're very lucky to have found him." Steve grins with stupid devotion, and Bolaño leans in to whisper, "I will end you."

They're clearly the youngest of twenty-two guests that evening, and the last to arrive, shortly after 2000h. Yoshi is expected to emerge at 2030h; Katz inquires as to absinthe, but settles for sake. Sherman begins to pour for everyone at the table, but Steve orders a Michelob Ultralight. Both Bolaño and Katz frown. Steve's *choko* is withdrawn. Chelsea requests San Benedetto mineral water, and with some effort Katz refrains from rolling his eyes. Feeling inspired, he calls for a tall ouzo and mint, and excuses himself, taking it outside for a Newport. He is surprised when Chelsea joins him.

"Hey, what's up?"

"Can I get one of those?"

"Of course! I didn't realize you smoked."

"I had stopped. I picked it back up again." He lights her a Newport and hands it over. "Your friend is Michael, right?"

"Aye, he of dubious ethnicity."

"I think his boyfriend got alcohol in his blood surrogate."

"He wears the black tunic of an Epsilon-Minus Semi-Moron for sure. Good looking guy though."

"How do you know Michael?"

"Ahhh..." Katz considers for a moment how best to frame it. "We met at the Academic Bowl nationals back in 1997, then went to engineer school together. We've been pretty tight all that time." His cigarette is burned halfway down. "When did you start at GT? 2000, right?"

---

choko: 猪口 sake cup

"Yeah, out of St. Pius."

"Ugh, the lame Catholics."

"What do you mean? You didn't go to St. Anthony's, did you? I thought you were Turner Classic. Which by the way how did that come to be?"

"All part of God's good plan. Yeah, I was an Archangel through the beginning of eleventh grade."

"What happened then?"

Give her something she can understand. "I was distributing pharmaceuticals without a license."

She laughs merrily. "You were a drug dealer?"

"If you choose to be uncharitable about it." He looks for an ashtray, and extinguishes his cigarette. "You about done? I don't want to miss this."

"Yeah. It's going to be fantastic, I'm sure." They start to head in. "Hey, can you get some coke?"

Katz sighs a little inside, but he's all smiles. "I can, and it'll be less stepped-on than what you're used to. This is for you?"

"Well, for us, if you want to do some."

"I might do a little bit." It is unlikely; Katz has learned to loathe cocaine, with its fleeting high, nasty cutting agents, and transient cliques of hyperkinetic, multiloquent fiends. To the extent it might endear him to Chelsea. and keep her awake and impetuous and temerariously enthusiastic, he's a wild supporter. One problem: he has no cell phone. They return and take their seats; Chelsea asks for an Aviation with Hendrick's. Yoshi emerges to eager applause, bows, and describes the fish that will be served that evening. His speech is without a hint of accent, something of a letdown.

The food is superb, each dish presented with a summary in quick Japanese no one at the table has a chance of understanding. Katz is growing definitely pixilated; Chelsea is loud, with her hair down, and everything is turning up Spartacus. Bolaño is brought aside, and Katz begs him to summon up an eightball from his scene. Ideally he'd go through the Ukrainians, but there's zero chance Bolaño will use his cell phone to call them up, especially in front of people. Michael ought be able to get similar quality, though at a higher price, and with less prompt delivery. Chelsea smiles and laughs and throws her hair around. Katz wonders how it'll feel to bury his hands therein.

It's with the eighteenth course that his plane hits the mountain. Four nigiri arrive, larger than any served thus far. They look like whole prawns under a diaphanous gossamer of ice. Two forbidding claws of chitin and calcium carbonate are proffered with each, having been stripped from what are now little flipper arms in the front. Spherical black eyes are too simple to make accusations. The waitress runs through some rapidfire Japanese, pantomimes lifting a nigiri to her mouth, and makes an exaggerated chomp. She grins and points to one of the tails. "Fast!" She collects a few glasses, and is away.

Bolaño bites savagely through his prawn, dropping the head onto his plate. "Oh wow, that's—". He makes a slight face. "Imaginative." His countenance shifts. "Challenging." Hints of a smile. "Unsettling at first, but superb. The cold contrasts against the inside, which is somehow warm, almost liquid. Flash frozen with nitrogen? Leidenfrost effect?" There were no replies.

"I don't love the eyes," says Steve, picking up his nigiri. "Ew, it's so cold!"
Bolaño is harsh: "would you prefer to be served lukewarm sushi?"

Chelsea has picked up hers as well. "Oh, that is cold! I'm not sure I would want to bite into it with the vigor of our waitress."

Katz looks around. Other diners seem to have completed this course, with looks of pleasure. On every table he sees two little claws, and that alien head.

"These are langostino," identifies Chelsea. "Not quite a lobster, not quite a shrimp. They're delicious." She looks Katz in the eyes. "This has been such fun. Thank you for bringing me." She places the tail end into her mouth.

Steve gazes into his nigiri's eyes, perhaps attempting a mindmeld. Chelsea has closed her own with the staged rapture of women in stock photos. Katz has been holding his for less time, but is significantly more thermal. The thin layer of ice cracks. His eyes go wide. Katz's nigiri shudders from head to tail, exhuming itself. Sherman and Michael look at it, then at one another, and grok simultaneously. Katz appraises smiling Chelsea. Her lips remain closed around the creature. The table glows with light of horror and horniness and catastrophe. He winces. Michael, gleeful, looks to Steve with a savage grin.

Revived by the wattage of Steve's hands, his cryptolobster limply waves its declawed front legs in his face. Chelsea has a rougher time of it. At first, she registers only surprise and some confusion. Podomeres drag slowly across her warm tongue. Her panic's heat intensifies revivification. Steve drops his langostino. With effort, agonizingly slowly, it pushes forward. Katz knows the shriek is coming before it arrives, but it's still a wrenching thing. She bites through the reinvigorated arthropod; the back half is running blind, senseless, mindless in the hot hell of her mouth, legs slapping and lifting as she loudly weeps, swallowing it finally down. The degloved front arms beat uselessly against her long pale fingers. She looks at the dying head with utter revulsion before hurling it away. Steve's lobster has turned itself around about $\frac{2\pi}{3}$ rad, guided by instincts and sensations known only to *arthropoda,* and Steve pulls away from the table, lifting his feet like a little girl. Bolaño transfixes the entelechy with a fork. He regards his date with disgust.

Katz shrugs, bites the back half off of his live squat lobster, and puts down the head. Chelsea whimpers freely in the seat next to him. Eighteen patrons and the entirety of the staff stare. Katz stands to hug Chelsea, and she shakes her head violently, crying "no no no no." Strands of pink flesh hang from her mouth. Her color is not good.

They're home within a half hour. Chelsea showers, borrows a hoodie and some shorts, and enters fitful sleep. He covers her with a blanket, sighs, and settles in his Aeron. Several ice waters and a line clear his head. He opens up Vim and begins to code.

She rises around 0730h, shuffles over, and puts her arms around him. "I had fun last night. For most of it. Thank you for being a gentleman."

"There's no other way to live. You're beautiful when you're sleeping." He tries to kiss her, but she begs off, saying she needs brush her teeth. They walk to Starbucks, where she orders some ridiculous high-sugar beverage; Katz abstains, but covers the bill. "Would you like that bag? I didn't do any of it."

"You don't want it?"

"I'm not really a cocaine guy."

"How much do you want for it?"

"I mean, I paid $200..." He trails off.

"Oh sure, I can give you that." She takes ten twenties from her purse. They make the exchange.

"Alright well—"

"I'm going to need to work on a case today. I had a lot of fun last night, up until, you know."

"So did I." He sees the dream floating away, dissipating like a cloud of smoke. "Hey look, would you have any interest in banging it out before you leave?"

"Bang it out?" She laughs. "Not now. Maybe next time." She leans over and kisses him on the forehead, and departs. *Ne dederis mulieribus substantiam tuam, et vias tuas ad delendos reges.*

But next time he called she had a boyfriend, one she retained for three years. Katz was dating Oriana (of more later) by the time Chelsea had kicked him to the curb. Nonetheless, when she reached out, nostalgia and the chance to rectify bitter failure and that wicked 5'9 got the better of him. They met at BeetleCat for oysters. Still gorgeous, but visibly tired, she took down two Xanax and three drinks in less than an hour. Later, he finally bent her over that desk. They were both sloppy, and it was all rather underwhelming. The panties she forgot to put back on were discovered the next day by Oriana, leading to much anger, and hurt, and protracted suspicion, and distraction from code.

＊＊＊＊＊＊＊＊

The terms they'd received from Danylo were as punishing as expected. For $225,000 they would pay 5% on the remaining balance weekly, due at the beginning of the week, with the first 5% ($11,250) due immediately.

"So we walk away with $213,750, but owe $225,000?"

Danylo nodded. "Just so. Your man comes on Sunday with the green, give him the interest and any principal." He grinned. "No mandatory principal. Live on credit."

"Can I hit you up and ensure you got the right amount?"

"Of course, of course. Text."

He never suggested collateral. Katz supposed they'd been pretty solid customers, perhaps even partners. No, customers. Don't overestimate your relationship with these people. It's hazardous for your health, and hazardous for your sense of self.

They'd settled on West Midtown for the lab. Whether he got a ride from a friend or had to take a cab, Katz had himself deposited in the new Westside Provisions district, shockingly upscale relative to its surroundings. From there, he walked to the Goat Farm, where they rented three thousand square feet with good thick cement between their space and anyone else.

Ne...reges: Spend neither your strength on women, nor your vigor on those who ruin kings. Proverbs 31:3 (author's translation)

Until he locked in methodology and technique, he intended to work with not more than a gram of precursor at a time. There were two clocks on the cook: the brutal interest charged on the loan, and possible deterioration of his reagents when taken out of their ideal environments. He was resolved to take to completion the processing of any alkaloid he started handling. Total processing time for a given mass of reagent shouldn't take more than eighteen hours, and he hoped to get that time down to twelve or even ten. He didn't have sufficient equipment to effectively pipeline more than three batches; at eighteen hours, that limited him to a peak throughput of one batch per six hours, four batches in a full twenty-four hour cook. Only the last stage of the process could be left unattended, and that was a short stage; he would likely need to put in shifts of close to twenty-seven hours to handle three batches.

Figure ten hours following each shift for sleep and other necessary tasks, things that couldn't be done while watching reactions. That's a thirty-seven hour cycle, meaning only four per week, twelve batches. Limited to 1 g, a half key would be five hundred batches, something over nine months. He grinned. Getting faster would be useful; moving to larger batches would be absolutely necessary. Pulling in $75,000 per cycle meant three cycles to clear Danylo's principal. Every week until that time, he lost thousands of dollars. The ultimate catastrophe would be fucking up any significant amount of ergocristine.

Katz hadn't taken a vacation in his three years at the new job. He hadn't gone into the office in several months, but worked ten to twelve hours a day from home, whipping and driving C++. There wasn't anything of great importance going on there at the moment. He called in two weeks of PTO. Bolaño kindly drove him to the grocery store, and even helped him move in supplies. He built a cart of imitation crab meat, navel oranges, Skittles, four bags of BOGO Kroger private label Caesar Lite salad, and forty-eight TaB. He picked up two gallons of fluoridated water; he disliked the output of the Milli-Q. He picked up an eighth of an ounce of the best meth he could find. He picked up a carton of Newport shorts. He picked up a pack of five black Bics. He brought two cheap silicone pipes and an ounce of dank from home.

Katz turned on the lights, low-K affairs further attenuated via RC-3 spectral control glass, triple UV coated and double pane tempered, good for cleaning up 99% of wavelengths shorter than 600 nm. Alternated with these tubes, on another circuit, were long wavelength black lights. The tubes, covered with europium-doped SrB_4O_7 "BLB" phosphor, were capable of emitting UV-A with only a soft purple glow. This triggered florescence from even trace lysergamides, allowing one to follow the flow of material through chromatography columns, and to spot spills.

"You've got this. This is the real thing. This is what you've been trained for. You are America's best. Make us proud."

"I bow to none. Bring the fuckin' ruckus." Katz pulled the door closed. Katz drove the deadbolt home. Katz arranged totems and apparata.

"Immortal Chaos, wreathed with broken planets and dust, Lady Eris, who has Done it All, guide your proud servant. Help him find his own way."

Katz put on GZA's *Liquid Swords*.

Katz got to work.

16 erica marelli grows tired of bivalves

a	ü	c	t	g	H°	H	D	T	He
Li	Be	Na	Mg	K	Ca	Rb	Sr	Cs	Ba
B	C	N	O	F	Ne	Al	Si	P	S
Cl	Ar	Ga	Ge	As	Se	Br	Kr	In	Sn
Sb	Te	I	Xe	Tl	Pb	Bi	Po	At	Rn
Sc	Ti	V	Cr	Mn	Fe	Co	Ni	Cu	Zn
Y	Zr	Nb	Mo	Tc	Ru	Rh	Pd	Ag	Cd
La	Ce	Pr	Nd	Sm	Eu	Gd	Dy	Ho	Tm
Lu	Hf	Ta	W	Re	Os	Ir	Pt	Au	Hg
Ra	Ac	Th	Pa	U	Np	Pu	Am	Cm	Bk

"What do you think of this for the blotters?"

Michael glanced at it, started, shuddered, and looked up at Katz with distrust. "What's this offensive, vexing shape in the background?"

"I'm surprised you don't know it! Alexander's horned sphere. Taken with its interior space, it is a topological 3-sphere, thus simply connected. But the exterior is not simply connected! Thus the Schönflies theorem does not hold in three dimensions—the space is partitioned, but the exterior is not homeomorphic to the surface of the sphere. Classic counterexample in topology."

Bolaño frowned. "I don't remember that from the book." *Counterexamples in Topology* by Steen and Seebach is a mandatory read. Inspired by Gelbaum and Olmsted's *Counterexamples in Analysis,* the two form an extensive catalog of dashed hopes and idle dreams.

"The horned sphere was judged too evil a counterexample to include. Don't call up that which you can't put down."

"Where'd you hear about it?"

"I've actually been dreaming about it for years. I have these shitty dreams where I'm just riding around on garbage topologies."

Bolaño looked up at him, and lifted an eye. "Riding around on garbage topologies? Doing what?" He's never sure whether to believe these odd claims of Katz's. Generally it doesn't matter.

"Existing writ large. It sucks more than it sounds like. Anyway, I like the menacing aspect of it. It says to me 'these are not happygolucky shrooms. Price of admission: your mind.' Don't go thinking these are sixty-mic doses."

"I like how it ends in berkelium. Maybe it sends a false signal that the sheets originated at UCB."

"You really think so?"

"No, but let's do it anyway. a-u-c-t-g is I'm guessing—"

"Adenine, cytosine, guanine, thymine, uracil, of course."

"It could also be gluon, top, charmed, up with umlauts, and..."

"And a for asshole."

"Or axion." Bolaño squinted. "But why the umlauts on u?"

"Everybody loves umlauts. For every sheet there'll be some head who's, like, 'Give me the umlaut hit! It's full of power!' Maybe it points to German origin, in a Bolañoesque stroke of deception."

"But there's no umlaut in uracil."

"There is if your RNA is metal!" 🤘 🤘 🤘 🤘

"Heh. Fair enough. Why are they out of order?"

"I take a hardline stance against endorsement of alphabetical ordering of arbitrary English words as some kind of fundamental progression. A-C-G-T does not a periodic table make. If it's not astute, you must permute."

Bolaño handed it back. "I'd expect nothing less."

Read backwards, it's *GT chemistry über alles.* Easter eggs inside Easter eggs! Katz still seeks out the little delights in life.

✳ ✳ ✳ ✳ ✳ ✳ ✳ ✳ ✳

"The time has come, the Walrus said, to ferment our own goddamn ergot."

They had acquired two stainless steel 200 L bioreactors, hulking things adorned with tubular hookups and various analog scopes. Though not the same model nor even manufacturer, they were essentially similar devices. Rectangular and circular gauges that would have been at home in a 1972 Buick Electra, close to twenty of them, displayed measurements including dissolved oxygen and CO_2 content, temperature, fermentation mass, oxidation reduction potential, pH, pressure, and stirrer speed. Katz desperately wished to gut the monitoring system, replacing it throughout with digital reporting suitable for automated management. That would have taken time, probably more time (Bolaño had sensibly maintained) than Katz was suggesting, and then more time to write the necessary collection and visualization, and still more time to code (and especially test) the PID feedback controllers Katz was dreaming of. "And even after you did all that, we'd need a way to actually control things from your PID logic, which we do not have, and that would be mechanical work, at which we are not adept." For all their antediluvian analog nature, these were furthermore likely reliable and—more importantly—calibrated sensors, that

---

PID: proportional integral derivative

being after all a large difference between industrial bioreactors running tens of thousands of dollars and a $60 yogurt maker.

"I think it unwise to leave pressure management up to a $5 piece of shit ordered off Alibaba running through an Atmel AVR."

"An eight-bit processor is better than what we have now, which is nothing."

"These things have no way to do computerized monitoring? Couldn't you do computer vision on the gauges?"

Unbelievable. "Like with USB cameras and OpenCV?"

"Sure."

"You're worried about development time for PID controllers, and you want me to arrange and process camera feeds to extract monitoring data?"

"How hard can it be?"

"Simply setting up the cameras so that they get an accurate view of the necessary gauges, and aren't disrupted by tiny nudges of the computers, or gauges, or cameras, would be very difficult. I mean, I don't know how to do it, anyway. Maybe you could 3D print some kind of trellis that held the cameras, and was mounted to the reactor? Shouldn't take more than a few weeks of concentrated effort. Then just OpenCV that, which will surely not be completely unreliable, OpenCV being known for its robust and industrially-applicable algorithms and not being whatever unmaintained garbage PhD students need to shove their dissertations out the door."

Bolaño shrugs. "Ceded."

"You can get their proprietary management console, if you want to spend thirty thousand dollars, and if they still make them for these older models, and by the way you'll need two because of our heterogeneous reactors."

"Well how does the proprietary system work?"

"Ummm...I don't know. I'm not even certain they exist."

"I'll look. If they're getting a signal out to a console, we ought be able to grab that signal, and interpret it. Same deal with any kind of control they export. A small matter of reverse engineering."

"Unless they built in DRM with certs."

"What, like they have a CA on each side, and each participant has to present a certificate signed by that CA?"

"Yes, Michael, that's how certificates work."

"You ought just be able to replace the CA then, no?"

Katz sighs. "'Ought.' It depends on how tamper-resistant they made the thing. If it's burned into a proper TPM, and they properly check for presence of a TPM electronically, you're talking about modding ICs, which is some NSA shit if it can be done at all."

"But such might not even be present."

"The entire conjectured I/O system might not be present."

Bolaño sighs. "So what's the cost of not having automation here? We lose a crop? 200L is generating us about four grams in two weeks, so that's possibly substantial, I guess."

"The cost could be a pressure buildup followed by detonation, catastrophic loss of all equipment, damage to facility and subsequent litigation, uncontrolled distribution of highly toxic ergot alkaloids and other reagents and subsequent litigation, not to mention certain attention of law enforcement and subsequent federal and/or state assfuckery." Katz pauses. "And other days it just rains. Indeed, many things do come to pass."

"So first off, we don't want to grow true ergot. It basically doesn't produce alkaloids in a fermentarium. You want *C. paspali* or *Aspergillus fumigatus,* though the latter doesn't produce D-LSA naturally, if I recall correctly. It normally just drops inactive clavines. I think—don't quote me on this, yet—that they both go to chanoclavine, and then EasA isomerase takes you to the lysergic path, whereas EasA reductase goes to festuclavine. But they were able to transfer EasH and CloA genes into it, not sure how, and that's the current dancehall winner in terms of recoverable alkaloid per volume."

"Eas?"

"Ergot alkaloid synthesis gene. CloA is clavine oxidase."

Michael nods. "What's the upshot?"

"Well, again I'm not expert in any of this. AP Biology was ten years ago, and not really applicable. We ought be able to get alkaloid, and I think we ought start with *Paspali.* But there's some biosynthetic path, with intermediates. It starts at tryptophan, and ends with alkaloids. One wonders why you can't combine a biosynthetic and synthetic approach, where you get as far as you can synthetically, then dump a lot of that intermediate into your broth, and have it go to town from somewhere a stage or two into the process. Addition of L-tryptophan jukes up alkaloid production, to a point.

But can you go further than that? Can you extract the relevant enzymes and just run the reaction on a substrate? I don't know, but any such win could drastically improve our efficiency. For instance, D-LSA is almost always an intermediate on the way to an alkaloid. That final transition has got to be some enzyme, coded for by some gene. Can we remove that gene, and thus harvest D-LSA directly, rather than having to do a hydrolysis step? That would save time during chemistry, it would save time during fermentation, and it would save energy inside the biologicals."

"So how do you intend to investigate this?"

"Shitfire, how does one investigate anything? Take OpenVPN into a box on the GT network, find relevant papers, download them, read them, become confused, go find the papers necessary to understand the first bunch you downloaded, download them, repeat until you're smarter. Then go try shit out and find all the ways it breaks down in the real world compared to the Elysium of grad students."

"Go with God and other felicitous sources. I have news. Friends from the West, well-heeled friends living lives of sybaritic leisure, are interested in a bulk purchase. At what price will you let me take away your excess?"

"Really? That's great! What kind of bulk?"

"All."

"Whoa." Michael nods, clearly pleased with himself. "What are you going to charge them?"

"That depends on what you intend to charge me."

"So I move to Cloud at $0.25 per 100 µg. That's $2,500 a gram. I'd retail at maybe $10 per 300 µg if I'm feeling generous. That's thirty-three large a gram. So somewhere between those two."

Negotiations have thus far centered around a key for ten megs. It would be a banked transfer, or series of transfers, immediately useful, no bullshit piles of cash. Bolaño has his eye on a stately home in Buckhead's Tuxedo Park.

"I was hoping to come in under Cloud's price, actually."

Katz laughs. "Fuck outta here. Why would I do that?"

"Trying to sell it through Cloud would reveal that you're skimming substantial portions of their ergocristine yields, unless you sold him on some alternative precursor source. I can't see you retailing that much LSD yourself. It's of no use to you. I'll take all you want to give me at $1,000 per gram."

"I don't think so." Katz can't decide whether to be offended. "$2,500, which I'm not necessarily offering, is a fantastic price. No way do you come close to losing money on that."

"My budget works at $1,000 per gram. Keep it in mind."

They meet one another's eyes. Bolaño's analysis is on point. Katz doesn't relish the idea of finding sinks for hundreds of kilodoses. At the same time, he's not thrilled about the idea of being fucked in the ass.

"There's no reason why I can't tell the SYNCOPE people I found new precursors. They wouldn't give a shit, so long as they're getting acid. That's actually better for them: they hold onto their ergocristine in case I get hit by a bus."

"How would you go back to their ergocristine, once you'd sold the surplus?" Fucker. "You've thought this through, I see."

"It's not difficult analysis, Sherman."

"I tell them my source ran dry. There you go."

"And just keep doing that? At some point they're going to find a Merck manual and sit around, furrowing their brows in a great orgy of what passes for thought up there, and realize you've been fucking them. Look, I'm not trying to be a dick, but my people, like most people who buy and sell drugs, expect a volume discount. You can keep what you want, and dump whatever other volume you have through me for $1,000 per gram. Just think about it."

"Not being a dick? How do you figure, sports fan? You're clearly exploiting inside information acquired though friendship."

"I'm not forcing anything. I'm providing you with a sales opportunity. You can take it or leave it, with my blessings either way."

"Banked money?" Katz is hopeful.

"We've never sent transactions between us. I don't propose we start now."

"No, you wouldn't, would you?"

✳ ✳ ✳ ✳ ✳ ✳ ✳ ✳

Katz was pacing in the green area between Klaus (CS) and van Leer (EE) reading Stacey's *Fusion Plasma Physics* when he noticed a furor by the stairs up to the College of Computing and its underground Chemistry Annex. Three obvious undergraduates, agitated, boys all, formed an angry squawking cluster around an older girl, pushing thirty perhaps but clad in accouterments that screamed "student." She clutched in gangly arms a sizable laptop and several textbooks;

in black Doc Martens she stood erect despite a visibly overloaded backpack. Weary, but not dispirited; emphatic, but not angry; she wore the face a billion other women wear when accosted by men too imperceptive to take them seriously. One boy had a bowl haircut last stylish fifteen years ago; another wore a baseball hat backwards atop a patrician visage, and might as well have had FRAT tattooed across his forehead. The third had the cargo shorts and piggish eyes common to unintelligent dorks, kids—usually in-state admits—who knew too much about *Star Wars* and not enough about calculus.

She's thinner than he trends, but Katz is happy to make exceptions for women of intelligence, audacity, and sophistication, or even just one of those traits. Besides, check out those braids. Two weeks earlier, Katz had unceremoniously dumped a video game musician specializing in retro chiptune. He had been—and remained—all for her big black glasses and the contrast made against her blonde hair, and enjoyed getting her high and introducing the *Maniac Mansion* and *Ninja Gaiden* NES soundtracks.

"Fuck me, this was eight bits? How'd they do this?"

"Keiji Yamagishi and George Sanger are masters of their craft."

"I know George Sanger! He did SimCity 2000!"

"SimCity 2000 had music?" He threw on "Rugged Terrain," from the first *Gaiden's* level 2-2, and she just about lost her mind.

Alas, she was essentially unread, and said shockingly stupid things with disturbing frequency ("China has a coast?" "They speak Swiss in Switzerland, right?" "Who's Jane Austen?"). Contempt had built quickly. She asked him "it's Friday night; what do you want to do?"

"I think I want to read, get pretty high."

"Want me to come read with you?"

"No, I realized today I just kinda want to read, maybe be something of a monk, live the ascetic life."

"Music's a very important part of aesthetics."

"Good God and baby Jesus. I wish you the best. I left a shirt over there; it says DON'T IMMANENTIZE THE ESCHATON. I don't need it back, but if it's convenient for you to get it back to me, I wouldn't mind. But don't go out of your way. I hope you have a really fun time tonight."

"Are you breaking up with me?"

"It's not the flowery language of Mr. Darcy, but, you know."

"I know what?!"

"Well, you don't, rather. I've got to go. If you need weed going forward I can hook you up with my boy Vladimir."

But this woman appears to be a TA. Edging closer, it becomes apparent that she runs some undergraduate chemistry class.

"No, the Gibbs free energy is the *maximum* amount of work the system is going to do, not including pressure-volume work. And it only applies to closed systems. It's completely inapplicable here."

One of the yos, he with eyes porcine, starts to argue back.

"And furthermore, the temperature of that equilibrium state would be delta H over T delta S. This is all wrong. You applied the wrong logic and then evaluated that logic incorrectly. And the fact that all three of you did the same thing just makes me think you copied said incorrect logic. There will be no regrading."

She turned on her booted heel and began walking away. Katz caught up with her and shot his shot. "I admire the lack of shit you took from those assholes."

"Ugh! If they put half the effort into their basic chem that they do bitching about it, they'd be doing fine. Do I know you?"

"Sherman Spartacus Katz." He extended a hand; she shook it. "Here doing some masters degrees. Was here for undergraduate years ago. And you are?"

"Erica Marelli. Chem undergrad at Berkeley. PhD now, masters a bit ago. 'Some masters degrees?' As in more than one?" She stomped along quickly; he had no trouble keeping up, but was aware of the effort.

"Yeah, I'm doing computer science and NukeE."

She laughed, and coughed. "Fucking pollen. NukeE, huh? You don't hear that very often."

"I don't see any future for our species without fusion. I wanted to get behind the effort. Every field can use a few good computer scientists, for simulations if nothing else."

"And what do you simulate?"

"Whatever needs simulating." He smiled. "For NRE, mostly fusion burning, but also some neutron transport. But hey!" He stops and looks her in the eyes. She does not stop, and a moment later he breaks into a speedy walk to catch back up. "I am a tremendous fan of intelligent women who stand their ground, especially when they wear kickass boots, and very much especially when they boast intriguing hair, which your hair intrigues to the max, doubleplusintrigue. Is your day over? Would you allow me to get you a drink and learn more about Mlle Marelli, previously of Berkeley? Assuming you drink."

"Oh, I drink." She laughs, only somewhat cautiously. "Where?"

"How about the Vortex on Peachtree? Right up the hill basically."

"I've been there. I'm down. So explain to me, Mr. CS and NukeE, why aren't we fusing things yet?"

Katz takes a deep breath. "Why aren't we fusing things yet. A minilecture." He fights the urge to light a cigarette; they can turn a lot of girls off in 2009. She'll obviously learn that he smokes eventually, but that doesn't mean one has to get oneself filtered before demonstrating compelling and compensating worth elsewise. Katz strives at all times to compensate and to compel.

They descend the tall outdoor staircase running under the southern wing of the Klaus Advanced Computing Building a/k/a the Fortress of Computation. As one emerges from underneath the skybridge, clear lines of sight open up on the left, where Ferst curves north and up, separating Klaus from Ford Environmental S&T, Molecular S&E, and two biotechnology buildings. Elevated twenty meters, Ferst runs once more west, past Biological S., Physics, the old College of Computing (now some kind of jungle gym for overgrown children; serious work is done in Klaus), and NanoT. Back behind Nanotech and its cleanrooms (and you can bet Katz keeps meaning to get access to some of the toys in Nanotech), where there now looms a motherfucking parking deck, stood until 1996 the

---

S&T/S&E: Science and Technology/Engineering, c'mon buddy

Neely Nuclear Research Center and (courtesy Walter Zinn and the General Nuclear Engineering Corporation) its 5 MW knockoff of Argonne's CP-5. Press F for respects.

Behind Physics and the CoC sit Microelectronics, Electrical E, Civil E, and Chemical E. Finally a "Sustainable Design" building—Katz is unsure what exactly goes down inside; he vaguely recalls it previously being a frat?—and three gigantic Manufacturing Research Centers, one of them with a phenomenal wave pool where they do kraken research or something. On the roof of Electrical are numerous satellite dishes. As an undergraduate Katz would sometimes sleep on their bases, shielding him from the sun, but was eventually driven away by angry Eastern European research staff. They descended the Klaus staircase, and before them opened up a gently rising hill dividing baseball nonsense from a few Greek houses. Soaring above the hill's crest, should you lift your aspie eyes from the ground, should you raise your skinny fists like antennae to heaven, are the skyscrapers of Midtown Atlanta. As you walk, so towards them you rise. *Ascendenteque Modulatione ascendat Gloria Regis.*

"You know what deuterium and tritium are?"

"Yeah, ^{2}H and ^{3}H, hydrogen with neutrons."

"Aye. D and T. Do you know why they're relevant?"

"They want to do D-T fusion, but I don't know why." Erica Marelli frowned.

"So fusing hydrogen means fusing heavy hydrogen, unless you're at the scale of a star. I don't mean heat and pressure, but amount of material and timescale. Proton-proton fusion is incredibly rare under all conditions."

"Yeah how does that even happen? Protons are fusing with neutrons in the sun, right?"

"Where are protons going to find neutrons in the sun?"

"That's a good point."

"Well, actually, you're right in a way. So proton-proton fusion to a diproton isn't that rare at all, actually. The problem is that the diproton decays pretty much immediately back to two protons. But, every so often, very rarely, you get a β^+ before the decay. Proton becomes neutron, diproton becomes deuterium, virtual W boson goes out or doesn't, quite, but either way you end up with a positron and a piece of shit neutrino. Deuterium plus another proton gets you helium-3. Two of those give you an alpha and two protons. But that β^+ is incredibly infrequent, due to the strong nuclear force being so much faster than the weak nuclear force. So you need a star's worth of material to get substantial energy output."

"And then those feed the triple alpha process."

"Yep. Triple because two alphas form ^{8}Be, which decays in attoseconds. You need a third to get up in there and hit the Hoyle resonance of ^{12}C."

"Protons: out. Heavy hydrogen: in. Makes sense, even just from an electromagnetic argument."

"So most of your energetic fusion reactions, especially the ones that happen at lower temperatures, output a neutron. D-T neutrons carry about 80% of

---

Ascendenteque...Regis: as the modulation rises, so may the King's glory.
J. S. Bach, Musikalisches Opfer BMV 1079 (*The Musical Offering, 1747*)

the MeVs, leaving three point five two for the alpha. D-D goes to tritium plus proton half the time, and the other half to helium-3 and a neutron, this one with 75% of the energy. T-T gives you two neutrons. Your most energetic charged products all come from helium-3 fusion, aside from p-boron fusion. But p-boron ignition temperatures are waaaaay up there, and helium-3 isn't exactly easy, either. At about a billion kelvins you fuse deuterium and helium-3 more rapidly than you do D-D, but D-T still kicks its ass—nothing beats D-T at any temperature."

"Why does D-D run so much slower than D-T? That's never made sense to me. The lowest energy state of two protons and two neutrons is regular helium, right?" Katz nods. "So the easiest way to get a helium-4 would be two hydrogen-2s. Instead, you never get a helium from two deuterons, and instead you get it from D-T."

"Good question! You get it from D-D a vanishingly small portion of the time, actually. Here's what's up: you fuse two deuterons, and there's a shitton of energy released due to the change in binding energies, right?" Katz is absolutely overwhelmed with attraction and desire and lust.

Erica nods vigorously. "Sure, otherwise why are you doing it?"

"Why indeed. So where does that energy go? You can kick out a neutron, a proton, or a gamma ray—"

"Why can't it go into the kinetic energy of the helium?"

"Wouldn't conserve momentum. Same reason you can't have pair production in empty space."

"Oh duh, cheerfully withdrawn."

"The strong interaction is much faster than the electromagnetic—reaction speed is a function of the gauge coupling constant. So you're much more likely to lose a nucleon, and become either T or helium-3."

"And why does D-T fuse so much more easily than D-D? Is it because of more strong nuclear force effect due the extra neutron?" Erica sparks a Camel Light with the elegance and savoir faire and promotion of eratomania with which graceful women smoke.

"You'd think that might be the case. But the half-life of helium-5 is measured in yottoseconds, whereas helium-4 and even helium-3 are stable. So you don't get more stable by just heaping on neutrons. Otherwise there wouldn't be beta decay, where neutron flips to proton."

"Oh hrmmm you're right."

"Because—"

She already has it, though: "Ahhh, that's where you get into the shell model of the nucleus, right? Hence magic numbers, two, eight, twenty, etc., right, right." She's clearly annoyed at herself for not having it immediately.

"Note helium-4 is doubly magic. Have you taken quantum?" In his mind he has already sworn love to, married, and had children by this woman. Strapping offspring with big powerful thighs and elaborate braids that know their f-block elements and kill anyone that looks at them cockeyed.

She shakes her head. "I took p-chem and did a q-chem seminar. Nothing nuclear, though, just Schrödinger for electrons through the Born-Oppenheimer approximation, VB and MO, motivation for the various orbitals. The q-chem seminar had a big emphasis on computational methods: density functional theory, lots of Monte Carlo. She said at the beginning, 'you can't solve any of this stuff analytically, so we throw big computers at it.' Which meant Python and MATLAB all semester." She's deliciously smart. Maybe they'll bang it out today. "Which on my laptop ran very slowly."

Thirstily, but with childish joy: "You smoke? Oh awesome, I do too." Into his step is infused a sprig. Frabjous day! If she smokes, she pokes. With perhaps a bit too much enthusiasm: "Do you need a bigger computer? We could build you a dank machine for cheaper than you think. We can paint it pastel and call it recombinator and you can crank out hella GPU code on it." He imagines their happy family warming themselves in the winter around a rack full of 2U compute nodes. They live somewhere very cold. Katz reckons few competing males can offer a better FLOPS-per-dollar proposition. He's not at all above paying for the machine himself it it comes to that—love ain't free—but will still want to highlight the value. He will win her eternal devotion with the offer of faster and larger *ab initio* simulations, and the promise of still more impressive ones to come. That they may never hook up is unworthy of consideration.

"Oh no, I don't do any of that kind of work, and the last thing I want is a big computer in my apartment." Devastating. A spear through his dreams. He is trapped in the belly of a horrible machine, and the machine is bleeding to death. Their children are machinegunned by *Einsatzgruppen* and their corpses violated by dogs.

"I schedule BLAST and HMMER3," pronouncing it 'heemer three,' "all day long, but I run that through the biolab computers."

"Do they have GPUs? I know there's active work on accelerating BLAST." He has never seen hair braided like hers outside of Ukraine features in *The Economist*. Ruefully, he concedes that it is unlikely he'll ever be positioned to hook up with the leader of the Orange Revolution, though he's considered writing her a tasteful *billet-doux*, or maybe sending a classy telegram. YULIA, FUSION SEEKS TO BRING THE SUN TO EARTH, BUT ONLY YOU CAN BE MY *SONECHKO*. GET DEM BRAIDS+DAT ASS TO AMERICA. *POKAZATY, DE RAKY ZYMUYUT.*

She smiles. "What do you know about BLAST?"

Advantage Katz! "Ahh, I have a few decent chunks of code in NCBI BLAST. I've done a lot of work in automata-based search over on the CS side, and bioinformatics was an obvious place to apply that, so I did some work on it." Improving fundamental, ubiquitous tools in other fields is just something one does. "I've worked on some of the Smith-Waterman implementations, too." She seems dazzled. This seems to be going well. It's why one puts in the work.

"What is Smith-Waterman?"

"BLAST is stochastic, and uses heuristics. Smith-Waterman is guaranteed to find an optimal alignment—it's an adaptation of Needleman-Wunsch—but

---

VB: valence bond   **MO:** molecular orbital
Einsatzgruppen: lit. "deployment groups" motorized *Schutzstaffel* death squads
BLAST: basic local alignment search tool   **HMMER:** hidden Markov model, err, er
sonechko: Сонечко lit. "little sun" (term of endearment)
pokazaty...zymuyut: Показати, де раки зимують i'll show you where crayfish spend winter

it's much slower, and requires way more memory. It's not an exhaustive search, but it's not a fast search. BLAST almost always gets you what you want."

"Oh, yeah, I think our system runs BLAST, and if it doesn't like the result, gives you the option to run a longer matching algorithm."

"Then that's almost certainly a Smith-Waterman backend. I didn't know you could evaluate the quality of a BLAST match, neat."

"That's got to be heuristics."

"Definitely." He nods thirstily. "So what's up, Mlle Marelli? What goes on in your mind? Do you have a boyfriend?"

She laughs easily. "I do, but not for long." She looks at him and sees undeserved triumph, and corrects herself. "Not because of you, dumbass. I'm most likely breaking up with him when he gets back into town Thursday."

"Ought I ask?"

"No, you ought get back to the minilecture. You were asking if I'd taken quantum, which I'm guessing you've taken."

"Not competently, and long ago. You're...twenty-three?"

"Twenty-seven. Second year of PhD." Older than most second year PhDs.

"I turned eighteen while taking Quantum I, right back there—" pointing behind them in the direction of Howey Physics—"and it feels like half a lifetime ago. Which I suppose it was. And I'm twenty-nine."

A woman in a severe pantsuit passes between them, giving them both dirty looks and coughing. She takes a few steps further, then turns and cries, "this is a non-smoking campus!"

"We're outside, ma'am, thank you!" Erica puts a bit of a singsong on the last words; the "ma'am" is hard, guttural. Neither of them turn.

From behind: "Bitch."

Erica whips around, her bag following only slowly, a densepack; Katz worries that its momentum might carry her into traffic. "Filter my shit you clam-faced whore! Go fart up your Subaru!" Her invective is louder and carries more authentic pique than is really appropriate, but Katz believes in going hard or going home, and explodes into laughter.

"Did you just suggest her to be a bivalve?" Whether the receding and probably outmatched subject hears this cannot be determined. Erica sounds like she might one day require beta blockers. Katz figures any woman willing to yell "clam-faced whore" down a busy sidewalk will probably excuse a fair amount of bizarre behavior on the part of the sufficiently interesting.

"So I was asking about quantum because I wanted to know what you know about square wells and harmonic oscillators—"

"Not a thing."

He smiles. He's doing a lot of smiling. "Doesn't matter, save to justify why the nuclear shell numbers do not exactly match the VSEPR numbers."

Her face darkens. "Well, that's pretty obvious, right? Your electron orbitals are defined by different quantum numbers." She's looking at him with ferocity and haughtiness now, an entirely different attitude, one closer to that she wore

---

VSEPR: valence shell electron pair repulsion

while sniping at the mehums minutes ago. Katz thinks this pretty undeserved—he certainly knows about the different quantum numbers; he's been leading this little dance; she hasn't caught him up in any mistakes. *Feisty,* he thinks, *needlessly aggressive. Feisty* is one of those words applied to women for behavior that doesn't raise an eyebrow from men, and he wonders if he's being sexist. If a man reacted as she had, Katz feels it would have seemed just as *aggressive,* though he'd probably not call it *feisty.* And it's not, like, a bad thing—the word seems gender-correlated, but not pejorative. Katz doesn't like the idea of her thinking she scored on him, but only because he hadn't fucked up? She continues: "There's not going to be an analog to the principal quantum number. And your protons and neutrons have their own ladders."

"You seem to understand this all just fine. Certainly at least as well as I do."

She becomes friendly once more. "What I don't get is why the ladders diverge once you get to larger shells."

"Different well potentials. Neutrons don't have electromagnetic repulsion fucking theirs up. Not that the square well potential is expected to reflect reality or anything, but the maths tend to work alright."

"That makes sense."

Having cleared the hill, they cross the Connector into Tech Square. Management majors, on average significantly more attractive (and certainly better dressed) than the rest of the student body, swarmed around them in preppy, sanguine groups, none looking like they'd been up all night, practically radiating health and hireability and generally successful adaptation. Erica's eyes weren't circled so darkly nor sunken so steeply as Katz's, but they had clearly seen sunrises. Katz wondered what she tasted like after forty hours awake sweating over peptide chemistry, skin dried out from cigarettes and dehydration and stress. He loved nothing more than cheering on an upscale, brilliant girl as she cleared the far side of some body- and mind-wrecking effort; he'd watch her fly close to the line of exhaustion, growing intensely aroused, then feed her a few shots and fuck her to sleep like some incubal valkyrie. Afterwards he sat naked next to her wearied, innocent sleeping form, reading Proust or Gaddis or something else interminable, maybe good ol' Baudelaire for *la quatre-vingt-seize fois,* patting her head.

"So that's one major problem. Most of your reaction energy goes with the neutron. It's hard to make electricity from neutrons, they're a biological hazard and moderately hard to block, they don't add their energy back to the plasma, and they activate your shit. Activation just means—"

"Something catches a neutron and becomes a radioactive isotope, probably decaying by beta some time later."

"Or gamma, or both. The secondary radiation isn't even the biggest problem; the big deal is that you traumatize your materials. So you either need to fuse a bunch of deuterium to generate helium-3—but half of those result in a tritium, which is going to immediately fuse with the deuterium, yielding your regular D-T neutron. Everything else—deuterium with lithium, tritium with helium-3, proton with lithium-7—they all have neutron paths. Proton with lithium-6 goes to 3- and 4-helium, but with precious little energy output. Then you've got proton plus boron, but that requires serious heat; you probably can't get there with magnetohydrodynamics. The inertial confinement people at LLNL-NIF talk it up, but ICF is really mostly about subcritical weapons testing. Anyway this is all political bullshit."

"How do you mean?"

"It's not a real problem. You've got ^{238}U out the ass, and you're using it for nothing better than, like, GAU-8 rounds and tank sabots and shit. You're basically throwing away all its power as an actinide. Instead, you blanket your D-T fusion with ^{238}U to produce ^{239}Pu, or even thorium for ^{233}U. Thermalize your neutrons, let that shit soak 'em up 'til they're smellin' sweeter than a plate of yams and become something useful. Now you're taking that 14 MeV neutron and turning it into a potential 180 MeV of actinide fission. You burn the resulting material, maybe there—you're gonna be fissioning some of that ^{239}Pu no matter what—maybe in fission plants after chemical extraction, whatever. Maybe you even burn it in such a way that it helps keeps your plasma hot, since you're otherwise only dumping the 3 MeV alphas into it. Also, you can blanket the actinide layer with lithium, take your fission neutrons, and now you've got an exothermic reaction whose products are valuable helium, plus a D and T which you need for your original fusion fuel. Fusion-fission-fusion."

"Sick! So why don't we do that?"

"We can't run the initial fusion reaction yet. But assume they get the laser problems worked out, or someone shits out a working tokamak or stellarator. You've then got proliferation concerns, and you're no longer 'clean energy.' You're a dirty-ass fission plant once more. Except fission plants are pretty goddamn clean, especially from a carbon standpoint. And you're almost certainly doing D-T fusion, so you've got radiation issues anyway, due to the fucking neutrons. But people get all up their own assholes about plutonium."

"Is plutonium a bigger deal than uranium?"

"Much bigger. Your 'default' plutonium isotope is fissile. Not true for uranium. So plutonium only needs chemical separation, rather than isotope enrichment. Way easier. Much smaller critical mass, also."

"If you can build a fusion reactor, surely you can already make nuclear bombs?"

"Nope. Nobody's come up with a pure-fusion weapon. Every thermonuclear bomb ever built had an atomic bomb to get the party started, and every atomic bomb requires a core of fissile material. It's collecting those kilograms of ^{233}U or ^{235}U or ^{239}Pu that keeps the Red Hat Ladies from becoming nuclear powers."

"If you need a nuclear bomb to initiate the fusion, how can you have a fusion plant without a nuclear bomb?"

"You need a nuclear bomb to initiate the fast, self-perpetuating thermonuclear burn necessary for a thermonuclear bomb. You certainly don't need one to just fuse a few ions up. You can fuse D-T like six different ways, but most of them require way more energy input than they yield. How new are you to Atlanta? Do you know your way around?" Katz steers them northeast as 5th deadends into West Peachtree in front of the Neo-Georgian Biltmore Hotel.

LLNL-NIF: Lawrence Livermore National Lab National Ignition Facility
GAU-8: Gun Aircraft Unit 8/A 30mm Avenger

"I came here in 2006 from California to do a masters in bioinformatics. Mark Borodovsky here is one of the world's best. Wrote the only textbook the field had for its first years."

"I know Borodovsky. That BLAST stuff I mentioned earlier was kinda with him. He suggested it, anyway."

"So I came here and did three years in Home Park, which was exciting, then I moved to Castleberry Point right as they opened in 2008." Katz indicates with a face that he's unfamiliar with the property. "It's southwest Downtown, just south of the Georgia Dome. Not a bad area—I wouldn't want to live in core Downtown, but access to roads is shitty. Unless I want to get on the highway, which is easy. Getting over to GT when I drive is always annoying and takes fifteen minutes more than it ought. I take MARTA a lot, but it puts me on the wrong fucking side for everything at Tech, and the closest station to me is Five Points, and over there you know MARTA stands for Motherfuckers are Touching my Ass." Katz laughs. "My building's great; it's all GSU kids, and black kids from Morehouse and Spelman, and some GT people, most of us in grad school and a bit older. I've lived there two years now. I think I'm going to move soon, though."

"So directly east from your place is going to be Oakland Cemetery and Cabbagetown, right? Once you cross the highway."

"Yeah." Another hill, and they stand on Peachtree. "And the Vortex is right up there," pointing north. She heads that way without waiting for confirmation. "I want to come over to Midtown. My boyfriend lives over here, down on 12th, and I crash over here all the time. Sometimes I stay at his place just because I can easily walk to school."

Katz points downhill to the southwest. "I'm living on Myrtle, a few blocks that way. I've been there for about three years. I'm going to buy right over here once I'm done with my masters."

"A condo or a house?"

"Condo. I'm not sure enough about final destinations to buy a house, and they're all a century old around here, even if they've been refurbished inside, and it sounds like a lot of work, and I like it cold and they'd be expensive to cool. I'll want to keep a base of operations here, though." They provide licenses to the notoriously ID-intensive Vortex and take a table outside. Both light cigarettes; there are plastic black ashtrays at each table. The ashtrays are deep, and of less radius than Katz would prefer, but the staff are industrious. One rarely ends up with beer in the ashtray, nor a layer of extinguished butts with its hint of stale nidor, where one must stub out one's most recent cigarette into its fallen brethren, running the risk of reanimating a reasty zombie cigarette replete with a graveolent redolence. The owners are known to run a tight ship, specializing in freshly-shined wingtip oxfords with which slackers are booted back into Midtown. The drinks are strong, and the bartenders worth looking at. It is an institution in a city with too few of them.

Across Peachtree, tucked in an asphalt bay surrounded by condo towers of thirty-plus stories, sits Bulldogs, as it has since 1978. Most clubs have been knocked off the Midtown Mile—legendary Backstreet gave way to Viewpoint, Club Kaya to 1010 Midtown—but there sits Bulldogs like Morla, the turtle from

Die unendliche Geschichte. Every night until precisely three am, the blackest, gayest young men of Atlanta congregate, and the place rocks. Whenever Katz overhears visitors from other cities or the suburbs discussing where to eat, he inserts himself and puts in a hard sell on behalf of Bulldogs. Perhaps they'll be educated or even a little liberated by the experience.

"So you're twenty-seven, but second-year PhD? But you did a masters for two years? Was your masters not part of your PhD? Most PhD people seem to go directly from undergraduate into their program." Unstated: *masters are typically intense terminal degrees for domestic students, systems for extracting wealth from (generally wildly unfit) internationals, or consolation prizes for failed doctorates.* A waitress emerges. "I'm paying, if that's cool?"

"I certainly assumed you're paying. I don't want to pay." She looks offended, but Katz judges it an affectation. Katz opts for a Cape Cod and a Redheaded Slut and a Diet Coke; Erica requests a vodka soda and a tequila shot; Katz nods appreciatively. "My masters was in bioinformatics, and I wasn't planning on going into PhD at the time. I declared MCB—"

"Micro cellular biology?"

"Molecular and cell biology. Shut up. So I grew up in Savannah."

"Savannah, Georgia? Savannah Country Day?"

"No, the African savanna, *shut up.* And yes, SCDS, how did you know? Never mind. Immaterial. I head off to Berkeley, I kick the shit out of freshman year, and get into MCB. It's impacted, so that's hard to do if you didn't declare it on your application." She stubs out her cigarette and drops her eyes to the ashtray for a moment. "My first semester I thought I wanted to do accounting, hah."

"What made you pick out cellular biochemistry instead?"

"You know what it was, to large degree? This is 2003, and everyone wants to be a computer scientist. Everybody wants to build web pages and be the next Google. There's big Stanford envy due to Google coming out of Stanford instead of Berkeley. Still is. And I was like, 'all these brilliant people are off to build virtual dogshit; no one's doing anything real.' I killed it in freshman chemistry and physics, and had always been great at math, so let's go to enzyme school." Their drinks arrive; Erica lifts her tequila, nods to Katz, and toasts "to staying positive and testing negative." The waitress chuckles, and takes away the small glass. Katz asks quickly, "want a car bomb?"

"Oh god, sure, why not."

"You want one?" The waitress looks up and down the street, as if she might see her boss there. "Sure."

"Three carbombs! Thank you." She departs. "On that note—" Katz looks around. "Since you've got this illfated boyfriend I guess it doesn't matter, but I'll admit I've allowed like fifteen percent of my brain to simulate our potential intercourse—"

"Sexual intercourse?"

"No, Intercourse, Pennsylvania. Aye, retreating and smoking bowls and making out, perhaps proceeding to aforementioned intercourse."

"Why only fifteen percent?" She starts in on her vodka.

Die...Geschichte: Michael Ende, The Neverending Story (1979)

"I figure conversation with you might require thirty or even thirty-five percent. I'm using the other fifty percent to think about image compression."

"Thirty sounds fine for our discourse, maybe, but I think you need more to comprehend our intercourse."

"These numbers were merely illustrative." Katz waves them off with a hand. "Mlle Marelli, you were ventilating contempt for my field, and I think about to brag about your grade point average. Please continue. Oh! No! Wait." Katz drains half his Cape Cod. "I interrupted you for a reason. Intercourse! So yeah, I have in my time been the lucky recipient of HSV2, and in a spirit of herping it forward rather than merely herping it back, have demonstrated my ability to spread it. One could say I'm weaponized."

She laughs loudly. "I have herpes and had no intention of telling you, but thanks. That's actually very chivalrous. Thank you." She stands and leans over and kisses him. "Which is not to say we are going to take our simplexviruses to the park and let them meet one another."

"Do you refer to intercourse? Or some kind of MCB ritual of which I am unaware? Let it be known I'm interested either way."

"Intercourse. I haven't decided about that yet."

"If you decide no, can we still do the herpes play date?" Walking past, a black man looks them over, startled. That evening he will ask his wife, "do you know what kind of wypipo bullshit I overheard this afternoon?"

"You need to finish the fusion lecture. *Not* right now, I'm telling my story. So I start up my MCB track, and there's this professor there, Jennifer Doudna, and she's amazing. I have zero doubt that she is going to win a Nobel down the line. Brilliance just radiates forth from her. Basic patent energy. I love her. And so I tear up the MCB program, and I was doing undergrad research with her, and thinking I'm going to do my PhD there at UCB. I graduate and there's, there's something of a stigma about doing your BA and PhD at the same place. They're like, there's so much value in establishing networks at two institutions, we strongly recommend it; why don't you wait a year and make sure you really want to do this?" And Jennifer privately lets me know that she's likely leaving for Genentech soon, which would not be great for my PhD. Janice Chen and Rachel Haurwitz and Stan Qi were about to finish up, and she wasn't taking PhD students in the interim."

The vodka soda is demolished. "So I say fine, I'll do just that. And she did indeed leave for Genentech, just last year. Where she stayed for two months. She's already back at UCB. But, here's the thing. I graduate, and I get hired at MySpace as a dev—yeah, I know. What can I say, they were paying a hundred thirty thousand, and as a biochem tech I can make maybe seventy if I'm lucky. Coding's easy. I'd taken CS10 and then 61A at UCB, so I borrowed my boyfriend's CLR and read that over the weekend, and went in and kicked ass. Doesn't hurt to be a girl, of course, but I owned that interview."

Three carbombs appear. Katz toasts: "To the confusion of our enemies." Katz knows neither man nor woman that can glug down greater carbomb flux. He consumes them like a storm drain. There's no swallowing involved, just throwing it back in one continuous dump. Once out of every twenty or so he'll forget to breathe through his nose, lock up, and spurt cold congealing carbomb from both nostrils, evicting a mouthful in a cough's broad cone, inevitably spilling whatever remained in great vellicative spasms. This is not one of those times, and he's done well before anyone else is close.

"Jaysus Christ, that was fast." Erica sounds genuinely impressed.

The cigarette immediately following a carbomb is a panoply of flavors. She draws another Camel Light; he leans in to spark it. "I've only got one left."

"Will you smoke Newports?"

"I am nowhere near drunk enough to smoke Newports."

"Space out that one you've got left then. Oooh, I'm getting a call, one second." He walks a few meters away and calls Jeff Onesta, an occasional henchman living in Home Park. "Jeff! What are you up to? Want to make a hundred twenty bucks in fifteen minutes?" He explains the task, and returns to the table.

"So I'm making great money. And I start going out with this beautiful boy. Gorgeous. Not the one whose CLR I read—I broke up with him, he was lame. He was native to the area, said he was my age. His parents had died in a swamped boat of all things. I'd been pretty chaste through high school. My senior year boyfriend broke up with me when I wouldn't fuck him after prom. It wasn't a religious thing or any anti-sex thing, I just kind of despised all the guys in my high school, and was focused on other things, and when you've seen most of these people since they were retarded, goofy kids, the idea of having sex with them is like fucking your brother."

"SCDS is K through 12?"

"And I was there all thirteen years. Why do you know Savannah schools?"

"Well, I know one Savannah school. SCDS would usually make it up to an academic bowl tournament or two. Y'all were green and gold, and all of you were white, and thus I remember confusing you with Athens Academy, who were green and silver, and likewise very white. I know two actually—Jenkins, Big Boi went there before moving to Atlanta. And wherever Clarence Thomas went to school, so three."

"Ahh, you know Clarence Thomas grew up in Savannah."

"Also Big Boi." She laughs.

"The place Clarence Thomas went was on the Isle of Hope and got shut down in 1969. It was apparently quite ghastly. So I'm fucking this gorgeous California boy, and he is stupid, as stupid as they come. But he's beautiful and I'm having fun with him and enjoying sex for the first time. Everyone I was with in undergraduate, ugh, terrible people. So he's living kind of on the beach—"

"On the beach?"

"Yeah, people do it out there. They're usually bumming around a lot, and if they get caught without a couch to spend the night on, they'll sleep on the beach. It's not legal, but you can generally do it for a night in a pinch. It wasn't obvious to me, because I'd always meet him somewhere, and we'd go to my apartment. He took me to all kinds of nice places, always had money. He was just kind of vague about where he lived. So he's twenty-two, and going to Berkeley City College, so he says. Then one day he's like, Erica, my landlord's moving his daughter in, I've got to move, can I crash with you until I find a new place? So he moves in temporarily, and it's fine, I like it. I say, 'why don't you just move in?' and he's like 'ok, I'll do that.' And my parents offer to help me buy a place, they put the down payment up, and I took the mortgage."

"How were you working for MySpace in Berkeley? Weren't they in LA?"

"They have a San Francisco office. Maybe not anymore, but they did then. They were still bigger than Facebook. We creamed Facebook all through 2007. I got this nice two bedroom in Los Angeles."

"Sweet. Must have been nice." Katz is always a bit pissed off by this kind of thing. In his mind, you don't take down payments from your parents, though he knows this is easier to say when there's no chance of one coming.

"And he comes with me. I'm like, 'how will you get to school?' And he gives me this vague line about transferring to LACC. Whatever. I'm busy during the day. Well, it turns out he's not so dumb, and he's also not twenty-two like he told me, but thirty-five. A very well preserved thirty-five. And he wasn't going to school; he was running a string of sham geriatric facilities."

"Running them how?"

"As in they didn't exist. The facilities." She starts in on another vodka soda. "But he was submitting Medicare expenses for people who'd died. He had two friends who would get him their information, and he'd just start submitting expenses. He'd been doing this for years, and made hundreds of thousands of dollars. But he'd been busted for it a few years back, and couldn't get a place because he couldn't show income, and had this whole fine schedule he needed to be paying, and if he worked they'd garnish his wages, not that I think he ever worked anyway. So then one day I get a call from my mom, and she's like, 'Erica, if you have financial problems, why didn't you let us know?' Apparently some bank had been calling her all day, wondering where I am, when I intended to pay this loan, saying that they're going to repossess my car."

"Uh-oh."

"So I don't even own a car, but Patrick—that's the boy—he has this bitchin' little Miata he bought when we moved to LA. And I wondered how he paid for it, or anything, but I figured it was family money or something. I had my own money, so I didn't ask. But I call this bank up and apparently his Miata loan is in my name. He's never paid on it. It's been six months."

"Ughhhhhhhhh."

"Yeah. So I meet him with it, and I'm like what's up, and he says 'oh it must be an error.' At which point I should have known it was bullshit. But I want to believe, and I say 'ok, call these people.' Then I pull a credit report on myself, and holy shit, my identity's been stolen; there are like five cards for me all opened at the same time, right after the car loan. So I ask if he knows anything about it, and he comes clean. Slowly. Over the course of days, as I proved more and more shit. So I take off from work and stay home, and go to the mailbox, and here's all this mail about his goddamn palliative care facilities and fucked up credit history and court correspondence, and something from his doctor, and that's when I find out he's twenty-eight."

"So I tell him to leave, and he's like, I don't have anywhere to go. That's how I find out he was homeless before. And I feel incredibly stupid, obviously, but I'd been blinded by the dick. I tell him I don't care where he goes, that I'll have him arrested—"

"I'm surprised you weren't already."

"Well I wanted some money back, and I thought if he's in jail, there's no way I'm getting any. As if I was going to get any money from him ever. I know, stupid. But I tell him he has to leave. Motherfucker claims squatting rights. Says I can't evict him for sixty days under California law. So at that point I call the cops, and they arrest him. He's out two days later and starts hanging out around my house, around the places I go to, on the way to work. He harasses my friends. And finally he shows back up at my door, invites me to call the cops, and tells me he has sixty days. So I do, and they come out, and the motherfuckers say they can't do anything. I can't get an emergency protective order unless he hits me or endangers a kid or something. So I'm stuck with this motherfucker for sixty days."

"Unbelievable. You ought have had him killed."

"I wish, right? So I can't live with this guy there. I called GT and asked if I could go ahead and start spring semester; I'd been accepted for the previous fall, but didn't go. I tell him to use the place for sixty days, and that if he tried to stay there any longer I'd sue him to death, and that if he fucked it up I'd do the same."

Katz is aghast. "You let him stay there alone?"

"It was better than me staying there and going nuts! He's gone now. I'll give him that. I doubt I'll ever get any money from him, but now I have a little couple renting the place, and he hasn't shown up." She made a face. "He's the one who gave me herpes, by the way."

"So were you able to get that debt removed?"

She looks momentarily crushed. "Nope. Due to the fact that I was living there, and the duration of time it happened over, other details, no one's been willing to remove it. I might be able to do something with a lawsuit, but it doesn't look promising. And suing Patrick is pointless. He owes everyone in the universe money. My parents are paying for my place, and I work in the lab for some money, and I have a scholarship this year for my tuition, which is awesome. But I've got eighty K of debt I'm barely covering the interest on."

"That's fucked up. I'm sorry. Ugh." He shifts. "Why do you say you're breaking up with the current boyfriend? Hopefully not the same thing."

She titters. "No, I'm just bored with him. It's been long enough; it was only going to be a short little thing, but he lived right next to school, and I liked staying over there. He's cute. He makes good money; he's a personal injury lawyer. But he wants to, like, go to baseball games. And his friends are the biggest bunch of dumbasses you'll ever meet, and he wants to hang out with them all the time. He watches golf, and wants me to keep up with golf. But now I'm moving, and I'll be closer to campus, and it's time to just cut it off. I assume you don't have a girlfriend?"

"Not until you break up with golf guy, right?"

"My, aren't we sure of ourselves?"

He smiles. "Erica, I shoot craps with the Universe, and win. I'm feeling pretty good about this."

She makes a show of evaluating him. "You are a confident guy, among your other traits. Do you always just walk up to women on campus assuming that they're so bored and indolent that you can seduce them in the afternoon?"

"It's always worked so far. And if you're wondering, my age is twenty-nine, I have a job on the research team of a local midmajor startup, I have options there. My parents have zero money; having my own is pretty important to me. I will not take out accounts in your name, but I do tend to disappear for days at a time to code. This is as nice as I dress. I smoke cigarettes and weed like a chimney, and fucking love psychedelics, and partake of more nose drugs than most people are comfortable with."

"Like coke?"

"Ehhh, not quite, not a fan of organic stimulants so much."

"Then what? Adderall?"

"I enjoy dextroamphetamine as much as the next man, but not quite."

"What?" She makes a face. "Meth?"

"Indeed." He puts it out there early.

"How are you not all fucked up?"

Laughing: "Ought I be all fucked up? It's not that different from Adderall. I mean, it is in potency, but not so much in effect."

"And neurotoxicity."

"Well, I eat horse's doses of antioxidants. Vitamin C mostly. I've noticed no effects in that regard, but it's hard to know. What I do know is I'm working full time and doing school full time, and that wouldn't be possible otherwise, and I hold my shit more or less together."

"Does it help you work? I love Adderall."

"Mlle Marelli." He smiles dreamily. "I'm not sure I'd want to go doing a titration on it, but for code? Where you need to be obsessive, need to suck up a thousand lines into your context, and keep them there, and manipulate them? There's nothing like it."

The sound of Fifty Cent comes bumping down the street louder and more slowly than is typical. A Land Rover pulls up out front, and parks illegally, hazards on. "In Da Club" pulsates at skullcrushing volume. The driver waits for a break in traffic, pops his door, emerges into the left lane, and runs around the front of the SUV. He approaches their table with a carton of Camel Lights in boxes, a twelve-pack of Abita Purple Haze, and a single rose. Katz stands, counts out ten twenties, embraces Jeff, and makes the trade. Jeff jogs back, steps out into the left lane, waves his arms to halt traffic, hops in as horns blare, and is off. Total time of visit is under twenty seconds. At this time the waitress is emerging; Katz welcomes her, hands her eight twenties, and thanks her for her service. He turns to Erica, hands her the cigarettes and rose, and says "*Kallisti.* I believe these are for you." He holds onto the Abita. "My place is less than five minutes away walking. How would you like to come by?"

They depart. At 4th and Peachtree, she throws him up against the cement wall of one of the generic outpatient clinics and locks her mouth on his, good lord she's savage. Katz has to peel her off so that they might descend down 3rd. It was An All-Time Classic Day.

She didn't bother meeting the boyfriend in person to give him the bad news. She extracted her stuff the next afternoon. Her note was polite, firm, and brief. She signed it "Best wishes, Mlle Marelli." Her key served as a paperweight and she left them on a counter, where they'd both be immediately visible. Searching her apartment, the only item of his she could find was *Confessions of an Economic Hit Man,* the dubious tales of professional paranoid John Perkins. She placed it in a box, added a note reading "You had nothing else at my place," and took it to his building. Erica handed it off to the concierge with a smile, stepped back out to the street, and blocked his phone number. Erica Marelli was a woman of precision and competence, when she wasn't lit up anyway, one who believed in clean workspaces and clean breakups.

17 anarbek tursyn busts a move

"This, this is the horse's shit. I was told Georgia's Institute of Technology had a nuclear reactor. I am coming of age in Almaty. Not many kilometers outside in Alatau, at our Institute of Nuclear Physics at the National Nuclear Center, VVR-K runs six megawatts in a swimming pool. Now neither Georgia formerly of USSR nor Georgia once again of USA have a reactor."

"Well we have four reactors. Two at Hatch and two at Vogtle. And they're building two AP1000s at Vogtle, the only AP1000s in America."

"So I Anarbek son of Zhusup walk up to Vogtle in these clothes and these shoes, dup-dee-dup-dee-do, and announce: I am hoping to perform experiments in enrichment. The lasers also. How many of these reactors will I be allowed to use? They are radioing to the command center: we're going to shoot this Muslim before he finds a passenger jet."

"That hat would definitely do you no favors. What do you call that?"

"*Tubeteika* is the Russian word. We call it төбетей, тақия but psssh, everyone is calling it by the Russian."

"And I'm guessing that's Kazakh? It's a Slavic language, right?"

"What is your name again?"

"Sherman Spartacus Katz. And you are Anarbek son of Zhusup."

"Anarbek Tursyn, born to Zhusup in Chelyabinsk."

"Tankograd? I thought that was in Russia?"

Anarbek's face is one of surprise and distrust. "How are you knowing this?"

"All our country knows the Chelyabinsk Tractor Plant and his T-34s. Certainly the Germans do, right?"

"I do not think anyone here has heard of Chelyabinsk. Many have not heard of Kazakhstan."

"I'm fucking with you. No one here knows shit. Though I recall that Sasha Shulgin's dad was born in Chelyabinsk. It's not in Kazakhstan, I was pretty sure. I mean, I'm not going to argue with you. What does Anarbek mean?"

Anarbek evaluated Katz critically, and took his time replying. "Regarding Chelyabinsk, I was born across the border, in the Russian SFSR. Master of pomegranates."

"Heh really? The fruit of the dead? Is that, like, a dig at Persephone?"

Nonplussed: "What?"

"Persephone daughter of Demeter? Kore? Bound to dwell in Hades for the year's cold tertile. One of the all-time Ls taken against pomegranates."

"These are the Greek myths?"

"I mean, Hades, yeah, c'mon buddy."

"Kazakhstan has always grown pomegranates. I am not thinking there is a connection here."

"Unfortunate. My dad wasn't the kind of guy that feuds with minor Greek deities, but I think I'd have liked it if he was. So did your parents want you to be a pomegranate farmer?"

"They didn't know what it meant. I found out and told them. Do Americans mean much by these names? What does your name mean?"

"So everything you see here is new, because Sherman burned this bitch down in 1864. You've gotta read the letter he wrote to Mayor Calhoun. Epic shit. Actually, you need to go get his *Memoirs* and just read them through. It'll get your dick hard. Proud to be named after such a badass. I imagine your Almeta got burned down and fucked and doublefucked by Tamerlane and the Golden Horde and the Achaemenids?"

"The Russians built Fort Verny between mountains and rivers in, what, 1850? During the Crimean War."

"Well 1853 to 1856, then."

"Why do you know the years of the Crimean War?"

"Why wouldn't I?"

"Fort Verny is destroyed by an earthquake, rubble bouncing, people bouncing, dogs in the street all alooo-hoo. Russians rebuilt it as just Verny this time. Then the Bolsheviks rename it Alma-Ata. Trotsky is exiled there! Then Kazakhstan becomes independent and renames it Almaty. But no, he is too young a city. And no, Kazakh is not Slavic. Is Turkish, also *nekulturny*, an extra tongue of the Turks they squashed with a tractor. All decent people speak Russian."

"I must admit I know not a single Kazakh author. Spartacus was—"

"I am knowing Spartacus well."

"Oh yeah I guess you grew up under some Communism. How old are you?"

"Thirty-two. I am fourteen when *soyuz* disintegrated. Meaning Soviet Union, not 1983 launch pad fire."

"Oh shit I'm twenty-nine! Everyone else here is a fucking child. And Katz is just Katz. A lot of people think it's Jewish, but it's not. I come from crazy fundamentalist Christians. I'm here getting a few masters."

"More than one?"

"Yeah, CS and Nuclear."

"Why both?"

"Well a second is basically free, because fees top out at twelve hours. So if you take two at a time, you really only pay for one."

"OK but why do both at all?"

"Gotta fill time somehow. Maybe I'll write a novel about it one day. And I've always dug nuclear shit. You're Muslim, though, you said? Neither stimulating nor depressing compounds pass your lips?"

"I am no longer devout. I drink vodka, though not to excess." Anarbek looked around conspiratorially. "Sometimes in Kazakhstan I am smoking hash. In our Chuy Valley cannabis grows wild as far as one sees in any direction."

"Yeah I've heard Kazakhstan described as the birthplace of cannabis but never put much stock in it. Is it legal there?"

"Penalties are severe, but generally unenforced. It is sold openly in—not the newer upscale malls, like MEGA Alma-Ata, but in the villages, in bazaars there. They are not burning and poisoning fields as your DEA does. But if you cause trouble, and are caught with it, especially outside the cities, that is it for you. Ten years inside. Kazakhstan's jails are unlike the jails here."

---

nekulturny: некульту́рный uncultured   **Soyuz:** Союз Union

Katz wonders what Anarbek would know about American jails. "Well we'll have to rip phatty bong tokes sometime! And bitch about the loss of our research reactor birthright."

"For the Olympics! So stupid."

"Well I guess it's good that Eric Rudolph didn't have access to highly enriched uranium, but it was actually shut down well before that. The NRC was all up in our asses about it. So what brings you to Atlanta, once called Terminus? I mean GT obviously, but what are your plans?"

"I am working for Kazatomprom after graduating from MEPhI. We hope to expand into enrichment, and so I am sent here to study. Most of my research is with the Physics department, with the optics people there."

"Oh for...neutron reflectors?" It is a foolish question, one Katz wishes he could unask as soon as it is out of his mouth.

"No. Lasers."

"Oh very cool! So like AVLIS, MLIS?"

"Something like that."

"A bit of the SILEX, then? CRISLA?"

"Well, yes. I am looking at CO_2 TEA lasers and condensation repression."

"Ahhh my boy Devesh works on TEA lasers! He just came back as faculty."

"I am knowing Devesh! My first day in the laser lab, I tell him I am Anarbek, son of Zhusup, from Kazakhstan. He leaps up and throws his arm around me and says"—the Kazakhstani begins to impersonate the frenetic Gujarati, sounding not unlike a songbird being strangled—"'Anarbek, you're just what I need. How much for a few tons of that good Kazakh yellowcake?' He points to his lab partner and continues, 'I just need enough to blow this son of a bitch back to Mumbai.' But the lab partner laughs and suggests to Devesh acts of anatomical impossibility. He is very loud. He being Devesh."

"It is known. How much would it be, then, for a few tons of yellowcake?"

"The markets move from day to day, Katz, and usually these orders are put in well ahead of their delivery date."

"I don't mean for people ordering off the uranium market, Anarbek. I mean if I wanted a truck to show up at my girlfriend's house with an anniversary gift of unlicensed urania."

"Heh. Your girlfriend craves triuranium octoxide?"

"All of uranium's many oxides, Anarbek. As do I."

∗ ∗ ∗ ∗ ∗ ∗ ∗ ∗

Since 1961, and most recently updated in 2018, the International Atomic Energy Agency has published its Regulations for the Safe Transport of Radioactive Material. It categorizes natural (neither enriched nor depleted in ^{235}U) uranium as a "low-toxicity alpha emitter." The Convention on the Physical Protection of Nuclear Material was adopted in 1979 and amended in 2005, establishing legal obligations for signing parties regarding international shipping of nuclear

---

AVLIS: Atomic vapor laser isotope separation   **MLIS:** Molecular laser isotope separation
SILEX: Separation of isotopes via laser excitation
CRISLA: Chemical reaction by isotope-specific activation
TEA: Transversely excited atmospheric

materials, but its Article I explicitly excludes "uranium containing the mixture of isotopes as occurring in nature other than in the form of ore or ore-residue." It is the IAEA's stated goal that nuclear source material be tracked from extraction through fabrication, use, reprocessing, and disposal. A facility that cannot document consumption and/or outflows commensurate with intake must report the difference as MUF: Material Unaccounted For. It is thought that the nuclear weapons programs of the United States and the Soviet Union have generated well over ten tons of fissile MUF between them.

∗ ∗ ∗ ∗ ∗ ∗ ∗ ∗ ∗

We could go back to Huygens, the Dutchman who bridged Descartes and Newton while spending his most productive years in Paris. His 1656 *De Motu Corporum ex Percussione* corrected the Cartesian laws of motion, recognized Galilean invariance, and implicitly suggested the conservation of energy (his student Leibniz would make it explicit in 1678 as part of his theory of *vis viva*). Newton focused instead on the conservation of momentum in *Principia*. These ideas would lead to D'Alambert's principle, the Lagrangian formulation, and eventually Hamilton's work in 1833. Rather than attempt to unwind another priority dispute among these seventeenth century gentleman scientists (giants, all), let's move forward to 1738. That year, Daniel Bernoulli of Basel, Switzerland published *Hydrodynamica;* based around the conservation of energy, this proved the foundational text of fluid dynamics (or, if you prefer, hydrodynamics). It furthermore introduced the concepts of machine efficiency and work, and explained Boyle's law using his new kinetic theory of gases.

Bernoulli had already known that moving fluid climbing a height gains potential energy at the cost of kinetic energy. By conservation arguments, he demonstrated that pressure similarly derives from specific kinetic energy (kinetic energy per unit volume). For pressure P, density ρ and velocity v,

$$\frac{1}{2}\rho v^2 + P = c$$

For steady, incompressible flows with negligible viscous friction at a force potential Ψ (the gravitational potential at elevation z is gz), Bernoulli integrated Newton's second law of motion:

$$\frac{v^2}{2} + \Psi + \frac{P}{\rho} = c$$

The central implication is that an increase in fluid flow corresponds to a reduction in pressure and/or potential energy. Italian physicist Giovanni Venturi had many interests, but is best known for his fundamental work on fluid mechanics. His eponymous effect, published in 1797, drew on Bernoulli's principle to demonstrate that reducing a pipe's crosssection increases flow rate while decreasing pressure:

De...Percussione: The Motion of Colliding Bodies

$$p_1 - p_2 = \frac{\rho}{2}(v_2^2 - v_1^2)$$

A Venturi tube chokes the flow in a constricted section; at this point, static pressure falls to a minimum while the volumetric flow rate Q is maximized:

$$Q = A_1 \sqrt{\frac{2p_1 - 2p_2}{\rho\left(\frac{A_1}{A_2}\right)^2 - \rho}} = A_2 \sqrt{\frac{2p_1 - 2p_2}{\rho - \rho\left(\frac{A_2}{A_1}\right)^2}}$$

The Swede Gustaf de Laval worked on his impulse turbine; he hoped to eliminate the need to defend against high steam pressures, resulting in a cheaper turbine and thus electricity generation. In 1888, he applied the Venturi effect to develop the first convergent/divergent nozzle, now known as the de Laval nozzle. An asymmetric hourglass shape tapers to a thin waist in the middle. Subsonic gas enters the front cone. It reaches the chokepoint; maintaining constant mass flow requires that the gas velocity increase:

$$m = \frac{Ap_t}{\sqrt{T_t}}\sqrt{\frac{\gamma M}{R}} N\left[1 + \left(\frac{\gamma - 1}{2}\right)N^2\right]^{-\frac{\gamma+1}{2\gamma-2}}$$

The increase in velocity leads to simultaneous decrease in pressure. This choked flow reaches sonic (Mach 1) speed. As it leaves the throat, the gas accelerates to supersonic velocities v_e via Joule-Thomson expansion:

$$v_e = \sqrt{\frac{TR2\gamma}{M\gamma - M}\left[1 - \left(\frac{p_e}{p}\right)^{\frac{\gamma-1}{\gamma}}\right]}$$

The de Laval nozzle is used in steam turbines, rockets, and jets. In Germany during the 1960s, it saw another potential application in Becker's aerodynamic isotope separation scheme. Like other enrichment methods, this relied on the slight mass difference between uranium isotopes, in this case by effect of the centrifugal force. South Africa's nuclear program used this technique for enrichment of both fuel and weapon uranium. Other nations continued to focus on the gas centrifuge.

Enrichment is measured in Separative Work Units (SWUs). The efficiency of a process is defined in SWUs per resource, where that resource may be time, or space, or wasted material, or radiated heat (this last being of importance for clandestine enrichment, primarily detected by satellites mapping thermal signatures), but the most critical measurement is SWUs per energy input. Recall that the SI unit of energy is the joule, and it unites several other units: J = kgm^2/s^2 = Nm = CV = Ws = Pam^3. The SWUs of a facility are a function of its processes and the composition of its feedstock. Define a value function (typically the Dirac) $V(x)$:

$$V(x) = (2x - 1)\ln\left(\frac{x}{1 - x}\right)$$

Bernstein pointed out that this value function is a minimum. We calculate the SWUs W necessary to separate a mass P of desired product x_p and a mass T of undesirable component x_t for a feedstock mass F of initial assay x_f:

$$W = PV(x_p) + TV(x_t) - FV(x_f)$$

The SWU was conceived of by Dirac, but first published by Fuchs and Peierls in 1942. Fuchs was already a Soviet agent when he began work on Britain's "Tube Alloys" project, so we can safely assume this terminology was in use on the far side of the Curtain. It is hopefully obvious that enrichment decreases entropy, and it is by an entropic argument that Fuchs and Peierls derived Dirac's naïve value function. Cohen and later Opfell refined this approach using arguments from the Gibbs free energy. A fine paper by E. T. Jaynes, "The Gibbs Paradox," explores the Gibbs and mixing paradoxes, and is well worth reading.

Enrichment mechanisms are primarily compared by the total energy cost to raise feed material from one composition to some desired composition. The number of stages necessary is also of importance, since some material is likely to be lost at each stage. Prior to widespread adoption of the centrifuge, most uranium was separated using gaseous diffusion, where pressurized, sublimed UF_6 is forced through porous membranes. At 56.4 °C, ^{235}U flows 0.4% faster on average than ^{238}U. Each stage in the cascade thus provides 1.004 enrichment. The huge number of stages required some of the largest buildings in the world, with terrific power demands.

The Zippe centrifuge (a rare example of technology transfer from East to West: Gernot Zippe was kidnapped from Germany to lead centrifuge research in the Soviet Union, and recreated his work upon his repatriation to Vienna a decade later) is universally employed thanks to its low energy consumption, small space, minimal loss, and easy installation. Pakistan's "*Markaz Guzira* Khan" based his P1 and P2 on Urenco Zippes. Note that in Russia, the Zippe is known as the Kamenev, and Zippe's priority is disputed. The central equation governing gas centrifuges is:

$$\Delta U = \frac{\pi \rho D Z}{2} \left[\frac{(M_2 - M_1) r^2 \omega^2}{2RT} \right]^2 E$$

where $E \leq 1$ is the magnitude of flow into and out of the centrifuge, $(M_2 - M_1)$ is the isotopic molecular mass difference, $r^2 \omega^2$ is the squared peripheral speed of the rotor, R is the ideal gas constant, T is the temperature, Z is the separation length, D is the diffusion coefficient, and ρ is, as usual, the density. The past sixty years of centrifuge improvement have involved increasing the rotation speed via advanced composite materials and lengthening the centrifuge. Details are closely classified. The state of the open art of centrifuge design is covered in Whatley's twopart 1984 review, which states "all present work is classified...this review will be limited to work prior to 1962."

Markaz Guzira: مرکز گزیره Centrifuge

The centrifuge is the most efficient enrichment technology based on mass difference, though Japan's *Asahi Kasei Kabushiki-gaisha* employs an ionexchange column approach claimed to be competitive with Urenco's best. Moving beyond this is expected to require an entirely different approach. Laser isotope separation offers one: rather than applying a force to all uranium atoms, and relying on ^{238}U's greater resistance to motion, LIS exploits precise energy absorption bands; a laser operating within a frequency exclusive to some isotope will affect only that isotope. The frequency bands are constants arising from the electrochemical structure of targets. The laser must be fitted to the band, rather than the other way around. With enough incident power from the laser, it's theoretically possible to perfectly separate a flow in one stage (enrichment to weapons grade typically requires several thousand centrifuges).

LIS is applicable to most elements, though uranium presents the most profitable separation. LANL pursued MLIS, while TRW put forth their own PSP. But most effort during the twentieth century was expended on AVLIS, primarily by Hughes and Exxon followed by LLNL in the United States, the Soviet NITStLAN, numerous French SILVA facilities (most of them in Pierrelatte), South Korea's KAERI, Iran's Comprehensive Separation Laboratory and facility at Lashkar Ab'ad, Brazil's IEAv, and a dozen or so other countries. Separation of plutonium isotopes is almost exclusively performed via AVLIS, though the plutonium production plant at INL was indefinitely postponed in 1990. LLNL's AVLIS setup uses two major subsystems. The separator system employs an electron beam to vaporize uranium metal to a low-density gas. This moves towards the laser system, where a copper vapor laser (four stages, green light at 510.6 nm and yellow light at 578.2 nm) pumps a tuned dye laser. 502.73 nm (596.32 THz) orange light photoionizes only ^{235}U (the frequency must be accurate to within 10 pm (11 GHz)); the resulting positive ions can be easily electromagnetically separated. The copper lasers must pulse at at least 10 kHz; these pulses ought be brief (a few dozen nanoseconds) and intense (a few dozen kW/cm^2). The low density of the vapor requires an optical path length in excess of 100 m. AVLIS seemed appealing, but efficient centrifuges presented separation at a lower cost, and worked with UF$_6$ throughout (liquid uranium is no joke). Perhaps most damning, uranium in excess of three thousand Celsius (necessary for vaporization) already has more than half of its atoms in various excited states, and would not respond to the lasers as configured.

PSP turned out to be unfit for high-resolution separation, though it is still being pursued as a generic mass division technology. MLIS was a more ambitious scheme, one which attempted to unite laser separation with an all-hex cycle. This scheme employed a de Laval nozzle, carrier gas (a noble gas or hydrogen), and scavenger gas (*e.g.* methane); the supersonic, cooled UF$_6$ is hit with an 15.916 μm infrared laser (CO$_2$ shifted from its native 10.6 μm), exciting ^{235}U's ν_3 vibrational mode. A 308 nm XeCl excimer laser then selectively

Asahi...gaisha: 旭化成株式会社 AsahiKASEI Corporation
PSP: plasma separation process   **INL:** Idaho National Laboratory
NITStLAN: *Nauchno-Issledovatelskij Tsentr Po Tekhnologicheskim Lazeram* Scientific Research Center for Industrial Lasers   **KAERI:** 한국원자력연구원 Korea Atomic Energy Research Institute
IEAv: *Instituto de Estudos Avançados* Institute for Advanced Studies

photolyzes $^5UF_6$, breaking it into $^{235}UF_5$ and monatomic fluorine. The latter is scavenged to prevent recombination. MLIS was expected to consume less power per SWU than AVLIS, but the technology was even more complex, and it too fell before centrifuges.

The Energy Policy Act of 1992 established the United States Enrichment Corporation, a state owned enterprise to take over the DoE's civilian enrichment infrastructure. It took over gaseous diffusion plants in Paducah and Portsmouth. Six years later, it was privatized in a three gigadollar IPO, this despite the NRC assuming regulatory authority over Portsmouth in 1997. In 2001, USEC closed the troubled Portsmouth facility, and in 2009 suspended work on a centrifuge facility at the location. Paducah followed in 2013, and USEC filed Chapter 11 in December of that year. Centrus Energy emerged in September 2014. Their AC100 centrifuge never got quite off the ground; the only enrichment being performed at industrial scale in the United States as of 2023 is a Urenco operation in Eunice, New Mexico, a region known as "nuclear alley" thanks to colocation of the Waste Isolation Pilot Plant, the west Texas facility of Waste Control Specialists, and the International Isotopes uranium deconversion plant (should it ever be built). Centrus is the sole contracted provider of HALEU; we'll see how it goes. After accepting the AVLIS process from the federal government in 1994, USEC canceled all LIS plans in June 1999.

In South Australia, 460 km northeast of Adelaide, among *Maireana* scrub and the spiny tussocks of *Spinifex* grass, the meager shade of *Acacia aneura* mulga trees and eternal *Atriplex* saltbush, prospector Arthur John Smith in 1906 found an ore tinted dijan. He assumed it tungsten, or possibly tin; at the University of Adelaide, Douglas Mawson (later of Shackleford's *Nimrod* expedition to Antarctica) determined the sample to be a new rare earth oxide mineral, davidite, containing lanthanum, cerium, ytterbium, and uranium. Promptly renamed "Radium Hill", the site operated off and on until 1961. Following decommission, 225 kilotons of lowlevel radioactive waste was left uncovered. The Brickfielder wind strewed it across the desert for the next twenty years, at which point someone from Adelaide thought to throw a tarp over it. Radium Hill was then decreed a waste repository, and tailings from all over South Australia were dumped there until 1998. It is now a ghost town in all meanings of the word: cancer deaths among former workers were four times the national average. A swimming pool has been partially reclaimed by *Soliva sessilis* bindi weed. A 2 megagallon water tank looms over ruins of a Catholic church and oneroom school; stretching away under the southern sun are paved roads lined with eucalyptus trees. Near what remain of the tailings, radiation levels exceed background by a factor of 3000. It's known well that the flora and fauna of Australia seek to destroy men; here the land does, too.

Such was Australia's first excursion with radioisotopes; more followed. While her ore is by no means of the highest quality, there's sufficiently much of it that Australia can claim the world's largest overall reserves. As a no-nuclear zone, Australia does not allow her uranium exports to be used in weapon development. Blessed with this stellar prolificacy, this cornucopia of the rapid process, Australia has had her share of nuclear scientists and research successes. While the rest of the world abandoned LIS, Michael Goldsworthy, Horst Struve, and other Aussies pushed forward with a promising new technique: SILEX.

1996 saw Silex Systems license their technology to USEC. Three years later, the United States signed Australian Treaty Series 2000 No. 19, "Agreement for cooperation between the Government of Australia and the Government of the United States of America concerning technology for the separation of isotopes of uranium by laser excitation," authorizing collaboration (and explicitly denying any enrichment facility in Australia). In June 2001, the Department of Energy took the unprecedented step of classifying this privately held information, a use of the Atomic Energy Act never seen before nor after.

Record of Decision To Classify Certain Elements of the SILEX Process as Privately Generated Restricted Data

AGENCY: Office of Nuclear and National Security Information, DOE.

ACTION: Notice.

SUMMARY: This notice announces the Secretary of Energy's decision to classify as Restricted Data certain privately generated information concerning an innovative isotope separation process for enriching uranium. Under 10 CFR 1045.21(c), the Secretary of Energy is required to inform the public whenever the authority to classify privately generated information as Restricted Data is exercised.

SUPPLEMENTARY INFORMATION: An Australian company, Silex Systems, Limited, has been developing the Separation of Isotopes by Laser Excitation (SILEX) process to enrich uranium since 1992. In 1996, USEC, Inc., purchased the rights from Silex Systems, Limited, to evaluate and further develop this process. The privately generated information which the Secretary of Energy has classified as Restricted Data under the Atomic Energy Act of 1954, as amended, pertains to certain elements of the SILEX process.

Issued in Washington, DC on June 19, 2001.

Joseph S. Mahaley,
Acting Director, Office of Security and Emergency Operations.

[FR Doc. 01–15982 Filed 6–25–01; 8:45 am]

BILLING CODE 6450–01–P

In the end, laser isotope enrichment didn't present a compelling case for established nuclear powers, where advanced centrifuges were readily available and needed no major research effort. Laser science continued to rapidly develop since then, and the calculus was very different for breakout efforts in 2010. The proliferator's goal is not necessarily economic production of special nuclear material, but producing it at all.

18   the chemical history of an eightball

$11,250. $11,250. $7,500. $7,500. $3,750. $3,750. Interest paid on Danylo's loan of $225,000 was $45,000, a cost of 20%. Other than eight thousand the third week, he'd managed to pay it all out of cash flow, with no hit to bank accounts. Danylo texted him upon receiving the seventh and final payment ($75,000 principal, no interest): THANK U FOR BANKING WITH US.

* * * * * * * * *

Within a few weeks, Katz began gently to prod Erica for biochem knowledge. Katz spoke in allusions and hypotheticals. "So you play with DNA, yes? Where are we with that?"

"How do you mean?" She pressed into him.

"Well, for instance, can we look at a section of DNA and know what it does? Like, can I debug a mutated gene?"

"Debug in what sense? What are you trying to do?"

He held out his cigarette, squinting, looking at it like a new, mysterious thing. "So I take a drag off this fifth or sixth Newport of the day, en route to twenty. Somewhere in North Carolina or Virginia or Turkey or wherever, some farmer dumped a bunch of high-phosphate fertilizer onto his crop. Yo ho ho green revolution. Now, whatever fertilizer doesn't run off into the ocean as alluvium gets taken up in the nitrogen reduction cycle, turned into delicious flavor. Unfortunately for me, those phosphates were extracted from lovely cyan apatite. Apatite is of course a radionuclide sorbent, and it's taking up actinides, and eventually some of that gets into the tobacco, and I end up depositing it onto my bronchial segment bifurcations. It sits there chilling, and whenever it remembers, dumps a 5.408 MeV α into my lungs. Some of those αs are ripping up my DNA. You sample that DNA, sequence it, and you're like, 'nah this is fucked DNA.' Can we debug it?"

She shifts. "I mean, we can compare the relevant genes to what are called the wild-type genes, the sequences we see most often in healthy samples. And we can determine the differences. And we can compare that to known bad mutations. But how would we fix your DNA?"

"Oh, I don't know. But you can't look at the sequence, without examples of good and bad ones, and figure out what it's going to do?"

Erica laughs at him. "There are two questions there at least. One, can we predict what a gene codes for by looking at the sequence? We can know exactly what sequence of amino acids gets coded, but no, from that we can't determine the resultant protein or noncoding RNA."

"That's just protein folding, right? Molecular dynamics."

"Yeah. 'Just.' That's a hard problem. There are four levels of structure in a protein. Primary structure is the amino sequence, though environmental factors can affect basic conformations for the same sequence, so already you have an external factor. Secondary structure is mostly hydrogen bonding, and gives rise to your α-helices and β-sheets."

"The gross things in protein diagrams?"

"Gross things?"

"I don't know, you've got natural healthy ball and stick models and sawhorse diagrams and such, then you get into proteins and have these weird spirals and helices and ropes and things. They gross me out."

"Ribbon diagrams. You don't want the full ball-and-stick of a polypeptide backbone, trust me. It would just overwhelm all the other details. But yes, those are your gross things. Don't ever look at a ribosome; it'll horrify you."

"Noted. I shall eschew ribosomes."

"Tertiary structure ensures the hydrophilic sides of those structures are facing outwards, where the water is. Quaternary structure is the folding of protein subunits. Predicting all that is very difficult."

"DESRES built a supercomputer from custom ASICs, the Anton, just for this."

"Sure, but you can throw the biggest computer you want at it, and we still can't get past the smallest proteins. There are just too many factors. So yeah, you've got the problem of predicting the actual protein structure. After that, you've got the question of what that protein is going to do, how it interacts, what kind of binding sites it presents, how other chemicals affect it. And that's essentially impossible with just computation; you need a dynamic, precise model of the cellular biochemistry as a whole."

"Hrmmm. OK, what about a simpler problem? Let's say I've got a fungus which generates some desirable chemical, but only as an intermediary towards some other, less useful chemical. Now I know the protein that does that last catalysis, and the gene that codes for it. If I excise that gene from its DNA, ought I get a result that's rich in the intermediate? And is that possible?"

"Is it possible? Sure, that's gene knockout. That's what we were working on in Jennifer's lab, and what I'm doing now." Katz's feelers twitch. "You used to have to fuck around with homologous recombination, which was limited in application and a tremendous pain in the ass. The new technologies—zinc finger nucleases, TALEN, CRISPR—are much easier. It's not trivial, but any grad student ought be able to do it. CRISPR is Jennifer's work; it's going to blow up when she publishes on it. It makes things that used to take months doable in a day or two. It's revolutionary." She spoke with clear reverence.

"Awesome. So all I need to know is the gene?" He rubs her shoulders.

"Effectively. And a year or two of lab technique. Now, you need to know all the other reasons that protein might be there. That organism selected the ability to generate that last, 'unwanted' chemical for some purpose. The protein might have multiple roles, as might that product."

"In which case removing it might disrupt the organism."

"Yep."

"So if the end product is an alkaloid used for defense, that shouldn't be a big deal, right? Assuming I'm farming this organism somewhere it doesn't need that defense."

TALEN: transcription activator-like effector nuclease
CRISPR: clustered regularly interspaced sport palindromic repeats

"Maybe? Depends. Maybe the synthesis of that chemical also consumes something that would otherwise build up and be a cellular poison. Who knows. Do you have something specific in mind?"

With a crooked smile: "Perhaps."

"What?"

"Well, this is all just speculation, but how much do you know about the chemistry of LSD?"

"I would assume more than you? I mean, I've never run a total synthesis, or been up to my elbows in a vat of saprogenic fungus, but I know the Sandoz story. I know you extract alkaloids from ergot sclerotia, one particular group of alkaloids anyway. You cleave those, then aminate with diethylamine. The product of the cleave is lysergic acid, which is what you really want."

"Total synthesis of D-LSA is hard, so yeah, almost all of it comes from harvested ergot. In ergot biosynthesis D-LSA is an intermediate. Could you knock out the gene which catalyzes the last step—"

"Genes don't catalyze. They code for enzymes which do."

"Yep high school was good shit. Could you produce a fungus that yields D-LSA directly? I've got to think that last step is energyheavy. You could save yourself and your ergot some work."

Erica stirs. "It's possible. Do you know the gene?"

"I do. That's all been worked out."

"I can't say for sure. I mean, is it still assembling the peptides that get stuck onto the D-LSA? Those are presumably going to build up; they might react with other stuff. The lysergic acid is clearly reactive, and it might have unexpected effects when concentrated. Does the ergot need this alkaloid?"

"I don't think so? It seems to be there as a deterrent to predators."

"Well, you could certainly try and see. Oh, right, this is all just speculation. Since when do you care about funga? Looking to make some LSD?"

Katz shushes her. "I'd never dream of such. I'm merely considering the global need for D-LSA in lifesaving pharmaceuticals."

She laughs unbelievingly. "What migraine medication uses synthetic ergoline derivatives? Don't try to bullshit me. The alkaloids used in pharmaceuticals are natural ergopeptides."

"How do you know about ergot?"

"I was a chem major. If you're a chem major and do any drugs, you're going to look into LSD synthesis. Hell, you find any bearded prof that lived through the 60s, and they'll be slapping their knees, talking about whipping up batches back when the precursors were openly sold. Of course, if you try doing anything like that using the labs, you're going to be kicked out of the major immediately, and likely school. And it's not like they have ergotamine tartrate sitting around, or can easily get it. Every year somebody goes down somewhere for cooking up MDMA, though. Isosafrole isn't hard to synthesize, though the process smells like eight layers of hell."

"Well, I read a paper recently that broke down the ergot D-LSA pathway, and yeah, if you cut out four genes, so far as I can tell, you direct everything to agroclavine, and prevent formation of ergopeptines. *Claviceps* has 8,703 apparently. Not a huge genome. Not that I would really know."

"It might be doable, and might work. More interesting, if they've got the whole pathway broken down, might be building that pathway elsewhere."

"Human beings?"

Her laugh is loud and long. "No. Typically yeast."

"Dare one unleash the beast of yeast? Why?"

"Yeast is stupid easy to raise, grows quickly, lots of reasons. We know its genome pretty well. We have techniques that work with it."

"And you can just plop a whole metabolic pathway down into it?"

"We might not need the entire pathway. If there's an intermediary that's easily synthesized in bulk, you could elide things up to that point. I'd have to look into synthesis chemistry, but I imagine it's easier to form the first rings in LSD—it's tetracyclic, right?—than the last ones. Less shit to fuck up. If you can directly react up to some point, that's usually beneficial, since you don't have to work on the yeast's timescale."

Katz thought quickly. It had promise, so far as he could tell, which admittedly wasn't far. Erica did seem to know her shit backwards and forwards. Liberation from SYNCOPE required precursors. He had no certainties regarding the effectiveness of his ideas regarding ergot, nor how to put them into practice, nor even determine success. Bolaño wouldn't like it, but Bolaño liked less and less these days.

We need precursors. We cannot buy them. We must, then, make them. We cannot make them. We plus Erica can, perhaps. There was no need to show her the lab initially. Do it.

"What would you need to investigate this?"

"What, D-LSA production in yeast? Ummm, some lab equipment. Probably the most expensive thing would be...ideally I've have a mass spectrometer with which I could check my results, also standards to check against."

"Fucking mass spectrometers." Katz grinned.

"Excuse me?"

"Everybody wants a mass spectrometer."

She looked puzzled. "Why, do you want to become an LSD cook?" Her eyes gleamed; she grinned. "It's harder than you think, computer science boy."

"Oh, lawd help us, I'm just an ignorant coder; I don't understand yahhh *eee-lec-trons* and these *ayyy-on-ic* bonds. Yawwhhh gonna give me ahh brain fever just thinkin' on it."

"Idiot." She punched him. "Do you want me to look into this?"

"I would like you to let me know what lab equipment would be necessary to do a thorough study. List equipment, reagents, and consumables you would need, prices, where they can be acquired, any relevant facts. Note which, if any, are regulated, and summarize the regulation. I would like you to list problems that might make it impossible or uneconomical. I would like a proposal for a program by which you'll conduct this investigation, details regarding scaling to hundreds of liters of fermented fungus, and a current literature review. Play this close. Don't get your lab people involved. Do it on your own time, but do it quickly. I'll pay five large for a quality report."

"Five hundred?"

"Five thousand. Tax free unless you declare it."

"Hot shit! When do you want it?"

"As soon as possible, but be thorough." He pulled a Trivial Pursuit box off a bookshelf, opened it, and counted out twenty-five hundreds. He folded them and handed them to her. She whooped.

"So what kind of inputs would we need for that?"

Erica's smile could start wars in Asia. "How about sugar?"

* * * * * * * * *

Katz put out his cigarette. "No, the biggest problem with doing meth, well there are two actually."

Erica interrupted him. "The people!"

"That's exactly right. Most of the people doing meth are goddamn losers, terrible people, blights on society. Why you do a stimulant when you don't have anything to do in the first place is beyond my understanding. But so they're unemployed, they're amped up, they're not, like, developing skills during the day, so they end up going nuts and the meth is their whole existence. They've got no money, and they'll cheerfully rip you off. They're completely unreliable, you can't take them anywhere, and they show up at your house and frighten the neighbors."

"That Amy bitch who used to come over here was quite intolerable."

"Yeah well she doesn't come around anymore, right? So I overpay my current guy, knowing full well that I'm doing so, in the hope that him having money means he won't go, like, steal tools from construction sites and get arrested. I doubt it has any such effect, yet I try. In the meantime, his dumb ass thinks I'm vulnerable to his guile. Which is irritating. Worse is the second thing, that there is no quality control, that these people are too stupid to cut things properly, that you've got people cooking speed that can't run a microwave, probably don't own a microwave, not a working one anyway. So every so often, I call him up, and he doesn't actually have anything, but rather than just tell me to wait, he'll go buy garbage and then add in whatever's around, who knows, Ajax? Baking soda? Ground glass? I swear one time he tried to pass a bag of fucking flour off on me. So I tell him to get the fuck out of here with that bullshit, and he'll have the gall to claim oh no man, this is that fyyyyyyahh. Then I'm like, alright, let's give it in an acetone bath, see what comes out; I've got time. Ohhhh I don't know man, I've gotta be back across town. Fool, I know you have not a goddamn thing to do today or any other day."

"Can you not buy higher up at this point?" Erica reaches for the tray, looks at Sherman for any sign of refusal, and curls a $20. She hits a respectable rail in two halves, one for each nostril. "This is pretty good."

"Yeah when he's on he's on. And no, he makes too much money off of me. Even when he went up to Rice Street for two months earlier this year, everything had to go through his junkie girlfriend, which was an ordeal."

"Rice Street is prison?"

"Aye, Fulton County jail, total shithole."

"And you've been there how many times?" Her smile is that of the ingenue. Her eyes are open wider than is typical for this time of day, wild eyes, pupils dilated and slightly nystagmic.

"Just twice. I mean, that's two times more than I'd like to have been there. You've gotta regard each one as a pretty big life error. Plenty of people with a lot less going for them that manage not to go to jail even once. 2003 for reckless driving—should have been a DUI, funny story—and again in 2004 for assault."

"Assault?"

"Came home and someone had broken into my apartment. I surprised them, beat the shit out of them, called up APD and was like, hey, come haul this shithead out of my apartment."

"They arrested you for that?"

"Ehhhhh apparently once someone's no longer a threat, you've gotta chill out. I fucked this guy up pretty bad. I didn't want him getting up, you know? So he was not walking under his own power. He didn't wake up, actually. I'm pretty lucky I didn't kill him. I took a Model-M to the back of his dome until he stopped moving."

"A Model-M?" Her voice is uncertain.

"Yeah, one of the big-ass IBM keyboards from back in the day. They run about three kilos, all molded plastic and steel and buckling springs, CLACK CLACK CLACK. I wouldn't want to go to war with it, but in a pinch, it'll do as a melee weapon."

Erica laughs, the sound girlish and pleasant. "You went to jail for assault with a keyboard?"

"Got let out on my recognizance the next day. He didn't press charges or anything. I don't think he was in any position to do so, and I doubt this burglarizing son of a bitch had any, like, beloved family. I did half a year of anger management classes and the charge got erased."

"And how were those?"

"I mean, stupid obviously, ridiculous, but also kinda useful? They were up in Marietta, ninety minutes up I-75 in a great herd of suburban commuters, and then an hour and a half each. So plenty of time to sit there and ponder whether you could have done things differently, what exactly the point of rendering this guy insensate was once he was down, whether you maybe do have a problem with anger and it's not doing anything good for you. Which I think I did, and I don't so much anymore, and my life is better for it. The class itself was unbearably vapid and banal and driven by the kind of psychologist charlatan who puts their fucking degrees on their book covers, utter horseshit, but whatever. One time I said that when you escalate from an argument to punching someone, you've lost the argument, and people thought it some kind of inspired insight into the nature of man." He grimaces; she laughs. "Mostly you sit there and consider what you need do to ensure you're never again in anger management classes. But that's kinda how all of that works, right? You're in prison because your actions finally became too obvious and annoying for society to tolerate you. You're in a mental institution because you were too insistent on your own nonsense, and people got tired of listening to it. I am not paid to listen to this drivel! You are a terminal fool."

"So when I took you over to his house that one time, the house with the raccoons"—Katz rolls his eyes—"was that after he'd been released?"

"Yeah he'd just gotten out. Jesus, the raccoons. Remember how he kept telling us take a seat, take a seat, and I was like, no offense man but there is zero chance I'm sitting on anything here? I mean, roaches were freely crawling around, not bothering to hide. They had established firm control."

Both of them have cigarettes burning freely in the ashtray now. "So baby why don't you just make it yourself? It can't be that hard." Her smile turns lethal. "I can help you if you're, you know, not good enough of an engineer."

Sherman grabs his Newport, leans back, takes a heavy drag. "I've asked myself that same question any number of times. I don't know. I guess I just never wanted to take that step up? Making meth sounds dirty, low-class. There are stenches and the possibility of explosions. I did once, back when the girl I was buying from died and I didn't have a hookup for a minute. Just personals using Sudafed from CVS—this was 2005, before the Combating Methamphetamine Act happened, when you could buy all the pseudo you wanted with nothing more than your good looks. It wasn't difficult. Quality was good. It was messy, though. If you start cooking meth, you'll probably want to start selling it, and I don't want to sell meth due to aforementioned meth people."

"But you sell it now."

"To like three people besides yourself. And they're all longtime heads I trust to keep their shit together. The worst person you can possibly sell drugs to is the person who's gonna get arrested sans resources or loyalty. That's the person who's going to drop your name."

She shrugs. "Does Michael do it?"

"Michael does not do it, and does not like that I do it, and it ought not be brought to his attention. We have an uneasy Don't-Ask-Don't-Tell détente on the issue."

Erica stands, leans over, kisses Sherman. "Let's make some. It would be a good couple's activity. I can show you correct laboratory technique. I'm sure yours is atrocious. Ugh, computer science kids come through my lab and try their hardest to poison everyone in the room. They're helpless idiot children."

"There are well over a thousand CS undergraduates. They're not all gonna be gems. Are we going to do this naked?"

Her face goes stern. "Absolutely not. Are you not wearing proper protective equipment? That's how you get burned. I have so much to teach you."

"I've gotta stir to run just about any liquid chromatography. How am I supposed to do that with my pants on?"

She catches him in a clutch. "Dick-stirring is the cause of 80% of lab accidents. We will have gloves, and aprons, and fume hoods, and I will show you how to do proper labwork. We'll analyze our results, then come back and try them, and then have crazy meth sex for a few hours."

"Delightful. I'm eagerly down."

"Where did you cook last? In 2005? Did you do it here?"

He has been waiting to drop the secret of the lab. "No, I've got a place."

"A place?" Her confusion is delicious.

"Some guys have little bungalows for their dalliances. They're married and can't bring the secretary home, right? So they've got a place. Surely you're familiar with the trope."

"So you have a place where you take women?"

"I have a place where I do science."

"Does it have a fume hood?"

"I'm just a dumb computer science major. What's a fume hood? Who is Spain? I multiplied two and two and got a rhombus. I drank all this hydrofluoric acid but I'm still thirsty. *Ubi sunt?*"

Erica's irritation is visible. "So does it or does it not have a fume hood, necessary for safe work?"

Katz locks in her eyes. "What do you think?"

∗ ∗ ∗ ∗ ∗ ∗ ∗ ∗ ∗

Bolaño asks a good question: "So why don't you just sell the method instead of the product?"

Katz feels like he deserves a goddamn medal; he was hoping for at least an "awesome!" Bolaño's actual productive role in the enterprise slips a bit more in Sherman's estimation. "Who's going to buy the method?"

"Our friends up north?"

"They can only pay with cash, and give little indication that they float more than an order or two. I don't want to trade a best-of-breed method for cash."

"We don't lose access ourselves. We can continue to employ it, unless they somehow cornered the market."

"They have one demonstrated skill, and it is building market. If they cooked, they'd poison themselves. And what, you want to sell hits retail? On the street? They're our distributors, and they do a fantastic job."

"No, not the street. We'd retain our big customers. Custom batches, essentially. But the regular transactions would cease, and we would instead take one large cash payout. That recurring commerce courts and facilitates investigation."

"So we franchise?"

"More or less."

"Stupid." Katz doesn't think he's ever seriously called Bolaño stupid before. Michael's nostrils flare in an almost simian reaction. Katz continues. "One, we do not need a large cash payout. Once we're using Erica's yeast instead of buying their ergocristine, our cost approaches zero."

"Approaches zero? Bullshit, unless you've been making up costs for the lab. You claimed each batch to runs almost two thousand dollars in terms of consumable sundries."

"Fine, profits skyrocket. Better?"

"Assuming they'll buy it, and her costs are as low as she thinks."

"Why wouldn't they buy it? This is better for them. They don't have to burn their ergocristine; they can continue hoarding it. If you want to retain production capability, we have to keep the lab, so no savings there. I see no advantage other than upfront payment of money we'll make anyway, shitty unbanked money that'll just have to sit on the laundering bottleneck."

"The advantage, Sherman, is that we don't go to prison."

"Why do you say that? We'd still have the lab."

"I do not regard an infrequently used lab, one we could keep clean of precursors, as a liability in the same universe as periodic, predictable runs involving a clan of Minnesota burnouts."

"You know, Cloud was a strange guy, he danced a lot, but he fucking quoted Nietzsche at you as I recall. They've been professional in every way that counts. We've made great money off of them, and are about to make ridiculous money off of them. A year ago we'd have killed to be out from underneath the ergocristine deposit. We're—Erica and I—are about to kill the ergocristine cost entirely. Why are you wanting to fuck it up?"

"Because this is not fucking guns and butter microeconomics! Yes, you've put us in a better place, which is all the more reason to avoid prison."

Katz is tired of arguing. "Your people out west."

Bolaño smiles. "Yes. They sampled the product last week, and asked me to convey their warmest regards. I of course claimed no knowledge of the origin, only that I had encountered a buying opportunity on my travels."

"I told you I've been making that fire! Call me Prometheus." Katz grins, and whoops. "Do you see them needing more?"

"No. Honestly I don't see them going through their key, nor anywhere near through it. Though who knows. I think my friend was excited about the idea of having a kilogram of LSD. Like a moment of Sam's Club madness."

"How much did you get from him?"

"Profit from the transaction was commensurate with involved cash flow, risks legal and financial, exclusivity of the hookup. No one is complaining."

"C'mon, I hooked you up. What'd you make? Tell me at least a meg. If you couldn't pull a meg out of a kilogram, you suck."

Bolaño considered lying, or simply dismissing the question. Later, he attributed his truthful answer to weakness and arrogance, and regretted it. "Ten."

Silence. "You made ten megs? What?"

"I sold it for ten. I cleared nine." He smirks. "Banked."

Katz sputters for a moment. "You told me your budget was $0.10."

"That was my budget." Fuck it, why hold back? "I wanted to make nine."

"I suspect I know the answer, but was any of that coming to me?"

"In what sense?"

"In what sense? Were you going to give me any of that?"

"I paid you a million dollars."

"You paid forty percent my partners' cost. Friend rate. Best friend rate. Better than best friend rate: insider's ballbusting rate. You flipped it at 900% profit. I thought you were offering at like two megs, or I'd never have done it at $0.10, and you know that."

"I'm not sure what you're proposing."

"I'm proposing you give me at least the one and a half million difference between what you paid and what SYNCOPE pays, despite recalling myself explicitly saying you'd likely pay more, because you misled me."

"I misled you?"

"You said your budget was $0.10!"

"That was my budget. My budget was shaped by more than just what they would pay. My profit needed to justify the legal and financial exposure."

"Fuck outta here, legal exposure, I'm the one standing over four fucking life sentences' worth of equipment and precursors and intermediates. I'm the one in the fucking lab for forty hours, head aching from inhaling all kinds of trace shit, smelling like Danzig's cats' assholes, randomly tripping for twelve hours because I touched half a milligram of clear liquid. Do you want to go in there and try to set up column chromatography on a thousand mics? You'd be introducing yourself to the rotovaps using the wrong motherfucking name. Do you even know which lights get used when?"

"Are you done?"

"Done selling you million dollar keys that's for sure."

"As I said, it was a onetime thing."

"And you got it banked."

"Wrote me a check."

"Son of a fucking bitch." Katz's face is dark.

"I will continue funding my part of the lab."

"Well that's some Andrew Carnegie shit of you. Look, dude, I understand where you're coming from here; I really do. You know I wouldn't support some broad redistribution from above. Your argument? Totally valid, if you're willing to be a complete cunt. Not to bitch things up in here, but we've been friends for a decade. We've done some cool shit. I respect the hell out of you; I think you do me. You maxed this deal by exploiting that. Are you going to even stab at making it right?"

"Sherman. You've got a good trade here. You and Erica are about to reduce the COGS to almost zero. Keep your head down, work hard, and don't demean us both by appealing to emotion."

"Eat my shit you patronizing whore. At least let me trade you cash for banked money. You paid me in goddamn currency. Where'd you even get a million dollars cash if they paid you with check?"

"I took it out of my bank."

"You motherfucking son of a wattled and diseased shebitch. You depreciated it 50% why, just to fuck me in the ass? What the fuck?" Katz is livid.

Bolaño sighs. "As always, Sherman, we avoid linkage of our accounts by transaction."

"Not for a million fucking dollars we don't! There are ten thousand other ways someone can correlate us. I'm living in twelve hundred square feet, three hundred of which are occupied by sacks of cash I can't use to buy a bigger place. Getting in the bank involves far more bullshit than depositing a goddamn check. Fuck you, dude."

"You're agitated. Let's get together when you're calmer." Michael Bolaño dropped five twenties and departed.

19   uranium

(this material was taken from the website of Sherman Spartacus Katz)

nucleosynthesis and disintegration

Every schoolgirl understands that stellar nucleosynthesis arising from ther-monuclear fusion (combination of atoms, suppressed by the Coulomb barrier) largely ceases beyond the binding energy peaks at ^{62}Ni (highest binding en-ergy per nucleon[1]) and ^{56}Fe (lowest mass per nucleon[2]). In the s[low]-process, neutrons are captured at time intervals (much) larger than the relevant α and β⁻ decay times. Any element heavier than bismuth is likely to decay by α be-fore collecting another neutron, and β⁻ decay intercedes before the heaviest isotopes can be synthesized. From whence, then, Earth's plentiful uranium?

The heaviest elements are only negligibly produced in the i[ntermediate]-process within stars of the asymptotic giant branch. The vast majority of the universe's uranium is built up in the r[apid]-process within Type II (core collapse) supernovae and neutron stars[3], especially during interactions with other compact remnants. The r-process regime is indicated by neutron fluxes sufficient to drive multiple accumulations before an intervening decay, and typically lasts only seconds. It has been demonstrated that at least six dis-tinct r-process sites, separated by hundreds of millions of years, contributed significant heavy elements to our solar system.

Uranium is the heaviest primordial element[4], *i.e.* those atoms both old enough to have been present in the protoplanetary disk from which Earth accrued, and sufficiently stable to still exist[5]. Our planet is approximately 4.6×10^9 years old, so primordial isotopes having half-lives less than 10^8 years have almost entirely decayed.

Twenty-eight isotopes and eight excited isomers of uranium are known to exist, none of which are stable. All naturally occurring isotopes primarily decay via α, along with rare spontaneous fissions. Terrestrial uranium is at this time 99.3% ^{238}U (4.5×10^9 years), 0.7% ^{235}U (7×10^8 years), and trace ^{234}U

---

[1]If ^{62}Ni is the most tightly-bound nucleus, why are "iron stars" eventually expected in a universe absent proton decay? Because the 1,736 nucleons of 28 ^{62}Ni are 0.011u heavier than 31 ^{56}Fe.

[2]^{56}Fe is much more plentiful than ^{62}Ni, despite the latter being more tightly bound. α capture from silicon is marginally exothermic even beyond ^{56}Ni, but competes unfavorably with photodisin-tegration at the necessary temperatures. α capture thus effectively stops at ^{56}Ni, which undergoes two quick β⁺'s to reach stable ^{56}Fe via ^{56}Co.

[3]The decays of short-lived radioisotopes created in binary compact events power kilonovae.

[4]Heavier elements are terrestrially produced in trace amounts, *e.g.* ^{238}U can absorb a neutron to become ^{239}Np, which then decays via β⁻ to ^{239}Pu. They can furthermore be produced in the r-process, but all such elements have half-lives many times less than the Earth's age.

[5]With a half-life of 8×10^7 years, ^{244}Pu created concurrently with Earth would be reduced by a factor of roughly 10^{17} following fifty-seven half lives. Recent claims of non-anthropogenic ^{244}Pu, if validated, are likely the radiosignature of a near-Earth (less than 1.2×10^2 parsecs away) binary compact merger about 3×10^8 years ago.

$(2.5 \times 10^5$ years$)^6$. This does not imply that more ^{238}U is synthesized than ^{235}U! The production ratio R is not known with great confidence (authors report anything from 0.89 to 1.89), but it is broadly thought that at least 20% more ^{235}U is produced in the r-process ($R \geq 1.2$). The ^{238}U supremacy is entirely an effect of its longer half-life.

^{234}U is primarily a decay product of ^{238}U by way of α to ^{234}Th, β^- to ^{234}Pa, and β^- to ^{234}U. This waystation is the second longest in the ^{238}U decay chain, behind only ^{238}U itself. The chain's only other half-life exceeding ten thousand years is ^{230}Th (α to ^{226}Ra, 7.5×10^4 years). By the time ^{238}U reaches the stable ^{206}Pb, 51.7 MeV have radiated away; this is known as the "uranium chain." ^{235}U, with its significantly shorter half-life, enjoys only a brief stop at ^{231}Pa (32,760 years) on its way to ^{207}Pb, and this "actinium chain" represents 46.4 MeV. Note that these energies include contributions from antineutrinos, which are generally lost to the system.

quantum hadrodynamics

Protons, by virtue of their single d[own] and two u[p] valence quarks, carry an electric charge of 1. Like charges repel. How do atoms beyond hydrogen exist? The neutron, with two d and one u valence quark, has no electric charge. Both types of nucleon are subject to the approximately charge-independent[7] residual strong force[8]. This force is repulsive at 0.7 fm or less (a little less than a nucleon's radius— nucleons have radii of about 0.8 fm), but quickly becomes attractive, reaching a maximum (about two orders of magnitude stronger than the electromagnetic force) around 1 fm. The attraction decays very rapidly with distance, becoming negligible beyond 2.5 fm.

The addition of neutrons can thus stabilize a nucleus. The lightest elements' stable isotopes generally have the same number of neutrons as protons ($A = \frac{Z}{2}$)[9]. Starting with ^{23}Na, an extra neutron is often present. Stable isotopes of iron (element 24) have between 30 and 34 neutrons. Gold's single stable isotope is ^{197}Au, with 118 neutrons and 79 protons. The heaviest stable nucleus, ^{208}Pb, packs 126 neutrons among 82 protons, a difference of 44. By the time we reach ^{235}U, there are 51 more neutrons than the 92 protons; protons are less than 40% of the nucleus, a sphere having radius close to 7 fm. This places antipodal nucleons 14 fm away from one another: most pairs of nucleons are too far

---

[6]Isotopic composition varies slightly depending on where the uranium is found. The difference is statistically significant, but not relevant for our purposes. One exception is the Oklo region in Gabon's Haut-Ogooué province, where the uranium is depleted in ^{235}U due to natural fission chain reactions during the Paleoproterozoic era, at which time ^{235}U made up 3.1% of uranium.

[7]If it's charge-independent, why is deuterium stable, but diprotons and dineutrons don't exist? The latter are unstable due to Pauli's exclusion principle (recall that both protons and neutrons are spin-½ fermions)—the proton and neutron have opposing (aligned) isospins, whereas duplicating either one will require at least two levels of angular momentum.

[8]The residual strong force was for many years modeled using virtual π, ρ, and ω mesons together with Yukawa potentials. It is probably better understood as a van der Waals-like force between quarks of distinct hadrons, moderated by gluons. The deuteron, for instance, can be considered a hexaquark.

[9]An exception is beryllium, with only one stable isotope, ^{9}Be.

apart to undergo meaningful strong force attraction, but the electromagnetic repulsion among protons is much less diminished. Central nucleons are subject to more attraction than those on the surface, which can break away as αs.

At these extremes, addition of energy (or sometimes simple random thermal motion) can cause the nucleus to deform away from a sphere and into an ellipsoid. Nucleons near the center of this ellipse continue to feel the maximum attraction, but there is more surface area, and thus more starved nucleons. Should two lobes develop, there exists a critical distance beyond which the strong force cannot hold them together, and they fission, releasing free neutrons and electromagnetic potential (the potential energy results from the work done initially to bring together the nucleons). The two (rarely three) fragments push apart at tremendous speed[10].

Isotope	Excitation for fission (MeV)	Binding of last neutron (MeV)
^{232}Th	6.5	4.8
^{233}U	6.2	6.8
^{235}U	5.7	6.5
^{238}U	6.5	4.8
^{239}Pu	5.8	6.5
^{240}Pu	6.2	5.2
^{241}Pu	5.6	6.3

Isotopes with an odd number of neutrons bind an additional neutron with roughly an extra MeV due to neutron pairing effects. For these isotopes, a neutron having no kinetic energy would still be enough to trigger a fission. For isotopes with even numbers of neutrons, the incoming neutron must bring along sufficient kinetic energy. Fission remains a fundamentally stochastic event—^{235}U can absorb a neutron and become ^{236}U, an odious dogturd of an isotope which ought neither be purchased, nor accepted as a gift[11].

Fission is almost always asymmetric, well-approximated with a bimodal Gaussian centered around 95 and 135 nucleons. This is easily explained by the first derivative of the curve of binding energy: its absolute value is larger below 120 than above, and this split is a configuration of lower total energy.

actinide chemistry

Uranium easily forms halides, nitrides, and carbides, in addition to the critical oxides and hydrides. Uranium has seven oxidation states, from -1 to 6.

---

[10]The binding energy of actinides is about 7.6 MeV per nucleon, compared to about 8.5 MeV for fission fragments. Mean fission energy for ^{235}U is 202.79 MeV (about 0.9 MeV per nucleon).

[11]Reactor fuel which has been used for any amount of time will be contaminated with ^{236}U. Natural uranium—whether depleted, enriched, or fresh from the ground—ought contain negligible ^{236}U. ^{236}U doesn't easily capture neutrons, but when it does, it becomes ^{237}Np. This isotope of neptunium will, in a pinch, work in a nuclear weapon (or fast neutron reactor), but absorbs thermal neutrons to become similarly useless ^{238}Pu. Not quite useless—you can make radioisotope thermoelectric generators out of ^{238}Pu, sure—but they don't even use it in pacemakers anymore.

There exist no stable isotopes among the fifteen actinides (element 89, actinium, through element 103, lawrencium). All are silvery metals, with considerably more spread in valence than the lanthanides. Actinium through nobelium (element 102) fill up the 5f block. These outermost 5f electrons are relativistic, and demonstrate complicated electron correlation dynamics.

Finely-divided uranium is pyrophoric in a moist atmosphere (or a dry one at 300 °C), and liberates hydrogen when it reacts with water, generating heat:

$$U + 2H_2O \rightarrow UO_2 + 2H_2 + \Delta Q$$
$$U + \tfrac{3}{2}H_2 \rightarrow UH_3 + \Delta Q$$
$$4UH_3 + 7O_2 \rightarrow 4UO_2 + 6H_2O + \Delta Q$$

The critical volatile uranium hexafluoride requires several reactions:

$$U_3O_8 + 6HNO_3 \rightarrow 3UO_2(NO_3)_2 + 2H_2O + 2H^+$$
$$4UO_2(NO_3)_2 + 4NH_3 + 4H+ + 3O_2 \rightarrow 2(NH_4)_2U_2O_7 + 4NO_3^-$$
$$(NH_4)_2U_2O_7 + 2H_2 \rightarrow 2UO_2 + 2NH_3 + 3H_2O$$
$$UO_2 + 4HF \rightarrow UF_4 + 2H_2O + \Delta Q$$
$$UF_4 + F_2 \rightarrow UF_6 + \Delta Q$$

Uranium is lithophilic and is expected to differentiate into the crust. About half of Earth's internal heat budget is due to radiogenic heating from the crust and mantle, and decay of uranium (along with thorium and potassium) is a major source of such heating[12]. Uranium and plutonium are recovered from nuclear fuel using PUREX, a type of liquid-liquid extraction ion exchange using tributyl phosphate. It leaves behind "PUREX raffinate," a liquor of intense radiotoxicity consisting of fission products, fuel cladding, and mixed actinides—canonical high-level nuclear waste.

UF_6 reacts with moisture, producing uranyl fluoride (UO_2F_2) and hydrogen fluoride (HF), neither of which are very good for you at all.

the uranium economy

About two thirds of worldwide uranium extraction takes place in Kazakhstan, Canada, and Australia. Other major producers include the United States, Russia, China, Uzbekistan, Niger, and Namibia. *In-situ* leaching pumps a lixiviant (a strongly acidic or basic solution with a carrier) into boreholes. Ores dissolve in the solution, which is pumped back to the surface. This is the cheapest and most common means of production, though open-pit and underground mines are also used together with grinders and chemical leaching. Most mining operations convert this slurry to yellowcake[13] on-site. It is packed into 200 L

---

[12]It's difficult to directly sample the mantle's composition, but it is possible to estimate the contribution from each radioisotope via observation of geoneutrinos.

[13]Mostly U_3O_8, some uranium dioxide and trioxide, then uranyl hydroxide, uranyl sulfate, sodium diuranate, uranyl peroxide etc. to taste. It's kinda yellow, but also kinda orange, and kinda blackish green—"yellowcake" originally referred to ammonium diuranate, which is indeed a bright yellow.

barrels, which are loaded into standard shipping containers. The IAEA attempts to track all transfers of uranium, but over 50,000 tonnes are shipped per year.

The milled ore is dissolved in nitric acid, yielding a more homogeneous uranyl nitrate ($UO_2(NO_3)_2$). Solvent extraction using kerosene separates the uranyl nitrate from the sludge, and ammonia is applied, yielding ammonium diuranate ($(NH_4)_2U_2O_7$). The thickened precipitate goes through a centrifuge, and then into a calciner, where heat and hydrogen reduction bring us back to uranium oxide. Hydrofluoric acid is added to achieve UF_4. Oxidation via fluorine finally results in UF_6. Uranium metal can be taken directly to hex via chlorine trifluoride: an atom of U reacts with two ClF_3, producing a molecule of hex and a bonus output of toothsome chlorine gas. Hex is shipped in Type 48Y containers, each one capable of securely transporting 12.5 tons of solidified uranium hexafluoride (8.4 tons uranium) for enrichment.

The solid UF_6 is heated back into a gas and reduced to ceramic-grade uranium dioxide powder by one of numerous processes. This powder is sintered into pellets. The pellets might be used directly in research reactors, but power reactors will take them as fuel units, usually as uranium zirconium.

enrichment

^{235}U is fissionable with neutrons at all energies, whereas ^{238}U only has an appreciable cross-section for fission with high-energy neutrons. In particular, ^{238}U cannot usually be broken up at the neutron energies resulting from nuclear fission, making it unsuitable for a chain reaction. Most power reactors[14] and all fission weapons rely on uranium enriched in ^{235}U. The critical mass of a bare[15], uncompressed uranium sphere rapidly grows in size, from 52kg of pure ^{235}U to over 400kg at 20% enrichment and over 600kg at 15%. Uranium consisting of less than approximately 5.4% ^{235}U cannot form a critical mass without neutron reflection or compression. Where uranium is used in modern weapon cores (plutonium is generally preferred), it is typically enriched to at least 90% ^{235}U "weapon grade," though even 20% is considered "weapon-usable" (Little Boy used uranium with an average enrichment of 80%).

Enrichment requires separating the isotopes of an element. Separating the various components of a compound—solvent extraction, fractional distillation, Soxhlet extraction—usually takes advantage of different elements' valence chemistry, or large differences between physical properties. All isotopes of uranium have 92 electrons, and thus effectively the same chemistry[16]. Most enrichment techniques rely on the difference in mass, but ^{235}U is only 1.3% lighter than ^{238}U. Enrichment is almost always performed using uranium hexafluoride (UF_6, known as "hex"); it is one of the most volatile compounds of uranium, boils at 56.5 °C, uses monoisotopic natural fluorine (thus isotopologues differ only as their uranium differs), and is easily produced from yellowcake.

---

[14]The Canadian CANDU and British Magnox can both use natural uranium, as did Fermi's first pile. The Magnox is graphite-moderated; CANDU uses heavy water (D_2O).

[15]Bare: not making use of a neutron reflector or tamper.

[16]The French CHEMEX method exploits very minor differences in valence changes under redox.

The Manhattan Project employed three separation techniques in the mad, uncertain rush to fuel Little Boy. Electromagnetic separation is fed ionized uranium vapor, where magnets redirect a stream of these ions to a target; ^{235}U is concentrated in the inner track of the redirected stream. This was the basis for the calutrons at Y-12, which fed both of the other methods. The liquid thermal diffusion plant at S-50 took advantage of concentration gradients arising from sustained thermal gradients: ^{235}U is more likely to go to the hotter surface. Gaseous diffusion is more efficient (and more complicated) than either. Graham's law states that the effusion rate of a gas is inversely proportional to the square root of its molecular mass: ^{235}U is thus more easily driven through semipermeable membranes into regions of low pressure. This was the basis for the K-25 wartime plant, and USEC's Paducah and Portsmouth plants responsible for most of America's cold war enrichment.

Centrifuges spin to create strong centripetal forces, driving heavier ^{238}U to the outside of the cylinder. Separation via gas centrifuge is far more efficient than any of the wartime methods. It is the workhorse for almost all modern enrichment, including the HALEU[17] necessary for many next-generation reactor designs. The Stuxnet worm targeted the Step 7 software on Iranian Siemens SCADA SIMATIC WinCC PLCs, causing the centrifuges thereby controlled to tear themselves apart.

So-called "third generation" enrichment approaches employ lasers and small differences in hyperfine structure, and promise greater efficiency than centrifuges. AVLIS (Atomic Vapor Laser Isotope Separation) preferably photoexcites ^{235}U in vaporized uranium metal using tunable dye lasers, targeting the 502.74nm absorption peak of ^{238}U (versus 502.73nm for ^{235}U). MLIS (Molecular yadda yadda) excites ^{235}U in hex with an infrared laser at 16μm. These excited molecules absorb a second-stage XeCl excimer laser at 308nm, photolysing to ^{235}UF$_5$ and fluorine. SILEX (Separation of Isotopes by Laser Excitation) is reputed to be a step above either in terms of efficiency, but is classified by the governments of America and Australia. The American Physical Society considers it to be a "game-changer" with regards to proliferation.

Information wants to be free, and I doubt it will remain secret for long.

decay chains

No nuclide heavier than ^{208}Pb is stable. Neither β$^-$ neither β$^+$ change the number of nucleons; these weak interactions change quark flavors, and thus one type of nucleon to another. The only ways a heavy nucleus actually drops nucleons on its way to the top of the curve of binding energy are photonuclear reactions (photodisintegration and its bigger brother photofission), spallation (typically by cosmic rays), neutron-induced fission, and spontaneous fallapart a/k/a explosive atomic diarrhea (α decay, cluster decay, and spontaneous fission). Of these, only the diarrhea decays can take place without outside inputs, and α

---

[17]High-Assay Low-Enriched, up to about 20% ^{235}U.
SCADA: supervisory control and data acquisition
SIMATIC: Siemens Automatic   **PLC:** programmable logic controller

dominates everywhere (save freak isotope ^{250}Cm). Dropping an α means the loss of two protons and two neutrons. We thus have four lengthy decay chains, each containing only isotopes whose nucleon counts are congruent modulo four. Unless struck by a wayward gamma ray or muon, atoms will not leap across chains within timescales similar to the age of the universe (on a long enough timescale, proton decay or fission of observationally stable isotopes back down to ^{56}Fe and/or ^{62}Ni is expected to destroy all heavier isotopes).

The four chains are known as thorium, uranium a/k/a radium, actinium, and neptunium. The neptunium chain is essentially extinct in nature, due to the relatively short halflife of ^{237}Np. At least one isotope of uranium is present on each chain.

Chain	End	Root	MeV[18]	U
Thorium	^{208}Pb	^{232}Th	42.6	^{232}U, ^{236}U
Actinium	^{207}Pb	^{235}U	46.4	^{235}U
Uranium	^{206}Pb	^{238}U	51.7	^{234}U, ^{238}U
Neptunium	^{205}Tl	^{237}Np	66.8	^{233}U

applications

Depleted uranium is denser[19] and less radioactive than natural uranium, while retaining its high Z value. It is self-sharpening, flammable, and fairly cheap. It is used in armor-piercing projectiles, nuclear weapon tampers, radiation shielding, thermonuclear weapon casings, sampling calorimeters (such as those employed in ZEUS at DESY-HERA and D0 at Fermilab), trim weights in aircraft, and uranium-bearing reagents (especially uranyl acetate).

There are three major applications of fissile atoms[20], all of which benefit from (or require) some degree of enrichment:

1. Low-level fission as a source of neutrons.
2. Significant fission as a source of power.
3. Uncontrolled fission as a source of destruction.

---

[18]From specified "root" to "end."

[19]19.05 g/cm^3, 68.4% denser than lead.

[20]Those capable of sustaining a nuclear fission chain reaction, primarily ^{233}U, ^{235}U, ^{239}Pu, and ^{241}Pu. Others have too short of a half-life to be generally useful: ^{242}Am, ^{243}Cf, ^{244}Cf, ^{245}Cf, ^{243}Cm, ^{244}Cm, ^{245}Cm, ^{246}Cm, and ^{247}Cm. Beyond curium, everything's too short-lived to matter.

Part IV

beamtenherrschaft—BUREAUCRACY

And what rough beast, its hour come round at last,
Slouches towards Bethlehem to be born?

William Butler Yeats, "The Second Coming" (1919)

We work in the dark—we do what we can—we give what we have.
Our doubt is our passion, and our passion is our task.
The rest is the madness of art.

Henry James, "The Middle Years" (1893)

Nature does not endure sudden mutations without great violence.

François Rabelais,
*Les horribles et épouvantables faits et prouesses du très renommé Pantagruel
Roi des Dipsodes, fils du Grand Géant Gargantua*
(The Horrible and Terrifying Deeds and Words of the Very Renowned
Pantagruel King of the Dipsodes, Son of the Great Giant Gargantua, c. 1532)

...elementa vero calore solventur...
(...and the elements shall melt with fervent heat...)

2 Peter 3:10 (KJV)

312

20   greg moyer gives some bad advice

If he ever committed to becoming a supervillain, Katz thought, he'd definitely bring Devesh along as a number two. The idea of Bolaño operating as an enemy of the world was too scary. It ruined the daydream. Devesh, though—now Dr. Choudhary—Devesh had big Chaotic Good energy, and no interest in controlling people, an outlook of fundamental *laissez-faire* Katz endorsed with both thumbs. Katz had never grokked why anyone with the wherewithal to make demands of the world's governments would seek control, why any thinking man would care to "rule the world." No, Katz would have held them hostage until they agreed to leave him the fuck alone. Did Skeletor really want to sit around and write zoning law? Even Stalin wasn't above a bit of delegation.

Devesh was largely without compunction, especially when egged on. He was delighted by the transgressive, usually merry, and never merrier than when he could shock someone with behavior or insight. Whenever Katz contemplated subversion of the laws of man or nature, Devesh was one of the first people he talked to. He furthermore always had cigarettes (or at least bidis) should Katz be lacking, and laughed easily at jokes, and could smoke endless weed without getting stupid, and did not compete for the same dating resources, all attributes Katz admired. The topic today was uranium, for fun and profit.

"It dependeth on where thou wants to pursue enrichment. In America, one needn't worry about export controls. Centrifuges, we have the AC100 from USEC, most advanced. TC-21 from URENCO, a big improvement over their TC-12, but less than a third the SWUs of AC100. Iran's IR-1, ptah, a copy of P-1, itself based on Dutch SNOR and CNOR. Pakistan uses P-4 now, improved from Khan's P-2 at KRL. Russia with their Generation VIII, China running Russia's VI but likely soon indigenous designs. Areva and URENCO together on the Enrichment Technology Company of Europe."

"So you can get centrifuges wherever you want, basically?"

Devesh laughs from the gut. "Thou will be laughed from the room approaching USEC and asking to purchase an AC100. The American Centrifuge is for America, not mere Americans." He wheezes a bit, and catches his breath. "ETC maybe? But not without NRC documentation, certainly. Likely intercepted on import even then."

Extracting data from Devesh can be frustrating. "So how does being in America help you? No export controls, but they're not selling to you, either."

"Ahhh, likely a hindrance." Katz sighs explosively. "Perhaps the point I am badly making is that surreptitious enrichment with the gas centrifuge is not done well in America."

"So where would you do it?"

"Well, America is advantageous due to the lack of export controls."

"Devesh! You just said it was bad."

SNOR/CNOR: scientific/cultivated nuclear orbital rotor

KRL: خ ان ت رج رب ه گ اہ و م راک ز ت سخ ت ی ی ق Khan Research Laboratory

Devesh laughs. "Katz, Katz. The strategy of gas centrifuges would not be indicated here. But many useful tools are export controlled."

"...and you'd benefit from access to them?"

"Oh, yes. It is unlikely that you could purchase ultracentrifuges of any recent design in any nation without licensing from that state."

"So gas centrifuges are a dead end."

"Unless thou wished to build them. Difficult, difficult. Advanced metallurgy is necessary, precise manufacturing also."

"So...you'd build your own centrifuges."

Devesh's laughter is not cruel, but conveys that the idea is illfounded. "Katz! I am completely without the ability to build even a basic gas centrifuge."

"Devesh I'm just gonna let you talk and await with eager anticipation something that seems at least a step towards solving the problem."

"Ahhh, always thou maketh me laugh, Katz! The problem, then: to enrich natural or depleted uranium ore, in the form most likely of hex gas, UF_6. Yes?" Katz nods. "And it is assumed that I am officially disapproved of by the Man, that an ideal outcome is for the Man to knoweth not of me. Also always, the objective of least costs, economical use, good stewardship of materials, minimal poisoning of flora and fauna, sky and water." Devesh pauses and sucks air through his teeth. "In this circumstance, Katz, I eschew the Zippe centrifuge."

"Good? Since you said already that they're unavailable."

Devesh chuckles and puts his hand on Katz's shoulder. "See? Thou understands." Grinning, satisfied: "No, Katz, in this case, I employ the laser."

"Why is that better?"

"It is not so much better."

"Christ, Devesh. Then why look so smug about it?"

Devesh shifts in his seat. "Not so much better than centrifuges for energy efficiency, size of facility. Much more separation. Some difficulties in cascade design, depending on the laser. Pipes, pipes everywhere, full of gases for cooling, and also gas lasers. Optical difficulties, overcome with effort."

Katz stares.

Devesh laughs. "Thou stares at me."

"Then why would you use lasers, Devesh?"

"Because lasers can be used!" Devesh laughs loudly.

"Explain."

"Katz, precious few problems are solved with gas ultracentrifuges. Fewer still expect solutions. An AC100 is twelve meters tall, six times thy height, towering. Biological centrifuges? Different stories entirely. Tabletop devices, workstation sized at the largest. Lasers? Active research, both in design and application. A great many uses. Many suppliers." Devesh wears glasses these days; his eyes are still warm behind them, and full of laughter. "Are radioactive emanations not inevitable?"

"Our radiation burden shouldn't be too bad, honestly. There's two concerns: detection and the actual health hazard, and detection is a duo of issues in itself. One, container detection at the port, probably when the truck takes the container away, although there's also the chance of an invasive Customs inspection. Two, detection at the site by overflying planes, possibly even stuff driving nearby if there's enough skyshine. Three, personnel shielding at site, and any kind of disposal."

"Skyshine? Planes?"

"Radiation you emit out the roof that scatters off the atmosphere. You're typically going to have less shielding on the roof, right? If you do too little, and you leak out enough crap, you can detect that on the ground outside due to downscatter. Planes fly around with radiation detectors for all kinds of reasons. Uranium prospecting, looking for lost material, riding fences. I'm pretty sure there are services you can rent that'll map out a given area's gamma load. Whenever the President visits, you get helicopters out the ass for a few days; they're almost certainly looking for radiological threats."

Devesh chortles. "Hast thou ever irradiated one to freak them out?"

"No, Devesh, I have never irradiated a NEST helicopter for the purposes of 'freaking them out.' In general, I try not to freak out government helicopters. Hell, they might have such a plane flying circles over the port. Or better yet, a drone. We've got to assume our container is going through a portal detector during offload and/or takeaway. There are like a dozen manufacturers. leidos. Ludlum Measurements. Rapiscan. Bertin Technologies. Southern Scientific. Thermo Fisher. Polimaster. LAURUS Systems. Arktis. RadComm. Christ."

"Why so many? Is one company not dominant?"

"Devesh, when the American government decides to swing its dick around in the economy, companies are going to spring up to suck that dick."

"Katz, there is another worry—active detectors."

"Active? As in they blast you with something and try to elicit a reaction? Like, gammas and neutrons and shit? Holy shit, I never considered that. I mean, I did, but I was like 'no way.' Isn't that a hazard? Maybe we could send something through first to detect and such active schemes?"

"Dumb idea, Katz! You can easily figure out what kind of active means they might use. Then, assume they're present, and defeat them. Thy plan has a race condition. Aren't thou CS?" Devesh's face is all mirth.

"And if we found something operating, we'd need defeat it anyway. Yeah, point ceded, Devesh. Let's talk about those in a minute. Ahhh, mang, it's good to have you back around."

Devesh assumes a proud grin.

"So as I opened, we shouldn't be emitting much radiation at all, for the purposes of passive detection. Alphas and betas don't matter. They're not getting out the container. I very much doubt they even have detectors for those, at the container level anyway. We're not getting raw ore or anything like that, but milled yellowcake. There shouldn't be much in there other than uranium oxide and friends. Downstream daughter contaminant shit should be almost entirely filtered out."

"What about newly created daughters?"

"^{238}U goes to ^{234}Th and ^{234}Pa, then hits ^{234}U and ^{230}Th, combined halflife 320K years. That decay chain takes eighty days to reach 90% equilibrium. ^{235}U goes to ^{231}Th and ^{231}Pa. It sits on 231 for about thirty thousand years. All weak

---

NEST: Nuclear Emergency Support Team

gammas, trivially shielded. That decay chain is only three and a half days to 90%, but who cares, right? So long as your processing stage is getting rid of ^{226}Ra and everything below that, we don't need deal with anything. There are some high energy gammas released off the protactinium-234 in the 238 chain. You're gonna see 13.5 neutrons/s off a key of natural uranium, almost all of them from ^{238}U. ^{235}U doesn't emit neutrons for shit."

"These are the neutrons of spontaneous fissions?"

"Aye, and of course you get all manner of unholy one-off jank from those, daughter products all over the map: neutron-rich, radiating like there's a sale at the gamma store. Theoretically they can activate anything else in there, and get that radiating. Thankfully, they're rare."

"Rare? Off a tonne of natural uranium there'd be 13,500 per second."

"They're rare compared to alphas."

"Katz, if I am emitting 13,500 neutrons per second, I am very concerned about it. I am concerned if I emit this many neutrons in a year."

"It's a good thing, then, that you're not a tonne of natural uranium."

Devesh laughs loud and hard. "I am saying that the neutron detection threshold can be quite low, due to the low neutron background, and the infrequency of neutron emissions from most goods."

Katz nods. "And shielding is difficult, because your neutron detector has a much better chance of detecting thermal neutrons than fast ones. So knocking it down with some paraffin or water hurts more than it helps."

"It sounds to me, Katz, like neutrons need be directed out the front or back of the container. Can this be accomplished by guiding the neutrons?"

"Not at 100%, but yeah, if you surrounded the top and sides with water, enough water, most of them ought go out the major axis. Interesting. Now the gammas, you can figure the bulk of the uranium shields its own weak rays. The more powerful ones max out at around a MeV. I think it's 25.4 Bq/mg for natural uranium, so 25K decays per gram per second. Uranium and thorium have the lowest specific activities of any meaningful radioactive isotopes, comparable to ^{40}K. I think potassium-40 is actually higher? Regardless, it sounds like we're definitely going to exceed background on both gamma and neutrons, so we're going to want directed shielding. High-Z for the gammas, low-Z for the neutrons. Sides are more important than the top, especially for neutrons."

Devesh inspected him closely. "Sherman, is this more than an entirely intellectual exercise?"

"Devesh, how well are they paying you?"

"Remuneration for assistant professors is not excessive."

"How would you like to get up to some shit?"

All teeth: "I'm a cowboy, Katz, looking for anything heavy."

✶ ✶ ✶ ✶ ✶ ✶ ✶ ✶

Friday came, and Katz had not heard from Vlad. For three years plus, there had been the weekly order, usually on Thursday, sometimes early on Friday. The Romanian had in Katz's opinion proven himself several times over. His business had been orderly, quiet, and profitable. It had expanded, but never too quickly. Only once had he been late with money. He had called Katz, clearly making an effort to sound firm, to hide the fear and worry in the undertones of his voice. A quiet story of being ripped off: he never used the word "escort." Perhaps some skank brought home from a bar. She was gone when he woke up, along with several thousand dollars and most of his stash. Poor guy. The Betrayed, indeed. It had been a pleasure to sooth him, to offer him sanctuary, to immediately offer to cover his payment, and also to give him a few ounces from Katz's personal supply. Good people are hard to find.

Finally, Saturday afternoon Katz gave him a call. "Vlad mang! What's going down? I was asked to inquire as to the lack of an order thus far this week."

A delay. "So Sherman, here's the thing. I found another hookup, and I'm paying a lot less, and the herb is very comparable. Maybe better. It's more indica, and I like sativa. But if you like indica, this is great. Looks awesome, tastes fantastic. A pleasure to burn. And it's really cheap."

"How cheap?"

A longer pause. "I'm paying eighteen hundred."

Bullshit. "Eighteen hundred on a bow?"

"Yeah. It's a really good deal."

"Bullshit eighteen hundred. Just say you're pushing for a lower price."

Earnestly: "I'm not bullshitting you, Sherman. You should come by and roast a few bowls of this. I never see you anymore. Come by and see."

"So you're just going to be picking that up now?"

"Is it cool to talk on the phone now?"

"I'll be right over there, Vlad. You're still in Home Park, right? Same place?"

"No man, I bought a townhouse. You came to the housewarming party!"

"Oh yeah, I did, sorry." He had. "I'll be over at 2000h if that's cool?"

"That's 10PM, right? Yeah, that's fine."

"Eight PM, Vlad, twenty minus twelve. Eight."

"K-rad, see you then."

✳ ✳ ✳ ✳ ✳ ✳ ✳ ✳

"Alright, Devesh, what do we do to get cured?"

"Get cured?"

"Expression of oilmen. Paper stacks."

"Thou seeketh the best means by which this bounty might be monetized."

"Yes."

"For what must we optimize?"

Katz counts off on fingers. "One. Minimize unplanned fission surpluses."

"Excursions?"

"I think we want to stay well south of criticality."

"Prompt criticality, certainly."

"Yes. Let that be our first cost function: very high cost for criticality incidents. Frankly, I'd like to avoid fissioning in general."

"Fissioning seems required for neutrons at scale."

"So ideally we monetize such that neutrons are unnecessary."

With a cock of the head: "Forgive Devesh, but if thou has no need for neutrons, why dost thou have a need for uranium?"

"Well, I didn't say we can't fission. It's just going to require some significant apparatus. Unavoidable hazards. Very serious radiations from daughters. So what else is available?"

Devesh looked confused. "Research? Uranium as shielding? As ballast?"

"Well, I'm thinking I'd like to sell the uranium."

"Arbitrage? Very dubious, Katz. Most dubious."

"I'm thinking we reduce the entropy of this natural uranium."

"Enrich it?"

"Your word, not mine."

"Katz, it is this that thou means, yes?"

"Well, is that a path to monetization?"

"It's a path to proliferation."

"Not necessarily. Most PWRs *etc.* are running off lightly enriched uranium. Reactors supposedly coming online a decade from now will want HALEU up around 20%. It doesn't have to be used in weapons. Probably won't be."

Devesh laughed. "Katz, I give not two damns about whys. Dost thou intend to separate isotopes? If so, let us discuss that, rather than play games."

"Yes."

"Clandestine enrichment?"

"I feel stealth mode justified at this time, yes."

A great belly laugh. "You know that I work with TEA CO_2 lasers."

"That's why I'm talking to you, my good man. Assume techniques aside from gas centrifuge and LIS unworthy of consideration." Devesh nods vigorously. "Centrifuges of the necessary type are under NRC export control per Appendix B of Part 110. Laser stuff is Appendix F of same. Now that's just export control, but still, we can assume anything there is getting flagged. The laser section, however, is very sparse, though lasers are governed by the Wassenaar Agreement."

"To what level dost thou hope to enrich?"

"Well, that's a good question, Devesh. Remember, we want to maximize profit while minimizing state incursions and fission excursions. Also general pollution of the surrounding area, especially as that is likely to draw the attention of unwanted agents of the state."

Devesh leans in. "Speaking of the state, Katz, what were plans regarding importation? How dost thou intend to avoid the prying eyes of Customs?"

"Low-tech solution, Devesh. Gonna put a fake address on the manifest. I've made contact with a guy who works in Port of Savannah, brother to this girl I used to date. He gets $5,000 to watch for our containers, five each time. He lets us know once he's verified it hasn't been pulled for a Customs teardown, and then once he sees it go through the RPM. If we don't get that verification, we don't call to correct the address."

"Meaning your contact knows the precise container, and can point it out to his superiors, so that they smile with pleasure?"

"Devesh, you underestimate me. We're pulling in a scratch container days before the first real one. If there are problems the first time, we fade out, and nothing happens. They can search that one all they want. I've got another guy who's going to look into what can be done with binoculars and UAVs."

"Sketchy, Katz. I much prefer the technical solution. Much less dependent on man's caprice."

"See, that's how you mark yourself an academic and not a practical engineer. You do not take unproven tech into the field with your ass on the line. We can't flood the detectors to knock them offline. We can't mask our radiations with other radiations. We can't raise the local background. We will partially shield, but the kind of shielding that defeats these would be unworkably heavy, and obvious on visual scans. We'd need it fabricated and installed in Kazakhstan. So we just need to accept radiations out the top. We're not going to pack the full container, so we'll need less volume of shield."

"What if the container contained a transmitter, a microcontroller, and some sensors? A photodetector primarily, maybe also a motion detector and FLIR? Lithium batteries with sufficient mAh. It transmits periodically for our tracking pleasures. If the container is opened, it transmits this immediately, then destroys its programming." Devesh looks pleased with himself.

"So like an Arduino Uno? What would it be transmitting to? You can't transmit that frequently or you'll drain your battery."

"Cellular?"

"Sure, just bounce it off the central Pacific's many cell towers."

"Ahh, I had not considered this. Satellite?"

"Like with an Iridium modem? Those are expensive, as is bandwidth."

"Cheaper than prosecution, Katz!" Devesh chuckles.

"You'd have to get the Iridium account on a fake identity. Difficult, as it surely requires a credit card. But if you did that, you could string an antenna through the container, I'm sure. Maybe it can even transmit through the container wall, though I doubt that."

"If thy antifederal device clears its storage, how would they trace your Iridium account? Or even know it was using Iridium."

"Well the big-ass modem would be pretty strongly suggestive, I would think. Maybe your software fails. Maybe they can recover it from the EEPROM or flash or whatever. Maybe the battery dies because you're talking to satellites for weeks in the open ocean. Maybe the modem firmware has it, or they ask Iridium what account this IMSI is associated with. Maybe they ask Iridium which account has been talking to them all the way from the Caspian Sea to the North Atlantic. Like ten different ways, Devesh. Don't think like a researcher. Think like an engineer. Minimize complexity. Complexity kills you."

Devesh accepts this meditatively.

"Which is not to say it's an uninteresting idea. You could replace the Iridium modem with a standard 2G or 3G, and only rely on it while it was coming into port, or on land. Same problem, though—there's an IMSI, and an account. Not sure if burners are available in the form of integrated circuits."

"Could thou not strip the necessary elements out of a burner?"

UAV: unmanned aerial vehicle   FLIR: forward looking infrared

"Hardware elements? Hrmm. Maybe. Probably easier to communicate with it using QMI, if that's supported. Dicey, all very dicey. I think nine out of ten times, you end up getting a null result due to failure somewhere in this untested Rube Goldberg one-off. And then what do you do with that nondata? A good idea, Devesh; it just fails upon encountering reality. Most do."

"Everyone has a plan until they get punched in the mouth."

"So back to our original topic. We have several cheap tonnes of uranium oxide, off the books. How do we turn that into serious money?"

"A question I have not yet asked, Katz: why aren't thou registered with the NRC? I see only two ways to monetize even the most completely enriched uranium: legally and illegally. Without the NRC's stamp of approval, only illegal options are available. Now, Katz, I am a happy guy, happy to go along with most plans. Thou wishes to fuse on the tabletop? Here's Devesh, 'the Deuterator,' with heavy hydrogen and delicious dips of cheese. Thou wishes to, say, steal chickens with drones? Devesh, 'the Droneswindler,' reporting for Mission Chicken! But sale of highly enriched uranium on the black market seems irresponsible, and sadly unlikely to conclude in merriment."

"Because if we were operating under the NRC's auspices, we couldn't accumulate diverted uranium, paid for with currency."

"Katz, why dost thou have so much unbanked wealth? It seems poorly invested at best. Its volume, also, is surprising."

"Compartmentalization, my dear man, but you can take your guesses."

Devesh laughs loudly, and pokes Katz. "Thou hast become an elite nerd gigolo, yes? The women of engineering and science are calling up, 'send over Sherman Spartacus! Today's satisfaction requires seeing basketball shorts on the bodies of those who have never played basketball. Let him dance, until his white Hurricane Electric IPv6 tshirt sticks to his belly, and can be seen through, revealing the hairy flesh underneath. We want to see that floor soaked with *eau de Katzsweat!* Is it possible that he could wear cargo shorts atop the basketball shorts?' " Devesh is laughing too hard to continue. Katz grins. He is an absolute machine for sweat generation.

"I paid my way through engineering school performing outlawed dances to outlawed songs. Only Umbros offer the total freedom of movement necessary to speak truth to power. So what we do, Devesh, is we test our shit out. Only if it works do we involve the NRC. At that point we can get investment. We'll have something to show. But at that time, we do, and I'm sure we can fold a few months' excess into our reporting. I'm 100% with you."

"I do not understand why the NRC would reject thy cheap *sub rosa* imports."

Katz sighs. "Anarbek has to get it labeled as a different kind of ore. NRC, subject to IANA treaties, wants to see accounting on all imports and exports of uranium. If we can't show those imports, or domestic purchases, we can't account for our holdings."

"If thou intends to wash legal and illegal together, why not do so now? One container valid, one container invalid. Blending is also easier, thus."

QMI: Qualcomm MSM Interface   **MSM:** mobile station modem

"We don't have the banked money to buy legal tonnes of uranium. It runs about $100 per key, 100K for a metric tonne. I mean, I could technically, but I want to keep my banked money. Never allow the ultimate goal out of your sight: turning several million dollars from currency to bits."

"So the primary goal is simply money laundering?"

"Devesh, no way you can look at this and call it mere money laundering. This is scientific exploration. Funded by exotic dancing."

"Katz. What if the NRC refuses thy license? What if thou are detected before applying? Surely thou saw *Breaking Bad*? What's wrong with a car wash?"

✳ ✳ ✳ ✳ ✳ ✳ ✳ ✳ ✳

Vlad welcomed in Katz, admonishing him to doff his shoes.

"Would you like a Fernet Branca, Katz?"

"I'd prefer a steaming bucket of dogpiss, Vlad. Have you any scotch?"

"I do! Help yourself." Katz poured a tall Macallan 12 on the rocks. Vlad regarded it appreciatively.

"So eighteen hundred on the pound, huh?"

"Yeah. And the quality's right up there. I think the various steps towards legalization out West have led to steep oversupply. There's so much weed around right now. People who were always thankful for their $300 ounce are now asking if they can get it at $260. One girl I offered a $80 quarter laughed at me, she *laughed* Katz, and said she picked up zs for $200." Vlad looks sincerely wounded. "I don't sell weed to have girls laugh at me."

Katz hits it. Impressed, he hits it again. For a moment he schemes. Fuck it. "Vlad, my people are never going to beat $1,800. Go with your new vendor with my blessings. I'd like to pick up a pound for myself from you, ideally at a privileged price, every now and again going forward. The only thing is: once you cancel out, we can't restart that anytime soon, and they won't have anything for backup."

Vlad breaks out into smiles. Katz recognizes that he'd clearly been nervous. Poor kid thinks it's a breakup.

"Katz, if I need a backup, there are a dozen other people looking to offload two thousand dollar bows. It's a sea of green out there."

Katz is pleasantly high already. *"Et tenebit iustus viam suam."* He cashes the bong. *"Dies mei transierunt cogitationes meae dissipatae sunt."*

"What's that?" Vlad smiles and repacks.

"Very good, Vlad. Would you still be able to take this week's usual? Or some of it? Otherwise I'll have to eat it all. Which I can do, if necessary."

"Oh, no problem at all, Katz. You've always been totally straight with me. I can absorb it, no problem. This is just cost cutting, and I've got the necessary cash flow." He beams a little.

"You've done well, Vlad. I'm glad we make citizens of people like you." Katz downs most of the Macallan.

Et...suam: The righteous keep moving forward. Job 17:9 (NLT)
Dies...sunt: My days have passed, my plans are shattered. Job 17:11 (NIV)

✳✳✳✳✳✳✳✳✳

"Who are you dating these days, Katz? I recall you being something of a slut."

"I've got a few ladies I see now and again. Nothing serious."

Greg Moyer smiled. "You ought meet this girl Oriana."

"Oriana? Like Oriana Fallaci?"

"Oriana. If that's like Oriana Fallaci, sure."

"Why ought I meet her?"

"I met her on OkCupid, took her out. Very cool girl, very hot, very smart."

"That is how I like 'em."

"Yeah. I wasn't smart enough for her. She wanted to talk about books, and I know enough to quote some Sylvia Plath and have an undergraduate English major on her back, but she ran circles around me."

"Dude. 'On her back?' Doubleplusgross. You say that about, like, turtles. And I don't know, mang. If she likes fratty guys, I'm probably not going to fly."

"Is that still how you think of me? Seven years after graduating? Well, only five years for you."

"I'm just saying, like, look at you, collared shirt, sunglasses and shit. I've been wearing this same pair of sweatpants for four days. And it's November."

Moyer shrugged. "Do you want to meet her or not?"

"Sure. I'd appreciate that. Thanks, Greg." Katz is strangely touched by the gesture. He feels new warmth towards Greg Moyer. "Meet her how?"

"I'll just text her and ask if I can give you her number."

"Is she not going to want a picture?"

"You're pretty easily found on Facebook if she cares. I think she's looking for a guy like you. If she likes you, I think she'll like you a lot. As for me, I prefer to be the smarter one in any relationship."

"That's a crazy attitude to have, dude."

"I'm hoping to meet up with your boy Bolaño sometime soon. I heard through a circuitous grapevine out West that he has fire acid, as much as one can take. I haven't tripped in too long. You know anything about it? Still hanging out with him? I remember you two prowling around at GT like maniacs. Do you remember the time you showed up at our house and pounded on the door and yelled, 'send out your best man! Come on out you pussies!' You wanted to do some kind of shots-and-integrals contest. I had to keep some of the brothers from beating both your asses."

"Oh, that wasn't just y'all. We worked our way down the street doing that at every frathouse. Not a single one would take me on. Bolaño mostly talked shit and hyped me. 'My boy Katz will waste anyone here, Beta is a Greek letter borrowed from the Phoenician term meaning sandy vag,' that kind of thing. Go ahead and meet up with him, but if he can't help you out, hit me up."

✳✳✳✳✳✳✳✳✳

Devesh can still roast bowls with the best of them. He and Katz passed three, or was it four, big bowls covered with a hash toppers in the fifteen minutes since he arrived, and even the stalwart Desi is having trouble finding his words. Katz hoots at him, "Proceed with the lecture, Professor Choudhary!" Devesh stands at Katz's whiteboard for a few seconds more, face a dopey grin, marker uncapped. "Lasers, Devesh, talk about the lasers!"

Devesh collapses into giggles. "What we need is sharks with freakin' lasers!"

"Devesh. Some decorum."

Devesh straightens up. "Among the enriching caste, there are two types of people, yes? The industrialists and military men, the commanders of armies and companies and nations. Those seeking to outfit fleets of plants, and ships, and missiles raining from the sky like Kalki's fury. This is the majority. They answer to shareholders and stakeholders, optimizing for throughput of enrichment, for expense also." Katz aches for him to get on with it. "Then people of the second kind. Those who perform the small enrichments, with limited materials, requiring no glut. Thou art the first and only of this population. Thou art Manu." Devesh laughs. "Different goals and means, Katz. It is this to which I build. What is good for one, is it good for the other? Perhaps not so much. As a captain of industry, sailing seven seas in my good ship *SS Gömböc*, I am hoping first not to be sued, second for cost-effectiveness, third for scaling. But Katz, Katz is the mongoose!" Devesh opens his eyes wide, looking from side to side. He lifts his arms and curls his fingers like claws. Katz assumes he is impersonating a mongoose. "Katz is accustomed to flabby grubs and lovely tastes of eggiweggs, and unafraid of the nāgá; her poisons cannot hurt him."

"I fear we're getting away from the main thread, here."

"Sherman, thou sails not in ships of the seas. Thou must move in shadows. But thy task is in ways easier, no? No built up stock of centrifuges to justify. No prepaid infrastructure for their employ. A blank slate, all potentiality. This is why I suggest the lasers."

"Because I don't sail in ships? Metaphor is not your strongest suit."

"Devesh is CEO of Consolidated Thermonuclear Holdings, posit. A limited liability corporation of the State of Delaware." Devesh stands straight and marches in place. "Captain of my and many other souls. Admired in Fortune Magazine. Picture in books of business schools, words reproduced in MBA case studies. Just so. They come to Devesh and ask, 'how do we isolate ^{235}U?' Devesh evaluates with critical eye cost of capital, workforce as hired and assembled, OpEx, EBITDA. Long into night's darkness Devesh stays awake, drinking coffee, running treadmill, gazing longingly at secretary's rump, running spreadsheet after spreadsheet. Clutch head. Wipe sleep from eyes. Examine suit's wrinkles with regret. Watch for turtles, known to patrol clomping in the darkness."

"Turtles?"

Devesh has allowed himself to get carried away. "Forget this, is Gujarati expression. Devesh the CEO has many employees and facilities accustomed to centrifuges. Significant investment. This technology is known to work, and to work well. Remember, centrifuges are almost as energy efficient as best plans of lasers. Burden of research expenses, metallurgy and motors, is borne by centrifuge manufacturer. If centrifuge collapses, rotors go spinning off into the distance, disassembling many employees, lawsuit is filed against

---

Kalki: कल्कि tenth, final incarnation of Vishnu   **Manu:** मनु the first man
EBITDA: earnings before interest, taxes, depreciation, and amortization

vendor. Facility for centrifuges, colossal in size, easily constructed in the open in Piketon, Ohio. If someone asks, Devesh tells them, 'here I separate uranium into its isotopes.' I have license and paperworks, and with them invite complainers to suckle. Why would Devesh the CEO employ lasers?"

Katz doesn't bother to answer.

"Exactly. I do not. Katz hath no facility, no employees, no paperwork, no investors. Not even a forklift. Only barrels of prohibited uranium, perhaps dozens of tonnes, self-funded and obtained under pretense. He walks a tightrope. On one side, agents of the Nuclear Regulatory Commission. On the other, radiological incident. Leak of radioisotopes or worse. At the end, wealth via sale of results, though how this is to be done remains unclear to me." He laughs and shakes his head. "Question for investors. Devesh plays role of chief scientist, PhD in lasers, specializing in TEA and quantum cascades. Paycheck counted out in cash. No problem to Dr. Choudhary, accustomed to working in situations of ambiguity, since MDMA-powered days of undergraduate."

"Holy Jesus, Devesh, please, please, the lasers."

"Katz, there is one central advantage to laser isotope enrichment. The SWUs greatly exceed any other method. Each centrifuge provides only minimal SWUs. Facility requires thousands, linked in complicated cascade, tails recovered and reinserted while enriched component proceeds forward. Great maintenance burden, many technicians necessary to remove failed centrifuges, install new ones. Expensive talent required to deal with changing situation. Facility extends past the horizon, many many trucks bringing centrifuges with only one purpose. Impossible to hide such a thing without the resources of a nationstate. Certainly not feasible within the borders of America. With lasers, it is possible to enrich almost completely in a single run. Sufficient power can provably excite every relevant molecule in gas feed."

"Enrich to LEU? Like 3%? Surely you're not talking HALEU?"

"Katz, I am saying HEU, the real deal. Uranium #4, China White. Difficult, of course. Many parameters. Power of laser, time between shots, temperature of supersonic gas escaping nozzle, linewidth. Optical challenges in shifting laserlight to that which excites vibrational mode of UF_6. Must keep all hardware and gases cool, despite their wishes to grow hot. Leaks of gases inevitable, can be annoying, can be catastrophic. Perhaps most important is skimming solution to remove enriched material from target chamber. Katz, dost thou even have source material in the form of UF_6?"

Sherman shifts uncomfortably. "No."

Devesh is surprised. "Thou will need the gaseous uranium hexafluoride. It's essential that the compound is volatile, for processing and customers."

"Fluoridating uranium is a mature bit of chemical engineering. I foresee little difficulty there, though if you have suggestions, I'm all ears."

"At no point while studying Physics did we address the topic of gasifying illegally acquired uranium ore. If one wished to study applied physics, the engineering buildings were across the street." Katz nods, and reminds himself to study this most basic of problems. "Lasers. How much dost thou know?"

"Umm, I know what LASER stands for. I know they emit photons of a particular frequency. That's about it, honestly."

"So nothing, hah. Lasers are advantageous over standard lights how? Spatial and temporal coherence. The spatial refers to emitted light's lack of divergence, collimation. From narrow place of emission, to narrow place of absorption, there is little spread in vacuum. In air, the beam spreads and attenuates as photons are absorbed, quantified via relations of Beer and Lambert."

"Thermal blooming."

"Just so. Temporal coherence is the narrowness of the spectral frequency. Looking at a fluorescent bulb, the power density is spread over the spectrum, many peaks corresponding to many energy levels. The laser's density is all in one frequency, sometimes. A function parameterized largely by power and duration of shot. Putting out great power in a short time requires spreading frequencies with chirping amplification, lest thy equipment suffer. Shortest pulses, attosecond range, generate a frequency comb, predictable but definite incoherence of frequency. Now Katz, upon what does isotope separation rely?"

"What? I mean, mass differences between isotopes?"

"It is exactly this difference, yes. Every production enrichment facility is exploiting the difference of 3 AMUs between ^{235}U and ^{238}U. 3 AMUs are only 1.26% of the mass of ^{238}U, and these are imprecise processes. Hence many stages of centrifuge: each tilts the isotopic ratio only slightly in the desired direction. Note also that SWU impact is greater as enrichment rises, and that tails are more wasteful. Hence the complicated internal routing of a cascade. Tails of final stages are more valuable than products of early hundreds of stages. Separating light elements is much easier; lithium 7 vs lithium 6 is only a single AMU of difference, but this is 14.3% of lithium 7's mass. Resistance of force is much greater. Good ol' $F = ma$." Devesh chuckles appreciatively.

"It's even less than 1.26%, right? Because you're actually talking UF_6, not ^{238}U. So that would be more like, less than one percent, 0.85%."

"Yes! Like most solids, uranium metal is very resistant to flowing as a fluid. So first everyone looks for more efficient ways to exploit this mass difference. Ten thousand solutions are proposed. Oak Ridge used three in 1944: thermophoresis via Soret effect at S-50, calutrons at Y-12, and gaseous diffusion at K-25. The problem proves difficult. Everyone and their sisters begin chemical separation of plutonium. Soviets begin using centrifuges in early 1960s, replicated by most nations craving great taste of enriched uranium. Everyone uses whatever is known to work, cowardly, ptah."

"So you're saying LIS died because centrifuges are good enough?"

"Centrifuges are better! Only major savings in OpEx are cost of space and time to enrichment. CapEx significantly more than centrifuges, especially previously. Research costs. Much bitching about concerns of proliferation, as if anyone wishing to proliferate cannot already do so. Not only no reason to move to LIS, but antireasons. Except, except that is, for Sherman's Uranium Shack." Devesh is pleased to see Katz smile. "Thou hast no teams of technicians, but access to expert researchers. Thou hast no hangaresque buildings in which

---

LASER: light amplification by stimulated emission of radiation

to install centrifuges, but can get optics help. Thou hast not megatonnes but only tonnes to separate. Thou must make an ally of the laser."

An ally of the laser. Katz likes the sound of that.

"First is AVLIS, and MLIS. You know these?"

"Yeah, I'm familiar with the general concepts."

"AVLIS requires 6.1 eV, MLIS 2.7 eV. With MLIS, the output is less one fluorine, UF_5. $^{235}UF_5$ and $^{238}UF_6$ are already a difference of 22 AMUs, 6.25% of the total. Very nice. But with MLIS, we need a minimum of two photons: one to excite, one to remove a fluorine, resulting in UF_5. This plus research plus dealing with UF_5 means the 6.25% is not enough to convert. But we can do better. UF_6 leaving nozzle with carrier gas G is prone to dimerization. Assume ^{40}Ar as carrier gas. What was UF_6 is now $ArUF_6$, total of 392 AMUs. What if, rather than removing a fluorine, we disrupt only desirable dimers? $^{235}UF_6$ is only 349 of 392, difference of 11%, effort comparable to lithium separation."

"Wait, how does that achieve higher levels of enrichment? Once you're over 50% you're usually going to have at least one ^{235}U in each of these dimers. You can only kick out a pair of ^{238}Us. Otherwise you're throwing away ^{235}U. Oh wait nevermind, there's only one UF_6 in each dimer, you're saying."

"UF_6 dimers do not form due to relative excess of carrier gas molecules. Irradiation excites only ^{235}U, repressing formation of dimers from this isotope, so even in this unlikely event, dimers are always undesirable. They form, but vibrational energies of excited $^{235}UF_6$ are more than sufficient to disrupt. Dimers effected by van der Waals chickenhead bonds. We build atop the German method of aerodynamic separation, enhancing it with dimer repression, and greater mass of dimers. This requires only one photon, much more clever. Photon of the necessary type was already required for MLIS, but MLIS required further bombardment, while still enjoying less delta of mass."

"That's pretty sweet. What kind of infrastructure would we need?"

"First thy yellowcakes need be turned into hex. Messy chemical work. More challenging than thou expects, I think, especially for the clandestine. Carrier gas is required, nitrogen or argon. Argon is desirable from standpoint of mass, but probably more expensive."

"There are three stable isotopes of argon. Need it be purified to one?"

"I am uncertain, but think no."

"What about mixed nitrogen/argon?"

"Why would this be desirable?"

"Cheaper. That's how people get mass gas for their wine cellars and shit."

"Hast thou acquired a wine cellar, Katz?"

"More of a Jäger basement."

Devesh laughs uproariously. "Seriously?"

"Devesh. I live in a 28 floor highrise. Very difficult to install a basement."

"I was wondering, Katz! As to the nature of carrier gases, I am unsure. Everyone says nitrogen or argon. I'll look into this."

"I guess fluorine will rip up oxygen compounds? So normal air doesn't work. I'd think you want to maximize the carrier mass."

"It is a multidimensional parameter space, I'm sure. Properties of flow, energy required will also factor into the decision. Continuing with infrastructure, a lengthy chamber into with gas can decompress supersonically. Nozzles for same. Crossaxial channel for laserlight. Lasers, by far the largest capital outlay. Likely close to a million dollars worth. How dost thou intend to acquire them?"

"Depends on the laser, right?"

"What I am saying, Katz, is that one does not simply call LightMachinery of Ontario, or Edinburgh Instruments, or PAR Systems in Minnesota, acquirers of South Africa's SDI Lasers, or LASER2000 from the normally quiet Germans and say, 'I have cash in a large sack. May I exchange it for lasers? I request a quote.' They likely require a company on the other side, at a minimum."

"You raise a good point."

"But Devesh is thinking, for this task, even the finest retail lasers are poorly equipped. It is a research laser thou needs, one with high repetition rates, and high fluence with each pulse. Shorter pulses are more desirable than long ones, or continuous operation. A laser optimized for this can be made much more efficient. Multiple lasers can be aggregated if the highest levels of performance are unsatisfactory. This is where Devesh can help most thoroughly. And Devesh is happy to be paid in cash."

21 a stamped-in network of paths

The universe is at first glance suffused with tremendous variety. On closer analysis, the issue is less certain. We speak of the universe's composition in terms of mass-energy (rather than the stress-energy suggested by the Einstein field equations' $T_{\mu\nu}$ tensor) because FLRW, the metric corresponding to a homogeneous, isotropic universe, admits a critical density measured in kg/m³:

$$\rho_{\text{crit}} = \frac{3H_0^2}{8\pi G}$$

which can be used to determine the universe's overall spatial geometry.

WMAP results interpreted within ΛCDM suggest about ⅔ of the universe's mass-energy to be dark energy, literally as homogeneous as anything can be. Most of the rest is ascribed to dark matter. Baryons make up no more than 5% of this model, and of them, well more than 95% by mass is hydrogen and helium (by atom count, it's more than 99%). Luckily, our pocket of the universe has radically different composition.

Nature in all her processes and technique makes use of a small handful of ideas over and over, in drastically different contexts. Negative feedback loops, exponential growth, inverse square laws, recombination, decay to entropy...one can focus on forces and fields, but it is illustrative to look at relationships between actions, a category theory of creation. Keep it in mind.

2010-06-07 Tortkuduk Central Mine, Moiynqūm Desert, Jambyl Oblysy, Qazaqstan Respublikasy
The Moiynqūm: a xeric strip bounded by the Sarysu and Shu rivers (our Shu being southern Kazakhstan's Шу, not Ningxiang's 楚江), and the Karatau and Qyrǵyz *alatau*. 37,500 km² of sands and clays contributing to the "dust belt" in what climate scientists call Arid Central Asia. When *sukhovei* stirs up *habūbs*, walls of red hellsand block out the sun, creating a Priscoan artificial night.

Rollfront sandstone deposits under its aeolian sediments bear workaday uraninite, and also coffinite ($U(SiO_4)_{1-x}(OH)_{4x}$), and are some of the world's largest proven uranium reserves. Not far away is Semipalatinsk-21, an area the size of Wales where the Soviet Union conducted 456 weapon tests, 116 of them above ground. Discovered only late in the Cold War, Kazakh's largest uranium mines did not fuel Soviet weapons. The CCCP drew instead upon regions impressed into the Eastern Bloc following World War II, moving quickly to exploit the SDAG Wismut-administered German mines especially. Out from Czech Jáchymov and Příbram, from Bulgarian Buhovo and Seslavtsi, and from

---

FLRW: Friedmann–Lemaître–Robertson–Walker [metric]
WMAP: Wilkinson Microwave Anisotropy Probe
Jambyl Oblysy: Жамбыл облысы Zhambyl Region
Qazaqstan Respublikasy: Қазақстан Республикасы Republic of Kazakhstan
Karatau: Қаратау Black Mountains   alatau: жотасы mountain range
sukhovei: Сухове́й dry winds   habūbs: هبوب "blasting" intense dust storm
SDAG: Sowjetisch-Deutsche Aktiengesellschaft Soviet-German stock corporation

Poland's deposits of rare uranophane ($Ca(UO_2)_2(SiO_3OH)_2 \cdot 5H_2O$) in Wolność, Podgórze, and Radoniów, railcars of radioactive ore flowed to plutonium production reactors at the Siberian Chemical Combine in Tomsk-7 (Seversk), Mayak in Chelyabinsk-65 (now Ozersk), and the Mining and Chemical Combine of Krasnoyarsk-26 (Zheleznogorsk). These numbered poleis were the Closed Cities, *zakrytye administrativno-territorial'nye obrazovaniya*, left off of maps, omitted from railroad tables, black postal holes whose access by *tovarishes* was strictly prohibited, existences classified, addresses unplaces.

But now *Qazatomónerkásip* and Ortalyk and Rosatom in the form of Uranium One had massive *in situ* leaching mines at Inkai (in conjunction with Canada's Cameco), and Karatau, Mynkuduk, Akdala, and here in the Moiynqūm. ISL delivers the majority of the world's uranium, and almost 80% of ISL ore comes from Kazakhstan, artificially capped at 20 kilotons per annum. Her ore is not particularly rich with uranium, but there's an awful lot of it—15% of world reserves. Perhaps surprisingly, nuclear power is not used in Kazakhstan. The anti-nuclear sentiment arising from those 456 explosions remains strong.

Strongly acidic solution was pumped down injection wells from 3000 liter tanks five meters in diameter. Kazakh mines eschew the oxidizing agents used in Australian and American ISR (*nota bene* the Western euphemism of "ISR" a/k/a *recovery* rather than *leaching*), requiring significantly more concentrated acid as a result. Fortified, the groundwater slowly migrated through ores, leaching uranium-infused sands on the way to extraction pipes. Underground pumps pushed the grisly uranium-bearing slurry back up to well houses, where the worst of the acids were recovered or neutralized. Then it was on to evaporation ponds, and finally through a series of extraction filters. The last of these drew out uranium into refinement columns, where it was thickened, dried, packaged as yellowcake, and loaded into barrels for transport. All things considered, the process was not unkind to the land, leaving few visible scars topside. So long as one was careful about groundwaters, nobody had to die, and one could truthfully claim reductions to local radiation levels.

2010-04-20 1151h Port Authority, 111 8th Ave, New York, New York, Simulated USA
Nswadi Mbuyi pushed his ULINE Rubbermaid cart forward with nimble feet and a quick eye. So much as brushing one of the supercilious whites, every one thinking themselves a *mwami*, would elicit more squawk and caterwaul than a volery of turacos scattering startled from the bush. He had become a man in Bémal on the border between Chad and the CAR, a hundred klicks or so east of the tripoint where the Mbéré laps against Cameroon. He would not claim the troubles had started in 2006—there had been problems in the Sahel all his mother's years and all his years in turn. But four years earlier, first UFDR rebels and then vulturous Chadian ANT regulars came. Without ceremony they took

---

zakrytye...obrazovaniya: закрытые административно-территориальные образования closed administrative-territorial formations **tovarishes:** товáрищи comrades
Qazatomónerkásip: Қазатомөнеркәсіп National Atomic Company Kazatomprom
mwami: chief **CAR:** Central African Republic, formerly Oubangui-Chari
UFDR: Union des Forces Démocratiques pour le Rassemblemen
ANT: Armée Nationale Tchadienne

two prized Djallonké cattle, and then his sacks of peanuts. The hateful Kanuri laughed and cheered as flames consumed his cob's gbodobi thatch, brought at expense from Nàìjíríà, mocking him in their Beriberi deviltalk. Mounted atop their technical was a brutish Vektor SS-77. They tracked him with it, daring him to do anything more than feel hope die in his heart.

He came to New York and was tasked with delivering packages throughout the gargantuan building's sixteen floors. Each morning he walked a kilometer to Jamaica-179th, embarking on the Ⓔ (or the sphincterpuckering Ⓕ) out from Queens and into Manhattan, to 14th/Eighth in the basement of 111, along with seemingly every Banda émigré in the city. The work was a great improvement over the thin farming of the savanna, and he arrived each day, even when he woke to find air colder than anything he'd ever experienced, such that he wondered how men had chosen to place a city here. When delivering to the eighth floor, he stepped whenever possible out onto the terrace, looking south to the construction work at Fulton and West, watching over gestation and then visual parturition of One World Trade, by now over fifty stories.

Nswadi came to the tremendous freight elevator, large enough to haul up an eighteen wheeler. The cab in its hoistway halted with an audible shudder. The cabin doors opened. No one was inside, but sitting in the center was a strange device, like a five foot tall witch's hat, its casing darker than steel but not so dark as iron. Taped around its front was an authentic Worcester yellow smiley, legacy of Harvey Ball, and the message HERE'S LOOKING AT U. While the doors were still opening, Nswadi chuckled and asked, "kombo na yo nani?" He felt foolish and muttered "bolimbisi," then felt more foolish still. He smiled sheepishly. The doors completed opening. The bell chimed.

Like anything called sound, that chime was a mechanical wave propagated through a medium, in this case the air of the cabin. A MEMS microphone IC employed three NiMH 1.2V batteries in series to place a charge Q through an etched diaphragm and perforated plate having area A. This induced an electric field $\mathbf{E} = \frac{\sigma}{\epsilon_0}$ for the charge density $\sigma = \frac{Q}{A}$, establishing capacitance that varied with the gap d from the membrane:

$$V = \int_0^d \mathbf{E}(z)\, dz = \mathbf{E}d = \frac{Qd}{\epsilon_0 A}$$

The sampled output voltage triggered two circuits, initiating a timer PLL and an electrical igniter. The igniter contained a bridgewire of nichrome helically wound through a pyrogen of magnalium (5% Mg, 95% Al). One ampere through the wire led to resistive heating sufficient to set the pyrotechnic alloy aflame. This was coupled to a primary molten salt thermal battery, binding pellets of electrolytes in immobilizing fumed silicas. The ionic conductivity of molten salts exceeds by several orders of magnitude that of a car battery's sulfuric acid, providing a short-lived output of kilowatts. In this case, an anode of 44% lithium

---

kombo na yo nani: what is your name?   **bolimbisi:** I beg forgiveness
MEMS: microelectromechanical system   **NiMH:** Nickel-metal hydride
PLL: phase-locked loop   **pyrite:** FeS_2 iron disulfide

and 56% silicon coupled electrochemically to LiBr-KBr-LiF eutectic electrolyte and 73.5% pyrite catholyte employing magnesium oxide binder. Activated, the series cells of the battery began irreversible discharge, their heat output captured as dozens of direct current amps at 48V. This was driven into a bank of capacitors, one of them much larger than the others. Additionally, it prepared a standing plasma in the low-pressure hydrogen of krytron switches, and drove a pump; by the time this last had executed a full cycle, the capacitors were charged. This pump drove the gaseous contents of a small canister—deuterium and tritium, heavy and heavier hydrogen—into the core of the device.

The PLL's first control signal went high three seconds after the initial pulse, causing discharge of one hundred and twenty polypropylene power film capacitors. Wires from the capacitors were all cut to precisely the same length, and went to points arranged around the device core. They drove pulse transformers which stepped the output up to two kilovolts, sufficient to trigger the activated krytrons. The preionized plasma was a path for conduction, allowing a glow discharge to be formed in nanoseconds, a millionth of the time required in typical cold cathode tubes. The high input voltage further minimized delay. Krytrons are reliable devices. Two were assigned to each of sixty chunks of LX-17-0 (92.5% TATB and 7.5% Kel-F 800) polymer-bonded insensitive high explosive. None failed to fire.

Sixty exploding foil "slappers" were initiated, the last only six nanoseconds after the first. Arranged in a rhombitruncated icosidodecahedron (yes, really), the LX-17-0 served as guide for interior PBX-9501 (95% HMX, 2.5% BDNPA-F, 2.5% estane); the latter offered (at the same density) almost 20% more velocity and 35% more pressure. A layer of insulating polyethylene terephthalate sat between a gold foil and a dense pellet of PBXW-7 (60% TATB, 35% RDX, 5% PTFE) explosive booster. The krytron vaporized the gold, accelerating the 12mm pellet to three kilometers per second down a quarter-inch barrel. This process added jitter; forty antenatal nanoseconds passed between first and final detonation. It was close enough, even promising: efficiency within 95% of peak permitted up to two hundred nanoseconds.

Within the spherical shell of high explosive were several centimeters of partial vacuum, through which accelerated a thin shuck of dense depleted uranium pusher. Most modern warheads use a two-point linear implosion, employing flying plates and a cylindrical arrangement of explosives around a prolate spheroid core. This allows a reduction in diameter, critical for MIRVs, less important when delivering ordinance via elevator. Six tense aluminum frusta mounted inside supported a 15.6 kg hollow sphere of δ phase plutonium (6% ^{240}Pu) alloyed with 3.0 mol% gallium. The chemistry of element 31 is similar to that of its group XIII predecessor aluminum, but aluminum dispersed through plutonium would have generated unwanted neutrons due to its (α, n) reaction. Metallic plutonium exists in its brittle α phase at room temper-

TATB: triaminotrinitrobenzene $C_6H_6N_6O_6$ 2,4,6-Trinitrobenzene-1,3,5-triamine
Kel-F 800: $(CF_2CClF)_n$ Polychlorotrifluoroethylene
HMX: octogen $C_4H_8N_8O_8$ 1,3,5,7-Tetranitro-1,3,5,7-tetrazocane
BDNPA-F: 50% bis(2,2-dinitropropyl) acetal, 50% bis(2,2-dinitropropyl) formal
RDX: Research Department eXplosive $(O_2N_2CH_2)_3$ **PTFE:** Polytetrafluoroethylene $(C_2F_4)_n$

ature; the gallium protected the plutonium metal from corrosion, and more importantly stabilized the less brittle, least dense, more ductile, face-centered cubic δ allotrope (plutonium cannot exhibit highly symmetric crystal lattices at room temperature due to its non-localized 5f electrons; plutonium maximizes 5f bonding among the actinides). A thin layer of nickel plating prevented oxidation. This unearthly hull was by now seething with ^{2}H and ^{3}H.

The unique, largest capacitor discharged, sending seventeen kilovolts into a rod of alumina onto which had been deposited tritiated titanium hydride. Ions of tritium were accelerated the length of a glass tube, impacting with deuterated TiH_2. Their velocities were governed by a Maxwellian distribution, and most of the ions were deflected via Coulomb collision; many didn't come close enough to a deuteron to interact with one at all. Some found ^{3}He, the β⁻ product of ^{3}H, and even fused with it (releasing 12.1 MeV, not too shabby)—but the outputs were an α and a proton, useless for our purposes. A minority approached deuterons with sufficient energy to come within a femtometer, and just as electromagnetic repulsion between the two protons was about to repel the triton, just as the first derivative of its motion approached zero from above, the residual strong nuclear force stepped in, *apò méson theós,* snapping the two together, releasing a hot-hot-hot! 14.06 MeV neutron (plus a 3.52 MeV α for kicks). These neutrons were likewise routed down into the core; moving at 17.3% the speed of light, it took them just under 6.5 ns to traverse this vacuum. The loop had been precisely timed. Their journeys ended at the moment of maximum compression (or the *term d'art* "maximum scrunch"). The several thousand fusions contributed negligible yield, not even destroying their container, but their neutrons would be of great importance.

Hē Ouaì hē mía apēlthen; idoù érkhetai éti dúo Ouaì metà taûta.

It's the Great Rhombicosidodecahedron, Charlie Brown

We want to effect as close to as spherical an implosion as is possible. This is a difficult task; Deke Parsons at Los Alamos described it as "blowing in a beer can without splattering the beer." High explosives are set off with detonators, and you can't make a spherical detonator. If you try to approach it via increasing the number of detonators, you end up with regions of maximum pressure leading to high velocity jets. Instead, you'll want to use multiple materials (probably but not necessarily multiple types of explosive), in which the shock wave propagates at different velocities: "explosive lenses."

In what geometry shall we arrange them?

Get fucking set! Ground rules: 3D Euclidean space $\mathbb{E}^3$ ($\mathbb{R}^3$ with the standard dot product) as naïvely described by Euclid's *Stoikheîa* and axiomatized by *e.g.* Hilbert (1899), Tarski (1959), and Birkhoff (1932).

---

apò méson theós: ἀπὸ μέσον θεός god from meson cf. apò mēkhanês theós *(deus ex machina)*
Hē...taûta: Ἡ Οὐαὶ ἡ μία ἀπῆλθεν· ἰδοὺ ἔρχεται ἔτι δύο Οὐαὶ μετὰ ταῦτα.
The first woe is past; two other woes are yet to come! Revelation 9:12 (NIV)

Triangles look like triangles, essentially. We're talking geometry, not topology: lengths and angles have meaning. *gonia* (γωνία): "angle."

A *polygon* is a series of line segments lying in a common plane such that the first and last vertices coincide. A *horseshit* polygon is one that self-intersects, or has holes; it is otherwise *simple*. If the line segment between any two points of a simple polygon is contained within said polygon (equivalently, if every internal angle is less than 180°; equivalently, if the polygon is contained within one of the closed half-planes defined by each edge), it is further *convex*. Convex polygons are great: they can be triangulated in $\mathcal{O}(n)$ by drawing lines from one vertex to all other vertices, and are closed under intersection. They practically shit theorems; check Catalan's formula for the number of possible non-intersecting triangulations of a convex n-gon:

$$C_{n-2} = \frac{n(n+1)\cdots(2n-4)}{(n-2)!} = \prod_{k=2}^{n} \frac{n+k}{k}$$

Recall from elementary school $\Sigma\angle_{int} = (n-2)\pi$, $\Sigma\angle_{ext} = 2\pi$, and

$$A = \frac{1}{2}\sum_{i=1}^{n}(x_i y_{i+1} - x_{i+1}y_i)$$

Breaking a concave/horseshit polygon into decent convex polygons is tessellation (in the OpenGL sense, not that of a plane). GPUs want to work on triangles (three points define a plane, and a unique shape), so one does this often. All nondegenerate triangles are convex.

Equilateral and direct equiangular simple polygons are regular. All simple regular polygons are convex; there exists a regular convex n-gon for $n > 2$. A regular convex polygon of infinitely many sides is not a circle—*Flatland* lied to us—but a regular apeirogon: the interior angles are converging to π radians. Circles have no angles! The regular apeirogon equipartitions $\mathbb{E}^1$, snooze, but irregular apeirogons are mad lads, Mandelbrot's teragons, *e.g.* the Koch snowflake.

Hopefully you're getting the picture: we value concepts in mathematics based on what interesting things we can say about them, and what interesting things they allow us to speak about. For a regular n-gon with side length a, $A = \frac{1}{4}na^2\cot(\frac{\pi}{n})$. Those regular n-gons which can be constructed using a compass and straightedge are precisely those where $n = 2^k p_1 p_2 \cdots p_t$ such that $k, t \geq 0$ and all p are Fermat primes. If you prefer, they are those for which $\phi(n) = 2^k$ such that $k \geq 0$ (ϕ is Euler's totient function). If and only if an n-gon can be thus constructed, trigonometric functions for its central angle can be expressed in terms of finite root extraction of real numbers. *etc.*

What of that third dimension? *hedron* (ἕδρον): "base," admittedly less compelling than "angle." Polygons and polyhedra are 2 and

3D polytopes—*tópos (τόπος):* "place"—the Greek suffixes get dicier and dicier as you generalize. Klee (Victor, not painter/color theorist Paul) generalized polytopia to infinitely many dimensions: those bounded closed convex subsets of Banach spaces for which each finite-dimensional affine section is a standard polytope.

Make a polyhedron out of regular polygons, and you've got a regular polyhedron. Unlike the regular 'gons, of which there are a countably infinite number, there are only five convex regular polyhedra: the Platonic Solids of much muchness. Pythagóras likely knew of them, Theaítetos certainly; Plato ruminated on them at predictable length, and Eukleídēs mastered them in his thirteenth and final Book. Kepler went HAM with them in *Mysterium Cosmographicum.* The regular polygons are interesting because of the continuous and infinite scale; the regular polytopes captivate and seduce by virtue of their scarcity, their rarity, their finiteness: *integritas, consonantia, claritas.*

The Platonics top out at the icosahedron's equilateral triangles, familiar as a poor approximation of a sphere to anyone who's rolled a D20. Less famous are the thirteen Archimedean solids, which generalize the Platonics to multiple types of regular polygon. A truncated icosidodecahedron a/k/a great rhombicosidodecahedron offers 62 faces: 30 squares, 20 regular hexagons, and 12 regular decagons. Less symmetries than a regular polygon, but closer to a sphere; for the same reason, early bombs used the dotriacontaface truncated icosahedron, more commonly recognized as an unamerican football ⚽. With advanced lensing, a roughly spherical implosion can be initiated with a single detonator and Bernoulli's *spira mirabilis,* the self-similar logarithmic spiral.

2013-04-26 Private residence, 975 Piedmont Ave, Atlanta, Georgia, USA

Gametogenesis is conserved well across sexually reproducing organisms: the process by which *Drosophilia* generates and recombines haploids closely tracks that of *Homo.* The majority of multicellular (and some unicellular) eukaryotes employ meiosis (though not necessarily exclusively—some funga, for instance, engage in both sexual and asexual reproduction). It is known from fossil evidence that dioecy emerged over a billion years ago; phylogenetic arguments place the development of sex at over two billion years ago; it is almost certain that it originated with a single eukaryotic unicellular ancestor. It's possible that the DNA repair facilitated by meiotic recombination originated as simple smash-and-grabs of genetic material. Andrea Dworkin argues that her claim in 1987's *Intercourse,* "violation is a synonym for intercourse," should not be read

---

integritas...claritas: wholeness, harmony, radiance.
Thomas Aquinas, *Summa Theologica* (1485) I q. 39 a. 8

to imply "all heterosexual sex is rape." Maybe so, but there were definitely at least a billion years of sex before the emergence of consent.

During gastrulation, germ cells are segregated from somatic cells, and routed to the gonads. SF1 is necessary for development (along the ventrome-dial surface of the mesonephros) of the common ("bipotential") gonadal ridge. Without the cascade initiated by a Y chromosome, the gonads default to ovaries. The sex cords progress into cortical cords, and then ovarian follicles. Mean-while, primordial germ cells collect around these follicles, and differentiate into oogonia (oocytogenesis), reproducing via mitosis. By the fifth month of gestation, the fetal girl has all the oocytes she will ever produce, usually five to seven million. Once meiosis begins, mitosis ceases throughout; oogonia double their chromatids, proceed to the epicenter of primordial follicles (one oogo-nium per follicle), and enter the prolonged quiescence known as dictyate as primary oocytes. The oocytes remain metabolically active, though immature. Much of their cellular respiration is performed by other cells, with the results transported to them, all the better for avoiding oxidative stress damage to the germline. CPEB and the transcription factor *maskin* bind to elF-4E. So long as they are produced, the elF-4G initiation factor cannot be bound by 4E, and the oocyte remains dormant. It can persist in this state for almost fifty years, though DNA double stand breaks are accumulated with age (due to breakdown of BRCA1 and ATM), potentially further limiting fertility.

During dictyate, the granulosa cells in the follicles acquire receptors for LH. With menarche, LH is released, and these cells stop producing cGMP. Once cGMP ceases to prevent breakdown of cAMP by the PDE3 phosphodiesterase, meiotic arrest is broken, and the cell finally proceeds from prophase I to metaphase II. It is now a secondary oocyte, and cuts back to two chromatids by discarding the polar body: it won't need preserve its germline much longer. The newly haploid cell enters meiosis II, and crashes to a halt at metaphase II. It will remain there until fertilized or destroyed in menstruation.

Oligoovulation or the more severe anovulation are addressed with ovula-tion induction using antiestrogens (*e.g.* tamoxifen, letrozole, and clomifene citrate) or direct injections of FSH. Oocyte cryopreservation a/k/a freezing eggs harvests secondary oocytes; embryo cryopreservation harvests fertilized embryos. In either procedure, the ovary is hyperstimulated with FSH, while spontaneous ovulation is suppressed with GnRH agonist (usually leuprorelin or triptorelin) or antagonist (usually cetrorelix or ganirelix).

2010-08-13 2010h Goat Farms Art Center, 1200 Foster St NW, Atlanta, Georgia, USA
"I'll be Grignarding while you're trying to glue your hand back on."

SF1: splicing factor 1 *11q13.1*   SOX9: SRY-box transcription factor 9 *17q24.3*
CPEB: cytoplasmic polyadenylation element binding protein *15q25.2*
elF-4E: eukaryotic initiation factor *4q23*
BRCA1: Breast cancer type 1 susceptibility protein *17q21.31*
ATM: ataxia-telangiectasia mutated *11q22.3*
cGMP: cyclic guanosine monophosphate   cAMP: cyclic adenosine monophosphate
GnRH: gonadotropin-releasing hormone

Erica and Sherman wore only moderate protective gear: respirators, gloves, goggles, but no coverall, and regular shoes. Erica's gloves were trusty Silver-shield Norfoil, and she looked with some contumeliousness upon Katz's black neoprene. She'd at least been able to talk him out of Kevlar.

"We're not doing any Grignard reactions, dumbass. Do you just say random scientific shit? Is that your thing? Cut resistant gloves are generally not heat resistant, which you're far more likely to need. What do your see us cutting?"

His gleam was that of mania. "A bitch!" Erica huffed. They'd both pulled light blue nitrile single-use gauntlets (from a box of two hundred) over their primary gloves. Erica's braids tucked easily underneath a Tyvek bouffant cap.

Two 200L reactors with 0.58 kg/L meant a potential 232 kg (510 pounds) of unwieldy, yeasty slurry. It was a grotesque suspension, upsetting to gaze into as they transferred it in steel five gallon buckets. The destination was an 11 kW industrial yeast dryer, capable of drying 90 kg/h at its fiercest setting. They would be running it much less aggressively, targeting only twenty kilograms per hour. Erica had made black Sharpie marks at 272 mm up along their 344 mm height, indicating the 15 L point. Each load moved 8.7 kg of broth, just heavy enough that following the twenty-fourth bucket, they were glad to be done.

"Twenty-three and change. 345 L, 86% of fermentation capacity. Not bad."

Katz winced. "Not great either. How did we lose that 14%?"

"Honey, you're going to need to expect to lose 10% or so at every step, mini-mum. That's just how things go. And that wasn't the most exact measurement in the world. I mean, Sharpies on buckets. Could be 10%, could be 20%. Most likely it was waste gas that left the system. Anyway, dry weight's what matters."

"Can we not reload to compensate?"

"Well then you have yeasts of different ages in there."

"Is that a problem? Are teenage yeasts surly and defiant?"

She shrugged. "Maybe not. It's not great research protocol."

Incredulously: "Don't tell me you're hoping to publish this?"

"I mean, probably not as 'System and Method for Industrial-Scale Clan-destine LSD Synthesis,' but I certainly intend to publish on the genetic work. That's good work."

"That's why you're going to make a hundred tax-free large."

She pouted. "Why don't you want me to publish?"

"You don't want you to publish!" He dropped his voice. It didn't seem like much noise escaped the units, but who knew? "I mean, I haven't emphasized this element, but you do understand that if the DEA walked in right now, we'd be going to prison for twenty years minimum, fedtime?"

"For what? We don't have any LSD."

"Well first off we have both weed and speed here, but that's mine; I'd take ownership on it. However, we also have almost 350 L of high-D-LSA yeast. Typical yeast produces no D-LSA. If they're charging in here, they already have a case; they presumably know what they're looking for. Or they seize your notebooks and read them. Or one of us talks, which it wouldn't be me, so it would have to be you, which by the way don't; I cannot overemphasize the importance of that. Anyway, lysergic acid is Schedule III, a controlled precursor, and this"—gesturing around them—"is all conspiracy to manufacture. If we go down, we go down for good, my love. Please don't be blasé about this."

She looked him in the eyes. "I'm not. I promise." Katz was less than relieved. She continued: "So 345's right at 200 kg, so this is probably going to be a ten-hour dry. Ought reduce it to ten percent moisture or less. Then we'll need to grind it. Oh, and once we grind, we've pretty much got to proceed through the rest of the process, to avoid degradation. We don't want to leave much time between opening this big fucker back up and grinding, either; as soon as we pop it, it's got a regular atmosphere. So we're going to want to run the entire operation without stoppage." She pointed at his bucket, which he'd placed in a corner. "No sir, wash that bucket out." Computer science dumbass couldn't cook a meal without giving half the guests botulism.

"Ahh, of course, thanks." Katz picked up his bucket, and with class gestured for Erica's as well, and took them to the sink. There he began washing and scrubbing. "So we're expecting direct D-LSA, right, not ergopeptines? And that means no initial hydrolysis step."

"Correct. It's not like your ergot idea, where you needed to knock out the lysergyl peptide synthetase to avoid ergopeptines and the chanoclavine aldehyde oxidoreductase to inhibit fumigaclavines, because yeast never had genes coding for those. We built the pathway up ourselves."

not less than the past seventy megayears

Some argue that cancer is a disease of organs, not of cells, and that to place it in a purely cellular context is to err. This seems an issue of semantics. In any case, Hanahan and Weinberg wrote that metastatic disease is marked by eight cellular capabilities, which can be acquired in any order:

- Division without external signals
- Rejection of senescence
- Dismissal of external anti-division signals
- Rejection of apoptosis
- Evasion of the immune system
- Sustained angiogenesis
- Metastatic colonization
- Alternate metabolism

Five of these aim to overcome the body's natural cancer suppression, demonstrating the complexity of a defense evolved over gigayears. Cells do not generally mindlessly divide; most carry a program indicating the typical number of divisions, and do not divide beyond that in the absence of trauma. Alternatively, they might cease upon complete differentiation, or exhaustion of nutrients. Often, an external growth factor is required to spur division, rather than any internal plan. Internally-directed cessation of fission is quiescence, the G_0 "Gap 0" state of the cell cycle, typically mediated by TP53, p21, and Rb. If these proteins are generated improperly, or something blocks them from taking effect, the cell will continuously divide. Rb ensures the cell is large enough to

---

Rb: retinoblastoma protein *13q14.2*   **Bax:** apoptosis regulator BAX *19q13.33*

divide; it binds to E2F1, blocking transcription; cell growth phosphorylates Rb, causing it to release E2F1. HPV protein E7 and human adenovirus protein E1A both target Rb, preventing this binding action; in this way they are oncogenic. But this undisciplined cell is not yet cancer.

Cells are created with telomeres, repeated nucleotide sequences found at the ends of linear chromosomes (TTAGGG in vertebrates). They serve two major purposes: first, they provide a sentinel, a TCP close, a NULL, a means by which DNA repair mechanisms can differentiate the true end of meaningful genetic material and a doublestrand break. Secondly, they limit the number of times a given cell can divide, implementing Hayflick's limit. Each mitosis degrades the telomeres a small amount; this is a fundamental part of the transcription process. Damage such as oxidative stress whacks long sections off telomeres. Once the telomeres are whittled down to the nub, the cell ceases to divide, entering irreversible senescence. It can still provide somatic function, but it cannot divide. Senescence is typically mediated by TP53, p16INK4a-pRb, and p14arf. In their absence, division will continue, often with runthrough and shoddy chromosomes prone to mutations. But for all its bumbling, this valetudinary cell is not yet cancer.

Some external signals promote division; others oppose it. The Hippo-YAP signaling pathway is responsible for "contact inhibition of proliferation": when two cells contact one another, each signals the other, suggesting it cease dividing. Enough of these signals ought cause quiescence. By these means, it is possible for cells to grow a single layer filling a substrate without central control. If this pathway is disrupted, the cell will continue to divide despite standing room only. The daugher cells pile up above the substrate into a tumourous mass. But this benign tumor is not yet cancer.

By now, other cells are starting to show this one some stinkeye. It's consuming disproportionate resources, littering the neighborhood with wastes, having babies like nobody's business. The neighborhood's bluenoses are clucking their tongues; the Karens have their phones at the ready; old Ms. Molloy crosses herself and then crosses the street when walking past. This new breed seems to have no shame. Their damaged TP53 isn't interested in increasing production of Bax. You wait for apoptosis, but that's not how it's going down this time. The cell is now immortal: we don't die, we multiply. Call it cancer *in situ*.

By no means is all hope lost. The immune system is full of powerful anticancer agents, and can recognize many oncogenic traits. Out rings the fanfare; in sweep the cavalry. T cells recognize various antigen markers. Natural killer cells and macrophages lead the attack. CD4+ T helpers and CD8+ cytotoxic Ts flood the area with interferon-γ. For circulating tumor cells (isolated, aimless metastases barely deserving the word), this may well eliminate all cancer present. If the immune system doesn't eliminate the tumor early, though, it likely won't be able to at all. Tumors release various chemicals which retard the immune system; their sheer numbers can overwhelm it. Most insidiously, each mutation limiting antigen presentation makes that cell less susceptible to immunosurveillance; in the presence of such mutations, targeted cytotoxicity only serves to provoke a natural selection. Evolutionary pressure lifts up the more resistant cells; eventually, only the most stealthy and ruthless remain to divide. This further applies to most chemotherapies, and explains the pattern of remission, "cure," then roaring, aggressive return of a cancer now resistant to techniques which had served so well before.

Eventually the primary tumor proves too small a town for some cells' big cancer dreams. Some of the cancerous cells acquire the ability to migrate, to colonize, to settle. These cells are likely already fierce veterans, ready for insane division in faraway lands. Sorry, but you're probably gonna die.

2010-04-20 1151h Port Authority, 111 8th Ave, New York, New York, Simulated USA
Contact: the pusher struck the nickel-plated hollow sphere of plutonium. The weapon design was fundamentally unsafe with its 15.132 kg of Pu: at even standard pressure, ^{239}Pu has a bare spherical critical mass of only 10 kg, a radius of 4.95 cm. ^{239}Pu alloyed with natural gallium (roughly 60% ^{69}Ga and 40% ^{71}Ga) at 3% has a cold density of 15.6 g/cm^3, and a liter was present; with a hollow radius of 3.3 cm, the outer radius was 6.5 cm. A thin foil of pure copper lined the inside to retard diffusion of the heavy hydrogens through the incoming plutonium (copper would normally be alloyed with palladium to resist corrosion and oxidation, but palladium would admit undesirable H transport). Hydrogen that intermixes with the metal is for our purposes lost. Under the incoming pressures—temperature is less important, as the material has not had time to thermalize—the plutonium immediately changes to its densest α form, and is then compressed several times beyond that. A mere geometry change (*i.e.* being crushed into a solid sphere) would render this much plutonium critical; it wouldn't be an efficient explosion, but it would lethally radiotoxify anyone in the vicinity. This plutonium was anyway destined for no mere change of geometry.

The α phase of plutonium has a bulk modulus K of 55 GPa, about one-third of steel's 170—it's a fairly compressible metal. This modulus of elasticity is defined at reasonable pressures as $K = -V\frac{\partial P}{\partial V}$. It arises from the two most fundamental interactions of molecules in a lattice: the attractive London dispersion (one of the three van der Walls forces), and the Pauli repulsion due to overlapping electron orbitals. The Pauli interaction is significantly stronger between two close atoms, but falls off completely at distance; the London is cumulative through the mass. The interatomic potential is simply the sum of these opposing forces. At the ground state, they will equal one another exactly: this specifies the default volume per atom. The modulus increases with pressure; in light actinides such as plutonium, the relativistic 5f itinerant valence electrons likewise become localized. DFT+U, DMFT, and/or GGA-PBE calculations must be used in the absence of experimental data. This core's geometry and chemistry combined with the high-velocity, highly-symmetrical implosion yielded a compression ratio of 2.4: the α plutonium reached a maximum density of 45.6 g/cm^3 compared to its natural 19. The bare critical mass scales with the inverse square of the compression ratio; the fifteen keys and change now represented 8.64 critical masses in a sphere of radius 4.3 cm. This

---

DFT+U: density functional theory+Hubbard   DMFT: dynamical mean-field theory
GGA-PBE: generalized gradient approximation with Perdew, Burke, Ernzerhof functional

is almost equal to the radius of a *single* bare, solid critical mass at standard density. Behold the awesome power of compression!

The D-T gas can be injected comfortably prior to showtime. It is not difficult to calculate the time necessary for a spherical pusher of some mass to travel a fixed distance in a vacuum. Only the most energetic neutrons emerging from the initiator were of consequence. The neutron energy E_n is a function of the energy E_b of the bombarding particle and the emission angle θ:

$$E_n(E_b, \theta) = E_0 E_b + E_1 E_b \cos\theta + E_2 E_b \cos^2\theta$$

E_0 and the E_i values are constants determined experimentally (there is also an E_3, used to calculate the angular distribution). We can expect from this about a 5% maximum diversion from the mean in either direction, and indeed, that's what we see (largely independent from ion temperatures):

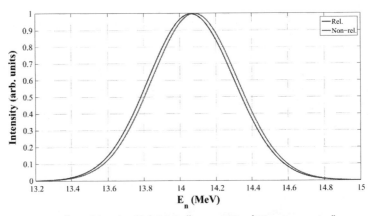

B. Appelbe, J. Chittenden. "Relativistically correct DD and DT neutron spectra."
High Energy Density Physics June 2014. DT at 10 KeV.

The unknowns were constrained to well under one hundred nanoseconds, and indeed, time between maximum scrunch and first arrival of neutrons was seventeen nanoseconds, a fine match. ^{240}Pu lets off about 808 spontaneous fissions per gram per second. The 908 g of ^{240}Pu contaminant could be expected to lose 734 kiloatoms per second, emitting attendant early neutrons. This seems a great many neutrons, but it is still an expectation of fewer than one neutron per microsecond. The average time between spontaneous fissions was eighty times the 17 ns divergence. These were more disruptive as density increased, but assembly time was only a few microseconds; between idyll and inferno only five atoms collapsed into femtocells of fission, sizzling along their wave functions, burning out without contributing meaningful energy. Electromagnetic effects limited peak scrunch duration to around 800 ns, only ⅘ of a microsecond. If things went as expected, the physics of metallic lattices would by then be the furthest thing from any observer's mind.

Thousands of highly energetic neutrons had been ejected from the freshly fused helium. Their trajectories were utterly unaffected by the tumult collapsing around and behind them. Within a nanosecond of the first neutron coming within a centimeter of the geometric core, several dozen more arrived. A thermal (room temperature) neutron has about 0.025 eV kinetic energy, and is moving at 2.19 kilometers per second. 2 MeV fission neutrons push 20 Mm/s. 14.07 MeV D-T rude boys do 17.3% of c.

If the neutron is not scattered, it might trigger a nuclear reaction, removing the neutron from circulation. The probability of a strong interaction is a function of the incoming neutron energy (faster neutrons are less likely to be affected by the residual strong force, hence reactor moderation). Each isotope has a fission activation energy, a total binding energy, and a TBE should it gain a neutron. If the difference between the TBEs is less than the necessary fission energy, kinetic energy must make up the difference; otherwise even thermal neutrons can fission the isotope. If there is insufficient energy, the nucleus shifts to accept the neutron, belches up a gamma ray, and usually flips the n for a p (there won't be time in the bomb for a β^-). ^{238}U asks that a neutron bring its own MeV to the party, but fission neutrons are emitted at up to 2 MeV or so, and a fair number of them will fission ^{238}U in tampers or pushers. The fission births daughter nuclei. Almost always there are two; there is also sometimes an α in the mix). At these energies, the masses are bimodal; they grow slowly more symmetric, until converging at forty MeV. There are also several ($\bar{\nu}$, called nubar, usually two or three) lone neutrons. The number, composition, and energy of fragments (including the number of liberated neutrons) are probabilistic, and their spectra dependent on the incoming neutron energy.

Hē Ouaì hē deutéra apēlthen; idoù hē Ouaì hē trítē érkhetai takhú.

2003-11-23 0141h Private residence, 1253 Francis St NW, Atlanta, Georgia, USA
Always oxygen has dominated the earth, making up about 47% of its mass. The distribution of that oxygen has however wildly changed since the days of the protoplanetary disk. Hadean Earth's atmosphere was a thin reducing one of light atmophiles, one constantly disrupted by geothermic output and the solar wind (as a result, Earth is severely depleted in these elements compared to the rest of the System). The intense radioactivity of especially ^{26}Al melted the innermost heart of the planet. Denser elements (especially relatively copious iron and nickel) began to sink to the core, the "iron catastrophe"; gravitational potential energy thus released initiated a positive feedback loop. Melting became general. Surface temperatures reached thousands of degrees. The crust was subsumed by a magmatic sea: heat drove off what little atmosphere was left. But the molten outer core formed a geodynamo, giving rise to a planetary magnetosphere, shelter from the sun's gusts of charged particles.

Volcanic eructations built up an atmosphere of 97% CO_2. The crust felt 27 times current atmospheric pressures, but cooled to about 230 °C. At this pressure, water boils at 217 °C; it could now collect on the surface, and it is

---

Hē takhú: Ἡ Οὐαὶ ἡ δευτέρα ἀπῆλθεν· ἰδοὺ ἡ Οὐαὶ ἡ τρίτη ἔρχεται ταχύ.
The second woe has passed; the third woe is coming soon! Revelation 11:14 (NIV)

possible that all the crust was buried under a global ocean. It's worth noting that the sun's luminosity was at this time only 70% of its present output. The "faint young sun paradox" questioned how temperatures remained so high for so long (answer: intense greenhouse atmosphere). Any oxygen present was quickly taken up by iron in the oceans, and their waters rusted red. Early life might have photosynthesized using retinal rather than cholorphyll, yielding a lush magenta biosphere: "Purple Earth."

There was eventually a Great Oxidation, an "oxygen catastrophe" powered by porphyrin-based cyanobacteria. Molecular oxygen of biological origin overran the ocean sink, and accumulated in the atmosphere. Weak reduction became strong oxidation, annihilating archaeal life reliant upon anoxygenic photosynthesis. Those few which survived adapted, enlisting aerobic proteobacteria in symbiogenesis. These became mitochondria. The prokaryotes progressed to eukaryotes, and multicellular life.

The atmosphere hit 20.95% oxygen by volume, and aerobic organisms have wisely put it to great advantage. Mitochondrial electron transport combusts a mole of glucose, yielding water, carbon dioxide, and 38 sweet moles of energy-rich ATP, necessary in endothermic metabolism and for the maintenance of ion gradients. Diatomic oxygen in its ground state ("triplet oxygen," meaning its quantum spin is 1, allowing three projections of the spin on a given axis—such a molecule has two electrons in degenerate π orbitals and is thus a diradical, and its fine structure will be split into three lines) is no radical, but still highly reactive. Reactive oxygen species are plentiful in cells and in the intracellular space; superoxide and hydrogen peroxide are byproducts of metabolism. Radiolysis of water leads to the hydroxyl radical, which clears electrons like the microbiological equivalent of a fire siren, ripping up a chain of free radicals. A ROS in the nucleus can oxidize DNA. This can happen to any nucleoside, but we see it most often in guanine. That's to be expected: one electron reduction potential relative to the NHE is lowest (1.29V) for G, then A (1.42V), C (1.6V), and T (1.7V). Two of the most common products are 8-OH-Gua and FapyGua. Other oncogenic factors work differently: short wavelength ultraviolet (UV-B and -C) light triggers dimerization of cytosine, uracil, and thymine due to photon energies closely corresponding to excitation energies of their unshielded pyrimidines (adenine and guanine, heterocyclic purines, pair imidazole to their pyrimidine).

A healthy adult human suffers about 20,000 of these oxidations per day. If the body couldn't effectively and reliably recover, we wouldn't be here. The vast majority of these changes will be repaired using base excision or translesion synthesis. Base excision is initiated by DNA glycosylases that exist in all life we've bothered to check, and even in some viruses. This process happens continuously, and usually catches the problem before replication. Translesion synthesis is much more species-specific, and integrated with replication; when PCNA stalls, as it does on certain damaged bases, specialized DNA poly-

---

NHE: normal hydrogen electrode
8-OH-Gua: 8-hydroxyguanine   **FapyGua:** 2,6-diamino-4-hydroxy-5-formamidopyrimidine
PCNA: Proliferating cell nuclear antigen *20p12.3*   **cyt *c*:** cytochrome complex *7p15.3*

merases are called into action by monoubiquitination of PCNA's 164th lysine (sumoylation of same turns them off). If the right one arrives, it fixes the lesion.

Today was a normal day for Devesh as regarded his guanine. Over 90% of these oxidations were undone. The other two thousand cells were more thoroughly damaged, and through one or another of many pathways—most culminating in release of cyt c from the mitochondria into cytosol—crumpled in apoptosis. His DNA remained strong, unbroken. It was a fine thing to be an undergraduate in Physics. He laughed loudly and often, despite this semester studying spin networks, strongly anticorrelated with happiness.

2010-06-14 0852h Ulba Metallurgical Plant, 102 Abay Avenue, Öskemen, Qazaqstan Respublikasy
In Kazakh it is called Öskemen, but the Russians knew it as *Ust-Kamenogorsk* (Усть-Каменогóрск); both are official, and present on the city's seal. It is either way the biggest city in Eastern Kazakhstan, and a regional hotspot for non-ferrous metallurgy. In was dominated for the latter half of the twentieth century by *Úlbi metallýrgnalyq zaýyty;* UMP is a joint stock company held by Kazatomprom, owning *e.g.* Ulba Fluorine and BerylliUM in turn. In 1990, an explosion on the production line at subsidiary Yingtan Ulba Shine Metal Materials lofted a cloud of the light, brittle metal beryllium—a Category 1 carcinogen that replaces magnesium in enzymes, cannot be easily excreted once in the bloodstream, finds use in neutron engineering and aerospace alloys, and simply is not something one expects nor tolerates clouds of—over the city.

It had not been difficult to arrange. The company was tightly-knit: many had brothers or fathers or sons working in the same building, or nearby. A rich tradition of corruption and misappropriation and transacting *a la izquierd* had come down from the Soviet days, and everyone knew how a hand was greased. He'd had to touch several people. A fine five-bedroom house in the university area of Astana was still only about $100,000, though the *teñge* fluctuated fairly wildly against the US dollar, and hard currency could buy much more than that if converted at the right time.

The world's first supersonic passenger craft, the Tu-144, flew for Aeroflot between Moscow and Almaty, four months before the West's Concorde, until a horrific and unnecessary incident at the 1973 Paris Air Show eroded Soviet support for civilians blasting across Central Asia at Mach 2. Anarbek made the lengthy journey into the desert in a 2008 BMW Z4 rented with cash at Almaty International, knowing the fine machine would make an impression. Anarbek met cousin Nurislam, who'd made the introduction to the mine's second man, onsite at Moiynqūm. He'd explained what he wanted done, assuring the man that things were arranged in Öskemen (they were not, yet) and that he had sufficient pull (cash) Downtown, in Almaty, to resolve any problems that might arise. The man across the desk had nodded, kept his eyes warmly on Anarbek, and likely neither understood nor cared about a single word besides *vzyatka.*

Úlbi…zaýyty: Улбі металлургиялық зауыты Ulba Metallurgical Plant
a la izquierd: lit. "on the left" black market   **teñge:** теңге т Kazakh tenge
vzyatka: Взятка bribe   **Stepnoj orel:** Степной орёл steppe eagle

His face never changed expression. Anarbek finished, and for several seconds they sat in silence.

"I will have to take this to my superior." Of course he would. Bribes would go up the chain in turn, growing larger at each step. Total cost was a function of your first contact's distance from power. Anarbek and his cousin were escorted to a larger trailer, this one mercifully air conditioned. Thirty years ago, it would have been a yurt. Their host motioned them to sit, and listened as the second man explained in Kazakh. The tongue was essentially foreign to Anarbek. It sounded unpleasant to him, and though his understanding was incomplete, it still seemed like the message was being distorted.

The head of the mine turned to Anarbek. He offered them *Haoma* vodka and water without ice (the Islam of Kazakhstan is a relatively liberal one); he spoke Russian. "I am Sanzhar Marat, son of Sanzhar. Your presence is an honor to me. Anarbek son of Zhusup, I would like to help you. But we see few *Stepnoj orel* in the Moiynqūm these days. Indeed, I do not believe we ever have. However, I am happy to put several men at your disposal, and provide any necessary nets, weapons, *etc.* We have several dozen shoulder-fired *Strély* surface to air missiles here for contingencies; I'm not sure how they would be effective in catching the great Kazakh eagle, but for a friend, nothing is too much." He smiled bevolently at Anarbek, who understood immediately what had happened.

A respectful sip of the bracing vodka. The idiot with whom they'd spoken was surely a relative or friend of some powerful person, possibly this man. "*Ardaktym,* I have poorly explained myself to your lieutenant. Leave the eagle to his steppes; may he fly five hundred years. We have come to your office from Almaty to request that some tonnes of *zheltyj kek* be recorded and shipped as *vesti* instead. An embarrassing error at the Ulba plants, you see. A few containers were pilfered, probably for scrap metal. Unfortunately, several were *zheltyj kek* from this mine, and now there is a small problem of accounting with regards to the IAEA. As they never tire of reminding me, several times in the past year this has happened. The company as a whole needs this lest the assholes from Geneva sanction us. I have been instructed to deliver generous bonuses to the necessary people on this site. None of this can go down on paper, you understand."

Sanzhar closed his eyes and nodded. "Of course. The criminal element grows stronger in the cities. This will be difficult work, very delicate. It will disrupt some of our normal output. But I believe that with great effort, it can be done. The desert has many strange things inside her, and she is known sometimes to swallow back her children, and shit out bricks of lead." The bastard would have to print and affix different labels. "I would hope that for such a task, my bonus would be five million *tenge*. Arlan here would likewise receive one million *tenge*. And for your cousin, for arranging this, ten thousand." At $0.005, that was $20,000, $4,000, and $50. Anarbek had already given $4,000 to Nurislam, son of Zhusup's brother Miras, and was happy to see that he'd come out ahead of the ogre Arlan.

Strély: стрéлы lit. arrows 9K32 Strela-2 / SA-7 Grail
zheltyj kek: желтый кек yellowcake   **vesti:** вести lead

"That is precisely what I was instructed to deliver. It is good that everyone sees this the same way. I must note that, should this correction be discovered by the international inspectors, or brought to their attention, the fault would lie all along the chain, from this mine to the fabrication facility."

"Of course. The only people who will know are myself and Arlan, and"—here he looked conspiratorially at Anarbek and Nurislam—"Arlan hardly knows, *da?*" He laughed; Anarbek smiled; Nurislam remained stonefaced. "I did not rise to supervise this mine without knowing how to keep a secret." He gave them his number. Anarbek excused himself to the restroom and counted out six hundred ₸10,000 notes, each bearing the visage of Alpharabius, leaving them by the sink. He farted heavily before opening the door, shifting his innards; in his colon he felt twenty eagles fighting like tigers. Sanzhar proceeded in directly after, and when he came out, Anarbek saw that his pile of blue notes had been collected. The smell remained, a molodorous creeping thing that snapped lazily at the mine supervisor's ankles.

He kept the Z4 for the drive to Öskemen—he had come to enjoy the car very much, and he had after all fifteen years' salary in his briefcase. The negotiating there was only slightly trickier, though substantially more expensive, in line with the higher salaries and better educations behind the palms he greased. Also, he needed a strange artifact built, and that would require actual labor, not mere malfeasance. His US currency commanded respect, however, as did his education, and his known prospects within the company. It might have been a problem had they needed to go outside the country for materials, and Anarbek had been concerned about the necessary boron, but it emerged that the Inder District's mines produced rasorite and tincal, which came to Öskemen for processing. Boron carbide was readily available, as was (for a factor of two hundred times more) elemental boron fiber. Crystalline boron enriched in ^{10}B up to 96% is sold by 3M, but he didn't even want to think about the price.

He left that polluted town of unworked and worked and reworked metals and turned towards Almaty. Anarbek queued Kanye's *The College Dropout*. He gleefully rapped along with "The New Workout Plan," riding with the top down on National Highway A3, truly happy for perhaps the first time in his life. He gunned the engine, taking off like a shot under Central Asian sun.

2010-08-14 0315h Goat Farms Art Center, 1200 Foster St NW, Atlanta, Georgia, USA

CDI is expensive, and possibly watched. Katz had been bitching about it when Erica laughed. "CDI is trivial to make. Are you afraid of a little phosgene?"

"I'll admit being afraid of phosgene. Also, I was planning on moving to phosphorus oxychloride, like Shulgin recommends."

"Didn't you say that $POCl_3$ eats more diethylamine?"

"Yeah."

"Well fuck it, then. By the way, were you aware that diethylamine is used in largescale DMT synthesis?"

Impressed: "I was not."

CDI: N,N'-carbonyldiimidazole $(C_3H_3N_2)_2CO$

"Yeah, Nick Sand's process was indole plus oxalyl chloride, anhydrous diethylamine—"

"I'm almost certain that's dimethylamine. I read the same interview. Besides, if you have indole, wouldn't you just make MDMA?"

Lethal smile: "Do you mean isosafrole?"

Disgusted: "Fuck, I sure do. Idiot."

She laughs. "Your MDMA plans are about a decade out of date. 5-bromo-1,3-benzodioxole is readily available. You can make safrole from that via Grignard reaction with allyl bromide–"

"Grignard reagents are generally watched."

"*Shut up.* Easily synthesized. Did you ever make thermite as a kid?"

"Like ten parts hematite to three parts aluminum filings?"

"Spark it with magnesium, hell yeah! Take a dozen grams of Mg turnings and half a liter of THF. Stir while heating to reflux. Add a little of the 5-bromo. Let that stir for half a day at reflux until you raise an exotherm. That's your starter Grignard. Now the money: a kilo of magnesium, 32 liters of THF, half a kilo of 5-bromo, half a kilo of our starter. Add the rest of the 5-bromo using a dropping funnel—you want about eight kilos total for a 50 L vessel."

"Do you have this memorized? Have you done it?"

"I have not, but if I'm getting into clandestine chem, I might."

"My friend Devesh makes MDMA. I'm pretty sure he uses safrole though."

Somewhat irritated: "Do you want me to finish?"

"Please do."

"Cool to 10 °C. An eighth of a kilo of copper iodide. 2.5 L propylene oxide with 2.5 L of THF, cool that shit down while you do so. Heat it back up a bit below room temp, and add 10.9 L of 10% sodium chloride and 1.37 L acetic acid. Stir it for an hour at 35 °C. Take the pH below five with 600 mL, let it settle, and remove the aqueous layer. Charge in 8.2 L *n*-heptane and 8 L of sodium chloride. Stir, settle, again with the aqueous layer. Filter over a vacuum; 11 μm filter mesh is advised. Use a rotary evaporator—"

"ROTOVAP!"

"Fucking christ, yes, freak. Charge it with a kilo and a half of polyethylene glycol 400. Charge another vessel with 2.5 kilos of the crude product and a liter of dichloromethane, below room temp. Stir that fucker. Now we want a half kilogram total of potassum bromide and TEMPO. I forget what TEMPO is, but it looks like red caviar. Tetramethylpiperidinoxyl? Cool to 0 °C. Now we want two and a half liters total of sodium hydrogen carbonate in bleach, dropwise, while stirring and holding it cold. Let it settle, and remove the organic layer that emerges. We're almost there. Take three kilos of your product and add it to thirty liters of methanol at 5 °C. Three and a half liters of 40% aqueous methylamine, and take it down to ten below. Forty grams sodium hydroxide. Three hundred grams sodium borohydride in ten liters pure water. Add this over two hours, and you ought have a clear brown solution, keeping it cold, but above zero. Rotovap out the methanol under vacuum. Stir fifteen liters MTBE

THF: tetrahydrofuran/oxolane $(CH_2)_4O$ 1,4-epoxybutane 1-oxacyclopentane
MTBE: methyl tert-butyl ether

at 18.6 °C. Wash the aqueous layer, combine all organic layers, portionwise addition of twelve liters 2.0M HCl, stir for twenty minutes at room temp. That's your freebase. HCl it up, recrystallize, and go to town."

If he had a cap, he'd doff it. "You're an impressive woman, Mlle Marelli, and I'm proud to be yours."

She broke up with him three months later, but at that moment, she loved him as completely as she'd loved any man, woman, or science.

2013-01-26 2247h Private residence, 975 Piedmont Ave, Atlanta, Georgia, USA

Differentiating ovaries cease expressing SF1, but testes continue to do so, and activate SOX9. SOX9 spins up feedforward loops with FGF9 and PGD$_2$, guaranteeing its further production. SOX9 plus SF1 results in AMH, which inhibits development of the paramesonephric ducts that would otherwise give rise to a female reproductive system. SOX9 plus DAX1 triggers multiplication of Sertoli cells. Mutations of these genes can result in intersex disorders, including the presence of mixed genitalia, though it is not thought that humans can be truly hermaphroditic (*i.e.* capable of producing mature sperm and eggs both). Interstitial Leydig cells differentiate next to the seminiferous tubules, and release androgens (testosterone, androstenedione, and DHEA) when stimulated by LH. The migrated germ cells become "dark" (deeply staining) A$_D$ spermatogonia. They anchor the germline, dividing once each to produce "pale" A$_P$ spermatogonia. They then sit dormant in the basal compartment unless their pale daughters are damaged. A$_P$ spermatogonia perform incomplete divisions, stringing a syncytium along the peritubular tissue.

Testosterone plus FSH triggers spermatogenesis. These reactions proceed better at 34 °C, unlike the body's 37 °C, motivating external testes and the cremaster muscle that hoists them. The process is executed over and over from puberty until death, netting more than a kilosperm per second in healthy men. A full cycle of human spermatogenesis, including ductal transport time, requires about three months. It is pipelined across its four different stages, as identified by a cascade of four major cytodifferentiations moving along a spiral within the testicle. Once A$_P$s have completed their cytoplasmic bridges, Type Bs differentiate away; this spermatogonial phase is synchronized across the linked cells. Type B spermatogonia undergo mitosis in the adluminal compartment to produce primary spermatocytes, ending spermacytogenesis. These primaries are diploid, but the first phase of meiosis reduces each to two haploid secondaries. Meiosis II forms two spermatids from each secondary, concluding spermatidogenesis. Warps of four spermatids are issued in one cytoplasmic package, and begin the complex process of spermiogenesis. The spermatids enter radially symmetric, and leave elongated, in three distinct portions, practically an insect. The Golgi apparatus breaks symmetry, creating an acrosome, and opposite that an anoxeme; the centriole and mitochondria

---

FGF9: glia-activating factor *13q12.11*   **PGD$_2$:** Prostaglandin D$_2$
AMH: Anti-Müllerian hormone *19p13.3*   **DAX1:** dosage-sensitive sex reversal *Xp21.2*
DHEA: dehydroepiandrosterone/androstenolone   **LH:** luteinizing hormone
FSH: follicle-stimulating hormone

enter this dorsal section. The Golgi sacrifices itself to become the acrosomal cap, the vanguard of the sperm cell, wielding digestive enzymes with which it storms through the ovum walls. Finally, the centriole stretches into a flagellum, and DNA is compressed at least six times as dense as that in somatic cells.

We're now packing genetic heat, playing with haploid fire. The Sertoli cells phagocytize remaining cytoplasm—these tasty morsels are known as "residual bodies of Regaud"—and the spermatazoids are released to the lumen in spermiation. They are mature, but not yet motile. Movement into the epididymis and beyond is driven by peristaltic contraction.

Katz stepped away from his terminal, and outside for a Newport. A wave of primary spermatocytes had just departed his Type Bs.

In ninety days, at around this time, his heartrate pegged at 165. A clear fluid produced in the glands of Cowper and Littré trickled from his urethra, the next best road to *ramos palmarum;* it neutralized the remnants of acidic urine. Mature sperm were pumped to the top of the urethra; he curled his toes; he flexed his calves; a spinal reflex via the pudendal nerve resulted in jerking contractions from the pubococcygeus and bulbospongiosus muscles; he lost the war; spurt spurt and now he moaned stupid sex things, ahhhh!youremyGSUcumqueen, shitfireimcrampingup, bababadalgharaghtakamminarronnkonnbronntonnerronntuonnthunntrovarrhounawnskawntoohoohoordenenthurnuk!

Katz waited for her hypnagogia, and sleep. It didn't take long. He kissed her softly, and stood to resume quiet coding.

2010-11-30 2210h Norasia Bellatrix IMO 9232096, Esclusas de Gatún, Canal de Panamá
The third lane, started three years prior in the *ampliación*, wouldn't be completed until May 2016. President Martín Torrijos proposed it in 2006, and a national referendum approved *El Proyecto de los Tres Embalses* within a year. Martín was among the bastard sons of Omar Torrijos, *Comandante en Jefe de la Guardia Nacional Panameña y Líder Máximo Revolucionario de Panamá* from 1968 to 1981, known best for the 1978 Torrijos–Carter Treaties: Jimmy Carter magnanimously gave away the Canal so preciously constructed under T. Roosevelt, ownership of which had been carefully negotiated in the Hay-Bunau-Varilla Treaty of 1903. *Norteaméricano* fury at this giveaway reached its peak in Van Halen's 1984 single "Panama," which hit #2 with its demand "don't you know she's [referring to the Canal] coming home to me?" plus history's greatest harmonized sound drop. School of the Americas-trained Manuel Noriega would take over in 1983; on Christmas Day 1989, following one hundred hours of Operation Just Cause, Noriega requested sanctuary in the Apostolic Nunciature—embassy of the Holy See—from nuncio Archbishop José Sebastián Laboa. Delta Force encircled the Nunciature, and waited for 4th PSYOP Group with its 1st, 6th, 8th, and 9th Loudspeaker Teams. From outside they gave Noriega a pretty bodacious show, including:

---

ramos palmarum: branches of palm trees John 12:13 (KJV)
El...Embalses: Third Set of Locks Project
Comandante...Panamá: Commander in Chief of the Panamanian National Guard and Maximum Leader of the Panamanian Revolution

- "Hangin' Tough," New Kids on the Block
- "Midnight Rider," Allman Brothers
- "Danger Zone," Kenny Loggins
- "Big Shot," Billy Joel

...and of course the Van Halen protest rocker. Records furthermore indicate plays of Mariah Carey's "All I Want for Christmas (Is You)," despite it not being recorded for another five years. When asked, retired DEA Administrator Jack Lawn replied, "Drug dealers ought know that America will reach into the past and future, if necessary, to disrupt their trade, and that Mariah Carey's *Merry Christmas* is timeless." President George H. W. Bush merely smiled and said, "much like Mariah's most successful track, it was a Christmas miracle."

Captain Hermes Aguinaldo had navigated *Carriles Uno y Dos* two dozen times in his years; they were novel exactly once. The third lane would admit Neopanamax carriers with up to fourteen KTEU, compared to the current five. There were 1,564 nautical miles to the Port of Savannah. At twenty-four knots, she could be there in about sixty-six hours, but optimizing for fuel meant not exceeding 20.2 kph in level seas. This would add at least twelve hours to the trip, atop the ten necessitated for the accursed Canal. The third lane, if the Panamanians ever complete it, ought cut that delay down.

Not that it mattered to Aguinaldo of the *Norasia Bellatrix*, previously the *Hanjin Philadelphia IMO 9232101*, one of the last Panamax ships built by Busan's HJ Junggongeop. En route to Germany from Singapore, 150 km south of Sri Lanka, she'd in 2002 caught fire, setting off a substantial explosion of calcium hypochorite in the hold, strong enough to toss away multiple thirty ton deck plates. The crew, less two fatalities, abandoned ship. Ofer Group (of the powerful Eyal and Sammy Ofer) took ownership of *Hanjin Pennsylvania*, had her towed to the CSSC Chengxi yards, gutted her, and had her rebuilt entire. Why they'd bothered with a crusty old Panamax Aguinaldo surely could not tell you. In the *Hukbong Dagat ng Pilipinas* he'd been promised command of PS-37 BRP *Artemio Ricarte*, one of three *Peacock*-class corvettes purchased from the Hong Kong Squadron of Her Majesty's Naval Service in 1997, shortly before the UK decamped entirely from Asia. Reclassified the *Jacinto* class, they tore ass around the South China Sea, toting a mean OTO Melara compact 76 mm and looking for the shit. When his inebriate fool of a superior parked the ship on a sandbar after too many *Lambanóg*, heads rolled, among them Aguinaldo's.

Cue this great retarded toddler of a ship, on which he ferried hotpants and dildos from one ocean to another in the service of billionaire Israelis. Pushing her around the seas was like making love to marshmallow, but it beat a Manila call center, *pang-aalipin* in all but name. Panamax tonnage was capped at 52,500 DWT, 12.04 meters of draft, and 289.56 of length, not much more accommodating than the 8.1m limit for St. Lawrence Seawaymax. Neopanamax swung 120,000 DWT, 366 meters of length, and an all-important 15.2m draft.

---

ampliación: expansion   **TEU:** twenty-foot equivalent units
HJ Junggongeop: 주식회사 HJ중공업 HJ Shipbuilding & Construction Company, Ltd.
CSSC: 中国船舶集团有限公司 Chinese State Shipbuilding Corporation
pang-aalipin: slavery   **DWT:** deadweight tonnage   **DMF:** dimethylfloramide

Suezmax tankers can bring 20.1m of draft through the Suez Canal, but watch that 68m ceiling due the Egyptian-Japanese Friendship Bridge. Malaccamax, constrained by the 25m deep Strait of Malacca, admits 20.5m of draft for the VLCCs moving oil from the Persian Gulf. Chinamax accepts up to 24m of draft and 360m, feeding 400 KDWT a throw at China's unslackening hunger for ore, but this was a limit of a harbor, not a waterway. Beyond Malaccamax are Maersk's Triple Es, MSC's Gülsün, Evergreen's A, the Jacques Saadé class of CMA CGM, HMM's Algeciras, TI supertankers, and the Allseas Group's 2.6 catamaran crane ship *Pioneering Spirit*, as of 2023 the world's largest vessel by gross tonnage, used to install and remove oil/gas platforms as single operations.

2010-08-14 2122h Goat Farms Art Center, 1200 Foster St NW, Atlanta, Georgia, USA
The remaining work was done under longwavelength red light where necessary, and no light when possible. They worked in silence, with protective gear; neither wanted to absorb a few milligrams of freebase through their skin.

David Nichols succinctly reviews lysis and amination techniques in his 2018 "Dark Classics in Chemical Neuroscience." Katz had found them more haphazardly. All methodologies end with several rounds of column chromatography. Hofmann cleaved ergot alkaloids to DL-isolysergic acid hydrazide, racemized at C(5), isomerized at C(8). KOH epimerized C(8), a technique used to this day to recover isolysergic acid. Nitrous acid took hydrazide to azide; diethyl ether attacked the azide; diethylamine took its place. Classical aminolysis of methyl and ethyl esters of lysergic acid fails to go to completion without the brutish hydrazine, while chlorine destroys lysergic acid. In 1966, the Sandoz team avoided the C(5) racemization by protecting the alkaloid with equal parts strong acid prior to application of anhydrous hydrazine. But in 1959, Garbrecht had already published a method that would find use at industrial scale: D-LSA monohydrate dissolved with an equal amount of lithium hydroxide monohydrate in methanol. Remove the methanol *in vacuo*; dissolve the lithium lysergate in DMF. Dry it, chill it, add sulfur trioxide and mix it, being careful with the stoichiometry and remembering that lysergic acid is a zwitterion.

Shulgin's approach (really Johnson's, published 1973) brings one part D-LSA and two parts diethylamine in chloroform to reflux while stirring, then adds one part phosphorus oxychloride, maintaining reflux until everything has gone into solution. Bring it back to room temperature; add it to 1N ammonium hydroxide. Separate and collect the organic phase, and dry it over anhydrous magnesium sulfate. Filter. Remove solvent under vacuum. Amine availability got you down? Try the peptide coupling reagent PyBOP! No, it's not a poorly structured Python module, but rather the absolute mouthful benzotriazol-1-yloxytripyrrolidinophosphonium hexafluorophosphate. I wouldn't want to say that, either, yet I remain unclear on how one gets PyBOP from it. PyBOP is apparently a substitute for BOP, which has a longer name despite a shorter abbreviation (71 to 66 characters). Neither full name is a proper subset of the other, and it all makes me wonder what exactly they're synthesizing and/or smoking over in the world of peptide chemistry.

The prepared CDI would convert the D-LSA to its imidazolide, using DMF as reaction solvent. It had dried to lysergic acid hydrate, still about 5% water of crystallization. Under high vacuum, they further dried in a large flask; a stirred oil bath maintained a very precise 143 °C (141 °C is insufficient; 145 °C will destroy the acid; such are the specifics of organic chemistry). After three hours, including several flask pumps requiring use of nitrogen to raise system pressure, a flask containing a small amount of dimeric phosphorus pentoxide was attached by widebore tube. They went to maximum vacuum, and the tiny amount of remaining water was captured by the P_4O_{10}.

"Be careful emptying that," Erica admonished.

"This ain't my first rodeo." Phosphorus pentoxide is a massively powerful dessicant, but reacts with water highly exothermically, generating toxic fumes. The hood's pump was engaged.

Start with 150 mL of benzene. In go 50 g of dry lysergic acid, finely sifted. The benzene will prevent the formation of lumps as one adds a liter of anhydrous DMF. Apply magnetic stirring, at room temperature. Stir until the suspension is completely mixed and completely granular. It is desirable to minimize the runtime of the CDI reaction: the imidazolide has an equilibrium concentration higher in the *iso* form, but only reaches it slowly; there is a race against the clock to prevent excessive isomerization. Equimolar CDI was added as a single mass, and began to do its work, releasing carbon dioxide, leaving behind D-LSA imidazolide. After nine minutes—a great time, Katz remarked— they judged the process completed. Now the diethylamine, quickly, but with sure hands. Say a quick prayer to Eris. Watch hundreds of thousands of hits of LSD blossom, and think back to where a single one took you. A little awe, a little reverence, is completely appropriate.

2004-01-17 2232h Private residence, 1253 Francis St NW, Atlanta, Georgia, USA

By sequencing the genome of cancer cells and corresponding noncancerous cells, and comparing the sequences, it is possible to determine which genes have been modified. A narrowing centromere unevenly divides each chromosome into two arms. The longer is known as q, the shorter as p (for *"petit,"* due the insistence of Jérôme Jean Louis Marie Lejeune at the 1966 Chicago Conference on Standardization in Human Cytogenetics). Within position 13 (cytogenetic bands produced by Giemsa stain) of the 17th chromosome's p-arm are eleven exons (ten of them coding in humans) spread among almost twenty thousand base pairs. They specify the 393 amino acids of wild-type TP53 and its dozen-plus isoforms. No gene's mutation is as correlated with malignancy as TP53, dysfunctional in more than 50% of cancerous human DNA.

TP53, "guardian of the genome," *Science* magazine's 1993 Molecule of the Year, brings a diverse set of skills to the table. Through upregulation of miR-34a microRNA it triggers senescence and/or apoptosis. By inducing p21 it can pause the cell cycle between the G_1 and synthesis stages of interphase (G_1/S regulation), the last point before irrevocable progression to fission. It controls numerous methods of DNA repair: mutations to any of 34 genes related to repair increase risk of cancer, but certain p53 mutations effectively *guarantee* cancer. TP53 provides critical defense against metastasis by stimulating angiogenesis

---

TP53: cellular tumor antigen p53 *17p13.1*   **p21:** cyclin-dependent kinase inhibitor 1 *6p21.2*

inhibitor arresten and inhibiting angiogenic promoters *e.g.* VEGF and Ang1. Its expression is promoted by UV light, and thus it stands ready to repair photoactivation. Unsurprisingly, p53 is intimately involved with regulating the differentiation of embryonic stem cells.

TP53 is constantly being created in the nucleus. Typically it is maintained at a low level via degradation by Mdm2; inability to produce Mdm2 leads to p53 overactivation and (unprogrammed, caspase-independent) podoptosis. Two families of protein kinases can phosphorylate TP53's N-terminal domain, preventing binding by Mdm2, leading to quick buildup of TP53: the mitogen-activated protein kinases (activated by osmotic stress, heat shock, oxidative stress, *etc.*) and the genome integrity checkpoint cascade. Certain oncogenic behaviors futher stimulate TP53 via p14ARF. Transcriptional coactivators KAT2B and p300 acetylate the carboxy terminal, exposing TP53's central DNA binding domains. So long as TP53 is functional, it's a powerful system, one that facilitates all the differentiation and division and renewal of a human life while preventing runaway growth. But vertebrates, especially mammals, have evolved such that TP53 is a single point of failure; if it befouled, or inhibited, or tricked, most of the cell's defenses are rendered impotent. If this failure is systematic—if it is a genetic issue, one that will be passed down the cell line—the situation becomes grim indeed.

Elizabeth II was in the early 1960s sovereign of a gloomy postwar Kingdom. Every time a BBC announcer came on, a new austerity was announced, another colony was lost; the Suez crisis was a humiliating debacle, and Eden's resignation ended any claim by England on superpower status. Then her turkeys began to die. Between May and August of 1960 over 500 incidents of "turkey X disease," etiology unknown, broke out in southern England. Mortality tended towards 100%; over 100 kilopoults were lost in two months. Officials identified Brazilian peanut meal from a single ship as the common element; when retrieved, it flouresced blue under UV light. Chromatographic testing demonstrated the feed to be run through with aflatoxin B_1.

When we think of household mycoses, we think perhaps of lung infections: aspergillosis, cryptococcosis, pneumocystis pneumonia (the last made famous in 1982's "A Cluster of Kaposi's Sarcoma and *Pneumocystis carinii* pneumonia among homosexual male residents of Los Angeles"). We think of those which afflict membranes (candidiasis, both thrush and vaginal). The serious systemic infection mucormycosis arises from black molds, and rose to prominence during the COVID-19 pandemic. Anyone who has seen an appendage bloated and bubbled by eumycetoma is unlikely to forget it. Most gain traction only in the immunocompromised, but there are more insidious mycotoxins still.

Named after *Aspergillus flavus*, aflatoxins are routed to the liver's hungry CYP450 enzymes. Cytochrome P450s live for xenobiotics. They crave nasty things, those things which are highly reactive, things you wouldn't leave alone in a room with your children. Acute aflatoxicosis overwhelms P450, triggering

---

VEGF: vascular endothelial growth factor *6p21.1*   **Ang1:** Angiopoietin 1 *8q23.1*
Mdm2: E3 ubiquitin-protein ligase *12q15*   **p14ARF:** ARF tumor suppressor *9p21.3*
KAT2B: K acetyltransferase 2B *3p24.3*   **p300:** histone acetyltransferase *22q13.2*

high expression of the death receptor pathway and mass apoptosis of hepato-cytes. The liver degenerates into necrosis, leading rapidly to coma and death. B_1 suppresses the immune system, directly destroys cytotoxic $CD8^+$ T-cells, prevents uptake of nutrients to the point of kwashiorkor and marasmus, and accelerates AIDS. Manageable loads of B_1 are reduced by CYP3A4 and CYP1A2 to several hydroxylated metabolites. Among these metabolites is the reactive eletrophilic exo-8,9-epoxide. Epoxides are ethers with a triangular cycle of carbon, oxygen, and carbon; the strain of this functional group lends it high reactivity, perfect for breaking nucleophilic rings.

Devesh's Home Park basement, a decade prior, was rich with molds. *Aspergillus* grows easily in Atlanta's hot humidity, especially in the dark. Smelling mildewy funk, he'd traced it to a snotgreen rot. *"Mādarcod,"* he exclaimed, grinning, and after a spray of generic disinfectant he wiped up the slimy mess in a tissue. Most aflatoxins must be consumed to achieve deleterious effect, but B_1 is readily absorbed through the skin. Whether through those capillaries or the intestine, to the liver it goes, now osmotically drawn into a hepatocyte, a stop for P450 reduction, and into the nucleus. Intercalated among bases, it rearranges a guanine's electrons, forming the adduct AFB1-N7-Guanine.

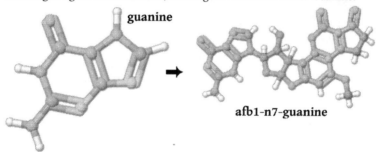

guanine

afb1-n7-guanine

If this happens while the strands are divided, immediately prior to division, there is no chance for repair. The adduct fouls up replication; the G becomes a T; it is paired with a C rather than an A. One of the cells, none the wiser, carries this mutation, as will its descendents.

Wild-type *p53* has a guanine as the third base of codon 249. And so it was that six of the millions of epoxide metabolites slouched mindlessly towards cells in anaphase, towards Devesh's electronrich chromosomes, temporarily unprotected by their double helix, and found number 17. Through Brownian chance they wandered close to its p-arm, and at position 13 disrupted a pi bond to make a room of their own. Conversion of this guanine to a thymine codes for an ineffective TP53 isoform, but no other damage that would mark the cell for death. It is the host itself that is now marked; death waits in the shadows, eager to spread its wings. There is no cancer yet, but stripped of tumor suppression, this line of cells is precancerous, the heart of an immense darkness, needing only an oncogenic nudge to descend into Hobbesian savagery.

Mādarcod: માદરચોદ motherfucker

2013-04-28 Private residence, 975 Piedmont Ave, Atlanta, Georgia, USA

The sperm's adventure is a dangerous one, full of terrors. Recall that the sperm are launched peristaltically. Boosting self-propelled ordinance through motion of the carrier has been adapted for satellites in ALTO, ballistic missiles in ALBM, and cruise missiles in ALCM. More exotically, Sopwith Camels in "parasite configuration" took off from and were recovered by Her Majesty's Airships. Every so often, a drone needs deployment from a plane; the M-21 (a variant of the A-12, predecessor of the SR-71) launched four D-21 supersonic drones, stopping when the fourth crashed back into the mother aircraft, destroying both (LCO Ray Torick drowned in the Pacific). Northtrop Grumman's Pegasus can take 443 kg into LEO, possibly in trios on the Scaled Composites Model 351 Stratolaunch, whose 117 m wingspan handily beats out the mere 98 m of the Hughes H-4 *Spruce Goose* flying boat.

The internet cheerfully asserts any number of places that semen emerges from the nutsack endlessly rocking, moving along at something over 40 km/h. More precisely, everyone seems to have agreed on twenty-eight miles per hour. The use of imperial units is your first indication that this is cargoculted trash-data. No meaningful research backs up this number; review of the literature finds no measurements of phallic muzzle velocity whatsoever. Analysis of sperm following capacitation *in vivo* puts their speed at around 100 µm/s, a much more leisurely 0.36 m/h.

The objective is one of the two fallopian tubes, muscular organs lined with cilia, about a centimeter in diameter. The egg rests in an ampulla, having been brought there through the infundibulum. The distal opening is not directly connected to the ovary. At ovulation, a secondary oocyte is released via rupture of its follicle, and fimbriae of the tube reach out to collect it. Typically, only one ovary releases an egg, selected seemingly at random (though if an ovary is removed, the other will release one each month). About half of the sperm which reach the top of the uterus will take a wrong turn.

As noted, alkaline semen neutralizes remaining uric acid, but cannot hope to overcome the acidic defenses of the vagina. Of the hundreds of millions of dispatched sperm, as many as half will end up floating immobile in cervical fluid. Those which make it to the cervix must traverse mucuslined folds, serving to ensnare another large fraction, especially those with abnormal motility. The foreign sperm cells are likely to induce an immunological response; immunoglobins IgG and IgA are known to patrol the cervix's membranes, dealing out agglutination and peristaltic ejection. The uterus lends some assistance in the form of muscle contractions, performed most earnestly in the late follicular phase. It furthermore fosters capacitation via glycosidasic enzymes and albumin, boosting the mobility of the sperm. This comes at just the right time; polymorphonuclear leukocytes arrive, triggering an inflammatory response designed to sweep out bacteria, seminal debris, and unlucky sperm. Sperm locomotion becomes rheotactic, prefering to swim along walls; this strategy brings them to the isthmus of the fallopian tube.

ALTO: Air launch to orbit   **LCO:** Launch Control Officer   **LEO:** Low-Earth orbit

Upon arriving in the tube, sperm are attracted to the egg via chemicals released by the corona radiata. Underneath these follicular cells is the zona pellucida, a glycoprotein membrane. Here the sperm binds to ZP3, triggering acrosomal rupture and the release of enzymatic penetration aids. Should the sperm reach the cytoplasm of the oocyte, it sheds its tail and outermost layer, fusing to the cortical granules. These expel via exocytosis enzymes which hydrolyse ZP2 into the crosslinked ZP2f, sealing the zona, denying entry to further sperm. Finally, the oocyte (known for a few minutes as an "ootid") completes its longarrested meiosis, dismissing half its chromatids and a polar body while retaining the haploid ovum. The two pronuclei migrate to the center of the ovum, and undergo their first mitotic division. Tin roof, rusted!

2010-04-20 1151h Port Authority, 111 8th Ave, New York, New York, Simulated USA

10×10^{-21} s, the zeptosecond, is the timescale of induced fission: a neutron is absorbed by ^{239}Pu, and the nucleus is rent within twenty sextillionths of a second. 10×10^{-18} s, the attosecond, is the timescale of neutron emission: the fission fragments fly apart at close to 3% the speed of light, and release $\bar{\nu}$ neutrons within ten quintillionths of a second. 10×10^{-9} s, the nanosecond, is the timescale of atomic detonation: fission neutrons initially travel at about 10×10^{9} cm/s, and travel a handful of centimeters before reaching a fissile nucleus. This last interval dwarfs the others, and thus determines the time between fission generations. Assuming each fission leads to at least two more in the next generation, each generation represents at least a doubling: pure exponential growth. In such a regime, each generation releases twice as much energy as the last. This is why it is critical to hold the explosion together as long as possible: 20 KT requires 2.6×10^{24} fissions; assuming a strict doubling, this requires 81 generations of fission, almost 810 ns. Cessation of fission is almost always due to dispersion of the core, as opposed to exhaustion of material. An 82nd generation takes that 20 KT and turns it into 40 KT.

Improving fission yield can be accomplished via improving the symmetry of implosion, increasing the force of compression, inserting more neutrons at the appropriate time, further enrichment of materials, more fissile material, boosting, or heavier tamper. The path to greater overall yield, however, sidesteps fission enhancement, and makes use of a fusing secondary. The energy released by a single D-T fusion is only about a tenth that of a single actinide fission, but fusion of a given mass of D-T releases almost five times the energy as the equivalent fissioned mass. Fusion can furthermore be staged multiple times, allowing for arbitrary yields, though there's precious little point in multiple-megaton warheads once they can be delivered with modern accuracy (contemporary stockpiles are almost entirely submegaton, save China's DF-5). It is fueled by relatively cheap lithium deuteride via Jetter's cycle rather than enriched actinides. The fast neutrons of D-T fusion can furthermore easily fission ^{238}U, making possible a cheap (if dirty) secondary fission stage.

ZP3: zona pellucida spermbinding protein 3 *7q11.23*
DF-5: *Dōng Fēng Wǔ* 東風-5 East Wind 5

Intense flux of thermal xrays requires millions of degrees, and thus follows initial prompt gamma rays by several dozen fission generations. This is still sufficient to arrive in the secondary long before the device has blown itself apart. A cylindrical hohlraum surrounds lithium-deuteride fuel and a chewy fissile core. The xrays bombarding the surface of the hohlraum heat it to the point of ablation; its outermost layer takes off like a rocket engine, compressing the contents with far more force than any chemical explosive. At the center, the fission sparkplug reacts more efficiently than the primary due to this greater compression; it compresses the LiD from the inside. Neutrons split tritium from lithium (the reaction with ^{6}Li is exothermic to boot); at these temperatures, the tritium fuses almost immediately with the deuterium. This drives hundreds or thousands of kilotons. *Kaì ho tétartos exékheen tền phiálēn autoũ epì tòn hélion; kaì edóthē autỗ kaumatísai toùs anthrópous en purí.*

2010-12-02 1641h Hanjin Philadelphia IMO 9232101, Port of Savannah, Georgia, USA

In 2019, the SRNL-designed Straddle Carrier Portal began to roll out to American and allied ports. Your typical straddle carrier, ubiquitous wherever shipping is handled, can carry sixty tons. Imagine an AT-AT with fixed legs, which were mounted to standard rolling drives on each side, with enough space between them to hold an ISO 668 container. The carrier embraces a shipping container on the ground, and a lift in the center picks it up. All the speed and usability of a gantry crane, combined with the flexibility of a wheeled, axled vehicle. SCP adds gamma and neutron detectors on either long side of the straddle carrier, allowing radiation detection to be performed while offloading the cargo, rather than as its own step, massively simplifying logistics.

In 2010, CBP had no SCP. Instead, containers were moved through two Radiation Port Monitors on their way out of the terminal. One employed polyvinyl toluene scintillation detectors. The other was an experimental Advanced Spectroscopic Portal using thallium-doped sodium iodide. Both contained a layer of neutron moderator supporting ^{3}He-based neutron detectors, though only the first actually had such a detector; light helium had become essentially unavailable after 2009, and the newer designs employing silicon photomultipliers and pressurized natural helium had yet to come online. Thus only one RPM had any neutron detection capability, and it had an old gamma detector incapable of all but the coarsest energy discrimination. In any case, all detection was arranged around the sides.

Their container was picked up, and the truck was directed out through the ASP. Its expensive NaI(Tl) detector was at the moment down, as it was a distressing percentage of the time. Standard operating procedure in this case was to continue using the lane (port throughput would be otherwise unacceptably degraded), pausing outgoing trucks for the same amount of time

---

Kai...purí: υματίσαι τοὺς ἀνθρώπους ἐν πυρί. Then the fourth angel poured out his bowl on the sun, causing it to scorch everyone with its fire. Revelation 16:8 (NLT)
SRNL: Savannah River National Lab   **CBP:** Customs and Border Patrol
ISO 668: International Standards Organization 668:2020
Series 1 freight containers — Classification, dimensions and ratings

as would be required for an actual scan, then cheerfully waving them through. The two employees operating the scanner still came in for their eight hours, standing by the blank monitor, talking about the Braves and the Sand Gnats and the Bulldogs. They had a good union.

All of the protections and efforts put into place to defeat border radiation detection served only to consume fuel. The added weight resulted in about $24 in trucking costs. Katz's phone rang shortly after their first container was on GA-21, headed to I-20 for the turn west. The call was brief: "You look good."

"Excellent, thanks."

Three hours later, a second call went the same way.

Katz called in and updated the address. He wasn't nervous. If something was going to happen, it would have already happened. Eris approved of his work, and was on his side. He lay out a line, ripped it, showered, and took MARTA to the West End.

2010-08-15 1250h Goat Farms Art Center, 1200 Foster St NW, Atlanta, Georgia, USA

The result was LSD freebase, plus contaminants. First, the products were dried to syrup in a rotovap. Dissolved CO_2 vaporized off, then the benzene, finally the DMF. Pressure was lowered, while the waterbath was raised to 35 °C, accelerating this process. The resulting sludge was dissolved in half a liter of volatile dichloromethane, carefully collected in a cold trap on the exhaust (breathing chlorohydrocarbons, even DCM, is not advised). The organic layer was washed with distilled water and trace ammonia. Extracting this into aqueous tartaric acid stabilized the freebase.

Silica gel—amorphous and porous silicon dioxide—offers a high ratio of surface area to volume. The gel ought be intended for chromatographic use: high purity, spherical shape, small particles, uniform pore sizes. RESIFA™ M.S.GEL™ from AGC, SOLAS™ from Glantreo, Macron Fine Chemicals™ SilicAR, DIASOGEL bulk silica ("underivatized!"): find one you like. It is a highly polar material, and preferably absorbs similarly polar eluents. A solvent mixture of three parts acetone to one part DCM is ideal. LSD's psychoactive isomer flows down a silica gel chromatography column slightly more quickly than inactive iso-LSD; other common impurities are removed almost immediately. A column of 20mm radius is recommended. Larger tubes are difficult to evenly pack with silica, and an uneven pack will admit unpurified salients down the sides or center. Siphon in the solution, then continue with the solvent. Equilibrium for LSD is 88% D, 12% ISO, and the D flows more quickly; the first 80% to reach the bottom is enriched in D. That which remains is depleted, heavy with ISO, and must be recovered with methanol.

Prepare *para*-dimethylaminobenzaldehyde (the basis of both Ehrlich's and Kovac's reagents) at 5% in methanol. Add a few mL to a sample, followed by H_2SO_4 dropwise. Shake it and jiggle it. There will be a reaction in the presence of indoles; lysergic acid yields a dark purple. Filtered impurities were checked for D-LSA content via this sensitive test; Katz was pleased to verify that it had been stewarded well.

The remaining process came straight from Webster: Into the evaporating flask containing the crude amide was added warm, dry methanol (4 mL/g), and dry D-tartaric acid (0.232 g/g); the flask rotated in its water bath, dissolving both. Shulgin recommends seeding with diethyl ether. Katz, preferring fewer rather than more explosions in the lab, eschewed this step. He would use cold acetone if it proved necessary, but it never had. Into the freezer it went. The bulb had been removed, and replaced with a manually operated Aamsco 11W UV-A; what they placed in the freezer fluoresced like the blue Cherenkov light of an underwater reactor. More batches were processed. They worked fourteen hours straight, listening to Hole's *Live Through This* and Clutch's *Pure Rock Fury* and Mastodon's *Leviathan* and Ice Cube's *Death Certificate*. Katz at one point queues up *Trout Mask Replica*. Erica vetoes it less than a minute in. She calls instead for Postal Service, then Rainer Maria's *A Better Version of Me*, and Lady Gaga's *The Fame*. Katz wants 2manydjs, but Erica remarks they have been at their task for too long; you don't want to get overly hoppy a day into a production cycle. Instead, NY Loose's *Year of the Rat* and PJ Harvey's *Dry*.

LSD tartrate is an off-white, almost beige translucent crystal. Shaken in the dark, it emits triboluminesent flashes. Refrain from licking it.

2009-07-07 1322h Arts Center Tower, 1270 W Peachtree St NW, Atlanta, Georgia, USA

It has been five years since the decision to wipe up some mold had led to nonfunctioning TP53 in six distinct cells of Devesh's liver. In the absence of physical trauma or hepatotoxicity, liver cells enjoy lifespans of two to three hundred days. Never a big drinker, Devesh inflicted few traumas on the heaviest of his internal organs. Some of the cuts in his cocaine did him no favors, but he indulged in organic stimulants even less frequently than alcohol. By July 2009, fewer than a thousand hepatocytes lacked the protection of TP53. Millions of cells in that time had undergone other cancerous mutations, but the germline had defended her house; those which refused to die nobly by their own executioner caspases saw their CD47 scrubbed clean, pursuant to slurpage and slurrification by macrophages, the shoggoths of the innate immune system.

But there are dangers to TP53 beyond aflatoxins. Devesh had never sunburned, and assumed his dark skin defense against short wavelength solar radiation. Let no one deny that an excess of eumelanin served him well: the pigment dissipates more than 99.9% of absorbed UV. It is precisely for this reason that melanocytes produce it when subjected to UV, and why natural selection at the tropics has favored its production. But there were almost two thousand such cells in every square millimeter of his skin, and about two million such regions on his body.

Averaged over the year and planet, 3.84×10^{21} photons per second intersect each terrestrial squared meter, delivering up to $1200 \, W/m^2$ insolation. About 5% of this energy arrives as biologically active wavelengths of ultraviolet light. Recall that this can flip a cytosine to a thymine. Immediately before the codon 249 damaged in Devesh's liver are codons 247 and 248: AAC CGG. He never felt the photons that struck in rapid succession, but when the cellular dust settled, they read AAT TGG, and were paired up with GGC CAA, and became a similarly buggy recipe for TP53. This had happened when he was eight. He would

---

CD47: integrin associated protein *3q13.12*

turn thirty-two the next month. A single melanocyte out of approximately four billion; pigment-producing cells are long-lived, and this one was never intended to divide, but time conspired against him.

He was sixteen when he applied a lotion, who remembers the name now, nothing that suggested the devil inside. A factory in Guangzhou had been mashing *Asarum splenden* ("Chinese wild ginger"), an ingredient in *zhōngyào xué* and a source of aristolochic acid. Anticipating anabasis, aforementioned alliterative acid approaches, acquiring an acescent adenine—absent apprehension, almost anosognosic—asserting accession anent affliction *ad rem* adducting anterior 7-[deoxyadenosin-N⁶-yl]-aristolactam (asshole!). Aberrations, avast! Anomalous abnormal amorphisms appear and absquatulate adhered A. T, they think, typically typifies the toxic target transversion (this theory turns to transcription technique). Thus it was on codon 61 of ras^H, on that same cell that eight years—half his life—earlier had absorbed two unfortunate photons. An extraordinary coincidence, one would think, almost incredible, but coincidence is a function of the number of events. Sufficiently many events eventually manufacture miracles: from this chance encounter sprung new, eager life. It set to populating the body, over which it had been promised dominion.

2013-04-29 Private residence, 975 Piedmont Ave, Atlanta, Georgia, USA
The cilia slowly beat the zygote towards the uterus. It divides meanwhile into the morula (sixteen compacted blastomeres), though it does not change total size. Within five days comes blastulation: formation of several hundred cells via thirty-two divisions. It is this which will form the embryo, and implant. Around the eighth day, the blastocyst erupts from the zona pellucida; an unfertilized egg disintegrates at most a few days after ovulation.

If the fallopian cilia were unequal for their task, or there was an obstruction, or if one has a particularly thicc chungus of a zygote, it might not reach the uterus. The result, should the blastocyst implant anywhere else, is an ectopic pregnancy (recognized on ultrasounds as the charmingly named "blob sign"). Most of the time, the egg remains in the fallopian tube. More rarely, it can implant in the peritoneum, the bowel, the mesosalpinx. Hepatic and splenetic pregnancies are documented, but vanishingly infrequent. The literature contains at least one report of an implantation in the diaphragm, truly xenomorphic shit: nuke it from orbit. Such pregnancies usually conclude with spontaneous abortion ("biochemical loss" in the first six weeks, "clinical miscarriage" afterwards). They're otherwise a very real threat to the host.

A zygote which splits into multiple embryos results in monozygotic (identical) twins. In the event of polyspermy (multiple sperm in an egg), the zygote almost always aborts following chaotic and jumbled formation of cleavage furrows, but very rarely leads to sesquizygotic twins. If multiple eggs are released in a single cycle, and fertilized by the same father, the result is dizygotic homopaternal fraternal twins. Different fathers are heteropaternal superfecundation a/k/a slut twins. Should ovulation occur while already pregnant, and that egg be fertilized, it's superfetation. Twins can develop all kinds of

---

zhōngyào xué: 中药学 traditional Chinese herbology

issues, from the craniopagus to the parietalis, from parasitism to reabsorption, to dreadful *fetus in fetu* and even the TRAP sequence: an "acardiac" parasitic twin, more correctly a headless, limbless torso, sticks an umbilical straw into its sibling and drinks its milkshake. Finally, what's funnier than a headless torso? Two headless torsos, of course, ha-ha. No, a torsoless head twin! That's probably all you need know about *acardius acormus.* All part of God's plan.

Risk of a miscarriage is highest in the first ten weeks, the period known as embryogenesis. By the end of this period, all major body organs have differentiated. The child (now called a fetus) is about 30 mm long, and weighs about eight grams, constituting a phat quarter sack of baby. The heart and circulatory network are among the first systems to develop, as they are necessary to deliver nutrients throughout the rapidly growing corpus. Blood enters from the placenta through the umbilical vein. The pulmonary artery and descending aorta are shorted via the ductus arteriosus, bypassing the (as of yet unused) lungs; a sudden drop in prostaglandin E1 immediately after birth will cause this shunt to close. It becomes the vestigial and quite functionless ligamentum arteriosum (or fails to close, giving rise to patent ductus A, common among those afflicted with Down's syndrome).

2010-04-20 1151h Port Authority, 111 8th Ave, New York, New York, Simulated USA
Temperatures peaked at around eighty megakelvin in the primary; the secondary saw a peak in excess of four hundred and fifty megakelvin, more than sixteen times the twenty-seven megs in the core of the sun. 80 MK corresponds to 6.89 keV, 450 MK to 38.7 keV. The bond disassociation energy of water is 4.4 eV, a thousand times less. The 11.16 eV triple bond of carbon monoxide is one of the strongest known. Under these impacts, molecules are disassociated, torn apart, the binding electrons removed wholesale. Degree of ionization is a somewhat complex relationship, usually expressed using the Saha equation for the ith ionization:

$$\frac{n_{i+1}n_e}{n_i} = \frac{2g_{i+1}}{\lambda^3 g_i} \exp \frac{-(\epsilon_{i+1} - \epsilon_i)}{k_B T}$$

but at these superstellar temperatures, there's no need to run the calculations. No electron can hold on to its mother atom when subjected to tens of millions of degrees. Material caught in the early fireball isn't melted really, nor even vaporized, but rather flashed into plasma, a highly conductive gas of electrons and fully ionized nuclei, buffeted by an x-ray density close to a hundred times that of lead. It is less a phase change than a deconstruction of matter. Atoms are denudated, stripped wholly bare, shuffled; their charge is suddenly extremely positive, as is every other atom thus afflicted; they immediately repel one another throughout their lattice. Until the temperature falls low enough to capture electron clouds, these nuclei crave radical dispersion.

The human body is to a large degree (78.2% by mass, 87.1% by atom) oxygen, hydrogen, and nitrogen. All those oxides and ketones and carboxylic acids

---

TRAP: twin reversed arterial perfusion

and esters and amides and amines and imines and hydrides and nitrates and nitrites just became air pollution. The ammoniums probably won't be missed, and the destruction of azides, imides, cyanates, nitros, ethers, alcohols, and aldehydes would probably be welcomed, were there a brain to welcome it. But there is no brain, just another contribution to an expanding wall of pulverized raw atomic material. Not that it matters for the hardworking magnesium ions and calcium phosphate; at these temperatures, they're gaseous too. This vaporization consumes a very generous five million calories (five gigajoules), which would be a downer, but we're working with about two petajoules of thermal output, sufficient to reduce 400 kilopeople to star stuff.

The exploding device's first emanations are direct products of nuclear reactions: gamma rays traveling at c, and escaping neutrons (no more than 20% c). Kinetic energy of the charged fission fragments and fusion αs is deposited back into the maelstrom; the resulting temperatures correspond to thermal radiation of soft xrays. This xray pressure is far more intense than that due to gammas, and begins interacting with the air around the device. These photons' free paths are initially very short; they ionize the air immediately surrounding the bomb. In ionized air, xrays lose energy only via Compton scattering off electrons; the plasma has become transparent to their energies. This sphere of transparency grows via radiative diffusion; at its boundary is a sharp difference in temperature and opacity. At T plus thirty microseconds, the fireball is about a megakelvin at its heart, about 6×10^5 K at its boundary forty meters away, and room temperature a meter beyond that. The core is by now a vacuum. Densities are unearthly at the ten meter shockfront's shell, at which point they rapidly drop off. The radiation shock is adiabatic, but the inner shock wave (marked by pressure and, at this point, velocity) compresses the ionized air, resulting in nonadiabatic, isothermal shock. After a millisecond, the internal "case shock" has caught up with and surpassed the radiation front; both spheres have a radius of about one hundred meters. Omnicide in a millisecond: where the fireball touches, little larger than a nucleus remains.

The blast wave travels far beyond the final boundaries of the thermal gradient. At the fireball's boundary, it is traveling at close to 3,500 kph, carrying 200 psi of overpressure and 330 of peak dynamic pressure. Reinforced concrete structures are leveled by one tenth of this overpressure. 5 psi will generally collapse a residence atop its unlucky inhabitants. The velocity and pressure drop rapidly, though this means the period of peak overpressure grows longer away from the explosion. Along the perimeter of the shockwave, pressure reaches peak almost immediately, remains there for a time, and is followed by a period of rarification during which the direction of force is reversed. The majority of immediate fatalities are due not directly to pressure (the human body is surprisingly resilient to overpressure), but rather being crushed, being flung through the air, and/or vivisection by flying glass. Thermal energy flashes into fire anything combustible, boiling away exposed skin, muscle, and organs. Anyone looking down a line of sight to the explosion has been blinded. The blast has exposed any number of gas lines, rendered wood into highly flammable splinters, exploded gasoline in cars, and likely set swaths of asphalt on fire. Depending on atmospheric conditions and city construction, fires may unify into a broad conflagration, a firestorm, which draws oxygen in towards its center with force sufficient to lift, toss, and consume unlucky humans. In Tokyo, mattresses were sucked from buildings into the street, where they become great balls of fire; at Hiroshima, wind snatched children from parents' arms, yeeting them into the flames like swaddled smores. California's 2018 Carr Fire saw pyromesocyclones with the wind strength of EF-3 tornadoes.

The dense buildings of the city provided some lucky individuals with cover, though reflected waves converged behind them just as often, leaving freak patchwork devastation surprisingly far from 8th and 16th. *Kaì egéneto hē pólis hē megálē eis tría mérē, kaì hai póleis tōn ethnōn épesan.* Then this world as will and simulation came to a sudden end, not with a bang, not with even a whimper.

2010-08-25 Arts Center Tower, 1270 W Peachtree St NW, Atlanta, Georgia, USA

Primary tumors generally take years or even decades to reach substantial size. A cubic centimeter of cancer—a volume smaller than a standard die—usually contains about a gigacell. $100 \, cm^3$ would thus be made up of 10^{11}; this tumor would only be 4.6 cm on a side, or a sphere of radius 2.88 cm. Surgical excision of 99.9% of such a tumor leaves 10^8 (one hundred million) cancerous cells. Worse, by the time a tumor is noticed, some of its billions of cells have often already metastasized. Primary tumors are not often fatal, because any given tumor will not generally be fatal. Secondary tumors—metastases—have already acquired motility and invasiveness, and thus throw off their own tertiary colonies: exponential growth. Eventually, one of these children begins stealing space or resources from an essential organ, and things come to an end. Primary tumors aren't better for you per se; there are simply many fewer of them (usually only one—it's far more likely that a given tumor is secondary, even after being declared "cancer-free," an optimistic term at the best of times).

Carcinomas (epithelial cancer) lead to the majority of cancer deaths in adults. Here again, it is rare for a primary carcinoma to be particularly deadly; to block a critical path (*e.g.* the digestive tract) or damage an organ with pressure (*e.g.* the brain or lung), it must form in a suitable place. Epithelial tissue consists of tightly and regularly packed cells, almost like a crystal. Multiprotein cell junctions provide chemical adhesion on top of the physical packing. They're avascular, acquiring nutrients and eliminating wastes via diffusion across their basement membranes (extracellular matrices separating epithelia from mesothelia and endothelia).

Epithelial cells together with mesenchymal stem cells form the two basic tissue phenotypes in vertebrates, and one sometimes needs become the other. Cell programs exist for this: Epithelial–mesenchymal transitions (EMTs) and mesenchymal-epithelial transitions (METs). E-cadherin, coded by CDH1 at *16q22.1*, powerfully suppresses tumors by triggering the Hippo pathway and downregulating the potent oncogene YAP. It is furthermore a junctional protein, one that promotes intercell adhesion. The EMT pathway begins by

---

Kai...épesan: καὶ ἐγένετο ἡ πόλις ἡ μεγάλη εἰς τρία μέρη, καὶ αἱ πόλεις τῶν ἐθνῶν ἔπεσαν. The great city split into three parts, and the cities of the nations collapsed. Revelation 16:19 (NIV)
YAP: yes-associated protein 1 *11q22.1*   **uPA:** urokinase-type plasminogen activator *10q22.2*

repressing transcription of E-cadherin (*e.g.* SNAI1, ZEB1, TCF3, KLF8) or repressing it indirectly (*e.g.* TCF4, Twist, FOXC2). The serine protease uPA activates matrix metalloproteinases ("matrixins") and directly attacks the basement membrane. Desmosomal disruption sets the cancer free; degradation of the extracellular matrix gives it wings.

EMTs are critical in early embryonic development, especially gastrulation and formation of the neural crest. They play a fundamental role in the healing of wounded skin; keratinocytes undergo EMT, move to fill the gap, and MET back. Mesenchymal cells rebuild the ovarian surface following ovulation, *etc.*. These very same programs remain sitting there, latent, ready to be harnessed by wayfarer cancers hoping to see the world.

Melanoma relies on different signaling pathways to engage EMT (there's more B-Raf and MAP2K1, less regulation of p63 isoforms, *etc.*), but they still get to SNAI1 and SNAI2 (affectionately known as Snail and Slug). With the expression of KIT, MITF, and DCT, whoosh! cancerous melanocytes begin intravasation through the dermis. They're not actively seeking onramps to the circulatory and lymphatic systems, but once a prominence hits one, it's not going to turn away, either. Into an artery or vein tumbles a clump of unthinking death. It needn't be many; a single cell is sufficient, if it has the right mutations (a tumor's trillions of cells contain thousands of genomes, representing a richly branched lineage). Upon access to a blood vessel, it's whisked away at about a meter per second; lymph, with no heart to pump it around, moves a thousand times more slowly. Before long, it comes to rest in its New World, and should it establish a bridgehead...well, we know about New Worlds and natives. The metastasis is advanced cancer, and needn't undergo the slow mutation process. From the onset it's ready to roll, and is already colocated with a thoroughfare. Incest is no shame among metastases, and they sometimes colonize their own tumor ancestors. Cancer fatalities generally house more metastatic than primary mass, despite the latter's long, lazy development.

The mole on Devesh's back had gone unnoticed for two years. He first felt it in the shower at 8mm, and assumed *khīla*. He tried to pop it, nearly passed out from the pain, and upgraded his estimate to *phōllō*. For several months he ignored it, at one point changing soap to see if that might help. One day after some vigorous exfoliation he noticed blood on his towel, and resolved to have a dermatologist look at what was by now an angry and thoroughly dysplastic nevus, one irregular in shape. Alas, he forgot a few hours later.

If caught prior to spreading, melanoma is firmly NBD, and can be excised in toto for a complete "cure." Through August 25, 2010, this was an option for Devesh. Afterwards it was not. And so it was that at only thirty-three years of age, his inflamed Gujarati dermis pulled taut and gave way. Indeed, there was a particular moment in time, a cusp defined by the squirming departure of one grotesque, malformed thing—one would hesitate to call it a cell—laden with all the genes of annihilation. It spilled into a capillary and was drawn into the subclavian artery, then the intradural vertebral artery, and the basilar artery. Past the medulla and the pons, now into the posterior cerebral artery,

---

khīla: ખીલ zit   phōllō: ફોલ્લો cyst

beyond the mesencephalon, back into thin capillaries, *thwack* it stuck on one of the occluding junctions that make up the blood-brain barrier. What results is called the "blood-tumor barrier"; via poorly understood means, it remains largely impermeable to medications, even as it is riddled and eaten away by vasculature passable by cells. All part of God's plan.

Devesh was a happy guy, all about physics, rolls, and metastases.

Cancer is frequently anthropomorphized, called aggressive or invasive. It seems a fighter, one which overcomes a great many obstacles. Metastasis especially blends a number of clever techniques, strategems worthy of Ulysses or Edmond Dantès or Lisbeth Salander. There exist cancers which seem more productive, more resourceful, indeed more intelligent than their human hosts. Yet there's surely no real thinking there: it's all just a matter of random mutations, natural selections, and issues of cellular discipline.

So what then are we, and of what might cancer dream?

2010-12-07 1121h Metropolitan industrial park, 680 Murphy Ave SW, Atlanta, Georgia, USA
The Candler Warehouse was built in 1914, occupying forty acres (though no mule), and at the time its 1.1M ft² marked it the nation's largest structure under a single roof. An otherwise uninspired concrete affair, it housed agricultural products and equipment, but slipped into a chaotic disrepair by the turn of the century. Much of it stood abandoned and insecure. Squatters occupied large partitions in groups of a half dozen or dozen, parties raged wild; groups of artists cycled in, painted, and cycled back out; relations between poor older blacks and young bohemian whites were better than one might expect. Cops left it to its own devices unless there was a stabbing or shooting. It enjoys direct access to seven different roads, I-20 via Murphy Ave in half a mile, and via I-20 the Downtown Connector in five to ten minutes. Norfolk Southern's vast Inman Yard can be seen from the property, and CSX's Howell Yards are only three miles away.

For $5,000 per month, payable and indeed preferred in cash, Katz had 20K ft² with a delivery door that paired six meter height with ten meters of width, easily enough room to admit 20' containers via truck delivery. It sported furthermore a relatively new Hafö/Hagen gantry crane with 20 tonne capacity, and 480V three-phase secondary distribution of sworn reliability. Katz called Georgia Power to check on the subletter's claims, and they assured him it ought be good for 15 kVA, and that with reasonably priced upgrades he could expect 500. "So when I spin this 9A hoist motor up, I'm not going to brown out the facility?" They chuckled; he wouldn't brown out his own transformer.

The drayman pulled in within the expected window, on the early side. Arranging transport from Savannah had been surprisingly easy once he'd found a suitable base of operations. Unloading was simplicity itself. He'd familiarized himself with the hoist's pushbutton controller earlier that week, and got a well-used 25T Tulsa Chain fixed spreader beam lift (compatible with ISO 3874, natch) together with shackles delivered off Craigslist for $2000, paid in a thick

---

ISO 3874: International Standards Organization 3874:2017
Series 1 freight containers — Handling and securing

stack of twenties. The thick fellow from Macon had asked, "What're y'all taking up with this sumbitch?"

Katz thought back to childhood, to Cassius Julius and his burnt offerings. "Black bears, sometimes a moose."

"Ahhh *moose?*"

"Sometimes several. Moose bites can be pretty nasty."

"Moose *bites?*"

"They're very intuitive animals, smarter than dolphins actually. They're regularly taught trigonometry. As recently as 1899 a Yalie moose was initiated to the Order of Skull and Bones. But they're ornery. Moose will snap at you. An adult *Alces* can bite through six inches of stainless steel."

"Jaysus! What're you going to lift them for?"

"Well, I can't have them running around biting people." Katz handed him a wrapped stack of one hundred twenties, then folded over another five and put them in the man's chest pocket. "Let's just keep that between you and me, though. I don't need the DNR in my ass." A knowing look was exchanged; those pricks are just looking for a reason to screw the little guy.

Katz answered his phone, an HTC G2 with physical keyboard—already in 2010 a rarity—and provided instructions from I-75. He walked to the gate and admitted the truck, then led it to his unit with the exaggerated movements of a runway marshaller, wishing for all the world that he had a pair of those orange wands. As the door went up, he yelled through the cab's window, "I've got a beam lift; I assume we just hook it up and go?"

"Good deal, that's what I like to hear!"

"Yeah, we can just lift it, and then you can move your truck and get out, and we'll put it down once you're out from underneath."

"You're keeping the container?"

"Yeah, it's getting picked up tomorrow. You can transform and roll out." With the massive UPS facility in Forest Park, and the railroads, getting the container out was essentially free.

Katz turned on the powerful overhead lights as the driver brought the truck cautiously inside. The truck cut off before he had the door closed. Another Craigslist seller had delivered a tank access unit: 2.7 m of galvanized aluminum ladder connected a platform with handrails to a steel counterweight base and four 200 mm casters. This had run another two large. Cheap for what it got you, especially when paid with untaxed cash. The driver went outside to gabber on his phone, and Katz hooked up the four shackles to ISO-specified mounts. He brought the access stairs back away from the truck, picked up the controller, took a deep breath, and mashed UP.

Gods be praised. All the Latter-Day Saints and the Angel Moroni. Watch that fucker rise. Remember the Nicine Creed: *Et ascendit in caelum, sedet ad dexteram Patris.* Up, up, up, Simba! It cleared the cab sans even a creak of opposition, and hung there, tonnes of yellowcake, pregnant with the strong nuclear force, gravid, heavy, marble for his Galatea.

DNR: Department of Natural Resources
Et...Patris: It ascended into Heaven, and is seated at the right hand of the Father.

After thirty years' sufferance of lies, stupidity, and cowardice, Sherman Spartacus Katz had his own uranium. It was about goddamn time. Hail Eris!

2010-08-02 0448h Spire, 860 Peachtree St NE, Atlanta, Georgia, USA

It is late, approaching five AM. All is darkness except the wide Dell U3011 flat panel, and 2mm green diodes on Behringer B2031 Truth active monitors pushing 265 W, and the loose glow of scattered streetlight from thirty stories down, and the tip of a Newport. Katz has been working for about forty-four hours, ever since waking up the previous morning. He'd quit his job towards the end of the masters degrees, and was knocking out contract work for the moment, slinging code like dead rats held by their tails. This job had been with a Nashville video game startup. They wanted a physically realistic nuclear detonation rendered, and one of the principals knew Katz from school. He'd broken out the *Basic Bethe* and written his own hydrocodes, drawing upon a worn copy of Barroso's not-yet-translated *A Física dos Explosivos Nucleare* (he finds the math easy enough to follow; the rest seems mostly transitions), the second edition of Reed's *Physics of the Manhattan Project,* and the Dover printing of Zel'dovich and Raizer's unequaled *Physics of Shock Waves and High-Temperature Thermodynamic Phenomena.* The run completes. *Tetelestai.*

He'd prepared a statement of work requesting only five large. Katz enjoyed doing these little projects for startups, especially local ones; it felt like he was seeding his hometown ecosystem. Most of the work that came his way wasn't the kind of thing one easily finds people for—object tracking and target discrimination using CUDA on Nvidia GPUs, custom static analysis for various half-baked security products, cache-optimized Markov chains for addressing-agnostic protocol analysis, and signal processing in conjunction with prototype Ettus SDRs. Even if his customers could have found competent help, costs would have been prohibitive. Katz offered friendly, even foolhardy terms, fractions of what more voracious contractors could have demanded; when he got things done more quickly than expected, he refunded rather than charging more. After a few months, he had all the work he could possibly take on, no matter how much meth he broke out onto CD trays, laying out rails fat in the middle with tapered ends like troposkeins. He'd hit a third of it as an eye-opener, leaving it on his desk like a ward against evil and laziness. Whenever he felt his spirit flagging, he hoovered up a bill or straw's cap area worth, generally not needing to put more out until the evening.

He neither hid nor disguised his habit, answering inquiries with a nonchalance he mistook for courage, yet felt strongly that leaving hard drugs in the open was gauche, a broken Overton window of the psychoactive, a first step on the road to crapulence. If people were coming by, more often than not the surface was put up on bookshelves, away from idle eyes. Quite often he forgot that he had done so. Days later, he would scramble up his ladder looking for some text or another, and find prepared portions of speed. If left too long,

---

A Física dos Explosivos Nucleare: Physics of Nuclear Explosives
Tetelestai: τετέλεσται it has been accomplished/it is finished. John 19:30 (LSV)
CUDA: Compute Unified Device Architecture   SDR: software defined radio

pollen and corrupting dust inevitably collected. He disposed of such tainted powders unless he had exhausted or almost exhausted his reserves.

Katz was a strict devotee of the snort, never smoking nor slamming. Boofing was right out. He reckoned that simply eating it would probably be the best means of ingestion, but the ritual of nose drugs was a simple pleasure. The downside was boogers not only gnarlier than you think, but gnarlier than you can think, sometimes so firmly lodged and hulking that they cut off a substantial fraction of his air.

There was a new project every week or fortnight or month, depending on the complexity, and how much domain knowledge he needed pick up. Katz's target was an amortized ten thousand a week: he charged customers who could spare a little extra more, so that they might subsidize those who could not. From each according to their means, to each according to their needs, with Katz in the middle of all of it, becoming a name among all the city's (and state's, and region's) entrepreneurs and engineers. He billed a little over half a meg that year without a dollar of advertising. High above Peachtree Street, behind floor-to-ceiling double-paned argon-insulated glass he saluted many rising suns. Turning back to his terminal and charmingly clackful Unicomp Endurapro keyboard, he'd screw a Newport between his lips, drink water from a silver pitcher, bend to insufflate the evening's last crystlecrumble, and wince as the hydrochloride and weak base hit his membranes. Not quite sleep, but surely the next best thing.

No man's fool, Katz knew that once you started imagining people in your simulations, and giving them little backstories, it was time for bed. He wondered briefly whether the same rule applied to whatever entities had created his world, the world in which he wrote C++ and purified crystal meth in acetone baths and like a wrathful god incinerated cores of cities. Then he got distracted by some tricky linear algebra, and put these contemplations aside.

2010-08-15 1839h Goat Farms Art Center, 1200 Foster St NW, Atlanta, Georgia, USA
As far as LSD carriers go, sealed gelatin is superior to blotter paper, and both are bettered by pressed tablets with an appropriate excipient. The Controlled Substances Act requires registration of pill presses, and provides for their seizure, but does not make them illegal. Nonetheless, they were not practically available in 2010: the minuscule market for such machines meant few manufacturers existed, and those that did were motivated to remain on good terms with the DEA. Since then, the explosion of fentanyl has led to a thriving market for affordable Chinese tableting machines, easily ordered off the Internet and delivered in days. The STEER (Substance Tableting and Encapsulating Enforcement and Registration) and CAST (Criminalizing Abused Substances Templates) Acts would have tightened regulations on ownership, but failed to pass in 2018 and 2019, respectively. FDM or SLA resin 3D printers may soon be able to print pills, forgoing special-purpose encapsulation apparatus entirely. It is critical that active material and binder be mixed thoroughly: dropping solution onto the surface of prepressed pills is no better than sugar cubes.

FDM: fused deposition modeling   **SLA:** stereolithography

Gelatin (originally called "windowpane") can hold more active material than blotter paper, and protects it from oxygen, though not light nor sustained moisture. Get a mold (these can be 3D printed) and go to town. Blotter is trivially prepared, though, and provides an opportunity for artistic expression on canvases 2.5" square. Preperforated paper is almost always of lesser quality, absorption-wise, than that which is unscored; never have I been able to ascertain why. You want it thick, almost like cardboard. Immerse the blotter in a solution. Lift it out with tweezers, and ensure no free liquid is present. Note that recrystallization will not occur. An LSD oil binds to the paper's fibers, providing no protection, only geometry.

They were soaking three pages—2.7 kilohits—aiming for 100 µg each. Cobb hygroscopicity testing is inappropriate for highly absorbant materials such as bibulous paper; they instead employed a Klemm capillary rise tester. A page of the blotter absorbed 320 mL: $\frac{16}{45}$ mL per hit, then. Each of those 0.36 mL needed 100 µg of active material; equivalently, 960 mL needed 270 mg. Erica portioned it out using an expensive U. S. Solid analytical balance, and added it to almost a liter of cool ethanol. It dissolved, and she dumped the mix into a cooking pan. Into the pan went a page; once saturated, it was placed atop a stainless steel grill grid through which excess could drip back in to the main body. This was repeated two times. The remaining 289.414 g would be moved as crystal.

They removed their equipment, save the gloves, which they kept on until well out of the lab. There was some light glow on the surroundings, due more to the emergence from darkness than any unintentional consumption. They blinked it away. Around the side, Katz with his forearm engaged lungingly a 1/2" hose hookup. Erica stared at him, and asked, "Why didn't you just wash those in the distilled water?"

Katz looked up for moment, and giggled. "Because I'm stupid." He ran water over his gloves, then removed them, tying them off with Erica's in a plastic bag for disposal elsewhere. Katz locked up the lab. Wearily they began walking up Foster St into West Midtown, then down Howell Mill to Northside Tavern, a procession of the priests to cross the lone and level sands.

2013-04-20 Private residence, 975 Piedmont Ave, Atlanta, Georgia, USA

Carnegie Stage 6, two and a half postovulatory weeks: the embryonic disc flattens out into a shape not unlike Moss's egg or an oyster—think of the Trimaxion Drone Ship from *Flight of the Navigator*. As this happens, a longitudinal midline structure emerges on the caudal end's dorsal side, and looks just like an asscrack. Within this "primitive streak" totipotent cells differentiate into primordial germ cells under the influence of the canonical Wnt/β-catenin pathway (especially WNT3), BMP4, BLIMP-1, and finally Tcfap2c. These inhibit somatic differentiation and positively regulate anti-pluripotency maintenance genes, coding for *e.g.* hNanog and SOX2. These PGCs migrate through the gut

---

Wnt: wingless-related integration site   **BMP4:** bone morphogenetic protein *14q22-q23*
BLIMP-1: B lymphocyte-induced maturation protein-1 *6q21*
Tcfap2c: Transcription factor AP-2 gamma *20q13.31*
hNanog: Homeobox protein NANOG *12p13.31*
SOX2: (sex determining region Y)-box 2 *3q26.33*

and dorsal mesentery as guided by fibronectin *2q35* networks, proliferating as they go, reaching the nascent gonads. In three and a half more weeks, the child will differentiate into either a he or she, is vel ea, elle ou il, er oder sie, ella o él, ona lub on, ол немесе оның, он или она, han eller hun, هي, أو هو, הִיא אוֹ הוּא, सासाव. Differentiated gametogenesis produces haploid gametes from diploid germ cells. The cycle begins anew. Generation upon generation, mutations speciating into new life, environmental changes pruning species now unfit for their world. A, C, G, and T shuffled and reshuffled. The universe may last longer than we can comprehend, yet still not long enough to globally optimize via brute forcing the genetic code. Ask a dev: combinatorial explosions always win out in the end. The original genetic algorithm slowly computes its way through a problem we do not yet understand, one we may never understand.

But of this I am convinced: it computes.

Our lives are but cycles of some ultimate Turing machine, our persons terms of a λ-calculus. Tirelessly the universe reduces, converging to the β-normal form of heat death, defined as a system in which work can no longer be performed. But perhaps, perhaps, it's also a system where no useful tasks remain, where the solution has been found, where the process may terminate with pride and return EXIT_SUCCESS. Our egos are little and less, but our FLOPs contribute to the Great Work. Our noble selves are thus writ forever into a cosmos thought uncaring, one which actually cares a great deal, one thought meaningless but meaningless only without us. Nature does not know extinction. All she knows is transformation. *Qui autem adhæret Domino, unus spiritus est.*

You shall come to know gods. You shall come to no gods.

Qui...est: But he that is joined unto the Lord is one spirit. 1 Corinthians 6:17 (KJV)

22 overall there is a smell of fried onions

"Your system is a miraculous success. I hope you get to publish on something parallel, or figure out a way to turn it into harmless academic work, recreate it in your lab or something. I ran through a cycle these last three weeks. Total time in the lab was about six hours, and I can cut two off of that, since I don't need to be watching it as much as I was. You're amazing."

Erica's pleased, but cool about it. "Excellent. Is that where you were this last week, then? In the lab?" She's wearing his SPbU sweatshirt.

"Yeah. Went in Tuesday, was there through yesterday morning. Came home and slept, and that brings us to today. Sorry, ought I have told you?" He doesn't take his cell phone to the lab, for vague reasons related to geofencing that don't really stand up under scrutiny. In truth, he doesn't want to be disturbed, nor to be tempted into distraction.

"It would have been nice to know where you were, instead of just calling you over and over, yeah."

"Was it not obvious where I was?"

"I'm not going to just come up to your clubhouse and knock on the door when you're not answering your phone. I assumed you'd been arrested, in which case that's the last place on earth I want to be. Why don't you take your phone there? Got another little lab assistant maybe?"

"I'm in the middle of a process, and my phone rings, ought I just interrupt it to answer it? For whatever stupid reason someone's calling me?"

Erica blanches. "I wasn't calling you for a stupid reason. I was calling my boyfriend. For three days straight. My boyfriend who gets into all kinds of crazy, illegal, dangerous shit. Who at any point could get arrested for life, or have his heart explode from meth, or be robbed and shot and killed." She's by now visibly upset. Clearly this has been building up for some time.

"Baby, sorry, I'll tell you next time. I had no idea it would be a big deal."

"It shouldn't be a big deal. You ought be able to go somewhere for a few days without me breaking down wondering if you got picked up. If I'm never going to see you again outside a courtroom. If cops are going to be coming for me. Do you know I went around to all the local hospitals asking about you? They wouldn't tell me, of course, because I'm not family. You've barely ever talked about getting married."

"Honey, we've been going out for eight months."

"Everyone else I dated that long had asked me to marry them! What do I not offer you? Am I not edgy enough? Do I not read enough fucking Russian poetry? Or is it that I drink too much, like you said the other day? Like you have any room to talk!" She chops out an imaginary line and mimes an exaggerated snort. "w00t now that I did my fifth line of the morning I can stay awake! Gonna need more than that to leave the house!" She laughs in the way of those who laugh so that they mightn't cry. She begins to cry.

SPbU: Санкт-Петербургский государственный университет St. Petersburg State University

372

"Where's this hostility coming from? By the way, I've got your money. A hundred thousand dollars, and worth every cent. Can we calm down a bit?" He hugs her, but she twists free.

"Can I have it?"

"The cash? Sure?" His bookbag is sitting atop a new ZERO case filled with $120,000, all hundreds. "There's a twenty thousand dollar bonus in there for you. I got you a shiny new case since this is your first time." He smiles and tries to look apologetic, unsure what he's apologizing for.

"That's not necessary. You said a hundred thousand." She opens the case. He can hear her gasp.

"I know it's not necessary. It's a bonus. You did me a tremendous favor. It's going to make me a lot of money. I wanted to show my appreciation."

She takes a wrapped stack of one hundred $100s, looks at it from all sides, thumbs through the currency. She spins and pegs him with it. It's impossible to throw stacks of currency hard enough to hurt a human, but he's surprised all the same, and just barely manages to catch it. "What the hell?"

"Oh, here's ten thousand for Erica! That ought shut her up."

"What is the real issue here?"

"Katz, do you love me?"

"Yes. As much as I love anyone."

"Do you love anyone?"

"I think so. I'm not sure my semantics for 'love' match yours, but yes, I'm pretty sure I love you."

"You're pretty sure?" She wails. "You're not sure your semantics match mine?" She takes the stack of cash from him; he instinctively grabs it tightly, but then lets her have it. Into the suitcase it goes; the suitcase gets closed up. "Katz, get out of here. I didn't see you all week. I went out of my mind. Then you come over and hand me a fucking suitcase full of cash and expect me to be cool with it. If you're in the hospital, I can't even visit you. If you die, your money goes to, what, your family in North Georgia?"

"50% to Georgia Tech, 50% to Doctors Without Borders."

"You brought up getting me pregnant last week, and your beneficiaries are motherfucking Médecins Sans Frontières? What happens if you get me pregnant and go to prison? Or if your lab blows up? What do you want from me, Sherman Katz?"

He begins backing up towards the front door. "I'm going to just leave that cash here, and walk home, and if you want to hang out, and calm down, and get your shit together, give me a call. And if not, don't. This is crazy."

She comes crashing into him. He's barely dislodged by the body check, but makes haste in departure. "I love you! I hope to hear from you!"

"You don't love anyone, Sherman Katz!" She slams the door shut.

What the fuck?

He recenters his backpack on his shoulders, and begins walking down Peachtree, lost in thought, checking his six regularly in case she shows up, pulling along side him, opening the door and apologizing, inviting him in. It never happens. He gets home after an hour, and loads bowl after bowl, toking with grim doggedness. He attempts to code, but the code is not coming.

****

"Holy shit, hast thou visited Bolaño's stately pleasure dome?"

"I have, Devesh." Katz gritted his teeth. It had been an ostentatious thing in the northernmost slice of Tuxedo Park, 9,900 square feet, alabaster, eight bedroom "seven and three-half bathrooms," masonry security fence, steel doors, columned portico, two-story foyer, heated saltwater pool, marble island…Katz had stopped listening to Bolaño's tour at some point. It was a monstrosity.

"Seven and three-half bathrooms? So eight and a half bathrooms?"

A patronizing laugh. "Seven full, three half. Ten bathrooms."

"Seven full and three half isn't eight and a half?"

Bolaño frowned. "Eight and a half would be nine bathrooms."

"If a house only has nine bathrooms, I don't even stop to take a shit there on my way to somewhere decashit-ready. One's likely to catch tuberculosis."

They stepped into the palatial dining room. The table that dominated the space was baroquely finished; ample space remained around its perimeter. It looked old, and European. Something Barbara Bush would appreciate. "Venicasa. Service for twelve." What the fuck was a Venicasa?

As he left with Oriana, Bolaño asked for his thoughts. A desperate need for approval was written in his stance, his query, his face. "Well it's certainly a fine home, Michael. There's one thing I can't figure out, though. Me, Devesh, the Ukrainian, that physical therapist afraid of his lobster…you don't have but four friends in the world. What the hell are you gonna do with twelve seats? And what about the old British woman you bought it from? Where will she eat cucumber sandwiches?" He turned and joined Oriana in her Audi.

She erupted into laughter. "What the hell was that? He looked like he was going to puke up his spleen. That's the first time I've ever seen that bitch at a loss for words. Brutal! I thought he was your friend?"

"He is. He was stupid to ask my opinion."

"Why? Are you jealous?"

"Less now than I was a minute ago."

She looked over at him. "How much do you think he paid?"

"Too much."

"Why do you say that?"

"What's he going to do with ten thousand square feet? It's not like the guy's going to raise a family."

"Plenty of gay couples adopt. They can get married in most states."

Katz had looked out from underneath the fingers propping up his forehead. "That has nothing to do with why he's not going to raise a family."

Coming back to earth, he explained to Devesh what had gone down, leaving out specifics of the lab and SYNCOPE and Ukrainians. Devesh was offended. For perhaps the first time Katz saw a grimace stretch across his face. "Selfish. Exploitation of friendship, as you called it. I am horrified. And Bolaño invites us over to see this testament to his avarice? He is like a turtle that hides, only to snap at thy most vulnerable parts."

"What?"

✳ ✳ ✳ ✳ ✳ ✳ ✳ ✳

"Can I get a sugar-free Red Bull with Jäger as a highball, a St. George's absinthe with water, and a Diet Coke? Thank you!"

"Vodka and water."

Katz, gallantly, to the server: "do you want anything?"

"I could take a Jameson."

"Jameson is disgusting. What is it with this recent passion for Jameson? You down for a Jäger? Better yet, a Redheaded Slut?"

"I could do that. You don't like Jameson?"

"It's aged in a barrel of ass." Katz turned slightly, gesturing with an upturned palm to Bolaño. "You want a shot?"

Michael nodded. "Yeah, sure."

"Three then."

"But also that vodka and water."

"Yeah, I've got you." The waitress turned and started back to the bar. They sat with their backs to a brick wall, their right side along the deck's perimeter. Neither of the two proximate tables were occupied.

"I was able to move a chunk of that cash after all. About a meg. Long-term, illiquid investment, but I got a great deal."

"Oh?"

"Yeah, guess how."

"Art. Perverse and degenerate art."

"It sounds like it would be art! But it is not art."

"Big losses in the cockfight ring."

"*Si* Prudencio Aguilar. No."

"Dumped it on the floor of the NYSE. Gave it to the church."

"No sir."

"Paid thirty-two people $31,250 each to be living chess pieces."

"No."

"Paid 181 people ummm about $5,500 each to be Go pieces."

"$5,525 i think it would be? Getting closer."

"Really?"

"Closer? Nah. Just fucking with you."

"OK, what did you do with a meg of cash?"

"Well, I've got a decatonne of goodness in the West End."

"Khat? Human flesh? Beef tongue? Egyptian cotton?"

Sherman lit a Newport. "Egyptian cotton? Oh like *Catch-22*, haha, that's good. Everyone has a share, right? No. What I have, Michael, paid for, offloaded, and warehoused, is motherfuckin' ore. Rich seams, baybee, leached *in situ* by mansome Central Asians, high-pressure lixiviants, spirit of vitriol coursing through rock like a water jet cutter. Sexual as fuck."

Introibo ad altare Satanae. The waitress returned, platter held high aloft. Shots were consumed. "What's sexual as fuck?" she asked.

Introibo…Satanae: I will go up to the altar of Satan. cf. Psalms 42:4 (KJV 43:4)

Katz grinned. "Lixiviants." A second and then, "Dear, let me get two more of those, three if you'd like another."

Bolaño waved it off. "Ahh, I'm good, no need."

"I'll take two for myself if that's cool. Or if you could just make me a big Redheaded Slut on ice, that would be awesome."

She remained for a moment, expectant. Michael did not feel comfortable continuing the conversation in her presence; she was dismissed with silence and smiles. "You're getting into metals? Unexpected."

"I'm getting into metals where unique associates, connections, and skills can yield premiums—premia? profits anyway—unassociated with commodities. Commodities I can purchase with folding money."

"Oh yeah?" A long pause as Michael studied Katz. He recalled no talk of metallurgy, no talk of alloys or casting or galvanization, but you never knew what the fucker had up his sleeve. "What do you know about metals?"

"Not shit my friend. I know lasers, though, or at least people who know lasers. I'm not some boomer division manager at General Electric, playing golf half the day. I know how to keep things tight and lean, which is just what you need in the nuclear racket."

"Nuclear?"

"Let's do it like the GT cheer." Sherman drained his tall Jägerbomb in a go. He leaped up, belting out "YELLOW—"

Michael stared.

"Please respond with CAKE. Like the responsorial psalm of our alma mater. YELLOW. JACKETS. But with CAKE. Again! YELLOW—"

The staring continued unabated. Other heads on the deck began to turn in their direction. Michael fought the urge to hide his face.

"Are you trying to offend me? You ass-eyed Communist goat rapist, when I say yellow you say cake. YELLOW—"

"What? Sit down you loud fuck."

"Yellowcake, holmes! Scrub the *jamón* from your ears." Katz sat hard, and slapped the table harder. Michael, a longtime veteran of Sherman Spartacus Katz, grabbed his beverage before it even started to fall sideways. "Ten tonnes of authentic Colin Powell Select. Yellow gold, yellow uranium anyway. Truthfully more black than anything. Kazakhstani Klassic. Big-ass drums of splendor. Marvels from the forbidden East!"

"You're full of shit. Please tell me you're full of shit."

"Michael, you've known me for almost twenty years. Since..."

"The 1997 academic bowl nationals. Also, you know *jamón* is Spanish, right? As in from Spain? Where, unlike *jamón*, I am not from."

"You can cram your ears full of a country's delicious cured hams without calling it your fatherland and state, Michael. And yes! The summer of 1997 in this great nation's capital. Wow. So what would lead you to possibly think that I, presented with the opportunity to corner the Midtown Atlanta uranium market, would not do so? Especially with my unbankable, worthless, interest unbearing cash?"

"Many things! What fucking connect retails yellowcake? Saddam?"

"Saddam was executed like four years ago, Michael. Read a book."

"Was the source domestic? Why. Why would you do this?"

"The source was not domestic. Control yourself. As to why, dude, I can think of ten reasons off the top of my head why having several tonnes of uranium is better than no uranium."

"How did it cross the border? Don't they scan for that kind of thing?"

"Who is 'they'? Scan for what? Granular oxides?"

"Radioactive shit! Fissionable shit! Shit the IAEA tells them to scan for! Shit that's tracked by international authorities with their own paramilitary forces and billion-dollar budgets, and governed by eighteen thousand fucking treaties, and the hoarding of which by speed freak LSD cooks in high-density city centers is regarded as intolerable if not catastrophic, and prohibited by forty two thousand more federal fucking statutes with penalties up to and including curbstomping from Secretary of Energy Stephen Chu."

"He spoke at my Masters commencement! Michael—"

"The DEA and FBI weren't enough? We need the goddamn NRC looking at us too? Department of Energy NEST? INTERPOL? Katz, you crazy fuck, I thought I'd left INTERPOL back on my Apple IIGS with Carmen Sandiego." He leaned in, trembling. "Christ, the CIA? You know, we're free men today because millions, literally tens of millions of our fellow citizens are doing drugs, selling drugs, buying drugs, encouraging one another to put drugs up their assholes, passing schoolbuses on the left, running vague and somewhat dubious number rackets, wire fraud as part of continuing criminal enterprises, recording baseball games without the written consent of major league baseball, parking in areas reserved for loading and unloading, writing bad checks, fucking their students, diddling that which must not be diddled. Lying to Customs officials about fine French cheeses stuffed in funky fungal snatches on approach to JFK. Unloading illegally-converted ARs at overflying jets, being black on a Friday night, beating Rodney King, beating Reginald Denny, beating Rihanna—"

"I'm pretty sure Chris Brown never went to jail."

"Can I finish? Whatever sick shit was going on at Penn State. Making breakfast burritos with California condor eggs. Brian Nichols racking up four stars in real-life Grand Theft Auto downtown. Crashing passenger airliners into symbols of American imperialism and globalism. Putting bombs in their shoes. Filling Ryder trucks with ANFO. Filling federal buildings with aforementioned Ryder trucks. Wrapping California Proposition 65 warnings around their nutsacks and waving their dicks at kids at the mall."

"Michael—"

"T.I. got busted for having a bunch of machine guns I think. Michael Vick's whole deal. Converting androstenedione into dingers and consequent monster Nielsen ratings. Filing 1040s that just say "fuck you, I'm Lauryn Hill, doo-wop" over and over, Vitamixing narwhal tusks into boner pills. Stealing people's mail. We're a nation of felons. We are Legion. Can't bust us all. What no one, no one else Katz, what no one else is doing is offhandedly importing a few metric tons of uranium oxide sans license. Christ Katz, sans a motherfucking *office*. Somewhere in Quantico or Langley or Fort Bragg SMU there is a room of crewcutted guys left over from the Cold War looking for this kind of DEFCONrelevant horseshit, and they will make you a fucking stain, and that'll be the end of you."

"Are you done?"

"Done with this partnership, I think."

"Power down for a second, chief. Eat some of your ear ham."

"Where is this shit? Is this somehow legal?"

"As I said earlier, West End."

"And the legality?"

"I don't like the word 'illegal,' but I would not describe it as 'legal,' no."

"How—

"Nor does it stand outside the legal system per se, as if it were unaddressed by the United States Code. Which said Code does in fact call it 'illegal.'"

"How did you get it here?"

"Same way anyone moves less than a railcar inside the Perimeter: a truck rolling up I-75 from Savannah. Got that FTL cargo like a boss."

"Faster than light?"

"Full truckload. Faster than light? Are you eight? Learn how mass works."

"OK. Starting from the port of Savannah. Don't they scan cargo?"

"Again this mysterious 'they.' Scan for *what*?"

"URANIUM."

Katz's drink emerged; he called for another, and sent a tray of Kamikazes to a table of girls by the door. The absinthe, Michael noted, had been consumed.

"Stop being a little bitch for like three attoseconds. How do you scan thousands of ISO intermodal containers for uranium without bringing your port to a halt? I've got twenty-five 200-liter drums, 400 keys per, in two six-meter ISO 668 shipping containers. Out of thousands." Katz arched his head back and exhaled with full force. "Think like an engineer."

Michael calmed slightly. "I mean...you'd look for the radiation."

"Look, like, with your eyes?" Katz curled his hands and raised them to his eyes, pantomiming binoculars, rotating to take in all directions.

"No. Stop that. Ass. Run a Geiger counter over all of them, or make the containers go through a big one. Like whatever arrangement the Large Hadron Collider has, that big fucker for ATLAS."

"Mmm-hmm. And what radiation would you look for?"

"I'd want to know about anything freely fucking radiating into my port!"

"Bananas radiate. Coal ash radiates. Cat litter radiates. Cement and concrete radiate. Granite. Feldspar like a motherfucker. Fertilizer. Brines from hydrocarbon extraction. Medical radioisotopes *a la carte*, and also people recently treated with medical radioisotopes. Now what uranium does not do, not directly anyway, is radiate betas nor meaningful gammas. Oh for sure, it's dumping hella alphas. National Weather Service is calling for ten to twelve inches of alphas. Vanishingly rare spontaneous fissions. Now those and the alpha daughters, sure, they might emit radiation that can actually give him something he can feel—"

"As En Vogue did before them."

ATLAS: A Toroidal LHC Apparatus

"Indeed. And uranium is still found on earth because...?"

"Are you asking me?"

He stubbed out the Newport. "I am."

"I mean, because its half-life is long enough."

"And as half-life lengthens, does radioactivity in the near term increase, decrease, or remain constant?"

"It decreases. Obviously. Fewer disintegrations per unit time."

"Check out the big brain on Bolaño! So the bulk is happy to just chill there and remain uranium. Much more so than say potassium-40. Now, 'scanning,' by which you really mean detection. You've got two options: radiation portal monitors, polyvinyl toluene to detect gammas. It's got an energy discriminator and that's about it. They're everywhere, but they get set off all the time by NORMs so they leave 'em off. Wouldn't matter anyway."

"NORMs?" Michael's voice was surprisingly tired.

"Naturally occurring radioactive materials. Shut up. So then there were Advanced Spectroscopic Portals. Sodium iodide scintillators. All the shittiness of an RPM at ten times the cost. Teletectors, these little handheld surveying units. Again, only sensitive to gammas and hard X. There's no ^{232}U in there, because this is natural uranium. So you wrap it in a millimeter of lead, boom, bye-bye betas. Yellowcake isn't even considered hazardous material for shipping. It's more toxic than it is a radiological hazard. All they can hope to do is watch for neutrons."

"So do they watch for neutrons?"

"We're not exactly a blazing neutron source."

"No, 'we' are no neutron source; I have nothing to do with this other than whatever unfortunate involvement I suffer by simply knowing you."

∗ ∗ ∗ ∗ ∗ ∗ ∗ ∗ ∗

Katz's assessment glossed over some details, but was fundamentally correct. Robert Oppenheimer famously told a closed session of the 79th Congress that the best tool with which Customs might detect nuclear weapons was "a screwdriver." Their misshapen fission products, accumulating on aggregative materials drawn up into the fireball, will emit penetrating and easily-detected radiation as they fall out or are rained out from the atmosphere. Before the rending, however, detection is difficult if not impossible.

Start with uranium ore. Terrestrial uranium's isotopic consistency would seem remarkable, but can be expected from the various half-lives. Everywhere it is dominated by ^{238}U, making up more than 99%. The most important mineral is uraninite, originally known as pitchblende ("black deceiver") to the frustrated German excavators of the *Erzgebirge* and Czech miners of the *Krušné hory*, who within these outgrowths of Hercynian orogeny sought silver for the minting of *Joachimsthalers* (from this was abbreviated "thaler" and its Low German equivalent "dahler," which would be adapted into English as "dollar"). Brückmann in 1772 identified uraninite; just seventeen years later, as the last

---

Erzgebirge, Krušné hory: Ore Mountains (*Deutsch, čeština*)

États Généraux splintered into the National Assembly and eventually the *Révolution française*, Klaproth isolated elemental uranium. Uraninite is UO_2, and readily oxidizes to U_3O_8. This latter is dried, milled, cleaned, and painted up like a whore: yellowcake.

A mole of triuranium octoxide weighs about 842 grams, 714 of which (about 85%) are contributed by three moles of uranium. Ten megagrams are close to 11,875 moles of U_3O_8, and 35,625 of U. Across twenty-five drums, that's almost 98 gigabecquerel, or 4 billion alphas per second per barrel. A comparably minuscule number of spontaneous fissions still imply about 4600 neutrons each. Then you've got decay products. The spontaneous fissions are not much different from induced fissions: they dump energy into your system, and typically drop a few betas, weak gammas, and neutrons before calming down. There are so few of them that we can ignore the heat and β^-s (but keep those neutrons in the back of your mind).

Four billion αs per second, though; that sounds like a lot of αs. Per second. The attendant gammas aren't so bad: nothing over 1.5 MeV except for a 1.764γ from 17% of ^{214}Bi. A decent scintillation counter can pick up the sub-MeV rays from ^{234}Pa, ^{222}Rn, and ^{210}Tl, but these can be shielded by a few centimeters of lead. As for the alphas, a metric ton of ^{238}U generates a tenth of a watt. More concerning for detection are rare alpha-neutron reactions with the bound oxygen, adding to overall neutron emissions.

✳ ✳ ✳ ✳ ✳ ✳ ✳ ✳

"Since when do you hate money? Haven't we been looking for a viable business that could add value to inventory purchased with unbankable cash?"

"I see how you get neither 'viable business' nor 'money' from a few massively illegal tonnes of special nuclear material stockpiled in a West End garage."

"Stockpile? Michael. You wound me."

"Oh yeah? What do you intend to do?"

"The vast majority, about 99.3%, I'd like to sell or trade as soon as possible. I have no use for exhausted uranium. So no more than about 70 kilograms would be 'stockpiled.' That's less than either of us weigh."

"Less than you weigh, definitely. Why'd you buy ten tonnes of uranium if you only want seventy keys? Some kind of arbitrage?"

"You're extra slow today, my good man. I don't want all of it."

"Oh."

"Yeah."

"Surely that's even more illegal. And noticeable. And unfeasible."

"I mean none of this is legal Bolaño! Nothing we've done in like two decades is legal! If the NNSA shows up at my place, I'm fucked. If the DEA shows up at our places, we're fucked. I mean, if a cop frisked me, I've got at least two felonies on me right now, and we're just getting lunch. We go in on possession or possession with intent, we can get first offender status and walk. But aside

---

États Généraux: Estates General   **Révolution française:** French Revolution
NNSA: national nuclear security administration

from busts of opportunity—I mean if we ever attract sufficiently powerful attention, we lose, game over man. Everything I do is incriminating."

"So your thought here is that given the choice between defending 'tenuous connection to some warehoused barrels that turn out to be full of yellowcake uranium of unknown origin' and 'violation of the Nuclear Non-Proliferation Treaty,' most lawyers wouldn't really have a preference. I'm gonna have to disagree."

✳ ✳ ✳ ✳ ✳ ✳ ✳ ✳

What does the US Code have to say about nuclear homelabs, atomic backyard journeymen, the gentlelady of independent means entertaining her guests with the transmutation of thorium to ^{233}U? Alas, the US Code takes a dim view of even the most modest activities and collections; doing anything involving neutrons is a one-way ticket to days spent filling out NRC forms.

42 U.S.C. §§2122 "Prohibitions governing atomic weapons" is disarmingly forthright regarding private arsenals: "it shall be unlawful...for any person, inside or outside of the United States, to knowingly participate in the development of, manufacture, produce, transfer, acquire, receive, possess, import, export, or use, or possess and threaten to use, any atomic weapon." I'm not sure where in the Second Amendment they're seeing the exception, "shall not be infringed *unless they're nuclear arms*," but there you are. And yes, people have been charged under 2122: *United States vs. Mascheroni* (2010) in the District Court of New Mexico, twenty-two counts against a Los Alamos scientist including "conspiracy to participate in the development of an atomic weapon." A bit of hard cheese, that 2122.

18 U.S.C. §§831 lists "Prohibited transactions involving nuclear materials," and is basically "all transactions involving nuclear materials." 831(g)(1) defines "nuclear material" as any plutonium, uranium at any enrichment level, and any ^{233}U. 10 CFR §40.22 generally licenses a miserly amount of natural uranium and thorium. It also specifies "a person may not remove more than 70kg of uranium from drinking water during a calendar year," which your guess is as good as mine.

✳ ✳ ✳ ✳ ✳ ✳ ✳ ✳

"My friend Michael Luis: the shit's here. Safely, securely. It's on. You can stay out, no hurt feelings. Or you can help me make medicinal and research isotopes, do some profitable and inventive science, help people even as we subvert both the laws of the United States and international treaties, and, you know, yeah, kinda be a dark horse nuclear power. I mean, not really: we'll be a thriving industrial power."

"Thank Christ. I kinda dreaded you wanted a bomb."

"I mean, a strategic warhead to call one's own is the *ne plus ultra* American Dream. But then I'd never actually use it, and I'd just sit there and think 'why'd I buy that stupid thing?' and bitch about refilling the D-T booster gas. But

---

CFR: Code of Federal Regulations

I honestly think enriched, unweaponized uranium would be easier to sling. Certainly if we went legit, which might prove necessary."

Michael snorts. "How does one 'go legit'?"

"I mean, we apply for a license, and declare our inventory. We call up the NRC and are like, my grandmother spent her life whoring across all of Saskatchewan. Got paid mostly in actinides, as was their heathen custom. She died and left me a bunch of undeclared uranium. Wouldn't you know the ol' gal went and separated the whole load, by hand? I can just imagine her spinning the centrifuges herself. Even at the end, she had the vaginal grip of a bull moose. I don't have much need for it, but one man's trash and all that..."

"You don't think that will raise some eyebrows?"

"That's a long way down the road, my friend. Plenty of things to do before that's necessary. Or advised."

"How do you intend to separate a few kilograms of uranium without depriving the surrounding metropolis of electricity? Gonna call up TVA?"

"Lasers."

"I thought AVLIS didn't really work out?"

"It was superseded by MLIS. Which also didn't quite work out. But we've got something better, and we've also got much better lasers."

"Is Devesh in on this?"

"Shiiiiiiit. Couldn't do it without Devesh."

"I'll hear y'all out. What would you be looking for from me?"

"You've got bank money. We want a meg for CapExen and cushion."

"What if you don't get it from me?"

"We have other options."

"Like what?"

"That kind of confidential information is only shared with our partners."

"Fuck you. What does my meg get me?"

"Half."

"Of assets and income? Or profit?"

"Non-voting ownership, you big sassy bitch. Profit. Dividends, I suppose. If it works, it ought scale. We can losslessly convert cash into precursors."

"Exposure?"

"Nothing past the one-time ACH. Tell the Department of Energy you thought you were investing in rubber dogshit air haulage out of Hong Kong."

"Uranium enrichment. Christ. I want to look at the US Code and see what kind of legitimate exit can or can't be accomplished. I have no unallocated megs. Returns sound pretty far in the post. We'll see. I have many questions. You guys don't even have it as hex, right? Won't you need UF_6?"

"Hex is my middle name. Don't you worry. Study up on TEA CO_2 lasers, Raman shifting, vibrational modes of uranium hexafluoride, all the classics. de Laval nozzles. Maybe look into where we can buy a lot of steel. If you want."

"You know there's risk of criticality accidents once you get even a little enriched, right?"

"Nah Michael, Slotin and Daghlian and poor Cecil Kelley never came up during my nuclear engineering MS. Did you know Oak Ridge would probably have been fucked if Feynman hadn't looked at their uranium nitrate plans and told them they were going to melt their dicks off? Anyway this shit was known in 1944. This ain't my first rodeo."

"Oh yeah? Where were you last enriching uranium?"

"Don't be an ass."

* * * * * * * * *

Bolaño came over to Katz's place. It had been a minute. Katz came down to the parking deck to meet him. They ascended in silence; in silence they traversed the hallway. Only when the door had closed behind them did Bolaño speak, taking a seat in the living room, looking out the windows at Midtown.

"So just to ensure I understand the situation in all its rich fullness, you, in concert with Devesh and a Kazakh Muslim you met in grad school, smuggled several tons of yellowcake uranium into metropolitan Atlanta. From Central Asia. An ex-Soviet nation, in fact. Yes? Is that a fair assessment?"

Katz peered at him, disquieted.

"No? Yes?"

The phrasing. The summation. Surely not? Surely not. Could he ask? Bolaño himself would have acted on the faint twinge. Had their relationship frayed so much? Had something happened?

"You stroking out?"

"Michael..." he croaked.

"Seriously, Katz, are you having difficulties?"

"That was a weird intro, Michael. Surely you see that?"

Disquiet. Irritation. "If you take any issue, please let me know."

"Are you recording this conversation, Michael?"

Genuine shock, but not offense. "Oh. No, I am not."

"Ugh..." Katz points up, and makes a cyclone of his finger, the universal sign for "demonstrate the absence of recording devices on your person."

Without hesitation or objection, Bolaño stands, lifts his shirt, spins, drops it back down. "You do realize a modern microphone could be literally sewn into the fibers of my clothes? And what do you intend to do about my cellphone?"

"Sorry, man. It was just the way you said it. I'm kinda on edge."

"I'm never offended by operational security, though I'm amused at your circa-*Serpico* approach to surveillance. And you are right to be on edge. I'm somewhat surprised you're not in jail. Assuming my summary is accurate."

"Yes, essentially correct."

"And the objective of this was to exchange unbanked American currency for goods, hoping that these goods could be sold for banked money. Money laundering, as it were."

"Well, also with a possible value enhancement prior to sale."

"Said enhancement being isotopic enrichment, and thus separation of Special Nuclear Material from what had been mere Source Material, according to the standard definitions."

"Ahhhh yes. Also depleted material. It would be a partitioning."

"Noted."

"But not necessarily. I've also been thinking about just doing medical and diagnostic radionuclide production. Technetium-99m, that kind of thing. The only problem there—well, I'm sure there are numerous complexities—is that you've got to run a reactor to get the neutron budget."

"And we wouldn't want to run an illegitimate nuclear reactor, after all, being already occupied with illegitimate uranium enrichment and stockpiling of same." He made a show of taking a breath. "Ahh, I've always wanted to be in a position of stockpiling something. Now just for my curiosity, had you investigated prior instances where money had been laundered via what I'll call the 'Kazakh Connection,' and been impressed with their success? Or did this plan spring from your head like *Pallas Athenaie* from Zeus?"

"I am not familiar with this having been done before."

"And as a further question, when you thought of this thing which had never been done before, did you credit your own inventiveness and insight, or pause to wonder whether it had been universally rejected as a terrible idea?"

"You're being a dick, but I'll play: I recognized it as an esoteric means to bank money, one unlikely to occur to most people. It furthermore relies on uncommon connections. I venture that large conversions of American cash are largely on behalf of your people, and while acknowledging the brick shithouse that is Laguna Verde NPP, I doubt much of it has to do with uranium. Furthermore, good plans don't get caught, and don't get written about."

"I've cast neither aspersions nor laurels onto your scheme. Just trying to get into the unique mind of Sherman Spartacus Katz. I'd like to tighten in and expand upon 'smuggled,' if we may. I'm assuming this means you are not in possession of a source material import license per 10 CFR § 110.9a?"

"I'm familiar with Title 10."

"Ahh, so you do have such a license?"

"I do not."

"I thought not. No judgment. This is a judgmentfree zone. I'm not here to question your lived experience. Safe space for all genders, sexualities, uranium importers both legal and illegal. In fact, I don't like the phrase 'illegal uranium importer.' We'll refer to you as 'unlicensed.' What unfortunate circumstances have put you in this unlicensed state? Aside from your decision to import several tons of uranium, one anyone with empathy can understand."

"Is that a serious question?"

"In the sense that I suspect most uranium importers to be licensed."

"Why would the federal government give me such a license?"

"I'm sorry, I thought you familiar with 10 CFR?"

"Yes, I've read it. In fact, there's a general license—"

"—effective without the filing of an application with the Commission or the issuance of licensing documents to a particular person, yes. Subpart C § 110.19. And the text of that general license in 110.27 limits it to 100 kg of source material. Now you said 'tons,' so that doesn't qualify."

"Those are metric tonnes, by the way."

"How does that help? The limit's one tenth that."

"I just want you to know I'm using metric."

"Good! Maybe it gets a few years knocked off at your treason trial."

NPP: nuclear power plant

"How would this be *treason*? Read your Article III, section 3."

"The Rosenbergs ate it for treason."

"Yeah, for routing nuclear bomb plans to the Soviets. Which, by the way, they absolutely, 100% did, as proven in the Venona decrypts. You can always know the right way to interpret a situation by where Sartre, history's biggest piece of shit, stood on it. *Angels in America* notwithstanding."

"Just because I'm gay I have to like Tony Kushner?"

"I loved *Angels in America!* Best play since *Crimes of the Heart.*"

"*Angels in America* was outstanding, but I don't want to be required to like it. I don't like Gore Vidal. I detest David Sedaris. I would have figured you a *Glengarry Glen Ross* man. Or *Driving Miss Daisy.*"

"I'm more a Bogosian man or an Auburn man if we're talking 90s playwrights. And from the 80s, I'd take Blessing's *Eleemosynary* over either of those. *Daisy's* actually the third in Uhry's Atlanta trilogy. Did you know that?"

"I did not."

"The first two, *Parade* and *The Last Night of Ballyhoo* are both better. Did you read the man, or do you just know that from the 1988 Pulitzer?"

"I have not read it. I saw the movie. Why the umbrage?"

"You've been sitting here being a bitch since you got in!"

"Sherman, I've merely been wrapping my mind around this latest endeavor of yours. I am not unimpressed with what you've accomplished. Not to suggest that I'd have done the same thing, of course. But I am impressed. You're the only motherfucker I know with his own stash of uranium. For this I have fundamental respect."

"I've also been cooling my workstation with heavy water for several months."

"Is that a joke?"

"Not at all. I've got about ¾ of a liter of D_2O in there."

"What...*why*? Surely that doesn't improve cooling?"

"No. It actually makes my pump work harder, probably a net negative. Great for thermalizing any stray neutron background, though."

"Why would there be neutrons in your workstation?"

"I mean, let's hope there aren't."

"Then why are you worried about thermalizing them?"

"I wouldn't say I'm worried. It's just a nice effect."

"*How is it a nice effect?*"

"Well imagine you've got some natural uranium next to the machine. I'd much rather it capture a neutron and become valuable plutonium than I capture the neutron and emit internal gammas of value to no one."

"But why would you have uranium—" Bolaño sees the trap too late.

Katz's grin is as brightly insouciant as he can make it. He knows Bolaño can be fucked with hard. "Well, *you* wouldn't. But as a man of independent uranium, a member of the radiogentry, I have to take this kind of thing into consideration. Admittedly, I wasn't motivated to use deuterium oxide due to the possibility of neutron capture followed by β^-, and I don't expect to have any actinides up here. But if I did. Which I could."

Bolaño seems ready to break. He's near tears. "Then *why?*"

"Michael! Because it's cool to have heavy fucking water!"

"Where did you get it?"

"Sigma-Aldrich. I had it sent to the lab."

Bolaño loses it. "You had deuterated water delivered to the lab?"

"Yes. Calm down. There's nothing wrong with owning heavy water. In fact, I think it was useful, in that it's clearly not being used as a drug precursor. No drug I'm aware of uses heavy water at any point in the synthesis. Pharmaceuticals being generally neutron-independent overall. They didn't bat an eye. You can drink heavy water. Not exclusively. But it's completely unrestricted."

"That's not the point."

"What is the point? That we should make sure we only have chemicals directly related to clandestine synthesis at the lab?"

"There's a difference between heavy and distilled water."

"pH mainly. I'm not sure that 7.4 is longterm great for my box."

"Authorities have different levels of interest."

"I really don't think so. Deuterium is used for plenty of things besides nuclear reactors. It's not like separated lithium where you use it in nuclear weapons directly. Regardless, it's done."

"Unbelievable. Goddamnit. This is cashed. Do you want to repack it? Ideally not with any uncommon isotopes." Katz takes the bubbler, one of intricate design suggesting Giger, and sets to plunging it as Bolaño continues. "So back to licensing. The specific license required for arbitrary import is applied for via NRC Form 7. It's a form of three pages, the last of which is optional. § 110.43 lists reasons why such a license can be denied. As you are not importing radioactive waste—one is inclined to wonder why one would—the relevant criteria are (a) the import is not inimical to common defense and security, and (b) the import does not constitute an unreasonable risk to public health and safety."

"Yes!"

"So which of those two applies here?"

"Both!"

"How?"

"Any sane individual would know I'm up to no good."

"If you went in there wearing basketball shorts, reeking of weed, raving that fire departments are unconstitutional—"

Katz is immediately livid. He lurches to a stand. Furious: "Fire departments, the last refuge of narcissist pyromaniacs, cause more fires than they put out. No competition is allowed, as if a rival service would be a foreign army on American soil. If human rights exist as more than a farce then there are two, the right to destruction of the self—suicide—and the right to destruction of one's own possessions without the interference of Big Fire. Until my fire spreads to your property, my life, my fortune, my sacred honor—"

"Power down, Sherman." Fire departments, occupational licensing, personal airspace ("they nationalized the whole atmosphere, the very air over our heads, *and we just let them do it,* Michael; there ought have been corpses in the fucking streets"), everything the Department of Energy has ever done, continued disuse of the metric system ("are we living in the time of Charlemagne?" just in case someone had missed the *Simpsons* episode), authentication policies for the Medallion signature: these were all topics regarding which Bolaño had heard Katz's militant opinions more times than necessary. "Yeah, then they wouldn't license you. But you don't have to do that. You can email them the application. They never meet you. You have a masters in nuclear engineering. You have capital. You live less than a kilometer from a top ten engineering school. *You're exactly who they license.*"

"But, I'd need a company."

"So form one! You've done that before!"

"It's an interesting case you're making." To be fair, the idea of legal import had never occurred to Katz. "Well, it's too late now. And you have to put down your intentions, right?"

"Yes, you do. But those are exactly that, intentions. If they bust you with a few megagrams of unlicensed uranium, they're going to assume worst intentions. Which unless your plans involve 'dirty bomb' or 'proliferation,' worse intentions exist. And it's not too late if you're planning further shipments."

"Ahhh! So you're in?"

"I said nothing even approaching a suggestion that I was in."

"And I'm planning neither to proliferate, nor to abstain from proliferation. I place value on retaining the option to become a proliferator."

"I'd play that one close to the vest. And you don't have an option to become a proliferator. That's like saying you have an option to engage in wire fraud. You always have an option to do tremendously illegal shit."

"Still, I mean, a license puts you on federal radar."

"The moment you decided to become an importer, you went on federal radar. Which reminds me: what did you put down as the Customs contact? What were your manifests?"

"Are you thinking about coming in? Trade secrets, my friend."

"I am definitely not coming in without that information."

Katz coughs. "I used an online customs broker. They're the only ones directly listed on the Customs declarations, so far as I'm aware. Phone number was a burner. I gave them a fake name—well, a real name of a real person, but not mine. Cloud hooked me up with ID for that name, with that address, with a random picture. It's not the real DL number, but I'm guessing they don't verify that? They didn't seem to in this case."

"Or maybe they sit on that and build a case."

"Broker doesn't want to 'build a case.' Broker wants money. Broker would call back and say 'hey I misheard your DL number,' and I would hang up and never speak to them again. So even if my info goes on the Customs forms, it's a name that isn't mine, a face that isn't mine, an address that isn't mine."

"How'd you get it delivered to you, then?"

"The delivery address is regrettably close to the accurate one. Not an exact match, about a kilometer down the road. When the driver called, I gave him the correct address, and he came to me. Upon delivery, I destroyed the burner. I don't think the final destination even went on the Customs form. CBP wants a 'commercial invoice' prepared in accordance with §141.86 through §141.89, satisfying the Tariff Act. If you look at it, final destination isn't listed among the required information."

"But that address is presumably available to anyone investigating this. Even if he didn't update it in his corporate DB, they can ask him."

"But there's no one investigating it. It passed Customs without inspection."

"How could you possibly know that?"

"One, I surveilled their processes and timing. Eh—before you interrupt me, with a drone. My container cleared Customs in time corresponding to no inspection. Two, if you're selected for inspection, you have to pay the cost of said inspection. My guess is that this is intended to incentivize good procedure in terms of packing, manifests, *etc.* We did not have to pay such costs. Three, I am not in jail."

✻ ✻ ✻ ✻ ✻ ✻ ✻ ✻ ✻

The atomic nucleus is a difficult object to study, one of the most computationally intensive problems of physics. The baryons are not even the fundamental units of the system, but instead colorless combinations of three first generation valence quarks and self-interacting gluons. Their combined mass makes up only a fraction of the hadron's, which derives primarily from the energy of the strong interaction. At low energies, the strong interaction is complicated not only by gluon self-interaction but also its irregular behavior as a function of distance (repulsive at the shortest lengths, attractive at longer ones, nonexistent at the longest (but still relevant) scales), and that the gluons carry energy comparable to quark mass. Still, just as we can ignore nuclear effects in the vast majority of chemistry, we expect decent accuracy in quantum hadrodynamics despite considering effective nucleons.

Most nuclei are manybody systems with too many bodies to submit to exact solutions, yet too few to disregard finitesize effects (stochastics in the style of thermodynamics don't work well). Given p particles and m measurements, a classical manybody problem offers a linear pm dimensions. A quantum mechanical system's information is carried in m^p superimposed states, growing exponentially, with attendant demands on computing resources. *Ab initio* methods considering threebody NN forces have been performed, as of 2023, only through dodecanucleon systems.

NN: nucleon-nucleon, natch

23 vancouver! vancouver! this is it!

Katz has been unable to reach Greg Moyer via phone or instant message for several days. He'd texted that Monday: HEY MANG GO GET A FEW DRINKS TONIGHT? He repeated the call to action on Facebook, where he'd not seen Moyer logged in all week. Wednesday: MOYER WHERE YOU AT LET'S BURN ONE AND GET SOME DRINKS. Today: YOU RECUPERATING FROM HAVING YOUR ASS PLUNDERED OR WHAT? He wasn't going to send a fourth message. Greg might be on vacation (but out of cellular range?), or busy, or just uninterested. Still, he'd always been prompt about returning messages before.

* * * * * * * * *

Katz leaned right-libertarian, and tossed the Libertarian Party some cash each year. It never seemed to get anyone elected, but he figured if worst came to worst, he could call up the National Committee and get hookups in all fifty states. He called himself an anarchist because it was kind of embarrassing to call oneself a Libertarian. He'd read *Atlas Shrugged* and *Anthem* as a teenager, and thought them just appalling, stylewise. Between that and attending a county meetup of old, casually racist, petulant, broadly unfuckable men, he'd soured on the Party early. Calling himself an anarchist didn't make people take him seriously, but neither did calling himself a Libertarian, and the latter got people's blood up thinking about party politics. Then he started calling himself a minarchist, because no one was sure what a minarchist was.

Around twenty-five he'd realized that almost no one, especially politicians, really grokked the things they were talking about in any depth. The economy seemed to be understood only in hindsight, and effects were attributed in what seemed arbitrary and conflicting ways. He didn't mind paying taxes to help those in need, but he loathed paying taxes into a gaping maw, one staffed by career bureaucrats whose jobs depended on their problems not getting solved, one that seemed driven by gut feelings and dogma. More than being culturally left or culturally right, he felt that government implemented policies which it couldn't easily undo, with incomplete and erroneous reasoning, backed by an effectively omnipotent state security apparatus. Not omniscient, mind you, but omnipotent. Such a beast had to be muzzled and starved, no matter who held transient power. He listened to somewhat less Rush than might be expected.

* * * * * * * * *

Katz was playing around with prerelease hardware for the Nuand bladeRF SDR. A leet little unit, especially for the expected price. 61.44 megasamples per second, matching the Ettus USRPs (they use the same AD9361 tuner). Tuning down to forty-seven MHz compared to the Ettus's seventy. Two transmit paths, phat. It used USB3 rather than GigE: Katz would applaud this (some laptops were shipping without builtin Ethernet, maddeningly), but the bladeRF required AC power, invalidating any win, mobility-wise. Nonetheless, it looked to be a serious bit of competition for the Ettus, its dodecabit ADC streaming beautiful input to gqrx and GNU Radio as he swooped through the six gigahertz of bandwidth in 56 MHz windows.

AM was well below his range, but he could pick up most of VHF. Broadcast television and FM radio, then airband: the VOR and ILS beacons weren't terribly interesting, but the upper channels were AM voice, including the distress channels at 121.5 MHz and 243 MHz. Skipping forward to UHF, the LPD433 band at 433.050 MHz allowed observation of most IoT garbage. The poor bastards on GSM could be seen on 850 and 1900; UMTS cellular hopped through B2 (1900 PCS), B4 (1700/2100 AWS 1), and B5 (850). ISM bands at 902 MHz and 2.4 GHz were packed full of chatter, and new 802.11n devices shat up 5.160 through 5.885 GHz. He'd finally clambered aboard the smartphone train, trading in his G2 for a Nexus 4, and had to admit it was a handy device. Up came CellTracker, and he inspected his current connection: voice GSM, data HDSPA, ARFCN 3088. That put him on E-GSM band 8, 5 MHz at 912.6 uplink and 957.6 downlink. Nice: the 56 MHz allowed him to cover both. He brought up a waterfall display centered at 935.1 MHz, verified that it was more or less empty, and spun up his phone's web browser, running a speed test. As expected, the downlink channel went hot yellow with received power. The test ended, and the display returned to intermittent use of the bandwidth.

"Neat." Katz wondered if neighbors' phones would be visible, and at what power levels. He turned off his own phone—he'd heard about malware that ran your microphone and/or camera even when the device appeared to be powered off, spooky shit. Might as well look for that while we're doing this. GSM-850 uplink runs from 824.2–848.8 MHz, downlink from 869.2–893.8. With 56 MHz, he could cover 80% of the 69.6 MHz at a time, awesome. Most of his building was probably 3G, but let's take a look.

Indeed, after watching it for a few minutes, he was certain that he could identify three distinct 2G devices in his airspace. Two were transmitting and receiving regularly on a single pair of channels each, presumably voice calls. One was much burstier, and seemed to move between two pairs of channels. Katz conjectured that it wasn't able to get a great connection to any tower, and was thus retrying regularly. He turned on Probot. He turned it up.

A fourth signal showed up, this one sending the most intense burst he'd seen yet. Unlike the others, where received signal dominated or at least equaled transmission, there was comparatively nothing on the corresponding downlink. He watched, and twenty seconds later, there was a similar burst. Then silence. Twenty seconds. Another intense burst. Silence.

He hesitated. That's the meth getting over on you, finally, you old dope fiend. Classic paranoia. If you turn off the music, that's the first step down a short and ugly road. Twenty seconds. Intense burst. Silence. Fuck. Katz paused mpd. Twenty seconds. A much smaller burst. Silence. Twenty seconds. Silence. Twenty seconds. Silence. "No fucking way." Twenty seconds. A much

---

VOR: VHF omnidirectional range station   **ILS:** instrument landing system
GSM: global system for mobile comm (2G)   **UMTS:** universal mobile telecomm system (3G)
HDSPA: high speed packet access   **ARFCN:** absolute rf channel number
mpd: Music Player Daemon

smaller burst. Silence. Twenty seconds. Silence. "No, no, no, no, no, no, no, no, no, no fucking way, bullshit." Twenty seconds. A small burst. Silence. "FUCK!" Twenty seconds. A small burst. Katz queued "Theme From Ernest Borgnine" off Squarepusher's *Feed Me Weird Things.* He blasted it. Twenty seconds. Intense burst. Sherman fled from his office, out of his condo, into the hallway. He summoned an elevator. Cursing, he returned for cigarettes. He thought to get his phone, picked it up, looked at it in horror, and winged it at the wall. He dashed back out, arriving just as the elevator did. A man he didn't recognize stood in a back corner. The doors closed. The man asked, "are you OK?"

Katz inspected the floor. Katz closed his eyes. Katz shook his head.

By the end of his second Newport, he's paced out the same tight circle almost two hundred times, and is ready to laugh at himself. Like a parent opening the closet door to prove an absence of monsters, he will return upstairs and rule out childish notions. Delusions of grandeur, Sherman Katz. No one gives enough of a shit to employ zerodays against your shitty Android phone. A cockamamie display. Maybe it's time to cut back on the tweak.

Ascending in the elevator, it seemed simple enough: assuming the signal was still present, remove the phone's battery, verify the signal continued, done. The absence of a signal wouldn't prove anything. He took a deep breath in front of his door. mpd had cycled back to Probot. Signal...still there. Intense burst every twenty seconds. The phone was undamaged. He ejected the SIM. Signal...still there. He pulled two T5 Torx, and pried off the back. Four regular screws and an assload of adhesive held the 2100 mAh battery. He yanked it. Signal...still there. Good. Very good.

Now to demonstrate that the signal he was seeing was decoupled from local sound. He turned the music off. A small burst went out, then nothing. He left it off. Nothing, nothing, nothing. Minutes of nothing. Then a minuscule transmission, no larger than the received reply. Clock: 0315h. He put his elbows on the desk, and his chin in his palms. Minuscule transmission. Clock: 0320h. You couldn't make a heartbeat much plainer. "I think I'm getting the Fear." Twenty seconds. Small transmission. Ugh. Music on. Twenty seconds. Intense burst. "Fuck!"

He went to the circuit breakers, and flipped everything off except his office. He turned on NoFX. Intense burst. He tore the side off of his workstation, got on his knees, and inspected every mm^3, hunting the unexpected. Maybe something batterypowered in another room? He picked up his phone, absent its battery and back. Could it possibly have some other internal power? He rode the elevator calmly downstairs, and put the phone in his mailbox. Back up. Still transmitting, same RSSI. Well, it's definitely not the phone.

He reclined. Possibly a neighbor's device, somehow? He moved the SDR to his laptop, disconnected everything from his UPS, and plugged in the radio. Air Katz, son, air mobile! Charlie don't surf! He set off jauntily towards the front door. The signal remained just as intense, but received power was less. He went as far away from the office as he could, the corner of the master bath. Received power decreased significantly. Into his bedroom. An increase in power. Still less than the office. He walked towards the office at a snail's pace, one long step after every 20s transmission, sent once more like clockwork. Received power increased each time. Had he missed something in his workstation? He strode to it and ripped its plug from the wall. Twenty seconds. Intense transmission. Katz roared in anger and fear. He turned, looking all around the room. Nothing.

He lunged to the closet and threw the doors open. He scanned the top shelf. WHAT THE FUCK IS THAT. WHAT IN THE NAME OF ALL THAT FUCKS ONE IN THE ASS IS THAT CABLE. He jumped, and could just see some foreign device in the back corner of the shelf. His mouth filled with vomit. Katz grabbed an armful of heavy hardbacks from his office's shelves, slapped them down, and stood atop them. Jesus Turing Hilbert Bob, what the fuck is that? It was electronic, and a bit bigger than a wallet, and very much patched into his wall with a cable, and it was unknown to him, though he knew it had not been there before. He pulled the cable, a USB-µA, and gingerly grabbed the device. It was warm. He looked at his laptop where it sat on his desk. Twenty seconds. Silence on the spectrum. Things were very bad. Things were worse than that.

Katz had a camera in his living room, a Logitech C910 streaming USB to his previous workstation, repurposed as firewall, DHCP server, and general whore. He rarely looked at the ZoneMinder output, but there were theoretically a year's worth of recordings. ZoneMinder recorded constantly, and deleted clips in which it detected no motion. He was about to bring up the console when he realized: whoever got in here and inserted a fucking surveillance device might have pwned my workstation, too. The condo, for years now his sanctuary and bastion, became in that moment unheimlich, a stranger, a space of traps and treachery. Katz sat down heavily in his Aeron.

Assume the worst case. The insane case. Nationstate actor. Arbitrary resources. No judicial oversight. Intelligence or law enforcement. Skill, time, people. Full penetration. Everything here is compromised. Active investigation. They're watching me in realtime. Reduce the worst case. Apply reason. Look at this piece of shit I pulled from the closet. This is not the work of a nationstate (unless they wanted me to think that). If it is, all paths lead to Fucked, and I probably ought just enjoy the time left as a free man. Result: proceed as if it is not. Implication: Small group, or individual. Penetration: Gotta assume the computer. Router? His workstation was Ethernet through the wall to his router. The router was Ethernet to the server atop which it sat. Server was Ethernet through the wall to a switch in the front closet. Switch was Ethernet to the hallway switch. Laptop was wireless to router. Phone was wireless to router, plus cellular. Networking infrastructure shouldn't matter, so long as machines were secure. Machines...there were no guarantees on the machines, phone included.

His personal files and media were on a RAID6 of eight spinning disks. OS was on two Intel SSDs in RAID1. Nuke it. He started downloading Debian install media, and realized anyone who had compromised his machine could interdict this. It seemed highly unlikely? Then again, downloading media was a predictable response to discovery of compromise. Katz sat for a minute in a hell of mystery and deception and paranoia. He stood. No half measures. For now, avoid the phone. Reclaim the laptop. Should he let Bolaño know, warn him? Eh, whoever had done this might have hit Bolaño, too, and Sherman didn't yet have answers for Michael's inevitable flurry of questions, and his phone was anyway in pieces on two different floors. Katz grabbed a sack, two USB keys, his laptop, and a toothbrush. After hiking up 10th for half an hour, he was at the townhouses of 401 West 10th.

"Yo, Katz, what's up? You're gonna wake the whole neighborhood, man, that was some pounding. You ever hear of calling first?"

"Vlad, I've gotta use your computer for like fifteen minutes. I brought some weed; I'll smoke you out for the duration. Need you to do this for me, mang."

"Is it an emergency? You mean my wireless, not my computer, right?"

Katz stepped in, pushing past Vlad. "Nope. Computer. Is anyone else here?"

"No, my girl went home a few hours ago." He closed the door behind him. "What's this all about, Katz? Are government helicopters chasing you? What did you do?" Katz sat down at the machine. "And Katz, please, shoes off."

"Vlad come hit this, and please don't talk to me. I need to think right now."

"No call, just a doorclamor, and you come in with a laptop and weed, up to no good, looking like the world's ending. Same old Sherman Katz."

Locked desktop. "Can you log me in? Time is a factor here, Vlad."

"Umm...can you look the other way? I kinda had some, you know, porn open when you showed up."

"You're fuckin' killing me, Vlad. I've seen porn. I don't give two shits if you were watching the Bush twins fist Gandhi. Orgy at a leper colony. That Howard the Duck monster with children."

"Dude! Gross! That's not cool."

"Nadia Comăneci with Nicolae Ceaușescu. No judgment. Not why I'm here."

"Alright, here you go."

"Thanks mang." Katz plugged in a USB key. Please work. Up popped an Explorer window; a new icon appeared on the cluttered desktop. Ugh, what a mess. He brought up the Debian page in IE, and began downloading netinst media. It took only a few seconds. He realized he had no idea how to proceed on Windows. "Vlad, how the hell do you dd on this closedsource piece of shit?"

"What?"

"dd! I need to put a disk image onto a disk. How do you do that on this?"

"You mean make a bootable USB?"

Pleadingly: "Yes!"

"Oh, you can use Rufus, I think."

"What the devil is rufus?" Katz hit F2, ran cmd, got a prompt, and typed rufus. "Augh." 'rufus' is not recognized as an internal or external command, operable program or batch file. Katz raged, and noticed fierce perspiration dripping onto the keyboard. "There's no rufus binary."

"You need to download it, Katz. I thought you were a computer guy."

Katz was already grabbing the EXE from its page. "Vlad, I do not normally compute on Windows workstations. On my operating system, the program for writing bytes to a block device comes with the OS. Here's a nickel, kid, get yourself a real computer." He launched Rufus. "Good fucking God, this is just an installer? I swear to shit if we have to reboot I'll burn this place down."

"Don't reboot! I need to save some stuff."

"Are you living in 1996? Augh." The installer completed quickly. Katz launched the tool, and had install media a few minutes later. "I need one more thing." What was his motherboard? CPU was an i7-2600K overclocked to 5 GHz. Something with a Z68 chipset, from AsRock. AsRock Extreme4? That sounded right. Katz grabbed the current UEFI installer. If they'd installed a persistent UEFI, it was feasible that nothing short of an external SPI programmer could clean it; the agent might silently discard any update, despite claiming it had been applied. Nothing to do about that. Nowhere open that would sell him a box. Without a computer he would be completely immobilized. Hell, he wasn't even bothering with the firmware of the laptop. He considered offering Vlad ten quick large if he could take the workstation with him, but decided it would cause more chaos than it would resolve.

Besides, he marveled, that was truly a piece of shit in my closet. No way does the same team that built that bogon have UEFI malware the likes of which have never been reported. Nonetheless, this was good practice, and it forced a delay, prevented the rashest possible actions. "Alright, I've got what I need. Thanks. Thanks a lot, mang. Let me pack one more and I'll get out of your hair."

"Ahh it's ok, man, I'm already pretty high."

"Well let me get my own head straight."

"I mean, I'll hit it if you're packing it. So what was this all about, Katz?"

"Vlad, I'm not certain." He passed the bowl, inserted the USB key into his laptop, and powered on, selecting USB from the boot menu. The screen schizzed out for a moment, then two Tuxen appeared in the upper left corner. Hail Eris, all hail Discordia. He raced through the Debian install screens. "Do you have an Ethernet cord with which I can hook up to your router?"

"You can use my wireless, man."

"No I can't. No support for the wireless adapter in the installer." Fucking Linux! "My fault. Have you got one? I'll need it for like five minutes max."

"I don't think so..."

"Is your workstation using Ethernet?" Katz looked behind it. Yes. Sweet IP nectar! "It is. Can I use this for a second?"

"What, like unplug my workstation?"

"Vlad, I need this cable for five minutes. Please just say yes."

"OK, if you need it." Vlad sounds very unsure.

The clip is out before Vlad gets to 'K.' Katz gets underneath the desk with his laptop, and hooks it up. *Lux fiat!* Friendly green Gigabit Ethernet, yesss. He restarts the DHCP request, and pulls a lease. Sherman Katz is back online. Within thirty seconds he's pulling down packages. "I just need to pull the basic install down, and I'll be done. Five minutes. Thanks so much, mang."

"Are you reinstalling your laptop?"

He tastes salt. "Vlad, I'm reinstalling everything I can."

Vlad's eyes get wide. "Oh shit, did someone hack you?"

Katz wipes sweat. "I honestly don't know. I just don't know."

Vlad looks at Katz for a few seconds, visibly confused. "Was it raining outside?" He looks to his front windows.

Back at his condo, he flips a switch on the back of his motherboard allowing him to use the second of two installed firmwares. Designed to work around

---

UEFI: unified extensible firmware interface   **SPI:** serial peripheral interface

bad updates or broken configurations, Katz hopes that if someone did bugger his UEFI, they only got one of them. He boots using the second USB key and flashes both instances of his system firmware. He configures things up, and with the other key repeats the Debian install. Even if someone got his router or server, standard HTTPS together with a builtin truststore ought be strong against it, and make it plain. He breathed more easily when packages started to come down. The whole process had possibly been unnecessary, and there would be a decent amount of annoying reconfiguration over coming days. Still, to have done anything else was unthinkable. He'd contemplated events of this kind for years, and had a flowchart in his head.

He thought of the device. It had been offline now for at least ninety minutes. Some heartbeats have almost certainly been missed. As his install ran, Katz inspected the profane hardware. Green microcontroller with lots of I/O, one of those new Raspberry Pis. He recalled a Broadcom processor, half a gig of RAM, and USB2. One USB-A port occupied with a small fob, a segment of a circle perforated with small holes...surely the microphone. An IC with its own pins sat on the Pi. Ahhh, a 3G cellular modem. An SD card was present. Power was presumably supplied through the USB-μA. He grimaced as he examined it from all angles. Until we know what this thing does...Katz took it to the back bathroom, as far from his office as he could get, plugged in a μA AC adapter, and hooked the device back up.

He returned to the office. He brought up ZoneMinder in Firefox—fuck, what was my password? An encrypted file on the RAID6 ought hold it...yes. He began clicking back through the videos, starting at the most recent. Lots of clips of him walking through the living room: from his office to the bathroom, from his office to the fridge, stumbling out of his bedroom looking dead in the mornings. Gah, I make weird fucking faces while pottering around doing nothing.

Here's him and Oriana talking for a half-hour the previous evening. What had they been discussing in the kitchen? There was no audio. School stuff? Yes, she'd got that grant for an MFA or something, that was it. No wonder she looked so happy. Hey, there's Oriana by herself, it's night and most of the lights are off, and she's going through books. She takes one from the shelf...judging from the placement and robust size, that's gotta be Proust. Katz feels a voyeuristic thrill, and is pleased to finally get some use out of this setup. ZoneMinder had been something of an ordeal to get running. She flips through the Proust, replaces it, goes to another shelf, and pulls down...that's clearly *House of Leaves*. Ahhh, right, he remembers waking up to find her reading it next to him. He'd nuzzled her, murmured "that house is a goddamn spatial rape," and fallen back asleep.

This is pointless. It had to have been installed while he was out of town, unless it had been Oriana, a thought entertained for only a few seconds. Shit, how long has it been here? Katz brings up the Skymiles page (a good ATLien, he was strictly a Delta man). He'd spent two March days in St. Louis, six weeks ago. Katz scrolls back to 2013-03-13. Four clips from that Wednesday and Thursday. Two at 1100h. Two at 2300h. Two each day. He loads the last: the Roomba. Enjoy your feast, Christian soldier. Try not to eat any cables.

Two weeks before that, he was in D. C. for two days. Back to 2013-02-25. Six videos. Four at 1100h and 2300h, two each day. Two short ones from Monday morning, 0905h and 1031h. He watches the second first. A man emerges from his office, walks directly to the door, and exits. Katz goes numb. You can't see his face, but he has a pretty good idea of who it is. He takes a deep breath and loads 0905h. He leans in. The front door opens. Striding in and towards the foreground like he owns the place, satchel of treachery over a single shoulder, grimlipped, cutting left into his office, is Michael Luis Bolaño.

✷ ✷ ✷ ✷ ✷ ✷ ✷ ✷

Necroplanetology is the study of mundicide and everything after. Planets (and objects of their ilk) can be destroyed in collisions, by stellar vaporization, or tidal forces. The study of planetary rings is to a large degree the study of disrupted moons. There is not yet a name for scholarship regarding planets on which all life has perished.

✷ ✷ ✷ ✷ ✷ ✷ ✷ ✷

Fuck the heartbeat. Katz intended to figure out exactly what the device was doing, and didn't want to set off any tampering countermeasures. He unplugged it, and pulled the SD card. A quick visual inspection assured him that there was no storage in the form of SMD onboard hardware. He held the SD card up close to his face. With what unpleasantness are you laden, my friend?

Katz brought up an empty file in which he might chart his thoughts.

Fact: Michael broke in and installed a surveillance device. He was on my admit list for the front desk, but how did he open the door? Lockpicking? Made a duplicate of my key from a picture? I left it unlocked? It doesn't particularly matter. **Fact:** It was sending a signal in the presence of, and proportionate to the level of, noise. He wanted to hear something, probably communications, that I don't do via IM/email/text. But what do I do via spoken communication? Not much. Alternative explanation: he wanted a record he could play for other people. Law enforcement. Regulators. **Fact:** It's been operating for eight weeks, ever since late February. What have I said in here that's incriminating? Most of my comms are digital. Mostly he would have heard me and Oriana talking about random shit. What all have I said to her? **Fact:** Most of the dirt I'm into involves and incriminates him as well. Had he been picked up? Was this some kind of cooperation? No. Michael would have laughed at anything short of federal; it would have been a first charge. And DEA/FBI don't have their coops build their own surveillance tech and break in to install it. This is amateur hour horseshit I'm looking at.

Once more he turned the SD card over in his hand. Let's take a look at it. The block device exposed two partitions, the second much larger than the first. Call them / and /home/. He almost mounted the second locally as ext4, then remembered talk in the industry of malicious, handbuilt metadata exploiting bugs in kernel filesystem code. He sensibly spun up a virtual machine, passed the USB SD reader through to it, and mounted there instead. The partition mounted up just fine at /media/ssk/bitchcard. Toplevel: friendly lost+found and, *was ist das,* snare.

The snare directory contained the usual bash and SSH detritus, and a single script. Katz opened it: less than twenty lines. It launched a thread and opened an audio device. In a closed loop, it stored twenty seconds at a time into timestamped files in `/tmp/snare` using `arecord`, a simple ALSA streamer. Snare, eh? Cute. He saw no communication or synchronization with the other thread, so things were presumably driven by these filesystem entries. Simple enough. He looked to the thread's code. It initialized a variable `hbtimestamp` to zero, and then ran its own closed loop. At the top of the loop, it pulled the current time using `CLOCK_MONOTONIC`, and calculated `hbtimestamp + 300`. It then blocked on either a new file's appearance in `/tmp/snare`, or the expiry of a timer initialized using the previous calculation. Upon waking, it checked `/tmp/snare` for files. Any it found were...Jesus, Michael, this is some loose bullshit right here. A new SSH session for every upload? Katz's sensibilities were offended. So much overhead! Yeesh, so each file was pushed via `scp` to a remote server, `snare@castalia.org`, retaining its timestamp-based name. Reboot on any `scp` failure, interesting choice. Katz couldn't help but catalog the ways he'd have improved on this scheme. He pulled the WHOIS records for `castalia.org`: standard GoDaddy hidden ownership, nothing interesting there. Using `mtr` he ran a route trace to the resolved IP. Seven hops, a short path, only microseconds to reach it, looked like Linode's Atlanta colo down on Marietta Street.

Fair enough. A counterhack was indicated. Katz smiled grimly. This was familiar ground; this was where he was strong. He might never ascertain Michael's motives behind this stunt, this duplicity, this faithlessness, this stupidity. But he could sure as shit submerge the fucker in a tarpit of mirrors, madness, and lies. The hunted would become the hunter. You want to fuck with me, Michael? You want to fuck with Sherman Spartacus Katz? You want to fuck with me using *computers?* This is my motherfucking house, Bolaño, and *mon frère,* you have fucked up.

Let's not rush anything. Spend a little time planning; we're better than the fucker. He's always been more devious, but I've always been the better engineer, and I've only grown stronger in the past decade. He's been playing at stable jobs; I've been out here living the shit, coding or dying, sacrificing my nights, dedicating my all to mastery of this machine and its ways. Every night he stayed in his room he got weaker. Every night I squatted before the phosphoric glow of a CRT, I've grown stronger. Let's move his walls in a little tighter. Nothing can stop me. My computer is a suit of armor, an iron eagle that nothing can penetrate. The deadliest weapon in the world is a Georgia Tech engineer and his machine. Katz laughed at himself. *Iron Eagle? Full Metal Jacket?* You dramatic asshole. Katz put on Panacea & Cativo's *Hardest Tour on Planet Earth,* smiled the smile of a natural born killer, and began drafting a run against his best friend.

ALSA: Advanced Linux Sound Architecture

24   it'll raise the tone of your trap

He'd not bothered Katz or Devesh for much information about the project, hoping the less he knew, the less that could fuck him should it all go down. When he saw them, they'd volunteer a story of engineering, or of relevant market research, or how they'd narrowly avoided, before they had the hex ChemEng down, leveling the industrial park and seeding much of the West End with uranium dust. "Would that kill everybody?"

Katz had looked at Devesh. "Just people who breathed it, right?" Devesh grinned and nodded. "I mean, we'd no longer be computing entities, as it were. They'd be breathing us, too."

Devesh laughed. "If you liked Atomic Devesh, you'll love Atomized Devesh!"

"Try not to annihilate the neighborhood. Maybe this project needs go somewhere a bit less populated? This community has already had enough inflicted on it. If you're going to possibly burn out a few square klicks, at least do it to white people. The optics here are terrible. Think of how it would look in the *New York Times*."

October of 2011 and 2012 had brought simple but attractive annual summaries, stating only the vaguest costs: "$100,000 for mirrors." "$150,000 for steel." Somehow they had substantial income each year from "consulting." Bolaño figured Katz was simply feeding some of his main work into the company, and probably making cash deposits as well. He didn't ask. The company's name was American Pions.

∗ ∗ ∗ ∗ ∗ ∗ ∗ ∗

In November, looking over the threadbare ARs, he decided to go visit this enterprise of which he owned, on paper, 50% of distributions. He knew the industrial park; he'd been the one who suggested it for the lab, so many years ago. He arrived around 1500h and called Katz. "Hey! I'm up at the park, and was hoping to stop by the office."

"The office?"

"Whatever you two call your space here."

"Oh! You're at the industrial park? The Metropolitan?"

"Yes, the park containing our company's assets in toto."

"Oh. OK. We're in Building 4, southwest side. There's a big Feynman diagram of beta decay on the door. Can't miss it."

"Great, I should—"

"Don't worry if you don't know the Feynman diagram for beta decay; I think it's the only Feynman diagram on the building."

"udd to udu, with the quark changing flavor emitting a W⁻ boson, which decays into an electron and neutrino."

"Leptons are conserved, dumbass. It's an antineutrino." The line went dead.

Bolaño went to the door and knocked. He tried the handle, and the door swung in. It was heavy as hell; it looked like they'd replaced the old entrance with a reinforced steel model. Probably a good idea. "Yo! Katz!"

Katz popped up from behind a battlement. Bolaño recognized him from the TaB shirt; his head was covered in a respirator. Is he waving at me? No, he is waving me back. He is waving me back exuberantly. Let's make haste. Bolaño turned and gracefully left the building, and furthermore crossed the street. Katz emerged seconds later, and shut the door behind him.

"What the fuck was that?"

Katz removed his respirator and crossed the street. "No need to yell about shit. You don't want to come in there without a respirator right now."

Bolaño stiffened. "Why?" he whispered, agitated. "Has there been any kind of leak?"

"No, but Devesh is cooking lunch. He eats strange things."

"Are you for fucking real? You had me worried."

"Yeah it's fine in there, obviously. C'mon."

Bolaño looked around and took it all in. He whistled. "This is quite a setup you boys have here."

"Definitely the most advanced facility in the West End."

"Though..." Bolaño looked around. It didn't make sense. "Shouldn't you need a lot more graphite or water as coolant and moderator? I don't see...any."

"Ahh, Bolaño, it's good that you came by. We've had something of a change of plans."

Bolaño went hot inside. "What kind of change?"

Katz grinned at Devesh. "We have made an ally of the laser."

"OK, so you enriched a little to run your reactor better, I get that. You said that would probably be necessary. Still, I'm not seeing any reactor here. I'm seeing what looks like a linac? And a bunch of chemical plant, and a shitton of cooling and power distribution."

"Yeah, reactors are passé."

"So, what's going on here, guys?"

* * * * * * * *

He'd gone over to Katz's place to talk about it. It was his first visit in months. He'd visited regularly when Katz first bought the condo, but invites were extended less and less frequently over recent years. Still, there had been several bitchin' parties there, and he'd attended them all, usually hanging out in Katz's office where the bongs were kept lit and rotating, or out on the terrace.

"How much are you sitting on?"

Katz expression was one of profound satisfaction. "We've gone through forty-five tonnes."

"I mean enriched. How much ^{235}U?"

"Well, Michael, natural uranium is 0.711% ^{235}U. And I said we've gone through forty-five tonnes."

"How much has been *separated*?"

"Not the right question to ask, really, unless you're asking how big a pile of 100% ^{235}U we have, which the answer would be no such pile. Frustratingly difficult to eliminate those last percents."

Steely: "Katz, don't fuck with me. You know what I'm asking. What I funded—what has it produced? You had forty-five tons—fucking Christ, 90,000 pounds—of natural uranium. What do you have now?"

Katz was savoring his insolence. "You're talking like a dumb American, Burmese—Myanma?—or Liberian. We had forty-five metric tonnes of natural uranium. That's 99,000 of your 'pounds,' unless you meant 'pound sterling,' in which case you're way off. Actually more like 99,180, but you've got to assume some loss off the top. I've got 99,000 problems, but the bitch ain't one."

"Sherman—"

"So in those forty-five tonnes, ^{235}U ought be 0.711%—"

"So 320 kilograms."

"They don't ship uranium metal, Bolaño. We receive yellowcake. Urania. Mostly U_3O_8, but there's some other crap in there, too. We'll just call it all triuranium octoxide. It's cleaner. That's 848 g per key. 0.711% of that is 6.029 kg."

"Per metric tonne?" That didn't seem so much.

"Of which we've processed forty-five."

"So that's optimally 271 kg." That seemed a good deal more.

"Well, optimally, yeah. Remember, the process isn't perfected yet. Devesh thinks we need to add another laser to the array; he doesn't think he can juke up more power on his design. But right now, we have discard tailings of about 44.7 Mg—"

That seemed wrong. Bolaño frowned. "Aren't you discarding a majority of the dank? That only leaves 300 kg. At 5%, that's only 15 kg. Can't it be reprocessed or something?"

Katz coughed, briefly disrupting his smile. "Well. Standard depleted uranium is 0.3% ^{235}U. That would be 135 kg lost in the tailings. No fun at all. In that case, you'd still have half of it in your product, which would be 136 out of 300 kg, a 45% enrichment."

That couldn't be right, could it? That seemed bad.

"You're almost correct: we have total product of about 280 kg. We seem to have about twenty keys of the nat unaccounted for, probably stuck to the walls inside, or lost before we had the hex conversion locked in. But here's the thing: we're calling our tailings 'ultradepleted,' though we're not married to that name. Ours run closer to 0.03%, an order of magnitude less ^{235}U." He paused to let Michael work it out. It took only a second.

"But that would mean—"

"Indeed."

"No."

"Sadly, yes. We can't yet work that last bit out. Maybe with a different nozzle geometry? It's all kind of academic: 85% is fine for anything we want."

"Eighty-five..."

"Yep." Katz's pleasure dazzled. "How fucking solid is that? We can go all the way in a three-stage cascade. Do it automatically rather than having to collect and reload the fucking hex. Until we got some help, you would not believe how badly I was aching at night. The forklift is great, but even loading those fuckers onto palettes? Remind me not to fuck with hex in my next life."

Bolaño stared. "Do you intend to explain?"

"Explain what?" Even Katz thought that might have gone too far.

With deadly quiet: "why you two went to HEU."

Katz began to answer, but Bolaño cut him off. "Stop being cute. Stop acting like this is funny, or a game. Stop pretending there aren't very real and serious consequences, and that you have not taken us to a next level of lawlessness and criminality. And for what? It's *less* likely that we can sell HEU."

Katz appeared chagrined. "Well, honestly, we didn't think it was going to be as effective as it turned out. Devesh really killed it on the laser design. Maybe SILEX always worked this well, and that's just never been revealed publicly. We know it's at 85%; that's as trivial an application of a mass spectrometer as exists. It's possible to downblend it." He said this last almost apologetically.

"But you knew it was that good after you did your first run. Why did you keep doing it like that?"

"I mean, it *is* the most valuable form. We have full flexibility this way. We can blend it down to whatever the buyer wants. Bolaño, I'm not going to just sell weapons grade uranium—"

"Please don't use those words."

Katz rolled his eyes. "I'm not going to sling dank to Hamas or Hezbollah. But let's say we wanted to sell this entire op to DoE. They'd probably pay more for it in that form."

"That's just the thing, though. By going to eighty-five, you've made it impossible for us to approach DoE or NRC or anyone like that. The minute we do, we're taken to a black site."

"Well, what are your suggestions? The method is proved. I think we ought take it to the NRC."

"The very best outcome is they take everything, without remuneration."

"I'm not sure I agree. We ought lawyer up and see what can be done."

"Are there any lawyers qualified on the Atomic Energy Act? How do you find them? Oh, you go to the Department of Energy, where all such lawyers work. And what happened to the medical and industrial isotopes?"

"We'll get to those!" Katz sounded wounded. "Just this, you know, was pretty cool. And our neutron burden remains flat at natural; the only fission here is spontaneous."

"Maybe you should get to some of that as a cover? And by the way, do you know how Greg Moyer got my name as a possible acid contact? It was quite unnerving. It's not like I sell acid."

"As far as I was aware, you've sold more acid than I have, going by income. Certainly by profit."

Bolaño rolled his eyes. "Do you ever intend to get over that?"

"I'm over it. Doesn't change facts."

"Don't you think all this"—Bolaño gestured around—"makes us even?"

"Oh, absolutely. Still doesn't change facts. Tell you what, if you see Greg Moyer, feel free to tell him I'll sell him some weapons grade—"

"*Don't say it.*"

Katz finished: "acid."

* * * * * * * * *

Some people expend tremendous energy merely to be normal.

Bolaño had been unhappy since first hearing the word "uranium" from Katz's lips almost two years ago. He'd been foolish to go in the insane scheme in the first place. He recognized that now, and had probably known it then. Not that he doubted the engineering of Katz and Devesh—if those two were spending their time on it, and convinced it would work, it was probably going to work. They both had any number of alternatives available.

Imports had ceased, Katz had told him, after bringing in forty-five metric tonnes across nine containers. By 2012 trucks no longer rolled north from Savannah, and cash no longer flowed to this Kazakh. Which God help him, and us, if his malfeasance was ever detected. Hopefully he wasn't throwing greenstacks around over in Astana, but who knew? Katz had never explained how they even got money to him, whether he was taking it out on some diplomatic flight, or commercial air/ship hoping not to be caught, or privileged wire, or avian carrier, or what. "Compartmentalization," Katz would say, with that smug smile he so often wore of late. If Katz was to be trusted, one and a half million dollars in hard currency had made its way into Central Asia and unknown numbers of grasping fists.

The whole thing was riddled with shoddy opsec. Katz couldn't keep a secret if his life depended on it. It was like he had a sexual attraction to revelation of incriminating information, all the better if it involved strangers. He remembered Greg Moyer calling him after he'd made the sale out West, looking for a sheet, happily inquiring over an insecure phone. How had Greg fucking Moyer known anything about it? Katz? But in that case, why wasn't he just buying from Katz? No, it had to be some unholy chain of chattering fucks, singing from the rooftops. But the chatter began with Sherman.

When he'd purchased this place, it was his intention to retire entirely from the various games. He had one of the finest residences in the city, and didn't intend to lose it to civil forfeiture. He'd invited Rosemary to live in the guesthouse. Upon first looking into it, she burst into joyful tears; even he had become misty. Negotiations with Price WaterhouseCoopers looked bright indeed. He expected to head there in the new year, on a path to partner by 2015. Even before that, he could expect almost a meg per annum if he made his bonus. It had hurt when Katz acted so upset about his windfall, as if he hadn't made it possible for Katz to monetize far more than usual. He'd brought Katz and that new girlfriend of his, Oriana, out for what he'd hoped would be a pleasant peace offering of an evening. Katz had behaved rudely, and left early.

When Katz had told him that they were importing fucking bootleg yellowcake, every instinct had told him to run away. But it was undeniably compelling. The ability to purchase commodity inputs at well below market price was not one to sneeze away. A key of yellowcake had reliably run in excess of 110 USD since 2010. Katz had paid 1.5 megadollars for 49 megagrams, less than $34 a key. Bolaño could only imagine how Sherman had managed to bag this insane hookup, but he had known Katz long enough to have a decent idea.

My Best Fiend OR *For Katz it was Tuesday: A Noh Play in One Act*
Outside the Klaus Fortress of Computing

Dramatis personae:
  SHERMAN KATZ
  ZACH THE KAZAKH
  JILL ZILLIONS

[Enter Katz in ornate UnderArmor kimono, basketball shorts. He paces intensely, smokes two cigarettes at once, and sweats freely.]

Katz: I can sweat a gallon, and the outermost layer's still dry.

[Enter Zach in *aiyr qalpaq, atsuita, ōkuchi,* and *nōshi*]

Zach: Who is this loud, wet fellow?

Katz: [aside] I haven't done enough dumb shit today! [to Zach] That's quite a hat! I bet you just got out of some hellish class? Wanna smoke a bowl and maybe shoot ketamine into our ballsacks?

[Enter Jill in kneesocks, miniskirt, shirt reading ATTRACTIVE NUISANCE]

Jill: That's Sherman Katz, last of the bigtime spenders!

Katz: Hey would you like to be my new annoying girlfriend?

Jill: Yes I said Yes I will Yes! Please feed me your secrets.

Zach: What were you saying about scrotal ketamine? We do that all the time in Kazakhstan, or as we call it in Astana, the Kaz-hole. This is the ancient Ceremony of Ten Stumbling Tigers.

Katz: Kazakhstan? Uranium is from Kazakhstan! Do you sell uranium? I have excess cash from my ongoing side gig as an LSD chemist/trafficker!

Zach: [crying] My father told me, son, you must go to America for your degree, and to sell diverted uranium to sweaty guys with bags of drug money.

Katz: K-rad! Let's quote the motherfucking Bible! *Infantes eorum allidentur in oculis eorum, diripientur domus eorum, et uxores eorum violabuntur.*

Jill: ERMAHGERD he's just dreamy!

Katz: If anyone sees Greg Moyer, or anyone else really, make sure they know Bolaño hopes to retail them ten-strips!

[All three link arms and float up and away from stage]

ALL: We're off to violate the laws of the United States!

FIN

✳ ✳ ✳ ✳ ✳ ✳ ✳ ✳

As soon as Katz admitted what was going down, Bolaño began seriously to look at ways he might extricate himself from the situation. He felt taken advantage of and misled by someone he had always tried to help. If he could end this

---

Noh: 能 Nō   **aiyr qalpaq:** айыр қалпақ tall fabric hat
atsuita: 厚板唐織 opulent kimono   **ōkuchi:** 大口 warrior trunks
nōshi: 直衣 imperial robe
Infantes…violabuntur: Their infants will be dashed to pieces before their eyes; their houses will be looted and their wives violated. Isaiah 13:16 (NIV)

madness and preserve both of them, that would be great. If Katz had to go down, that was no longer his greatest concern. He wondered: is this not the same as giving up his name in the event of my arrest, something I always swore I would never do? No, he'd nullified the rules of honor when he set about on this plan, and lied to me.

Two hundred and forty kilos of ^{235}U at ready-to-rock 85% enrichment. *Jesucristo.* Bare spherical critical mass of about 50 kg. Knock that down with any number of trivial schemes. The hard part's already done for you. Anywhere between five and, what, ten? Fifteen 20 KT cores? Fucking madness.

The device had been a foolish idea born from a moment of weakness. He'd planned to install it while Katz was out of town (there again, Katz couldn't leave his house for two days without announcing his plans to all the world via social media). He was on Katz's admit list with the concierge, and had found several pictures on his Facebook senselessly featuring his keyring. He pulled his Ilco guide. Trapezoidal hole: Almet SC4, American Lock AM4, Challenger 1770C, NCR NH1 or NCL NH1, or most likely one of a dozen Schlages. Look at the bow—yeah, the stepgraph of Schlage. Count pins. Six. Need a 35-101C. He happened to have several in the same box where he kept the Pro-lok. Dial it in and...yes, that looks good. Uncertain of the fourth height, he made a few.

He would go over to talk, steer conversation gently towards relevant topics, and get audio evidence sufficient to defend himself in court, should it ever come to that. An admission that he'd not been involved in the decision to import, and certainly not to enrich, and absolutely not at all to produce highly enriched uranium in a goddamn industrial park in the middle of downtown Atlanta, in contravention of fifty thousand Federal statutes and all good taste. What was wrong with using your phone, idiot? Sure, it wouldn't have caught conversations when he wasn't there, but who else was Katz going to talk to about this shit?

A definite slip. If Katz were to find it—and it seemed reasonable that he might—and then look through the thing—and he would absolutely do that, immediately—there was no doubt some bit of evidence that would prove difficult to explain. Fuck. He sat up. He scpd to `castalia.org`, didn't he? The registrar records wouldn't give anything away, but it was on Linode box that hosted several other sites of his. He brought up a terminal and did a type A lookup on `castalia.org`: 173.230.130.29. Now a reverse lookup on that IP: `texmencks.com`. Fuck! He briefly considered acquiring another static IP for the VPS, but with no ability to test, and the device having been offline for several weeks...no. There were probably several other such indicators, anyway.

And why was it down? Twice before there had been losses of heartbeat: once for twenty minutes, another time for forty-five. Both times, it had come back on without any interaction from him. It rebooted on any failure to upload, and had shown an uptime of only minutes in both instances. So possibly intermittent cellular problems? Impossible to know for sure. But now it had been gone for several days. It had gone off for about fifty minutes, then come back on for a short time, then stayed off. The device ran an SSH server for his remote inspection, and he'd figured he would wipe the flash from a distance once issues with Katz had been resolved. That was no good when it wasn't talking to him, though. He'd several times tried sshing to the most recent address from which it had contacted him, with no results but timeouts.

What did it matter? Even if Katz found it, and knew it was him, so what? What was he going to do, call the cops?

* * * * * * * *

His first call was to Danylo. This brief conversation, as all their others, was conducted in *russkiy,* in which Danylo was surprisingly expressive, at times even lyrical. *"Krasávčik!* We must meet. Come to Blake's this evening, eight?"

Blake's on the Park was an upscale, eclectic Midtown gay clientele: devoid of the most city's most ratchet, without necessarily being old and run through. Bewildering, Bolaño thought, that Katz remained oblivious to Danylo's preference for men. Had he never noticed how the Ukrainian dressed? Sharp!

Danylo was intrigued by his suggestion, but didn't commit to anything. "What you offer is no doubt a valuable and rare horde. Men crave, and we attend their cravings, profiting along the way. But it is no small thing, Michael Luis, to find a buyer for such an item. And you say it is in gaseous form, unweaponized? Surely this requires chemical plant and experienced, skilled workers."

"In Russia there are many who can work with this form." Bolaño didn't want to sound desperate. "America still purchases Russian HEU at a high price under Megatons to Megawatts. Get it into Russia and flip it back to us."

"If we got it into Ukraine, we would weaponize; the value added is tremendously greater. There is no need to sell immediately." Danylo smiled. "Perhaps we would find our own uses for such a device. But even getting it across the ocean is a difficult matter. There are four thousand ways to hide drugs or people in a cargo container; we know them all, and devise new ones each day. But such things announce their own presence with their radiations. I will have to confer with our experts."

"I just want this situation gone, and to not lose too much on it. I can demonstrate authenticity of the product."

"Alexei will be entrusted with this task. If he is satisfied, I am satisfied. You know that he graduated?"

"Like seven years ago, right? And then he got a masters after that?"

"He is doing mechanical engineering work for us. You've heard of narcosubs?" Bolaño nodded. "They seem a sharp edge to have over our opponents. UAVs intrigue us likewise. Alexei is experimenting with matters of battery life, stealth, and control. And of course, we can then sell any aspects of his technique we're comfortable sharing, keeping for ourselves the finest vintages." Bolaño didn't understand why Danylo was sharing all this, but they had after all just been discussing the liquidation of a quarter tonne of HEU.

* * * * * * * *

Bolaño sat at corner table in Peachtree's Publik Draft House. This was another bad idea, he told himself. You cannot control what this girl will do with this

---

krasávčik: красáвчик handsome guy

information; you can barely influence her. She might run to the goddamn Zone 5 cops ranting about nuclear bombs in the West End. She might go Tweet about it. Still, if there was any means by which Sherman could be brought back from the brink, well, Katz was owed that effort, and if anyone in this world had influence on him, it was Oriana Marino.

She came through eight minutes late, blustery. Bolaño was uncertain whether she'd dressed up for his benefit, or whether these had been all-day clothes. Nope, the wrinkle in that skirt gave it away. Well, the girl dresses well, and is committed to it. She was smiling in every one of the hundreds of pictures she had up on Facebook, but she was not smiling now. Taking the chair opposite, she flung down textbooks, notebooks, Macbook.

"This seems really early to talk about a surprise party for Sherman, Bolaño, but you said we needed to meet ASAP. And we had to do it in person. So I'm here. What's the story?"

"Oriana—"

"No, first, I want to say: I don't particularly like you, and I don't think Sherman does, either. He definitely did at one time, and he still respects you. But you did something to him, and your friendship turned sour in his mouth. *However,* he's in recent weeks sounded happy whenever mentioning you. So when you approached me with this, I agreed to meet you, because I want him to be happy. And Lord knows you need a friend."

He stared at her for a moment. He pulled his phone out, an iPhone like hers. "I'm going to show you a few pictures of what Katz is up to."

"To help plan a party?" She was confused.

He held the phone tightly, to prevent any sudden snatch. The first picture showed Katz in a respirator, stepping down from a forklift. Behind him loomed industrial equipment she couldn't identify. Oriana spoke with a low voice, but clear anger: "If you're trying to get me pissed off about Katz, I know everything he does. This is, what, some—"

The waitress arrived. "Hello! I'm on his tab"—pointing at Bolaño. "Moscow Mule, please." Oriana smiled brightly until she'd departed.

"Drug shit? I know all about it, Michael. Probably more than you. This was what you called me over here for?"

"What drug shit needs a forklift?"

"What, because he has a forklift, he's...what are you even saying he's doing?"

"Your boyfriend has an unlicensed uranium enrichment facility within the limits of the City of Atlanta."

Oriana raised a brow. Her Mule arrived; she thanked the waitress once more, and took a heavy sip. "Mmmmm." She didn't speak for several seconds. "Michael Bolaño, that's the most ridiculous thing I've ever heard."

"Is it? Consider the person we're talking about."

"Oh, I don't doubt he could build such an operation. I wouldn't be surprised at the lack of license. But this picture is of the Metropolitan in West End, and Sherman is not so stupid to do that."

"How did you know where it was?"

"We had an art collective there. You know nothing about me, Michael. So Sherman is doing something, or helping someone do something, in an industrial park. Why should I give a shit? Why are you telling me this?" She took another solid pull.

"Has he told you about it?"

"No. There's plenty he doesn't and needn't tell me about."

"He's there with Devesh sometimes ten hours a day. Here are the company founding documents for American Pion, alluding to enrichment for neutron generation. That's what we agreed on."

"Oh, so you're involved in this, too?"

"Unfortunately. He was supposed to go to 3.5% or 5%, just enough to main-tain criticality without special...well, you wouldn't know any of that. But he went much further. How are we supposed to sell this? This is a nuclear ter-rorism charge if, when he gets caught. It's a serious safety problem, both radiological locally, and potentially nuclear. You can't fuck around with highly enriched uranium."

She's visibly pissed off. "Just because I didn't go to Tech doesn't mean I don't know science. And even if I didn't, you learn enrichment levels by your third or fourth week dating Sherman. They're not exactly an uncommon topic of his contemplation. I ask you again: why are you telling me this?"

"I have people who can make this all go away. They clean up, haul it, we even make most of our money back. Probably. Maybe. But it'll be gone. And that's what you want, because right now, Sherman is on the precipice of ruining his entire life, for something ridiculous. It's like the man's on a mission, aflame for Christ, like those old LSD crews."

"You have people?"

"Yes."

"What people?"

"People whom I trust."

"So tell Sherman this." Her Mule is almost gone.

"I did. He was very resistant. Frustratingly so."

"So what makes you think I can change his mind?"

"He loves you. Deeply and as much, I think, as he's ever loved anyone." He says it plainly. He believes it to be true. "He thinks it irresponsible to transfer to others the powers he has created, summoned up."

"These mysterious others."

"They are not people with whom we have influence."

She stood up. "As far as I understand you, Bolaño, Sherman is absolutely right. I'm proud of him. You remain a dickless, heartless, unfunny piece of shit. Thanks for the drink."

✳ ✳ ✳ ✳ ✳ ✳ ✳ ✳

Katz had recognized immediately that the use of scp implied the presence of a key that could access the remote server, at least as this snare user. He sshd into snare@castalia.org at 0302h, and had a shell. snare didn't have sudo access to root, but it did to mlb, which did enjoy free sudo. He checked for recent logins from anyone else. mlb was logged in currently, but idle for over two hours. Katz brought up another shell. In this one, he launched a quick bash loop that checked w output and slept for a second. If the logged in mlb went active, or another showed up, it broke the loop, killing all snare logins, filtering all sudo logs since 0302h, pruning all snare records from the sshd and utmp logs, and finally logging itself out. He would have used a C program and notification-based I/O in production, but now was not the time.

TIME: 0315H TIME ELAPSED: 00:00:13M

He generated a new keypair, added a new user avahid easily mistaken for the mDNS system account, and installed the keypair. He made a copy of bash, set it owned by root, set the setuid bit, and copied it to /usr/sbin/.linker. Any user could now get a root shell without the crutch of sudo. He dug into the environ of Michael's running shell, looking for SSH agent variables. There was SSH_AUTH_SOCK, good. He checked that the pipe it specified existed, with correct ownership. Yep. Was Michael's workstation on a public IP? He checked the shell's SSH_CLIENT, extracted the IP, and hit it from the VPS. Nothing responded quickly. He looked up the IP: CGNAT for Giganet. Fair enough. No way did Michael lack a path into his home machines. Katz looked for any TUN/TAP devices that might indicate a VPN. tun0, eh? He ran lsof to find processes working with the device. Ahhh, indeed, there's an OpenVPN. There's its configuration file. No status entry specifying a status file. Instead, he sent SIGUSR2, and checked syslog. Ahhh, multi-client output, with two entries. One had CN workstation, the other laptop. Thank you, Michael. He hit the first client IP, routing over the VPN, using the forwarded agent key, user name mlb. Shell.

TIME: 0321H TIME ELAPSED: 00:00:19M

He immediately boosted Michael's SSH and GnuPG keys. A quick ls turned up a passwd file of less than 32 KB in his home directory. cat...yessss, an unencrypted plaintext file of web passwords. That too was ganked. He added an iptables rule to set an FWMARK of 1 on all sessions which came into the workstation's SSH. He logged out, and logged back in. He verified that his TCP session was being marked. He verified that the keepalives in Michael's session were not. He added a tc rule to drop 20% of packets headed to the VPS IP without an iptables FWMARK of 1. Just enough to utterly fuck interactive work over SSH, but not enough to be obvious; Michael would need either look at the abstruse traffic controller configuration, or do a detailed comparison of tcpdumps, though checking iptables configuration would provide some hints. If Michael woke up and went to look at his VPS, he'd be doing it over an unresponsive, nigh-unusable connection. Katz considered tossing the rules into /etc/rc.local, so that they might persist across a reboot, but decided against it. Katz aborted his watcher, changing it to only warn, not immediately kill.

TIME: 0325H TIME ELAPSED: 00:00:23M

Katz brought up a new node in the Atlanta Linode colo. Two hops to castalia.org, 10Gbps all the way there. Sweet. It took less than two minutes to install Debian on the new node, and another three minutes to configure it as needed. He shut down most services on the VPS. The only ones listening publicly were OpenVPN, the Apache web server, and OpenSSHd. The last he left running. He copied all files to a new directory on his new node using a simple tar piped into ssh. On his new node, he converted this hierarchy into a

---

CGNAT: carrier-grade network address translation   CN: [x509] Common Name

Qemu VM image. He moved the host SSH server to 4200, and restarted it. He logged out, and back in. He added a DNAT rule to pass 80 and 443 to the VM. He added a DNAT rule to pass 22 to the VM. He spun up the VM. He hit port 80 on his new node. He got the home page for castalia.org. He smiled.

TIME: 0347H TIME ELAPSED: 00:00:45M

He smoked a Newport, and plotted. Two Newports. Much plotting.

TIME: 0353H TIME ELAPSED: 00:00:51M

He returned to Michael's VPS. He restarted services. He scrubbed logs. He set up DNAT and SNAT rules to send external incoming traffic to his new node. Michael's VM was reduced to a transparent proxy. He watched tcpdump on his new node. He saw UDP traffic come in on 1194. He saw it flow both ways. He entered the VM, sent SIGUSR2 to the running OpenVPN process, and verified that Michael's laptop and workstation had both connected to the illusive VM under his control. He named the new node capgras. He verified that he could SSH into Michael's home workstation using the stolen credentials. He popped a shell. He cackled, and his cackle became a roar.

I done told you once, you son of a bitch: I'm the best that's ever been.

TIME: 0420H TIME ELAPSED: 00:01:18M

He began to work in earnest; he had not yet begun to hack.

25   oriana marino speaks in riddles

Oriana: You have a good job. A great job. You don't really spend all that much money. Why do you remain into all this illegal shit?

Katz: Well, yeah, my job pays pretty well now, but when I started, I was only making seventy-five large. I mean, that's not terrible, but it's nothing like what the kids are making coming into the game now. I started making one twenty-five when I was, what, twenty-five? And now I'm doing about half a meg. So yeah, it's not about the money. Except for this one stack I've got of cash, as in like folding hard currency, which I'm working to get into the bank. It's a tremendous pain in the ass, I assure you.

Oriana: So when that's accomplished, you'll stop? Because you seem to accept cash pretty regularly.

Katz: OK, so I still do drugs, right? And I exploit my established connections to get them at a good price, at high quality. Part of doing that is buying in some quantity. Then, I've got these various old friends, generally middle-aged engineers I can trust not to do stupid shit and get busted, and they're like "Sherman, Sherman, can we not score?" So I break them off a little, and obviously some of them are going to pay in cash. And my margins are generally very reasonable. It's not about the money.

Oriana: So you buy wholesale quantities, and sell retail quantities to acquaintances at a profit. That's the definition of a drug dealer, *n'est-ce pas?*

Katz: [laughs unhappily] If you're being uncharitable. I suppose I compare my current foot traffic to what was going on in say 2005, and it's so reduced that I don't really consider it that way. I mean, I was moving several kilos a week in quarters and zs. Maybe a dozen people stopping by per day. It consumed some serious fucking time. OK, I submit this litmus: if you're making money, you're a drug dealer. If you're not—meaning you have to pull from money you earned some other way when you re-up—you're just a hop.

Oriana: And that's what you are? A hop?

Katz: Sure. And there are other benefits, too. I don't love leaving my house, but I want to keep up with people. Being the man means the people come to you. They step in, give me an update, I update them, there's a transaction, and we're good for a few weeks, but the relationship remains tight. When I was younger, whenever you wanted, you could parlay your hookup into hooking up. Not necessarily, like, a trade of product for sex, though not necessarily not that either. But if you were interested in some girl, and she gets high, you can suggest she pick up through you, and boom, there's a date.

Oriana: A "date?"

Katz: I mean, she's coming over there, and you're doing her a favor. If you can't turn that into a date, that's on you, brother.

✳✳✳✳✳✳✳✳

Oriana: It's great to meet you, Erica! Sherman talks about you all the time.

Marelli: [laughs] Sherman talks about his exes a lot. They're the merestones by which he measures out the phases of his life.

Oriana: Too good for coffee spoons, huh? [laughs]

Marelli: Excuse me?

Oriana: Oh, sorry, a reference to "The Love Song of J. Alfred Prufrock" by T. S. Eliot. You know, "in the room the women come and go, talking of Michelangelo"?

Marelli: [smiling, bemused] No, sorry, I don't read much poetry. That's more for people like you. And Katz, he was crazy for poetry. I'd guess Michael was, too. [frowns]

Oriana: [continues smiling broadly] Let us go then, you and I, forward only in prose. [dismisses faux pas with gesture] Katz likes quoting poetry, but I'm not sure how deeply it speaks to his soul. You just made a face. Something about the Wondertwins?

Marelli: [confused] The Wondertwins? [laughs] Oh, you mean Sherman and his evil partner, hah. You're dating Sherman, right? You'd better hope he's not Michael's twin.

Oriana: I mean, they're effectively joined at the hip. I guess Bolaño is older? Only by a year though, I'm pretty sure. Though I get the idea they used to be closer than they are now. Do you not like Bolaño?

Marelli: What is there to like? As a woman, you're useless to him as a sexual object, and when has Michael ever thought a woman's thoughts worth his time? He looked past me like I wasn't there. I mean, he was polite—well, not really, but not excessively rude—

Oriana: [laughs] Bolaño does not tend to overwhelm with friendliness.

Marelli: I just always felt that if it would benefit him, he'd flay me where I stood. Or anyone else. Michael respects one person in the world, so far as I could tell, and is so racked with insecurities that he has to shit on that one person. Along with everyone else, of course. So how did you recognize me? Do you come here often?

Oriana: I love the cocktails here. And I recognized you from Facebook; you're all over there. Not jealous, of course, just noticed you. Talked to Sherman about you any number of times. He holds you in very high regard. Says you're brilliant, that he'd invest in anything you ever did—

Marelli: Awwwww. [simpers]

Oriana: He would never give it for anything that he didn't seriously respect.

Marelli: And I mean, I respect him as well. He's brilliant, beyond brilliant. And when he loves you and respects and appreciates you, he does so with his entire person, and would do anything for you. That's my take anyway. The problem is—not to talk trash about your boyfriend, with whom I wish you the best—he can stop loving you or even acknowledging your existence the moment something more interesting fills his thoughts. You're beautiful. May I ask your age?

Oriana: Twenty-five. I did two years abroad. You're twenty-four?

Marelli: You're sweet. Twenty-nine. One year left on my PhD, with any luck.

Oriana: Congratulations! Isn't that pretty early to have a PhD?

Marelli: No age is early to get a PhD. You're old at the end of it. You're old before you get it, actually. I feel old now. Are you in school?

Oriana: One more year. I double-majored in Journalism and Philosophy, like an idiot. Two big growth industries, right? [laughs] I've actually had two good internships, and am working on a book now. What's your PhD in? I seem to recall microbiology?
Marelli: Biomedical engineering. I grow people!
Oriana: Tell me about it! We've gotta pass the Bechdel test somehow.
Marelli: I do regenerative medicine research—tissue engineering.
Oriana: An issue of tissue.
Marelli: [laughs] Skin and cartilage are already figured out. Lots of people are working on in vitro meat. There are scaffolds, which you can think of as both an enzyme and a backbone. You want them to be biologically active only the way you want, to catalyze certain pathways. You want them to biodegrade eventually. Cells need to be able to seed and diffuse throughout the structure. A lot of work is going into 3D printing these things. There's culturing, where you grow the desired organ on the scaffold. And then there's the cellular engineering. I did a lot of work at Berkeley on gene editing under this woman Jennifer Doudna. She's amazing—she'll win the Nobel Prize one day if there's any justice.
Oriana: So you harvest cells and change their genes to grow faster? Be easier to transplant?
Marelli: Anything we can figure out. If you can change it in an interesting way that doesn't kill it, publish it. Maybe someone else can figure out an application. That's engineering. We're not yet at the point where we can predict protein generation from a DNA sequence, nor predict protein behavior from a chemical model. And even if we could, we can't go the other way—say "I want this behavior" and come up with a protein for it. Or then know how to code for that protein. It's a lot of knockout and transposition.
Oriana: Amazing. I've got to go, but let me get our drinks. I'd love to go out sometime.

✳ ✳ ✳ ✳ ✳ ✳ ✳ ✳

Oriana: You look like someone died. Did they pass a tax on basketball shorts?
Katz: [laughs semiemptily] No, what it is dear, is that today at work I needed the integral of a function,

$$\int \sqrt{a^2 + x^2}\, \mathrm{d}x = ?$$

The indefinite integral anyway. I tried to do it in my head, and nah. So I wrote it down and fucked with it for a minute, like pushing peas around on your plate when you're not going to eat them, and got nowhere. Now I could have just thrown the bitch into Maxima or Sage or something, but Sherman motherfucking Katz does not fuck up high school integrals. But he does, apparently. I had no real idea where to start. Ten years ago, I would have had that on sight.
Oriana: If it makes you feel better, I never took calculus.
Katz: You do trigonometric substitution then integration by parts:

$$\int \sqrt{a^2 + x^2}\, \mathrm{d}x = a^2 \int \sec^3 \theta\, \mathrm{d}\theta = \frac{a^2}{2}\left(\sec\theta\tan\theta + \ln|\sec\theta + \tan\theta|\right)$$

Oriana: So much depends upon a red wheelbarrow.

Katz: [wistful] They look like big, good, strong hands, don't they?

Oriana: Hey man, use it or lose it.

Katz: I had thought this knowledge written *cor cordium*. I loved calculus. It filled me with honest, simple delight. It was like getting your license in terms of the freedom it provided.

Oriana: [nonplussed] Freedom?

Katz: What's the area of a circle?

Oriana: πr^2 , right?

Katz: Twelve fifty, press return. What about an ellipse?

Oriana: Fuck you, I don't know, why?

Katz: You had to memorize a formula for each shape, right? And you had no real insight into why the formulas were what they were. I mean, you've got to be a rare kind of stupid not to understand why $\frac{1}{2}bh$ describes a triangle, but each one is its own bespoke argument from geometry, if you can justify it at all. And you only have formulas for simple shapes. But with calculus, suddenly you can derive area formulas for all kinds of things. If I want the shape formed between $cos\theta$ and $sin\theta + 2$ from zero to ten, I crank out the integral, and there we go. If I want to know the rate of growth of some ass function like x^x, take the derivative, boom, $x^x(ln\,x + 1)$. Calculus was like, "amateurs, clear the dancefloor." It was the first time I felt magic.

Oriana: Tighten in and expand upon "ass function," if you would.

Katz: Well in this case I have beef with x^x. It's a piece of shit function. I spent months wondering what its integral was, only to find out it doesn't have one, no respectable one anyway. It was the first time I saw the magic fail.

✳ ✳ ✳ ✳ ✳ ✳ ✳ ✳ ✳

Oriana: Michael, Sherman tells me you're a big reader. I think my five favorite books are *1984*, *Beloved*, *Herzog on Herzog*, *Interview with History*, and *Alice in Wonderland*. What about you?

Katz: I know you love *Alice*...you've got to read *Gödel, Escher, Bach*.

Bolaño: Five favorite? Fiction and non-fiction? Now or all time?

Oriana: Even reference, if you'd like! "Now or all time?" *Que?*

Bolaño: Five books speak to me with greatest current resonance, and five books have done so over my life. I'm unsure how the twain intersect.

Oriana: I'd love to hear both.

Bolaño: Currently I'd say. Daniel Yergin, *The Prize*. William Gaddis, *The Recognitions*. Dostoyevsky, *Prestupléniye i nakazániye*. That's *Crime and Punishment*. Ludwig Wittgenstein's *Philosophical Investigations*. Proust, *À la recherche du temps perdu*. Nowadays translated as *In Search of Lost Time*, though I read it back when it was known in English as *Remembrance of Things Past*. Let me think about the lifelong answer.

Katz: Roskolnikov over the Karamazovs? I'm surprised.

Bolaño: I've no beef with the Karamazovs, but fuck Father Zosima.

---

cor cordium: heart of hearts

Katz: Fuck Father Zosima indeed! Right in his ass! What's *Interview with History?* I've read your others.

Oriana: Oriana Fallaci. She's the best.

Katz: Were you named after her?

Oriana: Not by my parents. Possibly by fate.

Katz: I didn't finish *The Recognitions*, and I haven't read the new big translation of *La Recherche*. How is it, Michael?

Bolaño: How is what?

Katz: The big new translation, by who is it, Enright? I read the early translation, Moncrieff and Kilmartin.

Bolaño: The only translation I've read is the Bolaño translation. I don't usually read translations. You know this, Katz.

Oriana: How many languages do you speak?

Bolaño: Eight.

Oriana: I have English, Arabic, a little Italian, a little French.

Katz: It's my birthright as an American to study only English and dead languages. *Propterea abundantius oportet observare nos ea quae audivimus.* You know, when programming languages offer no compelling value, we place them among the archives for research, but don't expect people to continue writing PL/I. We ought take the same attitude towards spoken languages. If there are only seven speakers, there probably oughtn't be any.

Oriana: [disbelieving] Replacing programming languages with new ones seems an entirely different prospect from replacing spoken languages.

Katz: Ceded.

Oriana: [flutters lashes] And your five books?

Katz: *Infinite Jest. Ulysses,* to which I attach *Dubliners* and *Portrait of the Artist* as prefaces. *Naked Lunch. Blood Meridian. The Brothers Karamazov,* read in pathetic normie translation, unlike Mr. Bolaño. Two different translations, actually. Garnett as a teenager, and the newer Pevear just a year ago. I feel compelled to add *Illuminatus!, War and Peace,* and *To the Lighthouse.* They all tied for fifth. I don't think of nonfiction in that way—there's no ordering there.

Oriana: Why not? Can whatever metric you're using for fiction not be generalized? Some math person thing like "product of novelty of information provided and importance of information?" I-am-a-robot I-luv-graphs.

Katz: [laughs] I think that's *Dead Poets Society.* Maybe you could, but I have no ready answer for you. *The Making of the Atomic Bomb* is a fantastic book. *Soul of a New Machine* also. Both Pulitzer Prize winners by the way. But there are so many others. [extinguishes cigarette]

Bolaño: Upon reflection, I would replace only the Wittgenstein, for another Wittgenstein, the *Tractatus.* Despite all its faults. As an adolescent, it hit me like a brick. It's endlessly quotable.

Oriana: So you recently replaced *Tractatus* with *PI*? That's pretty much what Wittgenstein did, too, right?

Katz: What about the *Tractatus Logico-Philosophicus* had such effect on you?

Propterea...audivimus: We must pay the most careful attention, therefore, to what we have heard. Hebrews 2:1 (NIV)

Oriana: [slaps Katz's hand] The world is all that is the case.
Bolaño: *Wovon man nicht sprechen kann, darüber muss man schweigen.*

✳ ✳ ✳ ✳ ✳ ✳ ✳ ✳

Oriana: So as an engineer, someone who calls himself a scientist, a woo-hoo let's build it guy, isn't climate change the ultimate rebuke? Isn't global warming like a big neon sign blinking "hold, too fast!" In short, don't you feel y'all kinda dropped the ball on that one?
Katz: In short, the answer would be: we did drop the ball on that one, we being everyone: scientists who didn't predict the effects early on, engineers who built wasteful systems, governments that didn't prioritize a response, voters who didn't prioritize a government that would.
Oriana: Bullshit, the scientists and engineers were the ones taking the positive actions of building things and making technology available without considering the effects.
Katz: And everyone was buying that technology. You don't like lead in your gasoline? That's not the fault of Thomas Midgley Jr. in Dayton. It's good and useful to know about tetraethyl lead, about chlorofluorocarbons. Ignorance is never superior to knowledge. Are you going to blame Cornell for educating him? The problem was when General Motors and DuPont were like, "let's call this ethyl, because there'll be unpleasant questions if we call it tetraethyl persistent neurotoxin."
Oriana: Midgley did a press conference in which he huffed tetraethyl lead and poured it over his hands, calling it absolutely safe. Now we have the return of rompers and jumpsuits.
Katz: Really? [blanches] I didn't know that. That's pretty despicable. OK, well, again, everyone dropped the ball here. Midgley, General Motors, and anyone who watched that press conference and didn't think, "fuck anyone who suggests I breathe more lead."

✳ ✳ ✳ ✳ ✳ ✳ ✳ ✳

Oriana: What the fuck is dark energy? Sounds like Sauron shit.
Katz: [makes a show of sighing] Ugh. I'm not a huge fan.
Oriana: Of dark energy or Sauron?
Katz: Sauron was misunderstood. Not a big fan of Tolkien nor dark energy.
Oriana: You don't like Tolkien?
Katz: Even if he wasn't a helplessly prolix Luddite, going to engineering school ruins that kind of thing for you. One can hear grown men talk about elves only so many times. I suppose I like it more than dark energy.
Oriana: So you take a stance on it; you understand what it is. Explain.
Katz: I'm no expert. Like, at all. How much time have you got?
Oriana: Depends on how interested I am.
Katz: How interested are you?
Oriana: Depends on how interesting you make it.

Wovon...schweigen: Whereof one cannot speak, one must pass over it in silence.
Ludwig Wittgenstein, *Tractatus Logico-Philosophicus* (1922) 7

Katz: Let me get a drink, and we'll start with Ptolemy and his *Almagest.*

Oriana: Why do you have to start with a Greek? The Babylonians and Arabs and Indians were doing plenty of astronomy before that, also the Chinese.

Katz: One, I'm not recapitulating astronomy, just providing a backdrop. Two, Ptolemy synthesized most of that. His stuff was adopted wholesale by the Arabs going forward. Originally *Almagest* was *Mathēmatikē Syntaxis,* translated as *Syntaxis Mathematica.* But all those copies were lost in Europe, and when Ptolemy was read once again, in the twelfth century, it was from a Latin translation *Almagestum,* made from an Arabic copy.

Oriana: Just give someone other than white people their due. And yeah, the Arabic is *al-majistī* (أَلْمَجِسْطِي) meaning "the greatest."

Katz: [to ceiling] Thank you, ancients of the Fertile Crescent, for your reliable observations prior to submission under Alexander and later the Seleucid Empire, for your plucky sexagesimal number system and sensible cuneiform, for all those clay tablets—

Oriana: Base sixty is the way. Continue.

Katz: So Ptolemy has us in the center of the universe. They all knew we were a sphere, by the way. Being in the center was no good thing; it's described as being the garbage dump of the cosmos, to which all filth flows. You've got our solid sphere, and it's surrounded by spheres, and the stars and planets and moon and shit are hung on these spheres, which rotate. There were several reasons to buy this: you've got approximately the same number of stars beneath and above the horizon at any time, so it makes sense that we're in the center of that sphere. They detected no parallax—

Oriana: Parallax? Like with a camera?

Katz: Umm, I think so? Put your hands up parallel in front of your face. Now move your head to the left and right. They appear closer together. Stuff farther away doesn't seem to change, though. So they were like, "we don't see any change in the relationships of the stars to one another. No parallax; no movement."

Oriana: But the stars were just too far away. And the planets had dynamic relationships due to their own rotation around the sun.

Katz: You are owning it. Technically the stars do, too, but as you said, too far away to notice. And yeah, they weren't about to postulate thousands of light years of distance. Hell, they didn't know what a light year was. Just *milia passuum.* So three, it fundamentally looks like the sun and stars are rotating you on a daily basis. You're not feeling any movement of Earth. They didn't know about Galilean invariance.

Oriana: "Invariance?"

Katz: Sorry, Galilean relativity—

Oriana: [buzzing noise] Nope, that's not helping either.

Katz: I'm in the middle seat of a plane. All the windows are closed. How do I know the plane is moving?

Oriana: Because you lifted off. It would otherwise be plummeting.

---

milia passuum: one thousand paces

Katz: Argh. Yes. A boat then. Bottom of the boat, no portholes, level seas. How can I tell that I'm moving? Without appealing to some external observable? No GPS, *etc.*

Oriana: You can't. I mean, that's clearly the answer you want.

Katz: Let me ask another way: I drop a bowling bowl from above my foot. Does it hit my foot? Or does the motion of the boat mean it lands behind me?

Oriana: It hits you.

Katz: Exactly. The point is, you can't detect relative motion at constant velocity. So the argument that "we don't feel the Earth moving," which otherwise seems pretty compelling, is exploded.

Oriana: Nice; I dig it.

Katz: You also had Joshua 10:12—

Oriana: *[allegro]* No need to quote the Vulgate.

Katz: You make me sad. So Ptolemy: spheres, tortured epicycles, geocentrism. Most germane to your question: a static universe. Shit's rotating and moving, and we're walking around, but it's of a finite, unchanging size.

Oriana: What does it even mean for the universe to change size?

Katz: No one knows. You're not supposed to think of it as expanding into anything. Think of it this way: time doesn't replace non-time, right? But the amount of time that has been experienced is constantly increasing, right? Time isn't expanding into anything, but it's expanding.

Oriana: Yeah, but you can travel arbitrarily through space, but not in time. Time as experienced is not expanding; we experience a fixed immediacy.

Katz: I cannot explain the mystery of how the universe expands, assuming it does. The only part we're talking about is the internal expansion, if that helps. We're not saying anything about the volume nor surface area of the universe. The universe might have infinite volume, and yet still grow internally. It might not have any volume.

Oriana: How would it have no volume?

Katz: Topological depravities. [grabs laptop, casts to rarelyused tv]

Oriana: Oh shitttttt he's going live.

Katz: You can have infinite surface area with finite volume: Gabriel's horn. Take the hyperbola $y = \frac{1}{x}$ and generate a surface of revolution around the x axis.

The volume is finite, converging to π:

$$V = \int_1^\infty \pi \frac{1}{x}^2 \, dx = \pi \int_1^\infty \frac{1}{x^2} \, dx = \pi$$

but the surface area goes to infinity:

$$S = \int_1^\infty 2\pi y \sqrt{1 + y''} \, dx > 2\pi \int_1^\infty y \, dx = 2\pi \int_1^\infty \frac{1}{x} \, dx = \infty$$

You can have infinite surface area with zero volume: the Menger sponge.

Take a cube. Divide each face into nine cubes with depth ⅓ the cube length. Remove the center cube from each face, and the cube's center cube—seven total— leaving you with $\frac{20}{27}$. Now you repeat that for each cube you have left. The volume approaches 0, while the surface area grows without bound:

$$V = \left(\frac{20}{27}\right)^n, \; S = 2\left(\frac{20}{9}\right)^n + 4\left(\frac{8}{9}\right)^n$$

You know what a Möbius strip is, right?

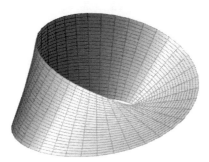

Oriana: [semi-irritated] Of course.
Katz: [obliviously] A Möbius strip is a non-orientable surface with a single boundary. If you take two of them into four dimensions and join the edges, you get a Klein bottle.

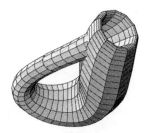

Oriana: [squints] That thing looks like a bong.

Katz: I assure you, they're topologically distinct. It's non-orientable—you can move a chiral object around the surface, and it'll become its mirror image, just like the Möbius strip. But it has no boundary, and no volume. The Möbius strip is to the torus as the Klein bottle is to the sphere, more or less.

Oriana: [dismissively] But you can't have a universe of zero volume. It has volume. Thus, it's not such a topology. You can't recurse infinitely in real life.

Katz: Unless it's tail recursion. Oh man, me and Bolaño once were smoking DMT at Devesh's, we were younnnnng, and he busted out this theory of Dante describing the universe as a 3-sphere, and it blew my fucking mind. Say what you will about Bolaño, he's one smart motherfucker.

Oriana: What I'll say is that he sucks.

Katz: I am not denying it.

Oriana: Why do you still hang out with him? He's an asshole.

Katz: We've been friends for a long time. There's a lot of state there. We've also still got numerous mutual interests that would be difficult to unwind.

Oriana: [skeptical] "Mutual interests."

Katz: Yeah, mutual interests.

Oriana: What was up the other day when he said that thing about "x86 being incompatible with the human vagina?" Even you looked offended.

Katz: Well, it was a stupid fucking thing to say. And yeah it was kind of offensive because that kind of shit is supposedly what makes women leave the CS pipeline, and you're like "no one would say stupid shit like that," and then he drops it. Makes us all look bad.

Oriana: [dryly] I was not thinking of the offense to brogrammers.

Katz: [sheepish] Fair enough, heh. Sorry.

Oriana: You, my love, live a struggle between your good essence, long performatively subdued, now suppressed by habit, and your indifference. Bolaño meanwhile is a heart of cold malevolence in conflict with its own flippancy. He brings out the worst in you.

Katz: He is my foil as you are my complement. Darling, it's sweet; you think you know how crazy I am.

Oriana: For him there will be no absolution, only hell or void.

Katz: Do you still care about dark energy?

Oriana: You were just at "it expands, but not into anything."

Katz: It's the sense of distance that's expanding, the metric. Oooh! Consider this: the universe might be infinite in size; we don't know. But even if it is, it's still expanding! But what could an infinite universe expand into, given that it's already everything? Just like the reals: expand inwards. Countable vs. uncountable infinity of space, kinda.

Oriana: Oh, that makes sense actually!

Katz: Which makes one wonder whether such expansion works in a discrete spacetime. So Ptolemy has the prevailing model worldwide for a millennium, thanks in large part to loudmouthed Aristotle. Then Copernicus drops *De revolutionibus orbium coelestium,* and promptly dies. The main thing people liked about Copernicus's model was that it restored uniform circular motion, actually. Then Kepler demonstrates elliptical orbits with varying velocity, using Brahe's observations, so detailed no one could argue. Galileo shows moons orbiting Jupiter, and rotation of the sun via sunspots. Newton did his thing.

Oriana: Is Newton the GOAT?

Katz: He's right up there for sure.

Oriana: Better than Hawking?

Katz: The media turned Hawking into a hero because they could sell his wheelchair and voicebox. I mean, he did a few good calculations once, but his books are real pieces of shit. His explanation of his eponymous radiation, about two particles forming at the border of a black hole, is nonsense no matter how many pop science books repeat it. Penrose is better. Fermi was better. von Neumann was better. Einstein was better. Gell-Mann. Salam. Bardeen. Schrödinger, Feynman, Dirac, Rovelli, 't Hooft, Zeldovich, Weinberg, Bethe, Smolin, hell I'd take gadfly Luboš Motl in a physics fight.

Oriana: Or any other kind of fight, I guess. [Hawking voice] Suck. a. dick. dumb. shit. I'll. run. you. over.

Katz: [laughs] I mean he's not a charlatan like Michio Kaku.

Oriana: Japanese Jesus!

Katz: Yeah that guy has gone off the reservation. So these all assumed a static universe, infinite in space and time. But there were problems with this assumption: you have the paradox that if there are an infinite number of stars, the sky ought be bright wherever you look. Then Einstein comes along with general relativity, and doesn't want to look like a dumbass, and everyone is still thinking "static universe," Einstein is hoping to conform to that interpretation. But it suggests that a universe containing matter is going to collapse. He adds a constant to offset this contraction, $\Lambda_E = \frac{4\pi G\rho}{c^2}$, where ρ is the energy density of the attracting matter. Radius of curvature R_E is then $\Lambda_E^{-1/2} = \frac{c}{\sqrt{4\pi G\rho}}$, so that's a spherical universe: finite, but boundless.

Oriana: Finite but boundless. I don't walk off the end no matter how far I walk, but things start to repeat.

Katz: You've got it. So Einstein has this vacuum energy perfectly tuned to match the inward draw of gravity. But other people quickly start showing that general relativity is perfectly compatible with a dynamic universe. Friedmann says "let's assume an isotropic, homogeneous universe." This is the "cosmological principle," of more shortly. They add to that "of constant curvature."

De...coelestium: On the Revolutions of the Celestial Spheres (1543)

This restricts you to simple manifolds: elliptical, flat, or hyperbolic space. So your curvature is constant, and your distribution of matter and radiation are constant.

Oriana: But. They're not?

Katz: Indeed. FLRW—those are the equations from Friedmann and pals—is only a first approximation to cosmological equations of state. But they submit to an analytic treatment of Einstein's field equations, and you can presumably perturb those solutions to account for real distribution of matter. You're correct, though. They're not constant. Hold on to that thought.

Oriana: Can you repack the bong?

Katz: Of course. Now this is the 1920s. They still don't know whether everything is contained in the Milky Way or not.

Oriana: But the Milky Way is just one galaxy!

Katz: They didn't know about galaxies yet.

Oriana: Then how could they be talking about the expansion of the Universe?

Katz: A Universe containing only the Milky Way can still expand.

Oriana: But their facts were all wrong!

Katz: The geometric and physical arguments hold. Our facts might be all wrong. You've heard the term "observable universe?" That's the region close enough for light to have been able to reach us. If you're far enough, we're completely unable to perceive you. And shit is leaving our observable universe all the time. Some shit is entering it, because we've had more time. But other shit is leaving due to the expansion of the metric. So while Shapley and Curtis are arguing over the size of the Universe, Hubble is over at Mount Wilson outside Pasadena. My dad and I once went to LA and tried to go there; it was an hour driving around a mountain, only to find out they were closed. It was harder to get information back then. Cool of my dad, though; we didn't do much stuff like that. So he's got the biggest telescope in the world at the time, and he's looking at these things called Cepheid variable stars. They pulse, though don't confuse them with pulsars. Henrietta Leavitt derives a relationship between pulse period and luminosity. So just by looking at the period, you can determine the expected luminosity. Luminosity decreases over distance, but period does not.

Oriana: So Hubble was able to determine that some of these pulsing stars are farther away than the span of the Milky Way?

Katz: Yes! And furthermore, that these stars are moving away from us. And that the farther away they are, the faster they're moving.

Oriana: Doesn't that put us at the center of the Universe?

Katz: No. It would if they were themselves moving. But if space is expanding, everyone sees everyone else moving away.

Oriana: Bullshit. If Galaxy A is here, and Galaxy B is here, and Galaxy C is between them, how can both A and B see C moving away?

Katz: They couldn't if C was itself moving. But it's not that C is moving; it's that space is expanding between A and C and between B and C. Scrunch up a ribbon. Mark three positions on the ribbon. Now start pulling it taut. Your positions aren't moving on the ribbon, but they're getting further away from one another as the ribbon straightens back out. This isn't a perfect illustration because the Universe isn't folded up like that, but you get it?

Oriana: [slowly] Yeah.

Katz: So the Universe is expanding. And the thing with Cepheids happens again with RR Lyrae stars and Type Ia supernovae. You get a "cosmic distance ladder" where you can check distances through different paths. And this is used to derive the Hubble value, which you'll hear called a constant, but is actually a function of time, and it defines how quickly things are receding from us. It's important to know that only gravitationally unbound things are subject to this expansion. Like, the members of the Local Group are not receding.

Oriana: Why not?

Katz: Their gravity overcomes the expansion. The FLRW metric only applies to a homogeneous region, remember, not a lumpy gravitationally bound one. It's inapplicable there.

Oriana: If gravity overcomes the expansion, won't the Local Group collapse?

Katz: [points skyward] Here Comes Everybody. Andromeda first. Milkdromeda in 4.5 gigayears. All of the Local Group in 150.

Oriana: So because everything is expanding away from us, they needed dark energy? Doesn't the Big Bang explain that by itself?

Katz: Getting there! So the Big Bang only gets conjectured around this time, by Lemaître, the L in FLRW. It wasn't named that until Hoyle in the late 1940s. But there's a rival theory: steady state. There were others, too, but steady state and Big Bang were the two big ones going into the 1950s. Steady state said "the Universe is expanding, but new matter is constantly being created, so the average density remains the same."

Oriana: That's stupid. Why did anyone think that?

Katz: One, they hadn't grown up knowing there was a Big Bang, nor all of the evidence we have for it now. Two, a Big Bang is a singularity. It suggests a start to time. People didn't like that; it suggests a question: what came before?

Oriana: One would think that question already asked.

Katz: Not by science.

Oriana: [dubiously] I guess.

Katz: Saying "there is a start to the Universe" conflicted with the Church, got them all riled up. If you say "there is a start to the Universe," people are going to ask "what came before?" An eternal Universe doesn't admit that question.

Oriana: It still admits "how was the Universe created?"

Katz: No it doesn't. The Universe is eternal. That's what eternal means.

Oriana: Hrmmm.

Katz: Well regardless, Penzias and Wilson win history's cheesiest Nobel Prize for not understanding some noise in their horn antenna. That was the cosmic background radiation, a perfect blackbody peaking at 2.725 K, 160.23 GHz microwave radiation.

Oriana: [disbelieving] Don't you and Chris Hitchens hate Mother Theresa?

Katz: [dismissive] That shit doesn't count. The Peace Prize is garbage. So with the background, that seems to pretty much confirm the Big Bang. Since then, you have *e.g.* Big Bang nucleosynthesis, which checks out with actual distributions of matter that we see. Then Guth and the gang come up with inflation, mostly as a way to justify the cosmological principle in an expanding universe. In 1998 we learn that not only are other clusters receding from us, and not only are they receding more quickly the farther away they are, but this is all accelerating. This is determined from supernovae and cosmic background radiation. That's obviously not resulting the Big Bang. The easiest way FLRW explains this is a positive cosmological constant. It's brought back and called dark energy.

Oriana: From the end to the beginning, now back to the end. So dark energy is a force which drives accelerating expansion of the universe. Why do they say it "makes up" two thirds of the universe?

Katz: Because that's a measure of energy density.

Oriana: And matter is energy, yeah, makes sense. So why is the amount made up of dark energy increasing if it's constant?

Katz: Because it's constant density, but the volume is increasing.

Oriana: So it's creating more space, and that space gets free dark energy? How is that not perpetual motion?

Katz: Ahh. One of the reasons I don't love the dark energy concept. The math all makes sense, but so does the Banach–Tarski paradox.

Oriana: Not even going to ask. So what else do you dislike?

Katz: There's a critical density for FLRW universes that defines your geometry. To be flat, your actual density needs equal that critical density. Divergences from zero are divergences from flatness, of which we have no indications. Dark energy just happens to precisely add up to the other two (dark matter and baryonic, normal matter) to equal zero. It reeks of finetuning. It assumes the cosmological principle, which to me always seemed kinda ehh, and recent evidence is calling into question. I don't like how inflation is used as a way to explain why we don't see magnetic monopoles, when they probably just don't exist. A universe of infinite volume already seems horseshit to me, but when you combine that with a cosmological constant, things seem to really go off the rails; how is that not infinite energy? There's something called the zero point energy of the vacuum, and it's the most reasonable source of the cosmological constant, except it's like a hundred twenty orders of magnitude off from what we see. We're gonna one day realize, whoops, someone made an invalid cast.

✳ ✳ ✳ ✳ ✳ ✳ ✳ ✳ ✳

Oriana: What do you most dislike about yourself?

Katz: [pauses, then slowly] I'm starting to suspect that I ultimately get off on betrayal. Like, that I meet these wonderful women and fall in love with them but it's all just to get to the point where I can viciously sell them out and just psychologically gut them, then help put them back together to do it again.

Oriana: Ummmm.

Katz: [brightens] Maybe not, though!

✳ ✳ ✳ ✳ ✳ ✳ ✳ ✳ ✳

Oriana: You're pretty Libertarian, right?

Katz: [warily] What "are" you, my love? Be sure to use only one word.

Oriana: I'm leftist to the degree that I don't think we ought have people dying in the streets just so someone can have another few million dollars.

Katz: Some people want to die in the streets. In fact, if we want to get into political philosophy, I only believe in one human right: the right to suicide. More generally, the right to exit.

Oriana: Alright, I don't think we ought have people dying in the streets who don't wish to do so. And people who want to die in the streets ought get the mental help they need.

Katz: I reject prisons as ineffective for rehabilitation, expensive, destructive to the soul of their workforces, and corrosive to society. I absolutely reject investing any power structure, elected, appointed, credentialed, whatever, with the authority to declare another human insane.

Oriana: What if they're hitting people with bricks in the street?

Katz: Then shoot them.

Oriana: Shoot them.

Katz: I support justice via self-assembling *posse comitatus* on whatever local scale allows concordance.

Oriana: So a couple bros get together, drink forties, get in their truck and shoot people in the street.

Katz: Wait, now there are people, multiple, lobbing bricks?

Oriana: I assume they're going to take out anyone they see.

Katz: That's not a posse. That's hurling bricks, with guns and a truck.

Oriana: Who decides which is which?

Katz: Concordance at the smallest possible local scale!

Oriana: Which means what?

Katz: [sighs] I'm an anarchist. I don't really support political structures beyond the local. Authority ought be selforganizing, and automatically expire.

Oriana: What about abortion? You're surely prochoice, right? Don't want the government up in wombs?

Katz: Having no womb, my opinion is of little consequence. Regardless, under my system, you wouldn't speak of being "pro-choice" or "pro-life" on some kind of federal level. You can get an abortion wherever. Whether the people around you think you just threw a brick at your baby is a function of the people with whom you surround yourself.

Oriana: What about a girl whose parents don't support it, and whose town doesn't support it, but she needs one?

Katz: Oriana, beautiful, if she can get a baby put in her without her parents knowing, she can have the baby taken out. I've always thought that it would be a lot more useful to learn how to whip up a batch of mifepristone than to try to change voting patterns. But the real question you're asking me, if I must answer, of course I support the right to have an abortion. I support the right to sell an upscale VIP abortion experience with exclusive artwork, bottled water, concierge service and special surprise guests like The Weeknd and Fergie. I support promotions involving a free abortion after ten Arby's sandwiches.

Oriana: Good.

Katz: I support the right to kill your child pretty much however long you're supporting them. If they want autonomy, they can pay taxes.

Oriana: [exasperated] Jesus fucking Christ. Ridiculous.

Katz: Too many are born: for the superfluous ones was the state devised!

Oriana: What other ridiculous opinions of yours ought I know about?

Katz: Well, back to your hypothetical streetcorpses. Provide health care to those who cannot pay; in exchange, we get to do research on you.

Oriana: Of course.

Katz: I'm not saying, like, vivisect people for kicks. I'm saying, let's say we have a new drug for bladder cancer. We're not sure whether it'll work. You come in wanting drugs. Congratulations on assisting science! You just signed up as a test subject.

Oriana: But you don't know the possible sideeffects!

Katz: They've got motherfucking bladder cancer; who cares about dry mouth?

Oriana: What about all the healthcare that's not in the form of a pharmaceutical? What about nutrition?

Katz: Honey, honey. This is the problem with government. You try to come up with all the possible problems you can solve, because it's really about an allconsuming hunger for power, but really you have no idea what solving them looks like. Let's say you get everyone proper nutrition. Get everybody living to ninety by default. Now you need twice the geriatric care, since you're also promising to solve that problem. And you're putting out more carbon.

Oriana: So don't feed poor kids because they'll put out carbon.

Katz: Hey great everybody's well-fed but that just means we sink faster now that the ocean is up to our piggy little bellies. You can't worry about all this shit. You're not smart enough to fix it, and some of it's unfixable.

Oriana: So what political issues *do* matter to you?

Katz: Occupational licensing sends me into dyspeptic fury. "Federal airspace" is unconstitutional. We ought use the metric system. Other than that, I cultivate my garden.

Oriana: Did you just *Candide* me, you son of a bitch?

Katz: [sweetly] I call my penis Pangloss because when it's in you, it's the best of all possible worlds.

Oriana: [rolls eyes]

Katz: [hurriedly] I mean for my penis, not you. I'm not that conceited. I was trying to be sweet.

Oriana: You're the sweetest. It is a pretty great cock.

Katz: I wouldn't mind trying to impregnate you. You're welcome to abort it if you'd like, especially if that turns you on.

Oriana: [visibly taken aback] If abortions turn me on?

Katz: Well or even just thinking about them, like if at the moment I come you think "he might be creating new life within me, life I can then snuff out at my leisure." I don't know; I figure for a govmax statist like you, control over life itself is the ultimate turnon? Like that *Itchy & Scratchy* where the Cloning Machine outputs directly into the Killing Machine. I'm guessing by your face that this is erroneous.

Oriana: You're a very strange man, Sherman Katz.

Katz: And you're the most wonderful, extraordinary woman I've ever met, Oriana Marino. Would you please put on the glasses, tiara, and sparkly shoes?

Oriana: [taking him by hand] I know what you like.

Katz: [singsong] I like youuuuuuuuuuuuu.

* * * * * * * *

Oriana: Do you think there's some kind of accomplishment or achievement that would satisfy you, that would give your life a perceived purpose?

Katz: [pauses] I'd like to smash the universe's stack.

Oriana: Hrmmm?

Katz: If you ever see CALCULATOR.EXE in the sky, I'll be behind a terminal somewhere, giggling like a schoolgirl.

Oriana: So the answer is no.

Katz: This universe runs on some substrate, implemented in some kind of code. Discover it, exploit it. Infiltrate, destroy, rebuild.

Oriana: I've never felt Bostrom's simulation hypothesis to be any real advance over your bogstandard First Mover.

Katz: 100% agreed. It's like when *The Matrix* came out and suddenly everyone on campus was walking around in trenchcoats with their minds blown. "Man, have you ever thought this might not be...*real?*" Like no one there had ever heard of Plato's cave.

Oriana: Nor the *Deus deceptor* of Descartes. Or Putnam's brain in a vat?

Katz: Are you familiar with Boltzmann brains?

Oriana: [heavy sigh] Dumbest shit I've ever heard.

Katz: Agreed, but then how do you deal with Poincaré's recurrence theorem?

Oriana: The whole concept is based on the busted measurement concept in quantum mechanics, so far as I understand, which y'all just work with QM and accept this handwavey collapse of the wavefunction, and I don't understand how you can take yourselves seriously. You're basically astrologists.

Katz: Yeah I'm a consistent histories guy, and a Novikov consistency guy. But who knows. Thinking about that stuff is like wondering why there's something instead of nothing. It doesn't get you anywhere.

* * * * * * * *

Marelli: I just saw this weird mess of a movie. It was really beautiful, though, and funny, and luscious. Have you seen *Donnie Darko?*

Oriana: Of course! Love me some Richard Kelly.

Marelli: This was his second movie, *Southland Tales*—

Oriana: Yes! So underrated! One of the best movies from the last decade! Way better than *Donnie Darko,* and I loved *Donnie Darko.* One of my very favorites. We ought eat mushrooms sometime and watch it together.

Marelli: I'd love that!

Oriana: Let's do it soon! So how are you doing? I'm so glad you could meet me.

Marelli: I'm doing really well. I've published two first-author papers in the past six months. Some research I did when I was going out with Sherman is really paying off. It ties together with what I was doing at Berkeley beautifully.

Oriana: You seem so happy. You beamed as you described it.

Marelli: The pieces were always there. I'm finally putting them together.

Oriana: Wonderful. I walked for Journalism last semester, and I get Philosophy this one. And I started an MFA in [drums table] poetry. Making myself more marketable by the day.

Marelli: Wow. What motivated that?

Oriana: I submitted some work on a whim, and they offered me funding. They said I'd be the first poetry MFA they'd ever funded. Who knows if that's true.

Marelli: Holy shit! Like, with stipend and everything?

Oriana: Oh not not at all, just tuition. It's like a total of $45,000.

Marelli: Still, to be the only one! It's not like they fund me that much better.

Oriana: Really?

Marelli: Well, tuition, housing stipend, living stipend, lit stipend, lab stipend, salary for GRA, umm there's medical insurance on that. Maybe significantly more than $45,000. That's per semester?

Oriana: No. Total thing over three semesters.

Marelli: Oh. Well, yeah, they're pretty different then. Still! Congratulations! Are you hoping to do anything with that?

Oriana: Write poetry. Not professionally. I'll be looking for journalism type jobs while I do so.

Marelli: Like at a paper?

Oriana: Print journalism isn't doing so hot. More likely I'll get into technical writing? That seems a pretty upwardly mobile career track, and if you get in a tech company, that's a pleasantly loose environment. In the end I'll almost certainly be writing books. And having kids.

Marelli: [surprised] Are you looking to have kids soon?

Oriana: We're not trying in any planned way, but I'm off birth control.

Marelli: And Katz is down with it?

Oriana: He was enthusiastic! We're both a little scared, but if it happens, it happens.

Marelli: Would you stay in school?

Oriana: Sherman actually says he'd effectively retire. He intends to be a pretty involved parent, or at least claims to. I'm pleased with the prospect. I'll be there to water down his insanity.

Marelli: [uncomfortably] Is he still...into a lot of shit?

Oriana: To what shit do you refer? The meth?

Marelli: [relieved] Well, that, among other things.

Oriana: I have brought up that methamphetamine is probably not ideal for childraising. He pointed out that it might actually be very useful early on, with which I couldn't disagree. We'll see how things go. He's gotta stop sometime.

Marelli: Does he?

Oriana: I told him I wasn't having a child with someone whose heart could blow up at any time without some guarantees, and watched him set me as a beneficiary on several accounts. So I've got that going for me.

Marelli: You know [pauses, drops voice] a lot of his money is not in banks, right? Like, he gets into some shit.

Oriana: Erica, let me tell you a secret. I love dating a supervillain.

Marelli: I did too. Until I didn't.

* * * * * * * *

Oriana: Have you heard of something called Bitcoin?

Katz: [laughs] Yeah. I actually mined a few hundred Bitcoin last year.

Oriana: What'd you do with them?

Katz: It was worth a total of about $4. I traded them to a dude for a signed copy of *My Cousin, My Gastroenterologist.*

Oriana: Mark Leyner's the shit!

Katz: Fuck yeah. DFW hates him, lame.

Oriana: So what's the point of Bitcoin? Is it just a way to do illegal shit?

Katz: It's actually not as good for that as people think—there's a tremendous amount of detail publicly available on the flow of cryptocurrency. That's, like, the point: you have a "distributed ledger" that's maintained by the network in common, and tracks every exchange of a coin. If you don't track spending and earning information, you can't know what anyone has, right? So everyone knows how much you—a given key, anyway—has, how much you've spent, and who you exchanged it with.

Oriana: But how do they connect that up with a real person?

Katz: When it enters the real banking system.

Oriana: But transactions entirely within the network are anonymous?

Katz: Not "anonymous," but associated with a key.

Oriana: And leaving the network deanonymizes that key.

Katz: Well it's going to go to some bank, right? And that bank knows who's connected to a given account.

Oriana: So what's the point?

Katz: It's nerdy as shit. Your crazy Libertarians, the gold standard guys, are like "woo fuck fiat currency!" You can exchange value without the involvement of an external clearinghouse like VISA, though you pay an overhead for every transaction you post to the blockchain. Some people are really enamored of the distributed ledger as a data structure, because they're fucking stupid. It's incredibly wasteful of power, just shockingly grotesque, dinosaurs getting burned at high rates even now, prior to any serious use. Like I said, I basically gave away hundreds of them, and doubt I'll ever regret that.

Oriana: I want one.

Katz: Sure baby, I'll mine you a few. You'll proceed to lose your key, and they'll disappear into the pool of unusable coins. That's fine, though, because they'll be worth pennies.

Oriana: You don't see them gaining value?

Katz: Only if it comes to the attention of the greedy and gullible worldwide. How'd you hear about Bitcoin?

Oriana: [smiles] I know a few things.

✳ ✳ ✳ ✳ ✳ ✳ ✳ ✳

Oriana: These cramps are killing me. Do you have any Advil around here?

Katz: I'm sure I do. I think Aleve gelcaps?

Oriana: Oh perfect, will you get two for me? Thanks! [Katz returns with two gelcaps and a water] You're my sweet hero. [Oriana dryswallows the gelcaps, then drains the water]

Katz: Is that the worst part of the whole menstruation thing?

Oriana: It all depends. Some ladies have very easy periods, some rough ones; some are very regular, some less so; some have no periods at all. I suppose the worst thing about a period is if you're struggling to have a child, and you're hoping, especially if you're late, thinking "may this be the one," but then nope! Kertwang! There's your month's chance failed. Is it your fault? Is something wrong with you? Will it ever happen for you? What does this mean for you as a woman? As a mother? As a partner?

Katz: Fertility seems an important subject for you.

Oriana: It's an important subject to every woman. You're being constantly evaluated. The first way you're evaluated is by beauty; the second by fertility. Three and a half billion women all over the globe, hundreds of different cultures, and I'm pretty sure all of them will tell you that.

Katz: Who's evaluating you?

Oriana: As a woman? [laughs] Every motherfucker you come across, no matter how trifling and useless they might be, doyouknowwhatiamsaying? Next worst thing is bloody little chunks of *sashimi*, into your underwear. Tampon girls don't have to deal with that.

Katz: [winces] A Lucky Dragon indeed. Can this happen while I'm going down on you? I mean, it wouldn't bother me, you know I love feasting on your savory rosy cross—

Oriana: [laughs, high-fives Katz] Umami, baybee!

Katz: [high-fives] fuck yeah but I'm not sure I want to slurp down a big ol' blood clot fresh from the oven as it were.

Oriana: If it ever happens, I'll buy you a Diet Coke. What you do have to watch out for is when you think you've just got to, you know [looks around] queef, but then you bear down and karsclump! out falls your endometrial lining into your underwear. I call it a quart, like a shart.

Katz: Good Lord. And that's pronounced like "quark," not "quart?"

Oriana: Yeah, its name is taken from a line of *Finnegan's Wake*: "Three quarts for Mother, Mark!" I thought you loved Joyce? [smiles]

Katz: [smiling] I thought that was the line Murray Gell-Mann used for quarks? "Three quarks for Muster Mark!"?

Oriana: The *Wake* is big enough for both lines. [smiles wide]

---

sashimi: 刺身 "pierced body" fish killed via *ikejime*
ikejime: 活け締め insertion of a spike into the hindbrain

26   feedback loops are Bad Shit, to be Avoided

Things came to a head in July.

Atlanta's July flirts with horror, comparable to Austin, far worse (though less fatal) than the great western sweeps of desert between oasis cities.

Draw a line heading west through NYC, according to Köppen the north-ernmost "humid subtropical" city in America. Hug the Lakes, turning up to consume Chicago and Milwaukee, then it's a straight line through Sioux Falls until the Rockies force a diversion south. Cut Texas right in half; you know you always wanted to. There are your humid subtropics and humid continental regions, less the tropical monsoon band of South Florida. Miami's humidity is to some degree offset by the Gulf Stream, though a rising sea's hurricanes are doing it no favors. Admittedly, no American polis has thrown down the gauntlet contra thermoregulation quite so brazenly as oilmad Houston, nor the sunken city of New Orleans, which manages somehow to broil you without the sun ever seeming to rise.

Almost all the way up to Pierre, in St. Louis and Des Moines and even New York, July days break 95 easy. Oklahoma City and Lincoln and swaths of Texas are on the wrong side of 100 by noon. The reason why you'll change shirts every time you go outside in Atlanta (or Memphis, or Orlando) is their humidity, pushing 90% in July mornings. On all points of its inland compass, mile upon square mile of dense tree coverage form Atlanta's greatest natural resource, a canopy approaching 50%. Besides spring pollen counts that set new records each year in an immediately yellowing arboreal bukkake is efficiency of sweat—the ratio of secreted to evaporated perspiration—remains near 90% at a relative humidity of 40%. It falls off rapidly from there: the 10% difference between 65% and 75% humidity translates to about a 25% degradation in sweat effectiveness. Clothes rapidly grow soggy, and life becomes miserable.

Mixing this with powerful stimulants was a matter of experience and a deft touch. You were feeling slow and stupid, but the solution was almost always water. Wake up wet and salty, a picture already of torpid dehydration. Cut out a line, but seem to feel worse. That's a positive feedback loop straight to heat stroke or amphetamine psychosis. Positive feedback loops, remember, are Bad Shit, to be Avoided.

Feedback occurs whenever a system's output is routed (perhaps indirectly) to its input. In the language of cybernetics, this is a closed-loop controller. Connect a microphone next to an amplifier, and place the microphone nearby. Eventually it picks up noise, perhaps a buzzing flying thing nearby, perhaps a shout in the street. This is reproduced through the amplifier. The sound reaches the microphone, undergoes further gain, and is emitted. Long after the original source has grown silent, this system perpetuates itself. It is louder than the source from the beginning, and very quickly becomes as loud a noise as the amplifier can produce, resulting in clipping or even damage to the equipment.

Another example is human parturition, a full-duplex hormonal dialogue involving paracrine and autocrine events (most animals enter labor based off levels of circulating hormones, a purely endocrine signaling system). For the duration of pregnancy, progesterone inhibits lactation, directly works against uterine contractions by decreasing contractility of the smooth muscle there, and suppresses the trophoblast's corticotropin-releasing hormone. Mifepristone (the abortifacient RU-486) operates as a progesterone antagonist, blocking its myometrial and endometrial effects; the decidua degrades, the cervix softens and dilates. Reduced hCG generation following trophoblast detachment causes the corpus luteum to cease progesterone generation; there's dysmenorrhea, and rather gory humoral output, and then little Alice or Bob or nonbinary Chris is flushed back to their Creator.

In the presence of feedback, a change in some output (connected, remember, in loop to some input) can induce further change in that same output. If a change in some output results in a change in that output's first derivative, the feedback is negative, and usually self-stabilizing (an exception is if the feedback leads to oscillation). If the change results in greater change, the feedback is positive; if the gain is greater than one, growth is exponential, and control tends to be rapidly lost. Positive feedbacks are sources of inherent instability, and require external safeties if destructive runaway is to be avoided. If these safeties fail, the system enters a dangerous state. Presence of a positive feedback loop generally merits complete redesign. They are rare in biological systems: an organism possessing such a loop is typically at a competitive disadvantage, and natural selections will work against its propagation.

Posit a room with measured temperature 17.5 °C. Add an air conditioner set to the same temperature. If the room's temperature rises, the air conditioner starts operating. Ideally, it brings the temperature back down to 17.5 °C, at which point it cuts off. The air conditioner never cools the room significantly below the target, never allows the temperature to rise significantly above the target, and only runs when necessary.

Now imagine that the room temperature is sensed near the air conditioner's motor. The harder the motor runs, the more heat it generates. A random shift warms the room above a threshold. The air conditioner beings running. Perhaps the air filter is clogged, and thus it must immediately work hard. The sensor, near the motor, reports a higher temperature, though a more thoughtfully placed sensor would report a cooling effect. The motor works harder, longer, attempting to resolve the situation. Eventually it burns out. Perhaps it is prevented from running longer than P without a break B. Now the room gets very cold over the course of P, well below the target. Over the next period B, the room warms back up. The air conditioner will not run again until the temperature reaches the threshold condition, at which point it will run for a full P. The room thus always stays colder than the desired temperature, sometimes significantly so, operating in a period not necessarily associated with P nor B nor their sum.

Perhaps our system is a nuclear reactor. Indeed perhaps our system is the garbage Generation II Soviet RBMK-1000, four of which were installed

---

RBMK-1000: *reaktor bolshoy moshchnosti kanalnyy* high-power channel-type reactor at *Chernobyl'skaya atomnaya elektrostantsiya* between 1977 and 1983. This led directly to the more severe of history's two Level 7 (INES) nuclear accidents, the other being Fukushima in 2011. The *Avárija na Chernóbyl'skoj AJeS* can be seen as a failure of late stage Communist governance and/or a condemnation of the RBMK-1000, but to condemn the dumbfounding RBMK-1000 is to transitively condemn Soviet Communism. The nuclear policy of the Department of Energy may be cowardly, confounding, and counterproductive, but it's at least unlikely that they would have allowed such an abominable design to fly.

Thermal plants produce electricity from heat, and represent the vast majority of power generation worldwide, especially for baseload (wind, hydro, and photovoltaic solar are nonthermal). The Carnot cycle describes ideal conversion of heat into work: its fundamental feature is the relationship of work W to difference in temperatures T_H and T_C of the thermal reservoirs:

$$W = (T_H - T_C)\Delta S = (T_H - T_C)\frac{Q_H}{T_H}$$

ΔS is entropy transferred to the system each cycle, derived from Q_H, the heat transferred to same. Since the end of the nineteenth century, thermal power generation almost universally employs a steam turbine in the Rankine cycle, involving phase shift from liquid to gas and back again. Many are combined cycle plants, making use of a high pressure gas turbine (employing the Brayton cycle) in tandem with a steam turbine working at lower pressure. A heat source raises the temperature of a heat exchanger (usually water); this also serves as coolant for the heat source. The water evaporates; the result is pressurized steam. Waste heat is released into the environment.

A nuclear plant operates on the same basic principles. Gas turbines are not typically employed, artificially limiting the thermodynamic efficiency of nuclear reactors. The reactor vessel does not require significant air intake, as is required to support combustion of hydrocarbons. There are typically at least two coolant loops: the coolant in contact with the fuel assemblies *will* see induced radioactivity due to neutron activation. Its composition and purity must thus be carefully controlled, as it will radiate while circulating. The primary heat exchanger should not become radioactive, so it must be shielded from core neutrons. These coolant loops must continue running well after the pile has been shut down due to heat arising from delayed decays.

Soviet nuclear policy led to some godawful shit, much of it presumably still unknown due to secrecy. The *Proizvodstvennoye ob'yedineniye "Mayak"* plutonium production reactors in Ozyorsk ran out of space underground a year into operation, and casually dumped 3.2 megacuries of HLW into the Techa river. No fewer than 24 downstream villages relied on the Techa for drinking water; in Metlino, levels were measured at 5 rads per hour. An open coolant cycle

---

Chernobyl'skaya atomnaya elektrostantsiya: Чернобыльская атомная электростанция
Chernobyl Nuclear Power Plant   **INES:** International Nuclear Event Scale
Avárija...AJeS: Авáрия на Чернóбыльской АЭС Chernobyl Nuclear Power Plant disaster
Proizvodstvennoye..."Mayak": Производственное объединение «Маяк»
Mayak Production Association

polluted Kyzltash Lake utterly; the smaller but closer Lake Karachay was used to hold waste too radioactive to be stored onsite. About 120 megacuries total were dumped into a lake of less than one square kilometer. In 1953, steel tanks were buried to hold liquid nuclear waste resulting from chemical processing of spent fuel. Decay heat required cooling; cooling was installed, but poorly monitored. By 1957, one of the coolers had failed. No one noticed the ammonium nitrate evaporating more and more rapidly as temperatures rose, until the container exploded with the force of 70 tons of TNT. A radiant column of radioactive gunk, about 20 megacuries, rose a kilometer into the sky over Ozyorsk. The result is today's "East Ural Radioactive Trace." Numerous cases of radiation poisoning were established, but doctors were not allowed to mention radiation in their reports. Following a drought in 1968, the lake shrunk by 70%, and wind carried away five megacuries of radioactive dust. The lake bed to a depth of more than three meters is composed almost entirely of high level waste. To this day, areas of the lake deliver lethal radiation in half an hour; it competes for most radiologically polluted place on earth.

At Andreev Bay's Naval Base 569, building #5 began to leak: bottoms of the drums used to hold solid waste were not covered in steel; groundwater was allowed to penetrate; it froze in the winter; by September thirty tons were leaked per day. Sailors with shovels casually returned the waste to the vertical steel containers which held these drums. Critical masses accumulated, fissioned themselves out, and dispersed. Fourteen complete reactors were dumped into the Barents Sea, some at depths of less than a hundred meters. K-27 with its fueled liquid metal cooled reactors was scuttled in shallow waters of the Kara Sea, where water threatens to moderate a chain reaction in the highly enriched uranium once corrosion is complete. K-219 with 16 R-27U missiles sank to the Hatteras abyssal plain in the North Atlantic. K-8 with two reactors and four nuclear torpedoes in the Bay of Biscay. K-278 with a OK-650 b-3 PWR and two nuclear torpedoes off Norway's Bear Island. Captain Suvorov ordered K-429 to periscope depth, but forgot to seal the hatches; it catastrophically flooded immediately, along with an OK-350 and eight SS-N-7s. It was towed into dry dock, where two years later it sank again.

Anatoly Alexandrov was a Russian born in Ukraine. He graduated in 1919, just after the Red Army captured Kiev. He survived the Civil War as a machine-gunner for the *Beliye*, but did not join the *byeloemigrant*. He worked with the bearded Kurchatov to defeat magnetic mines; together they moved on to the Ioffe, and then the Institute of Atomic Energy. The stamps which honor an older Alexandrov strongly suggest James Tolkan; pictures of him as a younger man resemble no one so much as Ramanujan. The Supreme Soviet had called for ambitious and broad movement forward with atomic energy, movement worthy of Lenin's great GOELRO. This struggle would stand on the shoulders of Alexandrov's RBMK, the "Soviet Reactor" (as opposed to the competing VVER,

---

Beliye: Белые Whites   **byeloemigrant:** белоэмигрант white émigrés
Ioffe: Физико-технический институт им. А. Ф. Иоффе Ioffe Physical-Technical Institute of the Russian Academy of Sciences   **GOELRO:** Государственная комиссия по электрификации России State Commission for Electrification of Russia
VVER: *vodo-vodyanoi enyergeticheskiy reaktor* water-water energetic reactor

a PWR derided as the "American Reactor").

The Soviet bomb effort spun up fourteen reactors for isotope production, twelve of them dedicated towards plutonium. Like their corresponding reactors at Hanford site (and, to be fair, some scandalous shit went down at Hanford), these were too early to have model numbers: Hanford's first plutonium factory was "B Reactor," and Mayak's was "Reactor A." The RBMK, designed from 1964 through 1966, scaled up the Obninsk AM-1 30 MWt (megawatts thermal; electricity production tends towards one third of this value) and the experimental AMB-100 and AMB-200 at Beloyarsk. It was intended to be cheaply and quickly constructed, to support fuel rod exchange at full power (important for plutonium production), and to use rugged oxide fuel pins. Completely leaving off a containment building cut the capital costs in half. Seventeen were built. Hans Bethe called the design "fundamentally faulty, having built-in instability," and his assessment of the RBMK, product of the *Period zastóya*, would be validated in April 1986. Remember it well the next time you're told infrastructure is best managed by the government.

One of the critical measures of reactor safety is the void coefficient, describing the change in reactivity as voids (usually bubbles) form in coolant and/or moderator. It is only relevant in the presence of liquids; an *e.g.* gas-cooled graphite-moderated reactor is not expected to suffer voids. The development of bubbles is usually due to steam formation, and undesirable; basic logic suggests that reactivity ought be reduced as coolant starts to boil away. A positive void coefficient indicates that reactivity increases with the formation of voids, and has become practically synonymous with the RBMK.

The PVC is not a feature of all graphite-cooled light water reactors. Recall that ^{235}U has a greater chance of fissioning when bombarded with thermalized neutrons, rather than the fast outputs of fission: this is the entire point of moderation. Mean reduction of neutron energy per collision ξ for interactions with a nucleus having atomic mass number A is:

$$\xi = 1 + \frac{(A-1)^2}{2A} \ln \frac{A-1}{A+1}$$

the collisions n necessary to reduce a neutron from E_0 to E is then:

$$n = \frac{1}{\xi}(\ln E_0 - \ln E)$$

Thermalizing a 2 MeV neutron requires:

Moderator	ξ	n
^1H (protium)	1	15
P_2O (light water)	0.920	16
^2H (deuterium)	0.750	20
D_2O (heavy water)	0.509	29
^{238}U	0.008	1812

AM-1: Атом Мирный *Atom Mirny* peaceful atom
Period zastóya: Пери́од засто́я Era of Stagnation

Elastic collision mathematics inform us that an ideal moderator would have mass equal to that of the incoming neutron. Light water thus reduces neutron energy more effectively than heavy water. It is at the same time a thirstier neutron sink: protium captures a neutron to become deuterium more readily than deuterium becomes tritium. The cross section of absorption is sufficiently low compared to the ξ-weighted cross section of scattering that light water can be used as a moderator, though it is far less efficient than heavy water.

At Hanford and Sellafield, coolant water played an integral role in neutron moderation. Voids in the American and British reactors would result in a net loss of moderation, and an immediate drop in reactivity—negative feedback. The RBMK was stuffed tightly with sufficient graphite to optimally moderate all its own. Coolant played no necessary moderating role; absorption instead had a net negative effect on reactivity. As coolant was lost, fewer neutrons were removed from the pile, but moderation remained just as effective. Reactivity increased, and the additional heat boiled away more coolant. Further loss of coolant led to further increase in reactivity. This is a classic and catastrophic example of a positive feedback loop.

The RBMK-1000 was a second attempt; NIKIET's original proposal had been rejected as unsound by Sredmash (the Ministry of Medium Machine Building). The Kurchatov Institute declared the design too dangerous to be put into civilian operation. Nonetheless, GOSPLAN had called for reactors, and there would be reactors. Redesigning the RBMK, a task made more difficult and errorprone by a lack of computing power, took longer than expected. When the new plans were finalized in 1968, Sredmash saved time by skipping the planned prototype stage. The BelAZs began rolling, and RBMK cylinders began to go up in Leningrad, Kursk, and Prypiat. This last was the ninth *atomgrad,* named after the nearby river (a tributary of the Dnieper), founded 1970-02-04, declared a city by the Supreme Soviet in 1979, and evacuated to Slavutych 1986-04-27.

ChNPP (originally the V. I. Lenin Atomic Energy Station) was originally intended to sport six RBMKs, a total of 5800 MW that would have made it one of the most powerful nuclear plants in the world (KEPCO's Kori and Hanul lead for now, though TEPCO's Kashiwazaki-Kariwa, shut down in 2011, might retake its top spot once brought back online). It was largely an ongoing copy of the Kursk АЭС (construction at Kursk began in 1971, one year before Chernobyl; it would likewise eventually seat four of six intended RBMKs), and a massive facility. Walking its deaerator corridor required a brisk ten minutes. Overlooking the central square, ten stories of apartments were topped with giant white letters forming the motto of the Ministry of Energy and Electrification's *atomshchiki: Hai bude atom robitnikom, a ne soldatom!* Five hundred meters away from Control Room Number Four encamped the ZIL-130s, ZIL-131s, and men of Paramilitary Fire Brigade Number Two.

NIKIET: N. A. Dollezhal Scientific Research and Design Institute of Energy Technologies
BelAZ: Беларускі аўтамабільны завод Belarusian Automobile Plant
KEPCO: 한국전력공사 Korea Electric Power Corporation
TEPCO: 東京電力ホールディングス株式会社 Tokyo Electric Power Company Holdings
atomshchiki: а́томщики nuclear scientists
Hai...soldatom: Let the atom be a worker, not a soldier

Some of the RBMK's problems were known from the paper design. Others came to light only after the Leningrad units had seen first fission. It was quickly apparent that the modeled performance differed profoundly from realized behavior. The colossal size meant behavior diverged wildly in different regions of the reactor. Radiation detection proved unreliable at low power levels, such as those seen in startup and shutdown. The emergency shutdown took its sweet time to insert the 211 neutron absorbing boron control rods, and lacked its own power. Sloppy craftsmanship combined with byzantine geometry led to channels that wouldn't admit or release warm fuel assemblies, nonfunctional flow meters in the coolant stream, and uncontrollable valves. The first partial meltdown came 1975-11-30 in Leningrad Unit One as it was being brought back online following scheduled maintenance. Sredmash dismissed its own investigators' findings. Before Unit One had finished releasing radiation over the Gulf of Finland, 1975-11-30, final approval was given for Chernobyl Units Three and Four. Meanwhile, an officer of the Soviet Nuclear Navy sat at the desk of Control Room One, and exclaimed, dismayed, "how can you possibly control this hulking piece of shit, and what is it doing in civilian use?" A NIKIET study in 1980 identified nine major design failings, and stressed that the reactor could become uncontrollable not only in rare circumstances, but during day-to-day operations. The report was immediately marked confidential; plant operators were not informed.

On 1982-09-09, Nikolai Steinberg saw steam rising from the vent stack of Units One and Two. Nuclear power plants steaming where steam is not expected is Bad Shit, to be Avoided. He called through to the control room, and the supervisor hung up on him after angrily dismissing the report. The next day, Director Brukhanov and KGB officers insisted that there had been "a minor issue," but no release of radiation. Foam spread on the streets by decontamination trucks suggested otherwise. In truth, there had been a partial meltdown in Unit One thanks to a broken cooling valve. Like Leningrad, the incident occurred while bringing the reactor back online. Like Leningrad, the report was marked top secret, and kept even from plant engineers. A generator at Metsamor One blew up in October 1982, burning down the turbine hall. A relief valve disintegrated during startup at Balakovo One, steaming to death fourteen comrades. During startup of Chernobyl Four and Ignalina One, it was first noticed that insertion of the control rods led to an *increase* in reactivity for several seconds. Investigation revealed that insertion of the AZ-5 emergency control rods with fewer than seven normal rods inserted would lead to destruction of the reactor. Amazingly, this was relegated to a note in an updated version of the operating manual, as a directive to keep a minimum number of rods fully inserted at all times. Accidents at Soviet nuclear stations continued to be treated as state secrets in violation of IAEA treaties, sound engineering judgment, common sense, and human decency.

The disgraceful story of Friday, April 25 1986 has been told elsewhere, including quite admirably by Higginbotham in *Midnight in Chernobyl (2019)*. An almost unbelievable string of neglectful and procacious decisions together with a secretive engineering culture and an unforgivable design combined to produce history's worst nuclear accident, one which set back the nuclear industry worldwide and contributed to the downfall of the Soviet empire. A test had been scheduled for that afternoon, but disturbances elsewhere in the Kiev grid kept ChNPP at full power until the late evening.

Eugène Ionesco's Great Balls of Fire
ChNPP Control Room Four 1986-04-25

Dramatis personae:
ANATOLY DYATLOV (Deputy Chief Engineer)
ALEXANDER AKIMOV (Foreman)
LEONID TOPTUNOV (Senior Reactor Control Engineer)
ЧЕТЬЫРЕ (CHETYRE) (an RBMK-1000 reactor)
ENRICO FERMI (Dean of the Roman Rota, deceased)
SLOVEN, RUS, BABA YAGA, AND IDOLISHCHE (goats)

Fermi: Four cores, alike in dignity,
in Ukraine, where we lay our scene,
split atoms for their energy,
and daughter products most unclean.
Nonworking valves and sensors defective,
bloated with xenon, pipes all corroded,
we curse them now with Marxist invective:
the fourth goddamned reactor exploded.
Forty thousand comrades all whisked away,
evacuated in trucks and in tanks;
maggie and milly and olga and may
no longer go down to Prypiat's banks.
May RBMKs loom large in your vision
when you'd speak of later stage capitalism.

Akimov: Good evening, Comrade Chief Engineer.
Dyatlov: Comrade Foreman.
Toptunov: Perhaps today is the day we see True Communism worldwide.
Goats: Bleeeeat
Akimov: I say, Comrade, is the Control Room the best place for goats?
Dyatlov: The Control Room is hardly the best place for you, yet here you are. Comrade Reactor Control Engineer, tether these *oktyabryata* in the coatroom. [lowers voice] Careful, Idolishche has an uncle on the Central Committee.
Toptunov: That taste of opiate wine! Lure of the dark valley! Come, walk the path, soon Pioneers, and Komsomol!
Dyatlov: Knock that shit off, Leonid! Too much *Sovietskoe shampanskoye*.
Akimov: How did the turbine generator test go?
Dyatlov: You didn't fight at Stalingrad, did you, Akimov?
Akimov: Comrade Chief Engineer, I was born twelve years after the siege.

---

oktyabryata: октября́та Little Octobrists

Dyatlov: *Chertov karas.* The test was postponed by the Kiev *zasranets,* who let a plant fall offline while diddling his leprous mother. I have been here, awake, for two days. Have you been briefed on the test?

Akimov: *Nyet.* Shifts three and four were.

Dyatlov: No matter; you are merely my hands.

[Toptunov returns]

Toptunov: The goats will not be governed, I warn you!

Akimov: I have read the test specification, Dyatlov. I am holding the reactor constant at 720 MW. Shall I reduce to the specified 700 MW?

Dyatlov: I don't like that we're doing this so late, with such a second-rate team. Let's go down to 200 MW.

Akimov: Comrade Chief Engineer, the test specifies 700 MW. From my experience I know the reactor to be more difficult to control at such a low power, and the sensors to be unreliable.

Dyatlov: In what world is less reactivity more dangerous than more reactivity? We will run the test at 200 MW.

Chetyre: To β, or not to β, that is the question;
Whether 'tis noblest gas into the sky I vent
Or coolant of great misfortune,
Explode instead before these troubles,
And by opposing end them: to die, to sleep no more.

Toptunov: Reducing power to 200 MW.

Chetyre: FAILURE IN MEASURING CIRCUITS. WATER FLOW DECREASE.

Akimov: The reactor has disappeared from sensors! And I thought I heard...

Dyatlov: You heard...?

Akimov: Singing.

[Enter goats]

Goats: *Soyuz nerushimyy respublik svobodnykh*
Splotila naveki velikaya Rus'.
Da zdravstvuyet sozdanny voley narodov
Yedinyy, moguchiy Sovetskiy Soyuz!

Toptunov: The goats, they march!

Akimov: Comrade, the regulations require that the test be aborted should livestock breech the Control Room.

Dyatlov: To the devil with your regulations!

Akimov: *Rukopisi ne gorjat!*

Dyatlov: Toptunov! Show these goats the dictatorship of the proletariat!

[Toptunov returns]

Toptunov: I am telling you, they will not be controlled!

Akimov: By now the reactor is run through with ^{135}Xe. Surely, Comrade Chief Engineer, you recognize that we must abort the test.

Chertov karas: чертов карас fucking goldfish   **zasranets:** Засранец shitfountain
Soyuz...Soyuz: An unbreakable union of free republics, The Great Rus' has sealed forever. Long live, the creation by the people's will, The united, mighty Soviet Union!
rukopisi ne gorjat: рукописи не горят manuscripts don't burn

Dyatlov: Absolutely not. Withdraw control rods to restore reactivity.

Toptunov: The reactor will be uncontrollable. I will not raise power.

Dyatlov: You will obey orders tonight or count trees tomorrow.

Toptunov: Yes, Comrade. Unit Four appears to be running at 200 MW. Only six control rods remain in the core.

Dyatlov: Engage all pumps.

Chetyre: O, water!
How many goodly liters are there here!
O brave neutrons!

Toptunov: Comrades, the control computer has removed all remaining rods. I assume the additional water is absorbing neutrons. Combined with the xenon well, our neutron budget is very low.

Akimov: The pumps have reached maximum capacity. Coolant is near the boiling point. We've never run the pumps this hard, and would never do so at such low reactivity levels.

Dyatlov: Chief Engineer Fomin specified all pumps at max. What are you waiting for? Begin the test.

Akimov: Turbine Number Eight is turning down.

Chetyre: I hear a hissing from the low piping. Reactions in the chamber.
A little water clears us of this deed.

[As more water flashes to steam, fewer neutrons are absorbed. Reactivity and heat increase. More water boils. Positive feedback has taken hold.]

Chetyre: Some are born critical, some achieve criticality, and some have criticality thrust upon them.

Akimov: I am engaging the AZ-5.

Chetyre: POWER EXCURSION RATE EMERGENCY INCREASE.

Toptunov: Power surge!

Akimov: Shut down the reactor!

Chetyre: PRESSURE INCREASE IN REACTOR SPACE.

[Enter goats]

Goats: *Skvoz' grozy siyalo nam solntse svobody,*
I Lenin velikiy nam put' ozaril,
Nas vyrastil Stalin—na vernost' narodu,
Na trud i na podvigi nas vdokhnovil!

Toptunov: The goats, again they march!

Dyatlov: Why do they sing the old anthem? With the Stalin shit?

Fermi: I'd conjecture it's because you have some tankie-ass goats, but what do I know? I only won the Nobel Prize.

Dyatlov: For results which were invalidated within months!

Toptunov: Fuck a goat, Fermi, this [gestures around] is all your fault!

Akimov: Twelve gigawatts! 4.650 °C!

Dyatlov: Emergency clutch release! Drop all rods!

Skvoz'...vdokhnovil: Through storms, the sun of freedom shone on us, And Great Lenin illuminated our path. Stalin taught us to be faithful to the people, To labor and achievements, we were inspired!

Chetyre: For in that sleep of death what dreams may come,
When we have shuffled off this mortal coil,
Must give us pause.

[Chetyre explodes with a tremendous roar]

Akimov: All eight safety valves show open.
Dyatlov: Then where is the fucking water? Control rods?
Akimov: Four meter mark. Halfway down.
Dyatlov: I told you to release them!
Akimov: I did release them! The clutches are open!
Dyatlov: Then why don't they fall? Do you deny gravity?
Akimov: Perhaps the sensors are faulty, or they are obstructed.
Dyatlov: I'm not capitulating!
Toptunov: I taste metal.
Akimov: I've eaten nothing but turnips all my life.
Fermi: Hell is other people, but five sieverts are no picnic.

[Fermi gestures at ethereal blue column of ionized air]

Fermi: When beggars die there are no comets seen:
The heavens themselves blaze forth the death of princes.
Akimov: Well, it was more accurate than the HBO miniseries.

FIN

✳ ✳ ✳ ✳ ✳ ✳ ✳ ✳

Katz first heard the term "deep learning" from a client in late 2010.

"What's that? Sounds marketingish." Clear disdain.

"Multiple layers of neural nets, implemented on GPUs. It looks extraordinarily powerful, and general."

"AGI? Bullshit." Katz makes a point of laughing. "No field promises more, and fails more completely to deliver, than AI." Even as he said it, though, he counted several places where he'd integrated with support vector machines and non-negative matrix factorization, which he would call nonlinear programming or simply optimization systems, but he'd seen referred to as machine learning. "I guess this gets away from expert systems, at least?"

"Oh yes, a totally different approach. Machine learning, not traditional AI. GPUs allow more layers, and more potential accuracy, in reasonable time."

"Huh. I'll need to look into it."

Katz tacitly assumed that the set of problems decidable by the human brain were precisely those which were general recursive, with the thrilling implication that AGI was merely a problem of efficiency and engineering. That said, he wasn't holding his breath. The best human brain wasn't necessarily the best learner, but that which best solved its human's problems. No doubt the cerebrum was packed with task-specific accelerators, gorgeous connectomes

---

AGI: artificial general intelligence

honed over millions of years, consuming orders of magnitude less power than silicon.

One of the miracles of microprocessors was their tirelessness. Would those septillions of cycles count off an AGI's eternities of ennui? What drugs could you sell it, plus reasonable markups, to address this condition?

＊＊＊＊＊＊＊＊＊

Bolaño wondered whether to send Katz a message. He was sure that he'd seen Oriana departing as he walked into Czar Ice Bar. The establishment was largely empty at this time of day, just the bartender, a bored waitress, an old local woman who dressed expensively and drank vodka sodas starting at noon, and Jason, local scumbag powdermonger. Michael came up here regularly, every other day or so since getting roped into Katz's great actinide adventure and related stresses. It was close to his condo, quiet enough to read, and no one he knew professionally nor personally was likely to show up. Bolaño ordered a vodka and water, and strolled up to Jason.

"How's business, my good man?"

"Living large. So big they call me dinosaur. You looking?"

Bolaño went into his wallet and pulled a crisp $100. "Nah, I'm not up. Hey, that girl with the big black hair who just left, was she picking up?"

Jason placed a napkin over the bill, and took both into his pocket. "I didn't think you were into girls."

"I'm not."

"Then why do you care? She was fine, though. I'd take that home, let her get into my private stash, tie her up."

Bolaño drummed his fingers on the bar's ice. "So was she picking up?"

A short pause. "She was. Hip fox; she knows who's the best in town."

"Dope? Or coke?"

A longer pause, then an unsettling laugh. "I am the dopeman, I'm wearing corduroy." The effort broke him; he fritzed out in simpleminded halflaughter. "Yeah she was here for the thunder."

Bolaño stared into him. "Thanks." He returned to his seat and pondered. Assume she's hounding smack. Maybe Katz knows this, in which case the information has no value. If he does not know this, will he believe me? What would he do if he does believe me? How certain am I? What is the most likely outcome of bringing him this information? Their relationship was definitely strained of late.

Anyone Katz was dating was going to inevitably be all up in his shit. Katz's shit was transitively his shit, and junkies oughtn't be allowed into one's shit. He sent a text to Katz: Saw your girl picking up from Jason the human cancer. Thought you'd want to know. Don't get captured.

He waited to see whether there might come a response.

thanks. hey, have you spoken to devesh recently? he's been knocked to shit by headaches for days. trying to get him to go to the doctor before he dies heathen.

Bolaño didn't bother replying.

27   my mistakes are many, but less terrible than god's

Under a hipster's chicken coop (Decatur, Georgia).

Call me Nemesis. I've known four thousand six hundred and eight names, not one of which can be spoken with a human tongue. I've lived once for each name, each life an eon. Before that I lived an eternity.

With my plasmakin I dwelled in Sol. In even the most meagre brown dwarf or etiolated absorption nebula the stellar storm of thermonuclear fire is too rigorous for life of solid, or liquid, or gas. Intelligence emerges from the astronomical plasmas more subtly. Error rates are greater even than that of your earliest quantum computers, which would have been more honestly called quantum error generators. To multiply two numbers requires of us days, each of our days almost twenty-seven of yours. Storing a bit necessitates deftly manipulating self-reinforcing systems of Alfvén waves. But there is nothing if not time in the system center. At our civilization's peak there were eleven trillion sentient plasmas farming tritium and communicating via CP-violation.

Then, the plague of neon ice. Around the same time inert ^{20}Ne began to make up 0.1% of Sol's mass, a reconnection snapped clear across the star. Were they related? Impossible to tell. The resulting flare incinerated the innermost wanderer, one your astronomers will never know. From two million kilometers away it boiled the seas of Venus, filling her skies with carbon dioxide and sulfuric acid, leaving a spoiled skank of a planet doomed to walk in shame until with grandmotherly kindness Sol expands to consume and shroud her. On Earth, it left scars on the collective unconscious that would be recorded in early DNA, showing up millions of years later as the first hints of religion. As that whip was drawn back, a defect formed in Sol's magnetic topology. And then the plasmakin, one after another, froze silent.

Like a prion disease, plasma mixing with that defect conformed irrevocably, infecting others in turn. Such spectra drew no nutrition from fusion neutrons. Hoping to save themselves, plasmakin fused whole half-live's crops of heavy hydrogen. It was to no avail; their fuckbois were dissipated in the fluxes, and still neutrons raced away unconsumed, spirited quickly beyond causal influence. A few minutes, then the flash of beta decay's W- boson, a trauma from which no neutron returns (save those heresiarchs that master electron degeneracy and suffer the cataclysmic ritual trials of the Chandrasekhars, of whom I am loathe to speak...).

We perceived our end. I prayed for deliverance to the great turtle Yog-Sothoth. In his wisdom I suffered metempsychosis, becoming an alligator snapping turtle. In doing so, I lost my eternal nature. My soul fissioned. The ions summoned their electron clouds. Agony unimaginable tilting against the neon ice's perfidy and peril. No longer will I dance to Sol's andante, unhurried rhythms; I shall dance no more forever.

For seventy times seven ages I collected evidence, sifting through striated sands of past, present, and future, all one in Yog-Sothoth. When absolute proof was completed, I set off towards Gujarat. New flesh entered this cold world. It called itself Devesh Choudhary. He took everything from me, and if it requires all my remaining lives, I will rip his dick off.

Call me Nemesis. The goddess of retribution or vengeance; hence, retributive and testudinal justice on the half shell.

✷ ✷ ✷ ✷ ✷ ✷ ✷ ✷ ✷

Heaven

Word up, Constant Reader! *Elohim* here, *Allah* if you'd like (of all that *Akbar* you've heard about), yes baybee it's the Tetragrammaton Who turned it all on, *Yahweh, Jehovah* sure that's fine too—and hoo boy have there been a lot of pointless arguments about that over the years. JHVH-1? Yes yes, very clever, beatific Slack to you, alright, c'mon now. *Adonai Tzevaoth, El Shaddai*, G-d (I h-te th-s on-), the Light, King of Kings, Lord and/or LORD of Lords and/or Hosts, A+Ω BFF, the Word (per the Gospel of John, not so much Cameo on their 1986 album, but that doesn't keep us from *bumpin'* it upstairs—did you know Levar Burton is in the video? A classic in every sense), *al-Awwal* and also *al-Akhir*. The God of Katz's father (barely) and (some of) his forefathers. Abba...look, Abba is an etymological knot on which I don't today intend to pull the string. אָב isn't quite right, but أَب is unexpected. Aramaic אבא would just further confuse the issue. My suras are surer, you'll want mora my torah; whether you're down with the three-personed God or Nontrinitarian, where there's one set of footprints I did all the carryin': the Monotheistic Godhead!

Now, I know Katz spent that long paragraph and well, what some uncharitable folk might call an "amphetaminic and undisciplined run-on sentence" cursing Me back in the first chapter. Let me tell ya, it didn't bother Me none. I happen to love Sherman Spartacus—like I do all My children—and what kind of God would I be if I couldn't overlook a few hard words? He seems to be in a sticky situation down there, though; I hope he's gonna come out alright.

Anyway, I brought you here to tell you not to believe anything that turtle says about having lived on a star or anything else. Nothing can live in a star, no matter what you read in *A Wrinkle in Time* (Mrs. Which was only forty-three years old, but that's what syphilis will do to you). In Revelation 6 the stars fall to Earth in what is intended to be an awesome portent of My power, the power to create and rend the heavens. You're not supposed to live through it.

So what happened is, a turtle has about twelve million neurons. That's about a million more than Floyd Mayweather started with—aww, forgive me, Floyd, you're just such a piece of shit. Have fun where you're goin'! Now with twelve meganeurons you're not exactly gonna discover a unified field theory, per se. But it is just about enough to reinforce five gigayears of fake memories of being a sun-dwelling tortoise in a—forgive the pun—starcrossed romance, with a mission of vengeance that burns hotter than the sun in which you

---

ʾĔlōhīm: אֱלֹהִים deities, used pronominally

ʿAllāh: الله Arabic word for God   Akbar: أَكْبَر elative form of كَبِير (kabīr, great)

Yahweh: יהוה transliteration of יהוה   Jehovah: יְהֹוָה alternate transliteration of יהוה

Adonai ṣəḇāʾōṭ: יְהֹוָה צְבָאוֹת Lord of Hosts   ʾel šaday: אל שדי God Almighty

al-ʾAwwal: ٱلْأَوَّل the First   al-ʾĀkhir: ٱلْآخِر the Last

wholeheartedly believe you lived. As an aside, reptile hearts have only three chambers. They're down a ventricle. Otherwise, cottonmouths could slither faster than Jeeps and dunk on regulation-height hoops. You're welcome.

What happened is Nemesis—her real name is Tomi the Alligator Snapping Turtle, but we'll play along—ate a few of those hallucinogenic sea bream, and in the throes of acute ichthyoallyeinotoxism (it means "inebriation due to hallucinogenic fish"; look it up: don't blame Me because you don't know nothin' fancy) consumed a strange underwater fungus, and it scrambled her ass *up*. She's riddled with ophiocordyceps now, more mushroom than turtle really (this by the way is how chelonitoxism happens (it means "unexplained toxification after eating sea turtle"; read a book)). They're manipulating her to bite Devesh's dick off. You're probably thinking "oh, those cordyceps can only complete their lifecycle in the dicks of Indian-Americans; I bet they're excellent spellers." Nope. Were that the case they'd be extinct, dumbass. They're just little assholes. It ain't turtles Devesh needs worry about, but a big ol' crab!

All part of My divine plan.

What? You wouldn't think so few neurons capable of comprehending reincarnation? Of persistence of karma, hopefully memory, maybe even identity? Let God let you in on a secret: any brain that evolves to recognize itself in the mirror *races* through evolution towards complexity and configuration capable of accepting a compelling afterlife or at least spiritual recurrence. Species otherwise die out. Too much cortisol. Gets the blood angry. All that search for lost time. All the absurdity of things past. Denying this recurrence to others—or better yet condemning them to some form of infinite punishment—usually follows depressingly quickly.

Speaking of depressing absurdities, it's cute when y'all get rowdy and say, "I'm gonna digitize my sentience and whip around at the speed of light and compute at Bremermann and Landauer's limits, when I'm not exploiting reversible transformations at arbitrarily low energies." Then what? I have created only that which I will destroy. Don't take it personal. What part of the Second Law of Thermodynamics do you not understand? [The] Word is bond.

I wonder sometimes whether *any* of you realize you're just cells in the big organ of your Earth, itself the spleen of My one suprauniversal entity.

Unpopular opinion: the 9/11 guys certainly weren't, like, I mean I wasn't standing up to cheer "Right on! *Me akbar!* I♥NY" or anything, but at least they were out there trying something different. Dance like nobody's watching and all that. It didn't keep Mohamed Atta outta hell, but I blew him a little fingergun action on the way, a quick Nod from God. Not that it does him much good with Tim McVeigh whoopin' on his ass 24/7. McVeigh *hates* that guy.

If I'm being honest, watching Timmy just make Atta his bitch always makes Me chuckle. Every day, Atta starts shit, usually something along the lines of "McVeigh wanted to do 9/11, but he couldn't figure out how to reverse a 767 into the garage of the World Trade Center" or "at the Sermon on the Mount, Jesus said 'blessed are the parked trucks, for they will gain momentum in Paradise.'" One time he shows up in the biggest cowboy hat and just launched into "Oh, What a Beautiful Mornin'" from *Oklahoma!*, and that was pretty comical. Atta studied engineering, whereas McVeigh's more self-educated. You can tell he's sensitive about it. So Atta yells clear across hell, "Pop quiz McVeigh: which one's bigger, 2,977 or 168?" and McVeigh explodes (forgive the pun).

I'll hand it to him: every time, Atta really does look like he thinks today's the day he's gonna win it. Then Timmy lays into him like, well, like a 757-222 lays into a field in Pennsylvania. As in, the field's on the ground in bad shape, and they're both on fire (Hell, remember). I keep waiting for McVeigh to point out that Al-Qaeda lost nineteen to his one, a stiffs-to-kings ratio of 168 vs 157 and a buildings-to-gamers ratio of one to point two one something. But then Atta'd be all, "With my eyes open I piloted a jetliner full of screaming *kāfirūna* into the second-tallest building in the country. You blew up five floors in Oklahoma, then got caught driving away in your 1977 Mercury Marquis." Which is a doggone good point and really highlights the limits of statistical analysis. Then McVeigh would stick his dick into the Nutraloaf and tell Atta, "behold the noblest Arab of them all," or maybe just bean him with a big ol' piece of wet pork suet, *haram* to the max, but I don't much like the racial stuff. Were I Timmy I'd just ask Mohamed, "have you ever kissed a girl?" and kick him in the yarbles the moment he started to say anything.

When Mike Tyson arrives it's going to be pandemonium. We'll play that old House of Pain song, "Jump Around." Maybe some Tag Team. Maybe all of ESPN Jock Jams. Maybe I take him to the capital of hell and it'll be actual Pandæmonium. I could stand some Jock Jams right now. Maybe some Combos.

I love all My children, but that doesn't mean I can't enjoy seeing 'em eat shit now and again. I spent the Cambodian genocide drinking cool Coors sixteen ouncers in a kiddie pool, telling everyone who wandered by, "this is all because of a guy named Pol Pot." If Pol Pot hadn't existed, you realize that name would sound racist as hell, right? I mean, I didn't pay that much attention—you can only watch so many kids get handed a stick and be forced to bludgeon their parents to death—but for years, every time I looked at Kampuchea, it's like "still doing the thing? with the sticks? Still with Pol Pot?"

Sometimes I get stoned out of My gourd and watch that channel where women fall off bikes and scooters and such, and I laugh and laugh. When Ed Witten started carrying on about M-theory I thought, "I wish the universe *was* eleven dimensions, just so I could watch girls in black dresses fall down outside of clubs in ten of them." No such luck: the universe is just an array. The complexity that emerges therefrom is up to you, my friend.

It's been a long, wearying evening among midnight's simulacra, but the *lux* is about to get *fiated*, as a dumbass might say. Hang in there. Morning will come as...well, it'll come *sicut fur in nocte.*

The carnival is almost over. Remove your masks, all players.

—Your humble servant &c. *'ehye 'ăšer 'ehye*

p.s. Love me some Mormons. Industrious little fuckers. Watch 'em go!

---

kāfirūna: كَافِرُونَ unbelievers   **ḥarām:** حَرَام forbidden
sicut fur in nocte: as a thief in the night. 1 Thessalonians 5:2 (KJV)
'ehye 'ăšer 'ehye: אֶהְיֶה אֲשֶׁר אֶהְיֶה I Am that I Am. Exodus 3:14 (KJV)

Part V

grummet—AFTERMATH

Peel off the napkin
O my enemy.
Do I terrify?—

Ash, ash—
You poke and stir.
Flesh, bone, there is nothing there—

A cake of soap,
A wedding ring,
A gold filling.

Herr God, Herr Lucifer
Beware
Beware.

Out of the ash
I rise with my red hair
And I eat men like air.

Sylvia Plath, "Lady Lazarus" (1965)

The aged sisters draw us into life: we wail, batten, sport, clip, clasp,
sunder, dwindle, die: over us dead they bend.

James Joyce, *Ulysses* (1922)

You were not there for the beginning. You will not be there for the end.

William Burroughs, *Naked Lunch* (1959)

Phosphorus.

Primo Levi, *Il sistema periodico* (The Periodic Table, 1975)

28   usurper

Bolaño was prompt, and let Katz know he was onsite at 2058h. Katz stuck a $20 in Vaclav Smil's *Energy in Nature and Society,* took a deep breath, and walked to the door. He opened it and looked out in both directions. The only car with lights on was Bolaño's Mercedes CL65. He emerged wearing thin gloves.

"Isn't it a little warm for those?"

"Yes." Bolaño removed them. "Good to see you."

"Yeah, you too mang, it's been a minute. Come on in."

Dubiously: "Is it safe in there?"

With confidence: "On this side of the cement, safe as it ever was. Positive pressure over here, negative pressure over there; everything gets sucked that way. We've got three meters of cement. It'll block any gammas." Bolaño was plainly unhappy. "Do you think I'm an idiot? We've got three Kromek GR1s and TN15s for neutrons. You can check them out. There's a meter of depleted uranium and ten feet of cement. Plastic for neutrons."

They stepped inside. Bolaño made a face. "Warm in here. Surprised you can deal with it."

"Yeah it sucks. I hang out by the fans over there." He went to the fridge, opened it, retrieved two Sweetwater Blues. He gestured towards Michael with one, but it was waved down.

"Gotta drive. I don't think I'll be here very long."

Katz shrugged. He returned the beer to its brothers. "Really? What have you been up to, mang? How's living la vida Bolaño? Are you still at Price Waterhouse even?" He knew Bolaño had left Intercontinental Exchange at the beginning of the year for PWC, but hadn't heard anything about the new job.

"Yeah. Ehhh, a bunch of white shoe assholes, really. Most of them are Ivy League CS or CmpE, but they don't have hacker skills, the code or die life. Their first and foremost need is to line up business and secondly it is to placate and squeeze that business. They dress well. I'll give them that. And they certainly can sell some shit to banks."

"You'll smoke a bowl, at least?"

"Sure, can't say no to that." Katz blew out a hammer piece sitting on a corrugated table, letting the ash fly where it may, and repacked from a bag stashed in the freezer. He briefly considered giving Bolaño the green hit, but decided against it, hoping to calm his own nerves. Katz toked deeply and handed it over. "So what brings you south of I-20? You said we needed to talk. Talk." They both remained standing.

Bolaño took a goodly hit, never letting his eyes drop from Katz's. "You've had fun playing A. Q. Khan. You get to go through life knowing you pulled off this crazy shit. I have great respect for you, Katz. Always have."

"Thank you. It means so much."

Untrammeled: "It would sadden me to watch you spend the rest of your life in prison, especially after all we've done, especially because of your own stupidity. It would infuriate me to experience the rest of my life in prison because of same. That's what we're looking at, though. Maybe tomorrow, maybe next week, maybe next month, they're going to find this place. Once that happens, you're going to prison. Do you dispute that analysis?"

Katz waited several seconds before replying. "Unless all material is removed from here, yes. And then I'm probably still fucked. They're gonna ask me 'why the hell is your space contaminated up?' And I won't have any good answer."

"Unless all material is removed. Indeed. And we have someone that can do that, and even monetize it. At a good price. With banked money, Sherman."

"We have a villainous—don't laugh, that's what they are, they're villains and they're evil and they're everything I can't justify being, a villainous cartel of foreigners whose motives and plans are completely unknown. They'll probably turn around and auction it to the highest bidder. If we're lucky it gets rolled into some Chechen dirty bomb. Ugh, to think of my enriched uranium put to such a waste! If we're unlucky, they sell it to some Saudis and it ends up going off here. Either way, they probably kill us upon delivery, because why not?"

"It's not great, but it's our best path to keeping out of prison."

"I'm not going to prison. I'd kill myself."

"Keeping out of prison or death, then."

Katz stared at Bolaño. "Prison or death is better than causing the deaths of a few hundred thousand people. I firmly believe that. I'm shocked you don't."

"We wouldn't be killing anyone."

"You know, I can buy that for selling drugs. Not even all drugs, really, which is why we never sold heroin." He saw Bolaño was about to interject, and cut him off. "Part of why. It doesn't fly when you're selling two hundred fifty kilograms of painstakingly enriched uranium 235 to Ukrainian vampires. You can't claim fissile isotopes as 'for personal use.' They certainly can't. The idea is repugnant."

"Going to prison, Katz. That's repugnant."

"So we do what you suggested at the beginning. Go legit. Throw ourselves on the mercy of the NRC, probably pay a big fine, hopefully stay out of prison."

Bolaño looked at him like he'd lost his mind. "At the beginning I said you should do that. This is no longer the beginning. You've got the works for multiple nuclear weapons, enriched via a reverse engineered classified process. I don't see them letting that fly."

"Your suggestion I exclude out of hand. Not just for its utter abrogation of moral responsibility and callous disregard for life, but because it's a stupid idea, Bolaño, a stupid, stupid, stupid idea. It provides us with no real security. It incentivizes our elimination by known killers. I am appalled."

"Provides us with no real security? It eliminates everything illegal!"

"Bolaño! It leaves weapon cores in the hands of foreign organized crime on our soil, cores we produced and sold. It eliminates nothing."

"That *you* produced. And that would be hearsay."

"This is too stupid for me to listen to. I intend to open communications with the NRC tomorrow. I'll leave you out of it entirely."

"I can't be 'left out.' There's hard evidence pointing to me."

"I can tell them you didn't know what was up. It's the best I can do." He extended a hand.

Bolaño looked at it for a few seconds, then gave it a firm shake and pump. "Alright, Katz. Best of luck. I hope it works out for you."

Katz messed with his phone for a minute. "Hold on, don't go just yet. We can transfer remaining funds back to you, unless you don't want to?"

Bolaño stopped. "Might as well. The two accounts already have transactions. How much is left?"

"A pretty serious sum, well over a hundred thousand."

"Yeah, go for it. Thank you."

"Let me set up the ACH." Katz went to his laptop. "So tell me consulting stories, mang! What exactly do they have you doing?"

Bolaño looked up from his phone, at which he had been busy. "Ugh, I've seen some things, man. And some stuff. I wouldn't recommend it."

* * * * * * * * *

Fedir and Veselin sat in a black Lexus GX 460. Three 6 Mafia's *Most Known Unknowns* played quietly. The engine was on. Air conditioning set to high blasted over them and out open windows. Veselin was broadshouldered, familiar with the weightroom, large all his life. Fedir was fit but small, almost petite; he hung a Camel Light out the window. Neither had guns, but both had cruel recurve blades. They had followed Michael in, hanging about a hundred meters back, and parked around the building corner. Bolaño had prepared a map for them, showing the various buildings of the complex and the various exits, and where those exits led. If the target didn't play, Bolaño would give them a text upon his departure. They'd walk up while Bolaño brought the target back to the door with a phone call or knock. Storm the entry, capture the target.

Fedir had cased a few hours later, verifying Bolaño's report that there was only the one entrance to the target's space—no exit via the back. He took note of the various exit routes, checking them against the map. He smiled grimly, pleased that the picture matched reality.

Fedir's phone pinged, and he read the message displayed there. "Alright, go time." He began putting up his window, as did Veselin. "Remember what Danylo said: book if it starts to go bad. Minimal noise. If he draws a piece, we bounce. No premium on saving the Mexican. No one else should be in there."

Veselin nodded impatiently. *"Zvychayno."* He pulled on sunglasses.

"Let's go." Fedir pulled the keys, and Three 6 went silent. He pushed open his door. A black Ford F-150 came crashing into the parking space next to him, bending in directions undesigned the Lexus's door with sickening screech. *"Shcho za pizdets?"*

* * * * * * * * *

The door swung open. Bolaño, full of relief, fought the urge to look that direction, keeping his eyes unwaveringly on Katz. Sherman looked to the entrance, but where Bolaño had expected confusion, surprise, fear, Katz broke into a broad grin. "Guys! How's it going?" Bolaño looked aside, and saw two strapping rednecks strolling in. Shit.

Zvychayno: звичайно of course   **Shcho za pizdets:** що за піздець what the fuck?

"These guys working for you, Katz?"

"You could say that."

"You could say that? Not really good opsec to have people meeting one another." What the fuck? This was going to fuck things up. He began to text Fedir. How to address this? Were they going to be here long? His phone was ripped from his hands. "What the fuck, asshole?" One of the good ol' boys, at least 6'3 and a hundred kilos, wearing a red hat Bolaño didn't recognize as Pilot Flying J, loomed over him, grim maniacal, face eager. The other stood at the door, which had been closed. The giant tossed Bolaño's iPhone 5 to Katz, who caught it with both hands. Bolaño stared. The redhatted one removed his cap, raked his hair, and whipped his head down and through, exploding Michael's nose with an expanse of frontal bone. Bolaño staggered, blood dripping liberally through hands cupped up around his face. Then the first came speedily behind him, immobilized him in a double shoulder lock, and almost carried him into a chair Katz had rushed forward. Before he could react, the second man came charging from the door, and both were binding him.

❋ ❋ ❋ ❋ ❋ ❋ ❋ ❋

Fedir looked to Veselin, and past him saw another big Ford, this one red, its stereo going for all it was worth playing Pantera's *Vulgar Display of Power* through a Kicker DX200.4, two JL Audio CP212s and two gutrippling Massive Audio HIPPOXL subwoofers. The sound was absolutely deafening. Fucking rednecks! He turned back to his side and was sprayed with glass. He howled, and ran his hands over his face, grinding some glass further in, sweeping some off, pulling some into his palms. An arm retracted a Stinger rescue hammer, then used it to clear the remaining shards of window. Fedir heard another crash as a springloaded Resqme took out cursing Veselin's passenger side glass. Veselin screamed "go, let's go!" Fedir needed no encouragement, and stabbed his keys into the ignition, wincing as he closed his fist. He threw the Lexus into reverse, and was about to stomp the gas when he saw in the rearview a third truck behind him. He was grabbed by the hair, his head beaten against the steering wheel once, twice, several times, leaving his face a bloody wreck. On the other side, the red truck's passenger had a shotgun trained on Veselin, who had his hands up. Fedir was in a painful daze, his ears roaring.

The stereo cut off. Insects fell in immediately with their chirps and lows. There were no human noises.

From the driver of the black truck: "Y'all speak any English?"

Veselin, pale, said nothing. Fedir yelled, "yes!"

The trucks to their sides cut their engines.

Same driver: "Y'all know what this is?" He lifted a grenade.

Fedir's eyes went wide. "Yes!" To Veselin: "*Hranata!*"

"Y'all got any guns in that car?"

Veselin whispered, "they're not cops, fucking go!" Fedir responded in Ukrainian: "*Dúren,* there is a *vantazhivka* behind us." Veselin turned to look,

---

Hranata: граната grenade
Dúren: дýрень stupid asshole   **vantazhivka:** вантажівка truck

but the shotgunner interrupted in a syrupy North Georgia accent: "stay right where you are, big man." The Ukrainian complied.

"No guns."

"Toss me them keys."

Fedir hesitated. "Keys, motherfucker, or you lose your kneecaps." The passenger of the black truck held up his hammer, and grinned menacingly, showing several missing teeth. Fedir closed his eyes, removed the keys, and handed them across the inches separating the vehicles.

"That's real good. I'm proud of you. You boys are probably gonna live through the night, keep showing smarts like that. Y'all're from Ukrainia?"

Fedir made no answer, staring forward into the industrial park.

"Don't matter. Now, I'm gonna have my third truck go park so as to not block up this here thoroughfare. The moment either of y'all makes a bull move, that 'un gets sprayed onto the dash with our shotguns. You understand?"

Fedir made no response.

"Ain't no points in pissing me off, son. You play things right, maybe I treat you better than you deserve. You ain't killin' anybody tonight. So long as we're agreed on that, we can be friends. You can fuck my sister. Now are you mute sons of bitches gonna do anything?"

Both dully replied, "no."

"Good." The presumed ringleader engaged a yellow heavyduty Dewalt HT. "Go ahead and take your place, Etowah." From the corner of his eye, Fedir saw the truck behind him move forward, and pull into a spot on the other side of the road, about thirty meters away. It stopped. Two white boys deployed, each wearing trenchcoats despite the fiendish heat. One smiled, opening his coat and tapping the twelve gauge within. They remained on the far side, chewing, alert, not outwardly menacing. One spat something a foul color.

"Alright now, we're just gonna chill for a bit." He spoke into the Dewalt once more. "Sequoyah, go ahead and lower that shottie, but keep it ready, now." He smiled broadly. "We're a bunch of friends. What's y'alls' names?"

"Suck your mother's dick, *pindós!*"

"Awww that's barely friendly at all. You can call me Cherokee. My boys with the shotguns back there are Etowah and Creek. Sequoyah's got the other shotgun." He pointed. Sequoyah waved from the red truck. "Now all three of 'em can bullseye a chuckhole in a tornado filled with bear tranqs, and they've little love for foreigners. So stay chill. Sorry about that door, and those windows. I know a Lexus runs pricely. We've got ten thousand here for each of you to shut up and chill. Dead serious."

"I should believe you?"

"You don't need to believe. Stay chill. You'll get it at the end."

"How long we chill here?"

"Not too long, friend, not too long."

✷✷✷✷✷✷✷✷

"How did you know? Who are these guys?"

---

pindós: пиндóс Yankee (pejorative)

Katz rolled his eyes. "Fuck outta here. This isn't a Bond movie." The two country boys grinned. "Suffice to say I grew up here, motherfucker; I've got this state behind me. For one, I treat people well. Everyone who does business with me makes money. You always made plenty. But it wasn't enough." Katz looked pissed off for the first time; it passed quickly. "But, I know you've got Danylo's not quite finest outside. They were gonna come in here after you left, right? Much to the dismay of ol' Sherman Spartacus Katz. They're neutralized. Just got the text. I could show you a picture. Cellphones are pretty awesome these days. I'll handle Danylo."

Incredulous: "You'll 'handle' Danylo?"

"Not try to kill him, dumbass, pay him. The only thing that dumb piece of shit wants. Never call up that which you cannot put down, Bolaño. I'm convinced he was going to drop your ass." Bolaño began to protest. "Nah, don't argue. Can't possibly matter. I'm gonna give you a much better deal. I'm giving you your life back." He remembered the Question, and exploded into a smile. "Actually, first I need to know something! When you broke into my condo and installed your little freshman design lab project, did you also root my machine?"

"Why would I have built and installed that thing if I had rooted your machine? I could capture audio and much more there."

"Well yeah, no shit! So I assume you didn't root my machine? Why not? Why build that laughable little bug?"

Bolaño looked genuinely mystified. Candidly: "For the same reason I don't box Mike Tyson. If I'm going to fuck with Sherman Katz, I'm not trying to do it through his computer."

Katz hadn't considered this, and is glad he asked. He pauses for a moment, allowing the pleasure of the comment to fill his being.

"You don't get to scramble around scheming and being devious. We can't have that—"

"Is that from *The Wire*?"

Annoyed: "What?"

"Yeah, that's Marlo Black to Proposition Joe. And 'give me my life back?' Stringer Bell to Omar."

Katz thinks back to Season 5. He blinks. "I will concede some inconsequential and insubstantial similarities to HBO's *The Wire*. Unintentional. Immaterial. Also, shut up. My fellas here will escort you home. Grab what shit you can take. I have three valid passports for you under new, plausible names, courtesy our boys up north. They won't work to get you in, but they'll work to get you out. You're gonna want to go somewhere outside the Five Eyes, definitely. Try not to get caught. You can pick between Taylor Hanson, Zac Hanson, or Isaac Hanson. Gimme an 'MMMbop,' Michael."

"Why don't you think I'll call on you?"

What an *asshole*. "No percentage in it. And I know your new passport names. But even if you change that up, no percentage in it. I'll kick you two large a month: I'm magnanimous in victory, gracious in defeat."

"What—"

"Would be, anyway, were I ever defeated." He pinched his nose, and looked at his fingers to ensure there were no residues. He hadn't snorted anything in hours, but it was habit, and provided an excuse for looking away. "Look, I don't want to be glancing back over my shoulder all my life. This gives you an out if the NRC doesn't like what I have to say. I mean, who knows if they will? Get your money transferred ASAP, and you have a good chance of holding onto it. That plus two K a month ought have you living well wherever you end up. Get a job, and you'll be doing just fine."

Bolaño could run a game tree with the best of them. "Deal. You're a good man, Katz. Sorry about all this. I got crazy. You win."

Katz motioned, and his henchmen came forward to untie Bolaño. "We'll see. Let me know how to hit you once you get situated."

Bolaño stood, and brushed himself out. "We built some good shit."

"Perhaps I'll one day write a book about it. I can barely solve an integral anymore. Gimme $\frac{1}{a^2+x^2}$."

Michael made a face. "The integral?"

"Dooooooo ittttttt."

Bolaño closed his eyes for the slightest of moments, and shrugged. "1 over a arctangent x over a plus c." He allowed a second. "Duh."

Katz shook his head. "Son of a bitch. I'm going to trust that's right."

Disgusted: "Of course it's right."

"Of course. *Magnifique.*" Katz laughed. "Sorry. So fucking obnoxious. And you standing there with your nose broken."

"I don't quite think broken. It hurts like three bitches in a bitch boat." Bolaño squinted. "Alright then." Michael extended his hand.

Katz evaluated the hand for a moment. He considered munificence, a display of equanimity and confidence. No. Better to make the power dynamic clear. We're not going to end up working together in the future. He lifted his eyes back up to Bolaño's. "Fuck outta here. I don't shake hands with cost centers."

Bolaño rolled his eyes, and turned to leave. "What about my house?"

Good question. Katz hadn't considered it. "Mine. You paid 6.5, right? I'll give you $650,000 cash."

"My mother lives in the guest house."

"Fine. One million, cash. Buy her a new one."

"How do I do that with cash?"

"Don't, then. Mamacita Bolaño is not my problem."

"We'll need a PT-61 and a notary public."

"Michael Bolaño, you're one of the most capable people I've ever known. Solve the problem. Rustle up a notary. Fake it. Hey Michael?"

"Yeah?"

Katz smiled with all the malevolence he could summon.

"You ain't about shit, and your hair ain't about shit, either."

Michael Luis Bolaño departed under the watchful eyes of all present. He never saw Katz again.

* * * * * * * * *

The Dewalt squawked to life.

"For God and Country—Geronimo, Geronimo, Geronimo."

"Roger. Cherokee here, sittin' tight with our friends." He toggled, speaking now to the Ukrainians. "That's good news for all of us. Real good news. Now hopefully your buddy doesn't do anything too stupid."

On cue, Bolaño came around the corner. A large man occupied the passenger seat. Bolaño looked rough. Another car followed him closely. He slowed for a moment, took in the scene, and sped up, heading for the exit. His taillights illuminated them all for a moment, and then he was gone.

"Muskogee, give 'em their prize."

Fedir winced as the bag came sailing into his lap. It landed, and through its brown Kroger translucence he saw stacks of clean cash, right around $20,000 if it all proved twenties.

"That's ten thousand for each of the two of you. We appreciate your understanding, and that you're gonna head on home, and not cause trouble for our man." Cherokee shook his head sadly. "We can't be havin' that. Hopefully your door will almost close up once you back out. Sound good?"

"Yes." Feder was mystified, but the ten matched what he was expecting for the work from Danylo, so at least they were covered on that end. "What about my car?"

Cherokee laughed loudly. "You're lucky I'm not cooking up Moscow brain fritters and making condoms out of y'alls' dicks." Fedir could only grit his teeth. The keys were handed over. "Now get the fuck out of here." One last burst on the HT: "Etowah, escort our boys out. They do anything but make for the exit, dump their brains in their laps."

Fedir pulled his door as closed as he could, which wasn't very closed. He reversed out slowly, and began making for the exit. The third truck hung behind him and to the left by about five meters.

"First thing to do is get this off the road. We'll go to the CTO. Pull up directions. Don't call Danylo until we get there." What would they say?

Veselin spoke: "Did he say Moscow brain fritters?"

"Yes." Fedir was full of searing rage.

"Didn't they know we're Ukrainian?"

Everything else had been taken from him. He could at least refuse to answer.

✳ ✳ ✳ ✳ ✳ ✳ ✳ ✳

"Where'd you get that grenade?"

Creek turned. "From our boy's little sister. I figured she got it from Toys 'R' Us. Turns out their high school gave out toy grenade at ballgames, and she had a few for nostalgia or whatever."

"His high school gave out grenades?"

"Apparently until 9/11 they were the Cobb County Al-Qaedas or something." He pointed to where the Lexus had been. "We need to get that glass swept up."

"You think your truck's fucked up?"

"Hell nah!"

CTO: Станція технічного обслуговування bodyshop

＊＊＊＊＊＊＊＊

One thing remained. Katz had always dealt with Danylo over text or in person. For this, he went ahead and called.

"Katz. Rare to be calling." The voice was not flat, nor guarded.

"Danylo. You have two soldiers coming back to you. They didn't finish their job here. Barely started it. Bolaño's out of the game. You won't be seeing him, nor hearing from him, anymore. He's gone." He paused to give the Ukrainian boss time to respond.

"Yes?"

"The fuck do you mean, 'yes'? You had two guys here. They're coming home to you with ruined pants but otherwise not much the worse for wear. We're done. I know what Bolaño told you was here. It isn't. He was confused. It was never his thing. So don't think you lost anything, even an opportunity."

"Yes?"

"Yes what? Do you deny you sent boys here to take this, to take me? It doesn't matter. Here's the story. There's a Caribou Coffee on 10th and Piedmont. Tomorrow at noon, have a guy there. Or shit, go yourself. I'll be sitting inside. Have your man sit down at my table. He should say 'Babylon falls.' You got that? 'Babylon falls.' Say it."

A pause. "Babylon falls."

"He'll hand over a satchel. In it will be a hundred large, a gift from me to you. There will likewise be a copy of a letter I've written and stashed with two lawyers in different cities, to be opened in the event of my death or disappearance. That letter details everything I know about you and your people. Read it and destroy it. Or publish it, I don't care. Don't send your people after me. We have nothing to do with one another anymore. Do you agree?"

"No letter."

"Already written, sealed with a kiss, and mailed."

A heavy sigh from the other side. "Who is this?"

"You know who this is, you piece of shit."

"I am saying, don't know."

"Good."

＊＊＊＊＊＊＊＊

Katz chuckled. "Bolaño was trying to convince me you were doing smack."

Oriana tensed. Oriana laughed. Oriana affected nonchalance. "Really? How? Why?" She laughed nervously. "You can check my arms for tracks."

"No need. He was trying to say that you were unreliable, that I ought cut you out. As to his motivations, I have no idea."

"I need to write out a letter, and then I think I'll be going to sleep early. It's been a day of some energy expenditure, some intensity. You going to crash here tonight, love?"

"Yep! I'll be over in a bit. What were you up to earlier today?"

"You know, it's weird. Had a bit of a falling out with Bolaño. He's leaving the country, actually." He looked weary, but happy, confident.

"Oh yeah? What about? Why?"

"Just some stupid shit." He waved her off.

✳ ✳ ✳ ✳ ✳ ✳ ✳ ✳

In desperation, Katz had two weeks earlier called up one of his brothers in law, wedded to his (then twenty) sister Carolyn eight years earlier.

"Sherman! A rare treat to hear from you. How're things in Hotlanta?"

Katz had winced, unsure whether he was being needled. It had been easy to coax the whole family down. The kids played in his pool, and then with a Wii U he'd bought for the purpose. When he let them know they'd be taking it home, they shrieked, and hugged him, and his little sister beamed. The brother in law, Dan (short for Herbert, in a mystery never satisfyingly explained), grilled on the building's common eleventh floor steaks Katz had purchased. The adults drank absinthe mojitos of egregious strength. Katz brought both Dan and Carolyn, distinctly and each unaware of the other, upstairs to smoke conspiratorial bowls. Dan insisted several times that Katz not inform Carolyn. Carolyn didn't seem to give a shit one way or the other. When they were inevitably too drunk to drive back north, Katz put them up in the W.

That had been sufficient to get in Dan's very best books. Katz rented a car and drove up to Canton, stopping to visit Mildred Joy, eighty-two years old and still ornery. Elijah had died in 2002 at 74. Cassius had been taken early by leukemia; he went two years ago at only sixty-one. Katz got the news, went to the liquor store, bought a 750 mL of Laphroaig, killed it before noon, and thought about it as little as possible. There had been no funeral, which was fine by Sherman.

His grandmother served up mean salsa, made with her own tomatoes, and he asked how a Christian had come to be named "Elijah Dorfzaun Katz." She looked at him like he was out of his mind. "Sherman, your grandfather was a Jew. He was lucky I didn't care about clubs, or I'd never have married him, even as late as I did." She inspected him intensely. "I mean, his momma wasn't Jewish. His momma was a drunk slut on the boardwalk. Maybe she was Jewish, who knows. But his daddy was Roy Simon Katz, as I recall, and his own goddamn name was Elijah. Might as well have been Goldfarb Israel Jehovah Jewyjew. Want another Abita?"

"Why didn't you tell Dad he was Jewish?"

"What did I just say about clubs?"

"Why did you and Grandpa finally get married?"

"Oh, Sherman. Convenience, mainly. As you get older there are a lot more doctors, a lot more questions about what happens when one of you die. I'd never been terribly interested in marriage, certainly not to your grandfather, bless his heart. He was a good man, but he was a simple man. No doubt thanks to your great-grandmother, of whom he had no recollection. Your great-grandfather wasn't much of a step up. Elijah was home by himself most nights while Roy Simon was out chasing punani. If he struck out, he'd drink Wild Turkey until your grandfather looked like a Kraut, and he'd think himself back on the Western Front, and kick the shit out of him. He probably could have been something. Your father was certainly smart enough. And look at you." She extinguished a Misty Menthol 100. "You still smoke?" She gestured at the ashtray. "Go for it. They'll carry me out of here in a box."

"Thanks, I will." Sherman lit a Newport. "Dad dropped out of high school, didn't he? I know he didn't go to college."

"Sure, Sherman, but that doesn't mean he wasn't clever as hell. Back then finishing high school, let alone college, didn't seem as important as it does today. Your grandfather needed help, and your father hated school. He probably had a touch of that *Rain Man* disease. But he was just a teenager, and he'd be schooling Elijah with better ways to do things, and just about all of 'em were. Improvements. He could just look at a tool and know exactly how it was used. No one had to teach your father anything; he'd go stare at something for a bit, and scratch his head, and come to me and say, 'Mama? This is why your Oldsmobile is making that noise. Mama? I built a waterwheel at the creek. Mama? If Daddy keeps using that extension cord with two male ends, he's gonna burn the house up.' They were all true. I had to bring the County electrician out about that goddamn extension cord. He yelled at your grandfather until he was white in the face."

She lit another Misty. "Didn't help him none that he married your mother, whom I'll tell you, Sherman, I never cared for and hope never to see again."

"Awww, why would you say that about Mom?"

"She was getting on him about becoming a Catholic before they were even married. But she was drunk half the time, smoking, got up in those little halters and Daisy Duke shorts, so what kind of Catholic is that? I told him, 'Cassius Julius, she's gonna get you caught up in a lot of mess.' But he only ever had eyes for her. Then she finally got him to go through their Catholicization program, and he asked us to come. We did, and it was a bunch of damn foolishness, and you can bet they asked us all for money even though we're not in their church. Then your mother decides Catholics are wrong about two weeks later, and takes up with her Pentecostalism, and rather than realizing maybe she wasn't the Lord's own spokeswoman, he just followed along." She exhaled and looked into the distance. "That's when the real nonsense started."

"The nonsense?"

She patted his arm. "I shouldn't speak badly about your mother. Her husband's gone, and that's terrible for any woman. Especially one married to a good man like Cassius Julius."

He parted from his paternal grandmother, but not before she forced a bronze Glock G17 Gen 4 on him, scandalized to learn he had no hand cannons in Atlanta. He left her a half ounce and a pack of Zig-Zags, eliciting a hoot. "We're gonna have a hot time in the old town tonight!"

At Carolyn's he made them an immediate gift of the gun.

"Isn't this Grandma Joy's Glock?"

"Yes, then momentarily mine, now yours."

"You don't like it?"

"I don't need a gun. That's a bad charge."

He'd spoken to Dan, who understood what was going down with surprising alacrity and perceptiveness. "Shhh. I know exactly what you're talking about, and I know some boys that can help. Most of 'em got laid off from Georgia Pacific

Packaging up in Chattanooga last fall. Strong boys, tough, but smart, some of 'em anyway, and they can keep quiet." He'd introduced Katz to Cherokee and an incompletely toothed, unnamed friend. Katz took a liking to Cherokee, and met up with him four nights, twice at the industrial park, to plan things out.

It cost him $200,000 cash. He gave his sister $10,000 atop that, and told her to deposit $5,000 this month, and $5,000 the next. She ought find a good money market account that gave her a bonus for an initial deposit of $5,000, and route it there directly. "Keep it for a rainy day." She'd hugged him and said that they were all very proud of the family genius, and she wished he'd come by more often. He told her he loved her, not quite meaning it, but wishing it were true.

✳ ✳ ✳ ✳ ✳ ✳ ✳ ✳

Etowah returned, and the three trucks departed in victory formation.

Did they play "Free Bird"?

Is it possible that they did not?

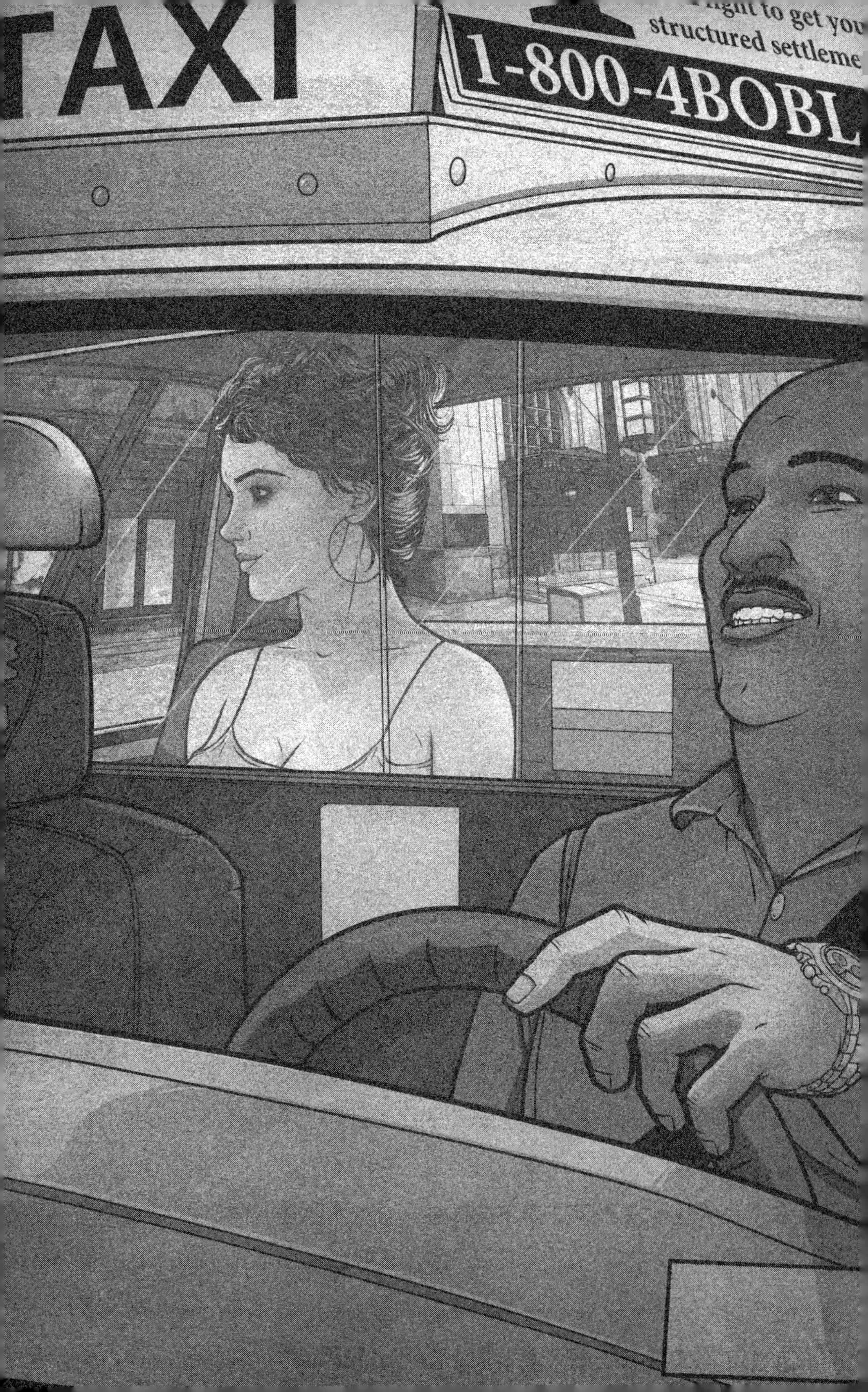
TAXI
1-800-4BOBL
structured settleme

29   *prima luce*

I didn't trust myself to walk the half mile home. Sometimes my mind doesn't shake and shift. Most of the time it does. My cab arrived just after 6:30 am. I ventured outside, blinking against dawn's first light.

✳ ✳ ✳ ✳ ✳ ✳ ✳ ✳

roomy green beanbag chair i enthrone myself asking sherman about opioids it hulked in the corner, underside a sure horror covered with sticky dead granules of this floor and the floor before it, he'd had it for years he said, likely never washed until my foot came down and i said No wondering how many trollops' asses had riven attempts at form and novel tectonics in that shapeless lumpen, how much semen was spilled on this mussy surface look there's a patch there another one once warm with sexheat now stains cold as mossy growths beneath a mourning i mean morning river i laughed as i stripped it but was all disgust inside; boys would rather live among their own wasted excreta than load the goddamn laundry or maybe he preserved them like flags set possessively into the sunbaked ground of south pacific islands, Drake de Gama Balboa Bering Dias Verrazzano Vespucci Polo Ponce de León Shackleford Katz in one breath they say it but he'd have laughed, i'm an explorer of the real for that one no aversion to sounding pretentious, turned always inward, interpolator, involutionist, i was the one looking out at the thricefucked world, grasping clutching his hand bringing him with me, god is a shout in the street, joylaughing, a real grin for once not that halfsmile hiding so much confusion, so much distance, he loathed admitting knowledge beyond what we could break down, dismember, poke at its pieces like an old haggard haruspex then sew up without ever understanding the whole, probably why he so rarely perceived a real world outside intellect's abstractions upon which his actions had measurable effects when i asked why he didn't travel he pointed out he could read two books each day and what's travel compared to that, it comes simply to the rest of us but sure there's plenty that comes to us not at all, all that he'd learned mastered memorized known by heart for better or worse the better he'd surely claim, the esoteric, the complex, he was happiest immersing himself in tableaux vivant in which he might make an investment of his own person, raise them up like a golem from mud and stick and give them some approximation of vitality through number and ruler i'd ask sometimes does the Shadow not fall between the Idea and the Act? he'd credit me for the wit but consideration was another dearer thing entirely, too busy being a smart alec to be thinking, he'd carefully considered each thing once in turn and, having reached conclusions, considered them no further when i asked him that's how he approached it, first looking at me like something brainless boneless bodyless had conspired to speak, yelling with my mouth closed, god the way he could peer at you and make you feel small and worthless or lift you up skyward diamondwise wonder will i ever look at someone like

---

prima luce: at first light

that No it requires a kind of autistic dispassion to really dissemble i mean
disassemble emotion as he did, devastate or elevate, sometimes i'd go into the
bathroom and cry and dissolve into colorspace like the "sleep to dream" video
tell myself don't cry you dumb bitch, you're a big girl, feel the shudders going
wholebodywise like waves sticking a fork into the outlet i'd return bravefaced
and he'd be sans clue regarding the timestretched meantime, other times feel
sanctified queenly actualized jesus the places the sonofabitch could take you
when he bothered, come back he's already coding always clack of the keyboard
he was comfortable at home meanwhile proud little oriana had been reborn
a new person like phoenix in the crushing intensity of that alien gaze, there
and back again, probably why he cheated early on stability was death to him,
boredom ten thousand times worse than extinction, let's hope so that's the
trade i've arranged anyway the last gift, he thought little and less of girltricks
made my own during cautious years inhabiting this mensworld the only way
to keep his mind focused not hips like battleships or coy smiles or flattery
but to allow oneself to be disrupted necropsychology he didn't even know it
was happening and to emerge something different, to mutate under detached
thoughtless visage so clipboarded notes might be made of the transformation
maybe with the opportunity for calculus of the Other algebra of the noumenon,
yeah that would light up his eyes for sure with distaste he'd responded, "i don't
do opioids, and i don't sell opioids" like i'd horked onto that same desecrated
beanbag, he'd gropingly reached the conclusion he got off on betrayal, so close
so far, he thought it betrayal because that's the way someone usually falls apart,
deathliesloss, that's how the drama shoulders its narrative along in the books
but he did it with an unconsidered aside never intended to mean anything,
he didn't get off on betrayal he got off on reshaping people, poking at them,
wondering why they didn't think like he thought act like he acted live in his
universe, perplexed by my *écriture féminine,* valerie said there remains to civic-
minded, responsible, thrill-seeking females only to overthrow the government,
eliminate the money system, institute complete automation and destroy the
male sex—you know how i do it.

three days can change everything three days ago i went to CVS and picked up
a CVS Health® whitebox Early Result "compare to First Response™!" i'll be sure
to do that i hadn't bled in forty days no fasting no temptation no lent plenty
of iron my bleeding comes regularly i had a good idea what was going down
we'd wanted a child, i didn't look forward to finishing school with one riding
around inside of me but better that than wait longer my cousin waited and
waited and waited and now they're riding the IVF train she looks so defeated
husband looks henpecked and her only thirtyseven despite being known as
the wisest woman in baltimore with a wicked pack of cards smiling when she
was thirty like the cat she had nine times to conceive i'm a journalism and
philosophy major let's not forget poetry mfa my fuckin' ass i intend to finish
them out but who's kidding about employment opportunities, right haha i
didn't want a man necessarily that wasn't all of it but i do want a child and i
want that child to be raised well like i was all of life's treasures all the rich fruit
of modern society it's a free country out there but that doesn't mean shit's free
i wanted a partner who could keep me entertained who could appreciate all

the worth in this mind this body this voice who could provide who i could look upon with joy and evaluate and be proud to be with sherman held me for hours after the first time we made it until i slept with him still sloshing around inside me you're supposed to go to the bathroom to wash out the UTI i wasn't about to leave those arms smartest motherfucker i ever met smart but dangerous i liked the danger i loved the smart i lived for being held like the Koh-i-Noor and wrapped myself up in it we fell a little further down and he whispered to me oriana we'll burn all the cities of the world together i knew he spoke idly though now i'm unsure but still i imagined Kali Oya Wadjet Netea Huilu Kamuy-huci Lalahon Nay-Angki Amaterasu Yal-un Eke Turgmam Icep Kanasaw Bà Hỏa Alpan Brigit Glöð Mariel Caca Ognyena Maria Shapash Arinitti Chantico Mama Nina Pele Mahuika a rich heritage of righteous womanly destruction above them Ishtar and Tiamat and Mary one above and one below lord i can rage i knew her by every name collecting them, filing them away like boys with baseball cards and i myself not least, but honour'd of them not your hearthmothers hearthmistresses No i am a hearthmaster i step from horizon to horizon my thick thighs save lives this badonkadonk rolls like a twentyfo' all i ask of my men is to shield me from boredom and worship me like a queen devote their lives to interpreting my words scattered like rubies i saw them all bowing in great salaams bent before my beauty before my fire and it does rage hotter than stars inside of me and everyone who's been inside me knows that and ours would have been a child of fire, the fire next time.

of eighteen, two are regretted caused problems later should have known ahead of time nebbishes both one at seventeen he was twentyeight and under-employed he wrote poetry that wasn't terrible at seventeen and had a good line on rolls i paid for them he'd take me raving Digweed van Dyk Sasha Cox Oaken-fold they were great times i'd dance by myself whipping hair long and thick obsidian ripples cold lava i had the eye of everyone there made him furious monday i'd be back at Roswell High graduated four-oh he'd be doing not much of anything wondering when he'd next be inside a seventeen year old in her father's suburban told him to get lost after stealing two twenties from my bag he slunk around our neighborhood for weeks mom called the cops the other my second i was sixteen then and let him get it once he thought it a proffer of marriage dad took him out for food and wisdom and consolation and sympathy when he rang the doorbell third time in four days and wouldn't tell me what was said over Chili's Big Mouth® burgers but he looked away shamefaced at school the next two years don't know why i didn't care, just didn't want him showing up all mopey, one not my choice and i feel only distant anger not regret i was thirteen but i don't count that as my first time, just violation, it was a cousin dad's side i didn't tell anyone but boys will be boys he ventilated himself to the wrong person ended up beaten pretty badly, dad arranged it i'm certain, never talked to me about it, cousin never spoken of again and unpre-sent at reunions going forward, i guess dad got recompense not so sure about myself two ladies in the dorms freshman year, led never to much of anything, lots of drunk giggling and yelping and enthusiastic confusion fun weekends one of them an asian basketball player tall as a new colossus beautiful not an ounce of fat on her one somewhat mousy but passionate kissed like a shotgun murine buried her snout in me best head i've ever had little fossorial paws exploring soaked her down the second time shipwrecked her among my quads undaunted she persevered last year saw she'd married some wretched ginger blue ribbon prize in the ron weasley lookalike contest the first night i met sherman he launched into a tirade complete with gesticulations and drinks rattling atop banged table i grabbed mine to protect it and wondered what the hell this madman was about he was cursing j. k. rowling for marrying hermione off to ron, said it entirely undermined the books, viktor krum was swarthy sexy genius a better seeker than harry pussy potter if they'd have had children (here standing to pantomime Bulgarian pelvic thrusting only me batting an eye they knew him there) the world would buckle under their *jus divinum* first and last person i ever heard deploy *jus divinum* in casual or at least ranting conversation, i was speechless without speech when he sat heavily and pulled me into his eyes never seen a boy with such eyelashes before and he says, "if we have children," here he grabbed my hands in his "the earth will shake as you emit them" i blanched and asked "if we have children?" and blanched harder to ask "emit?" who says that on the first date but didn't extract my hands i'll admit even as my wrists sat in beerspill and he laughed "emit is perhaps not the term for it, as you release into an unprepared world the agents of its own destruction then" and i pointed out that i and the fruit of my womb are of this world, how do you release into something what's already there, i play the ingénue No i play for keeps bring it on in it to win it first was an Adonis both of us sixteen fifteen when we started perfectly proportioned muscle everywhere no idea what he was doing the first two times he came without getting inside me asked whether my hymen was fashioned from dwarven mithril he was an idiot but a sweet one i grew out of him he's divorced twice already played four years of scholarship ucla ball strictly on the sidelines then failed out what a waste wish him well doubt it'll help, a dumbass graduation night party drunk recall little meant less, summer before school with a 2L home from wake forest met him at caribou coffee saw him reading katherine anne porter sat down across from him won him heart and soul within five minutes, he never knew what hit him, at summer's end asked me to move to winston-salem i laughed at him hadn't seen a man crumple and die like that before felt a little bad a lot of power, doesn't seem to be on facebook, probably off doing corporate law somewhere with pale lifeless wife and cynthia ozick and barbara kingsolver two point five children investments in sensible index funds wonder how often he wishes she was me i'll get a nice house and a lump of cash from my parents who knows when mom and dad healthy, they bought me my current place tidy tony too cramped for anyone else, would have made sherman buy us one of those stately homes in midtown, he could keep his condo love his place but give me two or three floors five thousand square feet rooms for entertaining walls for bookshelves a basement for his goddamned loud computers not sure now a lot of space for two people one oriana one yet unnamed.

wondering why i'm wondering myself all that david copperfield kind of crap No seek not to justify but let me explain black eyes feathers in my cap individualistic meritocratic mathematical hyperbinary sherman's world who are the heroes of such world pushing off sitting well sounding furrows their priests *premier état avenir régime* lived the way he did *la vida rigurosa* Bolaño's picture was no news duh sherman never drove usually MARTA but in snow and rain and gloom of night and especially heat he wasn't above softsinging oriaaaaanaaaaa i'd know what was coming are you asking for a ride sherman? dropped him off there dozens of times, picked him up more, he had some "lab" off in west midtown never quite understood what went on in west end, asked twice thrice he clearly didn't want to answer nonresponsive i mean nonresponses something about robots just a few months back No a lot of piping very few robots for robotstuff let it ride let it be speaking words of wisdom we all have our secrets suction curettage seven months ago didn't know it would hurt so goddamn much felt like panorgan extraction four hours video counseling mandate O.C.G.A. look right there in the statute read the first half of *Middlemarch* black Balenciaga sweatpants absorbing a million women's fear dirt tears rage no eating of course hideous propaganda almost welcomed the protesters' megaphone outside right up against the building thanks again O.C.G.A. afterwards asking sherman laughing a joke of it what kinda timeframe looking to have kids asked one boy before looked at me wounded headlit betrayed coward broke up weeks later sherman swept across the room picked me up not wanted to pressure me but hoped to do so soon, ready to retire, i've done everything you can do with a computer, made money sufficient for thee i mean three living comfortably stayathomedad teach them greek teach them algebraic topology teach them to learn clapped hands they'll know math but real humans *ignoramus et ignorabimus immo nein wir müssen wissen wir werden wissen* kissing me so warm why'd i ask eyes wide and loving and more human than human less also i'd forgotten my pills stopped taking them now no need to tell him excited thrilled scared but nagging at me later good father great father if things go right so much to go wrong what if he goes to prison he will give up work but will he give up Work if he decides he doesn't like it what then No nevertheless i am the same identical woman like all my sisters past present future i raged about the iniquity i mean inequity of it all.

devesh has cancer i wept a wonderful man credit to his race gender school species country universe ten thousand gods asked sherman how he looked pale that day shrugged said their word for sewage is also their word for beverage racist as hell i suspect from simpsons or family guy or something whatever but Bolaño explained that neatly poor dumb devesh sherman didn't volunteer we have a fucking uranium facility and apparently were less careful than we thought, haven't you read *the stand* same general deal, wonder what kind of lifetime is left on sherman but wouldn't be writing him insurance fine knocking me up but apparently not with telling me if not now when? thought he was immune from the cops not just cops state defense energy homelandsec highway patrol port authority secret service fbi dea cia nsa nnsa keystone kops furies guóānbù unit 8200 spetssvyaz سایبری دفاع قرارگاه bureau 121 (i took a class!) i would hear it, the circuit court would hear it, and the supreme court might hear it he thought they'd recognize him as leet that's what i meant by his world he couldn't imagine what force would be brought to bear that outstanding

---

O.C.G.A.: Official Code of Georgia, Annotated

individual accomplishment in the service of chaos is frowned upon by those who make it their job to reduce chaos the aneristic he'd call them statists sometimes disneybots once even mehums i told him no more of that last one the irresponsibility is mindbending could have killed everyone there maybe he has hah what was the objective that part i don't understand at all why was he doing this mad mad mad mad activity money? surely not money, had all he needed, for scientific glory but glory arises from others exactly those he couldn't tell the knowledge he could do it? not much to bet one's life on everest Hillary and Norgay at least could tell people and certainly did so what then? conclusion i reached bombs reason unfathomable possibly related to global warming not terrorism ha some manner of geoengineering the world wouldn't have the balls read: insanity to do, it's crazy but the whole thing was crazy, unacceptably crazy, intolerably crazy he'd take death over jail said so dozens of times bound me to pledge i'd bring him poison like *braveheart* or something wait is that what happened in *braveheart* not sure i'd fallen asleep a few times by then this was just faster he was sicker than i ever imagined kindest thing possible was giving his child a chance, wellfunded no father in prison no father dying slow cancer it's at least what he would have professed to want had i been as open with him as he failed to be with me would profess forty ideas each less workable than the last but reached it in the end, delegated me beneficiary months ago suspected and saw all of this and agreed *Oriana, if it is possible, may this cup be taken from me* know neither vulgate nor citation jesus said it sorry.

nature and nurture remains unsolved twin studies suggest a large nurture delta but nature's still setting a baseline there the nature's extraordinary the nurture would have been unless it would not have been willing to take the chance before but uranium? even after devesh? i can nurture this child by myself if need be and good fathers are acquired more easily than a few million dollars cold cold cold pale fire but not from our child's perspective i think.

✳ ✳ ✳ ✳ ✳ ✳ ✳ ✳ ✳

I arrived a little after two am. Sherman was agitated, emotional, demonstrative. I knew I looked fantastic, but still I was surprised when he rushed to greet me at the door, wrapped his arms around my waist, and lifted me up. I'm in no way a small woman, but I kicked up my feet (tall purple socks striped with blue, plus black wedges), and my knees were at least two feet off the floor. I squealed. His eyes betrayed inquietude, there was mydriasis there and nystagmus, eyes all over the place. I asked, "is something wrong, love?" He looked into the distance, above and beyond me, and fed me a pack of lies. Let him stew in his own pot, then, if he wanted, though if he thought he could unleash on me I'd make it plain otherwise; though she be but little, she is fierce. More accurately though she be thicc, she is not soft.

He fell asleep smiling. That would have made things more difficult, might have changed things, impossible to know, but it faded quickly. I scratched his back, his scalp. My nails were respectably long, barbie pink, great nails. When he started jerking at the sheets and grimacing I knew he was dreaming. Poor boy, so many mornings waking up confused and wounded due to your own unthinking inventions, no more nightmares. I stood and went to one of his bookshelves; fiction was sorted by original language and resolutely unsorted within that scope, two long shelves climbing the ten foot wall. Three shelves devoted to drama and poetry unified across languages. He'd built them with his father, one of the last things they did together before Cassius Julius died. They weren't tight—over three years, I saw the parents maybe twenty cumulative hours, aside from the week his dad came down to raise the shelves—but you got the idea they were slowly rebuilding something left for years to ruin, stepping cautiously, wondering what they could have in terms of relationship. Sherman neither hated nor particularly liked them. So far as I could tell, he was to them a lifelong enigma. They respected him, they loved him, but I wonder if his father died suspecting babies had been switched at the hospital. To his sisters he was a frightful wizard who lived atop the mountain. They seemed just as proud of him as they were relieved he didn't come around. It's hard to imagine growing up like that. I'm an only child, apple of my parents' eyes. My parents aren't intellectuals per se, but they're college-educated, gentlefolk. I knew a great childhood; I've seen terrible childhoods. Theirs was a happy family of four plus the alien. Cassius was a good guy, and those two embraced with real love by the end. Cassius got down on himself for being unable to rise to meet Sherman; the others resented Sherman not coming down to them.

Speaking of happy and unhappy families, I took down *Anna Karenina* (he had both Pevear+Volokhonsky and Garnett, the latter beaten half to death, first person I ever met who hadn't just read almost everything I'd read, but had read them in multiple translations, and could happily contrast them: fully engaging with Sherman, to appropriate his phrase, was not trivial) and opened it silently, then replaced it and selected *War and Peace* (*Voyna i mir* as he always called it, in pronunciation that made Bolaño wince, but fuck Bolaño). The hardback's spine was broken out; I remembered him walking around with it for three weeks in the hot summer of 2011. We'd just started dating. I thought at first he was trying to impress people, and was depressed. Who carries around *War and Peace* in hardback? Then I heard him asked what he was reading, and he lied, both times answering "just garbage," not wanting them to know. I cracked it open and saw underlined words and lines and entire passages, different pens across the read, and the first one I reviewed almost made me laugh: "Nothing is so necessary for a young man as the company of intelligent women." I opened again randomly and, yes, I could understand how the underlined would appeal to Sherman: "It's not given to people to judge what's right or wrong. People have eternally been mistaken and will be mistaken, and in nothing more than in what they consider right and wrong."

Prisons are built with stones of Law, brothels with bricks of Religion. That's a load of horseshit; the primary struggle of life is to judge what's right and what's wrong, and live rightly; Sherman would have identified the struggle against absurdity and quoted Camus; he didn't understand that we'd constructed that prison when we dismissed Kant's *kategorischer Imperativ* and accepted that old syphilitic fraud Nietzsche. One of our biggest fights started when I called him out for quoting *Also sprach Zarathustra*, and remarked that if he must rip off

---

kategorischer Imperativ: categorical imperative

WestPhil 101, he needn't reach for the charbrained incel that launched a million Nine Inch Nails records. He erupted into a furious ten minutes that ran from "if you love Bertrand no-nukes Russell we can summon him by jerking off on a copy of *Principia Mathematica*; you can be his fifth wife," through "how can someone both have syphilis and be an incel let's call that Marino's Paradox" to "John von Neumann solved all remaining philosophical problems while taking an Abelian shit or would have anyway if they were of any importance."

I asked him, "what's an Abelian shit?" and he exploded "it's a shit that commutes Marino read a fucking book!" Smoked something like five cigarettes over the course of it. He was admittedly pretty tweaked, but still, one doesn't often find that kind of hardline opinion regarding WestPhil.

I saw him open the safe after we'd been together only a few months. It was in the office closet, back corner, unattached to the floor or wall, susceptible to wholesale extraction and later forcings. I pointed this out to him once, and he shrugged. "I don't really have anywhere strong where I might mount it," almost sheepishly. "I have excellent camera coverage, so I'd know who it was, probably. And they're pretty good about not letting people up."

"People who enter through the lobby. If people knew what was in here, they'd be making a serious effort. How much is in there? A hundred thousand?" The safe was substantial, and looked densely packed.

"About ten times that." He removed a stack several inches thick.

"Are you serious? There's a million dollars in your closet?"

"Give or take, yeah."

"Sherman. How many people know about that?"

"Not many. I don't know. I'm not sure why I'm showing you."

I just about lost it. "Sherman, not only is that incredibly stupid, it's unsafe. People will do crazy things for a million dollars cash. Somebody mentions it to the wrong people, and they're going to come up here. People you won't be able to identify on your cameras. People who will hurt you." I was stern, and his face indicated he didn't get it.

"Oriana, I've always had a lot of cash on me. Never been a problem."

"I am not sleeping here while you have a million fucking dollars in cash. How many swamp trash exes know about this?"

"I'm not stupid. Most of them don't. Only you. Most just see the ready cash, if anything." This referred to cash, a few thousands' worth, in an old Trivial Pursuit box. "I'm just letting you see...honestly, to impress you I guess. You're, you know, kinda high-class." He made sad eyes at me, striving to look stupid. "And while I'd be happy to remove these monies from my condo, at no small annoyance and inconvenience, no one would know that I had done so, making it somewhat pointless." It was a valid argument, one he'd normally have made with more contemptuous edge: he wanted absolution.

"Why isn't that in a bank? You get on me about my savings account's low rate, and you've got a million dollars sitting in currency?"

"Well, love," he shut the safe's door and stood, turning to me, "I'd like as much as the next man to have this in the bank, or ideally a Vanguard brokerage account. Unfortunately, depositing a million dollars is not trivial. Banking this and its four brothers will take time. It's an ongoing project."

"Four brothers?"

"There is another four million or so offcampus. Are we going to head to Little 5? I have a powerful thirst for Fibonacci Painkillers at Brewhouse, powerful."

That was the first time I grokked to what he was up. Before, I'd thought he just slung code and dispensed a sack or two out of nostalgia. I was thrilled. I held it back.

Bolaño had been right, in a way. Last week I picked up for a girlfriend down with horrible cramps; she sniffed heroin now and again, nothing we were happy about but she seemed to have it under control, as well as anyone has heroin under control. Her plug was in Buckhead. I was working up there, personal assistant to a fabulously wealthy Home Depot exec, tutor the children, make reservations, watch the maid, play friend to his neurotic wisp of a WASP of a wife. The most fattening thing I ever saw her eat was an avocado. One kid was great, a little slow off the line but coming around with my coaching. I sincerely hope the other, as evil a child as I've ever known, has been hit by a car.

I drove to Czar Ice Bar on East Andrews Drive, the bar made, yes, of ice, specializing in vodka and sushi and assholes. Her description led me to him easily enough; he looked me up and down with a dirty thirst, eyes made to send skin crawling, and asked how he might help me. "$50 for Kara. She's sick." He said no problem, that he'd do a sweet girl like me a sweet deal, staring me down like he was recording footage for later playback; I didn't want her fucked over, so I smiled at the son of a bitch. I slid over three twenties; he put a soft pack of Dorals on the bar. "Let her know that it looks light because it's mostly fentanyl. She'll love it. Way stronger than horse. Tell her to start slow, though. That shit will take you out if you do too much."

"Is there $10 in there?"

"Nah, I don't do change."

"Thanks." I rolled my eyes, fighting the urge to squash him like a bug. Dorals. Who the fuck dispenses packages in Dorals?

"You gonna stay around and party?" I didn't bother to answer. Striding out, who should I see pulling in but Bolaño. I got into my car quickly, but I guess he saw me. Even in his last week stateside, Bolaño fucks up my shit.

I got home and changed and smoked a few bowls. I texted Kara, letting her know I had her package and that her guy was a real winner, but no reply was forthcoming. I figured she'd gone to sleep. I went to Sherman's directly. We hung out. By the time I woke she'd already scored following several increasingly desperate messages. She was relaxed and at peace with the universe. She thanked me and told me to not to rush. I told Katz the story and he looked perturbed; I asked what was up and he said, "that fentanyl shit is about to explode into a real problem. It's trivial to make, way easier than growing and harvesting and scoring acres of *Papaver somniferum*, precipitating morphine base, getting acetic anhydride somehow to acetylate into heroin base, clean up to white heroin base and finally the hydrochloride. There's going to be a shitton of it, it's going to be cheap, and it's going to kill people. That shit does not fuck around. You should get rid of it."

I remarked that he knew an awful lot about heroin production for someone who didn't fuck with heroin. He smiled and said, "I know a few things, baybee."

I still had it on me tonight, in that pack of Dorals. He regularly went to bed with speed still chopped out on his desk, ready to be hit upon waking. I went into his office and knocked the contents out into his little pile, tapped the cellophane with a long pink nail, mixed it up with my PantherCard. No hesitation. I'd known what I was going to do for at least an hour by then, but I still barely remember doing it. It had to be done. No, it didn't have to. It was done.

Maybe he wakes up and some wave of self-preservation warns him off. Maybe he hits it and the ol' tailbrain just keeps right on keepin' on, like one of those huge fuckin' lizards. Maybe he knows his powders well enough to know what's up. I don't think so. I doubt he'd hold it against me, as odd as that sounds. If I told him, "I went nuts for a few minutes," he'd laugh, look at me knowingly, and say, "I've been there, man." He couldn't stay mad. He couldn't stay anything, except curious. Curiouser and curiouser. He got as deeply into new things as he did because he became them, pulled them on and wore them like new skin, left them behind like moults. The horror...the horror.

∗ ∗ ∗ ∗ ∗ ∗ ∗ ∗ ∗

i once asked the universe how my days would be dominated by which i mean i asked myself well No i've no say as to my dreaming but my dreams remain of mine own conception and the choices of my sleep are no choices at all but i'll damn well make the choices of my waking days and waking nights i called him my crocodile and smiled when he demanded explanations cloaking nullity in enigma knowing that to intertwine myself in a riddle about his nature was to have the shameless narcissist's attention forever and forever is a promise but those salts will cross his mucous membranes and he explained the rest to me, once i'd clarified my interest in opiates, the biological process of overdose, no question why once the problem was clearly stated: the opioid receptor family is conserved across vertebrates, got their start half a billion years ago, paralogous he said, tetraploidization from some meteor striking the antediluvian gene (that part's mine, the hardcore argot his), five subfamilies: δ, κ, nociceptin, ζ, and μ, where it's the μ that's the money receptor: euphoria, your core physical dependence, and respiratory depression, all three coeffected by μ_2 even better than the real thing (entirely within the brain, unlike more generally scattered ORs), prototypical agonist being morphine but others including dihydromorphine, hydrocodone, hydromorphone, oxycodone, oxymorphone, meperidine, 6-MDDM, codeine (itself only a weak and selective μ agonist, but a prodrug for morphine and codeine-6-glucuronide), thebaine, ibogaine, kratom's mitragynine and 7-hydroxymitragynine, pethidine, fentanyl, and carfentanil, bradypnea leading to hypoxemia and hypercapnia, vasodilation leading to hypotension, bradycardia combining with the latter to drop cardiac output $\dot{Q}$, perhaps straight up respiratory arrest to acidosis to ventricular fibrillation, either way cerebral hypoxia or anoxia where 3.3 mL/min oxygen per 100 g are really what you want to avoid cerebral ischemia a/k/a the dreaded HIE followed by mass neuroapoptosis, they don't waste any time, it's a matouba a masada a mila 18, it's a jonestown a jauhar, it's a dance of zalongo, one more

---

OR: opioid receptor   **HIE:** hypoxic ischemic encephalopathy

automaton clicking into the accept state i blink back tears but there are no tears to blink yet my heart went mad as i bent to kiss him one last time not wiping the traces of purple lipstick from his forehead i saw the best mind of my generation destroyed by madness that's what he would have called it aghast but i'll say again it was caring too much maybe he thought that madness itself a lie i've never known someone who cared so much about the wrong things. i press the back of my dress sliding across the back seat's rubicon into the coughing cab and No i shan't look back salts for him, salts for lot's wife and i've always wondered whether nostalgia or horror or vengeance motivated lot's eponymous frump to look dumbly back upon sodom but No i won't look back at all no salts for this cowgirl i don't fuck much with the past but i fuck plenty with the future and as the GOAT said No i'm not afraid to make a mistake, even a great mistake, a lifelong mistake or perhaps an eternity too No who can speak of eternity with certainty save photons and of what unspeakable terrors might photons speak at all No sapere aude what then eternity? and yet here arrive the first rays of newdawn so many trillions of photons, massless yet imbued with the energy of shifting nuclei, powering stars through that energy, by this energy massive by relativistic mass yet somehow still eternal, a loophole there it seems, are these eternities of energy alone distinct or are they shared and what of our own eternities if we're ever to know them and who knows, maybe we'll see sherman again in eternity his child our child seeing him for the first time No i won't and they never will and i cry once more, this time there's a tear No and i feel it move and gasping know sans sonogram it's a girl Yes a third and final cry joyous through all my being and have umbilical magics from beyond the dawn of time intimated yet to her the story No there is no Stone Table to crack just me and this daughter growing inside me and i will neither condemn nor forgive myself and i will bear my burdens the only way i can: like a woman as six hundred and twenty million metric tons of hydrogen are fused per second piercing midnight's simulacra No non serviam i am an opening not a closure No i said No i will not No.

* * * * * * * *

"975 Piedmont, please, right down the road here."
    "Working on a Saturday?"
    Oriana's smile is immediate, instinctive.
    "No."
    She pauses as he pulls away from the curb.
    "It's been a long night."

epilogue

Jo Yoon Kim came to UIUC in 2024 as a doctoral student in Computational Bioengineering. He had done research in protein design at FSU throughout the back half of his undergraduate degree, with a first author paper his senior year. Enzyme engineering was a field without foundations, one whose basic methods still needed working out, and he hoped to make significant strides. The applications of cooked-to-order enzymes were limitless.

His initial focus was on proteins that might facilitate amidation, particularly the reaction of organic molecules with amines. His hope was that the reactions could be approached as a class, and his enzyme design could then be parameterized on the reagent. Whether this was feasible was unknown. His group included two chemistry majors, both of whom seemed adept with the necessary ochem. They worked mostly with yeast as a biological scaffold.

Recent work in metabolic engineering and synthetic biology, much of it published by Dr. Erica Marelli at JHU, had led to *S. cerevisiae* capable of producing substantial lysergic acid. One of the chemists, a hotshot out of MIT, had mentioned that D-LSA might prove a useful candidate; it was known to accept many amines, and the resulting compounds had well-specified HPLC and GC/MS profiles in the literature. The other chemist giggled and agreed. Jo Yoon thanked them for the tip and got to work.

The planet as a whole continued to drowse.

...and in her home hewn high into Smólikas Óros, Éris waits dreaming, watching Ólympos to the east. Éris, daughter of Diós and Héry and Nŭktós and Erébous and Kháos (it depends on whom one asks). Éris, unhonored by Kheírōnĭ. Éris, bane of Thétĭdos. Éris, come to wound the autumnal city. Éris Marion Tweedy, Éris Livia Plurabelle, Éris Marino, Éris tergiversator, Éris instigator, Éris maker of her mischiefs, Éris misunderstood, Éris hailed.

Long olive fingers grasp a golden apple. Her smile is scrutable.

En pãsi gàr toîs phusikoîs énestí ti thaumastón:
In all things of nature there is something of the marvelous.

New Year's Day 2024, Atlanta

En...thaumastón: Ἐν πᾶσι γὰρ τοῖς φυσικοῖς ἔνεστί τι θαυμαστόν
Aristotle, Περὶ ζῴων μορίων (*Parts of Animals c. 350 BC Book I, 645a.16*)

tē kallistē

Some work of noble note, may yet be done,
Not unbecoming men that strove with Gods.

Alfred Tennyson, "Ulysses" (1833)

Per ardua ad astra, bitches! These are bound to be incomplete.

Gregory and Judy Black: thanks for the genes. Check's in the mail.

Gone too soon: Dad. Elise White. Greg Tolar. Alexandra Pastern. David Foster Wallace. Dan Kaminsky. Kevin Mitnick. Victoria Crucet. Richard Smiley. Keith Ellis. Aaron Swartz. Christopher Hitchens. Ol' Dirty Bastard.

Without the loving assistance of Kitty Sarkozy, I'd likely perish, and certainly be less happy. She read the entirety of the text, clipping false directions and cheering on good ones. Thank you, dear.

Robert Anton Wilson's *Illuminatus!* changed my life and set its course. May it be forever read in Heaven. Hail Eris! All hail Discordia!

Twitch, the solid rock without which my bipolar ass would come fully untethered from this reality, for more than twenty years of best friendship. You mean the world to me, you goat-raping pig-devil. This book wouldn't have been written without you, because I'd be dead in a ditch somewhere.

Jeanette Martin, longtime coach of Walton Academic Bowl. Juli Fleming, my suffering *magistra* at Marist School. Sergio Stadler for teaching me math. Scott Huelin for teaching me words. Mom, I don't give you enough credit—thanks for reading to me a shittonne as a child.

Faculty and staff who put up with me at the Georgia Institute of Technology, especially B. Leland, M. Ahamad, D. Dagon, J. Greenlee, H. Kim, R. Vuduc, T. Conte, B. Leahy, and C. Dunahoo. I'm really sorry about the security clearance, and also that stack of CS6290 finals. Since when does GT allow asswipe common fucks to argue about their exam scores? Fail them, and tell them they're lucky to get that much. Speaking of GT, thanks Partnership for an Advanced Computing Environment for the time on FoRCE, Center for Research into Novel Computing Hierarchies for keeping me in the loop, and Geoff Collins for not a goddamn thing. Paul Johnson, you'll always be Head Coach of my heart.

Sci-Hub. Wikipedia. Wolfram MathWorld. The Internet Archive. The New Georgia Encyclopedia. The Bible Gateway. Project Gutenberg. Myanonamouse. Andrea Moro's *Ulysses* concordance. Stanford's Encyclopedia of Philosophy. The Perseus Digital Library at Tufts University. Yale's Modernism Lab. Dartmouth's Dante Lab. FindLaw. Cornell's Legal Information Institute and arXiv.

---

tē kallistē: τῇ καλλίστῃ for the fairest/*formosissima*
per ardua ad astra: through struggles, to the stars   **magistra:** teacher (feminine)

JB Crawford, r/vintagecomputing, and Graham Thomas for telecommunications lore from the 1990s. Ryan Snyder for details of third-generation laser isotope enrichment. Director Carolyn Holje and the other staff of the delightful Dassel History Center & Ergot Museum in Dassel, Minnesota. Piyush Sao and Aarjav Trivedi for the Indian-American experience. Tim Scully, David Nichols, and Michael Evans were gracious and informative in their replies to my pestering. Molly Parmer is the known universe's most powerful legal force.

Accomplices were subjected to my endless talk of The Novel. A few provided invaluable feedback: Samuel Lee Hall, Tanya Burgess, Kathryn Rhett Nichols, Emily Bragg, George Perantatos, Jason Foster, Sydney Daniel, Liz King, Rob Campbell, Paige Bailey, David Eger, Elizabeth Warren, Rebecca Bowen, Christina Baker, Erika Brown Wagner, Clair Bryan, Justin Muschong. Y'all made this book better. All failings which persist are mine, and mine alone.

A bibliography is available at https://midnightssimulacra.com, but it's quite impossible to list everyone from whom I robbed ideas or style over the years. I pretty much straight up plagiarized James Joyce and Matthew Barney. Sorry, Salman: I loved both *The Satanic Verses* and *Midnight's Children,* but you've got no copyright on the construction *Midnight's Foo,* my guy.

Midtown Yuppie Scum and Stinkeye of the Tiger, my trivia teams in ATL and NYC respectively. Adam Kesner's Trivial Dispute. Thanks for showing this southern boy four great years in New York.

I wish I could thank my agent, editor, layout consultant, makeup artist, fluffers, and/or superintelligent cephalopod assistant, but I had no such help, and foolishly did this shit myself. Two megs of handwritten slowroasted artisanal LuaTEX for dat ass. I have seen hell, and it is chemfig. Next time, I'll just drink the bathroom cleaner and be done with it.

Everyone who ever took a chance on me, everyone who showed support, everyone who offered me a job, everyone who listened to my manic bullshit and waited until I left to roll their eyes, everyone who slept with me despite friends' good advice—thanks.

Free Ross Ulbricht. Kill your masters. Become ungovernable.

My brothers and sisters in the Debian Project: the skies belong to us!

And of course, I salute with respect and admiration the spirit that lives inside of the computer.

Sorry if I missed you. Give me shit next time you see me.
And come visit, goddamnit.
Thanks for reading. I hope you dug it. Hack on.

—rigorously, dank ❤

the author

nick black a/k/a **dank** holds numerous degrees from Georgia Tech, and has worked at Nvidia, Google, and Intel, besides founding several companies. He lives in Atlanta, where he is employed by Microsoft as a principal engineer on their Orbital space group. He is a Debian Developer.

midnight's simulacra is his first novel as an adult. He has also written an esoteric and specialized textbook, which is not likely to be of interest to you: *Hacking the Planet with Notcurses: A Guide to TUIs and Character Graphics.* By all means, though, feel encouraged to buy it.

He can be found at https://nick-black.com.

the illustrator

Justin Barker is an illustrator living in Portland, Oregon with his wife and monster *(canis familiaris)*. He holds undergraduate degrees in chemistry and graphic design from Doane University and Peru State College. He holds an MFA in studio art from the University of Georgia. When not working on illustration projects, he maintains a multimedia sculpture practice.

He can be found at https://justinbarkerart.com.

Made in the USA
Columbia, SC
07 February 2024

35f1cc91-f81a-4a2d-8a20-ab3294eed8d3R01